SOVREV

THE FAITH ENDEAVOR

ALEXANDER SYLAZHOV

SOVREV

THE FAITH ENDEAVOR

REDSTAR
BOOKS

First published in 2013

ISBN: 978-84-616-3498-9

Published and edited by Alexander Sylazhov.
Cover art and illustrations by Alexander Sylazhov.

For more information feel free to access the author's website at:

www.asylazhov.com

Dedicated to my family, who have always guided me through the walk of life with knowledge, wisdom, principles and, above all else, love

CONTENTS

BOOK I

'The Faith Endeavor'

"A spectre is haunting Europe; the spectre of Communism."

- First sentence of 'The Communist Manifesto.'

PROLOGUE

I awoke from a profound slumber, a sensation of immense satisfaction emanating from my every pore as I stared deep into oblivion. Enveloped in darkness, I didn't need light to know my bedroom had not been ravaged by the passage of time. It remained exactly as I had left it.

A tall figure lying next to me suddenly came alive and sat on its knees, studying me with irradiating fondness. Her sheer beauty threw aside the black abyss of darkness surrounding us; a woman with pale skin white as snow and perfect Slavic features, thin and slender, a radiant Tsaritsa with long majestic hair, colored black as the obscure limbo enveloping the room.

Her soothing voice, so elegantly exquisite and full of Russian grace, resonated throughout my body in total harmony as the last remnants of my hatred vanished into nothingness. Her Eastern throat produced a string of sounds so delicate and harmonious it shattered my paranoid perceptions of danger, my constant state of emergency, dissipating every condescending trace of abhorrence toward the human race.

The unique voice described her essence perfectly; the words produced by her throat flowed in the air seamlessly, the sounds fused together inseparable, tightened in one never-ending word that lingered through the air, a passionate melancholic tune I hoped would never cease to play. The sounds generated by her magnificent voice thrillingly raised the hairs on my body, caressing the very insides of my being in an unbearable yet blissful manner, pronounced slowly

1

and patiently as she whistled into my ear, leaving nothing behind except a numb and absent mind. My body thirsted ever more for her touch, and decided to leave the worries of the mind aside in order to experience its astounding marvel.

Lying once again beside me, she began to caress my feet with hers. The perfectly formed limbs playfully toyed with my skin, the delicate toes and soft arches incredibly warm to the touch, comforting and arousing me. Soon, we both began gasping in anxious pleasure as the imminent prospect of carnal release became apparent, and she gently positioned her tight young body on top of mine. Our mouths fused in one endless passionate kiss, succumbing to the temptations we had sought. Each thrust sent me deeper and deeper into the tendrils of a world I hoped would never cease to hold me, as tightly as her loving embrace.

• • • • •

The world was now a magic place, a true utopia, an unpolluted paradise immune to the evils of man. We had released all of the woes which clouded our passion, and proceeded to rest peacefully still embraced, communicating with our minds now that our bodies had done their part. Her Slavic voice spoke words of beauty, of faithfulness, of true fidelity toward me. I marveled at the discovery that she loved and wanted me more than I did her. I dragged her warm, naked body nearer and she comfortably positioned herself submissively next to me, in a fashion as if she had always done so. My beautiful Russian Queen caressed and kissed me once more, sunk in her own undeniable happiness.

But it was inevitable. No matter how perfect, how faithful, I had to search for the absolute truth in her. She had never asked why I left or why I returned to her side. I ig-

nored what would make her accept me so easily, so lovingly after my obvious departure. Or was it the other way round? At this point, I no longer knew. I didn't know who had abandoned whom. I began to think about how perhaps, it had been something mutual.

I was so intrigued by this that I decided to question her, to interrogate her until nothing but the truth filled the air of the room.

"How long have you been here, all by yourself?" I asked.

"I've always been here. I never left. I was patiently waiting for you. I knew you'd return someday. And now that you're here, I'll never let you abandon me again."

"I never abandoned you," I said, insulted. "You did. You banished me. You kicked me out and locked the door. You changed."

"I never changed!" she yelled, surprised. "The world did. Don't you see? We can never go back to the past, no matter how marvelous it could have been. Nobody can! But we can remember it here, together. Love me like you used to do. Make love to me with the same passion that used to drive your motives. Love me for who I was. For who we were."

"NO!" I shouted, so loud she flattened herself against the wall next to the bed. "IT'S A LIE! YOU'RE LYING! NOTHING'S WHAT IT SEEMS! TAKE THOSE THINGS OFF YOUR WRISTS!" I proceeded to take her jewelry off, those disgusting yet deceitfully beautiful signs of change, as she wept and collapsed to the floor, helpless. Only a few moments ago I was blinded by her inviting warmth, omnipotent beauty and the harmony of her lovely voice. But nostalgia on its own could never maintain this model forever. My perfect utopia, my only chance for redemption was but a shadow of her former self, lying shattered in the room's corner, passionately weeping. "I didn't want to. I'm sorry. They made me. YOU

made me. Nobody liked me for who I was. Not them, not you ... Don't you remember? You disapproved of me. I thought that maybe changing would bring you back to my side ..."

"I would have never done such a thing. Look at you. You're a mess. You look like a tramp, a rich prostitute. I don't need those expensive clothes and jewelry to like you better. I've always been attracted to your natural beauty, to your clear reasoning, to your fair personality. But you became corrupted ... I didn't want any of this ... Why couldn't you stay just the way you were, when we first met?"

"Even if it were possible, we couldn't go back to that now ... They won't let us. We'll be isolated. What kind of living is that? Going against the current, thinking every human being is stupid and undeserving of choice? That's the lie! You want to live that lie again! Nothing like that will ever happen again. We can live together side by side, loving each other more than ever before, in this new world. The outer appearance might change, but love doesn't have to. I'm here for you, like always ..."

"There's a thing even more pathetic and sad than living in the past, and it's reliving it in the present. You leave me only one choice. The one thing you taught me, the only thing about you that will forever stay with me ..."

"NO! PLEASE! DON'T DO THAT! DO NOT FORGET ME! THAT'S WORSE THAN LEAVING ME AGAIN!"

"I won't forget you. That's impossible. You can't destroy the past. But you can modify it. It can be remembered its own way."

"Don't do that. You know I no longer do it. Don't take it out on me, you'll regret it, you will ..."

"Yes. You can't do it anymore, but I can. Don't worry, you won't miss me. The love of the people, the love of abundance, the love of excess will make you get over it. Everybody

wants you now. You'll find a better suitor. Someone more adapted to this new world."

"I won't. I don't need it. I only wanted you ... You made things special. You wanted to change this awful world, and even if you lost, you deserve my love and admiration. You already have it, you always will! I ... I love you."

"I must leave now, to let you get on with your things. For us, our past will be very hard to forget, but everybody else will easily get over it. They already have! Nobody remembers us anymore. We're already carcasses of history, another marriage ending in failure. History warned that we would fail, but we wouldn't listen, we were too proud, too young, felt too immune to the evils of the world. But we were mistaken. And now we're paying for being so idealistic. But it won't happen again. As long as I'm away from you, I won't make the mistake of being so naïve ever again. Your intentions are good, but not enough. We are not good for each other. We fuel our innate pureness, a pureness that can't survive in this world. Your offspring always dying at birth is an example of that. We're not meant to be together, and we're not meant to change the world. The world will change when it's ready. The world will remember us when it's helpless. And you and I both will die before that happens."

"Stay ... just stay ... Live the rest of your life here with me. Forget about the world. We don't need it."

"I won't. You're nothing but a memory to me, a memory I will dispose of soon. I hate living in the past and you know that. You've been nothing but trouble the whole time, so now I'm moving on. I'm looking for someone who's not so easy to corrupt, so eager to get off on power like you did, forsaking me in that way. Who did you think you were? You're no better than any object in this house. You're just a prop in the

background, a decoration, easily replaceable. But you also were the perfect companion, the very best of lovers. In any case, you're no longer useful to me. I need someone focused, cold, detached, like you once were. You were a warrior whose blood boiled with revolution. Now look at you. You disgust me. You follow anything that happens on the outside, like a sheep. You believe anything they tell you, swallow every single corrupted idea."

"No ... please ... come back ... I'll do anything ... Don't leave me again ... You know I can't deal with solitude ... I'll collapse, I'll shatter from the inside out. You can make it all better again, if you stay."

"I already gave you two chances, more than enough to see that you speak lies."

"IF YOU GO THROUGH THAT DOOR, YOU WON'T COME BACK! YOU'LL CHANGE AS WELL! YOU'LL BE JUST LIKE ME! WHY DO YOU PREFER THAT INSTEAD OF SIMPLY STAYING WITH ME?! WHY?! YOU'LL BE CORRUPT EITHER WAY!"

"If I become corrupted as well, I do not want it to be with you. You don't deserve that. I couldn't ever bring myself to wish such a thing."

"But I don't care ... You know I don't ..."

"I know you don't. But I have to do this on my own, without you. Goodbye, my love. Enjoy your life. Or at least, try to."

She was left crying on the floor next to the bed, banging her tiny fists on the floorboards. I opened the door, knowing well that once I had stepped into the unknown, I wouldn't be able to return. I glanced back one more time at my loved one, who between sobs, managed to formulate one last sentence before my departure:

"Never ... forget ... me ..."

· · · · ·

I woke up to the sound and feel of my own heartbeat; seconds after, countless clocks and alarms of different kinds started to drill themselves inside my head. Each activated after an interval of a second or two counting from the previous one. Their acute vibration resounded in my heavy skull as more and more of them joined the commotion.

Everything was pitch black; my muscles hurt and my head was pulsating, blood aggressively boiling through my tense veins. I didn't know where I was. My head was banging violently as if something would burst out of it. I felt like I was rotting inside, noting the scent of vomit in my mouth and breathing the putrid smell of dried blood in the room. My stomach appeared to be twisting itself, squeezing all the fluids out like hung clothes. My throat was sore, itchy and dry, as if I had swallowed sand.

I got up from the cold floor I was lying on and wandered clumsily searching for a light, but it was simply all dark; I started to shake at the thought of my location being unknown. I could have been kidnapped, drugged, raped, held captive. I did not remember anything recent prior to this. My inherent paranoia instantly thought of searching for wounds, expecting to feel a scar, stitches or even missing limbs, and felt relief knowing my body remained completely unscathed.

I searched for a light switch on the cold walls with trembling hands, and was glad to find out my sight had returned when flicking the switch. Even so, I couldn't see very well. Drowsy and on the verge of collapse, I clumsily tried to recognize the place I was in without success.

I walked further on, rubbed my eyes trying to get accustomed to the light and became confused at the fact that I recognized the room I had just walked in as a bedroom. Even though darkness covered most of it, different objects like beds and wardrobes could be distinguished, eerily mimicking bluish figures. I tried to look for someone else inside the room but I was clearly alone. The sensation of why would I be looking for any of my former comrades struck me as I had either forsaken or come to bad terms with all of them. An electric feeling traveled throughout my torso when I came to this realization, and my old phobias intensified; schizophrenia, Alzheimer's syndrome and hallucinations from my own conscience in general were my main sources of panic. The situation at hand could be proof that I had lost the fight. I had finally given them room inside my mind.

I halted my thoughts abruptly when a screeching sound, that of an old door in need of oil, stabbed the silence in that eerie house. It came from a very nearby room, so when I left my current position I noticed I was in a small corridor, leading to a hall. The screeching noise was heard again, coming from a white door which I presumed was the one to the main entrance.

I froze instantly when I heard a sound like someone trying to force it open and adrenaline instantly flowed throughout my whole body, preparing myself for anything that could happen beyond that door; I decided to open it first and face whatever waited on the other side.

Blinding, piercing lights appeared everywhere I looked at, revealing my ghastly whereabouts. It was a passage way, similar to a tunnel, which for some reason reminded me of the Saint Petersburg metro. However, it was different in many ways. Gigantic chandeliers hung from the white ceiling, which had to be a hundred meters above my head.

Large white pillars with Victorian era carvings stood imperiously sustaining it. The ceiling was decorated in its entirety with Greek paintings. I analyzed them more intricately and discovered they actually displayed people having all types of sexual encounters. It resembled a painted Kama Sutra, except that it even displayed scenes involving animals and homosexual couples as well.

The same case could also be applied to the carvings on the pillars; they were sexually oriented, in the shape of women, twisted and confusing, not at all influenced by Greek art. The floor, which featured a pattern comprised of black and blue lightning bolts, almost resembling a zig-zag, was covered by a red carpet with one yellow stripe at each side, unusually bright and clean, as if nobody had ever dared walk over it. At the extreme end side of it, something could be seen, probably a door, but it was too distant to be appreciated. It had to be at least 300 meters away; holding my heart almost with my very hand, I took a deep breath, fearing all sorts of ridiculous painful deaths coming ahead. I walked slowly toward it and with a watchful eye calculated every step with unnatural attention.

Walking past the imposing pillars, which adorned the entire corridor, I noticed portraits of people could be seen between them. I approached one to see the inscription below the painting, carved in bright gold.

"May Our Rest Dwell Evenly Nowhere."

I ignored the meaning of this quote and the identity of the person in the portrait. There was no name either. On the faint possibility that it could be a quote by a philosopher, artist or intellectual, my eyes always recognized a warlord when they saw one. Portraits were supposed to immortalize

and improve upon the features of the individual with an artistically neat perfection, but there was nothing here to admire in terms of beauty; the face reflected a feeling of self-indulgent insanity, his eyes lost in a void of twisted derange, the ugliness of his facial features almost mocking the viewer, inspiring nothing but raw fear and sparking curiosity. It reminded one of shadowy figures such as Vlad the Impaler and Ivan The Terrible, immortal icons from grim times when humanity entertained itself with torture and the blood of others more than today. In the background beneath him, a dark harbor could be seen, similar to Vladivostok's, looking heavily industrialized and developed more than ever before, a green and venomous sky announcing a dreadful storm.

Taking my mind off that horrible piece of artwork I headed toward the doors, not caring one single bit for the other portraits at both sides of the passage way. I wanted this to end without recording a single image of it all inside my head. I wasn't really there. I wasn't there at all.

When I was at a certain distance, I recognized the distant object as a set of large double doors, painted gold. As I was about to reach them, a mechanical sound began to travel through the quiet atmosphere of the passageway; I instantly jumped, looking at every direction, searching for something out of place or someone coming right for me. Even though the entire place appeared to be completely still, it wasn't sound what struck the most feral fear into my mind, but the absolute certainty of being watched; I could feel a certain presence in the area.

I continued toward the doors and reached my destination unharmed, feeling as if several hours had gone by. I kept looking over my shoulder to scan the deserted, endless corridor, which stretched as far as the eye could see, uselessly

vast and tall. I faced the doors again and focused on finding something suspicious. Immediately, I noticed a panel next with several buttons, each with different symbols. The mechanical sound appeared again, and finally revealed its source; the doors opened, showing they were in fact elevator doors. I quickly turned around, and looked at the end of the corridor as if the noise I was making could somehow alter the unbearable calmness of the place.

It didn't matter, since as of now I could continue exploring. There was no reason not to. How long could I remain hidden in that deserted place, without food or water? Although the place looked like a museum or an art gallery, I could perfectly be in the home of a rich and eccentric madman, bound to come looking for me anytime soon. I had to move and attempt to escape instead of waiting to be found. My eyes headed once more toward the panel inside the elevator.

I got overridden by nerves when I noticed no normal symbols were painted on the buttons; no numbers or letters of any kind. In their place, different drawings were painted in white over the black buttons, lined up vertically in columns. There were twelve in total.

I began looking at them frantically. One had a drawing of what appeared to be a cage. Another, what looked like a triangular slope, then a dome, a saucer, a string of ovals ... Nothing made sense. I had no way of telling what each button did, or where they would take me, given this was an elevator at all.

What to do now? If I pressed any of those buttons I could face a slow and painful death. Or maybe they would take me somewhere where it would occur. I had no possible way of knowing, no other choices. The only alternative was starving to death in the long corridor.

I kept staring at the buttons; the slope, the cage, the string of ovals, the dome, the saucer, thinking carefully about what they could represent. The cage, a trap. Maybe being trapped indefinitely in the elevator. The string of ovals, something to do with chains, another reference to entrapment. The dome and the saucer, absolutely no idea. The slope, maybe falling to a certain death. Then I saw a glimmer of hope.

A drawing of a rectangle, possibly representing the elevator, was located somewhere in the middle between two straight vertical lines. Among such dubious possibilities this was the only one I could decide for.

I shut my eyes and pressed the button quickly, expecting to instantly be shred into pieces. However, an eerie, slow piano tune started to play as the elevator made another mechanical sound and pulled itself upwards with a violent motion.

The trip upwards was long, confusing and fearsome; I looked at the right side of the elevator facing the doors, and noticed a gap where the wall the elevator was climbing could be seen, clearly motioning downwards, as the various imperfections in the stone wall let me see. It somehow made me sigh in relief, as it indicated my ascent. Even so, I didn't know what these doors would let me see and where I was heading toward. Somehow, the thought of descending farther from where I was seemed claustrophobic and hopeless.

After a while the temperature began to rise, and motion sickness started getting to me. The heat gradually increased, waves appearing before my eyes. The elevator was now a blurry stain, as my eyes sunk in their tears. I felt faint, and leant against the right side of the elevator, trying to recover, but eventually collapsed, sitting abruptly on the floor.

But I had to remain alert. I brought myself up by wiping

my eyes and breathing slowly, so as to recover some energy. I couldn't doze off. My eyes instantly directed themselves toward the opposite gap in the wall, to the left side of the elevator, as it was the only thing in the place clearly moving. I was glad to see the elevator hadn't stopped, but it was taking too long. I must have been at least 200 meters underground.

I got up and staggered, holding on to the wall, but managed to finally stand still. My vision was clearer and my body was getting accustomed to the heat. Unexpectedly, my bowels cringed with fright and confusion when I looked at the left side of the elevator again.

The gap in the wall. It was clearly indicating a descent. The elevator must have changed directions without me even noticing. Instinctively, I checked the opposite side. It motioned upwards. I couldn't believe it. Just as I was about to draw conclusions regarding this confusing realization, the doors opened with a screeching metallic sound only comparable to that of a circular saw.

The moment had come to embrace what I was seeing. Having reached my destination, curiously unaware of the dangers I was putting myself in, I remained perfectly oblivious to the risk of the unknown. Any word that describes an absolute lack in logic was what I felt upon stepping on these unearthly grounds, this alien landscape where reasoning proved futile.

I was fainting; I leant on a hot rough stone wall to keep myself standing, and I would have otherwise passed out had it not been for the extreme need to grasp the reality of what I was witnessing.

I found myself in a dome of titanic proportions, built entirely with raw brown stones as in a cavern; before me was the only human contraption in the place, a large metallic

catwalk that hung above a sea of bright flaming liquid, acting as a bridge allowing pass to the other side of the dome. There were black figures moving among the bright liquid but I couldn't analyze them steeply from where I was. I calculated the sea of flames had to be at least a hundred meters below.

At the end of the catwalk there was a door. I began walking toward it, trying not to look down. The metallic catwalk, unbelievably hot from the fumes, forced me to run so as to avoid scorching my feet.

But the thick air and the hot despair made me stagger once again. I collapsed, shaking, feeling as if my head was being crushed, immediately cringing in pain when coming into contact with the hot metal. I crouched trying not to touch the catwalk with my knees, and started to vomit copiously, my hands wrapped around my torso. Blood started mixing in with the vomit, just like I feared. I was passing out.

Suddenly, the catwalk produced the same screeching sound the elevator did earlier, giving me only the necessary time to look at the now broken banister. The portion of the catwalk I was on gave in, and I slid down trying to hold on without success.

As I fell screaming in terror, I visualized the ceiling; a cross, similar to a cross potent but with dangerous curvy sharp edges similar to a biohazard sign was carved in the dome above, a dot at its core where the arms did not reach. Between each arm lay small joint-like structures, curved, separated and not touching the arms, as if the cross had been shattered. The content of this cross-shape was a blinding yellow liquid, like the molten metal in the pool below. I seemed to be upside down in a place where the laws of gravity did not apply.

Before even pondering the impossibility of this fact, my body touched the engulfing flames, burning at a thousand degrees, each nerve succumbing to the ruthless, damaging heat, my skin melting away like the last strings attaching me to reality.

But I was still alive.

In a vortex of pain and insanity, I moved through the molten liquid and breathed the charring vapors, hoping to somehow save myself. Inexplicably, I retained the ability to see. I witnessed the black figures lying around me, moving through the molten liquid just like me, but gracefully free of pain. The black figures were humans; humans indulging in savage acts of sex and lust, as their charred skin and sparkling muscles shone between the boiling liquid and the floating ashes. Consumed without dying, these figures didn't seem to notice my presence and danced circling me, viciously interacting with each other as the only need left in my shattered mind was to finally die, desiring to vanish from existence, wishing only for the excruciating pain to wither away ...

• • • • •

A bluish, dark blur emanated from my room after my spring back to life and thought, and my eyes gradually opened to grasp the sour taste of reality. My mind virtually sunk again, preferring that insane and perverse illusion my subconscious had engineered. The result left me not knowing whether I was awake or dead, lost in a black void or awaking from a trance.

The dream had ended abruptly and without warning, al-

most seeming as if something out of the ordinary was bound to happen, a deadly and invisible forecast. The catwalk collapsed, and the illusory trip had finished seconds after my demise at the hands of those pleasure seekers engulfed in flames.

I tried to get up and immediately felt the decadent state of my body. All my muscles and joints seemed to hurt no matter how delicately I moved, direct consequences of all the stress I had endured during the last week. I managed to stand up and headed toward the kitchen, my eyes still hurting and my sight blurred, drowsy and wanting to completely vanish from existence in the exact same way I had had in the dream. It was the kind of night you would just want to slip into a coma to escape reality for an indefinite period of time, be it days, months or years. Anything was better than awaking under the circumstances I found myself in.

I hadn't forgotten anything during my tortuous deprivation of consciousness. The guilt of the tragedy would never be erased. Without wanting or knowing, my mind found itself remembering every source of discomfort and pain, why I was in that particular state of mind. I started to remember my random misadventures, anything that could have transpired up to now, every person, feeling and situation; my friends, affairs, dreams, desires ... and Her.

She was the cause and consequence of everything somehow. This certain individual was the only one who managed to completely eclipse every single personal demon I could have ever faced before, the only one who I allowed to shed some light into my rancid view of the world, the only one I fully welcomed into my being; she was infatuation incarnate.

The key moment where my fate would be sealed by external forces neared. My enemies wanted to punish me for incidents that had spiraled out of my control, but they didn't

know that their actions would punish me far beyond their expectations; they would destroy everything I had worked so hard to create all these years, something that was secret even to my most trusted acquaintances. They would finally uncover the truth behind me.

I couldn't go anywhere. All the places I could stay in had been ravaged and corrupted to the point of being unrecognizable. There simply weren't any more places I could deem safe. I needed to come up with a plan; an alternative that would obliterate every chance to be defeated, a strategy to redeem myself before these vicious unavoidable stalkers. And I only had three days left to think.

Looking at the perpetual daylight outside of the window, provided by the restless yellow streetlamps of Montenade, I started to remember my life when she wasn't a part of it, one month before I first saw her.

CHAPTER I

Capitalist Utopia

"Freedom in capitalist society always remains about the same as it was in ancient Greek republics: Freedom for slave owners."

- VLADIMIR LENIN -

Soviet Politician, Marxist Writer and Theorist, First Premier of the Soviet Union, Leader of the Bolshevik Party and of the Russian Communist Party and Father of the Glorious Union of Soviet Socialist Republics

---

Everything began three years ago, on the 13th of September, at approximately 07:00. I woke up struck by a frightening, energizing willpower strange in my tame and routinary behavior. I felt each cell in my body working relentlessly, preparing to traverse a day which would put to rest all doubts and fears I could have had accumulated throughout the summer; for ahead of me lay the very first day of school in my third consecutive year in Loynne's Island. I was starting 1st Grade of Scientific Baccalaureate, having passed 4th Grade of State Compulsory Education the previous year, what many people called "The Bridge," meaning it separated true students from thugs and Kannies.

I set my sights on the day that was to come. I dressed up slowly, still sleepy, with an unusually high mood and thinking nervously about the usual stuff that preceded a school year; wondering what kind of classmates and teachers I would

have to cope with, what would once again drive me to the edge in a personality toughening experience rich in stress and social competition, and a long row of other disturbing what-nots which cannot normally be predicted in social environments. My complete calmness before this storm was paradoxically even more upsetting.

During that time I had only lived two years in Loynne's; a majestic island in the middle of the North Atlantic Ocean located approximately 3,000 kilometers away from every continental landmass or archipelago. Rapid economic changes transformed this 10,550 square kilometer island into a paradise state, where millions of people worldwide went for diverse purposes; some to study on exclusive scholarships, others seeking shelter and a new life, running away from the cruel realities of the uncivilized mainlands, eager to take part in keeping the world's only true welfare state alive. Loynne's had been described as a fusion between Earth's greatest capitals and islands, a fast-growing megalopolis, a melting pot of cultural diversity and freedom of expression, the new navel of the Western World.

On the other hand, my country of origin was ravaged by its transition from Communism to capitalism. A mixture of poverty caused by economic blockades from the West, inner corruption, negligent management on the part of the State Administrations, constant propaganda bombardment from the "free world" and probable sabotage from the US had managed to finally topple our Communist project, culminating in a failed coup d'état on the part of the Communist supporters that, unlike Russia, had exploded in a full-fledged civil war. Divisions spread and everything that had once held us together in ideology and country disappeared overnight, very similar actually to what happened in many Soviet satellite states. My nation had resisted for a few more years but

without important support from allies and subsisting through international aid, it remained isolated from the rest of the world. The change was bound to happen sooner or later, and the decrepit State had finally caved in.

My parents, who will remain as nameless as my nation, had fled to work with some friends of my mother's on the outskirts of the country, where the peasants were still humble, simple and submissive, and where the riots and battlefields had not yet arrived. They would live there until the civil war had subsided and the Communist radicals – it was after all, an inevitable matter of time – had been vanquished. The fate of the nation had been sealed and had dictated capitalism would be fully embraced. The people had formally abandoned our ideology and its cause.

In The Motherland – like in so many other Communist nations – you couldn't buy anything but everyday expendable products with common currency. They were more like coupon tickets. Food, basic necessities, nothing that fell into the category of private property. Cars could be "owned" but actually belonged to the State, same as houses. People couldn't buy plane or train tickets in order to flee the country. You needed proper government clearance and paperwork to do such things, and in that chaos, no plane or train would leave the country. The only way was through a fake passport. As such, my parents had devised a strategy months before, when it was already apparent that things would head in that direction. They contacted criminals who smuggled people into Western Europe and asked for forged documents that would enable us to live in Loynne's Island, arguably the best place to live in the world. Reluctant at first – getting smuggled into Loynne's was incredibly more difficult and costly than any other place in the world – the gangsters accepted on the condition that my parents stayed in The Motherland, working

until all debts had been paid. I would be the one sent to Loynne's Island alone, as an insurance policy so that my parents did not even think of escaping or not paying once they reached the island. For further control over my person, I would stay in an apartment block owned by one of their contacts, who would act as my landlord. If I escaped or ran to the authorities, the gangsters would do anything in their power to have me deported and then everything would be ruined; maybe even worse, we could be assassinated.

I know obviously what you must be thinking; that no responsible or caring parent would do such a thing, not even out of desperate naivety. But this was a completely different country, which operated on a completely different framework to the one Westerners are accustomed to. Our criminal countrymen were seen as anti-communist freedom fighters, beloved by idealistic rebels as the strongest anti-government force in the nation, and were as such obeyed and respected. Following the traditional "vor v zakone" or "thief in law" code of honor, they were perhaps the most trustworthy element to be found in the global criminal underworld, the perfect Eastern equivalent of an old Sicilian crime family who hated the law and exploited the peoples, but still provided services to them and kept them by their side with favors, not force. The gangsters weren't to be messed with, and they would gladly eliminate their enemies or teach lessons to anyone who challenged them, but under the circumstances inside our Communist country they were largely suppressed, and thus were even seen as victims by some. A part of the population idolized and praised them because of their ability to get Western consumer goods, drugs and other capitalist garbage, but this obviously came at a cost, as the gangsters were not philanthropists. Despite that, anyone who approached them was immediately considered worthy of respect and held in esteem

in some degree, as the only test of loyalty the criminals required was a demonstration of communist hatred. They needed all the sympathizers they could get. Thus, they would gladly help people deal with their problems, not to mention helping in getting people out of the country. My parents, swallowing their Communist ideals, used this to their advantage.

The criminals forged a passport and a Loynner ID card using the documents of a tourist that had lost them on his stay there, which were virtually foolproof and perfect for the chaotic time and place they would be needed. These documents were enough for me to use and get new ones in Loynne's when I met their contact there, someone who would see to it that I had always existed as a resident of Loynne's in their databases. All I needed to do was speak perfect English, which I did excellently. My new name would demonstrate a blend of Unitedstatian and Russian heritage, very common elements in Loynner society, and thus I legally became Sonny Zharostin.

Loynners would almost never venture abroad; much like Unitedstatians in their golden era, they didn't need to. They were considered guests of honor if they did, having a reputation of being rich and spending lots of money. Traveling around with Loynner papers granted you access to virtually anything.

The strategy went even better than planned by my parents. I boarded a train headed into the heart of Western Europe. I took another train and finally a plane, the very first one out of the hundreds that were headed to Loynne's Island. Even if the ruse ran the risk of being exposed, I would be traveling on the plane with a secondary set of documents that would enable me to sneak past authorities momentarily. The first thing I had to do was meet their contact at the airport,

who would be waiting for me ready to register me on the Loynne's Island Police Department as a permanent resident with Loynner nationality, something which would eventually grant me new and truly legit papers after a year had passed. After all, the passport was everything I really needed, all else was secondary and could be replaced. The work of the criminals was so perfect and accurate it fooled every type of authority. The worst thing that could happen to me was being shipped back to The Motherland, and by the time that happened, at least the armed uprising would have been over.

But choosing Loynne's Island for my destination had proven costly, and my parents warned me that we would not meet in at least five years, perhaps more. Thousands of immigrants must have done something similar, but none of them seemed to have chosen Loynne's as a destination like my parents did. I trusted I was the only person from The Motherland on the island. The world wasn't used to heavy immigration, and as such wasn't as controlled as it is today, where immigration rarely goes on and most Western countries have been taken over by racist neo-fascist parties. It was a moment when Loynners didn't quite know that an outside world even existed, with different cultures and peoples. Racism and ignorance were widespread, as were classism, social prejudice and paranoia. No Loynner wanted foreigners intruding in their perfect paradise, except if they were tourists loaded with cash. My following school years and social life were plagued with this prejudice, translated in the form of Kannovschina. That's my personal term for bullying as performed by Kannies, who as you may deduce, acted as self-proclaimed undeniable kings of the school who nobody dared oppose. In the Soviet Army, a phenomenon in military hazing dubbed "Dedovschina," meaning literally "rule of the grandfathers," was established as the most bloodthirsty and brutal

form of bullying ever in a nation's military. They say the Russian Army is more dangerous and vicious during times of peace, and it figures, as Dedovschina still remains unsurpassed as the most psychologically devastating form of bullying in military organizations worldwide. It is rare for my Soviet Russian comrades to disappoint me, but I will never forgive the invention of Dedovschina in the army. I knew it all too well in school in the form of Kannovschina, which while being nothing in comparison to Dedovschina, still scarred us heavily, and nobody who had been through it was left unchanged, for better or for worse.

Kannovschina was an integral part of school life in Loynne's at the time, for foreigners and Loynners alike, but to a much lesser extent. Locals were considered righteous and deserving of living in Loynne's whereas foreigners would be denied any type of help or integration. Thus, many ethnicities ended up forming hermetic and tight groups trying to survive this ignorance. I remember that learning the island's motto, "*Fortuna Et Libertatem*" – "Fortune and Liberty" – was an eerie foreshadowing moment for me as it made me think of the hypocritical nature of Western democracies, and it would be engraved in my mind at all times. Compared to my country's motto, "United through Motherland, Strengthened by Socialism," the Loynner motto fell under the weight of its own meaningless message. Fortune and liberty are what every human being thinks he wants, a meaningless pursuit that leads to nothing except a vapid existence. Nothing described a country better than its national motto, and Loynne's Island proved to be yet another shallow piece of rock destined to be remembered throughout history as a primitive example of a superficial society devoid of dignity.

But on this day, I didn't ponder about those relatively recent subjects which strangely seemed incredibly far away. On

this day, I looked forward to going to school and catching up with my acquaintances, as you can't say I really had true friends. A strange blend of inner peace and anxiety took possession over my body as I took a good look at myself in the mirror.

I was tall for my then 17 years of age, 1.84 meters to be exact. I had short black hair cut in a military style and gray eyes. My skin tone was described as being complicated in essence, people often referring to it as grayish or a shade of "dirty pale." I was big and stocky, but not very athletic; I suffered from asthma since I could remember, certain breathing issues impaired my stamina, and had uncontrollable allergies with fast temperature changes, a reason sports in the cold Motherland weren't an option for me. As a result I opted for a more static, intellectual living, since my mind related sports to unpleasantness and unbearable doctor appointments. Moving to Loynne's had however cured my asthma almost completely and even endowed me with increased aerobic stamina. Not that it meant I was especially good at anything, but I was nonetheless achieving normal results, and having so much spare time made me engage in weight-lifting exercises that added to my bulky frame. The only sport I could be said to excel at was fast, brute wrestling, where I didn't rely at all on stamina and used sheer strength and size to take an opponent down. Despite this, I wasn't a conflictive person, and would always rather use diplomacy and dialogue instead of violence.

I walked up to my hulking wardrobe, too massive for the few garments stored inside. I hated fashion. I wasn't used to not wearing my uniform, which comprised my main outfit during the Motherland days. I almost never took it off, just like my schoolmates, not even after classes. We loved our uniform, as it was not only comfortable and versatile, but

good to look at. All of us felt a strange union by wearing our red and white uniforms constantly, and it had become a symbol. But there wasn't such a thing in Loynne's; boarding private schools were the only ones with uniform norms, and public ones let the students dress as they liked. I hated the fact of always having to come up with a new combination of clothes, and of being pressured into having a gigantic set of clothes to choose from like everyone else seemingly had. As a response to this, I had created several "uniforms" of my own design, filled with Communist iconography in order to combat the empty capitalist symbols people pathetically adorned themselves with.

My usual one consisted basically of a red shirt with a yellow Hammer and Sickle on the back and a "USSR" inscription in Cyrillic above, which transliterated read like "CCCP." At the front, on the right part of the chest, it had a Soviet Red Star with a Hammer and Sickle on its center. It passed for a sports shirt, and many people must have thought it was some Eastern European football team. Nobody was sure of what it meant, nor ever bothered to look it up. Loynners were ignorant as that. I even remember some people even asking me if I was Turkish, confusing the Hammer and Sickle with the Muslim star and crescent. It was only natural, as they couldn't understand how a T-shirt did not bear the insignias of a millionaire European football club owned by Russian oligarchs and comprised by Latin American playboy jocks.

My alternatives to my Soviet red shirt included an urban splinter camouflage one, a plain black one – which I sometimes wore in conjunction with a woodland camo military vest – a Soviet Airborne Troops Telnyashka shirt with blue and white horizontal stripes people often mistook for a rugby polo, a khaki Soviet Afghanka winter jacket for rare cold days, and a woodland camouflage Spetsnaz jacket which had origi-

nally come with Russian Federation patches and icons, but I had covered them completely with old Communist symbols to capture the true Spetsnaz spirit, which will always be Soviet. Don't get me wrong, it wasn't like I didn't admire the modern Russian Federation, as even though it was capitalist and had abandoned Communism, it always acted in a friendly manner toward those countries not ashamed of their Soviet pasts, like Belarus and Transnistria, and still supported greatly Communist nations such as Cuba and my former country. Russia was also a friend of any enemies of the US and Western Europe, never a bad thing, and particularly Latin America, where it was maintaining a strong presence to stop US imperialism in the region. But still, I couldn't bring myself to like non-Soviet Russian symbology revived from Tsarist times, as I considered it empty and nationalistic, and which I also associated with the collapse of Communism and its widespread rejection. I also disliked wearing anything bearing modern Russian symbols since it attracted attention from the *nouveau riche* Russian crowds at school, a sorry and ultrashallow Westernized bunch only interested in the things of New Russians, that is, money, status and expensive brands. Wearing Communist clothing was a way to stay true to my ideology and distance myself from these people. Luckily for me, they were so ignorant they didn't even recognize a Soviet flag as part of the history of their country, like most Loynner denizens.

Most of my army wear was based on the Soviet TTsKO camouflage pattern, the acronym for "*trekhtsvetnaya kamuflirovannaya odezhda,*" meaning "tricolor camouflage clothing," and the KLMK pattern, that is "*Kamuflirovannyi Letnyi Maskirovochnyi Kombinezon,*" which means "Camouflage Summer Deceptive Coverall." The TTsKO camouflage was adopted by Soviet and Eastern bloc forces in the '80s and

has evolved ever since, but I obviously preferred the old fashioned Soviet designs. I had nearly all of the available patterns, including several variations of woodland green, desert brown and gray urban splinter. The KLMK, commonly referred to as Beryozka – "little birch tree" – was a pattern consisting of white or yellowish tan shapes over light green, developed in the 1960s by the Soviet Union specifically to counter the widespread use of night vision technological devices by NATO, and it was so effective it's still used in the present era. The shirts, jackets and trousers I wore were all fashioned after these camouflages, and most were proper army surplus I had bought while scavenging at local Sunday flea markets, where people from ex-Communist countries used to sell their heritage to the highest bidder.

My jackets and trousers, being standard army issue, were resistant and full of pockets. This came in handy, as I liked to keep my most precious belongings secure and very nearby, never in my backpack where they could be easily stolen, as I had learned the hard way. All of the trousers I wore ensured high mobility and versatility, much needed to traverse the uneven mountainous landscape of Loynne's. I had several full-length cargos as well as cargo shorts frequently used to combat the high Loynner temperatures. I never wore jeans, since I considered them to be a shameful symbol of the Soviet collapse, aside from too uncomfortable and restricting.

For the Physical Education classes I mainly wore track suits so often associated with Eastern Europeans, in different colors but mainly red and olive green. These track suits served several functions, as they proved to be comfortable clothing well suited for PE classes and protected my identity as an Eastern European caricature. I had other types of Communist clothing at home, but would seldom use them as I had learned my lesson the hard way regarding their popu-

larity with Kannies. The clothes that I wore outside had extensive field testing and mixed in well with that urban hip-hop/Kanny military kitsch that for some reason was the fad at the time.

As for footwear, I almost always wore my expensive SKAR boots, one of the few luxuries I had allowed myself to own. These boots, used by SKAR patrolmen, riot squads and Special Forces alike, provided high mobility as well as protection and were lighter than they looked. I had them only because I found it impossible to get a hold of actual Spetsnaz boots in good condition. For Physical Education classes, I resorted to wearing different types of regular white sneakers I had bought around supposedly trendy shops, and even so did not prove popular enough with the Kanny regime.

Finally, the cherry on top of my uniform was a pair of US styled dog tags which almost always hung from my neck. Along with the SKAR boots, they were the only foreign element adorning my uniform. The dog tags, one written in Russian Cyrillic and the other in English, indicated aside from my name, a mixture of data found in several US military units, such as blood type, designated military branch and religious preference:

ZHAROSTIN

SONNY

O NEG

SPETSNAZ GRU

ATHEIST

Obviously inaccurate and not meant to be taken seriously, my ironical dog tags seemed just a piece of trendy military fashion to onlookers, as many Kannies had started to adopt them, but nobody knew they were in themselves a form of

protest. My decision to make the Spetsnaz GRU my designated military branch was not an infantile make-believe on my part to look cool, but another protest in itself at how Unitedstatians always looked up to the most elite military units as role models, in their case the Army Rangers, the Navy SEALs or the Delta Force. Not a single youngster in the world was safe from their influence and fame, and anybody who played a military First Action Peril video game wanted nothing but to one day become what they perceived elite Unitedstatian soldiers to be. It was strange, given that no US forces remained abroad as they had to be retired due to the heavy budget cuts, and as such one would think their exaggerated fame would evaporate with time. But thanks to propaganda, it didn't. Years later, the standard was still that Unitedstatian military forces were the best of the best in the entire globe, and video games – together with films and TV series, albeit in a minor degree – were to blame. It was a fact that the US military had found in war video games the perfect recruitment tool, and making foreigners enjoy themselves with top-notch games while at the same time being indoctrinated into hating enemies of the US was the best form of passive political propaganda. Latin Americans, Arabs, Russians and Chinese were common targets to shoot at, ethnicities and nationalities vilified with a clear xenophobia in mind and shown as wanting nothing but the complete and utter destruction of the US, always the victim in these fictional digitized wars. It was a fact that the US had reduced its global presence and decreased its military budget, but it was far from being the poor abused underdog portrayed in Unitedstatian books, films and video games; the famous right-wing strategy to gain support through victimization never went out of style.

After dressing up and regaining some consciousness, I took a couple of minutes to reminisce and stare at the pic-

tures I had decorated my room with these last two years; photos of Soviet firearms, landscapes of The Motherland, prominent and revolutionary Communist figures, tanks, helicopters, armored cars, assault rifles, and propaganda posters against the West written in bold Cyrillic fonts. On the wall my bed had been placed against, parallel to the threshold of the door and facing the barred window from where you could see the little patio where I used to hang my clothes, I had placed a gigantic Soviet flag, almost touching the ceiling. Below it, were the portraits of all the Soviet leaders in order, from Lenin to Gorbachev, and directly below them the portraits of Enver Hoxha, Todor Zhivkov, Gustáv Husák, Erich Honnecker, János Kádár, Wladyslaw Gomulka and Nicolae Ceauşescu, to my eyes the most prominent leaders of the Warsaw Pact States; Albania, Bulgaria, Czechoslovakia, East Germany, Hungary, Poland and Romania. Each portrait had the name and occupation of the displayed personality, along with a small flag of its respective nationality.

The adjacent wall, which faced the gigantic wooden wardrobe, had the Soviet and Motherland flags juxtaposed forming a cross, and the portraits of the Fathers of Communism, Karl Marx and Friedrich Engels, hung beside them. On top of their portraits was an excerpt of the Communist Manifesto, printed on a yellow cloth which curved downwards; the inscription in Russian Cyrillic read; *"Let the ruling classes tremble at a Communist Revolution. The proletarians have nothing to lose but their chains. They have a world to win. Workers of the world, unite!"*

The rest of the room had the pictures I described before, surrounding the terrific and organized presentation I had set up in quite a randomized manner, photos placed without criteria or any particular order. It didn't mean they were less important, however. Josip Broz Tito, Mao Zedong, Ernesto

"Che" Guevara, Fidel Castro, Hugo Chávez, Ho Chi Minh and Kim Il-sung had visible and privileged positions on the wall.

Mikhail Kalashnikov, designer of the very best assault rifle known to man, also had a corner reserved, his portrait surrounded by photos of his creation. The same could be applied to Mikhail Mil, Artem Mikoyan and Mikhail Gurevich, designers of aircraft such as the Mil Mi helicopters and the MiG fighter planes, the most versatile, efficient and fearsome military vehicles which had forever instilled a virulent panic in NATO officials at the prospect of a war with the immensely superior Armed Forces of the glorious USSR.

I had another area dedicated to Yuri Gagarin, the first human to go to space, as well as pictures of his space comrades Alexei Leonov and Valentina Tereshkova. The greatest Marshals of the Soviet Union were located not far from the Cosmonauts, from Voroshilov to Zhukov, the vanquishers of the Nazi enemy during one of the Soviet Motherland's most perilous times, the Great Patriotic War.

Nonetheless, not all of my icons were politicians, revolutionaries, soldiers or arm designers; as I had my very own chess corner, brimming with pictures of Anatoly Karpov, Boris Spassky, Mikhail Tal, Tigran Petrosian, Garry Kasparov and Mikhail Botvinnik, the greatest chess players to grace the Soviet Union and the world. Viktor Tsoi, frontman of my favorite music band, Kino, was one of the figures I revered the most because of his austere lifestyle and his politically charged lyrics, instilling Soviet youths to make necessary changes in their nation and prevent it from collapsing, which as we know, inevitably happened. In any case, Tsoi was a revolutionary in every sense of the word, and I might add a patriot. It is wrong for a stagnant system to not be revolutionized by the new generation, and he proved himself a leader and a visionary with his own cultural form of protest.

Regarding the visual arts, I had of course chosen to pay tribute to Socialist Realist paintings, and countless works of Isaac Brodsky, Aleksandr Gerasimov, Mikhail Khmelko and Arkady Plastov adorned my wall, the last one being the creator of my favorite Soviet painting ever, *"Vesna"* — "Spring" —. Cinema played an important role in Soviet art and society too, as it boosted the morale of the Soviet people during periods of hardship with patriotic content and eased the tediousness of labor via comedies; thus, the portraits of filmmakers Sergei Einstein, Sergei Bondarchuk, Andrei Tarkovski, Lenoid Gaidai, Eldar Ryazanov, Georgiy Daneliya, Nikita Mikhalkov and many more greeted me each waking hour as well. A screenshot of the film *"Oktyabr: Desyat Dney Kotorye Potryasli Mir"* — "October: Ten Days That Shook the World" — by Sergei Einstein and starring Vasili Nikandrov as Lenin, was centered around the filmmakers, and I had done so to honor the film's status as the pioneer in modern Soviet cinema. I also had posters featuring the cover artwork of all-time Soviet favorites, such *"Beloye Solntse Pustyni"* — "White Sun of the Desert" — the most popular Ostern film ever made, ritually watched by Cosmonauts before flights and so loved that virtually all of the phrases spoken by characters eventually became everyday catchphrases. *"Brilliantovaya Ruka"* — "The Diamond Arm" — by Leonid Gaidai and starring comedy icon Yuri Nikulin was also so immensely popular virtually every single phrase uttered in the movie became a catchphrase in Soviet society. Soviet cinema was indeed one of a kind, as it was not only brilliantly crafted, but one could sense the artists' love for film-making and not the money end-goal of cinema in capitalist societies. Artists in the USSR were the most genuine of all, as they knew they would never become as disgustingly wealthy as those in the West, and as such were incorruptible, immune to the decadence of West-

ern art. Lenin had so famously said "of all the arts, the most important to us is the cinema." If you ever watch a Soviet film, you'll understand the true meaning behind Lenin's words.

Countless other prominent figures of Socialism and Communism to name them all completely covered the walls. I loved the imperious and imposing look they gave, Cold War at its highest, making the person who entered the room feel intimidated by such glorious images of power, struggle and discipline. The never-ending urge for Socialism governed the room's atmosphere, the faces of those who had rebelled against injustice were what I met each waking hour. And they made me go on. They granted me strength, fueled my ideology, forged my courage; they were the ones who increased my resistance to the venom of Western life, but there was something else. I praised them *voluntarily*. It was my own free will and decision that stuck their portraits to the wall. The power to do so lay inside me. I often pondered over these questions trying to place myself in the shoes of an average human being, with no knowledge of anything I just described, driven by selfish animalistic impulses. And day after day, the question always answered itself; no one seemed to care being like me, and I fed from that feeling. Attributing to myself the maximum quality of uniqueness as a human being amongst these pathetic sheepish individuals effectively gave me enough strength to keep carrying the glorious banner of Communism onwards, forever.

I knew that decorating my room in such a manner was dangerous, especially when living in a place provided by anti-communist gangsters, but I couldn't help myself. My expression for my ideology needed to surface, and it was impossible to keep it bound and restrained. It was a natural extension of something I had basically known this all my life; that Com-

munism was the fairest political and economic system ever crafted by man, efficiently serving society as a whole, and not just an elite of oppressors who starve and exploit their underlings for personal gain, a system which ensured free and universal healthcare and education, a system which promoted culture, sports and intellectualism. Make no mistake though. I was fully aware of the crimes and killings committed under Communist States, about the repression some leaders chose to exercise, but to me they were necessary procedures that helped shape the world in the form we know today. Rapid industrialization is not possible without harsh measures, and a fragile state cannot survive for long without a swift and accurate police response. Both China and the Soviet Union, under the leadership of Chairman Mao and Comrade Stalin, had been transformed from agrarian imperialistic wastelands to industrial world superpowers, and even though China and Russia lead very capitalistic economies in modern times, the Communist successes of Mao's Great Leap Forward and Cultural Revolution and of Stalin's Five-Year Plans could not be denied. But the world was a different place now. Soviet Communism had left its juvenile murdering stage behind since the sensible times of Khrushchev, who denounced crimes under Stalin's regime and introduced policies of Peaceful Coexistence with the West. And starting with Gorbachev, Communism set to have a more transparent and humane approach more similar to Marx's view than to Stalin's theory of Socialism In One Country. Soviet leaders like Gorbachev put more emphasis in a modern and humanitarian Soviet Union, even though ironically, these much needed reforms that youngsters like Viktor Tsoi demanded led to the downfall of the USSR.

In any case, global communications now prevented massacres and repression to go unnoticed like they would have

before, and people were more rebellious to injustice that did not have a point. However, I had never been a sensitive type who cares too much for the deaths of others, even less if they were traitors and enemies of the State. What's more, there was nothing that I didn't despise more in the world than a defector, someone brainwashed by the illusory wealth of the West, someone who would throw out of the window all of his ideals and principles for commodities and capital. I was quite sure that the reason we lived in such a catastrophic world was due to this and the widespread hatred of Communism in general. Anti-Communism during the 20th century had instilled but the utmost fear in the people, making capitalism rise, the right-wing unstoppable and unopposed, left free to pursue their goals while people still dwelled in their misery, while in places like Africa, Asia and Latin America military interventions, civil wars and ethnic cleansings kept the continents weak and separated for corporations to exploit like colonies. I sure was aware of the injustices under Communism, but those injustices were man-made, and man is corrupt. Many Communist regimes disgraced themselves and lost sight of what they stood for. Stalin, for example, vanquished the Nazi enemy and turned the USSR into a massive superpower, becoming the most cunning and ruthless rival of the US even if he did resort to widespread preventive repression to ensure victory. Other regimes, however, got lost in unnecessary cruelty and endless power drunkenness for the sake of it. But I was not worried about this. Nothing could compare to the crimes committed under capitalism. They always said that a child died every few seconds in Africa, and that was always under capitalist conditions. I was sure of my ideology.

But, as I said before, the world was now a different place, and hopefully a peaceful Communist global revolution

neared. The financial reactionary dragon was dying, the people were rebelling, and soon they would create a successor to this failure, be it a new form of Communism from that of the 20th century or a completely new ideology. Perhaps, at long last we would think of a political system where people could be satisfied and lead intellectual lives simultaneously, where rulers would be more transparent and could not harness as much power, being nearer to the people. New theories were already rising regarding the undeniable damage capitalism was causing to the world, arguing that the issue could be solved through Socialist reforms in order to resurrect the world from its lethargic financial chaos and bring economic balance once and for all, suppressing the wealthy elites who possessed the capability to end the recession four times over and imposing limits to individual and corporate wealth. But the right-wing would not stop their deluded and selfish agenda. The liberty for one individual to be insanely rich while the rest of the world starved and dwelled in misery needed to be respected, like the liberty for medieval monarchies to exist in 21st century democracies. In any case, it was a great time to be left-wing; in a highly polarized world divided by left and right, the left seemed to start having a voice, that is, in the rest of the world where poverty was widespread. Needless to say, no general left-wing mindsets could be found in Loynne's Island, where its conservative and anti-Communist citizens got their political indoctrination from both the media and their love for mindless consumerism. Heavily influenced by right-wing Unitedstatian media ever since the Cold War, Loynne's had remained a staunch ally of the US, or better said, a disgusting backyard like Cuba had been under Batista, a territory deprived of any sense of national pride or dignity like Puerto Rico. The legacy had remained engraved forever on the ultra-shallow culture of Loynne's, as not only people

were of mixed Unitedstatian and Hispanic descent, but looked at the US as the ultimate defender of freedom, the "good" guy, mainly from getting their image of the US from TV series, films and conservative pundits. It wasn't weird that many Unitedstatians had chosen Loynne's after the decline of their empire became obvious. After all, what other country would bear to welcome such obnoxious, paranoid, angry and ignorant peoples?

As I stared at the pictures, a thought which had haunted me since abandoning The Motherland occurred to me once more; even though I praised and loved each of the faces and images that greeted me each day after waking up, I also knew their time had gone by. All of them had been dead for quite some time. And most importantly, let us not forget that history should never repeat itself. They had their time, obtained triumphs and committed mistakes, and had passed through history as legendary icons. But that's all they were, icons. And we shouldn't get stuck admiring the same faces all the time. New ones need to emerge to replace the old, and sincerely, I was itching for new ideological leaders or revolutionaries to admire. I had begun to think that maybe, I would never again admire a hero. Communism needed to rise again but in a new form, more suited to the needs of the present era. This had been my ideology for quite some time, and to be honest, I didn't know at the time what to make of it. Struggling against the poisons of Western life had made me blur every single line of dissent amongst leftists of any kind, and as such focused my admiration on every single Communist figure, even contradictory ones like Stalin and Trotsky. My recent confusion regarding how Communism should be practiced did not matter to me at this moment. My only concern was for capitalism to be finally destroyed. And embarking on that endeavor meant I should learn from every single Communist,

Socialist and anti-capitalist that had bothered to develop theories on how to topple the reactionary system once and for all, in hopes of finally creating a new society.

Coming to Loynne's Island also made me understand my sociopolitical perceptions of what can be achieved by capitalism better. In Loynne's, everyone seemed to be almost on the same level economically, a much higher level than that of any other country. The luxurious lifestyle in Loynne's surpassed that of any other average citizen in the world; in new societies like these, the old rules changed. Nobody was starving in the streets, asking for change or mugging people. The island setting granted better control of the limited territory, a feature impossible in overwhelmingly crowded massive lands. The abundance of wealth, allowing citizens to afford incredibly luxurious possessions and amazingly comfortable lives, and the free health care and educational system also threw out of the window Communist rants and thoughts about capitalism impoverishing the common citizens. The widespread atheism was a featured also shared with Communism. People simply didn't have time to believe in gods in such a technologically advanced land geared toward vice, sloth and pleasure. It seemed outdated, a belief of our cranky and uptight grandfathers, a laughable fairy-tale designed to scare us into being "good." Which takes us to another matter; crime was extremely low in Loynne's. Even though some kind of local criminal organization with links to the government had to exist by common sense, you didn't see these big moves in the open, and the petty crimes were practically non-existent, from pick-pocketing to vandalism. Robberies and murders were extremely rare as were drug trafficking and gun smuggling. A government special police force, the SKAR – Special Knowledge Assault Regiment – monitored these activities closely.

The SKAR acted as an undercover police assault unit, border patrol, anti-vice operations and counter-smuggling at the same time, having the right to interfere in whichever way they deemed necessary. The "Knowledge" in "SKAR," was a way of telling people that every single form of information was monitored and controlled by their jurisdiction.

Most SKAR agents entertained themselves watching a young and promising gangster rise gradually in the criminal ladder and kept a close eye on him until they decided it was time to bust his bubble, eventually bringing him behind bars; if things got out of hand, they shot him dead. It was highly unlikely that anybody would care or interfere in any way, and a common Loynner myth was that black helicopters flew at night with the lights turned off, invisible to the naked eye, to dispose of bodies in the middle of the Atlantic.

But the supposed abundance of this welfare capitalist system didn't make the average citizen smarter, morally superior or inherently good; people in Loynne's, driven by arrogance and greed, were usually ignorant straight-forward brutes, living only for their job, which enabled them to afford their expensive lifestyles. Culturally, Loynne's was poor, extremely poor; the museums, the monuments, the landmarks of great historical value and the dead leaders of other countries had been replaced for the futuristic and the meaningless. Expensive and overly elaborate buildings such as twisted looking auditoriums or shopping malls were the only places you would find of Loynner criteria, the things they could afford with capital.

Historically, Loynne's had started out strong, but its contemporary history had been rendered stagnant by the nature dictated by the times, which hadn't been kind to her; the island had first been discovered by Columbus on his second voyage and named Luana, and sighted by Amerigo Vespucci

on his third voyage, who referred to the island as the "Solitary Giant" for its unusually isolated location and size. Later it was shortly conquered by the Portuguese and turned into a neglected colony they officially named "Ilha da Luana," not because of Columbus but because of the daughter of one of the commanding officers who had a daughter with the same name. When the settlers came across the inhabitants of the island they named them "Luanos" as a result. They basically consisted of nomadic tribes of hunter-gatherers and fishermen. The Portuguese slaughtered the natives when they proved to be hostile and refused to convert to Christianity, and fierce battles had ensued as the Luanos seemingly had very strong religious beliefs and deities, even though no statues or carvings could be found. Their legacy dying with them, the Luanos had been the only cultural heritage of Loynne's, and after their onslaught nothing could be known about them. The only thing that could be considered their direct legacy were the various areas across the island named after violent incidents, such as the southeastern town of Fatal Coast in Arias, the western Bloodied Mountain in Servatori, the northern Genocide Bluffs in Kalysand and the Death Glen west of Kalysand Lake. All of these places had witnessed countless deaths, and not only by the hands of the Portuguese invaders. One area of Death Glen, for example, contained a narrow pass between two large hills where the Luanos had ambushed a large Portuguese military unit from above and stoned them to death, first blocking the pass with large rocks and then proceeding to almost bury them alive. After the Luano annihilation at the hands of the Portuguese, the island was invaded by a British armada, poised for conquer and ready to take territories away from the waning Portuguese and Spanish empires. As the conquerors were unable to pronounce the island's name correctly, they kept calling it differ-

ent nicknames until it was usually referred to as "Loynne's Island." When their turn arrived to experience decadence, the British lost the island to the unstoppable expansionism of the United States. Loynne's thus became a British colony until the rise of the United States, and it experienced several skirmishes with the Unitedstatian Navy for control of the island culminating in the War of 1812, when hostilities ceased as a result of the aftermath of the war. Tensions began once more in the 1880s, with the increasing expansion of the US Navy and its vulture-like victory in the 1898 war against Spain. After this war, the building of dreadnoughts brought the US Navy up to par with European countries such as Britain and Germany, which had already signaled a turn of events in global power shift. In 1907, the so-called Great White Fleet of the US Navy demonstrated its reach in a 14-month circumnavigation of the world. The brainchild of US President Theodore Roosevelt, it was meant to demonstrate the US Navy's global capacities. By 1911, the US had begun building superdreadnoughts at a rate that began to rival the British Navy. In 1914, shortly before the First World War broke out, the US Navy began to circumnavigate Loynne's Island in a way meant as a message to Britain, and soon the British Navy mobilized to deter the Unitedstatians. A standoff was produced, but with the outbreak of the war, each side retreated fearful of provoking an even major conflict. US President Woodrow Wilson was committed to a neutral United States, and not willing to stain the global reputation of the US as an aggressive and opportunistic nation, promised British Prime Minister H.H. Asquith that US forces would cease navigating near the island. As WWI raged on, it became clear that tensions between the US and the UK on the Loynner affair would need to cease. Loynne's was thus granted independence in 1916 by the UK, which was fearful of getting dragged

in a naval engagement with the US right in the middle of the war. This was done too so that the British government could rid itself of responsibility should the US want to invade it eventually. The move to grant Loynner independence further hurt the reputation of H. H. Asquith, who went down in shame as a useless wartime leader and was thus replaced by David Lloyd George, who arrived too late to change the status of Loynne's as a British colony and the treaties with the US. The island, though independent, proceeded to become a symbol of dispute between the United States and the United Kingdom, which wanted its overseas territory back. WWI had exhausted Britain's resources and will to engage in a new conflict, and the US as the strengthened victor didn't want to start a new conflict with a former ally after the aftermath of WWI. In a treaty signed by both countries, Loynne's was to be considered neutral territory, and neither country could use the island to perpetuate their power through the establishment of military bases or otherwise, under the threat of war. This applied as well to all other countries interested in conquering Loynne's. That 21st of May when Loynne's was granted independence would later be known as Sovereignty Day, and the forthcoming celebrations which lasted one week long brought forth the Sovereignty Week holiday. As a result of its special international status, Loynne's was neglected until after the collapse of the USSR, when Russian capitalists started investing on the island. Turning small fishing towns into luxurious resort cities, oligarchs from all over the world saw the potential started by the Russians and started transforming the island into what it is today. On the condition that no country could claim full sovereignty on the territory and appropriate it for its own interests, the island was afterward forgotten when neither country wanted to spend too much in the modernization process of such a virginal land, which

would have required enormous amounts of time, effort and capital, all without having the certainty that people would be willing to travel to such an isolated place. Like the dispute over the Argentina Malvinas Islands, at the time it seemed wise to leave Loynne's be, as it didn't have any valuable resources worth starting a massive conflict for.

After the Cold War, however, Loynne's experimented a boom brought forth by Eastern European oligarchs and businessmen. Interested in exploiting new places and investing in tourism, Russians had arrived in big numbers to the island. The result was incredible. Small towns became full-sized cities comparable to those of developed countries, and the Russians started using their respective equivalents to refer to different local areas. Confused by the new names used by Russians, Loynners were unable to get accustomed to them and began producing hybrid ones they were able to pronounce. These new names began to sink in with the population and became the official ones, not to be changed again.

And that was it for Loynne's. That was its entire history in a nutshell. No heritage, no legacy, no culture, unless its obvious Anglo-Saxon one counts. Nothing that tied this land to an ancient culture or sociological historical chapter of any kind, as its original inhabitants had been erased from history and the island never played a significant role of any kind during the two World Wars or the Cold War. It was the shallowest place on Earth, a rock in the middle of the ocean ravaged by colonialism and industrialized by tourism, a land devoid of grace, littered with post-modern capitalist inventions and influenced by the vapid non-culture of the United States.

As I said before, Loynne's drank socially from the most vile junk to come out of the US, to make matters worse. From TV shows to films and music, the decaying Unitedstatian Empire seemed to be giving its horrible swan song to the

world in hopes of once again regaining its old status as an undeniable superpower, hoping to achieve this through its media. The rise of countries like Russia, China, Brazil and India showed clearly that we were in a transitory state where the cultural hegemony of the US was not only withering, but destined to disappear when the country inevitably collapsed. For the first time ever, subcultures around the world now were influenced by trends from other countries other than the US or England, especially Russia, where its growing influence gave people renewed hopes through patriotism and generated negative responses to anything Unitedstatian. What's more, in a bid to stop the heavy immigration of Unitedstatians to the rest of the world, countries thought of strategies well in advance and stopped the madness before it was too late; they all knew how self-righteous and stubborn Unitedstatians were, and nobody wanted their culture infested by people demanding an imperial measuring system, firearms for everyone, Fahrenheit degrees, month/day/year dates and sports no one else in the world played or understood, like what they called "football." It also helped greatly that many countries in Europe had already turned neo-fascist. They knew what they had to do, and preventing the disaster, entire nations repelled most immigrants immediately, but surprisingly, they didn't even need to make an effort. Blinded by their overzealous patriotic brainwash, most Unitedstatians did not want to leave the country considering it the worst type of treason, insisting that the US was still the best place to live in, even if a third of their overall population was living in misery. Those Unitedstatians who had successfully established themselves abroad posed often as Canadians to avoid the shame of looking like traitors even to fellow immigrants, and adapted to the laws and culture of the country they lived in, much like they had forced immigrants to do during the

rule of their empire. Also, they never used the demonym "American" to refer to their nationality when abroad, since foreigners treated it as a sign of arrogance, and had as such adopted the "Unitedstatian" demonym even between themselves. It was a glorious thing to witness the Eagle in agony, and now I could only seek the complete collapse and downfall of the nation as revenge for the demise of the USSR, for the damage they had caused to Communism and the oppression they had exercised in Latin America. China was the new undisputed superpower, and I was glad. Even though little Communism could be found in regular Chinese society, their Communist hierarchy was enough for me. It was to my eyes the official heir of the USSR, and I hoped only that the Dragon could finish what the Bear had started. It was a well-known fact that China was the one responsible for keeping the US afloat economically with its aid – even though the US engaged in free trade, its enormous military budget ate away all resources – but China's plan was one I could perfectly comprehend; they wanted to weaken their enemy in military might. First they had waited until the US was on the verge of economic collapse, and watched as it dismantled base after base abroad, starting with Guantanamo Bay and eventually cutting off support to Israel. All 737 military bases they had once possessed across the world began to be dismantled after countries started treating them as foreign invaders, enforcing their sovereignty as nations. Then they continued watching as the US performed much needed cuts in its armed forces, reducing the number of nuclear warheads and forcing its almighty pacific fleet to retreat. Many Unitedstatian military vehicles and weaponry were as a result sold to the Chinese. As the only country left in the world which still aided them, the US had sold its skin forever, and the whole world was expecting anxiously and with glee its glorious inevitable de-

mise. Eventually, the dispute would be settled between the Russian Two-headed Eagle and the Chinese Dragon, bringing forth the Cold War of the future.

In any case, the Unitedstatian imperialist foreign policy was far from over; aside from its Space Deterrence program, with the aim of policing the world without overseas occupation, the US was setting its sights on its nearest prey, Latin America, the CIA being still very active and already planning the overthrow or assassination of democratically elected leftist leaders. Ricardo Valdés, the new Cuban president in charge of preserving the Socialist Revolution, had already warned about the Eagle's new intentions in Latin American soil. A clear revival of Operation Condor, the public began calling it "Operation Vulture," and the peoples of America began rallying against the newest form of overseas Unitedstatian terrorism, while simultaneously fighting the domestic threat that were the hordes of pro-imperialist right-wing Latin American oligarchs.

But no one in the world seemed to be suffering more from the sickening interventionism of the US government than the Unitedstatian citizens themselves; each and every one of them was monitored at all times by the government, and the skies were littered with automated drones armed with cameras and automatic sniper rifles aptly named "Eagle Eyes," in charge of securing the nation against terrorist threats, able to dispose quickly and efficiently of any suspected hostiles. The US government was like a cockroach with a superb survival instinct, and now that it couldn't police the world as before it concerned itself with policing its domestic territory, spending millions in military drones in order to prevent riots, upheavals or civil wars of any kind. US citizens could be poorer than ever, but nobody was willing to challenge the integrity of their nation yet; the infamous "American Dream" still made a

good job of brainwashing people, while omnipresent magic words such as "freedom" and "democracy" justified any activity the government could be involved in. If I still held a grudge against Unitedstatians, it should be noted that it was because of how stupid they still appeared to be. It was enough to call someone "un-American" or "unpatriotic" to dissuade them from questioning anything related to their nation. They loved "America" more than anything, even if their own country was to blame for sinking them into complete misery. The truth was, a Socialist Latin America was on the rise, and with Brazil being one of the biggest superpowers in the international arena, Latin America was unwilling to bow down to Unitedstatian bullying anymore. With China as a powerful commercial and political ally, there was nothing the US could do, except continuing its decline until it finally did us all a favor and disappeared, maybe fortunately turning into a friendlier and helpful ally instead of the disgusting world bully it had been until the rise of China.

This makes me remember something; if we must acknowledge what the worst feature of Loynne's was, it definitely had to be the fact that for it to exist, the rest of the world needed to keep plunging into chaos and poverty evermore. Not even the booming Socialist Latin America was safe from the effects of the global recession. The gap between rich and poor widened more than ever in almost every country, and the unstoppable population growth we were experiencing only managed to make resources scarcer. The elites became fewer but wealthier, the poor more numerous and weaker. We had been warned, but we never listened. The future was Loynne's Island, a shelter for the lucky citizens of Earth with its overabundance of resources and relatively modest population. Why would anyone living in Loynne's care for the outside world? Just like the US at its peak, Loynners didn't need

to care. As long as money kept rolling in, and the high living standards remained, all was well in paradise, and the rest of the world could go down in flames for all they cared.

I moved to the kitchen to have a little breakfast, very little because nerves and anxiety before school – remnants of Kannovschina-related traumas that I had not yet learned to eliminate – shattered my hunger. Being almost strictly carnivorous, my diet was not very varied. Fruit and dairy products were the only thing I consumed that wasn't meat, as vegetables and salads made me nauseated. I could never understand what was tasty in them. In my country, the meat industry was well-known and agriculture wasn't widespread. As such, large barbecues involving veal or chicken were the country's signature food.

To ease my hunger for the morning hours, I had my usual ration of digestive biscuits and milk, a meal that could keep me going until the time for a chicken croissant arrived. As my hunger was usually shattered by anxiety, I almost always ate at the school canteen before the first class of the day started, when it was empty and without little kids piling up and bashing their heads in to get first to the counter. And by the way, I'll get to the croissants later.

I looked at the clock, which read 07:49, and decided to leave. I crossed the street, where the bus stop was located near a low-level restaurant called "The Gecko Bar," a typical slumhole where the usual Loynner and Brit drunkards used to frequently get their shots. These were the streets of Montenade, or better said, the main road. Whitedale, the neighboring town, was further on directly eastbound, as were the rest of the little towns which followed in succession. To the west lay Pilgrim Coast, the luxurious resort town where I attended high school, an absolute landmark on its own. Pilgrim Coast had started as a small fishing town and eventually

developed to a luxurious tourist destination for people from all over the world. Although usually associated to the Cristobal Atoll resort city because of its proximity, Pilgrim Coast had its own mayor and remained in fact separated from it.

Although not big enough to be considered a full-fledged resort city like Cristobal Atoll or Saphron Bay – each measuring roughly 100 and 200 square kilometers respectively – Pilgrim Coast was the biggest in its class with its approximately 40 square kilometers, and brimmed with activity and businesses of every sort, housing a large beach area known as Crosshair Beach which was one of the most popular points of interest in the entire island, as well as several hills and craters, visited by millions yearly. The clean streets filled with palm trees, bushes and flowers, the luxurious cars and the brand new colorful buildings contrasted heavily with towns like Montenade, which seemed rough and underdeveloped in comparison. All of the towns like Montenade were virtually the same in terms of looks, and colloquially speaking, they seemed like a bunch of houses in the middle of nowhere with a road put in between. It gave you a nice cozy feeling of vastness and peace, without making you feel stranded or exiled from civilization. The weather was usually dry but nice, and some rocky hills and mountains without a hint of grass on them colored the horizon. There were also a few palm trees which had been planted around for tourism's sake, but they felt awkwardly out of place and fake.The architecture of these towns was however, the worst part. Many buildings were unfinished, unpainted or simply abandoned. This was due to the fact that owners of partly completed buildings would not pay taxes as proper ones did. This gave the towns of the easternmost coast of Loynne's a particularly third-world look. In The Motherland, a Communist society stuck economically by thousands of blockades from the West, we wouldn't even

dream of such a thing. Buildings could be decaying, the paint peeling off, the bricks showing, but it was due to the years of economic stagnation and not something devised purely to save money at the expense of beauty. Why would wealthy people that already lived off the rent without working want to save even more money by living in such conditions?

Curious behaviors like these were abundant in the southeast coast, things not usually seen in other areas of the island. Other common practices of the southeast included the choice of living in garages. Some Loynners who only lived off the rent – so as to not say most of them – leased the upper floors of their homes to immigrants, students, young couples or whomever was willing to pay, whilst they limited themselves to living in twin garages that passed as a full house. I never really understood this style of living, and I never actually knew anybody living like this, but I would see it around often. I could see them basically letting the car into the garage and then parking it outside in order to bring some tables and have dinner. Stuff like this was what made me think Loynners had some mental challenges by default. Being middle aged and living in a garage while your tenants lived comfortably in your house, that I could not understand. It showed nothing but a clear and rigid mentality of not wanting to do anything with yourself, to live marginally only to earn profit that you would spend in luxuries far beyond your means like cars or gadgets. In Loynne's, it was more fashionable to have the latest car or phone than having a nice place to live in.

Nearing the bus stop I met my friends Gordon and Claude, both immersed in a subject that had been driving me psychotically insane lately; the growing industry of digital entertainment.

I had met them on the same year when I moved from the Motherland to Loynne's Island. Since I didn't have any

friends back then, and I was feeling alone and rejected by a society in which I didn't feel comfortable, I started to befriend them. At the time I was happy to know I could talk to friendly people and not just athletic stereotypical jocks or socially insecure drones that try to do the same thing everyone else does. But as the years passed, I began to understand that they had created a lifestyle adjusted specifically to their social circumstances. The whole video game thing with Gordon was but routine now, just a minor disturbance. I still remembered when I just arrived on the island and was new in town without any friends, and now I was underestimating them? It was clearly unfair I thought, but lately I was realizing how repetitive, uninteresting, hollow and freaky they could turn out to be. A life dedicated to avoiding the problems you encounter can't be good at all.

Gordon greeted me cheerfully as I approached him. He was one of the few students from my high school who lived in Montenade, and his residence was located nearby Rot Volka, in the easternmost chalet of Thomas Drive. Physically he was fat and short, measuring approximately 1.70 meters, positioned in a stance reminiscent of a toad, with his legs bent slightly inwards; plump and heavyweight looking, with dark eyes, overgrown curly hair which he never combed and a badly shaven beard, one was forced to think about the hours of dedication to virtual entertainment he must have spent to neglect his appearance in such a manner. Gordon used to have a standard military crew-cut before, pretty much like everyone back then, me included. Having a crew-cut was a symbol of sympathizing with Kannies and their regime, whereas weird hairstyles or long hair of any kind was seen as infringement of the unwritten rules punished by a subsequent Kannovschina treatment. For my relatively long natural hair, which wasn't particularly shaped after any style, I

had been ostracized, ridiculed and harassed by literally almost everyone I came across. I never had my hair grow long again after that, and instead, tried to maintain a trace of individuality leaving it spiky on top and gradually military shaven on the lower part. For some reason, it made my fake status as a Russian seem more believable.

"Hey dude," Gordon said, without looking at my eyes, smiling faintly like he tended to do. I shook his hand, a plump, fleshy mass, drenched in disgusting cold sweat.

"How are you doing?" I asked with my usual whisper of frustrated boredom, knowing what replying would unleash upon me.

"Fine, fine. I finally reached 485,000 points in SternSpielt, man. Feelin' that shit, dude, totally feelin' it. I'm a Galaxy Lord now. I have a fleet the size of the guy that's 45th on the spaceboard. I'm gonna totally own his galaxy by the time school finishes. I sent him all my elite space top commanders. He's gonna feel the sting now. Look I'm playin' right now!" he said, as he pulled out the world's most expensive and powerful wireless phone, the Hipps-Tear Cellu-Light.

SternSpielt – meaning "Star Game" in German – was a revolutionary game everyone was into; it consisted of resource management nonsense and algorithm ridden space battles. Besides, it was free of charge, spread worldwide and translated into every language possible; a total wet dream for people like Gordon.

"Oh, yeah ... terrific," I replied with a sigh, knowing I would not be able to make Gordon shut up. During these moments I only thought about what I could do to distract him from his rants, but no matter what I came up with he would always go back to the same subject, so I had learned to stop trying, stop caring; I had absolutely no way of escaping from these torture sessions.

"Yeah, I have managed really well, you see, if you consider how many resources you spend in daily trips through space trying to avoid space pirates you'll notice you can save up to a million in fuel per night, given you have a fleet as large as mine, but then there's compatibility options and management features in your GamEsprit system too you know, like—" This slang was what pissed me off the most about these gamer types. Gordon proudly owned a GamEsprit, like everyone in Loynne's and much of the European market, something that would consume every minute of his spare time; *gaming* – the word was so hard to take seriously – constituted a 24/7 habit. Something that I had always wished to know was how on Earth the *gamers* themselves could cope with studying and playing so much at the same time, and playing SternSpielt was Gordon's way of saying "*I play even when I'm not playing.*" To these people, in their culture, someone like that was considered an utter complete undeniable God; as you may assume, Gordon here was one of those Gods.

My ears had, as a matter of fact, been shut and sealed at that moment, my eyes fixed on the road, trying to scrutinize the purple bus in the distance, the only thing that could save me from this daily ordeal. "*Why don't you shut up, you slimeball arrogant sad bastard,*" I thought, being at my very best behavior nodding and saying "yes yes yes" to any piece of incomprehensible gibberish he said. Claude joined in and engaged in a deep and meaningful conversation with Gordon about intergalactic fuel, battle cruisers and space-tech R&D centers, gaming terms which I thought I would never be able to understand or care about. Claude was a thin and tall boy, dark skinned, with spiky brown hair and dark eyes, which always seemed to be lost, spaced out, wishing to vanish from wherever he was standing that wasn't his house, apparently.

He was a sly silent type, the kind that surely analyzes every-thing he sees without ever interacting with his environment, forming a documentary of sorts inside his learning center. If Claude appeared in a movie, he would have been a prop, not an extra. He dressed like every person in Loynne's Island did at his age, expensive sneakers, sports pants and shirts, all clad in multinational corporate logos, and carried a suitcase-like folder for his school belongings. These were the kind of clothes that you would wear in Loynne's when you didn't know what your true identity was, or when you didn't even have enough character to pretend you had one. If you wanted to take the case of not having an identity even further, you could dress as a Kanny, sporting expensive and colorful sport shirts and shorts, usually by Unoq, a major global mega-corporation known for its sponsor of football, basketball, tennis, formula one, any kind of sport. Their logo, a curvy check mark over a leaping lioness, was featured on everything that was of Kanny liking. They wore these stupid baseball caps to the side and without placing them fully against the head, so that they were loose and about to fall any second, but never did. Shaven legs and military buzz cuts were also their thing, and some of them even had funny shapes or writ-ings in their shaven skinny numbskulls, like "100% Mafia," "KANNY KING" and more.

Kannies were jocks, high-handed bullies, fake, pretentious wannabe street thugs with loads of money and parents who maintained their parasitic existence since they did not work, or if they did, they were waiters, janitors, construction work-ers or gardeners. The Loynne's Island Ministry of Education had an extremely varied and diverse system to suit people like these, the kind who can only exchange workforce for money, neglecting intellect and ignoring they are able of any creative process. I did not regard them as people in any way.

They were simply animals one step higher on the evolutionary ladder, but clearly below intelligent human beings. Some
people never develop a sense of morality, a conscience, a
philosophy, an ideology. These people were exceptional. At
the peak of civilization, with its modern technology, abundant resources and widespread free learning sites, they remained stuck in centuries long ago forgotten. I blamed Western civilization and its clear cultural decadence.

Kannies also seemed to be completely similar in biology;
their bodies were slim and athletic, their skin suntanned and
smooth, their jaws square and thin, some of them looked
cunning like foxes, others smart as donkeys. But what surprised you the most was that in most cases, unless they had
some facial hair or different height, you could not tell them
apart; they were both a memetic and genetic stereotype, an
example which had to be avoided and above all, a social class
and fad which served as nothing but handwork for the economy; they were the ones who served us in restaurants,
cleaned our rooms hotels, mowed the grass and watered the
plants each morning. This does not mean I regard people
who do these jobs as worthless, as I respect all kinds of workers; a profession does not dictate character, and all workers
are worthy of admiration as long as they do not get sucked in
by mediocrity. Lenin once said 'any cook should be able to
run the country', and I think it describes my mentality quite
well. However, Kannies did not have any respect for their
professions, and only did jobs like these to get money for
their flashy cars and going nightclubbing with their bitches,
attracted by professions which did not require a lot of prepa-
ration. As such, they were job-slaves often recommended by
relatives – almost all Loynners were inexplicably cousins
between themselves – so a cousin in the Ministry could recommend a slightly retarded brother for a Ministry job like

garbage disposal which was really well paid and didn't involve too much hassling around. Kannies with shitty jobs done usually by immigrants were actually considered lucky by people at school, looked up to because of their economic emancipation. Many of these Kannies trafficked with drugs and actually bought them with this money, generating an illegitimate source of income that proved quite beneficial and easy. If the drug trafficking went wrong, they could always get money from their jobs at the end of the month, and relax, converse and chill in a luxury hotel where they did everything they wanted except for actual work. This was the Loynner general mindset; do as less as you can, never do extra hours, if you brake it blame an immigrant, and go to the doctor often to get medical happy holidays for your stressful life.

My thoughts on these subjects, following classic, orthodox Communist doctrine, were that these people served no purpose to the state. Actually, most people didn't. In this world of greed and luxury, nothing of real value was produced. Everything was vapid, fake, and meaningless. Kannies came to mind as mankind at its worse, but the general population was spiraling downwards gradually like it had never done before. The current state of welfare we lived in was a bubble about to pop, not with a gradual and weakening whimper, but with the loudest, most violent bang.

The 202 line finally appeared in the distant horizon and I smiled at the sight of it, as it meant one part of the day had finished; listening to Gordon's confusing rants about virtual entertainment, thinking the kind of trains of thought I just described and dying in the morning cold. I didn't refer to the bus as 'Purple Wonder' for nothing.

When entering the Forge Monsoon bus I noticed Gordon was still talking to Claude about SternSpielt, and continued to do so for the remainder of the ride. Claude limited his

actions to listening, as usual, and letting out an occasional line in a monotonous, boring tone. It really seemed like he didn't enjoy the offline life too much. I paid for the ticket in cash, as I never used sliding cards like the rest. I paid the driver with 1 cross and 5 palms, the currency of Loynne's; 100 palms were worth 1 cross. Palm coins came in values of 1, 5, 10, 20 and 50, and crosses in 1, 2, 5 and 10. Notes came in values of 20, 50, 100, 200, 500 and 1,000 crosses. As for me, I had never seen a note higher than 50, which was the most common note in circulation for lower-middle class working people and jobless youths. Notes of values higher than 100 were only used by the extremely wealthy, usually for purchasing high-end consumer goods or cars, although this practice was now heavily in decline due to the high usage of debit cards.

Gordon and Claude seemed to momentarily forget all about me while entering, which was a nice cue for me to find a solitary seat, plug my earphones in and admire the landscape of Loynne's. I could finally listen to my music in peace and sink into the wonders of my exclusive world provided ironically by a Hipps-Tear Hipp-Man music player, the world's undefeated, unbeatable best portable music player ever made. Having a high resolution LCD screen with touch capabilities and designed to be worn like a wristwatch with a removable strap, the little square silvery device was what saved me from listening to this kind of gamer gibberish, and plus I had found it on a bench so I had never been a Hipps-Tear customer to begin with. I would have never paid that amount of money on a stupid toy in my situation.

Listening to Kino's *"Zvezda Po Imeni Solntse"* — "The Star Called Sun" — I sat back, closed my eyes and breathed deeply, the Soviet rock band always sending me to a state of relaxation, if not nostalgia. I chose to play this song on this special

day as it made me remember the very first scene of the 1988 film *"Igla"* — "The Needle" — a very famous Soviet film by Rashid Nugmanov about drug addiction starring Viktor Tsoi. Kino always accompanied me wherever I went, and when I wasn't listening to Kino's youthful but sorrowful rock I enjoyed the greatest, most patriotic military marches performed by the Red Army Choir. I liked the duality of enjoying these two different sides of the Soviet Union, the rebellious one and the disciplined one. Anything from the glorious USSR fueled my will to go on and cope with the boredom and frustration of my miserable Western existence.

The ominous voice of Tsoi shut me off from reality as the Forge Monsoon drove smoothly into Arias Road, 22.4 kilometers of drive remaining until we had reached Pilgrim Coast. The ride to the resort town lasted approximately 25 minutes, as the road was pretty straightforward and without stops.

I looked through the window to entertain myself. Though surrounded by the grasp of capitalism, it was more uplifting than the poverty and misery the late Motherland had been subjected to in its last years. It was joyful to watch the island's geography, seeing the mountains in the distance, the luxurious cars, the lack of poverty, the cleanliness; passing through the majestic Saphron Highway, which connected the main touristic districts in the South, vehicles of the main car manufacturers freely accelerated and displayed their raw horsepower. A white Madison Escapade, a luxurious and titanic SUV, roared as it passed the bus by and cut its path. Madison's main competitor, Washington, another United-statian car maker, responded with the Escalator, a six-wheeled monstrosity. It was now a trend for the wealthy to own 6x6 luxury SUVs, and the Escalator was the pioneer in the field. There was a funny ad for it, which featured the

eponymous vehicle climbing a very tall mountain in the shape of a mall escalator, with the tag line "Reach for the Escalators," and had become a sort of running gag with Loynners.

Several expensive vehicles of Germanic and Scandinavian precedence sped up and kept up with the Monsoon. It wasn't rare to often see the respective flagships of the main car manufacturers. *Großdeutsches Wagen*, or simply GDW, the leading German automobile maker in the world, had then delivered a sporty car known as the Prinz Sportlicht, a powerful and versatile two-door convertible that's still heavily in use nowadays. GDW always baptized its cars after the titles of royalty hierarchy. The model in question gracefully sped up and disappeared from sight while turning left and heading toward Saphron Bay, giving a loud and echoing roar.

After a while, an ominous and dark-blue sedan occupied the GDW's place as it drove past the bus and shone as the morning sun reflected the palm trees on its magnificent pearlescent paintwork. It was the work of Hades-Larsson, a Swedish luxury car maker. The model I saw was a Drakkar V1. Hades-Larsson often named its vehicles after Viking longships, and classified them with the letter V, standing for "version." The smaller the number, the better and more equipped that version of the car was. As you may assume, a Drakkar V1 was the definition of success in car form.

All vehicles in Loynne's were certain to have four-wheel drive, or in the case of large Unitedstatian SUVs, six-wheel drive. It was almost a necessity and not a luxury, given that wherever you went in Loynne's you were sure to find a difficult slope. As such, vehicles were also required to have a certain minimum of horsepower or they would not be allowed in the streets by the Traffic Department. Powerful 6x6 SUVs or sedans with four-wheel drive were as such amazingly ordi-

nary in Loynne's, and it added to the island's glamour that inexpensive low-tier vehicles were not seen anywhere. The US exported plenty of vehicles to Loynne's for this reason, and made sure to make new models each year so as to incite Loynners in selling their older unpopular models and buying the shiny new iterations. Without even realizing, Loynne's was helping in keeping the US economy afloat with this spending excess. The most common SUV brands were Forge, Madison, Washington, Montana and Chevraun, each with their own flagship best-selling series, which came in various different versions: from Forge the Patriotic Duty, from Madison the Escapade, from Washington the Escalator and the Browser, from Montana the Stampede, the Tusk and the Charge, and finally from Chevraun, the Suburbia and the Plateado. The six-wheeled Unitedstatian monstrosities were such an ordinary sight that they added to the general pro-Unitedstatian feel present on the island.

During this bus ride there were a couple of landmarks you would see. As the Monsoon drove through the Pilgrim Ring Highway – a highway system obviously in the shape of a ring, connecting Pilgrim Coast to the easternmost towns like Montenade – large deserted sections could be seen at both sides of it. Bunkers from times when Loynne's had been the scenario for several territorial disputes were a common sight, as were several wind power generators scattered across the dry hills. Then there was the world famous sign, a gigantic field on the slope of a hill burned to form "PILGRIM COAST" in massive lettering. Many tourists backpacked their way there and took photographs to mark their complete sightseeing tour of the town.

Passing through the busy Dakota gas station and the second-hand car lot, you knew Pilgrim Coast lay just ahead. In any case, this could be considered its secondary and much

less glamorous entrance, only used when traveling from the unimpressive southeast. The main way was usually thought to be via Saphron Highway, another highway system designed to take people through Saphron Bay and Cristobal Atoll, the most luxurious resorts of the South. Cristobal Atoll was the neighboring archipelago of islands connected to the mainland by two gigantic bridges, Citadel Gate Bridge in Pilgrim Coast and Gatling Bridge in Saphron Bay. My school was just a few blocks away from Citadel Gate itself, positioning us at the southeastern limits of the town.

The bus made its way through the district of Waverly Heights, an exclusive neighborhood mostly owned by Russian businessmen. Expensive cars were often parked outside large villas, the best of the best from high-performance manufacturers. GDW König models – sturdy and lavish SUVs – were often seen parked beside the hyper-powered sports cars. Traditionally rich business people often preferred GDW or Hades-Larsson SUVs rather than Unitedstatian six-wheeled monstrosities, things they considered to be distasteful products aimed at the *nouveau riche* and the imprudent.

Further on, passing the Paradise Land resort hotel and the Pilgrim Coast Academy of Dance, was the area known as Little London. As the name implied, this medium-sized district of Pilgrim Coast had been slowly conquered by the British, the Irish and anyone Anglo-Saxon, including Australians, Canadians and New Zealanders. Sometimes it was even home to Unitedstatian exiles too ashamed to admit to their nationality, humbly trying to stay off the radar as Canadians. The district had a heavy emphasis on Indian Tandoori and Chinese restaurants, something Anglo-Saxons seemed to have taken into their culture due to colonialist experience, increasing the diverse population to Asians as well. Pubs where everywhere you looked at, accompanied by all-inclusive deal

hotels which knew how to market to the British and their love for staying as much away from the outside world as possible. Cheap all-inclusive deals were said to keep the island's economy afloat at all times, no matter how dire the economic climate could have been.

And then, beyond a myriad Irish pubs and Chinese souvenir shops, lay the marvelous Paradise Plaza, a landmark on its own, representative icon of the island's culture of luxury. This was the easternmost district of Pilgrim Coast, and its most important one, as unlike the rest it didn't simply serve the purpose of tourism or residential suburbia.

Paradise Plaza brimmed with the diversity so well-known on the island. Roaming the streets were people from all countries, races and religions. Some looking freshly arrived from a plane and combing the streets for work, others carrying on with routinary Loynne's paperwork. Under the morning spell, the people seemed to operate on mechanical instinct switching their brains off, wandering to and fro always making me wonder what their motivations could be. At this point, the Monsoon stopped at the Paradise Plaza bus station. This was yet another landmark, the core of all activity in the city and its main transport route. A park was located north from it, where a huge fountain themed after the Greek god Poseidon stood imperiously overlooking the station. The fountain had to be at least 7 meters tall, and featured a statue of the god of the sea sitting on a throne-carriage with a trident in one hand, as three horses seemed to pull it forward with vast strength. Loynners had a fascination with Greek architecture, and most constructions were fashioned after exotic Greek designs.

Paradise Avenue, one of the busiest and most important avenues in Pilgrim Coast, was home to the bus station and a large business-oriented block. The largest mall in Pilgrim

Coast was located on that block, the Méndez Center, which featured all kinds of stores and businesses. Also, the gigantic Citadel Highway surrounded the entire district; my school was located a few meters away from it, and it lead directly to the eponymous bridge, the connection to Cristobal Atoll.

Arriving at the school's nearest bus stop, one block away from the Méndez Center, I got off the Monsoon shaking off Gordon and Claude as fast as I could, who fortunately were too absorbed in their conversation to notice my absence and soon mixed in with the other students. I walked down to the school, which was divided into three smaller buildings named West Wing, Main Building and East Wing. The whole building was painted vanilla, with sets of small yellow tiles on the outside grounds and red ones on the roof. The floors in the interior where usually comprised of huge cream colored tiles, while cheesy yellow tiles covered up to half of the white walls. For security measures the school featured white bars protecting the windows and its entire perimeter was protected by a tall gray brick wall with a towering green fence. The Main Building had upper floors protected by balusters, and from the street level you would see the students piling up in between classes conversing and resting their arms on the balusters. The school's sidewalk, comprised of small gray tiles, was littered by different kinds of trees including the omnipresent palm trees of Loynne's Island, which I often loved to stare at during those boring long hours inside.

Right in front of our school was a barren area, the school's sports complex which was beginning to be built at the time, and at the end of the street there were several unfinished blocks, huge concrete slabs cutting off access. They would have connected the school to a system of roads that at the time was under construction as well. The slabs had been there for so long that they had become a sort of landmark, a

part of the school itself. Graffiti didn't usually last a lot in the most luxurious areas of Loynne's as it was often removed for the sake of beauty and tourism, but the graffiti decorating these concrete slabs had endured the passage of time effectively. The disturbing messages, written by what I thought were trembling hands searing with rage, often made me think what sort of stories these concrete slabs could have witnessed; written in four of the seven slabs was a red graffiti with the message "*LEAVE HER ALONE OR I KILL YOU,*" then one which occupied the remaining three slabs read "*SOCIETY BREEDS INSANITY,*" and occupying the same slabs below it another that read "*HALFWAY BETWEEN MEDIOCRITY AND CONFORMITY LIES TRUE HAPPINESS.*" Surrounding these messages, which for some reason had become incredibly respected and thus remained unmodified, were the stylized names of different crews of taggers.

Crossing the main gates and watching the usual crowd of students hanging out by the main stairs, I recognized a lot of people from previous years but decided to just ignore them; I hated meeting acquaintances randomly while they told me their lives and personal big stupid non-stories. It was just a formality after all and they would forget about me as soon as they broke visual contact anyway. Instead, I marched firmly to the Assembly Hall, a big room full of chairs which was used for important events, also the place where the principal would give the yearly lecture, welcoming students into the new school year. I mixed in between the crowd to see if I could catch a glimpse of any friends, and was glad to know Wolfgang Emmerich was there, among all the unknown people I had never seen in my life, transferred from other schools.

"*Konnichiwa, Doshi!*" Wolfgang said with utmost joy, greeting me with a quick and heartfelt military salute. Ob-

sessed with Japanese culture, Wolfgang often referred to me as *Doshi,* Japanese for "comrade," while I used the Russian equivalent instead.

He was a stocky looking guy, slightly shorter than me, of mixed Unitedstatian and Thai descent, and he always gave off the wrong impression of being fat when he was simply corpulent. An odd mix, Wolfgang had sparkling blue eyes, brown skin, shoulder length jet black hair and round facial features. He always wore glasses even though he didn't need them, and sported a unique Japanese haircut not very popular in Loynne's, which consisted of shoulder-length hair with a bun at the back, like a samurai. Given he actually straightened his hair to make it appear more Asian, Wolfgang was an example of someone immediately shunned because of his atypical appearance. His clothes consisted mostly of military cargos like mine, usually in woodland or desert camouflage, and olive green and desert brown T-shirts. Sometimes, however, he wore normal casual clothes, the kind you would see Loynners wearing.

His personality was particularly odd as well, given he always compared the events that happened to him in real life to those of his favorite video games or films. He was another video game freak, perhaps too much of one, but unlike Gordon, he was greatly interested in philosophy, life, human values and honor. This all led Wolfgang to get extremely interested in his Asian heritage and become obsessed with Japan's military culture, praising the samurai as the ultimate warrior. In his case, his interest for military culture derived from a scenario I did not share, which was being the son of a professional soldier. Wolfgang's father was a former US soldier of Danish descent who had decided to settle in Thailand after serving there in the Cold War, and soon met his future wife there. After Wolfgang was born they decided to move to

Loynne's. Like many people of Unitedstatian descent raised on the island, Wolfgang rejected and abhorred his ancestry; it seemed he had found refuge embracing his Asian heritage, later moving on to admiring and respecting Japanese culture. Although he didn't respect Thailand as much as Japan, Wolfgang had developed something for all types of Asian cultures and countries, much like I did with all the different Communist States of the 20th century.

Wolfgang, like everybody else, had been told a carefully constructed lie; specifically, that I was an ethnic Russian born in the Moldavian SSR from Russian parents, and that after the fall of the USSR and the republic's dissolution on the 27th of August, 1991, my parents had decided to move to Loynne's so as to escape the escalating violence of the War of Transnistria, all to safeguard a peaceful living for their son in a stable country. The Moldavian SSR had experienced such a similar scenario to the one my country was then going through that I never felt I was lying, and as such I could always tell this story with a straight face. Wolfgang, regarding this fictional story of mine, had thus always believed I was self-righteous on anything regarding Russia and the Soviet Union in general for not having been granted the opportunity to stay and fight for my country, to revive the USSR in that defining moment in history. He was right; there was nothing I would have liked more than to stay and fight for Socialism in my country. I had always resented being sent to the island, and I believed part of my refusal to integrate into its society was due to this.

"Glad to finally see a friendly face, *Tovarish*. Did I miss anything?" I asked, looking around in alert like I always did when in a crowded area. Like my comrade, I hated crowds and always preferred to be left alone. This was the reason we had started to befriend each other in the first place.

"Nah, we've been here waiting for the teachers to show up and tell us where we're supposed to go. I really hope we can be in the same classroom again, just like last year, *Doshi!*"

After a small interval, the teachers finally arrived neatly in two rows. The principal, a fat and balding man pushing 50 years of age, was at the end of these rows and placed himself behind the microphone.

"Students, future pride of Loynne's island, you've shown up once more to prove you are ready to take on one more year of learning, experiencing and in general, improving yourselves. I'm very proud to see that the quantity of people has increased since last year, I'm seeing many new faces, and I can assure you, you are definitely not wasting your time. Spending a year in one of the most brilliant schools in Loynne's Island is a thing you can talk about to show off: each year that passes, our students travel to the mainlands to put their knowledge and skills in practice, demonstrating the professionalism we possess. Your teachers will be like your friends this year; please, treat them with the respect they deserve. Our team has since developed and improved, and they are ready to teach you all they know about every-thing, life itself included. As students, your duty, no, your obligation is to honor them, respect them and feel overpow-ered by such vast knowledge, by the things they will enlight-en you with."

The speech, as every year before it, went on and on for an infinite, monotonous amount of time, decorated with im-portant sounding words only a third of the people there could probably define and praising the teachers insanely – often saying how they should be treated with respect from time to time. The funny thing was that he said nothing new; things

about how great the school was, how much we should study because life was hard without a professional career, how much effort and dedication it took to go forward and the usual.

After the principal's speech, the teachers took the students to their classrooms; it was usually chaotic and disorderly. I guessed that about four hundred students were in the massive room. Wolfgang disappeared between the stampede and I lost him from sight.

I ran around in desperation searching for him, since I had no other clues as to where the classroom was, or knew anybody destined to it. I never read the lists, mostly due to the fact that I couldn't possibly browse through all of the countless bulletin boards scattered across the Main Building's lobby. Typical thing that only happened to me. I began to consider quitting and exiting the building in shame when I noticed that the corridors were empty, but a booming grave voice relieved the pressure.

"Sonny! Over here *Doshi*!"

"I thought I lost you for good, *Tovarish*. Where were you?"

"I began following a group thinking they were from our class, and they told me they weren't, so I began asking people and nobody was from our class ... What should we do?" I looked straightly at him with open eyes, my head tilted downwards and my eyebrows raised, not quite believing we faced the prospect of having to check room after room in the entire school.

"So what now?" I asked, irritated.

"I think our grade is 1-B, but I told you, I asked around and nobody was from our class. Maybe nobody that's from our class came, you know how it is, some people choose to skip the presentation and just come on the following week."

"Yeah but I can't believe absolutely nobody came, there

must be a couple of them, how many people did you ask?"

"Three or four, what was I going to do Sonny, you know how this people are, you can't even talk to them, some of them didn't even acknowledge me and just walked past me!"

"Typical disgusting Loynners ..." As soon as I said that while turning on a corner, my eyes immediately recognized a familiar, frightening figure. The presence of Jason Clark Vega eclipsed the joy of daylight. Even though this fearsome sighting was to be expected, it was never welcome.

Jason Clark, commonly referred to as JC, was what you would describe as the undisputed king of the school. A star athlete, captain and striker of the football team, boyfriend of the hottest girl and everything else you can pull out of a cheesy Unitedstatian film. It seemed surreal, corny and made up, but that's the way it actually was. After all, every type of fiction has a real world basis, and it is an undeniable fact that violent dimwits — especially Unitedstatians — are encouraged to dedicate their lives to the military or to sports in a bid to channel their psychopathic bloodlust to more socially accepted occupations, turning into amoral mindless jocks whose behavior is celebrated and accepted by the establishment.

Jason's power came from several sources. Firstly, his father was a successful Unitedstatian oil tycoon who had been able to detect the financial crisis and move his operation to Loynne's. Secondly, his mother was a lawyer who had once been a hot high school queen in her youth, just like Jason's girlfriend, but was now a drunken surgically operated mess with a slit for a mouth and a saggy decaying face. The typical woman who knows when to cling to a man far more successful than she'll ever be after her looks are long gone.

There was not a thing in the world Jason didn't possess except for proper parenting, education and a good set of values, again, like most Unitedstatians. He did as he pleased

in every way; he could bang any broad he desired, even if his girlfriend, Monika Strössner, supposedly engaged in similar activities of her own. And that takes us to the third subject of his power.

Monika was a majestic blond of South-African and Germanic descent, perfectly tanned, tall, muscular and curvy, an Amazonian bombshell with a beautiful and deadly face with hazel serpent eyes, who spent her time running in the elite track team, playing handball, practicing kick-boxing and swimming. Her trophy room was as full as Jason's, if not more. Her parents seemed to be physically non-existent, much like Jason's, and her tomboyish desire to stomp and harass anyone who could rival her power had led people to speculate whether she was actually a repressed lesbian, though no evidence ever surfaced to support the theories. As a side note, she had a very suspicious looking tattoo on her right arm, her own surname with gothic fonts and a couple of SS lightning bolts in the middle, stylizing it as "ströSSner." The tattoo was simply an eerie demonstration of what went on in her mind ideologically. She believed herself superior not because of her success or economic class, but of her race. Fascist scum like her deserved no right to live.

Due to her sex appeal alone, most guys – and some girls – would have given anything to submit themselves to Monika's ruthless tender pleasures, but the given public image was that she and Jason were made for each other, forever. As such, she obviously didn't mess with people around the school circle. She picked her gigs elsewhere, in places far above the social ladder where Jason would have looked like a harmless little puppy. This was sometimes debated, as people pondered whether Monika truly ruled the school and Jason was the face behind it all. Her dominant nature and violent temper made her as fearsome as her loving partner. Jason and

Monika used to be inseparable, and even when one of them was alone, you could always find the other nearby.

However, Jason obviously remained unchallenged as legendary school bully. His strong athletic build, fast reflexes, violent mood swings, infamous amoral practices and dangerous and powerful connections all contributed to making his presence something to be avoided at all costs. I could only think of one person strong enough to challenge this character, and it was Mike Levanter, an imposing behemoth I had befriended on my first year. Even someone like him dare not challenge JC. At the possibility of beating him easily with one hand like I knew he could, he'd have to forever endure the torment of an all-out Kannovschina aside from police trouble and a fat lawsuit. And I say police trouble because of Jason's best friend Joakim Miller, the son of the Chief of Police. It was basically the reason I had to endure Kannovschina from Joakim and his gang on the 3rd Grade, but thankfully, not too much. I even ended up getting him off my back for good after a few months. Now that he and Jason had finally found true love in each other's arms, the alliance was indestructible and all powerful. This sort of corruption and "friends of the friends" alliances were widespread in Loynne's, but not as much as I figured they would be on my land of origin nowadays.

Luckily for us, Jason, Monika and his cronies were just entering classroom 101 and didn't see us. Had they noticed our presence, I could not have predicted the outcome. I had in fact overcome every type of fear and paranoia I had held back in the day, but the sight of Jason in a lone corridor with his lackeys was enough to give you paralysis. He was apparently calmer recently, but he hated people like me and Wolfgang with a passion; firstly for being immigrants, and secondly for being legal immigrants he couldn't kick out of the island with

his influence. Rumor had it that just out of malice, he'd frequently do that. I had evaded encounters with him for too long now, and I intended on it remaining that way. I was still trying to erase from my memory the few run-ins we had had in the past, although compared to other unfortunate bastards, mine could be considered a subject of envy.

Trying to locate more people who could help us on the floors above, we met with an older guy. He was considerably taller than me, rivaling JC's impressive 1.96 meters, completely clad in black, wearing a jacket with a white shirt and red tie. His pale skin and dark hair gave the impression that he shone against the yellow tiles of the school walls.

His attire was an extremely odd and brave choice for a student, and I wondered how he had even managed to survive entering the school without having a thousand Kannies harassing him. He acknowledged me with a stern, transfixed expression, and his mouth wrinkled into what I discerned to be a smile. He knew the way toward the classroom however, and pointed Wolfgang in the right direction without stopping his strange staring. He went away later, with a slow and steady pace, almost a glide. I ignored why he was there at that moment unless he was lost too, or why he knew to what classroom we had to go, but he proved useful enough. I immediately stopped caring about this strange and awkward moment when I remembered what I had to face next, and the usual nerves in the lower abdomen began to manifest themselves again.

The classroom was in the second floor, at the end of the corridor to the left; Room 206. We stood there a few moments looking at the door, taking a deep breath, expecting to find something comforting and relieving. At least JC wasn't there.

"Who's gonna go in first?" Wolfgang asked.

"Well ... does it matter?"

"No, but ... you go in first."

"Aw, come off it, Wolfie. Haven't you had enough years to be shy?"

"C'mon Sonny, cut the crap, just do it." I opened the door slowly, giving Wolfgang a general look of disapproval. He always made me face the situations he found uncomfortable the most.

There weren't as many people as I thought there would be, and they all stared at us as the door noisily creaked. I took a moment to analyze all of the faces and walked toward the first familiar person I saw. The other guys seemed the archetypical Loynner scumbags cut from the same sheet of paper by the same set of scissors, so no need to narrate much there. Not specifically Kannies, but also not outstanding either. Just simpletons, to give them a category. Simpletons interested in simple things, talking about generic, boring stuff. The classroom had also an unexpected superior female population, which was never a bad thing.

Ryan Mantis dedicated me a strong grin as one or two zits on his face dangerously turned volcano-white. He was one of the few people I felt comfortable with in my first year in the school; we were similar in a lot of things, like our passion for video games and computers – which unlike his, mine had been short-lived – had the same luck with the ladies – which back then was next to zero – and was a bit anti-social in general. We would always get together in breaks to have a chat, crack up jokes and laugh together or at least try to. A trademark of his was the unique quality to suddenly come up with a crude or right utter bad joke that incited people to belt him.

Ryan possessed the feature of being Unitedstatian, which sort of integrated him into Loynner social life by default, or at least, granted him some safety from the most brutal forms of

Kannovschina. He had lived in the US his entire life until the age of 12, and then his family moved to Loynne's. For some reason, he had always struck me as a visual stereotype, very representative of his culture. He hailed from Santa Monica, California, and as such was heavily influenced by any type of stupid Unitedstatian media, obsessed with skate-punk rock and dangerous TV stunts not to mention crappy music videos. Video games could also be thrown in the mix but the society we're talking about here was completely infected with them anyhow.

With about as much flesh as an average skeleton, a long and sharp face ending in an eye-gouging chin, dark blonde short spiky hair, blue eyes, complete constellations comprised of red and white zits across his face, and pubescent facial hair trying to be a full grown beard, Ryan was as hard to take seriously as Wolfgang or Gordon, perhaps more. He had this Unitedstatian geek thing going on, but also the other trendy Californian half that turned him from an awkward geek to a somewhat cool urban kid. One could even imagine him on his own TV show walking with his surfing pot-headed friends down Santa Monica Pier on an orange, subtly lit afternoon. Thus he remained in my mind a Californian caricature on two legs, an absolute archetype of his homeland. His choice in clothing emphasized this, as he only wore surf and skate themed T-shirts and cargo shorts, always sporting expensive skate shoes and hi-tops as well.

I also caught a glimpse of some other friends I had known in the previous years, such as William and Robert Nazareth, casually known as Billy and Robbie, two brothers who looked extremely similar in physical appearance, with messy red long hair, blue eyes, white skin, freckles and slim bodies. Their personalities were their most special feature though, as they didn't speak very often to strangers and never revealed

anything about their personal lives. Their hermetic nature and the way they seemed to analyze everything you could say or do was quite unnerving, but usually they just came off as mischievous guys always looking for the next laugh. Billy dedicated me a calculating and joyful smile, as if to say "so you showed up, huh?" while Robbie limited himself to acknowledging me sternly, almost by compromise.

I sat next to Ryan as he was nearer, and listened to the course tutor, who had just made a sly, sneaky entrance into the classroom. He seemed nerdy and freaky at first sight, wearing thick spectacles, jeans and an orange surfer patterned shirt with the text "California OC." I guessed he wasn't so bad overall, just a regular clown suited to comply with the functions of education and bureaucracy as a whole. I noticed he just limited himself to repeat what the principal had said before, but this guy was rougher and added that he would not tolerate any kind of odd behavior from students or among students. Another difference between pre-Bridge and post-Bridge classes; childish silliness stopped, along with a lot of immature childish bullshit. He gave a simple yet subtle example for this:

"I've seen people punching someone right in the face while on the inside, and later receive a stab directly in the heart on the outside. Be careful with what you do, and who you mess with, because tomorrow can be the day you realize you've gone too far. I will not tolerate any kind of irrational behavior inside this classroom, and you'd better be careful with what you do. You can chat for a while now if you want."

Surely, this course tutor wasn't like the rest. When he introduced himself more steeply and gave us his name finally at

the end of his speech, we knew this Unitedstatian physics professor wasn't worth taking too lightly; he had a black belt in several martial arts, had worked for important government researcher centers and had even contributed in improving several scientific theories, or so he said. His name was Tom Richards from Santa Monica, California. Ryan was in ecstasy; being his usual sycophantic self, he'd sure take advantage of his homeland for this subject.

Richards left us 30 minutes to spend talking until the presentation was finally over, so Ryan, Wolfgang, Billy, Robbie and I sat together for a little chat, and it was just a matter of time that we discussed what was in stock in class, meaning women. After all, what could 17-year-olds talk about given 30-odd spare minutes in the class presentation when there was nothing else to mention? However, I always kept those things to myself, I hated the archetypical image of a guy drooling over a girl who doesn't even know he exists, and if she does, she ignores him. You do that in secret unless you intend on actually dating her. Women don't deserve recognition just for having come up better than others genetically or for knowing how to put make up on.

None of them caught my eye, however. They were so stereotypical looking that the little glamour they could have had drained slowly at the very thought of it. Their visible g-string thongs, their tight tops, revealing skirts and high-heeled shoes meant nothing to me. I had to act the part with my crude little friends though, and acknowledge a Chilean girl sitting near from us had an absolutely bangable ass. Protocol was protocol, after all. I couldn't have been any less interested in any of those vapid whores. For me, it was insultingly obvious that they wouldn't suffice. I needed a female representation of beauty like all the other years before, so I picked the first good-looking girl with a huge butt and perky breasts

temporarily while I continued to search for something better. Don't ask; it's simply irresistible to have a muse, a woman that lights your life, a beautiful angel who makes catching as many glimpses of her as possible your main motivation to bear the tediousness of ordinary routine. Every man needs a woman to admire, and while in the past all my muses had been cynical nymphs who thought everyone else to be inferior it helped me psychologically, as it fed and kept my sexual drive on constant alert.

When the bell rang, we exited the school and walked directly to the corner; it was the typical September day in Loynne's. The people went home happily or to walk around Pilgrim Coast, enjoying the day before classes really started. We wouldn't be doing much in the following week anyway, simply getting to know the teachers, spending almost all of our parents' wages on expensive books we would be forced to discard the next year or sell to others for half the price, and have a slight yet accurate idea of what the rest of the school year would be like. Each year in Loynne's to me was simply terror, imagining what sort of people I'd have to be put amongst. The worst torture for any person in any workplace or classroom is always dealing with the monster of social relationships. This kind of Kanny phenomenon of bullying was also seen in the hotel business workplace though, and you would wonder whether this wasn't just a school or army problem anymore. You were outrageously lucky if the human beings selected for your compulsory integration in society's system weren't difficult types.

As we walked outside the school's perimeter the Nazareth brothers left quickly, almost dismissing us. I got the feeling that they didn't want to hang around Ryan for too long, leaving me alone with Wolfgang and him. I felt the tension of being stuck with them in the same spot, and given their awk-

ward and anti-social nature it was best to just break them apart to end the awkwardness. I didn't think they'd like each other as friends very much, although Wolfgang was always eager for more friends like me who would cope with his mental ravings and not laugh at him. Not taking any chances, I decided to go to Wolfgang's house, since I had more confidence with him, why not say it, liked more than Ryan at the moment.

"You going?" Ryan asked.

"Yeah. I'm going to Wolfgang's house now. I had already told him I would go with him after the presentation. Sorry, man. Maybe next time," I said, seeing Ryan coming.

"Oh, don't be like that man, hang out with me instead, I got nothing to do this afternoon. C'mon, man!"

"No, sorry, maybe another time, I really sort of like had an arrangement with Wolfgang. I can't just give him the cold shoulder like this."

"But ... OK. Fine. See ya later," Ryan said, looking rather disappointed, walking alone in the opposite direction. He left "duck-walking" sulkily in that stupid manner of his, a pathetic sight to behold. Duck-walking involves walking without moving your arms a lot, bending your knees slightly and having your feet pointing up as if only standing on your heels. We used to refer to this with the guys as duck-walking behind his back, and even though it wasn't something very noticeable to the untrained eye, it was enough for us to forever refer to him as "ducky" when he wasn't among us.

I remember thinking how odd it was of Ryan to ask me a thing like that. Up until then, Ryan had never shown any interest in developing a friendship that transcended simple school companionship, and I felt incredibly awkward when declining his request. I have to admit, Wolfgang was my safety blanket, and he had been for more than a year. Replac-

ing Wolfgang for Ryan as a best friend seemed a wrong move at the time. I wasn't prepared to change my social life, being so used to the stability of bottom feeders like Wolfgang. A tiny seed of fear grew in me whenever I thought of the possibility of being rooted out of my newfound peace. However, this year the atmosphere seemed different, like I had seen this all before, like it was all a predictable formula. The thought immediately brought boredom, but the seed of fear grew larger when I reminded myself of the uncertainty of social situations, especially when remembering my experiences on the 3rd Grade. For the first time since my arrival, I felt confused at the prospect of relative constant peace.

We walked together to Wolfgang's house, talking about the people in the classroom and our plans for the afternoon. Listening to my Hipp-Man and walking together with Wolfgang to his house was becoming a routine, since his apartment was a nice place to be, and his company always made me kill the alienation of Loynne's for an hour or two. We often discussed life's facts, ideas and concepts such as justice, duty, valor, pride, love, death and hate, so since I was the only person who was willing to pay attention to Wolfgang's mental ramblings, things he never talked about with anyone else, and he felt the same way about me, it was the perfect symbiosis. I actually felt relieved at least one person in Loynne's was willing to discuss these things with another human, and even more willing to look up to them in true honesty. Wolfgang was after all one of the few people who had to cope with personal ordeals similar to mine, and who wasn't an entire SternGeek like Gordon.

"Sonny, do you think I'll someday be able to engage in a relationship seriously? I mean, with a woman I love, and that she loves me too, and the usual ..." Wolfgang began, initiating one of our usual conversations regarding the opposite sex,

which were quite plentiful. Wolfgang in particular regarded women as a complete mystery, as at this point he hadn't even touched or kissed one.

"Of course, there's a girl out there for everyone, no matter who you are ... There always is." I said looking the other way, not believing much in what I had just said, as per usual when boosting Wolfgang's confidence.

"Because, I don't know, I can't seem to succeed, you know, as if I had something they don't look for, or despise ..." Wolfgang said with the sorrow of a teenage boy who knows and acknowledges will never achieve female attention, at least not in their current incarnation. This was too obvious, so I needed to stop lying and unleash the harsh truth for him to see.

"Look, I'll be honest with you. You need to begin to think like Loynners, not make them like you the way you are. Do you think they'll accept you if you insist? Of course not, this is something that took me a little while to learn. You need to work on yourself a bit, change yourself both visually and mentally so that you resemble everyone else in order to deceive them. It doesn't mean you have to become what they are. Cut your hair like they do, wear the clothes they wear, behave as if you were a Loynner ... It's pretty cruel to say it in this way, and it sounds bad, but you need to learn not to be yourself. This applies to everybody, including women. Women don't want you to be who you really are. They want the illusion of a strong and confident man who will protect them, somebody their friends will envy. In this society, you and I aren't really what most women would like for boyfriends. It's all about the status it brings. They're attracted to power, to social position, to royalties. Only a few women won't follow those rules. And those few women are the ones you're looking for, the ones that will accept you for who you are. But, I think that takes years. At this age women are very stupid, just as

men. I think that when people grow older, they start thinking about what they truly need in a person and do their best to secure that. We're surrounded by peer pressure, don't you see? At this age, forget about it. It's too volatile. Maybe in university, in your 20s ... around that age. But don't be looking for anything so serious at this age. You'll be sorely disappointed. And even then, you'll have to follow the same rules. Society doesn't want you to be unique; it wants you to adapt, to be the same as everybody else, to follow blindly the rules it lays for you to obey. Think of the organism that is society as one big oppressor. That's why I prefer to be left alone. When you fall in the viciousness of social circles, you're playing by rules that are not your own, and I hate the thought of that. I always laugh at the irony of the freedom these Westerners brag about, when there's nothing more oppressive, discriminatory and narrow-minded than their social behavior."

"I know ... So ... I sure do have to work on me then, haven't I?" Wolfgang said, destroyed.

"Forget it ... it's not worth thinking about. When you're that old, you'll have plenty of other things to worry about ... Let's just enjoy this time now that we can."

When we reached our destination, as usual, we had something to eat before going straight to his room to play online First Action Peril games and kill time an hour or two. Wolfgang only ate Asian food from bowls always using sticks, while I usually had a ham and cheese sandwich. Even though the area was luxurious, Wolfgang's apartment was austere at best; comprised by a small corridor you found yourself in when entering with a kitchen to the right and his parents' room to the left. The corridor was so small you'd find yourself immediately in the living room after a few steps. To the left of this living room was Wolfgang's bedroom. There was a balcony as well, that stretched from the living room to Wolfgang's

room and was opened via a sliding door.

Wolfgang's bedroom was the biggest room in the apart-ment, roughly as big as mine, with its wardrobe embedded to the wall and the floor completely covered in a blue tatami Wolfgang used to practice Aikido. Filling the room were a messy desk with a desktop computer, a flat-screen TV set with a GameEsprit Zwei console, a small bed with a Japanese flag patterned bedspread, a small wooden shelf filled with computer and GameEsprit games, as well as music CDs; and the finishing touch, two very iconic posters, a replica of the "*The Great Wave off Kanagawa*" by Katsushika Hokusai and an imperial Rising Sun flag with the Kanji words for "*Bushi-do*" at the center, in black, and two other smaller sentences I had never asked him about their meaning. Aside from this, he had two extremely coveted possessions he often bragged about; a Katana sword rested on the wall above the computer desk, unsheathed, the steel shiny and sharp. Wolfgang had procured this deadly weapon in an online bid, or so he said. I never believed him, as it was extremely difficult to get a hold of this kind of weapon in Loynne's. I always suspected his father had procured him during his time in Asia. The other possession was another weapon he felt extremely proud about; a replica Minebea PM-9, the official submachine gun of the Japanese Self-Defense Force. Wolfgang often practiced reloading and aiming with an identical airsoft version of it, and I had used it myself as well to practice firing from the balcony to the pool area below.

Unfortunately for my comrade I couldn't stand sitting there killing virtual avatars of people online for too long, so after an hour we went for a walk around the marina, which required an incredible amount of persuasive power on my part. Wolfgang's apartment was located in a building named The Sun Tower, which was in a small neighborhood called

The Pentagon, where the best nightlife Loynne's had to offer attracted countless British, Dutch and Russian tourists, who contributed in making sure the district never slept. We made our way passing by "The Aquatic Lounge," "Club Subterra" and "De Wallen's Gentlemen's Club," some of the trendiest and most expensive places in the entire island, places of vice and excess which Wolfgang and I completely rejected. During daytime, however, the neighborhood was nice and calm, housing the marvelous Crosshair Beach, a true global tourist destination. The name came from a small isle only 200 meters from the shore, where an old lighthouse had once been the vantage point of a mass-killing performed by an anonymous sniper. It was one of those Loynner myths impossible to corroborate or debunk. The sand of the beach was white and bright and the area was filled with restaurants with balconies that provided an excellent view of the beach below. We climbed the stairs to get up on one of the balconies, watching the people from above, all of them tourists from all over the world who came to the island running away from the reality of their home countries; gun violence, organized crime, gang warfare, vandalism, petty thefts and dreadful weather. Loynne's Island; Paradise Itself, a motto invented by the Ministry of Tourism, was a temporary safe haven for these tortured middle class tourists, but also the preferred destination of scum who would crave a type of narco-sexual tourism typical of places like Amsterdam and Bangkok; for in Loynne's, soft drugs and prostitutes were legal for tourists and residents alike.

Prepared for this, Loynne's Island had a very extreme and harsh policy toward illegal drugs and criminal organizations, making it safe to live in and enjoy its comfort, in fact, it was one of the safest places to be on the world. Prostitution was legal like in the Netherlands and Switzerland, something

which reduced considerably the number of mafias exploiting sex-slaves. Soft drugs were legal too, but hard drugs like cocaine and heroin weren't. In any case, they always made it to the island no matter how hard the SKAR Coastal Patrol Unit tried to prevent it, and many complained on how such a well-organized police force could be fooled by smugglers unless it willfully participated. Beneath the façade of political correctness, a lot of criminal and illegal activity could be felt in the heavenly atmosphere of the island, since drug barons and mafia capos helped keep the economic and political structure of the island stable, a sad but true fact. However they only used Loynne's mainly as a counterfeiting and money laundering haven. The workers and ordinary people were just pawns in a chessboard who helped guard the kings and queens in a seemingly never ending game of turf conquering and influence spreading. In any case, why did that matter anyway? As long as the Ministry was concerned, they didn't damage people's lives or mangled with their safety. Only a handful of a very "select" population did hardcore drugs like cocaine and heroin, and kids only did marijuana, ecstasy or acid. Everyone my age had already smoked tobacco or marihuana, and it was the only system that enabled me to discern the scum from the upstanding. That line was becoming grayer, though. I was surprised at how people that looked more innocent than Wolfgang sneaked during classes to smoke pot in the bathrooms, just like Kannies. The thought always gave me nausea and only increased my ever-growing feeling of isolation in a society where principles and ethics were increasingly more difficult to discern.

"'Paradise Itself' alright," I told Wolfgang sarcastically, following my current train of thought. We contemplated this supposed peace from the balcony; the tourists walking up and down in tacky beach clothes, the stunning foxy girls we

would never be able to get sunbathing, the Kannies returning in packs from an evening of truancy, the blazing sun reflected on every sea wave.

"Yeah, I guess. But what do you mean by that, Sonny?"

"Look at that," I said, pointing my index finger at an advertisement showing a stunning model, ignorance and shallowness firmly printed on her face, sporting the clothes that most Loynnerins wore. From the uselessly enormous sunglasses, to the tight jean pants and boots to the over-sophisticated and confusing layers of clothing she wore on the upper part, your reaction was of immediate rejection if you were like me. There was nothing good that could be imitated from this example. A destructive form of narcissism and compulsive weight loss were the only things you would learn from this monster. The island's slogan could be seen on top of it. The ad was sponsored by designer clothes manufacturer Dominique Bouche, its logo being a stylized D&B.

"Haha, F-M-S, yeah! Ridiculous isn't it? They try to show a stereotype which denigrates women, right?" Wolfgang asked as naïvely as he only could. Most of the time he didn't know what I was on about, and always tried to guess what I was probably thinking, without much success.

"Of course," I said frowning, pressing my teeth fiercely, hatred flowing through my body like a powerful electric current. "Do you see the way she's disgustingly looking at you? Her inability to smile or express the least trace of empathy? Her hair blowing with the wind? Look at her expensive Bouche clothes, her Bassa Donna sunglasses. It's exactly the stereotype they're perpetrating on the island, on society in general. Do you have any further doubts about why we can't get a proper girl over here?"

"No, not at all Sonny. I know they're worthless."

"Liar. Why do you pursue them all the time, then? I don't

see you doing anything except drooling for them when in fact they laugh at you behind your back."

"I don't Sonny, but it's hard, you know? They're shallow, I know, but they're so pretty. You can't help but want to cuddle them, to touch them, to be in bed with them and spend some time enjoying their company even if it's just talking. You just desire them. I find it hard to believe how it's so impossible to even find ugly girls out there. They're so perfect and slim and full of make-up. You can't help but fall in love with these dolls sometimes. 'Cause that's what they are, dolls. And dolls are always beautiful."

"But dolls are made of plastic. And they're hollow. Expensive artificial creations designed to be bought and owned by those who can afford them. Nothing but overrated prostitutes, even if they don't see themselves under that light. Never forget that the next time you supposedly fall in love, Wolfie. This is not doing you a great deal of good."

"It's all the same to me. I don't really care anymore, Sonny. I don't feel anything about this place, I've given up. I just don't belong here and you know it well. I don't care about this place or its women, and I ought to be in Japan. Think about what we could do in Japan, Sonny! There are so many interesting things there. The technology is so advanced, people are different, and they ..." Here he went again. Wolfgang had an absolute infatuation with the Japanese in every sense, an infatuation I could not share. He always talked about their sense of honor, their relentless willpower, their high intelligence and modern society. But I never agreed. To my eyes, the Japanese had mutated to a deranged form, focusing on primal instincts devoted to explore the most disgusting aspects of the human psyche. Through their "arts" and creativity, the Japanese animation and video game industry made it into the Western audience with a bang. Outcasts with a ram-

pant hatred against society eerily entertained themselves digitally raping virtual girls. Gruesome torture and bizarre sex became so intertwined there was no telling them apart. In fact, I had begun to despise what Japanese culture stood for in modern times so much that I no longer had Wolfgang's gift, a poster of the kanji word for "Bushido," stuck to my wall next to my revered Communist pictures. Just like pro-Western Russians, the modern Westernized Japanese didn't have any sense of ideology, honor or glory. It seemed to me they were worse than Unitedstatians or Europeans in the way that not only they consumed the most horrible aspects of human darkness for the sake of trendy post-modernism and papier-mâché values, but they in fact produced and marketed it. I didn't doubt for a second that people like Gordon existed because of this industry. But taking this from Wolfgang was different. I believed he could be talked into reason.

"Snap out of it, Wolfie. Admit it. They're amongst one of the most capitalistic societies ever, rivaling the US itself. Their screwed up society is falling apart morally with weird porn and sexual fetishes, humiliating TV shows, an absolute lack in ideology. They may have been honorable in the past, I do not know about that, but currently they're just capitalists making good business, sharing all of the features of a modern society. You know that the other day they were this much of killing off a poor guy who suffered a heart attack after a TV prank? They don't seem that perfect and mature to me. Don't you think it's a bit shameful, knowing their history? I wouldn't complain if those things came out of North America or Europe, and they do, but it's different. Japan is just home for global corporations, corporations which would take over the world if given the opportunity."

"Yeah, I know, but you're just looking at the negative sides. Look at all the good things they brought to society! Like

the video game industry, digital cameras, cars, robotic advances, medicine, they have improved your life in every way and you can't seem to acknowledge it. They're amongst the smartest people on the planet."

"I'm not saying they're not. But they didn't reject capitalism's flaws, they made them evolve, they perfected them ... Look, I know you can't judge a nation and their people like these, maybe someday I meet a Japanese guy and I become best friends with him, why not, I'm only saying what I honestly think. And don't even get me started on the Russian Mafia. I know what they're like, OK? Russians have always had this little touch of selfish feudalism in them, which hasn't withered away one bit since the times of Nikolai II. With capitalism, they only got that back in greater ways. I know everything you're about to say. Russians are filthy too ... There, content?"

"Yeah, I got your point. But you won't change my mind about Japan just by saying that. Besides right now those things are changing! Japan has a new leader now, who plans to eradicate all the Western Unitedstatian influence and establish true Japanism."

"Oh, I heard about him. He's a right-winger. He may stand up for Japan and its culture, but there's a fine line between nationalism and fascism. Considering Japan is still an empire officially, my bet is that guy is no good news at all. Extremism is always bad, from whichever political spectrum. We Communists learned that a long time ago ... Never forget *Tovarish*, Comrade Lenin already warned of this ... Imperialism is the highest stage of capitalism, any empire existing in our current sociopolitical model is in itself a reflection of an obsolete and outdated form of oligarchy, just like modern parasitic European monarchies ..."

"Say what you will, but I love Japan just as you love Rus-

sia, I love its culture, it's simply fascinating to me, and if the new leader will stand up for Japan I support him all the way, to the death. I'm loyal to Japan to the end. I'm sorry you are so close-minded. If you could understand it, you'd know why I love that country so much."

"I won't. And I may love the Russian Federation for still being Russia and standing up to the West, but I hate what has happened to it. I hate the way organized criminals and oligarchs throve under the new capitalist changes, the way corruption went unchecked and the way the ideology died down. Lenin once righteously said, 'freedom in capitalist society always remains about the same as it was in ancient Greek republics: Freedom for slave owners.' The current Russian Federation, like Loynne's, is ruled by oligarchs who exploit the workforce. That's why freedom is incompatible with capitalism. That's why the only nation you could say I've ever loved blindly is the Soviet Union, who despite having an elite, that elite ruled for the working class, and look what happened to it; disbanded and turned into a pile of developing countries with different flags and anthems, completely lost in petty nationalism, their silly little Catholic, Orthodox or Islamic superstitions and the ever widening gap between rich and poor, which is so representative of capitalism. The biggest disaster of the 20th century. And I most of all hate the way the Soviet and Warsaw Pact peoples embraced a system they stood against for 70 years so easily, a system that was met with no resistance whatsoever when it arrived. I just can't get why they fled their own Motherlands in favor of this Western land, this stupid promise of 'freedom,' everything their nations and political doctrines stood against. I wonder how low you have to get to want to defect. Betraying your own country and ideology for this? But I'm stuck here. It was the unstable political climate of a collapsing Soviet Union or

this. Obviously we settled for this, the lesser of two evils. Communism had already died down and there was nothing we could do to salvage it, no matter how we fought. Remember the Moscow 1991 coup? And there was actually nowhere we could go that resembled our former country. The rest of the Communist countries throughout the world were hit too badly from the collapse of the Eastern bloc, shattered by economic blockades imposed by the West, isolated from the world and hated just for choosing a different socioeconomic system, constantly bullied and pressured into accepting this deluded vision of 'democracy.' But this supposed utopia we found here never fooled me; Loynne's is as despicable as any other country in the West, or rather, the most despicable of all, because it leeches of others wanting to come here and escape from the harsh realities of capitalist injustice."

"Sonny, look at you ... I know what you mean, and I think similar to you in some ways, but in the end this island accepted you, and you find yourself here like the rest of us. You did everything you just described traitorous defectors did before you, complain about their land and defect, only to later live in the West in luxury ... like those communist pilots who flew their planes to the West and defected only to be rewarded with cars and houses, or those scientists that ended up living in luxury while criticizing their homelands ..."

"The age-old hypocrisy of the brain drain, Wolfie; those bastards received their education in the Communist East, only to be rewarded by their treason and defection in the West. Preferential treatment. You know what disgusts me most about those traitors? That they knew that their preferential treatment was only due to propaganda boosts and because of the nature of the Cold War, and thinking in a selfish and individualistic manner, risked defection as a gamble to access all of those luxuries in the West, not caring that

the system they ceased defending is the only hope for an equal society. A defection from the West to the East was considered noble because of all the idealism it conveyed; the other way round, it was merely a selfish gamble for luxuries. Traitors like those wanted this all along, that's all they were really after. They wanted the houses, the money, the cars, the hot women with silicone tits ... in contrast, my family and I simply abandoned a land that was devastated by violence and war, a land that was no longer ours. On the 23rd of May, 1991, the name of the country was officially changed from Moldavian Soviet Socialist Republic to Republic of Moldavia, and it officially seceded from the USSR. That's when it hit my parents. Imagine your country having a different flag overnight, a different anthem, different name, a different political system, a different set of principles ... you simply reject it immediately. You no longer consider it your land. It's normal."

"I am not blaming your parents for choosing this, but all I ask is for you not to complain when this land, bad as it may be, accepted you. But I do think that if your country needs you, running away is the most cowardly act of treason you can ever commit."

"Is that so? I would have loved to see you back there in that political climate. There are things you will never understand." How was I to explain Wolfgang that my true country had just been disbanded and was currently in the transition between Communism and capitalism? How could I possibly explain to him that I had lived through this transition, that I possessed more experience on the subject that I let on? But no ... Wolfgang needed to remain fooled like everyone else, thinking I was merely a new-born when my country collapsed, and not a teenager fully aware of its sociopolitical concerns.

"What I don't understand is how come you started to de-

velop this communistic ideology, if most Russians today are so capitalistic and Western-like?"

"Seeing the injustices of capitalism was enough; but there's also the fact that I was born shortly before the Union died. I always thought of it as the grandfather you never met as a child, that you love and look up to, but could never get to know. You only hear the stories of the generation ahead of him, parents telling you the most wonderful tales and anecdotes. This is what happened with me and the Union."

"And you really think that communism works? You think the Soviets would have fixed the world if the US had fallen and not the USSR?"

"I told you about this already, you know what I think. In my opinion, if the Soviets had won the Cold War and the United States had collapsed, we would be living in more equality to some degree, probably with an elite Nomenklatura of political leaders enjoying superior benefits to some extent, like China, but not so much as people will have you think. With the US out of the picture the other capitalist nations would have fallen instantly and joined the Communist Revolution. Life nowadays would be more oriented toward education and social services, people wouldn't die on the streets because they can't afford medical care, like in the US. People can say whatever they want about the Soviet Union, but over there your life was educating yourself until you became an adult, and either going to the army or university. Being parasitic scum was treason. And everyone had access to a house and free universal healthcare. Look at Cuba, the world's foremost superpower in health and university education. Many go over there from Western countries to get educated. And I love how the Unitedstatian pigs have not managed to bring Cuba down, disgusting fascist pigs ... All the destabilization attempts in Latin America have failed, Cuba being the

greatest example. The whole world, including the US, Canada, Europe and some parts of Asia are trying to destabilize Latin America. Their neoliberal model failing, they will see they will have to adapt to the times too. The whole world was sunk by that neoliberal wave of corruption and tax havens. The people allowed a few to hoard all the wealth, and look at the results. It's impossible to live decently anywhere except for in Loynne's Island, which is another bubble waiting to get busted. People are on the dole by the millions in Europe and the US, they don't have access to healthcare or education, they have even immigrated to countries they would have never even thought twice about visiting. The world is changing, Wolfie ... we will wake up to a new world ruled by Socialism, not imposed on the people by leaders, but directly preferred by the people because of its benefits. Forget about the way Communism worked in the 20th century ... this new century will see Communism and Socialism directly wanted by the people."

"Perhaps. But Sonny, you only speak of ideology, there is something very important you're ignoring. Look at Japan ... you're not looking at its code of Honor, the Samurai, *Bushido* ... Japanese warriors had the greatest honor code in history, and always fought loyally for their Emperor. True patriots. They gave everything for their land, and expected nothing in return. Tell me, what's more patriotic than that? Russians, for all their talk about Motherland, have never had such patriotic fervor. They could learn a couple of things from the Japanese."

"I know Wolfie, but ... the Japanese peasantry also suffered under the samurai, who were the Empire's workforce. I've heard the samurai could kill a peasant on the spot without any reason at all, without justification. After all, the samurai were like Japanese Cossacks. You see what I mean? It's

all a lie ... it was then in Japan and Russia, and it is now in the current Loynne's. This place is the perfect example that capitalism is the new god for the people. No Emperor. No Premier. Nothing. Just money. The economy will have to undergo certain changes. *Society* will have to undergo certain changes. We're living under laws that were written 200 years ago. A lot of modern everyday life things aren't even included in the constitutions of countries. How can you expect this to work? And then there's religion ... the ultimate progress-stopping power, the most systematic type of brainwashing, the maximum representation of humanity at its worst. If you want to see why the world does not work, look at religion first and at politics later."

"You're not considering the viewpoints of those people who love what you hate, Sonny ... they have different ideologies from yours for a reason."

"Different viewpoints, you say ... that's good. But from who, exactly? From lowlives without ideology or vision, looking to be richer, looking through the Berlin Wall to West Berlin, craving the free land of money? That's what people in East Berlin did, thanks to the propaganda of the West. Look at the nice West! Look how nice it is! Look how everyone's got a Hades-Larsson luxury car! Nothing but lies ... They went to West Germany, many dying on the wall, and then became poorer and even homeless. May I remind you that in a capitalist society a few have a lot while many have nothing? Nice dream. Well deserved for deserting our just Socialist ideology."

"Can't blame them, Sonny ... What if you think your own country is not perfect and that these so called hard-working communists are nothing but opportunists and liars?"

"A lot of them must have thought that ... yeah, I can't blame them. The only thing I can blame them for is for not

standing up for their own country and failing to make it better. If the old Communists have turned into bureaucratic idiots like the ones from the West, kill them! Change them! Run through the streets, burn everything, rise in arms, just like the Bolsheviks did against the Tsar! But never forsake your nation, your ideology! How could all these Russians embrace a new flag, a new coat of arms and a new system so easily? Didn't they feel shame and disgust at the West entering their homes? At the US and the Free West winning when our fair ideals should have been victorious?"

"A blend between capitalism and communism has to be created, Sonny, taking the best parts of each. Think about it, it can't be that hard, there's organizations for everything these days ... You just need a special signed permit from the Minister, and a bit of paperwork and that's it."

"And convince the locals to rebel against the hand that feeds them fancy cars, computers, mansions, a nice livelihood and stability? Wake up, Wolfie! Nobody wants that! They wouldn't even listen to us; they'd laugh at us and throw tomatoes at our deserted HQ! People love their lives, they won't die for anything, and that's how capitalism succeeds. The people who are alright turn a blind eye on those who are starving or dying from cold in the streets, but the poor don't have enough power to change the system not because they can't but because they don't want to. Even them, who are repelled and ignored, have been absorbed by this economic and political hellhole run by a financial elite who hoards the power. Societies require revolution to change, but that change brings forth a trauma; just as you wouldn't like to change your whole life upside down now out of being alright, not starving, you wouldn't like to change, there's no need after all. Immediately, you don't feel it. But every society does later on, like the world is now, and like Loynne's will be later.

The economy will collapse, capitalism will destroy what's left, and when a change is needed, it will be so swift and brutal that you won't remember how you lived before that apocalypse. No revolution, no armed uprising can eclipse what is to come."

"Sonny ... would you die for a revolution?"

"I don't know ... I haven't really thought about it. I don't think I make much of a soldier, and I certainly think I can be of more use alive than dead, not dying for a revolution which will certainly be crushed and change nothing. But what I'm sure about is that this world will need one if it keeps going like this."

"In Feudal Japan the Samurai lived and died for their *shogun*. Forged in the discipline of *Bushido*, they led a frugal and austere life dedicated to being loyal to the end, balancing philosophy and wisdom with physical prowess. This, to me, is the perfect type of warrior, *Doshi*. I very much doubt any of your Soviet soldiers could be as loyal and give their life for what they believed in ..."

"Perhaps not modern Soviets as in the last days of the USSR, but true revolutionaries would. Che Guevara himself gave his life defending what he believed in, and when offered a relatively privileged position in the newly established Cuban government he rejected it, saying there were still countries that needed to be liberated from the yoke of United-statian imperialism. That's how he died in Bolivia, captured and executed by the disgusting CIA-controlled puppet Bolivian Army. Dying to defend an idea, a just cause. And his men were willing to give his life for him just as the samurai gave their lives defending their emperor."

"Well, I guess revolutionary guerilla fighters and the Samurai do have a lot in common. But I still defend my model. No person has ever been able to achieve the Code of Honor the

Samurai developed. They were extraordinary, true warriors. I think their way of life should be made an example of in this modern and disgusting society."

"But what can you do about it?"

"Well ... you'll laugh, but ... I always wanted to create a gang ... Imagine it ... recruit people who have some skill at martial arts and Aikido, who know *Bushido*, and who have great discipline, principles and ideas ... not donkeys like these Kannies ... and no Unitedstatian obnoxious drones like Ryan ... People like you and me, who understand Honor ... We could have uniforms, I always thought of this red bandana or berets, armbands with the Japanese Rising Sun war flag, woodland camo fatigues and black boots. Nice, eh?" I gave him a sympathetic, friendly smile, laughing mildly, and patting him on the back said:

"Wolfie ... you really make my day at times ..."

" *'Kannan-ni atte hajimete shinyu-wo shiru.'* "

"What?"

"It's a Japanese proverb. It means 'a friend is known in adversity, like gold is known in fire.' It means that only in true hardship you know how much a friend is worth."

"Thanks, Wolfie ... it means a lot."

"It's OK, Sonny ... That's what I'm here for, *Doshi*."

"Well, I' have to go now. Do you want to tag along to the bus stop?"

"No Sonny, I have stuff to do, I'd like to, but ..."

"Yeah. Understood. You prefer to seal yourself shut in a dark room playing GamEsprit all day."

"It's not that Sonny, but it's just that I'm so tired lately. I don't have the energy anymore, you know? I have Aikido practice later on, and I want to be fully energized for it because when I get home I just go to sleep, it's even worse when I've been to school for six hours ..."

"I always walk this whole road by myself whenever I want to come here, which is pretty often, and you can't even come with me to the bus stop which is half of the overall road? Give me a break ... you would if you wanted to ..."

"No Sonny, don't take it like that, but today I'm very tired, c'mon, be reasonable ..."

"Alright, I'll catch you around at school. But don't expect much from me later on, alright?"

"Look Sonny, don't get offended, put yourself in my shoes!"

"Yeah, yeah, don't worry about it, I'll see you later Wolfie."

"OK Sonny, see you later ..."

I turned around and left highly offended. Lately, I had been thinking about how Wolfgang could probably not be willing to sacrifice as much for this friendship as I was. Beyond his words and ideas, I sometimes wondered whether Wolfgang was really a true comrade, which led to an even worse realization; that I didn't possess any true friends at all.

I turned to face Wolfgang again after a few steps, looked at him straightly in the eye and said:

"Never forget ... I'm your only friend, your only comrade here ... *Nikogda ne zabyvay, Tovarish* ..."

"Likewise, *Doshi* ... *Kesshite wasurenai* ..." Wolfgang bid me farewell in his usual way, with a dismissive and casual military salute.

· · · · ·

I got off the air conditioned bus listening to Kino's "*Pechal*" — "Sadness" — immediately absorbing the blazing heat of the 14:50 sun as I made my way toward the Rot Volka apartment block, the grayish-white building where I resided in apartment 2-F. Even though it was just one of the ten

apartments that comprised the two-story building, I had no neighbors; excluding my presence, the entire place was uninhabited.

There was an explanation for this: the building was, as I explained before, owned in some way by the gangsters or associates of them. It had surely been some kind of safe house for criminals to lay low or move merchandise without attracting too much attention. It was only natural for them to smuggle immigrants and make them live in relatively isolated places like this one.

I had had no contact with the landlord aside from when I had arrived and he drove me to the building the very first day, and I always left him the rent money in an envelope stored in the mailbox outside. No contact was required or encouraged, it seemed. I had simply followed his instructions, and so far he didn't seem to mind what I could be doing in the building all by myself, as he never visited or checked on me.

I felt the silence that reigned at this time in Montenade and became amazingly relaxed, businesses shut because of the lazy Loynner owners taking an afternoon nap and traffic being almost non-existent due to the same reason. It was virtually a ghost town, and I always took my time to walk so as to enjoy the peace and quiet reigning in the outside for a while before being ultimately scorched by the unforgiving Loynner sun.

When I got home, the first thing I did was throw my backpack in my room and lie on the couch in the living room. I was immediately absorbed by that cool feeling of darkness, and decided to open the green curtains slightly to let some sunlight in, but instantly closed them down again. The blazing sun outside often turned the house into a hellish greenhouse and as such it was better to leave it dark at all times.

The darkness also made me relax and retreat further into the hidden corners of my mind, forgetting anything that could have happened during my outings.

I had a very modest and austere-looking home; the white walls were peeling off in certain segments, giving a feeling of decay and abandonment, and the rough gray tiles which comprised the floor gave the apartment an atmosphere of being still under construction. The possessions I had bought with what little my parents could give me were a quite powerful laptop computer running the latest operating system of the time, the Hipps-Tear Rhino, at merely 150 crosses, and a printer for 40 crosses, both possessions bought from people advertising in a newspaper eager to get rid of them, as Loynners would throw anything old out of the window the minute something better hit the market. I had also bought an old 64 cm CRT TV purchased in the same manner from someone so desperate to throw it he sold it for 5 crosses, a cell-phone – which was actually free, I only paid 5 crosses a month for telephone services – and picture frames I had procured to put the pictures my parents sent me and fill the apartment with some life. I didn't have to spend much more money on the apartment, as it came with pretty much anything needed to live decently, from furniture to cooking equipment. As a norm, all apartments for rent in Loynne's needed to provide tenants with essential household materials, and it wasn't odd that even filthy Russian criminals had a fully equipped apartment too in order to hide their comrades in or smuggle immigrants like me.

Looking around aimlessly, I became surprised at how I didn't feel like doing anything: all I ever did was going to school and then right home again, to play computer games Wolfgang had recommended me only to stop after a few minutes, and watch whichever films were on TV in between,

besides of listening to music and reading books. In some way, I was living in the way I had craved for so long, left alone and enjoying my favorite hobbies; but something was changing, I could notice it awfully. I didn't want to be a peaceful little kid hiding from the world anymore, for that was all I had been doing up to now in life. Currently devoid of conflicts, there was nothing to hide from, nothing to fear. Slowly, I began to consider myself a person as pathetic as my friends were: people with absolutely no ambition, who would not disrupt their environment out of laziness and fear of progress. I started drawing comparisons and developing thoughts that shattered my pride. I could be better off than this. It was moment for a proper change. I had grown tired of my own lifestyle and fortunately acknowledged that a change was necessary, a change involving some sort of personal growth.

I had been living in Loynne's like this for three years. The Motherland seemed so distant, so ridiculously far away. I couldn't even remember what it was like to step on its soil, to stroll on its gentle, inviting sidewalks. To feel the clean fresh air and humidity of its green forests, the salty air of its deep blue sea. All I had now was the fake dry grass of the deforested South of Loynne's Island, where everything was so artificial that nothing seemed to give a scent. Everything smelled dry, hot, unreal, and gave you this drowsy feeling of lethargic discomfort. When I learned that the reason why the South was so desert-like was because the oligarchs had completely deforested entire areas in order to build hotels and apartment blocks that never saw completion, I was dumbfounded. It was a completely normal sight in the South to see cranes, constructions sites and half-finished buildings. Towns like Montenade and Whitedale, so as to not say all the towns of the southeast, were sure to have barely finished buildings like those. The north of Pilgrim Coast was like that as well, pos-

sessing separated areas which were going to become blocks, surrounded by unfinished deserted roads. In the South there was hardly any wildlife, except for a very small number of insects such as ants, cockroaches, flies and mosquitoes, which disrupted the artificial environment in urban areas, while in the extreme wilderness of the Southern Loynner deserts you would find only lizards and rabbits, which would hide quickly after being spotted. It was like that in Montenade, and in the neighboring towns scattered over the southeastern coast of the island. Simply put, the dry deforested South had no place for life; the imported palm trees and grass were no replacement to the original tropical biodiversity.

And suffering from the suffocating heat of this ravaged, deforested land, was I, once more alone in my apartment, which was always kept in strict darkness to deter the scorching heat from the outside world. Almost all Loynners had access to state-of-the-art homes with computerized temperature regulation, which constantly monitored and adjusted the temperature, but mine was obviously an exception. The heat, coupled with the social alienation and homesickness I had to battle each day, was the perfect illustration to the hell I was traversing.

The only thing that saved me from the torture of this searing after-school loneliness were my parents. They sent me every month an envelope with money, pictures, and always a letter usually written by my mother. These letters were what made me survive through Kannovschina mentally. Seeing my mother's handwriting and the photos would sometimes make me want to burst into tears and desperately return to The Motherland, but I always remembered my mission and that it would hopefully come to an end soon. This was especially intense and made most apparent the moments before leaving for school, those dark and dreadful mornings when the sun

rose at 08:00, and six seemingly neverending hours of social isolation and possible harassment awaited me. That had gone on for about two years, and there was still not a single day that I hadn't wanted to return home.

In her letters, my mother would tell me about the plan of getting a life in Loynne's instead of eventually returning Home, telling me we would be reunited again when they made enough money. The Motherland, she kept saying, had been stripped of its former glory, the land poisoned with the stench of capitalism, the peoples infected with its greedy consumerism and its superficial happiness. Such is an example, taken from the latest letter I had received during this time:

"Dear ********,

We are doing alright so far, the last remnants of the civil war have finally subsided and the country is recovering slowly but surely. We feel safe now and the democratic process at least ensures that we are not persecuted or questioned by authorities, which is what would have happened had the ultra-right nationalists won. As it was to be expected, the democratic party that won has a capitalistic center-right ideology, but at least will ensure that we are left alone. Even so, their economic beliefs will only widen the gap between rich and poor even more, and at the farm they're saying that we will experiment an even major economic crisis than during the worst years of Communism. Seeing what happened to other Communist States in their transitions has really opened these peasants' eyes, they're sharp as foxes. Production in the farm is at least at reasonable levels and we will continue to send you money. Make sure you spend it accordingly like you've been doing as of

now.

Your father and I miss you very much and can't wait to see you again. We only dream of being able to start a new life now that the world has decided capitalism and 'democracy' are the future. We do not share these beliefs but there's nothing we can do. We will have to adapt to the situation and so will you. I expect you are doing alright adapting to that strange new land. Your letters as of now have not been very optimistic. Try to be strong, ********. Life here is much harsher, we have to work countless hours and all for the little money we're able to send you. You have to be strong so that one day we may be reunited, like a family once again. I only live for that day and your father and I are doing this sacrifice so that it will be possible.

Love you,

Mom and Dad."

The last bastion of Soviet–styled Communism destroyed, my mother had begun to leave all romanticism behind, wishing we could definitely settle down in Loynne's so as to not feel the gradual destruction of something so dear and beloved. As such, I had begun to share this contempt; the same piercing sensation of abandonment and nostalgia. The Motherland would never be the same again. Mom often sent me political leaflets and photos of political rallies and demonstrations where the masses cheered in unison against capitalism and its new changes. They were small demonstrations, with the support of a few old-school idealists. The general population couldn't be bothered with revolution and struggle anymore; capitalism had already bought and appeased them.

I felt like a jealous, paranoid husband; my country was be-

ing raped and abused by its own people and the thought made me physically ill, nausea instantly invading my body. How could they learn to love the new tasteless flag so rapidly, the feudalistic coat of arms testimony of disgusting imperial times, the new generic and hollow anthem? How could they adapt so gleefully to symbols which bore absolutely no meaning?

I spent the rest of the afternoon entertaining myself with the vapid joys and easy life capitalism provided for those with the monetary power. I must say I felt quite guilty, like betraying the Motherland for her worst enemy, but at the same time couldn't help but feel she had betrayed me first. She had forced me out by embracing this foreign system, and I guess this was some sort of deranged, masochistic payback. In fact, the Motherland would never return to be the same again; I would often ponder this ... The Motherland itself was the same land, but now corroded and polluted by the very forces I saw and subsequently despised in Loynne's each day. I couldn't even cope with the thought of my nation engulfed in ads and people talking about newfound "liberty" and "choice." The self-righteous and widespread parades of racist neo-fascist parties, symbols of the ambiguous and moronic essence of "liberty," the kids owning stupid Pandoras or GamEsprits and sitting on their asses all day instead of becoming rocket engineers or chess champions, the Hades-Larsson cars owned by whomever was the new head of the Mafia. But no. I couldn't leave her. At least, not yet. If I fully replaced her with Loynne's, then the betrayed would be me. I needed to think about this, studying intricately every angle of the picture before reaching the ultimate conclusion.

For the time being, I simply thought of how my life as an individual seemed to improve; Kannovschina did make the first year of my Loynner life hell, and I was lucky the second

was a radical change, especially since I learned to adapt and get people to like me better. Each day I would come back home fearing for the unpredictability of the next, feeling nausea until I returned to school again to see for myself how the situation was coming along.

I felt rather relieved however, as each year I spent in Loynne's Kannovschina seemed to grow weaker, and people appeared to have become seemingly more peaceful, or better said less dangerous, which was enough to me. I ignored why such a strong fad like Kannovschina could simply start to wane like that. People at school seemed childish and oblivious, but more down to earth and innocent. Girls were as slutty and loudmouthed as ever, but at least didn't look like drug empresses who would call their hitman boyfriends on you. I noticed the change and a little glimmer of hope lightened my mood as I went to bed and tried thinking how things were slowly starting to look up for me.

Before I could be completely relaxed however, the buzzer rang. I picked up the phone and greeted, expecting to be talked to in a Loynner accent, but nobody seemed to be there. The silence of the afternoon streets was all that came from the phone.

My parents couldn't afford fast and expensive deliveries like those, if that had been the reason for the call. I headed downstairs, all the while remembering that from time to time strange mail had been delivered to the house sent to the previous tenant, someone seemingly Russian by the name of Anton Melianov. I had carefully stored all mail delivered to Melianov as he could be someone important to the organization. If they found out I had thrown all the mail away, I could have found myself in deep trouble. Unwilling to run into any unnecessary risks, I had decided to never open any letters and leave them untouched in a box I kept inside my ward-

robe. Still, I often wondered what could have happened to that Melianov person. He had to be either another person brought into the country by my gangster countrymen or member of the organization itself.

Once outside, I noticed a shabby package at my feet. I was surprised at how absolutely no one was around to make me sign for it. The bundle itself was extremely odd, as if it had been hastily wrapped by someone careless. It almost looked like a bakery bag. I brought it upstairs and placed it on the kitchen's counter to analyze it more steeply.

There weren't any addresses or stickers placed on the brown cardboard package, and it seemed to not have even been shipped by mail. Maybe it was meant to be a prank and I would find a very nasty surprise once I opened it. I tried shaking it slightly but nothing odd could be heard rattling inside, and it didn't smell of anything funny. What could be the worst that could happen if I decided to open it? The package was so badly wrapped that nobody would ever suspect I had opened it. With some finesse, I could open it without damaging it too much and take a look at what was inside.

Taking a pair of scissors and a knife from one of the kitchen's drawers, I ripped all the loose tape holding the box together surprised at how it was basically coming apart on its own. I needn't make any effort as the brown cardboard box completely collapsed between my fingers, revealing a slick dark blue attaché case.

I immediately opened it, rendering its contents obvious to me. I had never been so astonished at the sight of an object in my entire life; it had surpassed all my expectations.

A gigantic black revolver rested peacefully inside. I took a closer look; aside from the obvious size, this was no ordinary firearm.

The customized grip appeared to have been taken entirely

out of a handgun, replacing the revolver's original grip. Small and rugged with comfortable finger grooves, it resembled that of the Loynner Police Department and most specifically the one SKAR started to adopt based on the latest German and Austrian designs. This was a completely compact and lightweight grip, intended for obvious law enforcement tactical use.

Judging by the size of the gun alone, the caliber had to be a .600 Nitro Express, developed by the British, the largest caliber ever for handguns. Thanks to the outdated imperial system nobody uses, a lot of confusion can ensue with gun calibers, so I'll give you the proper metric system measurements, 15.75 x 76mm if I remember correctly. As you may assume, it's a caliber that surpasses the ones large assault rifles and anti-aircraft belt-fed machine guns use. It was a very rare caliber for a handgun, and the biggest one available for that matter. Only the biggest handguns in the world used this caliber; the Austrian Pfeifer Zeliska and the United-statian Thompson Contender. Judging by the size of this gun however, I wondered whether the caliber was even greater, maybe using the biggest one of them all, .700 Nitro Express — 17.8 x 89mm — only available in rifles.

The large barrel measured 30 centimeters in length, and had been outfitted with customized built-in iron sights and Picatinny rails to mount attachments, installed on top and below it. Analyzing its size, the cylinder had definitely been replaced and upgraded with one able to store an impressive seven rounds, increasing the size of a revolver which would have stored five on normal conditions.

It was an absolute work of art; there weren't even markings from any of the major arms manufacturers, not on the gun or the case, only a personal carved inscription that went all along the long barrel. The inscription read in Russian

Cyrillic the words *"Reviziya,"* meaning "Revision." But I noticed there was more; two numbers, a zero and a two, were carved right next to the name, slightly separated. *Revision 02.*

It made no sense. This was no firearm I'd ever heard of. Revision 02? It had to be a model designation or serial number, something akin to M2, Mk. II or Type 02. This was surely the second model of this type of handgun produced, or at least, a revision to the previous model, whichever version it could be. Maybe it was a message, a code or an encrypted signature. In any case, there were now no doubts about it; this had been specifically custom-made for someone. Whoever had requested it, had to be an arrogant individual poised on channeling his power in the form of an extravagant and undeniably expensive weapon. This gun was not meant to be fired, I was sure of it; it was a self-given trophy, a reward over some kind of victory or achievement. And it would have made a lot of sense if the nationality of said individual happened to be Russian.

I spotted some surprises I had ignored, eclipsed by the majestic sight of the weapon. An optical sight with a 5x zoom scope rested on top of the revolver, detached, as was the flashlight with integrated laser aim located below the barrel. A detachable stock for greater accuracy and recoil reduction had also been included, resembling the ones usually seen on VP70M handguns. Unlike the stock for those handguns though, the one here could not be used to holster the gigantic revolver, an impossible feat by any means.

Something bothered me immensely. This weapon was clearly geared toward tactical urban combat, enhanced with equipment usually used by elite police forces, the Picatinny rails with the flashlight and laser sight being an example, but the size of the gun alone was clearly intended for big game

hunting, as indicated by its titanic size, immensely powerful caliber and the inclusion of a 5x zoom scope. It was a gun designed to kill, not impair like the small caliber 9mm handguns of policemen, yet it had been modified for urban combat. With its titanic size, I doubted it could even be fired from a standing position, the recoil surely decimating one's joints. If it was indeed a 17.8mm Nitro Express, the recoil could be over ten times worse than that of a normal hunting rifle. This was not a gun to go waving around when sweeping rooms or to exchange fire with criminals behind a patrol car. In fact, I wondered how strong a person had to be physically and how experienced in order to fire it without suffering recoil injury.

I decided to pick it up, noticing first how incredibly lightweight it was, and secondly how unusually textured and rugged the material was to the touch. It wasn't made of metal, but some kind of carbon polymer, again, like most modern handguns and submachine guns used for tactical police units. Most revolvers are made of an alloy of zinc, steel, iron, magnesium, aluminum and brass among other materials like carbon polymer and wood. Why would this one be an exception?

Caressing it with my fingertips, I wondered if the entire gun or some of its parts could be made of some other type of carbon-based material. A gun this size would weigh about 6 kilograms or more, yet I doubted this could reach half a kilogram. In the case of the Zeliska, its weight helped in making the recoil minimally bearable. What would this one feel like? Could it then be that I had in my hands an actual police prototype, designed as some kind of lightweight and hyperaccurate sniper handgun to take down dangerous suspects from afar and ensure their death? I wouldn't have bet on it. Extraordinary sniper rifles already existed for that purpose, possessing greater range, magazine capacity and accuracy

than any handgun. But I couldn't ignore what I had in front of my eyes; a hunting revolver that resembled a portable rifle, clearly intended toward law enforcement use.

I then tried to open the cylinder to check whether it could be loaded, yet found it impossible to do so. I felt silly trying to check for openings and switches on a double-action revolver, but there was no way to open it. It definitely didn't feel like it was loaded, and as per standard procedure no gun ever arrived with loaded ammunition, but given the odd context it was safe to check. Baffled, I left the gun alone not wanting to ruin it with my tinkering.

I ignored what to do with it. Actually, there wasn't anything I could do with it; if the police found out, I would have been in deep trouble. Guns were heavily restricted in Loynne's, which made me think also how on Earth this package had arrived so easily to my doorstep. Something was amiss, but as long as I kept the gun I would be safe; who knows what would happen to me if the owner, probably one of the dangerous criminals who had smuggled me in, caught me empty handed? I admired it for some time and quickly hid it in the second drawer of my wardrobe, well away from sight; nobody would ever know of my new prized possession, no matter how much I was dying to show it off. And for some reason, I knew that somebody was bound to come around asking for it. I didn't think I'd ever move out of that apartment, so at least I'd be able to return it to the owner. I just had to cling to it and leave it unused, and I'd be safe.

I thought one last time about the gigantic revolver before lying down comfortably on the bed. Now that the shock of the surprise had faded, I couldn't help but ask myself a thousand questions, thinking only of how extremely odd the whole event was. Who could have brought it here? Was "*Reviziya 02*" a person's code name or a message? Who could Anton

Melianov be?

I did not know the answers to these questions, and even then I doubted they would be answered in the following days; all I could think of at the moment was how convenient it was for society that the revolver had come without ammunition; that is, in case it was unloaded.

- CHAPTER II -

Mir

"The time has come when the old world must make way for the new."

- **VYACHESLAV MOLOTOV** -

Soviet Bolshevik, Diplomat and Politician, First Deputy Chairman of the Council of Ministers of the Soviet Union, Minister of Foreign Affairs and Chairman of the Council of People's Commissars of the Soviet Union

---

"It appears that the 'Rifleman Organization of America,' or ROA as its most commonly known, keeps deluding the US into all sorts of paranoid fears blurting out that communist Iranian terrorists, allied of course with drug cartels from the United Mexican States, will brutally murder your children and make you watch. The new best-selling novel by Tom Millius, 'Duties of a Patriot,' not only successfully elevates right-wing stupidity higher by claiming that tax cuts in the armed forces will get a nuclear-capable country invaded by developing countries, but manages to convey the outrageous illusion that the right-wing always wants the best for the people. This, of course, is great for the gun merchants and other assorted murderers that deal in blood. If you fear your children getting murdered, don't look at Iranians or Mexicans; look at deluded fellow Unitedstatians, at serial killers driven insane by the social alienation of Western society and the lack of proper healthcare, look at lost

youngsters constantly engaged in gang warfare and petty revenge, look at personnel especially trained to kill, such as ex-Marines suffering from PTSD. Unlike foreigners, these factors are at your very doorstep and have easier access to guns and ammunition than you'll ever dream about in any other Western nation. My advice? Emigration is the only solution to escape from the natural selection society established in the US, and I seriously doubt the 5% or less of Unitedstatians who have a passport wish to emigrate. There are constant factors to keep them either deluded or terrified of leaving. The population is in fact so blinded by 'American' patriotism that they would never even think of leaving the country. 100 million people living under the poverty line have not been enough to wake them up, and the little migration the US has seen cannot under any circumstance be considered a sign that things will change. The US needs to change from the inside, but the government, the ROA and the Church keep deluding them and isolating them inside that theocratic, militaristic nightmare. The only thing which can possibly be done is keep denunciating this regime to the rest of the world, in hopes the people see the truth once and for all. As long as that deranged and unhealthy military patriotism and the gun culture exist, thousands will keep dying. This is something the world cannot turn its back on."

"Thank you, Michael. That was Michael Weinstein's report for the week on gun control in the US, a controversial topic that ensued after the rising number of shooting sprees in the North American country."

"More international news related to gun control; in Switzerland, a man killed thirteen people and wounded twenty-seven others using a hunting shotgun and a pistol. In a

country known for its high number of firearms per citizen and almost null gun violence, this has shocked the world as gun regulation laws continue to weaken in most countries. The United States is currently the only nation in the world where acquiring firearms is encouraged by the state. What has been dubbed 'the gun culture' by the media is growing exponentially, and with it the murders and mass shootings. Although studies continue to demonstrate that gun regulation laws result in reduced killing sprees, the ROA continues to deny the facts claiming that an insane individual will use anything he can find to kill, such as knives, in a bid to defend what they refer to as the 'freedom to keep and bear arms.' Currently, the ROA, which holds incredible political power in the right-wing US government, has started to support and fund the US Space Deterrence program, a military campaign with the objective of placing strategic satellites armed with ICBMs as a self-defense mechanism to what they perceive to be 'potential foreign threats.' China has voiced its opinion and has threatened the North American nation with cutting off monetary aid for good and imposing economic blockades to dissuade them from engaging in further projects. Highly dependent on commerce with China, without this foreign support the US risks a devastating economic recession unless it immediately begins radical cuts in its over-inflated military budget, something Washington has been very outspoken against ever happening. This is what a spokesman for the White House had to say:"

"No economic cuts that can jeopardize our ability to defend ourselves against foreign threats will be made. We have reduced significantly our presence worldwide in order to focus on a stronger and better America, to comply with the demands of law-abiding American citizens who wish to

be protected by our Peacekeeping Army units. Our military bases were dismantled and our foreign Army Units were called back home not because of an economic inability to maintain them, but because America deserves better, and the safety of every American is the top priority of this administration. Fortunately, our time assisting our allies throughout the world has helped in strengthening them against possible threats, and they have learned tons of invaluable knowledge from the efficient and disciplined American Army. God is forever with us, and He will ensure our Great Nation prevails no matter what."

At the time, the newscasts on the United States used to be mainly about gun violence, religious fanaticism and the right-wing brainwashing so common to this particular era. Watching these reports before going to school was my way to kill time, a routine I had begun to grow heavily accustomed to.

"Stupid Unitedstatian white trash and their silly paranoid delusions of being invaded by the King of England," I used to think as I watched these numerous reports of massive shootouts involving assault rifles, and smiled gleefully every time thinking that as long as they kept killing each other, they would rid the world of the their stupidity forever.

Regarding gun control, I was fully in favor; even though I liked firearms and was extremely proud of the achievements of Communist designers, I knew that the civil population should not be allowed to freely own firearms. Firstly because it threatens government control and the general stability of society, and secondly because it threatens the security of citizens themselves when they fall in the hands of bullied psychopathic teenagers or soldiers suffering from PTSD. I also loved how they completely ignored a very important issue, the probability of a new civil war or a political group

117

with an agenda looking forward to seize power. The entire country was a recipe for disaster waiting to come to pass. With such a vast armed population, a complete societal chaos would erupt when the growing numbers of poor people began to stand up for themselves and consider capitalism the enemy which had deprived them of their human right to live decently. But in a society such as this, seeing a homeless man was simply a normal everyday thing, something to avoid and ignore in order to look forward to becoming a millionaire, a film star, a singer or some such stupid ambition. United-statians never thought about how poverty might reach or affect them.

They also seemed incapable of facing the fact that in order to defend themselves they didn't need guns that killed, but guns that stunned or paralyzed; electroshock weapons, riot shotguns, flashbangs, CS gas, sting grenades or pepper spray, these are effective means to which dissuade an opponent giving you enough time to handcuff them and call the police. Ironically, these measures were legal in the US but prohibited in many countries for their useful offensive purposes, implying they could lead to an increase in crime. Most police forces around the world had access to them, Loynne's included, but citizens could not be allowed to use them. Self-defense mechanisms that kill are legal while self-defense mechanisms that save lives are outlawed, very coherent indeed. Lethal incidents concerning firearms aren't only related to crime or insanity, but accidents. How many children have shot themselves or others playing with their father's revolver, or how many fathers have killed a family member mistaking it for an intruder? My thoughts went to the *Reviziya 02* revolver immediately. I wondered if one day I'd change my mentality completely when the massive gun defended me from a life-threatening situation. But this was Loynne's. Nobody was

interested in owning a gun, and the restrictions prevented anyone from wanting to. That's what the SKAR was for. I would never find myself in an extremely life-threatening situation in Loynne's that involved firearms. On the other hand, in the US these life-saving weapons proved useless as police forces had to face up against insane people and criminals armed with perfectly legal assault weapons. If Unitedstatians wanted to resolve this issue, they needed to ban lethal weapons entirely and promote the use of non-lethal ones. End of story. But there were too many interests to simply outlaw guns so easily. The ROA brainwashed citizens into believing they needed to own guns to survive the crazy jungle of society, to keep the Iranian-Mexican Communist Muslim Nazi Jews from invading and keep the gun companies selling, and the hick Unitedstatian rednecks needed to hunt and perform other assorted useful activities so as to not get bored in the middle of nowhere in the desert or the forest – those who didn't live in cities, that is. It made me think once again how the geography changed the context completely. As Unitedstatian cities sprawled with gang activity, armed robberies and daily revenge shootings, the countryside people focused on ending the lives of pythons, gators and deer. Everyone needed something to shoot at, or better said, give their newly acquired firearm some use.

Michael Weinstein, the rogue Unitedstatian, was becoming a sort of hero to those Unitedstatians who were willing to listen and take the blindfold off their eyes, tired of the social decay and the religious fundamentalism around them. Of course, everybody from the right-wing hated him backing their arguments with the stupidest reasons ever developed by a human mind. Nobody in the US liked the fact that he lived in Cuba to promote alternative values while criticizing Unitedstatian ones. Talks of him being "an evil red baby-killer

traitor sent from Hell by Satan" were also off the chart.

Michael Weinstein was a young slender man clad in a black suit with a red tie, his short black hair perfectly combed. He wanted to end once and for all the stereotype of the left-wing as being composed solely by sandal-wearing promiscuous hippies devoid of dignity or personal hygiene, and as such led a very conservative lifestyle, choosing to marry and raise a family as well as dressing exactly like his enemies. This was not propaganda from his part. Michael Weinstein had long campaigned for a serious, intellectual and disciplined left-wing which could break apart from that morally and sexually ambiguous lifestyle the left seemed to celebrate, often saying that not everybody interested in the fight against oppression needed to be a drug-abusing, anarchic and hedonistic decadent without moral values or ethics. According to him, the left-wing was experiencing a serious lack of ethical values in the wake of a rediscovered sexual freedom which eliminated the need for the family, a supposedly conservative topic Michael Weinstein insisted on being the basis for society, and the only way to raise people psychologically healthy with good citizen ethics. The promiscuous and degenerate left, as he always referred to it, needed to evolve into a more serious collective leaving behind the infantile and lusty need for a decadent lifestyle. Children raised by families consisting of bitter divorced parents buying the offspring's love with possessions, promiscuous single mothers acting like teenagers and midlife crisis-stricken fathers who neglected their children in favor of sluts half their age were to him the main cause of the shallowness, the anti-intellectualism and the materialistic ambitions of the future generations. This was a social issue which he insisted needed to be analyzed in relation to the ultra-permissive freedom the Western democracies always advocated, and just like Lenin, Michael Wein-

stein insisted on freedom being a precious resource, so precious that it needed to be carefully rationed and not abused or exploited.

But as it was to be expected, he quickly became the most hated person ever in the US, forcing him to immigrate to Cuba, a country he chose so as to give example on how the US would be if it wasn't so self-centered, zealously patriotic, ignorant and violent. Since then, Michael Weinstein had often traveled to the US to give interviews on TV or the radio, putting his personal safety in jeopardy. Two attempts against his life had already occurred, fortunately without injuring him, but greatly shattering his nerves resulting in an increased paranoia. Even with the odds that high, he insisted on traveling personally to the US so that people saw he could not be restrained. He often said that if he died, his enemies would merely prove the veracity behind his ideas.

I turned the TV off ready to head out. One week had passed since the presentation as I awoke on another hot clear day and followed the routine you're already familiar with; coped with Gordon, took the bus to Pilgrim Coast, walked down to school and met with my new classmates outside of room 206, where my class was on the second floor on the West Wing of the building, at the end of the corridor to the left. But not without doing something extremely important first.

I had picked this routine up in 4th of SCE, when my liberated state from Kanny oppression allowed me to see what I was missing in the school. Always rejecting the loudness and blue-collar brutality usually found in the Kanny infested school canteen, I had learned to bring my own food and ignore the place entirely. But with Wolfgang as a friend, I picked new customs and learned new tricks, almost all of them regarding food.

The canteen was usually deserted in the mornings before the classes started, busy only with a sparse population of teachers drinking their coffees. For some reason, students never bought anything in the morning and instead preferred to slaughter each other in elbow fights at recess. As such, Wolfgang and I had learned to sit comfortably at the canteen tables usually occupied by Kanny kings in recess, and enjoyed a relaxing meal far away from the noise of the students in the outer corridors; and our meals were none other than the best chicken croissants in the whole island.

I had never tasted anything so absolutely satisfying in my entire life. It was the only good thing that Loynne's had given me. Simple, delighting and cheap – only 2.15 crosses – the chicken croissants had become one of the very few luxuries I could enjoy only at school, and nowhere else; for some reason, bars and restaurants in Paradise Plaza were picky about preparing chicken croissants, saying it was a low-level tacky meal that tourists never ordered, and as such never bothered to prepare them, although they did on request. Very few bars offered chicken croissants in Paradise Plaza, usually uncomfortable slumholes, but the schools had the order of doing it, maybe because it was a cheap and complete meal easy to prepare and hand out to students. Whichever the reason, I had become completely addicted to them, and my day was complete when the moment to relax and eat a chicken croissant arrived. The soft texture of the salty bread, the tender shredded chicken completely bathed in cold mayonnaise, the melted sandwich cheese, the nice hot smell – when I wanted it grilled, sometimes I ordered it cold and enjoyed it just the same. Everything about the meal was simply marvelous, astounding, unique; and I was able to enjoy this particular pleasure at school, the last place in the world I thought could make me experience something akin to true joy. I had tried

many bars, pubs, cafés and even restaurants in the search for the perfect croissant, but to no avail; Pilgrim Coast High School remained the undefeated champion in chicken croissant making, and I could not fathom why.

I approached the girl, a school employee whose name I had never bothered to ask. She was cute, a blonde and short girl with blue eyes and her hair in a pony tail. Everyone used to flirt with her and ask for free food with unbelievably embarrassing pick up lines, but not me. Always cold and detached, focused only on what I wanted, I had always treated her with a certain distance Loynners were not accustomed to, and ordered my food politely. The girl, who I suspected had become considerably bored of the routine, used to simply go immediately to the grill in order to prepare the croissant and hand it to me as quickly as possible, never smiling and never looking me in the eye. I liked exchanges like these to be devoid of human touch, but this was too much even for me. As a result, I had come to despise the girl's demeanor, and always thought of asking her why she had to adopt that attitude when cooking my meal. But I never did. I always fell under the spell of the croissant's flavor, eventually forgetting all about the girl whenever the coveted meal was in my hands ready to be devoured.

This time I ate quickly, not quite enjoying myself as I would have liked, and rushed to the West Wing as soon as I could before something awkward happened like the last time. I threw the tinfoil wrap they usually gave you the chicken croissant in – it was the school's main projectile, preferred by pranksters and little kids for its light weight and high velocity, and as such could be found wherever you looked at, in classrooms, bathrooms and corridors – and marched quickly to the second floor, licking the remnants of the wonderfully cold mayonnaise from my lips.

The nervous knot in my stomach loosened when I reached my destination. You can get a lot of information by just looking at people, and now I could get a glimpse of my future classmates better than at the presentation. Most of them suited the perfect profile I had in mind, meaning no fancy codes in dressing, no hidden intentions and spoke in low, balanced voices. These were semi-Kannies at best. Pure, true Kannies always alerted you of their presence with loud, incoherent slang. These guys were the perfect class companions; not the ones you'll hang out or be friends with, but nice stage props that wouldn't worsen your already unstable view of the world. I knew by the sight of them that they would leave me alone in every sense of the word.

I saw Wolfgang separated by an invisible social barrier from the other students, looking stern, frowning and visibly uncomfortable. His jaw was pressed forwards, a sign he wanted to get out of the place fast. I couldn't have blamed him. Two years from then I would have been him, there in the dark, ignored by all the rest if lucky, made fun of and maybe beaten up if unlucky. I knew he hated being singled out, and people used to do that just by looking at him, the open book effect. Everyone pretty much singled Wolfgang out for another reason, however. Even if you don't believe it, Wolfgang had an older brother who had successfully completed his education in Pilgrim Coast High and had left quite a mark behind. People looked up to him, to his charming easygoing nature, to his leadership skills, to his smart, witty dialogue, and to make matters worse he also had quite a reputation with the ladies. Wolfgang was the shadow of his brother, and there was no doubt it affected him. He never shone by himself, and needed someone who would appreciate him for what he was. People knew this, and seemed to instinctively abuse Wolfgang to make him shape up. However,

it was obvious he had taken these lessons the wrong way, and just like me had learned to hate the world instead of adapting to it, not wanting to become a mindless drone following the will of whatever social norm ruled at the time.

I approached him instantly as I had nothing to do with the other guys anyway, nor I found myself wanting to. I still didn't know if under the clean-cut appearances they could be hiding something funny, like I had learned with other Loynner classmates – more often than not they had turned to be extremely fake, hypocritical people. No wonder I never learned to like locals much. What I was sure about was that at the moment, my loyalty lay with Wolfgang. I stopped fearing being associated with him a long time ago, and was actually quite concerned about his well-being on this new year. He was after all the only person I could rely on, the only one I could truly consider a friend; or at least, I felt reassurance in thinking that way; knowing I couldn't even trust Wolfgang seemed quite a depressing scenario.

"*Privyet, Tovarish.*"

"*Konnichiwa, Doshi,*" he said, doing the hand gesture his favorite video game character used to do. He signaled me with his fingers mimicking a handgun and raised his hand as if he had fired, also imitating the recoil. This was the signature gesture of Makarov Cat – his favorite video game character – known as the "Gunshot Salute," performed when he recognized a foe as a worthy opponent. Wolfgang was apparently the only one who dared reproduce it in public, something not even Gordon had the balls to do. Wolfgang had never really developed a sixth sense that warns you when you're doing something odd in front of people. In any case I had started to like the gesture as well, and officially adopted it as my private greeting for Wolfgang. I made sure nobody was looking when greeting back, and "fired" at Wolfgang also

imitating the recoil. It was nerdy and childish, but it showed just how much we wanted to separate ourselves from the rest, and how we really depended on each other for survival. Even though it seems hard to believe, in Loynne's you would almost never develop a special type of chemistry with another human being, at least if you had the kind of mentality people like Wolfgang and I did. Back then anyone who stood out from the thoughtless masses of Kannies was worthy of being approached as a potential friend, but amongst these, only Wolfgang proved to show interest in my ideology and understand the driving force behind it, which was a blend between strong militarism and unbreakable codes of honor, something he understood in the form of Bushido. Anyone who transcended the shallow mentality of Loynne's with their own philosophy was worthy of my time, no matter what others said about them.

"How's it going so far today? Any new friends yet?" I said, half sarcastically.

"Hah. Not today, not ever. I never made any last year, why change now?"

"I was just saying! Don't get so clinically depressed. You never know when a new friend can pop up from absolutely nowhere."

"Why bother, Sonny? You know how people are here anyway. Remember last year? The guys weren't so bad, but you know ... not like anyone's sending us Christmas cards."

"Yeah, got you there. Never mind that. Do you prefer being laughed at by anyone wearing a Unoq sports cap up their ass like two years ago?"

"Yeah Sonny, last year was the best I had in school as a matter of fact. I don't even remember being laughed at once. Well, maybe once or twice."

"There you go! And you did make a friend. You've got it

right in front of you in case you're forgetting, you blind bastard."

"Haha, oh yeah. Sorry, Sonny ... sometimes it feels as if we've known each other for ages ..."

"Sure does ..." As we conversed, a loud Spanish-sounding voice began to echo nearby. Suddenly, two huge shadowy figures came into the faint light of the corridor. They were imposing, but different. One was athletic, shorter in height than the other – as tall as me – and agile in its walking. The other was gigantic and robust with big heavy arms, and marched decisively with stomping feet.

When they came nearer their features were fully revealed, and my eyes feasted on the information they irradiated. The figure on the left, the athletic one, was dark skinned, obviously Latin American, wearing quite not what Kannies wore, but in a similar way. He had a short curly hairstyle with sharp sideburns which blended right cleanly into a small beard that ran along his very square jaw, very well shaven. With a tiny nose pointing a bit upwards, ears fully clad in earrings and dark and beady eyes, his expression was that of infinite joy and cheer; his body, something Kannies would have quite envied.

The figure to the right, however, was none other than Mike Levanter, the friend I mentioned before who I had met in my first year in Loynne's, along with Ryan.

"Mike!" I shouted, approaching him to shake hands. "I can't believe you're in the same class we are!"

"What's up, Sonny boy? Yeah, I'm gonna keep you boys company for a few months. I plan to get a job and since my dad is being a real asshole lately, I prefer to be here than stayin' at home."

"You must be really passing through something hard. I mean, to prefer spending six hours in this hell-hole than at

home ..."

"Yeah, but I'm sure you don't have a dad like mine, Sonny boy," Mike said, as if he didn't want to touch upon the subject too much. I actually knew very little of his personal life, only that his father was somewhat abusive of his family. Mike Levanter spoke with a grave and educated voice, seemingly wanting to distance himself from the stereotype of urban Unitedstatian black slang. Highly intelligent but also street-wise, he was a tough character, big and strong as a grizzly bear, fat but muscular, sporting a shaven haircut, almost bald, brown round eyes and a childish smile which showed an overflow of happiness, but could turn into an aggressive ex-pression if he wanted. He was almost always seen wearing his Unitedstatian M-1965 field jacket and dog tags, items which had belonged to his grandfather, a US soldier who had gone MIA in Vietnam. Mike rarely took his jacket off, not even against the odds of facing brutal Kannovschina for not wear-ing a hundred different garments each week, but somebody like him didn't have to fear. Out of size alone, roughly 2.02 meters and weighing over 150 kilos, nobody dared utter a word, at least not in front of him. Also, nobody wanted to fight a former Boxing Champion of Loynne's Island.

I remembered very well the day I had met Mike for the first time; it was two years from then during recess, when I was in the 3rd Grade. Mike was part of the ragtag band of outcasts that got together during breaks to talk about video games, and it was only a matter of time before I tried to es-cape Gordon's claws and socialize with people who had wider interests. This is how I also met Ryan and the Nazarethes. After conversing with Mike for a while, I had been naturally surprised to see that a black Unitedstatian from California and I shared plenty of intellectual matters in common. We befriended instantly and since that moment, had always

maintained a close friendship, often falling for the philosophical aspects of life and having deep insightful chats over the reality of Loynne's. Mike had always been interested in Socrates, Plato, Aristotle, Nietzsche, Kant and Freud as he seemed to prefer philosophy over politics, and I used to seize the advantage to demonstrate my knowledge of Marx to him, which he always found interesting. He generally did not trust politicians or ideologies, but still identified heavily with activists such as Martin Luther King Jr., Angela Yvonne Davis and Malcolm X, also having great respect for the revived Black Panther Movement struggling against white-supremacists in the US. As such, Mike had become a symbol that made you feel respect toward the few Unitedstatians not brainwashed by petty patriotism and religious bigotry, as well as for comrades of different skin color, a representative figure who demonstrated their keen intelligence and good nature, virtues always suppressed by the propaganda of European and Unitedstatian racists. As it was usual with Unitedstatians abroad, Mike never spoke about his country probably out of sheer embarrassment, and instead tried to embrace the multicultural society of Loynne's.

"Fuck, Mikey! Never told me you knew some motherfuckers here!"

"Haha, yeah, this is my friend, Sonny. Sonny, this is Axel Guerrero. To put it simply, funniest fuckin' guy you'll ever meet in your life."

"Hey man, pleasure to meet ya! You new here too?"

"No, this is my third year here actually."

"Fuck, you look like you just been drafted from the fuckin' army man, this how you always dress?"

"Well, yeah ... What? Is it ... wrong?"

"Nah, nah man, just a bit weird, don't you think, holmes?! Wooooh, I'm fuckin' pumped today!! Haha, this school o'

yours, it looks like a fuckin' prison, man!"

"Better believe him, Sonny ... he knows."

"Not like I'm too fond of it either, Mike. It IS a prison," I said.

"From where I come from man, it was a prison but a grade-A fuckin' luxury prison. Know what I'm sayin'? A fuckin' boarding school, man! Like the third I've been kicked out of ... Man, you look like pretty cool people. Bet you're really popular around here, right?"

"Er ... you mean us?" I said, looking at Wolfgang with the corner of my eye, who was silently contemplating the situation, submerged in his silent social awkwardness.

"Yeah, you two! Let's hang out bitches, I seriously doubt I'll get along with anyone else in this fuckin' class at least. All fuckin' pretentious Kannies an' shit with their cocks up their asses. Know a few of them from boarding school too. Rich pricked asses who got thrown outta boarding school jus' like me, but without keepin' it real. STUCK UP FUCKIN' FAGS! ALL OF 'EM!" At that moment, whilst Axel Guerrero was shouting his heart out for everyone to hear, some of the people I described before seemed to notice his loud nature, and recognized it, not taking exactly kindly to it.

"Hey Guerrero ... you talking about us?" a serious-looking guy said with a monotonous voice, looking at him mercilessly with cold eyes.

"No, man. How can I be talkin' 'bout you? Wait ... what the shit, man! I didn't see you before! How you doin' over there! Haven't seen you since last term, when I got kicked out! Everythin' runnin' sweet, man?!"

"Not exactly ... Especially not after my girlfriend broke up with me for some odd reason. People told me you were involved."

"Me? Haha how can I be involved? I had my own girl-

friend man!"

"Too many girlfriends you had."

"Yo, how 'bout we chill for a bit, motherfucker. You know that's all lies. What. You callin' me a liar, man?!"

"No no ... easy there. I'm just saying ... take care of yourself ... that's all I'm saying." Axel's expression of cheer and joy vanished to turn into deep hatred and a cold murdering controlled rage. He stared at the guy and replied:

"You wanna start somethin' man? 'Cause it's fuckin' on the moment you say it is, alright?"

"Pff, yeah ... as if ..." The guy said, and turned his back on Axel and returned to his friends, who were looking from a safe distance down the corridor.

"Fuckin' assholes man. Jeez ain't givin' a guy a break ever. CUT A GUY SOME FUCKIN' SLACK, HUH?! So what if I got lucky with bitches, they came after me, not the other way round! Anyway guys, let's introduce the people that haven't been introduced yet, shall we? I don't think I know your friend, or that he knows Mikey."

"Oh yeah, look this is Wolfgang, Wolfgang Emmerich," I replied quickly. I was still wondering why someone so fly looking like Axel Guerrero would even want to do anything with us, and had I met him years before I would have guessed this was a prank. It wouldn't have been the first time.

Wolfgang shook their hands looking rather relieved and happy to be making new friends, and, following his naïve nature got friendlier in a matter of seconds. His stern facial expression withered almost immediately.

The bell rang. It was a horrible sound, a mixture between a normal school bell and an air raid siren, and I'm not exaggerating. Everybody entered the class with notable parsimony and proceeded to seat down in the same places we had done during the presentation, as per usual. General chatter ensued

on what to expect next, perhaps a fun and involving set of teachers like during the liberal 4th Grade, when teachers began opening up and befriending students. Maybe we would have a kind and generous obese math teacher like last year, who we could chat with and waste a good precious 30 minutes of class while he talked about how he hated the service at McReady's. Or even so, maybe a German teacher who would give us sexual advice on how to please our partners better. The previous year had been a wonderful and innovative experience, but when the class tutor strolled through the threshold with his frowning face and volatile demeanor, we knew we were in for a good time.

· · · · ·

We had had quite a busy day. The first class had been with the nerdy Californian teacher, Tom Richards. He was quite a character that turned out to be much more than what his looks gave away.

Tom Richards had moved to Loynne's Island at around the same time Unitedstatians started looking outside of the US for opportunity, and the "Unitedstatian Dream" was officially vaporized. The trillionaire military spending had ravaged the country beyond repair, and they found themselves almost slaves to Asian and European currencies. Such a big country, with such a vast military and world superpower status costs couldn't maintain its position globally competing with its old foe Russia and its newfound rival China. The US found itself defeated for the first time after a long "winning" streak. Unitedstatians were now spread across the globe still invading other cultures with their bizarre mentality and spreading the Dream no matter how many times they were told it had forever died. But the new Dream was Asian in

nature. It represented basically conformity with one's work and being thankful you had one in the first place. The new Dream wasn't power, stardom, fame and omnipotence anymore. It was aiming at petty materialistic possessions like the new Hipps-Tear device or the latest 216 cm VaniTV. It was getting one or two cars, a home if extremely lucky. It was getting a job as a waiter and having a hot Kanny girlfriend whom you'd eventually have Kanny kids with. It was drugs and alcohol and whores every Friday night. But never aiming for real power. You couldn't "make it" anymore, nor anyone was encouraged to. The new thinking was "make the best out of yourself, but the important posts are already filled." Loynne's was invaded by these people, Ryan and Tom Richards being living testimony of how Unitedstatians cut off their own stupid nationalistic, imperialist pride when they were forced to emigrate. As a Soviet Communist, I was glad this had finally come to pass, that our old nemesis had begun to experience the first signs of the eventual collapse that would get rid of their system, culture, society and nation. But spiteful as I was, I couldn't help but be bothered about something; the fall of a superpower always brought forth the dawn of a new era. And even though I was quite tired of the past, I was fearful maybe something even worse could arise.

Tom Richards had studied physics and chemistry in the University of California and graduated with major honors. The guy was a mastermind, but also extremely vain and a show-off; he wasted most of our time detailing how he had helped invent some space shuttle or biological weapon, how he had worked at NASA building rockets, how he had met the only Loynner owner of the legendary Sforza Contessa, how he had helped develop combat tactics for the US Special Forces and so on. As such, most viewed him as a joke and a clown due to the impossibility of his achievements, despite his bril-

liant mind. Being a US citizen as he was, the detail of politics, Unitedstatian culture and his hatred for Communism and all things Russian was quite apparent either way, although he "tried" to never take sides in politics. He possessed a mixed ideology of his own to criticize as fairly as he could how humanity failed in most of the things it did and how we would be better off becoming extinct as a species. He used to go around describing himself as a progressive conservative, a paradox I could not quite fathom. I had always thought he meant being progressive scientifically while being conservative sociopolitically. Tom Richards was obviously proud of his heritage, but secretly knew what was wrong with his nation, and the damaged it had caused the world. The brilliant professor, once lecturer at the University of California, was now an immigrant two-bit teacher for Science Baccalaureate in some school in Loynne's Island, coping with stupid children and Kannies every day. You couldn't help but feel sorry for the guy.

That was for physics and chemistry; for history and – unbelievably – language, we had a Russian professor still sporting what I thought could be his clothes from the Soviet era. He had an infamous hole in the rear of his torn jeans many used to perfect their projectile accuracy with. He was also quite big and fat, having to drink a bottle of water frequently between speeches and rubbing his forehead constantly with a handkerchief. His face was round in an oval shape, with a beard similar to Lenin's and a bald patch on his head.

Artem Arkazhov was the name. In personality terms, he was a loner, a pessimist, a nostalgic and many thought, a drunkard. Artem spent most of his classes talking about the past glory of Soviet Russia with great nostalgia, and with rampant hatred when it was the moment to talk about the current Russia. It was a guy I would have socialized with

more if it weren't for the fact that I wanted to conceal my identity as much as I could, and also because he didn't seem the type you'd befriend and hang out with. He rushed to the exit when the bell rang, as if wanting to vanish from existence as much as me, and never expressed interest in any student. He barely smiled. Many thought that inside his bottle he had actual vodka mixed in with a bit of water, due to his constant smell of alcohol. It was amazing how nobody ever seemed to mind his dirty and abandoned appearance. Artem had a rivalry with Tom Richards which was quite unhealthy, and they would often exchange dirty looks or even insults when shifting for the classes. It was actually kind of fun. Seeing Tom Richards being forced to leave the classroom for the Russian teacher was a show in itself; they hated each other for their respective nationalities and ideological background, and Richards despised even more the fact that Arkazhov was in charge of teaching History. He never praised the US in any way, and almost always evaded talking about the end of the Soviet Union at the hands of capitalism. However, he recognized the weak spots that drove the USSR to defeat, adding always that capitalism would drive the world to lose its identity and pride. I liked this teacher more than anyone, but I couldn't do anything else aside from limiting myself to hear what he said and picturing it in my head, it being the only link I had to a world I knew and considered home. Artem got me nostalgic every single class, and I was happy I was sitting in the front left corner of the class so nobody could see me obsessively drawing the Hammer and Sickle all over the table, shedding a tiny tear thinking about The Motherland or imagining deviously cruel ways on how to slaughter a Kanny.

Immediately after, we had German class, which I hated. German class meant that every single student was bound to ask me their doubts, as I had an unbearable penchant for

expressing my superiority in foreign languages to make up for my innate uselessness in mathematical sciences and sports. The teacher, an ill-fated old woman with a short temper that had depressive issues was named Edith; during Kannovschina – teachers suffered sometimes even more than students – she waged what can be described as an all-out war on Kannies, a zero tolerance policy concentrated on shaping up the toughest cases. Through a regimen of perseverance and humiliation, she had won. She was the only teacher who could criticize a student and make him laugh in sympathy. During this era she had somehow mistaken me for a troublemaker and supposed I had a superiority complex just due to being good at the subject. She was German teacher on 3th Grade, so you know of what period I'm talking about. Edith later seemed to be giving up, especially since Kannovschina mysteriously began to weaken considerable after 4th grade. She no longer was the ardent and terrible warfighter we had come to dread and fear. She had turned into a friendly face and unfortunately for me, someone who always needed my help and interaction in class.

After that, we had our very little break, the infamous recess. Basically a half an hour excuse for people to stuff their mouths with junk food, for Kannies and jocks to play football and freaks to gather in small assemblies to talk about Stern-Spielt, World Defender: Peace Corps and Realm of Witchcraft, the groundbreaking video games of the moment. Almost everybody was buying the new GamEsprit Drei because of World Defender, whilst Realm of Witchcraft concentrated gatherings of lifeless freaks in Gamer Abyss – no, not an expression – an actual popular video game store with computers to play that sort of games online with your stupid friends. SternSpielt, however, had people on a tight schedule and painkiller diet, as the game never stopped and was saved

via LoynNet, since you somehow could command ships to come back and forth the hours you wanted, and you had to make sure you made those times adequate for your advantage, as an unfortunate player could get wiped out by three or more others in a massacre that left you crying over the debris of your former fleet.

To be completely honest, I was into video games once; ironically, they were my only shelter from the scourge of Western life. I would sit in front of the computer every afternoon and forget about my suffering filling my mind with the wonders of a type of entertainment I would have never ever dreamed of in The Motherland. As good as any type of book or film, video games filled a gap in my life at the most precise and needed moment. I would have been driven to insanity without them. Having so much spare time and no friends dictated this type of behavior. Unlike Gordon, however, I looked for a perfect balance in quality, story-telling and entertainment. A franchise named "Gears of Deterrence" – Gordon's favorite – in particular astonished me for its understanding of the political, making me question what someone so stupid like Gordon could see in it. I also never played with people over the net. To me, it was the machine and me, the fictional world the game set for me to dwell in. If I had wanted to bear the shit of human beings playing that as well, I would have gone out and played football with some Kannies. Isolating myself in that virtual world, without obviously taking it as far as Gordon did – after all, fiction is just fiction – who had basically no other subject of conversation and who constructed his whole life around it.

However, over the span of a few years, video games had visibly changed. While most of them had in fact been a balance of personal empathy with the story, no matter how simple, and the smoothness of the gameplay itself, video games

were now – like anything the industry lays its eyes upon – a cold mass-produced source of wealth aimed at making more and more profit, not very much different from the music and film industries, which every year continued to release more and more creations of incredible low taste and talent. Video games were the entertainment industry of the future, a bid for points and competition in levels not reached even by professional sports leagues, while at the same time being used for customer espionage and marketing PR; the gaming systems of the next generation had sprung to life not long ago in their newest forms, involving updated reward systems that earned you points used for absolutely nothing, just status and bragging rights. The world had lost its barriers at least in the online life, where you could compare your status with every single player of any of the other systems. Everything was online, taking advantage of the newly established LoynNet intranet, a Loynne's Island only network service. The reason Loynne's had to create Loynnet in the first place was that the main superpowers – United States, Russia and China – had engaged in brutal cyberwarfare causing most countries around the world to establish their own parallel networks shut off from the big and chaotic 'Internet.' Countries like Brazil, Iran and India spearheaded this trend claiming that their cyberspace could be monitored by intelligence services of – mainly – the US. But this was not the only issue. Hacker collectives comprised of members of widely differing ideologies kept troubling the governments of both left and right, not caring one bit for the real issues at hand and seemingly wreaking havoc just for thrills, hacking the devices and accounts of innocent people, destabilizing networks and security grids and even going as far as engaging in physical terrorism through the practice of electrical outages. The growing threat of jihadist terrorism also seemed to be increasing,

unstoppable and undetectable. These threats were quickly dealt with as demonstrated by arrests performed by United-statian and Russian government agencies, but more hackers and terrorists kept appearing to replace those incarcerated or killed. It was time for the governments of the world to act decisively if they wanted to prevail, and as such the cyber-terrorist menace received top priority. Country specific cy-berspaces inaccessible to other nations were born out of paranoia, fear and deterrence. Long gone was the chaotic and disorganized freedom of the "World Wide Web" at the start of the millennium, and now each country in the world possessed its own private cyberspace in the form of intranets. LoynNet was one of those isolated networks born as an answer to the spying nature of the superpowers and their cyberwarfare, and the anarchic chaos of reckless hackers.

Not monitored by the government agencies of the world and available for free, millions of tourists visited Loynne's only to enjoy the freedom of surfing the net without the watchful eye of their respective countries. It should also be noted that LoynNet servers offered the best, fastest service in the entire world.

This unusual luxury also brought about another battle-field, that of the digital entertainment industry I so immense-ly loathed, greasing its gears to perpetuate vapid and mind-less forms of entertainment people like Gordon consumed. The launch of the world's new leading consoles was targeted to the population of the island, who would boost sales and increase the popularity of each system, while also waging war and competing with each other in the best capitalistic fash-ion.

Each console had unique system capabilities and were aimed at different target audiences, but only two of them were virtually the same and competed for supreme domina-

tion; the super-powered, impossible to afford and hyper reliable GamEsprit Drei by European based Vanity Digital Entertainment Corporation, praised by its free online service, top-notch graphics and multiple entertainment features, and criticized for its price, obvious spying applications and weak online credit card safety; by the hand of the Unitedstatian super-giant Hipps-Tear Enterprises came the Pandora, strong as its Vanity counterpart but without as much features and with an online service you had to pay for monthly. It also came fully equipped with its own Death Beep of Doom, a total halt of the console turned infamously well-known for its annoying beeping sound, which meant its complete utter destruction and subsequent return to the shop or throw to the nearest dumpster. Lastly, and no less important until maybe two years from then, was the Kabushi Inazuma, a sensor based and movements orientated console with an emphasis on fitness and childish kid-friendly games. This might have just been the last video game console attached to the era I talked about, that is, not featuring the bragging reward system and its sickening emphasis on social interaction. This console had sold fiercely as it was the first one to launch, but had been used to stomp paper since her cousins developed their own ways of sensor gaming, and combined with high definition graphics and ultra-high resolutions, it wasn't long before this console was considered "old" and left aside, its impact withering away along with the incompatible ideology of making fat lazy gamers move around. This console war discovered many things about our nature and idea of gaming, and it would be Vanity and Hipps-Tear the ones in the right; gamers wanted reward pat-on-the-back attaboy systems, encouraging them to be completion obsessive maniacs devoted to brag about how many Milestones – as these completion rewards were called – they had collected. Kabushi

sort of remained behind the scenes in the gaming community, orientated for bored adults who hadn't used a console in their life, kids who weren't allowed to play hardcore violent games, and girls. Hence Vanity's publicity slogan, "True Gamers enjoy Vanity."

With the Kabushi officially out of the competition only two remained, the GamEsprit and the Pandora. In this overly competitive capitalist world, everything seemed to head into a direction of absolute monopoly. Whereas countless devices had littered the markets a few years from then, usually three to two companies were left in the industrial arena, all others vanishing or merging with the giants. This happened with video game consoles, with phone companies, with computer brands and cars. Like democracy and its tendency to create a two-party system, capitalism seemed to generate a monopoly shared between two major rival companies. Vanity and Hipps-Tear were a perfect example of this.

So recess involved me just by the small passageway to the parking lot, right behind the football pitch, with the freak friends like Gordon concentrated on the upper part of the passageway and my closest friends like Wolfgang near me, at the lower part. The Cuban-Unitedstatian Axel Guerrero was now like a star in recess, but especially among freaks. His knowledge of video games and his Kanny coolness made him a god amongst weirdos, and a misfit amongst jocks and Kannies, however he didn't seem to care much, as his only friends there were Mike, Ryan, a few freaks more and me. His drugs and sex parties stories plus his rants about funny things that supposedly happened to him while fighting around with Kannies earned him a solid reputation and a leader-like role. Also, he was the only one to tolerate the burden of buying the food in the canteen, and as such everyone handed him the money to go and buy food, prompting him to return filled

with chicken croissants, ham and cheese sandwiches and other delicacies which made our sorry existence as exiled misfits more tolerable. Axel Guerrero indeed seemed to have a heart, and comradeship was amongst his best signatures; he would never leave anybody to rot at the hands of someone else, typically bullies, and also had strong moral values dubious of a person who would leave a female partner to care of herself in such evil ways.

I must admit, people might be anti-Communistic in tone generally, but when they show signs of comradeship like that you can feel there's not a world of difference among humans. Axel couldn't bear hearing about the Cuban Revolution, about Communism and Socialism, about nothing at all regarding those matters, except of course when it came from my voice of reason, only because I knew how to approach him and actually talk to him on the subject, a thing he always praised. Axel thought what almost everyone thinks, that Communists are power hungry megalomaniacs as anyone can be, shielding themselves on their just ideology and good intentions, all of which fail when put into practice. You couldn't really blame them; Stalinist Communism involved a largely arbitrary witch-hunt similar to McCarthyism, pointing at the person next to you accusing him of being a Communist if you were Unitedstatian, and a capitalist dog if you were Soviet.

Speaking to people like Axel actually made me open up more about who I actually was while interacting with locals. Axel was clearly apolitical and pursued a care-free, lavish lifestyle, the kind the higher ups enjoy. His proletarian status enabled him to enjoy this in a capitalist system, which he wouldn't have in a Communist one. He also clearly loved to say whatever he was thinking or feeling. This unleashed freedom of choice gave him true happiness and stability, whether

his home country was riddled with supposed corruptions and bureaucratic technicalities proper of emergent Socialist South American republics. I understood quite well the state of affairs in countries that had been abandoned by the fall of the USSR, destined to wander in a capitalist savage uncertain woodland. The kind of human mistakes made in this condition were to be expected. I had the following conversation at recess with Axel, a conversation which made me ponder on this even more:

"Was speaking to my cousin the other day Sonny. Shit ain't that shiny in my homeland. That prick Ricardo Valdés keeps censoring journalists, imprisoning and deporting those who don't shut up man, like me. I ain't ever gonna shut up and it's my duty to tell this to every fucker I can."

"You know I'm a Communist sympathizer, Axel. And as such, I'm going to defend him. You know what I stand for. Social and economic equality, the suppression of higher classes with better conditions and a worker's society where everyone is a true equal, a comrade. How can you oppose that in favor of Unitedstatian and European imperialism? Countries like the US and continents like Europe are simply trying to influence you all the time. Remember the Cold War? They had local dictators appointed in every part of South America to spread right-wing influence and suppress leftist ideals. That resulted in more deaths, censorship and imprisonment than you supposedly have nowadays. What you call 'censorship' or 'oppression', is a war of interests produced due to people like those right-wing pro-Unitedstatian agents or sympathizers, mercenaries that work to put the government in an unfavorable light in order to make your country a nest of drugs, prostitution and gambling, like Cuba was before the Revolution, the disgusting and corrupt backyard of the Unitedstatian empire. What kind of society is that? Yeah, I know

you like to like to have your fun but—" And then I stopped. I realized there was nothing else to add. He lived that kind of life and even so managed to be a good friend, more or less. Definitely not someone who would stab you in the back for personal gain. But was this enough to defend his actions? After all, he was nothing more than a womanizing sleaze, a drug supporting fun lover who treated women like objects and wanted nothing more than money to support this never-ending cycle, a perfect representative of the Miami ultra-right, the *gusanos*, and its undeniable criminal background. Where could humanity go with people like these leading it, the younger generation lost in a self-induced sleep of vice, lust and sloth? Judging by the decay in capitalist systems worldwide, my guess would be not very far.

"Look Sonny man, I feel you, I know what you're trying to say. But my people suffer 'cause of this shit, OK? They really do. Imagine you living there, would you be happy? You sure seem happy here talking about games with us and listening to your little Hipp-Man and eating chicken croissants every day. Well that shit ain't possible in my country, not without sling-ing some drugs or pulling off some tricks or some shit ... and it surely wasn't possible in yours neither, motherfucker!" This is exactly why my hands were tied with people such as Axel. People don't like to listen, to open their eyes and admit the true hard and cold reality that is the cynicism of capitalism. My thoughts went back to the never-ending green fields of The Motherland, only to die shortly after while thinking about the things that poisoned both from outside and inside. The drug trafficking, the disputes between different parties, the cult of personality and useless glorifying of leaders, the black markets and government corruption; it had all ended when the civil war rampaged through the same green fields. My country lay ravaged by death and economic decay, aside

from the general moral void that was sweeping the world. The youths grew violent and uncivilized, learning their lessons from the environment.

"This is capitalism," I thought. And people like Axel talking in that way only worsened my view on "freedom" and "democracy."

"Axel, this is not about material possessions. This is about the bigger picture, a thing many fail to see. Heads of corporations worldwide, celebrities, politicians, businessmen enjoy a life you will not ever even reach with your fingertips. A life you can only fantasize about in your mortal assumptions. To them, you're an expendable pawn, a number in the millions of statistics that buy their worthless products, to them you're money. What we aim to build is the suppression of all this injustice, but it's difficult when people oppose it so fiercely and only want to assassinate whomever is trying to lead the movement. Valdés is trying to unite Latin America in order to stand up to Unitedstatian interests, why oppose him? To feed the US with our resources and enjoy their consumerism and capitalist role-model? I just can't think of anything else. You'll see when these economic systems finally crumble. The US already ceased to be the dominant superpower a long time ago, it's actually not considered a factor anymore, and Europe will also experience this. Latin America and Eurasia are on the rise. You'll see what I'm talking about in no time."

"Ahh Sonny, Sonny ... your ideals are honest and true and shit, but face it, politicians lie, no matter if they're from the left or the right, governments are always gonna be corrupt, and corruption is gonna spread like bat shit all over, be it capitalist or communist. So shut up and do what I do, and just enjoy some sluts and good sex before you ain't got the enthusiasm no more. One day you'll be old and boring and shit, worrying more about a bank loan, car insurance or why

you can't sleep with your daughter's friends, instead of trying to save the world with communism. Look man, I told you, I feel you, I got respect for your beliefs just like you do for my shit, but I ain't ever gonna agree or believe in it. Forget it. Any guy with enough power turns into an asshole. Let's just forget this whole thing and forget about changing humanity and enjoy what we have nowadays! The video games, the drugs, the sex, the cars, the beach ... Why worry, one day we'll all be dead! You're not gonna be happy if you spent all your life worrying about how these fuckers should handle their shit. Let 'em rob us, see if I care. One way or another, every pig has his day." Suddenly, Axel's attention shifted completely from me to Wolfgang, who was nearby speaking to Gordon, and approached the guys completely halting their conversation. "Listen up amateur motherfuckers, gotta true Delta Hardcore story to tell! It was by the time I was serving with the Unit in Central Slovodnia, so there I was ... pff, you know, when you're there in the middle of fuckin' nowhere, surrounded by enemies ... hungry and terribly wounded. The situation was desperate; I didn't have any ammo left for the RPK and the enemy were closing in even further ... What is one to do in a situation like that, man? My strength at this point was extreeeeemely LOW. Imagine that. While resting against one of those makeshift tranches, some of them threw F-1 frags at me, others kept chasing until they got a clearer shot, but I didn't give up and continued to fight, I simply never bend over like a bitch and take it. I attacked a lone soldier whose rifle had jammed, and using my personal defense techniques I managed to pry the rifle out of his hands and slaughter the other soldiers. Yeah, that's how I did it. It saved my life, man."

"F-M-S, what happened next?!" asked Wolfgang.

"I selected the health menu to bandage the wound, of

course, of course. Did you know that if you have a Gears of Deterrence 2 save in your Stat Card the healing options are more complete, including those from Gears of Deterrence 1 and its expansion pack?" Axel told Wolfgang.

"Wow, that's so awesome! I want to buy me Gears of Deterrence 3: Cannibal Vipers. They say that it's the best game ever designed for the GamEsprit since Spirit Limit: Warrior's Patience."

"You oughta try an' play some World Defender Wolfie, shootin' them 8-year-olds and insultin' the fuck outta them while you do it is some good fun too!" The world of digital entertainment had been invaded by a wave of military shooters, always putting the player in the role of a jarhead US Marine ignorant of his actions repeatedly told to fight for supposed democracy and freedom, "liberating" other countries by increasing the body count to unheard of levels. These Unitedstatian military shooters, of which the World Defender series was the absolute king, were quite a thing. Addictive multiplayer modes made the players want to slaughter the hell out of each other while training themselves mentally for fighting the enemies of the US. The enemies you had to fight always were the tired formula of Arab insurgents, Hispanic guerillas, North Koreans and Russians. But people kept on buying these games. For some reason they loved to be in the shoes of a tough Marine defender of God, freedom, liberty, democracy, capitalism, and everything else that's holy in the West. Why other nationalities didn't complain also came as a surprise. Wasn't it time to move on, to forget about Unitedstatian imperialist foreign politics and shoot something else? I find it very unlikely Unitedstatians would spend their spare time shooting virtual versions of themselves in the shoes of foreign soldiers. This was what they forced the rest of the world to do. A kind of cultural deterrence, like Michael Wein-

stein always upheld, was needed to stop this Unitedstatian brainwashing abroad, a cultural deterrence capable of dissuading them from producing their stupid Hollywood films about the US being attacked and the glorious Marines coming for the defense of the nation. Why couldn't Russia produce a video game about a Unitedstatian invasion, inciting players in sympathizing with Russia in order to defeat the Unitedstatian invader? What kept countries from wanting to produce a propagandistic counterattack to stop Unitedstatian non-culture? And most importantly, why did nations like China still consume Unitedstatian trash with such glee? China was the biggest consumer of Unitedstatian idiocy, even if Chinese society was largely unaffected by their idiotic mentality. But it made no sense. Couldn't the Chinese rise up and claim superiority, produce films, literature and video games criticizing Unitedstatian values while making the consumer feel sympathy for Chinese ones?

"Why don't we talk about something that isn't games, please?" I said, scornfully. They didn't hear me, as usual, as Axel was extremely engaged in the conversation not only with Wolfgang, but with Mike and Billy as well. They didn't help either; continuously, more game names were poured into the conversation, making me remember titles I had worked hard in forgetting after Gordon was done with them and moved on to new ones, including "Evil Hills," "Manslaughter," "Neverending Story XVII" and "Call to Action," creating an image inside my mind of how much lifeless and addicted my friends were in reality. Was this a temporary stage of life? Or was it a fad? I had long ago surpassed the short-lived vice video games brought to my life, and wanted to start living in the flesh things they couldn't bring. I didn't understand how they could feel such an excitement over a thing that didn't make you feel alive, instead making you feel dead and bound

to the chair like a body inside an iron maiden device, bleeding and decomposing, losing more life each second that passes, escaping from the grasp of the living world and falling into eternal darkness sentenced to a numb and useless existence, surrounded by your own worthless, useless, good for nothing Milestones and your limp dick.

"Yeah, I remember Sorority Chainsaw. Wasn't it that one where you're this kid that goes around murdering people that piss him off at school?"

"No dude, that's Suburban Release, what I'm talkin' about is the one where the lead guy Timmy goes to the sorority manor to get it on with the chicks and they're all undead and he's gotta escape the manor, ring a bell?"

"Ah, yeah, I remember that one; it was one of the coolest, no dialogue and lots of sex, just the way I like it. Gears of Deterrence 2, don't make me laugh. Lame-ass conversations about nukes and shit, what the hell, nobody bothered to listen to that crap, what were they thinking?! It's only proof that gamers never talk about that aspect of the game with each other, don't you think? So fuckin' stupid, that game is at the top of my blacklist. All the war philosophical babble going on, a radio call every two minutes ... I just wanna friggin' shoot somebody!! Sheez, no wonder that game was so hated. Adapt to the market or die, baby! Well, that's why they released the sequel, didn't they? Yeah, they knew how to adapt alright. Keepin' the bar high up! Don't you think, Sonny?"

That's the kind of material I had to talk about during recess. Gaming 24/7, every day of the year. After this inane punishment that made me doubt whether the old days of Kannovschina deserved a comeback, we had our lovely computer class with our favorite teacher, The Perv. Being that the only name they used to refer to him, I've forgotten his actual name. Girls in class had started complaining about the teach-

er looking at their impossible to ignore g-strings and cleavages. These unwilling teasers had their benefits; for instance, their complaints had to go through the proper channels to be validated, and since it was common practice to denounce teachers for anything, students would be usually brushed aside unless their concerns were proven to be true. In any case, this waste of time granted us access to very beneficial rewards, namely free hours after break, making our recess last an hour and a half almost. Thus, our bonds increased through those free hours and even made our desires to commit truancy far more frequent, a temptation we failed to resist and usually succumbed to quite often, but didn't matter. There wasn't much you could learn from those teachers, and I knew very well what sort of knowledge would be useful to me in the future.

After this class we had math with an average normal teacher, not particularly interesting to talk about. This in turn made the classes infinitely more boring. Just like with the biology and philosophy teachers, he was competent but sorely uninteresting as a person, a simple bureaucrat successfully fulfilling his role, keeping a low profile and thus being undeserving of any mention.

And finally we had PE class. However, for the first weeks, we had swimming lessons, which made all of us want to get home as early as possible to have something to eat and sleep the afternoon away. It wasn't compulsory but you had to do a written exam if you skipped the lessons. Usually, people with medical problems or girls who didn't want to show their bodies could be found sitting at the benches overlooking the pool, comfortably enjoying the shade of the palm trees.

PE class, fortunately, was at the very last hour. When the pool lessons finished and we had to get back to the tedious obstacles courses and football matches, we would get sweaty,

dirty and skinned, itching to have the wondrous opportunity to go immediately back home, shower and forget about school for an afternoon and two days. If you were responsible and hard-working, you'd usually maybe take the rest of the day off, and finish homework and pending essays on Saturday or Sunday, but I never minded work too much unless it was a matter of life and death. I always left everything unfinished until the very end when it was essential. The therapy I submitted myself to each afternoon after class involved cleansing that awful social stench off my mind and indulging my favorite hobbies; I thoroughly enjoyed watching films and reading, any kind of entertainment would do in order to seize each passing second before the educational machine awoke again the next day. I was avoiding life, shielding on my mysterious nature and supposed busy and tortured lifestyle, using excuses so as to not involve myself too much in any way that would have disrupted the delicate microcosmos I happily dwelled in now.

An after-school routine usually involved walking with the guys to the bus stop, a pretty enjoyable routine except for the nerdy video game chatter; even so when they skipped that part, I loved being around Mike, Axel, Wolfgang, Billy and his rather silent brother Robbie. Ryan also accompanied us on this route. Although he could be considered a nice enough friend, he had always shown a sort of undeniable selfishness. He seemed to crave attention by making fun of others or making them feel bad just so he could muster some self-esteem, and it spoke of his nature as a person. Someone like him was a mediocre individual without higher goals, much like everyone else in Loynne's, but in his case it was different, as he seemed to be rather smart at times. As such, it was no wonder that he remained an outcast just like us. Unable to befriend other Loynners and confined to the isolation that

hanging out with the bottom feeders represented, he had obviously tried to blend in with his fellow immigrant compatriots and any person that wasn't from Loynne's. I pondered about this as well, often wondering why all my friends seemed to be Unitedstatian when I absolutely hated the nation and everything it stood for. I often thought that the Unitedstatians who decided to emigrate where above the level of those most mediocre who decided to stay, like the ROA gunfanatics and Creatonologist zealots. Billy and Robbie where the only Southern Unitedstatians I had ever known, as all others hailed from the West or East Coasts, but seemed to be somewhat different from your common ROA vigilante. I knew they were smarter and hid something, but never pondered about it further. They were good guys, and that was enough for me at the time.

I must admit though, there was another reason as to why I also liked to get away from the crowded atmosphere generated at the end of classes and walk this alternate route with my friends; my usual stop was always packed with Kannies from all the southeastern towns, and I dreaded waiting for ten minutes there alone or at the side of Gordon and Claude, who as you know I despised. These newfound friends became the solution to this and to avoid going to Wolfgang's house after classes all the time.

Ryan lived right in the middle of Paradise Plaza, in a building called The Crucible located next to the Community Center, so after school he simply walked there with the Nazarethes, who lived there as well. Axel lived in a town named Chaffield, which was nothing but a long highway filled with houses and businesses at both sides. Mike lived in the most important town of Arias, whose significance was only due to historical importance, also where the Mayor's Hall of the Arias Province was located. Arias Town, as it was called to

differentiate it from the Arias province, was a town built with the same materials and around the same time that Whitedale, Montenade, Asiz Valley, Desidelleo, Chaffield, Fatal Coast and all the southeastern places of preference of immigrants who could not afford to rent in Pilgrim Coast, like me.

The Montenade bus finally arrived at the bus stop, so I greeted my friends and marched home again, listening to my Hipp-Man tuned to the soundtracks of my favorite films, as I loved to do while on the bus. I had always been a fan of the world's greatest film directors, and had begun to take great pride in that. Lenin had so righteously said *You must remember always that of all the arts the most important for us is the cinema.* And what truth lied within those words. People with less knowledge in cinema than me were enough to offend me, and the fact that I enjoyed the most intellectual movies without faking it to appear more intelligent like some people did fed my dandling self-esteem as I commenced to make myself stand from the crowd in every human field possible. This also applied to music and literature, what I considered the greatest and finest arts and entertainment in human craftsmanship. I had the philosophy that a person needs to upgrade itself to its highest exponent, regardless of what the field is. I saw mediocrity in so many different levels a day, in the faces of so many that I had to live with the fact that people surrounding me were stupid, annoying, ignorant and uninteresting. Maybe in the same way I was to them, but with the difference that I possessed knowledge they would never harness, a gift to enjoy beauty they would never appreciate.

I stopped my train of thought when the bus pulled over at the second Montenade bus stop and continued toward Whitedale. I got off the vehicle and fortunately for me, my home was just a few steps away, one of the westernmost

buildings on Montenade, located one building away from the border. I walked looking at the distance, staring at the road to Whitedale as the almost empty bus slowly took off, the sun shining gleefully and casting a nice shade on the early after-noon feel of the town. This was the kind of moment that had made me forget Kannovschina so quickly. This and the sup-port of a select group of people I considered humane.

When I finally came back home, I checked the mailbox as per usual, left the bills for the landlord untouched and re-trieved my mother's response to my previous letter. I never read her mail outside, preferring to isolate myself in the dark recesses of my shelter to read such coveted replies.

Surrounded by my portraits, keeping a watchful eye over me as I lay in bed, I proceeded to retrieve the letter out of the cream-colored envelope and absorb its contents:

"Dear ********,

I'm glad to see you're finally doing better! See? Maybe not everything is that bad. I'm sure there's a lot of exaggera-tion in what you tell us. The pictures you've sent look abso-lutely beautiful. It's like a paradise. Your school looks very clean and colorful.

We've sent you some photos of a political demonstration that occurred last month. Communists and Socialist parties are criticizing cuts the government is performing on certain social services like health, education and welfare. They're reducing wages, privatizing services and firing people. It's horrible, and many have already lost their houses or their possessions to the bank. Was this what they wanted? People are complaining about how at least in Communist times they had food, health, education, a decent house and a little car. It's useless though; they send riot police teams to ap-

pease demonstrations all the time and there hasn't been word of another as of yet. People have always been very submissive here, I'm surprised we even had a civil war, but since democracy settled in the submission of Communist times has returned. The rebellious spirit was short-lived, and I doubt there'll be another act like this in months.

I hope you make new friends in school, perhaps a girl-friend? Have fun, ********, you need to be healthy and hap-py and enjoy your youth, but don't get into trouble or do questionable things. I know you won't, but it's a mother's duty to make you remember. I love you and want nothing bad to happen to you. Take care of yourself. I wouldn't know what to do with my life if you were gone. Sometimes I get so scared. But the thought of you being such a calm nice boy makes the fear go away immediately. I trust you completely.

Love you,

Mom and Dad."

I saved the letter with the rest on the third drawer of my night-stand. What was my mother thinking, getting a girl-friend in Loynne's? She was used to girls being like the ones she grew up with, hard-working, loyal, silent, submissive and simple, whose only purpose in life was to wash and cook for some husband. What would my mother say when she saw the disgusting Loynnerin sluts walking around with barely any clothes on, with the prostitute high heels, their bodies cov-ered in tattoos and piercings? I very much doubted my par-ents would like this Western nightmare. The Motherland was stuck in time and these things had not yet arrived there, but my parents would get to see these things for themselves pro-gressively when The Motherland fully morphed into a dis-

gusting "democracy." I still didn't know how they would react when seeing this dystopia, or if they would die out of unhappiness when finding themselves unable to go anywhere else.

Trying to distract my mind from this, I turned my computer on and opened the favorite instant messaging pro-gram of Loynne's Island residents during this era; ChitChat was a program where one could add their favorite people LoynNet addresses and speak to them in private. Bearing the standard of the best software for inconsequential conversation, nothing rivaled ChitChat in terms of popularity.

Due to the nature of the Intranets, one couldn't add or contact people outside of Loynne's, as the program functioned only within the limits of LoynNet. It was a shame for people like me that there wasn't a way to communicate with one's relatives abroad, but the program was extremely useful to keep in touch with one's closest friends and I used it often to talk to Wolfgang, the only person I had added there. Since I didn't trust any other person aside from him, I hadn't given my address to others. But even I knew I couldn't go on like this, alienating myself for years, not even Wolfgang was so anti-social. As such I had decided to ask Ryan for his Chit-Chat address that same morning and see if I could build trustworthy friendships with other people. Not surprisingly, after adding him he immediately appeared online.

"Hey!" I typed.

"Hello," he replied. It was kind of strange to be greeted like this in ChitChat, especially by someone young.

"So how you doing?"

"Fine, fine, just bored here. I was listening to the latest album by The Offdicks."

"Ah, yeah ... I haven't really heard anything from them, but I've sure heard about the band. Can you pass me a song from them or something?"

156

"Sure, see if you like these."

ChitChat allowed the user to pass several types of files from one system to another. Music or movie files, photos, any kind of data. it was pretty useful for almost anything, and popular as hell among teens and youngsters.

Ryan passed me a song titled "Cun't Repeat," and another one called "Cumming Out Swinging." The songs proved to be a guilty pleasure. Simplistic and devoid of musical talent as they were, they worked their way around my ears, thus they immediately went to my Hipp-Man. At least they were a nice and cheery alternative to listening to the Red Army Choir all the time.

I continued chatting with Ryan, in a mechanical way akin to compromise instead of real friendship. He didn't seem as friendly or sociable on ChitChat. It may have only seemed that way to me because of the loss in translation, but the reality is he changed when behind the safety of his screen. A sinister darker side to him always used to awake in moments of extreme intimacy and privacy, which warned me of his true nature and confirmed the suspicions that always dissipated when facing him in person. His charm and charisma had increased greatly since that fresh yet distant 3rd grade of Compulsory State Education. Retaining his lame humor and his craving for attention, Ryan had built a semi-bulletproof vest against outside rejection and disapproval. He would laugh loudly and snorting, ease tension with a lame joke and a grin full of yellow teeth, but when in the company of no-body except his very own self, Ryan changed to this acid and reclusive individual that seemed to want the destruction of the entire human race, a feeling I perhaps knew better than him. He reminded me of myself in several ways, and the fresh abuse we both experimented during Kannovchina surely damaged his emotional state somewhat permanently, as it

was clear that in only two years, not all was forgotten. I may have experienced Kannovschina for less than a year, as in my second year I truly did not even feel it except for a couple of rare encounters, but I knew Ryan had taken even more abuse than people like Wolfgang. His flimsy frame and his association to people considered bottom feeders helped increase this, while Wolfgang at least had a bulky frame, engaged in exercise and practiced Aikido. However, Ryan had a reptilian instinct of survival far bigger than Wolfgang could ever possess. He put his personal benefit ahead of anything or anyone else. He was the kind of person that used you while making you feel he was helping you, making great sacrifices on his part. Nothing but a self-righteous snake disguised as a whimpering lamb.

It got to a ridiculous point where he wouldn't even answer anymore, so I took it as an offense and logged off, feeling a bit of a prick for wanting to truly engage in healthy conversation with someone so awkward and arrogant. At least I liked the songs, even if they were the kind of five chord simpleton skate-punk garbage these Californian types seemed to love.

$$\bullet \bullet \bullet \bullet \bullet$$

We found ourselves in the basement, right outside of the computer classroom. The Perv always arrived late, inciting students to usually entertain themselves with whatever they could. The expelled students from Axel's boarding school were not the saints you thought at first sight. Far from Kannies, these guys were however smarter and definitely good students, but pranksters at heart. One of them threw a tennis ball around with such strength that it bounced completely around the corridor and hit Axel on the back of the head, making him jump in surprise. The others laughed at him

loudly. Mike immediately picked the ball up from the floor and raised it as if to say "come and get it." Everyone shut up almost in unison. The guy that had thrown the ball went to grab it, and just as he was reaching out for it Axel grabbed him by the shirt and started punching him on the shoulder, uttering a word for each hit.

"YOU ... NEVER ... DO ... THAT ... AGAIN ... HEAR ME?!"

The guy, of flimsy build and tall height, cowered and hid his head beneath his arms as he retreated, only to trip and fall on his back violently. His friends were going to intervene but Mike stood firmly making sure Axel was covered. Wolfgang and I felt incredibly uncomfortable. There was nothing to fear having allies such as Mike and Axel, but we weren't dumb enough to establish alliances and enmities this early. As such, we contemplated the scene from a neutral perspective. I for one knew that it wasn't worth sticking your neck out for people in Loynne's. They were backstabbing traitors who would sell you out the first time they could. I didn't fully trust Axel at this point. I couldn't say the same about Mike, but for some reason I couldn't trust him as much as Wolfgang. They were still school acquaintances, not proper friends. Wolfgang and I had been watching each other's backs for more than a year. I knew that my loyalty lay with him.

The Perv had finally arrived. He stood where he was, witnessing Axel kicking the guy that threw the tennis ball on the ground and Mike in bouncer stance with his arms crossed making sure nobody trespassed.

"What the hell is going on here?!" he uttered. Nobody spoke. Finally, he did the sensible thing and sent Axel and the other guy to the principal's office. The school severely punished vicious fights, which unfortunately encouraged Kannies to psychologically decimate their victims, who always remained alert and on the lookout for a possible beating, never

159

knowing when they could be attacked. Fights were rare, and when they happened they were usually devastating for the victim, but nothing surpassed the paranoid terror of the unexpected.

"Come on you two, break it up and get going. And uh, you there on the floor, you'd better go to the infirmary first." Axel and the other guy slowly walked through the corridor, both incredibly furious at the humiliations they inflicted on each other and their corresponding punishments.

The Perv opened the classroom with his key and we entered still commenting on the incident that had transpired, and I listened as the girls curiously attacked Axel's behavior instead of admiring it like they would have otherwise done. It was all in the social class, I thought; Axel was an outcast who hung out with freaks to them, and as such had no right to be admired.

We started sitting on random places and always next to our friends. Mike, Ryan and I sat next to each other while Wolfgang got left behind and was forced to seat on his own. I could see him gesturing through the corner of my eye but I ignored him. Sometimes his clinginess annoyed me.

"Right, all your computers on? Great ... today we're gonna learn how to design a website ... so ... uh ... mmm ..."

The Perv always spaced out for infinite amounts of time. Usually someone brought him back to Earth by finishing his phrase in the form of a question.

"... we start by opening FrontLine?"

"Uh ... yeah! Yeah. Please, all of you, boot up FrontLine like your classmate said."

"*What's wrong with this guy?*" I thought. He was beginning to get on my nerves, I hated this behavior in teachers. It completely urged me to shake them, to slap their faces until they finally uttered whatever they wanted to say. But I con-

firmed that what people had been rumoring was true. The teacher was slyly looking at the girls in the class, the g-strings very visible like usual. I could not really understand what he saw in them. Sure, they were interesting for a while, but there was only so much you could see. How utterly desperate he'd have to be to entertain himself with such simple pleasures.

"Sonny, hey Sonny ..." Ryan whispered. "Y'see this guy eyein' the fuck outta them asses?"

"Yeah. Can you really blame him?"

"Haha, not me that's for sure! I'd so do that Lyssandra chick, dude. Check those freakin' udders out. Booballicious."

"Hey! You two over there! You paying attention?"

"Yes sir!" Ryan replied.

"Good, 'cause, this part is really important here? If you could keep quiet and listen, that'd be great. Now ... as I was saying ... uh ... open FrontLine and ... er ... huh ... mmm ..."

"... select new file?"

"Uh ... yes, Lyssandra. That. Mm-hm-mm ..."

· · · · ·

As daily school life progressed, Ryan's company gave me a sudden urge to check on the current stock of females. I couldn't help but think about the Loynnerin girlfriend I had had in the summer, Lyria, but I actually didn't remember her at all, just the brief and lusty experience we had lived together and how she almost cost me my friendship with Wolfgang – we had raced for her attention simultaneously in a Cold War, and I had emerged victorious. She was shallow and devoid of culture, clingy and emotional, like most Loynnerins. Even so she had decent looks, and would have proved a status symbol among my colleagues at school. Back then I was still young and inexperienced regarding the opposite sex,

and thought I needed to do this with several women before finding one I would not let go of. However, none of the girls pleased my needs like I was hoping, they had all turned out to be photocopies; the same tops, same pants, same belts, and same thongs, even the same hairstyles and horrid earrings; the same way of talking, expressing themselves, gesticulating, thinking and interacting. This was definitely the end of the road for guys who looked for something different, for the truest romantic experience, I thought pessimistically as I walked past a group of giggling slutty 13-year-old types, wearing precisely what I described. Where were the Vera Alentovas, the Natalya Seleznyovas, the Zhanna Prokhoren- kos, the Natalya Varleys? What I would have given to have a girlfriend with the hypnotizing stare of Alentova, the cuteness of Seleznyova, the submissive humbleness of Prokhorenko and the enchanting smile of Varley! Those were true women! A thousand times more beautiful than anything the West could produce, women with both looks and solid, authentic characters, each possessing unique personalities forged in the glory of our Communist system. But I would never get to stumble upon superior women like these in Loynne's Island. Women with intelligence, values, honor, integrity, and a relentless faithfulness in love and marriage? I knew this was impossible. These were women who had been brought up in more decent, saner times. They had not grown up consuming the disgusting corruption of capitalism, just like me. But just like them, I had also been through the traumatizing experi- ence of losing my country overnight, and of having capitalism forced upon me. The more I thought about it, the faster my hopes collapsed.

To distract myself from these thoughts, I stared momen- tarily at Billy and Robbie when I caught a glimpse of them walking toward the canteen, always covering their backs

when carefully traversing school territory. In a serious military fashion, adding to the nerdiness, Robbie signaled Billy to come forward by closing and then opening his fist in mid-air, something often done by Special Forces units before clearing a room.

"There's something about them," I often thought, remembering how their appearance always struck me when I hadn't been even introduced to them. They simply weren't like the rest, their eyes shining with a as they seemingly passed judgements on everyone they met, with a special knowledge they didn't share with anyone else, reserved purely for their own kin. However, I oftentimes dismissed this side to them for the sake of socializing with them, having a laugh and talking about firearms. I was an individual who wasn't content with the superficial, shallow layer of a person. I had to dwell in deep, discovering the driving force behind the person's will, the rational fundamental thoughts behind their actions; I had unearthed the secrets behind most people, who were usually mere simpletons, but I had yet to fully uncover the secrets behind the Nazareth brothers.

I still remember well when I was properly introduced to them. The conversation had included a bit of Ryan, explaining the infamous story of Johanna, a Dutch girl of about 15, pale and freckled-face, with a set of blue shiny feline eyes and a weird penchant for letting just about anyone touch her. She never really anything by herself, yet she let people kiss her or touch her as she did nothing and simply sat still. She would however make no preference for any particular guy in the group and wanted them to fight for their touching rights instead of her pursuing their attention. It was all a childish game, sexual in nature and perhaps a sign of depravity, but still a childish game. I remember like it was yesterday when Billy told me more in detail at recess:

"*We all gathered 'round for the afternoon in Ryan's house as usual. We almost never, ever had anythin' to do after school. Yeah, homework an' all that shit, but we were 14 for fuck's sake. This shit I'm tellin' ya about, muss'abeen like two years ago, I reckon. Yeah, two years alright. Anyhow, we were sittin' in the couch, watchin' TV. Suddenly we started feelin' for 'er breasts an' bitch wouldn't move, jus' sat there, fixed on the TV. We could 'ave simply raped her, boy! God only knows! But we wouldn't go that far, after all we're not there yet. We were simply content to degrade the poor bitch and feel 'er breasts an' legs an' ass fer a while.*"

Billy explained this all to me as a strange thought ran through my mind; the realization that all my friends were lifeless losers with zero chances with women. I was one too. My luck had nonetheless changed when turning 15, and I left the lifeless loser club. During that era these stories came as a complete utter shock to me. It just seemed unreal. A pack of boys feeling a girl's ass, while she just sat there, content and oblivious? It seemed unlikely, a blatant lie. Either way I had no choice but to believe it, just like with Axel's stories.

Just as Billy began pouring more details into his story, Ryan passed by briefly like he used to do at every recess, to eavesdrop on the conversation. He snorted loudly, as he used to do whenever something amused him, and said "*yeah, that shit was alright, wasn't it Billy?!*" Billy simply looked at him and smiled until he left. When Ryan was sunk into another conversation, Billy told me almost in a whisper "*That pathetic fuckin' loser believed that Johanna favored him better. She didn't. I'll tell ya a little story. Ryan thought that Johanna gave him this sorta non-existent special attention, which was unique, just for him. In reality, Johanna would let any-*

*one feel 'er up the skirt. That's right boy. We did touch the
little bitch down there, quite frequently. Ryan did this only
once and believed they were automatically datin'. This mis-
communication allowed for a lot of funny Ryan moments.
For one, we touched her more just to piss him off. It was so
funny. He'd get all like, 'hey, don't touch my girlfriend!!'
Poor basterd. Then this other time, I think it was the last
time we ever saw 'er, he invited her over to his house to
sleep, dunno how he managed that. He got up like five times
in the night to investigate an' see if she was sleepin'. When
he thought she was, he tried to get in bed with her and rape
her. She obviously jumped in shock, all disgusted. Next thing
he knew, Johanna had built this little fortress of pillows
around the couch-bed. That was the last we ever saw of 'er, I
think. Can't be too sure. What I'm sure is that, goddamn,
Ryan was a fuckin' chump an' still is.*" At the time, this was
the most secret unofficial information I had regarding Ryan. I
would have never been able to guess that secret side of his
judging by his personality alone. I would have never believed
him capable of trying to rape a girl in the middle of the night.

Being there at recess with the guys was the closest I related to an actual utopia; it functioned but it was only held together by its obvious capitalistic nature, a society where nothing mattered aside from material possession and vanity, and
this was the point when I usually reminded myself of why I
hated such a land. All this abundance and riches kept its
people satisfied and blinded, while the outside *real* world
suffered from massive poverty, famines, war and economic
collapse. What I couldn't help myself from doing was com-
paring it constantly with the revolutionary, down to earth and
militant lifestyle in The Motherland, where such concepts
would never intrude our lives. There was no ideology to be
had in this Western "free" world. How could you develop one

in the first place? What was there to fight against? The constant feeling of society improving only in the technological aspects aimed at leisure, such as cell-phones, computers, TVs, gaming consoles, everything worked to keep its citizens consuming and detached from reality, vapidly living in a non-place, a surreal landscape impossible to reproduce anywhere else. The industry was decadent, turning anything of cultural significance into money-making franchises devoid of substance. These Loynners were fed countless movies, songs, video games and books all devoid of substance, originality or quality, and their society was obviously shaped around these atrocities. No intellectualism ever arose from these beings lacking in so many essential human qualities, everything revolving around the prospect of scraping a better living, of manufacturing and marketing comfort and leisure. In the process of living only for entertainment, society had lost its creative drive. The inane, synthesized and mass-produced electro-pop songs heard on the radio, the comedies devoid of laughter, the dramas lacking in emotion, the talentless icons, artists and the insanely wealthy celebrity socialite leeches; it all contributed to making this world pointless, senseless, doomed; stuck in a perpetual present where the only things that ever changed were technology, comfort, celebrity and war news, but never the core itself. Perhaps we had reached our peak as a civilization, as a species. But something between capitalism and our current society seemed unbearably related, inseparable.

Life indeed seemed to have reached its peak for me. Looking back three years from now, when the only things I faced were grim prospects of abuse and existential hopelessness, I had gotten more than I could have ever asked of this land; I had enjoyed experiences with members of the opposite sex, like my Loynnerin girlfriend in the summer, and I was sure

there were many more to come; I had managed to secure plenty of friends and acquaintances, even new clothes that enabled me to pass unnoticed in front of the judgmental scrutiny of the Loynner population, all without changing who I really was inside. But what was that lacking factor? Was it my undying nostalgic longing for my country? I could not possibly know at the time. I followed the mentality of taking life day by day and enjoying my newfound peace in Pilgrim Coast, trying not to think about how long it could last.

· · · · ·

Weeks flew by as October neared its end, and the pool days in PE class were finally over. The first month had passed by pretty quickly, and it was a good sign. It wasn't every day that I associated sunshine and palm trees with utter peace and inner calmness. In previous years, days like these only foreshadowed grizzly events involving hazing, either experiencing it by yourself or witnessing it on someone else, it involved paranoia, a constant state of alert, adrenaline and stress, the kind of life you expect to have when living in the wild, struggling for survival against vicious creatures guided by nothing except primal instincts; but this was supposed to be civilization, the apex of it. Such barbaric way of living should have been wiped out in natural selection by our very organisms, but it seemed we still had a ways to go in evolution. Small gangs of vicious-looking Kannies searching for prey came to mind instantly. Harassing onlookers, forcing you to always face down in submission, looking at your clumsy fleeing feet, as a comment involving your clothing or bodily features was more than you could hope to happen. Others weren't so lucky. I once had to cross paths with an unlucky Italian exchange student who had the nerve to be outspoken

and try to crack up jokes, completely unaware of Kannysm around him. His eventual punishment submerged him completely into a silent and evasive rodent, a shadow of his former self.

But everything related to that seemed to have never existed. At this moment in time, Loynne's appeared to be traversing a new era in individuality, where you weren't persecuted for your clothes, appearance or personality, and you could be whoever you wanted to be. Now that Kannovschina was withering, my only worry started to be that unusual lacking feeling which was beginning to develop in a much greater extent. The hunt I had started for a female symbol of beauty, admiration and respect still went on furiously, and I feared it would for many years. I sensed myself coming off age, my thirst wanting to be sated with something much more complex, of greater magnitude, something I had not come across never in my entire life, an ultimate sensation of bliss and happiness rolled into one, but those things don't just come any day at random. Thinking I should give up on this ghost chase and enjoy life more, I limited myself to listen to Axel rant again to get the depression out of me;

"Then after ridin' the shit out of her I say to myself; 'Yo Axel! You've done it again, boy! X for aXel baby! X marks the spot in yo' ass!' And bitch wouldn't let me leave 'cause, she just wouldn't man, you know, too clingy, and I was gettin' all berserker mode 'cause I arranged with the guys to play a football match against some Kanny fucks that were sayin' shit 'bout us. I was stressed, man! I just had to go and beat the fuck outta them Kanny dumbasses! But there she was, asleep, what was the sensible thing to do? I fucked her again man, when she was asleep like Cinderella! Rode the shit outta them buttocks, thong on an' all. I had to, man. She looked so damn cute you know with them fuckin' braces man, teenage fuckin'

tourist girls are the best kind, not too chubby and not too thin, great skin, amazing tits and scream and ride your cock like fuckin' cowgirls ... I remember I had a hard time making myself scarce but I'm sure she got it at the end. She did steal some money from my wallet and crashed a picture or two though but hell, the damn slut was worth it ... I just hate it when they get all emotional 'n stuff. One night stand, baby! Didn't you get the memo?! YEAH!! It turns up she was a virgin so that explains a lot. There's usually not THAT much blood after it on the sheets ... but she sure wasn't a virgin in the mouth and ass! I'll never understand that hymen shit bro. What I do understand is ... I ripped the motherfucker!"

Axel Guerrero began to serve as a stand-up comedian during breaks, a much needed respite for us "freaks." His charming attitude and magnetic personality were really entertaining, and the personal stories he narrated always provided all of us with a laugh or two. The veracity of these stories was in fact questionable, and most of the things he said for that matter were probably lies, but since they were fun it didn't matter.

"Damn Wolfie, haven't you ever asked a girl out or what? Stop playing Gears of Deterrence dude, you have to go out there and give those hotties out there all the Wolfgang Frankfurt wieners they can get!"

"Dude, I do try but, it's hard you know? I just don't know how to approach the right prey. These things wouldn't have happened in Feudal Japan ... How I'd love to live back then, with a nice and faithful Japanese wife ..." He said, his voice beginning to show that hint of self-hatred I was acquainted with.

"Oh ... did I just hear the forbidden word? Shut the fuck up with that weird shit ... Ugh, *wife*! Are you all up there?! Wolfie, the girls you put in pedestals and that you idolize are

the same girls that regurgitate my load every night! Look, jus' don't worry my friend, you don't need to talk, man! Uncle Axel here will do the talkin' for ya, and besides, he's gonna invite you to this big-ass sex and drugs party where you'll meet these incredible and fantastic chicks that will blow all your socks and cocks off! These babes just ask for one thing, somethin' to keep their love holes busy and filled! Haha! Nah I'm kiddin'. They only care about the blow I get 'em. But when they're down, you know, out cold on the floor, you'll make sure you can provide them with that, can't you? Not like they will *feel* anythin' but ... you WILL *fill*, right?" he said, looking at him with his eyebrows raised.

"Oh, yeah. If it's um, size, what you mean ... I think I've got that covered."

"Hahaha, don't be an idiot man! You think size matters to an out-cold overdosed bitch, bleedin' from every hole in her body? I was talkin' about you being able to get the Wolfgang frankfurt stiff enough for female consumption. Jeez, Wolfie. You don't get out much, do ya?"

"Yeah, I know ... but, like *mark-dwayne_87* says in the forum ... strong, positive attitude ... right?"

"There you go, man!! See how easy it is? You worry too much. Hey, you made me remember one of my boarding school days, man! Listen, one day, we were sooooo fuckin' bored man, like stab yourself to see how bad you bleed bored, with no fuckin' drinks, no fuckin' drugs, no smack, no blow, no weed, no nothin', and there was these stupid little girls in the windows in the girl dorm that was right in front of ours, separated only by this like little square you know the kind you see in campus. All the time with their woman shit these girls, like, gigglin' and being stupid you know the kind, almost as if to say 'come here and fuck the shit outta us,' so we snuck past the dumb drunk half-asleep watcher guys, and got into the

dorm. The girls started pillow-fightin' us when we got in, and I was all moody and morose and shit, thinking, 'I'm so pillow-fighting your face with my dick in a minute,' but then they began to lay down the kiddie shit and they poured us some drinks of their own private stash, right, so I go and sorta without them noticing obviously, I put some 'stasis I totally forgot I had in the drinks before it was too late, hahaha! It wasn't too long before they started blowin' us all off man, sheeez that was the last school I've been in ... God fuckin' bless that 'stasis that saved me in the last minute, I probably would have fucked at least three of them without drugs but, when you get your dick sucked by a bitch on 'stasis it's so trippy 'cause listen man, pay attention, they don't seem to notice when you go the full distance and shoot all your load down the sink!!! AWESOME!!! Fuckin' cum dumpsters man, all of 'em, I tell ya they swallow that shit like cough medicine, and they love it!!!"

I wasn't paying attention anymore myself. I generally shut up while Axel spoke and narrated his stories, but my mind was someplace else. I looked at the people surrounding me; Mike, Billy, Robbie, Ryan, Wolfgang, Axel, Gordon and Claude. I couldn't help but feel misfit and out of place when once I had felt immensely secure, right at home. Gordon, Claude, Wolfgang and Axel began talking about Gears of Deterrence 3 again when Axel finished his narration, and Billy, Robbie and Mike were sharing with Ryan family problems and personal dramas. Mike's parents had filed for divorce, and he was seemingly suffering the consequences by this point, so Ryan, whose parents had also divorced, was helping him to feel better with himself. Billy and Robbie just listened, since somehow they seemed interested in what they were saying, but stood silently behind Mike's gigantic figure, a calculating expression in their eyes.

Billy and Robbie were from Houston, Texas, or so they said. I never quite trusted they had been born and raised there, but nobody was asking either. They were into firearms a lot, often talking about the US Civil War, the Second World War and the Vietnam War, and classic battles such as the Alamo, Chancellorsville, Omaha Beach, Iwo Jima, Stalingrad and many others, clearly showing their passion for military subjects and knowledge of history. Billy was very loud and outspoken, laughing every two seconds and usually swearing a lot in a thick Texan accent, although he tried not to in front of people he didn't trust, a situation in which he adopted a cunning, sly and quiet demeanor, but never losing his smirk. He would always asked you daring questions to stimulate your thinking, seemingly not wanting people to speak mechanically and wanting them to dwell in his questions. His choice in clothes reflected his personality, often wearing desert combat boots, digital camo cargo pants and authoritarian-looking dark flight jackets with patches of the Confederate flag. Careful, this did not mean he was a racist or a white-supremacist, as he was very good friends with Mike. But he had an unsurpassed pride for his heritage and for the Confederate States, as well as a hatred for what he called the Union and I called the US. He argued both sides had used slavery shamelessly and that his side had been merely more conservative, but that it wasn't a question of racism or slavery, but rather emancipation from the oppressive US and their policies, which I obviously agreed with. This is how we found a common ideological ground against the United States. Billy didn't see himself as Unitedstatian, merely Texan, and wanted only for Texas to be either an independent republic or part of a Southern Confederacy.

Then, there was Robbie. The complete opposite of his brother, he was quieter and usually spoke when it was of

utmost importance, never saying anything about how he felt and never uttering a complaint. He was cold, closed in himself and never expressed emotion except for sudden short bursts of laughter, which usually sparked out whenever we made fun of someone or messed between ourselves. His choice in clothes was also completely ironical; colorful tacky t-shirts with drawings of palm trees and surfers, bright Hawaiian beach shorts and almost always flip-flop sandals or sports sneakers. With his white skin, freckled face, blue eyes and long red hair, he was the most Hippie-looking guy in the crowd. He seemed to silently agree with everything his brother said, but his true beliefs were a mystery, as he didn't seem so ideologically motivated as his brother. Still, the basic essence of the brothers was the same, no matter their individual character quirks.

Suddenly, Mike advanced toward me, surely noticing how I kept looking at empty spaces on my own.

"You alright, Sonny boy?"

"Hey Mikey, yeah, I'm fine, what's up?"

"Nothin' man, just checkin' up on you. I gotta admit these boys spend way too much time playin' video games, eh? And I should know about that ... but ... don't have much else to do up there in Arias Town, do I? It's a ghost town ..."

"Same deal with Montenade."

"But it's not so bad. If you control yourself, playin' this shit like Realm of Witchcraft can distract you for a couple of hours ... but it does make the posse addicted, look at this crazy motherfucker," Mike said, pointing at Axel with a jerk of his head.

"Yeah, well ... I used to play a lot of single-player video games before, Gears of Deterrence was a bit over the top, but at least wasn't hollow, and it did have a good anti-war message. Much better than that World Defender Marine Corps

propaganda machine ..."

"Hehe, I know ... Motherfuckers don't even try to hide it. I don't play that shit, I've had enough of that brainwash back in the old country ..."

"Do you still study Nietzsche on your own like last year?"

"Yeah, I do. I gotta say, those philosophy classes really opened my eyes. Have you noticed that nobody else got interested in any philosophers aside from you and me? You hear people talkin' about philosophy on their own? All sheep, man. The drone effect is worse than ever ..."

"We'll really achieve Übermensch status at this rate ..."

"Tell me ... When we studied 'Thus Spoke Zarathustra' last year, I dunno, it was as if I had woken up. God is dead ... what a thing to say. I had never believed in God so studyin' it didn't bother me as much as it bothered other people, who had problems goin' on with the subject after ... but yeah ... they can incarcerate you for sayin' shit like that where I come from. Or kill you."

"Nihilism is only for a few, Mikey. Most people need to feel that their lives have meaning, and that the universe revolves around their petty existence. We are nothing but a mote of dust in the vastness of the universe. That's the fact that scares them. Science has uncovered most mysteries, and philosophy together with psychology have managed to give rational explanations to our narrow human viewpoint. But still, look at the world, look at your country. Old religions prevail and even gather more followers, while new ones emerge. Organized scamming groups like Creatonology are free to operate, astrology and tarot still exist and maintain a strong presence in mainstream newspapers ... We haven't progressed at all. You know how I feel about this at least ... solely the fault of capitalism and the hyper-permissive 'freedom' of Western democracies."

"Well, but you saw what happened with the dissolution of the Soviet Union. People still held their beliefs even if the state didn't approve of them. They couldn't suppress the Orthodox faith. Now we even have Orthodox churches here in Loynne's Island ..."

"I know, there's one near my house in Montenade ..."

"Yeah ... but don't get depressed Sonny boy. You keep fightin' for what you think is right. As long as some people are cultured and awake, we'll have nothin' to fear, absolutely nothin' ... We have the arms to fight this idiocy. We just have to stand up for ourselves and fight for a better world. Problem is, when you're surrounded by people like these you might get discouraged ... but ignore them. I learned that there's only a few people you can really talk to in life, and Sonny boy, I'm proud to say you're one of them."

"Thanks, Mikey ... it really means a lot."

The air raid siren announced the end of the break. Mike gave me a supportive pat on the shoulder and pointed at the Main Building with his head, as if to say "let's come back to Earth." I marched once again to the torture chamber, amongst a sea of thoughtless, crude, loud and mannerless imitations of human beings that erased completely the effect of Mike's friendly words. I remained thoughtful, in another world of my own creations, ignoring everything surrounding me and still thinking about that void I couldn't ignore or satisfy.

Shattered by the whiplash of hopelessness I decided to put my headphones, hoping to momentarily vanish from that tortuous jail of mediocrity. I often did so when walking through the hallways, as it made me feel fearless and prevented me from listening to the idiocy reigning all around me, also deterring any attempts of provocation or insult toward me since it rendered me effectively deaf. I had actually

tried an experiment once, as two Kannies happened to coincide with me when walking to school one morning, and as we walked side by side I, pretending to be deafened by the music, turned the volume down only to hear them address me regarding my clothes, one of them truly interested in knowing why I dressed the way I did. This was usually a Kanny test designed to see what your response would be, and would usually end up in a very negative manner, so ignoring them was the best option, as they would assume you were too scared to face them. From there on in, it could escalate into a provocation if they decided to go from words to fists and push you around until you cracked, but in this case nothing happened. When they noticed I wasn't responding, one simply concluded that it was because of the headphones, and then they started talking between themselves about the nature of my dress-style, not being viscerally mean about it, yet clearly not sharing or understanding the motive. It was a tense and worrisome moment, yet I was amazed at how peaceful it had turned out to be. Most interesting was seeing how by pretending to be deaf, I could actually get to infiltrate a Kanny social interaction without barriers, and hear their ignorant thoughts at their purest state. It was also particularly strange to know that people would risk talking about another person in front of them in such an open manner, as if I were an animal exhibited at a zoo and not a human being. But then again, they treated everyone who wasn't like them in such a fashion.

The Hipp-Man thus saved me once again as Tsoi's melancholic voice raised the hairs on my arm to the tune of "*Skazka*" — "A Fairy Tale" —. I turned to climb the West Wing staircase when I saw a group of girls in a deep immature conversation like the ones they keep at that age, not bothered to know what the hell about, probably boys or hot singers.

Talking nonsense and screeching their horrible voices, the little girls where causing trouble for the people who either wanted to go down or up the stairs. Sunk in the sorrowful melody of "*Skazka*" and looking at empty spaces, I was already going to run them over out of sheer annoyance but suddenly stopped, standing completely still; I had seen something absolutely out of place. At first my heartbeat accelerated, feeling my head boiling, making me feel hot and filled with adrenaline and euphoria. I then raised my sight high enough to admire an outstanding but small figure coming down the stairs, and it took me several seconds to assimilate that it wasn't just a little girl. My eyes reflected the most distinctive female I had ever seen in my entire life; a mysterious Anglo-Saxon girl with incredibly white skin stood waiting impatiently for the girls to move, looking furiously frustrated but still shy, almost having problems dealing with the situation laid before her. It was as if she didn't want to act per se, but soon proved to have no problem dealing with people. She yelled hysterically in a clear Unitedstatian accent "*GET OUT-TA THE WAY!*" with a high pitched but delicate voice, causing the other girls to stare at her scared and annoyed, eventually obeying her command to move.

The little girl was very short, at around 1.50 meters tall, and in her perfect weight, not too thin and not too chubby. She held a dark purple portfolio between her arms in a strong embrace, and seemed to glide and flow as she moved about. The blinding paleness of her skin, especially noticeable in her extremely white feet, was visually striking, but it wasn't the only outstanding attribute she possessed; she had beautiful eyes, big and round, of an emerald green color I had never seen before, covered in blue make up; her eyelids were so low it gave her a faint air of superiority and disdain. Her hair was auburn colored with blonde streaks, long up to the hip and

very straight, combed in a middle part hairstyle. Her small and delicate fingers had their nails painted black, same as with her toes.

Her outfit was most curious, standing out immediately from the generic uniform all Loynnerins seemed to agree on wearing, and appeared to be more unique because of the way she wore it: she sported a black zipper hoody over a tight blue t-shirt, in a way so that the hoody was zipped half-way and pulled back at the right shoulder, fully covering her left arm but revealing her right shoulder and the skin of the arm below the t-shirt sleeve; a jean miniskirt with a black studded belt, in complete contrast to the tight black slutty yoga leggings with tacky cheap-looking plastic belts worn by girls all around, provided further amazement; her black open-toed sandals with white straps, with very short heels for that matter, were in direct contrast to the flat beach-bum flip-flops that were the Loynne's Island trend at the time; and finally, a studded bracelet on her left arm, matching her belt, signified her strong commitment to the trendy punk rock scene that was big in other countries, but nonexistent and completely unpopular in the island. But that was not all: in this state of absolute focus, devouring all the visual information this unique female provided, my every sense was enhanced, and thus I managed to notice something ridiculously insignificant about her outfit, something not easily seen and which I noticed in a fraction of a second as she moved the portfolio covering her torso downward; it was a Christian cross necklace with a US flag motif. I found myself feeling a strong ambivalence at the moment of noticing it, not quite sure of what to make of it, but for some reason I didn't consider it negative. In fact, I somehow liked it; and that's what scared me the most.

As she made her way through the staircase girls and

marched firmly and angrily in front of me, leaving the West Wing and venturing into the outside corridor toward the school's canteen, a sweet cherry aroma overwhelmed my nostrils, the smell of her perfume; I was paralyzed, and at that exact moment in time, I was convinced I had just seen the most beautiful girl that could have ever lived.

Coming out of the drowsiness the whole event had caused me, I eventually ran over the poor annoyed girls completely immersed in my own thoughts. Still looking over the shoulder and climbing the stairs while trying to record what I had seen, I began asking myself why it had affected me so much; she was just a little girl, what was there to be excited about? Just a little girl from school, like the dozens I came across in my daily life. I thought about how I could be becoming increasingly desperate, so much that I was willing to fall in love with just about anyone, like my comrade Wolfgang had begun to do. I tried to dismiss the incident, convincing myself that nothing had gone on, and looked at the timetable seeing I had chemistry class. I continued to move along heading toward the torture room, fearing my ordinary routine for the rest of the school year would consist of never-ending days like this one.

· · · · ·

"Hey, kids! Can I have a bit of attention here, please? Anyone? I'm tryin' to teach here, alright? What are you doin' in 1st Grade of Scientific Baccalaureate if you don't wanna study?! Go back to 4th of SCE or go hit the streets and get a job, but I'm tryin' to teach here, so either let me do my job or walk out … Now, am I right or what? Great … Anyway, as I was sayin', you got half an hour to finish that sheet, or else …"

Tom Richards proceeded to coax us into doing inorganic

formulation exercises as I found myself unwilling to pay any attention to his rants. I kept looking at the girls in class thinking that something could be wrong with me. I didn't feel the slightest bit of attraction to any of them, and I could have sworn some of the most beautiful girls in that age group were all cluttered up in my classroom. Younger girls, aged 13 to 16, could be found in my corridor in classroom 201, the one closest to the staircase. Some of those girls were absolutely attractive, maybe even too much, the ones Axel always bragged about banging when they were too drunk to care in parties. Yet, they were the same vapid whores who could be found in my class, just younger versions of them. Suddenly, without even wanting to, my mind thought once more about that little girl I had seen just an hour ago, and if I would get to catch a glimpse of her again. In an extraordinary fit of impulsiveness I headed straight for the corridor when the bell rang, in order to check whether I could accidentally cross paths with her. A rush of adrenaline flowed through my veins at this sudden decision, as I didn't exactly know what I was going to say to her in case we suddenly found ourselves facing each other.

Crowds of students had already occupied the corridor, but I walked among them quickly heading for the staircase. There was no certainty that her classroom was on the second floor; she could have been descending from the third, or going to the first floor, maybe even the basement. What if she was a Unitedstatian exchange student? They usually put them in the basement rooms. But no, I couldn't inspect the whole school and expect to come across her by luck. What would I say to her anyway? Nerves were not the only thing that mattered to me, but the first impression, what I could say to her in order to initiate conversation. I decided this was too much of a pointless hassle and that I would eventually find her

randomly just by carrying on with my usual business. There was no point in actively searching for her when I didn't even have a good reason to address her. I abandoned pursuit of this impulsive endeavor and headed back to class, only two lessons remaining for the day to finish. At least, now I had an interesting motive to wake up and go to school.

· · · · ·

When the classes were over, I headed home immediately, not wanting to talk to anyone, still thinking obsessively about the little girl. I couldn't remember seeing someone as delightful and warm to the eyes than the alluring nymph I saw at the staircase that moment, and yet another strange rush of adrenaline set my body ablaze just by remembering how good it was to merely see her descending the stairs, yelling at those annoying little girls with such bottled frustrated anger and walking away with a mixture of fleeing fear and dominant self-righteousness.

I lay on the bed looking at the ceiling – the only part of the room not covered with portraits, flags or symbols – smiling stupidly, my mind completely blank. I knew how idiotic it was to be happy because of that reason but I couldn't control it, nor could I see myself wanting to. One simple question was roaming my mind at that moment. One simple and decisive thing I had to do; how I would approach her. I wasn't shy while meeting girls, it was a fear I had long ago surpassed, but how could I do it? Under what circumstances? I didn't know her, she seemed shy and closed in herself, angry, lonely, as if she didn't want to be bothered by anyone or anything, so that made me retreat my thoughts on her a bit. I couldn't just approach her and attempt conversation. That usually scared them. I calmed myself thinking I would get to know

her eventually and that working on the seemingly impossible achievement could be a nice hobby to keep me going while I adjusted to this new year.

• • • • •

The first person I told my secret to was Wolfgang. We were sitting alone, apart from the cheery snobby girls in biology class; we were the only boys there, as all others had chosen to have an additional PE hour kicking balls in nets instead of wasting time in the biology lab.

"*Tovarish*, can I have a word?"

"Sure *Doshi*, what's eating you?"

"Well ... I'll be blunt. I like a girl. A girl I saw the other day. I—I can't stop thinking about her."

"You do? Mmm ... And ... who is she, what does she look like?"

"She's younger, that's the problem. I think much younger. Maybe two or three years younger ..."

"Damn *Doshi*, what's wrong with you?"

"Nothing's wrong! I just—I dunno ... she didn't seem like all the rest. She wasn't Kanny, she wasn't running around like an idiot, she seemed off, out of it, like she didn't belong here, like she was conscious of what was going on around her, just like me. I haven't seen her since. I wonder if I dreamt the whole thing up ..."

"Mmm ... you should be careful *Doshi* ... Use protection."

"What?!"

"If you're going to do anything ... use protection. Never forget."

"But I don't even... Why would you—Look, yeah sure." Wolfgang, as childish and inexperienced as he was, wasn't able to give me any better advice. I instantly dismissed Wolf-

gang's possible involvement in this case as he was in no position to help me. Advice from someone else was needed, but whose? I couldn't just ask anybody for help, I had to be careful as I didn't want the secret to be divulged. It was then that realized I was completely on my own unless I relied on Ryan.

I went after class to talk about this with him, who first asked if the girl was hot or not. I smirked and told him that she was simply the best thing I had ever seen.

"Wait, and where did you see this girl?" he asked.

"At the stairs, on the first floor of the West Wing."

"And what did she look like?"

"Well ... she was short, she had long reddish hair ... that's what I noticed the most, how long and straight the hair was. The rest I can't remember that well. I never got a good look at her face."

"Look, I don't have any idea of who this girl could be, she could be anyone. All girls have long and straight hair now, it's the fashion standard. What if you tell me when she is around, so I can take a look by myself? We'll see what turns you on then," Ryan said, grinning and biting his lips.

"Alright. But I don't think you'll be that impressed. She wasn't a bombshell, she was quite normal-looking. I mean, I thought she was beautiful, but even I know she was no Kanny goddess."

"Haha, never mind. Anything that has more than two holes and moves is worthy of a man's attention ..."

However, the next day I never ran into her, and obsessively tried to find her whereabouts without success. This happened again the day after, and the day after that one. My patience was ending, I was as anxious as ever, and the feeling of bliss and happiness died to give birth to anxiety and despair, but the mysterious girl was nowhere to be found. Ryan's patience seemed to be wearing off too:

"Where the fuck is this girl you talk about so much? She's a fucking ghost! She's never around, man!"

"I know, I'd really like to know where she could be ..." I replied each time Ryan asked. As a matter of fact, I was worried thinking that she could have been transferred to a different school or moved away. I began to wonder that maybe I would never get to see her again. But if there was something I hated was unfinished business, especially when the experience had been so unforgettable. Only time could tell whether I would lead this to an end or not. Ryan always tried to cheer me up; "Anyway man, there are a lot of other nice chicks here ... Also look outside this freakin' high school, man!"

I tried looking at a gang of 15-year-olds from the 3th Grade. One struck me like a thunderbolt. I looked at her from behind; with shoulder-length jet black hair, a skinny build easy to dominate and a genuinely striking ass, bubbly, round and enormous. But the feeling soon withered when I saw her eyes, the overall expression on her face. Static, reptilian and cold; immature, distant, unreachable. This was a nymph. A complete object of praise and worship, with absolutely no possibility of contact or interaction. She had to be admired not for who she was, but for how well formed she was. This applied to most girls in Loynne's, and judging by the look of things I'd go as far as to say the entire globe.

"See that one over there?" I told Ryan, pointing at another girl with amazingly sun-tanned chubby thighs squeezed in tight jean shorts.

"Haha, yeah, keep dreamin'! You have to aim lower than that Sonny. Much lower I might add."

"I'm not in the mentality to conform myself with what I'm given right now."

"Well, with that attitude, you're so gettin' a girl tomorrow, Sonny. Look, I'll tell you how it works; at this age, when we

don't have a driver's license for a car or a motorcycle, and if we're not dumb-looking Kannies who go to the gym or play football, we're screwed. So what you do is you grab the first fat ugly bitch that you get a hold of and you fuck her. You form a sort of friendship with her, never get too involved. Once they cling to being liked, you don't shake 'em off. Better to have somethin' to fuck so you can brag about with your pals even if she's fat or ugly or both. Just tell 'em she's thin and make her walk out the back door when your friends come in."

"That mentality will get you lots of girls, Ryan."

"I know! I know ... but does it really matter, when inside you know you're getting' laid? Grab the first girl you can and fuck her so hard so that then you gain experience for the proper hot bitches, when you're 20, maybe 30. That's the way you do it. Like a car, man. You start with a shitty Chevraun City Car from the '80s on its fortieth change of engine, you know, like the one my mom's got, and then you reach for the Escalators!"

"You sure love making stupid puns, don't you?" I said, trying to hide my exasperation.

"Hey asshole, don't tell me they don't cheer you up!"

We entered the classroom for our last class of the day, don't even remember what it could be now. When the bell rang, I walked outside with Ryan, constantly talking and telling me what clothes to buy to appear trendier, when she appeared out of nowhere, and a feeling of joy and surprise struck me as hard as they could. But it wasn't merely seeing her what made me feel such happiness; it was the fact that she had just exited room 201, the classroom next to the staircase on the very same corridor my class was in.

Grabbing Ryan strongly by the arm, I told him to follow me as we descended the staircase before we lost her, racing to

the first floor. And there she was, just a few meters ahead of us, mixing in with the crowds. She was wearing the exact same clothes she had on when I first saw her. I frantically told Ryan it was her, the girl we had talked about so much, the only subject of conversation we had had in weeks, just in front of us. Ryan's reaction was really what shocked me the most; he wasn't laughing, or cracking up jokes like he always used to, or even smiling. His answer resonated through my skull for a couple of seconds, as he took a deep breath, stared at her coldly and sighed:

"Yeah. I know her. She's my sister."

It couldn't be. This was impossible. I was still looking at her going toward the gate, descending through the wheel-chair ramp for a shortcut, and I couldn't do anything but stare at her beautiful appearance with a confused, worried stare. Everything around her had been erased or frozen, she being the sole thing focused on my retina.

I tried to handle the situation as carefully as possible, re-plying:

"Oh ... well ... she's still hot!"

Although not the best way to break the icy tension with, I wasn't able to come up with anything better; after all, what else was there to say after my unmasking? I thought I might as well be sincere. Ryan's facial expression didn't change until the next day, and I felt as if a sacred rule had been shattered to pieces. My world had been turned upside down, and a gallery of a million doors laid opened for me to explore. Hundreds of wonderful possibilities limited only by how well I played this, with Ryan as my own personal goose of golden

eggs, available in person five days a week. My second reaction was, as an idealist and Marxist, how opportunistic and capitalist it felt to leech of someone's friendship and goodwill for personal benefit. I remained silent until I noticed this had offended Ryan deeply, and decided to talk to him to make amends or smoothen the event. I couldn't. What I let out by instinct was the following:

"Ryan, I've spent weeks talking to you about her, didn't you have the slightest idea that your sister was who I was describing?"

"No! How was I supposed to know? When a friend tells you he likes some broad you never actually think he can be referring to your sister ... I thought she could be, dunno, some of them bitches in the East Wing, you know, them tiny chicks in Arts Baccalaureate that do artistic gymnastics ... and who are our *age* ..."

"Look Ryan, I'm so sorry, how could I have imagined she was your sister, as if I were trying to do this on purpose ..."

"Sonny, you don't need to tell me that ... I know you're not doin' this on purpose, I'd love it if you were ... at least it would mean you're jokin' or trying to piss me off ... but ... you really like her ... Now you're fucked ..."

"What do you mean by that?" I asked, offended.

"Sonny, now I know how you feel about her and there's no going back, you can't just pretend this conversation never happened, although I'd be more than eager to pretend myself ... Look ... let's see how this goes day by day ... just ... just try to chill until next week and we'll see how it goes ... I dunno ... whatever ... I'm just too tired ..."

"Ryan, don't tell her anything! I mean—"

"'Course I won't. Who do you take me for? But well ... if you want anything to do with her, I gotta tell you now that you're on your own ... This is your own mess, your own situa-

tion ... Deal with it yourself ... I won't help you in any way ..."

"I wasn't expecting help ... I mean ... friends don't do that."

"Yeah, yeah ... look, just try to sweep this under the carpet ... I dunno ... you really like her that much?"

"Well ... well, yeah."

"Oh boy. How much?"

"Like what you've been hearing for the past three weeks? Like, a LOT?"

"I know ... I know ... And you don't think there's a chance you can just let this go ..."

"You mean you're personally asking me if I can drop this?"

"Yeah."

"I don't think so. I mean ... like you said, now's too late. I'm really crazy about her, Ryan."

"Jesus ... let's just hope this is nothin' more than a crush."

"I'll see. I can't tell you right now what I intend on doing. I'll do what you said, take it day by day. Whatever will happen will happen, right?"

"Yeah ... good or bad."

"So, uh ... Ryan ... I'm sorry I couldn't go to your house the other day but if you want now we can arrange som—"

"NO."

"Yeah ... I knew it ..."

We exited through the main gate, talking about that subject over and over, with me saying I was sorry but at the same time trying to get as much information about her as I could, and Ryan helping me without the least bit of enthusiasm, not even disguising his disgust anymore. I remembered how joyfully he used to invite me often to the house before, offers I always refused as I had no interest in hanging around someone I considered to be awkward company. This was the groundbreaking moment I had been expecting for months since I broke up with my first Loynnerin girlfriend. A chal-

lenging task, almost impossible to achieve; and the reward for it was infinite bliss.

After a few lines of conversation, I noticed to my surprise that she had remained nameless. I proceeded to cautiously ask about her name, to which Ryan replied with scornful regret;

"*Faith,*" he said, as if out of breath. "Her name is ... *Faith.*"

"*Faith,*" I said to myself, audible enough for Ryan to hear.

"Sonny, we don't actually call her that, you dig? She's called Faith but we simply call her Faye. It's shorter and well, more Irish."

"Faye ... that's her nickname?"

"Yeah. What else can you call her? Fatty? Only I use that."

"Why is she called Faith?"

"Well, it's a long story, but ... summarizing, we're a mix, and we don't have the same dad. My brother and I share the same dad, but Faith's from another guy. My dad's of Irish descent, my mom Italian, and Faith's dad, well ... we never got to know the guy that well. My mom gets hysterical when we ask, so we don't anymore. My mom started dating Faye's dad when my dad dumped her for a slut half her age. It seems she started dating that guy out of spite, and then something happened and she dumped him and we moved here to start over again in a new country. The thing is, my mom's maiden name is Avellis. She's like an ultra-catholic nutjob, like all Italians, but she shits on God the first time that things don't go the way she wants 'em to, which is pretty often. In any case she believes everything, nice or shitty, is because God wants it like that. She named her only daughter Faith because she wanted to have faith in her, that she would be fortunate and healthy, I dunno stupid crap like that. The thing is, we call her Faye because it's more Irish. My brother Dave is actually called David, because it can be either Italian or English de-

pending on how you look at it. It's ambiguous. My name is not Italian 'cause my dad wanted to leave a mark of territory on his first son, I think. Then Dave is the ambiguous one in the middle and Faith the pure mark of my mother. In a way it looks good; it's like, from my dad's side to my mom's, gradually."

"I guess. Yeah, it's not bad."

"Anyway, I don't even know what I'm telling you all this personal shit. Up to now you've never been interested in my family. Why the change, I wonder?"

"Hey look, I'm sorry, I don't want to leave a bad impression on you with this, but like I said, I can't help it. I'm sorry it turned out like this. I always knew you had a brother but never knew you had a half-sister. I thought you were like Billy and Robbie."

"Well, you guessed wrong. And make that *sister*. We don't use *half*."

After a few moments, during intervals where Ryan wasn't looking, I unleashed my victory smile when it broke free of its social restraint, never wanting to let others know how I was feeling inside when in public. I tried to look the other way so he couldn't see me, but the happiness of the moment erased the fine line between logic, reasoning, bliss and desire.

Ryan and I parted after a tense walk, as I continued on to the Méndez Center shortcut in order to reach the bus station and he walked down to the Community Center area where his building was located around the block. It was interesting noting that although he appeared to be distant and upset, he had a tone of longing in his voice, as if reaching for me, trying to rescue me from the powerful influence of his sister. I would not be convinced. No matter how many times he referred to her as a childish snot, an apolitical boring midget, an awkward teen pop loving statistic, I could only rejoice in

my own happiness. The glory of remembering her beautiful face, a face which raced my pulse and elevated me from the boring ground of reality, made me forget about every single care in the entire world.

about beginning to like me as a friend. He couldn't fool me. I had been in his place before, when Loynners destroyed my self-esteem for a period of over two years and needed the company of just about anybody. But Ryan didn't have self-esteem by default, and as such he was the kind of person who always needed a sidekick, a security blanket, someone to keep him safe from the harms of society. To help remedy this he had chosen me as his new best friend, but for him everything was coming apart before even having a chance to ignite a friendship. *"Poor guy,"* I couldn't help but think. Poor, poor fool. Destined to be used as a tool without even knowing it, destined to become an unwilling intelligence gatherer, destined to be lied to, to absolute falseness in friendship. I knew what I had to do the moment he said "sister," and it was ruthless, calculating, cold, merciless acting and a lot of surreal naiveté. I didn't hate Ryan. He was half disgusting, half sad. I pitied him, even when I didn't know him a lot. I may have respected his streetwise wannabe aspects, or the knowledge I could learn from his urban ignorance. But it can't be said by any means I felt respect for him in any way; Ryan was a by-product of the pollution Unitedstatian mentality still irradiated in the world, a poor guy destined to live in darkness. I felt so sorry for him that I made my top priority befriending, culturing, teaching and getting along with Ryan; it was my duty as a young Communist to erase the brainwash he and many others had been subjected to, victims of this decaying capitalist culture and its empty legacy.

But I couldn't have my thoughts on Ryan too much when things with *Faye* needed development. There was no other

thought inside my mind except for the "when" and "how." I had to start planning my move and anticipate adversity at an early stage. My instant impression of this was that I wouldn't be able to talk much about the subject with Ryan, the greatest source of information I had under my possession, and the most unreliable one. In a split second, Ryan Mantis passed from an overlooked and not very interesting little character to an awesome, godlike figure of enlightenment, progress and evolution. I foresaw the Cold War coming between us, the tension and the mutual distrust this would mean in our friendship.

I got home grasping the taste of everything that had transpired. I knew by instinct this was a crucial moment in my life, a thing I would not allow to end up in a meaningless stunt. It surely was a very emotional, nerve-racking and uncertain situation, but all worries dissipated easily, for I had engraved in my mind the name of my new loved one after showing Ryan my true colors and softening his disappointment a bit. It was one of the few rare times Ryan let out something out of his mouth that wasn't foul, corrupt or disgusting; in fact, it was beautiful. The second time in the day time had completely frozen.

I smiled to myself quite visibly and closed my eyes for two seconds, trying to imagine the name in its written form; without question, it was a sign of the new finally replacing the old.

CHAPTER III

The Great Leap Forward

"I have witnessed the tremendous energy of the masses. On this foundation it is possible to accomplish any task whatsoever."

- MAO ZEDONG -

Chinese Marxist Guerrilla Fighter and Theorist, Father of the People's Republic of China and First Chairman of the Central Committee of the Communist Party of China

---

"Faith. Her name is ... Faith."

A million thoughts had materialized chaotically inside my mind, violently clashing with one another upon hearing the name from Ryan's lips. I had basically recorded the phrase inside my brain and played it in an infinite loop from the moment I first heard it. The sensation that traversed throughout my shaken body and mind was one of stark contrasts, a mixture of praise and loathing, soothing calm and frightening anxiety; I found it marvelous that she had been named with the English equivalent of my favorite Soviet actress of all time, Vera Alentova. But I also related it instantly to religious dogma, a serious incompatibility issue related to my ideology, and an issue I knew was very alive in her country of origin. Even though it was just a name, and usually people didn't feel compelled to make their names justice, I

wondered whether she could be deeply religious, or rather, religious at any level. In her country, the name Faith was only used by those most zealously loyal to religion, and the receiver of the name was likely indoctrinated beyond repair. If so, it would represent an enormous problem. In any case, these thoughts did not bother me as much as I'm letting on; for at that moment, I was incredibly more concerned on how beautiful the English variant of the name seemed when applied to a person. Beautiful and, in her case, fitting.

"*Faith,*" I whispered, imagining a situation where we were facing each other. When Ryan first uttered the name, it came as a jab to the face. It woke me completely up; until that moment, I had never really fallen in love. All previous instances had been rendered null and obsolete.

Alone in my house with nothing left to do, my mood high as it had never been, I could only think over and over again about the conversation that had taken place between Ryan and me. It was like regressing into childhood. I felt eerily nostalgic about a childhood that had transpired not long ago, when boys and girls were still a mystery to each other and a little thing such as a kiss would create a gigantic impact on your psychological state. This was one of those phases; speaking to your best friend about the girl you like and who you will never dare approach. I played the conversation in my head again one more time, from the moment we walked through Missionaire Drive to the corner next to Gamer Abyss, where he could go on further down to The Crucible, passing in front of the Community Center:

"Ryan, you told me that you wanted me to deal with this on my own, right? That you wouldn't help me ..."

"Yeah ... how could I forget?"

"Well ... look, I'm going to do that. But I first need to know something about her so as to make conversation. This is the

only thing I will ask of you. I promise."

"Umph ... Fair enough, if that voids any further advice ... well, um, she loves Green Köontz to death. That's a good startin' point. And ah, she loves pop punk in general you know this shit like Bad Alberta and those happy-go-lucky bands that are so popular right now, you know the kind ..."

"Yeah, I know ... I don't think she'll like the kind of music I'm into ..."

"What's that, Red Army orchestra folklore balalaika shit? Well if you want to get somewhere near her pants that's what you need to know ... and you would do yourself some good if you didn't mention politics ... she fuckin' hates the subject, it bores her, she's a little ignorant dork, she don't understand any of that, you'll get her bored outta her fuckin' little mind. And guns as well ... don't go thinkin' I don't know you ... and forget about army shit and communism anyway ... Hell man, clearly not a whole bunch of stuff in common, I don't understand why you even wanna approach her when you two are so different. I'm tellin' you now man, this is a bad idea, it's not cool, and you won't accomplish fuck all. Waste of your fuckin' time." Ryan was saying this all with his usual monotonous voice that usually gave a little jump and became high pitched, with his characteristic hybrid accent, a mixture of New Yorker Italian and Californian. The tone of his voice made me think I was pushing boundaries a bit too far. After all, we didn't actually know each other that well, we had only been simple school acquaintances. At this point however, our "friendship" became literally dangerous as its guise was removed. We liked each other enough so as to prefer our company to that of Kannies and Loynnerins, and he definitely wasn't bad company, but this thing was getting in the middle, and the worst part of it had to be how I couldn't care less. My mind was on Faith, not Ryan. In case you haven't noticed, I

never cared much about Ryan. The objective was the sister all along, pure and simple. Ryan was my informant and inside man. What I was trying to do was follow the strategy of becoming his friend slowly, so it didn't seem I was now more interested because of the sister situation. It was a good thing we managed to bond slightly more now that we were together in a class.

In essence, she loved pop-punk music, such as April Divine, Green Köontz and Bad Alberta, and was highly obsessed with Green Köontz's front man, Frank Boy Al. According to Ryan, April Divine was her source of inspiration for her dressing style and Frank Boy was her sex symbol. I was quite sure her bedroom walls had to be covered with posters of these artists in the same way Communist figures covered mine.

Like Ryan had said, one thing she hated was politics, and knowing how political and opinionated I was, he had warned me about sounding boring to her if I touched the subject too many times, like I so often did. On top of it all, she completely hated firearms and other types of bellicose topics. Video games were obviously dismissed as a talking topic, but music was a good thing to start with, as I had a wide taste, including some hit songs by Green Köontz. The hunt would maybe require more effort than usual, but nothing impossible. I was more than up to it.

· · · · ·

I let a cool-down period pass by before proceeding. After all, Ryan and I had been sucked into the kind of awkward moment you don't want to talk about immediately after. As it was to be expected, he did not mention her again and returned to his usual personality, the Ryan I had always known.

As for Faye, I tried to avoid her as much as possible; I would see her from time to time when going to class, crossing paths among crowds of people without her noticing me. I became paranoid at this, as I didn't want her to consider me just a guy from the adjoining class. I had to think what I should do in order to approach her in the best way, without the possibility of disappointment from her part. Little girls like her were sure to expect a prince, an idolized boyfriend surrounded always by an aura of mystery. This wasn't possible in a high school environment; not only seeing a guy every day of the year ruins the romance, but if she asked around people were sure to tell her who I was and end the suspense. I had only managed to do that with my distant girlfriend from the summer, Lyria, who lived in Nova Atlantica. How could I maintain the mystery of my identity and create atmosphere for the day we would finally meet? There was only one way, pretty much the only way there was back then to hook up with girls, and it was ChitChat. However, there was more to using Chit-Chat other than the will to maintain suspense and it was my loss of control over myself whenever she was near. When we crossed paths, that tingling sensation ran through my body like a wildfire, effectively stunning me. I used to think often about what I would do when actually facing her, when I had her beautiful face in front of mine and was required to formulate a sentence, but there was no use; I always became overrun by nerves. I would have to fight this anxiety first before embarking seriously on this endeavor, and the only one who could help me was Ryan, the last person on Earth who wanted to give me a hand on this. I waited until a window to attack him was open, making me able to subtly suggest he should give me his sister's ChitChat address. All I needed was a good excuse.

· · · · ·

"Alright, helloooooo, can I have your attention, please? OK? Now?" Edith was unable to make the class quiet, and was about to pull one of her little attention stunts. This required mocking the entire student body, making insulting impersonations of certain students or simply making an ass out of herself. It usually worked.

"Awwww, look at me!" she began, with an annoying nasal voice on purpose. "I'm a student, I talk loud and bang the table with my fists, look, look how loud I can get, teacher!" and she began playing drums with the table, moving awkwardly in rhythm with her mouth and eyes wide open. Everyone just burst into tears, to my surprise, even her. I had known her since first setting foot on the island, and she had always adopted a bellicose attitude with her students, never once showing empathy. It was understandable; she had lived through the worst years of Kannovschina, when teachers all but committed suicide *en masse* due to the constant harassment and the battlefield the classes represented. This incident, this spontaneous and genuine bond between teacher and student body, was definitely a first. The students had always loved her getting stupid like that because of enjoying laughing at her, but never laughing almost with her. Teachers were willing to sacrifice personal dignity to bond more with their students. Education seemed to be spiraling toward this more than ever before, enforced by these buffoons in teacher's clothing, all because the so-called Western democratic societies had stripped teachers completely off their power. The only way to make oneself appear not as the enemy was to become one of them. This was yet another reason why I didn't believe in Western democracy. Without anyone to dictate what should be done, to shape attitudes and ways of

thinking, the people simply laugh at their leader and end up doing whatever they want, lost in mediocrity and completely lacking in purpose. A Western classroom was a thirty-people representation of a Western nation, merely a cell within the larger organism.

After everyone was satisfied at the poor teacher's expense, soon after everyone was paying attention again, listening to her whiny, pedagogue nasal voice:

"We have a very special event coming up. I'll explain in detail so please don't interrupt. The Prometheus Project is adding Loynne's Island to its list of participant members, and it's a chance for several things you can take advantage of. First, you can learn German or any other language you want from the students arriving here. You can also make friends, go to excursions with them to places of interest and culture, and learn that not everything in life is sit chatting on ChitChat all day long. Or you can do it as long as you learn a new language. Anyway, never mind that. The thing is I need a list of volunteers that want to participate. These volunteers have to make the commitment of taking care of the arriving students, offering to let them stay at their homes and providing them with company at ALL times, no exceptions. Even in school. If any guest student reports claims of isolation, abuse or anything by the hosts, aside from making us look awful bad, it will ban us from the project and the visit will be over. They're very sensitive about such things. They don't take kindly to the um ... more improvised, sincere, chaotic nature of westernmost countries. Try to seem educated and treat them with respect, for Pete's sake."

"Oh, oh! Mrs. Edith! Can I volunteer?" Ryan asked.

"Mrs. Edith, Mrs. Edith lemme suck your saggy tits," some Kanny behind us said, in a low but audible voice.

"Shut the hell up you son of a bitch!" Ryan may have had

low self-esteem, but he certainly didn't take any shit, especially if mocked in public. He took the nearest pencil case, threw it with all his strength and hit a girl that was sitting right behind the Kanny. The case struck her right on the forehead. All the while this happened, the Kanny got up, ready to grab Ryan and hit him, when Edith let out a loud shriek and everything went back to normal in two seconds.

"HEY! Now, that's exactly what we don't want here! Both of you settle down or I send you to the principal's right away. You want that? It's no problem for me! I'm the teacher here, remember? Am I right or am I right?" She waited five seconds, then went on. "So Ryan, you'd like to volunteer?"

"Yes, Mrs. Edith. I'm willing to make the commitment." Ryan could be amazing when kissing ass. His manipulation skills were one of the few things I admired in him, even though most of the time they disgusted me.

"Alright. We'll tell you shortly who volunteered on their side. You never know, you might get any student of any country or gender. They don't discriminate and they expect people to trust each other on equal terms. You may go as a guest to a girl's house, or you might get a female guest. You might also get a boy. You never know, and that's what makes this interesting. But, I'm sure I don't have to say this Ryan, no weird things amongst visitors and hosts. You know what I mean."

"Yeah Mrs. Edith, but wait, you absolutely positive that you can get a girl at your house?"

"Why that's exactly what I said, yes."

"Alright ..."

· · · · ·

Edith, in her infinite enlightened wisdom, wanted three people to represent the school and give a speech in German,

French and Dutch, to welcome the new exchange students who were coming from Germany, Belgium, Switzerland, Austria and the Netherlands. Naturally, I was the first choice in my class to speak German, and I gleefully accepted the task when Edith looked at me. Mike spoke German very well too, but he lacked the accent. Wolfgang was picked due to his ability to speak French fluently, and the other person in the whole school who could also be up to the challenge, particularly for her convenient Dutch ancestry, was Viktoria von Östinsel. I was amazed at how Faye had managed to steal all my libido in a way so I didn't even desire this voluptuous, porn star-looking girl. Viktoria's main features were her enviable massive natural breasts, perky and well-placed, which rivaled those of the best endowed porn stars. A small sexy waist with gigantic thighs and a perfect bubble-butt complimented her exquisite figure. Her skin was moonlight white, just like Faye's, and her face very European with traces of Jewish, with lusty and voracious blue eyes and prominent lips, crowned by jet black hair that she always changed in style, never in color, from elaborate braids, childish pig-tails, pony-tails or straight as Faye's. The expression on her face was a constant smile which never faded no matter the circumstance. These features made her skillful at manipulating men into doing her bidding, but she never established any type of friendship with them, and romantic relationships or sex were completely out of the question. Not even JC Vega dared lay eyes on her. Men who as much disrespected Viktoria would find themselves in very uncomfortable situations, as her father was rumored to be in contact with very dangerous people, and aware of his daughter's looks, had obviously invested a lot in preventing anything from ever happening to her. It was actually quite astonishing seeing how nobody would even stare, whistle or yell obscenities at

her. Nobody dared. Even so, she never walked in the company of bodyguards or tough male friends. Viktoria's only friends were a group of girls that followed her everywhere she went, wanting to leech off her pseudo-socialite status. It's also interesting to note that she wasn't the most liked girl in the school; in fact, she was as despised as Monika Strössner. Everyone hated Viktoria for her family's enormous wealth, her striking porn star looks and her unceasing teasing nature. Needless to say, Monika and Viktoria hated each other with a passion, but never coincided in the same place, seemingly to avoid inevitable confrontation.

On this occasion, I had the indescribable pleasure of being addressed by Viktoria. A funny feeling overtook my body as the imposing presence of this famous character somehow told me I would get to experience this event perhaps once in my entire life. I saw her descend the stairs in the central building on the second floor, near the Biology Lab. She really was Aphrodite incarnate; wearing the latest in designer clothes, she knew how to make her hour-glass figure stand out. A very tight mini-skirt that outlined her curvy thighs and bubble-butt, a tight top struggling to keep her breasts inside and high-heels showing her sexy feet, Viktoria always dressed to kill and hypnotize men around her. Today was certainly no exception, and she had her eyes set on manipulating me.

I acknowledged her powerful beauty, but I felt immune to it. Now that I had designated her as my objective, Faye had already established absolute control over my sexuality. Such good looks were completely disregarded and deemed obsolete knowing what a disgusting, spoiled capitalistic brat she was. Knowing Viktoria was as visually striking as a porn star only raised my inflated charisma. Aside from defending my pride, my loved one and my ideology, I would outright ridicule this powerful and elitist social figure.

"Hi there!! What's your name, cutie?" she said, grinning profusely, her blue eyes, invitingly warm and delicate, putting all the effort into persuading me into doing something I had predicted from the first moment she opened her mouth.

"My name is Sonny," I said sternly, with my usual education and cold respect.

"Oh, great! Well, you obviously know who I am, right?"

"Ah ... as a matter of fact, no, I don't think so," I said, looking at random spots, trying to seem as if I were looking for someone and she was simply wasting my time.

"Ah ... well ... I'm Viktoria? Viktoria *von Östinsel?*" She put a very strong emphasis on her surname, visibly hurt by my supposed ignorance. I tried to carry on without causing an obvious incident. After all, it was really dumb to pretend you didn't know such an astonishing girl being a guy.

"Ah ... yeah, I think I know you alright. Sorry, my mind must be slipping ..."

"No problem, handsome! Look, they told me you're one of the three people who are going to give the speech to the Europeans, so listen, a tall and strong guy such as you wouldn't mind me taking your speech after so I can translate it to Dutch, right? I mean, it's pretty hard as it is, don't you think?" She then smiled and bit her lips, lustfully winking at me. I really appreciated the effort but something inside me was boiling at how this fake behavior didn't affect me in any level. I had scientifically dissected the exchange from such a cold, rational and psychological point of view that any potential respect, attraction or empathy for this individual withered before even materializing. I had to reward myself for such an outstanding feat, unleashing my anger at this obvious disrespect received from this pathetic excuse for a human being.

"That's the most predictable thing you could have ever

said."

"What?"

"That I'm strong, tall and handsome? It's as predictable as me saying you're absolutely beautiful."

"Oh why, thanks Sonny! That's really nice of you! But what I really want is to know if you could lend me your speech ..."

"Yeah, and why should I do that? What's in it for me?"

"What? Well, nothing, obviously! I just thought you could do me a favor ..."

"I've had to write this speech on my own, using my own words and skill, and you're just going to copy it and translate it to Dutch ... do you think that's fair?"

"Well ... yeah! I mean, it's not like they'll notice ..."

"It's not about them, it's about my work being copied. But what would you know, integrity and honor aren't things especially growing on trees here. And you seem to be no exception, *Viktoria*."

"Oh, so that's it ... Look, never mind *Sonny*. I'll ask someone else. Nice knowing you, (*stomme klootzak.*)"

"Likewise, *zhirnaya korova.*"

"What? What did you say?"

"Something you can't understand ... just like you did."

"I'll remember this one ... you, whatever your name even was! Be sure of that!"

"I'll be safe if you can't even remember my name."

"You'll see, when the time comes for you to ask me favors, you'll see then!"

"Why would I want a favor from you? I don't even know you."

"You'll see! You'll see! You're finished!" she kept shouting, while walking away. What a stupid bitch. She wasn't known for being very bright at all, but this event took the cake. Viktoria von Östinsel, what a joke.

When the day finally came, I felt like one of the enlightened favorite students teachers were usually in love with, but truth is, I wasn't really that popular among the student body, just maybe, liked a bit. Not admired. Most of them didn't know me, or I hadn't shown the truest side of me yet, and the popularity in question would slowly come.

I was waiting in the Main Building's lobby outside of the Assembly Hall, next to Wolfgang, who seemed very nervous. He had been designated by Edith as the third spokesperson when nobody else wanted to volunteer. He had reluctantly accepted the task when Edith bribed him with raising his grades.

"Big deal here, right?" I said, enthusiastically. It was the typical day at school I liked. A special, forthcoming event lining up, me taking part in it, the weather sunny and pleasant, and I wasn't in class due to my special skills being needed by the teachers' stupid activities. I saw several of my classmates going back to class, and I remember feeling an instant sensation of relief and self-importance.

"Yes *Doshi*, I'm a bit nervous really."

"Oh don't be nervous, *Tovarish*! It won't be that bad, just relax. Well, judging by those people coming in ... forget what I just said ..." To my own surprise, I was beginning to get nervous too. A delegation of Europeans headed straight for the main lounge where the thing was supposed to take place. There were adults and kids alike. It was fun seeing foreign kids around. Most of them were the typical pale, rosy-faced timid Jewish looking kids with curly light red hair. The girls, mainly, were actually quite attractive, and looked less timid and shy. Strange, huh, with girls? I wondered if they were the equivalent of Loynnerin sluts up there where they lived. Maybe sluts in Germany were actually difficult to tell from normal girls?

Moving on from this curiosity I continued my conversation with Wolfie, trying to calm him down;

"No worries *Tovarish*, this will be over before you know it. As long as we stick together nothing will go wrong. Come on, what are the chances that something truly terrible happens? Breathe deep, read your speech and forget about the whole thing as soon as you're done."

"Oh no ... I don't think I can do this. I'm gonna be horrible, I know it, *Doshi* ..." He said, genuinely concerned and no longer hiding his nerves.

"Why are you so afraid anyway?"

"I can't stand crowds, I mean ... all that attention. I don't mind being among crowds, but not when all the people in a room are watching me."

"I've got your back, *Tovarish* ... just relax. Everything will be alright. Not everyone in a crowd watching someone really cares that much. Just pretend nobody gives a crap about you and proceed with the speech calmly."

"Alright *Doshi* ... I'll give it a go."

I helped Wolfie's nerves by making fun of teachers, fellow classmates, and generic Loynnerins. I was not surprised to see how much he talked about women. After a while though, we sensed the call to action when the Germanic students started gathering for the special event, inside the big lounge. How sycophantic Loynner's could be, I told Wolfgang, in order to gather nice publicity and money for their silly little tourism megalomania. The room decorated with the respective flags of each country, and tables with typical food from the Germanic countries placed strategically next to the guests. The teachers, the principal, even the Mayor of Pilgrim Coast was there, since events like this, even if they took place in a simple school, meant a matter of life and death for local tourism.

Edith began the evening with her usual eccentric nature, welcoming the foreign students and teachers with her non-existent cute charm. Wolfgang, Viktoria and I had to wait standing next to her and the loud microphone, smiling like idiots in front of over a hundred people from Western Europe. I had a fun time getting the faces, and forming opinions inside my naughty little head. Some teachers looked like authoritarian Nazi SS officers, with shaven skulls and all. I wondered about the racist and fascist tendencies that Europe overflowed with, and if these kids suffered indoctrination at the hands of these authoritarian looking teachers. The Germanic students appeared to be normal, without racist tendencies, but also quite stone-faced, their intentions and thoughts impossible to perceive. Other teachers, probably the Dutch, looked like aging naturist hippie liberal trash with more than just a spare bong in the mountain-hiking backpack, ready to hitchhike to Mount Tyler or party at Club De Wallen's. The Belgian and Swiss students, quite frankly, looked like spineless shy little timid milky scarecrows, with freckles and Jewfros. I really wondered if that was a front and inside they were all a pack of morally deviant junkie perverts. The Prometheus Project was a sham in every sense. In a world polluted by discrimination, loathing of foreigners and heavy immigration laws, tolerant integration attempts like these felt not only forced, but deceitful.

Wolfgang had a nice time staring at the girls with curiosity and glee, but blondes had never been exactly my type. Even though they showed some signs of shyness, their eyes glowed with something else, something lusty and naughty. I had to give in to Wolfgang's pressure and got dragged once more into his opposite sex discussions.

"Look at that one, *Doshi*. I wish I had such a nice girl for myself."

"They all look the same to me, *Tovarish*."

"Come on Sonny, don't say that, you know they aren't all alike ..."

"I'm not being discriminatory to women, *Wolfie*. I got my sights on someone already. Someone worthwhile. I have a real objective at last ..."

" '*Koketsu ni irazunba koji wo ezu.*' "

"Ah, what?"

"It's a Japanese proverb. It means, 'if you do not enter the tiger's cave, you will not catch its cub.' "

"And what do you mean by that?"

"You have an objective. You have a tiger's cave to enter. All you need to do is risk, and you will gain. I have nothing to reach for, nothing to crave."

"I've got a proverb for you ... '*bez muki net nauki.*' "

"What does it mean?"

"Literally, it means 'without torture there is no science.' Basically it's a form of 'no pain, no gain.' The best teacher is adversity, hardship. All you need to do is simply search, like I did. I searched and searched, growing bitter and suffering by never finding what I wanted. Then, just when I gave up all hope and was willing to conform myself with my mediocre destiny, I found her unexpectedly, by accident. That's precisely the point. You need to search until you know what you need, and then the answer will reveal itself to you. '*Know yourself first, then know others.*' Isn't that what you always say, that Japanese proverb?"

"Yes ..."

"Well then? You know what to do. Stop worrying. Everything eventually happens, you won't die alone, you know ... it may seem like this drought will last forever, but that's just now. Eventually you will find a nice girl for yourself ..."

"Oh ... yeah, I'm sure of it."

"Shh, quiet Wolfie, I think it's about to begin ..."

The teachers were about to be done with their stupid speeches, and after the Mayor's turn to speak in a laughable cheap imitation of German, Edith grabbed Wolfgang by the wrist so as to direct him on where to position himself on the stage. Wolfgang looked at me once last time with an expression as if to say "What did I get myself into?" leaving the rest to fate.

"And without further ado, our very own students will now proceed to welcome you with speeches they have written themselves, using their best skills in German, French and Dutch to help make you feel more at home! They are all volunteers from various countries who decided to participate in this project to let others know of their experiences moving to Loynne's Island. Please receive the first of these volunteers, Wolfgang Emmerich, a student of Scientific Baccalaureate of Unitedstatian-Thai descent, with a warm applause, and let's hear his story!

Wolfgang, who had remained to Edith's right while she spoke, advanced to the microphone timidly, with the sheet of paper containing the speech in his hands. He spoke timidly and by the book, with his heavy booming voice, and earned a regular applause from the Europeans, an applause that felt forced and out of compromise, especially because of his imperfect German accent. He returned and only said "*better this way; I wouldn't have imagined what would have happened if you spoke first. At least it's over now.*"

"Please receive now Sonny Zharostin, a nationalized Loynner of Russian descent also studying in Scientific Baccalaureate, who will share with us his experience as both a local and a foreigner!"

My time had come. I approached the stand firmly, trying not to seem intimidated by the on-looking crowd. Knowing I

had to be defying in order to earn some respect, I raised my voice loudly and spoke with an energizing presence, trying to visualize all the charismatic Latin American natural born orators I admired and loved, like Hugo Chávez and Fidel Castro:

"*I stand here today to address you, our honorable guests. It is my greatest pride to welcome you to the Island of Loynne, a place recognized by its excellent weather, its abundance and wealth, its love for liberty and most importantly, its human heart. There is no place on Earth where you'll be as welcome as you will be here, for it's in our nature to promote friendship, respect and tolerance.*

I once was like you, an individual in a foreign land, an unknown paradise which scared me, an environment I did not understand, even though at the eyes of the law I could legally call this land my own. The people here accepted me with open arms and never looked down on my race, nationality, accent or anything that made me feel different. This is, I must stress, the factor we need to continue upholding across the entire world, a gesture of goodwill that will continue to endure for generations as long as we treat our equals with respect, remembering always how they feel and perceive the world, which is just like us.

I urge you, our guests, to dismiss any kind of preoccupation that can be worrying you. On this island, you will nurture your mind with new knowledge, feed your heart with the warmest human kindness, fuel your deepest passions in any way you desire. It is here that you will rediscover yourselves as new human beings, just as I did.

We have a saying in Loynne's, which goes 'in a borderless world, we are all foreigners'. This should be noted, as it describes our true spirit. Nobody has to feel discriminated

or out of place on an island where by being different, we all end up being alike. This is the message we intend to pass on in order to extend friendship and a sense of brotherhood all across the world. We are your neighbors, and we kindly embrace your presence.

Thank you for your time, and if you'd let me, allow me to express how great an honor this has meant personally for me. Farewell our guests, and may you discover the true essence of Loynne's Island through Fortune and Liberty!"

It was a shame that I was forced into regurgitating such meaningless drivel, but it had worked. Upon finishing my speech the crowd cheered joyfully and even the cynical Germanic youngsters found themselves sincerely praising the welcoming speech, not because of my perfect accent or how well and fluently I had spoken, they could have easily presumed I was simply German, but because of what I had said. The words, the charisma, the spirit … Those aren't things you learn at school. Wolfgang seemed detached, unresponsive. I was greeted with a heavy, heartfelt applause that went on for several minutes, and made people outside want to look inside. The stupid Gardening Course Kannies stuck to the windows, peering and trying to see what the ruckus was all about.

Edith gave me one of her usual proud smiles of "done it again, boy." The world was mine for five minutes. Wolfgang cleansed some sweat off his forehead and laughed heavily, looking at me. Then it was Viktoria's turn. She gave me a disdainful look as she walked toward the microphone, and I was thinking she must have had to ask people for help or used ChitChat to look something up and make a speech of her own. I didn't know what she had said in Dutch, but the result spoke for itself. It weren't the contents of the speech I was

sure, but the way she delivered her speech. Like most people of her cultural and intellectual level, she couldn't read at all. Stuttering, mumbling, reading the same line twice and getting confused earned her a mediocre and discreet applause that made her burst into tears. Seriously, nothing would have toppled the shock of my speech, not even her looks, which by being far away diminished the impact. Viktoria's forced and mediocre applause earned me her dirtiest of looks. The tears on her red and sunken face weren't an impediment to viciously stare at me. I happily stared back, grinning discreetly with my chin so high up it could have gouged out one of those beautiful teary eyes.

Viktoria was taken by Edith outside, and I don't remember seeing her again much that year, given she studied Arts in the East Wing like most lazy Kannies and Loynnerins who wanted to do as little as possible. Most probably, she had never felt more humiliated in her life. I felt a strange joy toppling such a supposed important figure in the school's social hierarchy just by refusing to be her servant, and all I had to do was simply be myself.

After we finished with the whole paraphernalia, we got to the food part. I headed immediately for the non-weird, corporate multinational food and began to ingest and digest as more and more poor Germans were drawn to the tastes of corporate megacapitalism. The teachers ended up eating their own version of German food so as to not look completely pathetic. I could see instances of them discreetly throwing it in bins at the slightest, or holding the food in their hands.

"Heeeeey!!! Hey Sonny!!"

"*Oh no,*" I thought. "*Not him ...*" But I had to dissimulate my lack of enthusiasm as much as possible.

"Hey, Ryan! How have you been!"

"Gettin' by ... Oh, sweet Jesus ... where am I supposed to

find her! So many hotties to look at! Seriously, I hope she's one of the hot ones ... hope it's not like that one over there ... Better ask the ugly ones since they're just a few, so I can shake the fear away quicker ... Be right back, man!"

"Er ... mind telling me who you're looking for?"

"For one of the Gerry girls, of course! She's stayin' in my house! What you think now, motherfucker! You jealous?"

"Depends on what you bring back home with you, jerk."

"It'll be one of the hot ones, believe me. The probabilities of having a *fat* one are very *slim*, hehe, get it? Fat, slim?"

"Umph, sure Ryan. Anyway, who cares! You already have a really hot teen right in your own house ... oh, but too bad you can't do anything with that one!"

"Oh, you goddamn fffuc—Look I'll be off before someone suddenly finds himself lyin' on his back. Bye," he said, and left heavily offended.

"Is Ryan always like that?" Wolfgang asked.

"What do you mean?"

"You know, always so obsessed with women ..."

"And look who's talking!"

"I only want a nice woman, you know that Sonny. I'm not interested in fucking them all like he wants."

"Yeah, well ... he's going through a hormonal explosion at the moment, from what you've been able to witness. But I think he's a good person at heart. I've yet to find out, honestly." Pissing Ryan off was a nice satisfaction anyway. I wondered whether it could even be developed into a hobby with enough dedication.

"What's he doing, is he actually talking to all the girls he can find?"

"Yeah ... he ... he tends to do that. He's a bit of a prick, you know. The more girls he can get, the better he thinks he does and looks. Give him a minute ... he'll make it worse ... much

worse if he's given enough time." We immediately turned our backs on the scene we had just witnessed, two seconds after I delivered my last line. Ryan dropped soda on a tall, tough looking but pretty German girl, which belted him right across the face and made him stagger and retreat scared. He had stained her all over, and later tried to help in the only way he could, which was sycophantically trying to clean her with a hysterical looking expression only he could produce. Wolfgang and I were trying to hide our amusement as much as possible, something hard enough with our faces bursting trying to repress the laughter. In the end, it turned out it had been that girl the one who was staying at his house, just like I had thought. So much for a first good impression.

Ryan had returned, not visibly defeated by his little stunt of embarrassment. He still had fight in him, which resulted hilarious.

"Way to go, champ with a 'u.' That's how you do it with the ladies."

"Shut up, you dick, at least I go after real women. Listen, Edith just told me a couple of things. Seems we need to go and show this girl a good time."

"Huh, is that so, I thought that's why you went through all this migraine to show *her* a good time! She sure had a good time with you and your face."

"Oh come on, listen it's just that we gotta you know, break the ice a bit. Edith said that since you and I are good friends in class we should go and take her out to see Paradise Plaza. No biggie, just one afternoon, I can handle her at school and at home. You explain shit to her in German or Australian or whatever it is she speaks and then we talk about certain things. You know a nice afternoon out. Come on man, I know you don't get out much."

"How do you know? I go wherever I like."

"Which is limited to your house and the school and back? Jeez, come on don't be lazy. And I'll dunno ... I—I'll do YOU a favor ... anythin' at all. Just please!"

"Oh ... no ... So ... hard ... to think ... about ... something in return."

"I know it's gonna be related to my sister, motherfucker, just do it quick so it's less painful for all of us ... come on, hurry up."

"Haha ... that was easy. Alright. Look I'll be your slave and translator for the whole afternoon if you give me her ChitChat address ... and pass me a photo of her."

"What?! Sonuva fuckin' bitch!!!"

"What is it going to be then? I scratch your back, you scratch mine."

"Oh, fine, jeez. God, it's only a stupid picture after all, no big deal. Just don't go around passin' it around to everyone like she's some kind of town bicycle."

"Why would I want to do that? Haven't you even analyzed the situation? You really don't know me if you think I'm going to do that to something I want all for myself."

"Yeah, yeah, yeah, yadda-yadda-yadda don't wanna hear it. Whatever. Just be there tomorrow at 17:00. And by the way motherfucker, my sister ain't home at that time 'cause she goes to school tutorials in the afternoon to better her grades, that's how much fun she is."

"Yeah, don't worry, I'll be there in time."

"Alright, see ya tomorrow. I'm goin' home, had enough of this Prometheus horseshit."

"Thanks, Ryan. It means a lot. I'll try to do my best tomorrow."

There was a certain degree of camaraderie and friendship even if Ryan and I secretly – and supposedly – hated each other. It was a very fine line, and we never crossed it either

into total rivalry or trustworthy friendship. I noticed there was a lot of it which was his fault. He didn't use to trust people up to a 100% like I did with friends like Wolfgang. Wise move, but spoke a lot about his true nature and character. He used people, he was a manipulator, he took what benefited him the most and then discarded the waste. Fair enough. The only thing I needed from him was precisely him needing me. Total symbiosis. As long as he needed me, he'd be willing to trade in goods for information or favors regarding Faye. Even though it was just information, I had managed to plant my stomping Communist feet in Ryan's homeland. I had *made* him comply. Not only that, but he basically invited the enemy into his very doorstep. He needed me at his house for this. I was about to do a little spying and intel gathering on my very own, under his very nose; there was no denying the pleasure I took from this win-win. Nonetheless, something made me afraid, that defeatist thought paranoia always brings along. The thought that most probably, no matter how much we helped each other, neither of us was going to be walking next to a girl anytime soon.

· · · · ·

The very next day at 17:00 I prepared myself for his stupid little stunt, my part of the bargain. The day itself was already dull; cloudy, cold and the streets largely deserted. I was in for some fun alright. However, I'd get a lot out of this, namely that talk with Ryan and the blueprints to his home, which I wasn't able to visit when I should have.

Arriving and setting a foothold in The Crucible proved strangely familiar, as if I had always done that routine. The enormous building was cream-colored like many others, and had the letters of its name hanging from the side in a stylish

italic font. There was a circular staircase at the center, and its corridors were safeguarded by walls that went up to approximately chest level. The building distilled a faint yellowish glow wherever you looked at, be it the exterior paint or the interior tiles.

There were three entrances; the parking lot entrance facing Paradise Avenue, the back entrance at the west side of the building facing the Community Center itself, and lastly, the main entrance was located at the east side in a small promenade between the two buildings that looked like a passageway. Bushes and flowers were piled at the sides of it, often with flies and dog feces as well. To the sides of this promenade were The Crucible and another building, their perimeter walls riddled with Kanny graffiti.

I entered through the Community Center back entrance, a ramp with grayish tiles which lead to the parking lot onwards and to the pool area to the right. The pool area was actually the best feature about the building, as it had big squares of white and red colors surrounding the three pools and large areas with grass, bushes and palm trees giving nice foliage. All of the balconies of The Crucible's residents overlooked the pools.

The parking lot area granted you access to the main lobby, which consisted of the elevators and bathrooms to the left and the receptionist office to the right. Onwards you would see the main entrance and the stairs, which lead you right to the pool area.

I took the elevator and stopped at the seventh floor. Turning immediately right, the Mantis apartment was number 75. I took a deep breath. I doubted I'd actually get to see Faye, for I knew Ryan would take precise measures against it. Then again, there was the probability, and nerves started wreaking havoc between my internal organization, damaging anything

short of strategy and plans.

"*What the hell,*" I thought. "*Vperyod.*"

I rang the bell pressing it for about two complete seconds, which was my first mistake. A loud, annoying metallic buzz almost shattered my ears. A bitter Ryan opened the door with that assface of his that I was getting used to see.

"Don't do that, man! *FUCK!*"

"What?!"

"That! Don't do that! Press it for just a quarter of a second! See?" he said, as he showed me how to gently press it in order for it to be less noisy and more tolerable. It seemed doing that in the Mantis residence meant annoyance and a change in mood for the worse. It however alerted them of strangers and people they weren't expecting. The bell wasn't exactly music to the ears and drilled and echoed its way throughout the whole house.

"Well sorry man, how was I supposed to know, I pressed it thinking you had a normal doorbell, not a submarine alarm."

"It's alright, I'm sorry ... Jesus, I'm just a bit nervous about this whole thing."

"Haha ... what's the matter? You wanna impress the Gerry hottie and you don't think you can do it? After that thing with the drink, I mean?"

"Ah, shuddup with the drink. That was nothin'. The problem will be the livin' together thing. That will decide whether she likes me or not anyway. I wonder how Dave's handling it. He's in some armpit in Europe, part of the Prometheus Project. Thinks that way they are gonna raise his grades, like that's gonna help him ... He's in the same fucking grade as my sister. 3rd Grade of fuckin' Compulsory Education ... can you believe that? It's the third time he goes to the same grade. If he don't do something fast he's gonna dunno, end up bad. A bum. Working at McReady's flippin' burgers ... maybe worse.

Well what's worse than a bum in Loynne's Island anyway ... there's so few that you're immediately singled out from society. How many bums are there here in the whole South, four, three maybe? Damn ... this ain't LA, You can't go and join a bum club under a bridge here so easy."

"Er ... OK ... And what does that have to do with anything?"

"Nothin', just' getting my cables crossed. Look, lemme show ya the rest of the house," Ryan took me and his neurosis on a small tour around the apartment, which consisted of a living room that led to the kitchen turning immediately left, and a corridor up front which lead to the balcony and the bedrooms. The walls were painted white and the floor tiles were of a dark grayish color, almost black, very elegant compared to the rough ones in my place. The living room was fitted with a wooden round table and four chairs, next to some kind of curtain. There was a couch, a lamp, and a silver 64 cm CRT TV similar to mine, probably one of the latest that were produced. There were several wooden shelves containing either books or movie boxes. It seemed tidy enough, and had this summer-like coziness. If I have to be honest, I liked the ambience from the first moment I went in. Space was a big issue for me in households, but the coziness sort of made up for it. The view to the balcony was splendid and simply filled you with life; the pools were right under, with its recognizable red and white tiles, palm trees and grass. The Crucible was actually a beautiful building, no matter how many times they said it was shitty, falling apart and old. Loynne's had this asset to its structures, which was a sexy summer look and an '80s Miami vibe to it.

"I noticed you have a lot of self-help books," I told Ryan while gazing curiously at the shelves.

"Ohh. Yeah. Never mind that. That's all my mother's. I

don't read a lot. I only have a couple of books. Readin' was like, never really my thing. I prefer movies. Too lazy to read."

"Right, right ..."

While looking at different objects in the room, I noticed that there was a collage of several photographs next to the phone, featuring the Mantis family and their friends. Some of them showed the Mantis brothers attending school events with costumes, or showed them at what I thought were beaches in California. I identified Faye immediately. In one picture she appeared completely suntanned and childish, maybe 11 years old, next to some other girls. I could only recognize her by the eyes and lips. Her hair was tied around the back and her overall appearance was kiddy and not precisely womanly sexy. It was but natural ... she had been a kid like the rest of us once. I tried to assimilate the fact that she had never been the girl she was to my eyes. Even so, I felt this strange attraction to everything that was related to her; her past as a child, as a baby, anything at all. You can't exactly say I was sexually attracted, but I was in other terminology, purely interested. The other most noticeable picture was one where she was at the beach holding an apple, looking at the camera with smiley eyes, and had an olive green cap. Her skin was also suntanned on this one, and she looked twelve or early thirteen. The Faye I knew didn't look like this, but it was nonetheless the same person, and I adored her in any incarnation she could adopt. Once I had looked at all the pictures, I immediately became aware of something I had not paid much attention; the Christian cross necklace with a US flag motif hung from her neck, in every photo. It must have been something relatively common in her homeland, it wouldn't mean she was religious, or at least, I didn't think so. I would have hated it if she had turned out to be a religious fanatic, but Ryan had never mentioned anything related to it, but he

may have been ignorant to her deepest passions. I moved on quickly so that Ryan didn't think I was way too interested in staring at his family pictures, and dismissed as well the possibility that the cross could bear any meaning whatsoever. To justify my reason as to why I was looking at the collage, I formulated a question:

"When will I meet your brother?"

"I dunno, when he comes back, I guess. Why you think Jenna's stayin' over here? I wouldn't have been able to if my brother was here!"

"Right ... so you traded him for Jenna?"

"I'd trade 'im for a sack of potatoes, and I wouldn't feel too sorry for him if I were you. He's gettin' a hell of a lot more than me by doin' that. He must be fuckin' a lot of tight German pussy right about now."

"He seems really savvy with girls from what I've been hearing ..."

"Yeah, well ... who gives a shit. Eventually we all get to bang somethin'. It's just a matter of when. I'm not worried, I'm just impatient."

"You mean ... you've never done it?"

"What me? Wha—how dare you! Of course I have!"

"Ohh, right ... just curious ..."

"What, do I look like a virgin? Do I give that impression?"

"No, you give the impression of being a closeted homosexual."

"Fuck you. Lemme show you the rooms," Ryan said, irritated. He went through the opening in the living room that led to a corridor with the three bedrooms and the balcony at the end. The bathroom, a small room which was on the living room area immediately next to Ryan's bedroom, was painted sky blue, to which I became disgusted at first sight. I hated sky blue painted rooms, it made stuff look like an old folks

home. It also reminded me of visiting houses of old distant relatives in The Motherland, with old people smell in every room and antique furniture. It made it look boring and stuck in time, or just simply tacky. The distinct smell of urine impregnated the air and suffocated my nostrils with its unavoidable, acid, piercing scent. There wasn't enough space either. The washing machine was ridiculous stuck between the short space between the walls and the toilet, making relieving yourself a hard task if you were my size. The Mantises were small and barely fit there, so imagine that. The bathtub was normal, of no significance in any way. Just a normal bathtub. But it sparked my curiosity knowing that was the place she took showers every day, washing and rubbing her tight naked body. I was getting gradually acquainted with what being Faye was like, and what her routine must have been. I always did that anyway with the houses of other people. Must have been a residue of wanting to know how normal "people" lived when I was younger.

"Mmmm ... I shouldn't be doin' this but what the hell. This is my sister's room. Don't get your hopes high, she's not here," Ryan said, as he opened the door. My enthusiasm had not waned when knowing I would not see her. At long last I would get to see her world.

"Uh, yeah, don't mind the decoration, it's just what you could expect of her ... fuckin' Frank Boy Al around everywhere and that dyke skater wannabe April Divine. Told ya she's a stupid teenie-weenie happy-go-lucky twerp." Although I know now the exaggeration behind it, I analyzed this as one of the most fascinating places I had ever seen in my whole life. This was it, where she saw the dawn and dusk of each day, and I had been allowed to witness it firsthand.

A bed with its own night stand, a dresser drawer and a desk filled the entirety of the room. If we looked at the room

in a north-south-west-east perspective with the door located at the south, the wardrobe was embedded in the southern wall, at the left of the door. The bed – with the night stand to its right – was placed alongside against the west wall, looking east, forming a small walking space between the night stand and the wardrobe. On the northern wall there was a small desk placed with a window to the right forming a very small walking space due to its proximity with the bed, and on the east wall a dresser drawer with a TV set on top, opposite the bed. The distance and walking space between the bed and the wardrobe could hold but a single person in width. The other walking space, between Faye's bed and the desk was larger, but either way not particularly big. In front of the bed there was an old silver 51 cm CRT television set resting on top of a white and pink dresser drawer. The small desk contained a mirror and several drawers filled with books, scribbled sheets of paper, pens, make-up and woman stuff like hair dryers. But on the desk there was an item of extreme importance; a dark red bottle in the shape of a cube bore the "Detènte" logo, with the subtitle "Balearic Cherry." I had finally gotten to know the name of the sweet perfume she wore. Without Ryan witnessing, I sprayed some on my hand and smelled it when his back was turned. There was no doubt about it; indeed, it was the same smell, that fragrance that had rendered me completely numb in bliss. However, it didn't exactly smell like when she had it on, as if something was missing. Quickly, I concluded that aside from the perfume, her own personal smell added to the unique aroma she irradiated. I became astonished at how well a woman could smell on her own without added products.

Moving on, the entire room was actually a bit of a mess. Clothes where scattered everywhere, the bed wasn't even made, and the desk was in disarray. Once again I found my-

self having no trouble with it. I accepted any flaws that came from Faye as a person. This was her room, and as such had to be loved by default, no questions or second thoughts ever arose. Ryan told me anyhow that the mess was always related to his mother Flavia, who was described by him as a nervous, childish and forgetful person who would intrude in Faye's room at all times in order to use her make up and try out her clothes. For what he was telling and showing me, Flavia seemed like the typical mother in a midlife crisis hopelessly clinging to any youth she could have ever possessed, and trying desperately to fool others into believing she could be her daughter's sister. That would have explained the massive amount of self-help books and its lasting impact, given she read them at all, a rather unlikely deed. I felt a strange pride in not judging Faye even if conditions seemed against her for some reason. At the time, I must have thought it meant true love, a calling, even destiny.

The last room – Ryan didn't want to show me his mother's bedroom – was shared by Ryan and Dave. It was rather in order, according to manly standards. Not worse than mine, at least. It had Ryan's personality printed all over it, and I guessed Dave's as well. Firstly, the walls were painted sky blue, but it didn't matter as you couldn't see much of them. The room was simply filled with too many things. Bunk beds lay against the right wall, covering it all. A desk with a computer and many wooden shelves on top, plus posters and flags covered the left one. The flags were from Unitedstatian baseball, hockey and football teams. The posters were from either games, bands or whatever. It seemed random and without much thought to it, totally suiting their seemingly chaotic personalities. Next to the computer desk there was a 36 cm TV on a small wooden stand, with an integrated VHS and a connected GamEsprit Zwei console. Several other ran-

dom possessions such as toy aircraft and cars also decorated the possible empty spaces they found. The dresser drawer was also built on the inside of the wall and was located at the right of the door, facing the bunk beds.

"Alright, so this is our room, that's our shit, etcetera, etcetera. I got some important stuff to show you though. Look, wait." Ryan sat quickly on the computer with a queer jump and browsed through several pictures, and I instantly recognized the Faye ones I wanted. Shame I couldn't make him pass them all, but I'd sort that out.

"What do you want to show me?"

"Wait ... um ... here I think. Yeah, that's it."

Ryan started showing me photos of a red-haired, short and somewhat chubby girl, who appeared to be about our age, with a very round face and glasses, freckled with pale, white smooth skin in a Germanic way. She was beautiful.

"Who's she?" I let out immediately.

"She? She?! Haha ..." Ryan was brewing one of his fancy showing-off antics, the attention seeking behavior so common in people with accumulated years of outwardly social repression from his peers. I followed his stupid ritual as this interested me greatly.

"She's Daphne. A half-Loynner half-German chick. She's got a sister too, Eva, but she's a stupid little brat, I think she's my sister's age, maybe less. If things don't work with Jenna I got more pussy to look forward to."

"Hm, you sure don't waste your time. You don't even know how the thing with Jenna is going and you already have another one stored up."

"That's how you do it, boy. But listen, let me tell you the story ... turns up we've been friends with these girls for ages, since they arrived to the island. Me, Billy, Robbie and Dave, but they moved away and we sorta lost contact. Well now

thanks to these wonderful social communication tools so handy to the average hormonal adolescent young male, I can have a shot at her ass again. Word is she's really interested in me. At least that's what I managed to gather from my conversations with her."

"So this is pure speculation."

"Sorta. But don't worry. I know when a girl is not interested. I'm not gonna waste my time with a battle I know can't be won."

"Oh yeah? Well ... let's see how it goes then."

"Yeah ... Hey, lemme show you the pics of when we went to Kalysand Lake last summer!"

Ryan proceeded to show me some of their adventures in a infamous excursion that had transpired when I was on 3rd Grade. I remembered everything Billy had told me about it one day at recess, about how Ryan had been a complete selfish dick who had not helped in any aspect and that Dave had slacked off just as bad. If I could find a political ally in him against Ryan that'd be an interesting thing, I suddenly thought. What I needed was people siding with me on my quest and with Ryan's popularity of selfishness I thought of it as quite possible. So far Ryan didn't seem as bad but he spread a foul air of corruption, he was hiding something, some dark side. Billy and Robbie did even so in greater fashion, but seemed more down to earth, friendly and loyal. It was evident there was some kind of ongoing in-fighting and distrust between them. With my arrival this seemed to have intensified, with Billy wanting to lead me toward his side, while Ryan did this in his own way. The thing with the sister seemed to trouble him greatly anyway, and was a major obstacle in his desire of me becoming closer to him than to the Nazarethes. However, I needed Ryan for information and help on Faye, something which the Nazarethes would not be

able to do. This whole train of thought was interrupted by the bell, which caused Ryan to jump merrily out of the chair in his own queer fashion and head for the door at light speed. Jenna had arrived. I wasn't actually ready for this. My mind was still assimilating and processing all the emotional information surrounding me, and another part of me was waiting for the chance to snag the pictures in Ryan's computer and put them in my music player's storage. I wouldn't risk it now as he would immediately bring Jenna in. And later Jenna would be there to maybe snitch if I did it in front of her. I didn't know her after all, so trust was non-existent. I'd have to fuck myself over this time and rely on the one picture Ryan promised to send. I still found it hard to believe he acceded to that.

"Sonny, Jenna ... Jenna, Sonny. Wunderbar! Now we all know each other. Fantastisch und scheize! I'd really better learn some German quick, it'll do me some good, know what I mean Sonny? The stiff frankfurt here needs to be put between some nice buns! Haha!" Ryan then began to mock the German language in an exaggerate fashion, and I couldn't see where this would get her closer to Jenna. I for my part, formally shook hands with her and tried to keep a low profile. The girl was sure pretty, but too tomboyish for me. She was tall and broad, had an athletic yet muscular body, and eitherways I wouldn't replace Faye as a symbol for beauty now that I had found one. All girls to me seemed shitty after Faye. None could ever hope to match her grace and power.

"Sooo ... alright. Listen let's head out so we can show Jenna the town. And uh ... Sonny ... please translate as I'm speakin'?"

· · · · ·

227

Jenna proved to be a nice girl, but didn't speak much. In her own fashion, she was shy. I wasn't sure if she was annoyed by Ryan's imbecility or if she preferred to keep quiet so as to not belt him. Either way, it proved to be a nice yet slow afternoon out. The rare cloudy weather and the lack of people on the streets helped my mood, which at the moment was a bit dull, if not awkward. Ryan talked the most and simply kept worsening it. His optimism was to be admired, however, as he kept his smile and winning attitude until the very end. When we got tired of walking around, we visited several shops located near the Church & Square, one of the main commercial and touristic areas of Pilgrim Coast, surrounded by banks, stores, restaurants and the eponymous church which benefitted from a rather large square to host festivities of any kind, but mostly religious. One of the shops, named Spin 'n Punk, was a tattoo parlor and a clothes shop rolled into one, and was accessed via some stairs leading underneath to a corridor. The tattoo parlor and the clothes shop were in front of each other on separate locales, but were a part of the same business. My eyes had simply never seen stuff like this before in real life. Dozens of leather spiked wristbands and studded belts kept piling up on the exhibit windows, and black shirts with band logos laid outside for you to browse. A lot of stuff was kinky in nature as well. Many sadomasochistic and leather oriented accessories like thongs or mouth gags were on exhibit. I wondered about sexuality even further, as my eyes studied several detailed cartoonish wax figures of people having sex, almost all of them Rastafarian for some odd reason. The Jamaican culture was present in the form of these little figurines, marijuana symbols and Jamaican flag shirts. I thought of this as crude an unnecessary, I hated drugs. They were a capitalistic recreation that damaged your health in the long term, turning the proletariat

into stoner-hippie degenerates which would not fight for the just cause of Socialism. I forgot about all of this however when I saw a Hammer & Sickle, in the form of a little metal box. Communistic symbols were not present in a lot of ways, and I wondered often if pot-smoking liberal slacktivist hippies knew the real deal behind my beloved *serp i molot*. Suddenly, Ryan broke the interesting atmosphere with his rants;

"Yeah, 'cause, like, I'm totally gonna be a real punk one of these days. Yeah, like in the videos ... Get a real fuckin' mohawk and a studded vest. That's how you do it. And them combat boots, with ripped jeans. That'll be so cool ... You like tattoos Jenna?"

"Look Ryan, I ... uh ... listen I'm going to go inside the shop."

"What you doin' man, I need you to translate for me!"

"You'll do fine. Just practice your German. She'll like it and you'll both get a laugh out of it."

"You think?"

"Sure! Speaking languages even if it's a half-assed attempt amuses people. Give it a go. It'll do you good some time alone with her, don't you think?"

"Yeah ... yeah, you're right!! I'm gonna take her for a spin 'round the Church & Square and Stockholm Avenue. You gonna be here? I won't be long."

"Sure, sure, just take your time *(annoying prick.)*"

I left Ryan alone with Jenna, letting him worm his own way out of this. I was a bit sick of the forced and awkward trio, and the consequences of the outing were very clear; Ryan wouldn't get the girl. She simply had no respect or interest in him. Jenna was taller, stronger and tougher. She would never be interested in such a flimsy guy. I forgot about them when I went inside to explore the store and see if I could buy anything with the little money I was carrying.

Browsing the shirts I immediately jumped at the sight of Green Köontz. The clean, brand new shirts with the artwork of several albums, *American Douchebag* included, could prove to be a most valuable asset in the war for Faye's attention. I was sure that the face of Frank Boy Al, with his distinctive hazel cat-like eyes, jet-black spiky punk hair and light stubble beard would work in some way to make myself appear as positive in her eyes. I took a closer look at Frank Boy Al, and noticed that although I couldn't possibly emulate his slim build, his white skin and his Anglo-Saxon features, I could actually make my appearance more similar to his.

I sensed somewhat that this would get me closer to her, but didn't actually think about her specific reaction. I just thought it was the right time to make a move regarding my own image. I wanted to get that shirt badly but my money wasn't enough. I had to simply come back another day. The spiked wristbands, the heavy metal bands belts, the posters, the flags, the shirts … It was all in abundance, and also quite expensive. It was after all quality material. I'd come back another day when I had the chance, with enough money for two shirts and maybe something else. If I wanted Faye to avoid thinking I wasn't in her world at all, I'd have to start with physical appearances. But even then I could never predict the exact outcome of this fallacious attempt at earning her sympathy.

· · · · ·

"So, that was a good afternoon out, guys. Had a lot of fun an' all … but, I must return home! Jenna, you're comin' with me, very soon if I'm lucky. Sonny, you're not. So listen, I'll catch you around at school tomorrow."

"Hey, I thought you had stuff to tell me. Remember that

you wanted to talk to me about don't-know-what?"

"Yeah man, sorry. It'll have to be some other time. With this bitch in the middle it's rather uncomfortable, and I can't just ignore her. Listen, I'll tell you tomorrow how stuff is goin'."

"Don't forget to give me 'you-know-what.' You promised."

"What? Oh yeah, that. What was it, my sister's ChitChat and the photo you wanted? Sure. I'll email the pic and send you the address with it."

"Right, thank you."

"No problem. But sort it out yourself from now on. Whatever happens, it'll happen. Just hope you don't smash your face too hard when you learn the truth. My sister is a kid. Finito. She's not serious and definitely not mature. Even if you do get her she'll confuse the fuck out of you with her immaturity. You're a very mature person, I've noticed. You'll be right in hell next to someone like her."

"Well ... thanks, but we'll have to see, won't we? I only want to tell you that I'm not the deranged pervert you think I am. I told you before, what I'm feeling is really honest, I'm not hiding it, and I want to follow it all the way through to the very end."

"Oh God, again with that shit. Look, I know, but even so I don't particularly care. We're all adults, sort of. We know what we're doin'. But she's not. You know ... I shouldn't even be sayin' this. But on the smaaaaall possibility something does happen with her, just—Oh, goddammit. Just forget it, I won't say it. Not till I see danger ahead at least. Let's save that awkwardness for an alternate forthcomin' future."

"Look, I'm sorry stuff has happened like this but we gotta face it, alright? I also don't want to ruin my friendship with you because of this. I just didn't know, OK? I told you before, if I had known, who knows what the situation would be like

..."

"Yeah, yeah, don't we know. There's a million parallel universes where that wouldn't have ever happened, and another one where you're feelin' my sister's peaches right now. Just save me the talks and let's just live it day after day. Whatever you do, Sonny, for the love of God, don't turn her into a slut."

"Oh yeah, as if that has any chance of happening ..."

"Who knows. I already told ya she thinks whatever the TV tells her, given she thinks at all. Maybe she fucks you and then dumps you and then goes on a fuckin' everybody spree."

"Well, that will depend on her, if she was raised well by her family she won't have a need for it. Listen I have to go or I'll lose the bus, we'll talk tomorrow morning."

"Alright, man. Bye."

I walked up that horrible slope from the Community Center passing through Poseidon Park. After one block, I would be in the bus station. Before reaching my destination however, I distinguished an odd figure, almost as tall as me and walking in a funny fashion as if giving little childish jumps; I rejoiced at the sighting of a character I had not seen or heard about for a long time. I couldn't believe all the ruckus from starting school had made me forget such an important character, who had basically spent an entire year accompanying Wolfgang, Claude and me in what would be an absolute improvement in my school life since that awful 3rd Grade.

Ettore Fratto was a foreign Loynner resident, a unique case with mixed ancestry and a disjointed, shapeless family unit. His mother was a working-class Italian immigrant, a born homemaker and a spinster; his dad had never been around, and he had never met him. He was an only child, and had lived in Loynne's as long as I, moving at around the same time. Before, he had spent a couple of years in the US, Portugal, Greece and Italy. Obviously, he didn't feel very identified

with any nationality, and all you could get from him when asking about his country of origin was an ambiguous "I come from various places."

Ettore was a wannabe intellectual, a person who had set the priority of his life to be learning as much as he could in the shortest amount of time. This could be disputed. He had knowledge of some things which was quite accurate, but most of the time I was sure even Ryan could point out his mistakes. He followed the pseudo-philosophy created by Ayn Rand, Objectivism, attracted by its concepts of selfishness and individualism, which he praised above everything else as the ultimate form of freedom. Reaching the conclusion that the world had to be clearly run by a shadowy political elite, akin to an Illuminati or freemason organization with Socialist inclinations, he loathed totalitarianism in its every form, capitalist or Communist, and longed for an individualist, neoliberal, free-market dog-eat-dog society based on general lack of altruism, unregulated economics, lack of government input in most fields, cynicism, paranoia, egotistical pursuit of happiness and blind worship of successful entrepreneurs, who are the gears that move the world according to Ayn Rand. This of course had always struck me as a completely illusory model prone to massive class-warfare, economic inequality, political instability and social ineffectiveness, causing nothing but conflict and misery for the irrelevant 99% of the population who according to Rand are too lazy and lacking in ambition to ever become omnipotent slave-labor using industrialists. Due to this, Tory and I would frequently hold intellectual and political discussions where our ideas always clashed fiercely. My vision of Communism always collided with his "Objectivist" utopian capitalist paradise ideology, and for good reason.

Another interesting feature of Ettore was that he was very

educated in his manners and way of speaking, very correct in his eloquence but awful in his pronunciation. He came of as an uneducated peasant who tried to appear more than what he was. But he was a friend ... and in all his weirdness, a very loyal one at that. Billy and Robbie were arguably his very best friends, always saying he was a brother and not a mere friend, something which prompted others to refer to this close circle as "The Brotherhood," like Ryan used to do scornfully when he felt left out.

"Tory! So good to see you! We haven't seen you at school this year!" We had nicknamed him "Tory," a joke on his distorted right-wing political ideology, and because it was the best nickname for someone with such an odd name.

"Hello, Sonny. Yes, that's correct, I now formally attend the Whitedale Secondary Education Institute."

"Whitedale High ... I heard it's like a death camp over there."

"You could say that. It's particularly rough at some points. However, sheer psychological skills are all you need to survive that hormonal testosterone jungle."

"Have you seen much of Billy and Robbie? I'm in class with them."

"Yeah, I heard about that, they inform me of everything. Billy says you're really close to Ryan ..."

"Well, I wouldn't say exactly close, but we hang out, in fact, I've just seen him."

"Mmm ... right, right ..."

"What about you, what are you up to?"

"Doing some paperwork, I haven't exactly started school like all of you have. I ... I have some business to take care of. Now, if you'll excuse me ..." that was yet another trademark of Tory. A particularly mysterious aura surrounded his person at all times, a try-hard suspense he always intended on

keeping up. At some points I felt sorry at his problem fitting in. Girls savagely used to laugh at everything he said, he was like the class' buffoon but not in a very good way. Along with Wolfgang, he was constantly ridiculed, even more so due to his inability to keep quiet and make arrogant corrections of others. He was the kind of person that never shut up if he had something to say, no matter how bad the social punishment could be. Wolfgang, Claude and I would always keep to ourselves, having learned our lessons, and found it to be the wisest way even if it was considered cowardly by Ettore. But as with Wolfgang, I was under the impression that he had not aged accordingly, or simply could not adapt to the cruel animalistic instincts of society around us. He was very naïve for such a dark world, even though he always tried to convince you of how aware he was of everything.

I took the Purple Wonder back home, forgetting about Tory as soon as he had appeared and concentrating on the digital surprise that would greet me once I got there.

· · · · ·

My eyes delightfully feasted on the one thing I had been craving more than anything else excluding Faye herself. Ryan had done good with the email, which only included the picture attached and the following text:

"green_mantis_07@hippmail.loynnet"

Faye was sitting down at what seemed to be a very exclusive jazz club, no doubt a classy setting. Behind her was what had to be Saphron Bay, due to the colorful neon lights illuminating the sea. You could tell because Saphron had the most illuminated skyline of the island at night, more so than even

Nova Atlantica, and the sea was inevitably irradiated by it, shining in shades of green, red, blue, yellow and white.

Faye was sitting down holding a glass with what I guessed had to be wine, or at least any red alcoholic beverage. Her curvy legs were crossed in a fashion I fancied unbearably elegant and sexy, the stance of a veteran seductress in the body of a teenager. She wore a black cardigan, with a jean miniskirt and short heeled shoes, this time in white. Her nails were painted black, something that for some reason I found to be exotic and irresistible. All Lollies painted their nails red or pink, which I considered to be slutty and of low taste. Such a delicate little girl wearing black nail polish seemed unbelievably unusual, establishing a contrast between her innocent appearance and enhancing her moody and depressing anti-social nature.

There was something else though, something which sent a worrisome shiver down my spine. I didn't think it could be a matter to lose any sleep over, but she was wearing the same distinctive cross necklace with a US flag motif I had noticed when staring at the collage pictures in her house. Could it be possible that Ryan was ignorant of her religious beliefs, that maybe she was the kind of patriotic religious zealot so common in her homeland? I would not have minded if she had worn a simple Christian cross necklace, but the US flag motif was rare, and shall we say very suspicious looking. Nobody that was not a complete Unitedstatian religious extremist would wear such a thing.

But even so, the magnificent sight of Faye eclipsed this matter completely. I can't count the minutes – or hours – I spent looking at it; analyzing her legs, her skin, her hair ... Everything about her was just too perfect, and no matter how hard I tried to brainwash myself against it, the fact was there. I was obsessed. I was clearly infatuated and above all else,

already thinking about it being true love. Even if it's hard to believe, in the very first stages I never thought of sex. I could only think of tender kissing, seducing her when her guard was down and going for a stroll or to the cinema, but never sex. She was a symbol of purity. Her obvious virginity had a certain effect on me, making me feel even more destined to be her first, and it stood as an icon of everything that was right about the situation. The anti-social sad behavior, studious nature, dramatic self-important air, teenage self-loathing and negative attitude toward the idiotic and mediocre world surrounding her was just too much to simply ignore. It was the kind of woman I had been looking for. The complete opposite of a happy-go-lucky imbecile whore. Simply put, I wanted to uncover every single secret and detail about Faith Mantis. Again, I went to bed waiting for a new day, with my new-found love now occupying the totality of my thoughts.

· · · · ·

It was finally Friday, and my body shivered with a delightful electric current of renewed vigor and relief. The day was worth living out of the possibility of seeing her once more. I couldn't wait.

That day I remember Gordon being more of an awkward dork than usual during the bus ride. Interrupting his First Action Peril rant about World Defender: Peace Corps 2, he signaled at the window, shouting.

"Hey! Hey! That's Sonny's loved one, Ryan's sister, ain't it? Hey Sonny, how's it going with that? Haha!"

"What are you talking about?"

"That girl, the little one! The one that looks like she's 12! That's your girlfriend, right?"

"No, I really don't know what you're talking about."

"Haha! Sonny's a pedophile! And he won't admit to it! Hey Claude, am I right or what? I mean come on, man! 12 is like, completely out of the question. How old are you, 17? 18?"

"She's not my girlfriend Gordon, and cut this out before I remind you that your 15-year-old sister is dating some 20-something Kanny scumbag."

"Geez, I already told you about that! I don't know if that's even true and I don't even care! And that doesn't deny the fact that you're totally nuts about a 12-year-old! Pervert!"

"Will you shout it too so that the whole bus can hear?"

"HEY EVERYONE! SONNY'S INTO KIDDIE PORN!"

"Shut the fuck up you obese piece of shit, will you fucking grow up already?"

"Oh come on Sonny! I'm just teasin'! Chill out man! Hey Claude, this guy hasn't seen that cutscene from Peace Corps, where the Muslims bathe in acid all those little girls accused of adulterous sex, maybe we should show him! See what happens to you, pedophile!"

The conversation went on for a bit more like that before Gordon's amazingly short attention span got bored of the subject and proceeded to talk to Claude about the same stupid game when we got out of the bus. Why didn't I simply break Gordon's face? What was deterring me? I was seriously getting softer. I now talked to Gordon out of inertia than anything else. One day, I knew I would simply ignore him without even explaining why to his stupid chubby face.

Other than this minor disturbance, the day went away rather quickly. Ryan, Wolfgang, Axel and Mike barely noticed my social absence, each one talking about their own selfish concern. Axel talked for all of us and more, so my quiet demeanor passed by slyly without gathering much attention. Although I didn't manage to even get a glimpse of Faye during that day, I went home anxiously thinking what it would

238

feel like to talk to her, thinking there couldn't be a greater pleasure on this reality that could surpass the joy of everything Faye unleashed in me. Every single dark thought, every single wish to perform horrible acts against humanity, everything was suppressed by her presence immediately. There wasn't foul hatred in my heart when her image clouded my vision, no need to persecute relentlessly an ideological enemy or to focus my energies on fleeing from Loynne's Island. I didn't want to think about what would happen should I continue to see more of her. A brutal change in my person was already present at this point, and I didn't even want to think what else she could awaken in me as time continued to pass by.

I logged on and remained on the lookout for her appearance. Ryan said she used to log on at about 16:00, but it was only 15:00. I cringed at the thought of waiting nervously the whole afternoon so that she didn't log in at all.

"//***Take me somewhere new***// has signed in."

The funny beeping sound announcing a friend signing in ChitChat broke the awful silence. It was one of those moments in my life where everything seemed surreal and too coincidental to be true, but believe me, it happened just as I'm telling you. Faye appeared out of the blue when I had been sitting down waiting for no more than a minute and a half.

The sudden, unexpected event left me cold and unable to react, so nervous that I failed to lift any of my trembling fingers. I pulled myself together eventually, seizing some time to breathe deeply, and bravely as I could, typed an ambiguous "hey" which claimed allegiance to no personality or category she could tag me as.

I could only look at the blank screen for immensely long periods of time. Nobody else was online. The atmosphere inside the house was of complete and deadly silence, as per usual when the TV was turned off, when my music wasn't blasting and my video games were hibernating. It was that part of the day where quiet and peace reigned, the sun subtly illuminating the living room and casting a cool shade in contrast to the blazing hell dominating the outside world.

I kept staring at the screen completely immobile, waiting for the coveted reply. Suddenly, a word appeared on the screen, startling me.

"hi," she said, in a little italic, blue font. "who r u?" I decided to not play it arrogantly or man-of-the-world, as it'd just appear fake and pathetic. I opted for a sincere, honest strategy, appealing to her personality directly and just sounding friendly.

"Hey, I'm Sonny, a friend of your brother Ryan," I replied. This might surely seem odd, but I used to write perfectly *even* on ChitChat. Writing idiotically like everyone else did seemed to me an awful thing to get accustomed to. Besides it simply came out faster like that.

"ohh kk."

"Do you want me to show you a picture so you can see who I am?"

"yeah k."

I passed her a picture from June of that same year, when the classes had finished and the student body had organized a dinner party, as it was tradition when graduating from SCE. In the picture, taken in a Pentagon Italian restaurant named Albanessi, I was next to none other than Wolfgang, who due to his inability to procure anything trendy found himself wearing a tacky orange Hawaiian shirt, blue jeans and white sneakers, while I failed in my own way by wearing something

I had bought at the last minute when knowing I was invited, the striped white and blue Telnyashka-like shirt people mistook for a rugby polo, and my black cargos with the PE white sneakers. Nobody in their right mind would have ever let us in a nightclub with those clothes, but fortunately for them Wolfgang and I would never shame ourselves by partaking in such mediocre and humiliating petty activities. Considering that I looked quite well-dressed for my usual appearance and that next to poor Wolfie my looks incremented dramatically, I decided to share this photo with Faye, who like most women, would feel glad that at least I wasn't Wolfgang, even if she wouldn't date me.

"wich 1 r u."

"I'm the one on the left."

"i dont recognize u at all," she said.

"Oh, but I'm sure you have seen me around at school," I replied quickly.

"where."

"Well, in the corridors. We're in the same corridor! My class is 206."

"oh i dunno."

She didn't really say much, and I was doing my best trying to be charming and interesting. How could I impress her without some interaction from her side? I wasn't used to this. Desperate times require desperate measures, I thought. And it was time for a drawback, to go to the rear for a while.

"So what do you like doing the most?" I asked, remembering that tactic had helped me one year ago with my ex-girlfriend, who had instantly gotten spicy, flirty and inquisitive, knowing all I wanted to hear were sexual teasing innuendos.

"what u mean what i like doin."

"Well, you know, movies, music, etc?"

"well i love music yeh ... i like green koontz and april divine ... dat sort of music u know ..."

"Yeah, well, and what kind of movies do you like?"

"action, romance, comedy, i dunno everything."

This was helping me to get an opinion on her; as I said before, I was a fan of quality cinema; I believe I mentioned the great "Igla" before. My favorite directors included the celebrated Sergei Einstein, Sergei Bondarchuk, Andrei Tarkovsky, Eldar Ryazanov and Leonid Gaidai among countless others. In the cold Motherland, film theaters could be attended, but in my time – when Communism was already declining – political pro-Communist films weren't being made anymore, and many Unitedstatian and European films started to find a way in. Going to the cinema was the most modern pastime of my fellow compatriots. The films were obviously censored in some parts, and only the most intellectual ones were picked for public viewing. As such, the films themselves were edited to appear to agree with Communist doctrine, or at least, not attack it.

With this pastime, I had learned to become a fan of many celebrated filmmakers, so I felt instantly that she was somewhat ignorant and simplistic, without a clear opinion of what was really going in the world, but I didn't want to press the issue about her level of mediocrity and preferred to attack the places where she was surely going to be willing to give conversation.

"whats ur favorite green koontz album?" she asked unexpectedly.

I was blank, immediately redirecting myself toward the LoynNet and other sources of information to have an idea of what to say. The only thing I knew about Green Köontz, was that they were a trio, the front man was the typical "handsome rebel rocker sellout" every single teenage girl fancied,

and they had generated some controversy with their *American Douchebag* album due to its perceived anti-Unitedstatian content. This is the album I told her was my favorite. I knew songs of this album like *Avenue of Stepped-on Emotions, War Boosts Album Sales* and *Wake Me Up When The Draft Is Over*, but that was pretty much it and either way considered it to be the kind of US media little girls like Faye consumed. In any case, knowing more about this band to have more subjects of conversation wouldn't hurt me, would it?

So there I was, downloading entire Green Köontz albums via LoynNet so as to listen to some songs and tell Faye if I had liked them or not. Most of them were fast, enjoyable and rhythmic, so I didn't even have to lie after all. I was really beginning to enjoy listening to that band, and I didn't know why I had never paid much attention to Green Köontz before. I was influenced by the retro feel of the '60s, '70s and '80s, and I was so used to the mentality that the new wave of music was utter garbage that I didn't even bother to develop curiosity for it. The same as with cinema, I hated new films and preferred to dive in older times. I thought whether I could experience more new things and stop being such a close-minded person, but for the moment, I wanted to be cautious.

It had taken some time, but the conversation was finally going somewhere. I was glad however, because I was learning some facts about the musical scene in the US. It seemed that the youths in the US were quite rebellious and not willing to tolerate the indoctrination of its barbaric government. Faye passed me the video for a song titled *Judas of Friggin' No-where*, a song about a teenager living in the punk scene in the US, in a dysfunctional social circle with a schizophrenic personality and other assorted psychopathic bouts. The video for the song lasted over nine minutes and featured the teenager

performing random acts of violence and sometimes love, all the while suffering from some type of mental paranoia. The song was ambitious, touching, particularly complex in both execution and concept for a five chord skate-punk sellout band, and made me develop a new kind of taste for this type of music. However, it wasn't long before my rejection alarms kicked in and made me feel that this wasn't really my style, that I was letting myself be fooled by my infatuation over Faye.

"Yeah, I liked the song," I opted to tell her instead.

"its gr8 its 1 of my favs."

"Is there any other particular song that you like?"

"c if u like this 1."

And she sent me a song by the Canadian band Bad Alberta, called "*Off*." She also sent the video link to VapidVidz.com for the song:

Today the teacher told me the world's just fine
So did my dad when I asked him late at night
So shut up and stop poisoning my mind
Neither my teacher nor my dad would sleep alright
Knowing what they preach is fuckin' lies

Turn the radio off
Turn the lies and the radio off
Turn the lies, the TV and the radio off

Turn the radio off
Turn the lies and the radio off
Turn the lies, the TV and the radio off

Today the teacher told me off in style
So did my dad when I said he shouldn't lie

Please shut up and stop poisoning my mind
How can anyone sleep soundly at night
Knowing what they preach is fuckin' lies?

Turn the radio off
Turn the lies and the radio off
Turn the lies, the TV and the radio off

Turn the radio off
Turn the lies and the radio off
Turn the lies, the TV and the radio off

Today the teacher told me I shouldn't think too much
So did my dad when I said he's out of touch
Just shut up and stop poisoning my mind
One thing I'm always sure of now
My teacher and my dad sleep easy at nights

Turn the radio off
Turn the lies and the radio off
Turn the lies, the TV and the radio off

Turn the radio off
Turn the lies and the radio off
Turn the lies, the TV and the radio off

This one was more sentimental and sensitive, featuring images of war and the usual tolerance advocating, give-peace-a-chance hollow hippie crap. But aesthetics notwithstanding, at least the message was alright. Despite this, I couldn't help but feel that Faye's likings were too capitalistic and influenced by Unitedstatian media, and wondered about her education, how culture or ignorant she could really be.

Yes, it was a fact that Frank Boy Al was her ideal man and that she dressed in a fashion similar to April Divine in order to express her passion and fascination for the commercial punk trend, and this could be capitalistic, a cultural trend I always associated with the ignorance, mediocrity and stupidity influenced and perpetrated by the Theocratic Empire, but something I'll never be able to explain rationally made me love her even more.

The conversation had to end at some point, and she eventually logged off with a flavorless and cold "bye". We had been chatting all afternoon long, but the one who was visibly changed by the exchange of words was me. I was sure she was still the same before and after that conversation, but my world had been turned upside down. I went to bed soon after, watching the downloads list on LoynNet, seeing how much I should have to wait for the Green Köontz discography to finally download. I was happy, glad and beginning to feel certain things I had been unwary of before. I picked up my music player, with the Bad Alberta song Faye had given me, and laid myself to sleep peacefully listening to that track repeatedly, thinking of her, of things to come, fantasizing about holding her in arms in a whirlwind of submissive and timid adolescent passion. I got aroused merely by thinking about how small, pale, shy, soft-voiced and delicate she was. I was feeling that unique sensation of blind love, already developing a sense of possession about her.

"*Enough,*" I ordered myself. "*You can think about this tomorrow, go to sleep now.*"

But I couldn't. Tossing and turning, fantasizing about meeting her personally and wondering what could happen in the near future, I was once again sunk by my youthful want of love, trapped in a lustful dream:

I was walking Faye home when I insisted unexpectedly on going to her apartment. At first she denied me the entrance, but I managed to convince her. I found myself in a small hall with a TV set and a couch, the walls painted blue, the lighting giving the impression as if the event was happening shortly before twilight. The end of time itself seemed near. The room was dark, subtly lit, with a lovely tense atmosphere, an eerie silence drowning us comfortably as we feared each other. Suddenly, "Skazka" started playing in the background as I approached Faye, her face timidly turning red, forcing me to get even more aroused by her little innocent girl shyness. The cherry aroma she irradiated was exquisitely addictive. Completely confident, I kissed her. She grabbed my hands returning the kiss, as the world rotated around us, our passion for each other growing larger and stronger with each demonstration of love. I caressed the impossibly white soft legs feeling the hot blood and adrenaline boiling inside her body, enjoying her heavy breathing and the exaggerate gasps of pleasure. I found myself staring deeply at true bliss, a colossal manifestation of love, ecstasy and passion wrapped around my body, fused with moral ambiguity and morbid curiosity, loving the dirty yet pleasant emotion it produced. I lifted Faye in order to carry her to the bedroom, place her on the bed and savagely undress her, revealing the most beautiful and breathtaking female figure I had ever laid eyes upon, the most marveling object ever produced in the vastness of the universe. I was prepared to label that divine body as my own and carry out the essence of the act, that which would seal our futures for all eternity.

Faith fused herself to my body as I lost all consciousness and identity, all traces of individuality dissipated by her

unreal kisses, every single earthly concern destroyed with each thrust. Nothing in the world mattered to me anymore, for Faith was with and within me.

CHAPTER IV

Mauerbau

"I like to say that the attacker always has the advantage."

- GARRY KASPAROV -

Soviet-Azerbaijani Chess Grandmaster and World Chess Champion

---

I opened my eyes painfully and felt the light bursting through my pupils. The dream had been so realistic I brought back with me the illusory flavor of her lips, the surreal taste of the coveted opposite sex. I was sunk by a strange anxiety which instantly accelerated my heartbeat, making me remember there was still a lot of work to do. The possibility of failure instilled an unpleasant and omnipresent fear in my mind, as if conquering her comprised my one and only duty. Even though it had never happened, my mouth still remembered the indescribable taste of Faye's lips, or better said, their expected taste fictitiously cobbled together in my mind.

I picked the Hipp-Man from my night stand and instantly played all kinds of miscellaneous songs in random order; during those days I almost only listened to songs by Kino, the haunting guitar riffs of *"Pesnya Bez Slov"* — "Song Without Words" — being the case as of that moment. Kino's music and Viktor Tsoi's lyrics kept me away from the real world and everything that preceded a school day: the rush to have a

shower and get ready, eating without pleasure and watching the news about how chaotic and irrational the world was becoming. The nature of the lyrics, filled with utmost sorrow and grief, sent me to a melancholic state where I felt immersed in the beginning of the end of the Soviet Union, back in 1989. I often pondered what life would have been like back then, if I had been mature enough to comprehend the socio-political context and the needs of the Soviet youths like Tsoi. I wondered if I would have been in a high school with politically motivated friends, concerned with changing the USSR and bringing it back to a state of glory and prosperity. But it didn't matter, nothing regarding that mattered now. The USSR was dead, and by the looks of it, forgotten.

However, unexpectedly and without any semblance of warning, the sadness was immediately swept aside as the entire world was drowned in a thundering melody, one which was all too familiar, sending an equally familiar shiver down my spine; the Soviet National Anthem had started to play:

> *Unbreakable Union of freeborn Republics,*
> *Great Russia has welded forever to stand.*
> *Created in struggle by will of the people,*
> *United and mighty, our Soviet land!*
>
> *Sing to the Fatherland, home of the free,*
> *Bulwark of peoples in brotherhood strong.*
> *O Party of Lenin, the strength of the people,*
> *To Communism's triumph lead us on!*

I stood up, my eyes fixed on the Soviet flag on my room, placed imposingly above the others. The Hammer and Sickle, present wherever I looked, seemed powerful and alive, and my whole body found itself shivering, filled with but the most

perfect definitions of pride and love for The Motherland. I saw Father Lenin's face next to Uncle Stalin's, producing an ecstatic feeling as if anything was well within my reach. It was as if they were my own great grandparents, the kind you mourn when you know they have been long gone. How wrong I had been in my assumptions. The USSR was not dead; it was very much alive, in the hearts and minds of all Communists and Socialists of the world:

Through tempests the sunrays of freedom have cheered us,
Along the new path where great Lenin did lead.
To a righteous cause he raised up the peoples,
Inspired them to labour and valourous deed.

Sing to the Fatherland, home of the free,
Bulwark of peoples in brotherhood strong.
O Party of Lenin, the strength of the people,
To Communism's triumph lead us on!

I closed my eyes and stopped looking at the pictures to imagine them moving, suddenly come to life; sequences of magnificent military parades, Mil Mi-24 helicopters at night patrolling over the Berlin Wall with ominous searchlights, armed groups of peasants battering the Winter Palace of the hated Tsarist oppressors; everything was glorious. Never had I paid such an emotional tribute to my ideology and my country than at that moment. How splendid was the beautiful red banner of Communism! How my love grew infinitely for the Party of Lenin, for the foreign Communist Parties of all comrades abroad! How honorable it was to be there at that moment, bringing Communism and the USSR back to life in my

little room!

> *In the victory of Communism's deathless ideal,*
> *We see the future of our dear land.*
> *And to her fluttering scarlet banner,*
> *Selflessly true we always shall stand!*

> *Sing to the Fatherland, home of the free,*
> *Bulwark of peoples in brotherhood strong.*
> *O Party of Lenin, the strength of the people,*
> *To Communism's triumph lead us on!*

Sunk in my euphoric patriotic pride, I performed a heartfelt military salute during the last sentence of the anthem, my body brimming with the most powerful force in the world, a force only Communism managed to produce in me. I never cried but this was an extreme exception, and at that moment my right index finger caressed my left eyelid and dried the little trace of a tear, as the most ardent defenders of Communism ominously hung on the wall, neatly positioned below my Soviet flag above the bed, portrait after portrait from Marx to Che Guevara, possibly the only place in the whole world where such heartfelt honest reverence was paid to them.

Marching to the subsequent military marches performed by the Red Army Choir, starting with "*Nasha Derzhava*" — "Our Nation" — I got out of the room and turned the TV on to watch the news, trying to come down to Earth and get something to eat, as there was still a whole day of school ahead. Flipping through the insane amount of free channels Loynner satellites managed to transmit, I stopped at CMN — Cox Media Network — when a startling header managed to open my eyes fully. It read; "*BREAKING NEWS: LIBERAL RAMPAGE*

THREATENS AMERICA." I let the only voice the US had anymore speak for itself. After all, it wasn't like anyone was actually listening.

"Welcome to another edition of CMN News, fully endorsed and owned by Robert Cox III. God bless his soul.

I'm your host Harry Dushbaugh. Today on domestic politics news, the United States of America has once again been unfairly accused of severe government corruption as well as of religious and moral hypocrisy in the wake of a new wave of liberal fanaticism, in conjunction with foreign leftist oppressive regimes. Taxpayers have a right to know about what is going on in Our Great Nation America and where their money ends up. Once again, the liberal media has brainwashed the masses into evil, occult and satanic communist fascism. Taxpayers demand an end to this crusade for evil in our country and are rallying the most powerful conservative forces to do a referendum on whether the ROA should claim full sovereignty over the government and lead the Greatest Nation on Earth against godless communism and Global Terror. Long gone is the disastrous communist presidency of Jerome Abdallah, of wanting to see his birth certificate to prove he's actually American and not Islamic, working secretly in conjunction with terrorist cells. Why he won in the first place is actually a mystery, as nobody confesses to have voted for him and everybody agrees that our current President Johnny Marshall is doing a great job in combatting these un-American forces of evil. Let us remember President Abdallah let our humanitarian peacekeeping Army units come home coward and introduced a socialist free healthcare bill for all citizens, the infamous WideCare, which we rightfully removed as soon as possible, as econo-

mists warned against the likely scenario where it would increase the country's deficit. Thankfully, the ROA is putting enormous pressure on the liberal prone politicians, who do not seem to see the American concerns regarding Homeland Security and National Defense through our own eyes. Introducing a communist health system, what's next, totalitarian ID cards? A DNA database? Cameras to monitor our every move? We can pay for our own insurance, pharmaceuticals and doctor bills, and if we can't we have banks, loans and casinos. This is America after all, the land of opportunity where everybody can succeed and become a millionaire overnight. That goes for you, good law-abiding American legal citizens. After all, we don't call it the 'best country in the world' for nothing. No illegal alien is going to benefit out of taxpayers money for free. That is communism, and in America, communism is not welcome.

May God bless us all.

On local religion news, another current of biased liberal attacks have resurfaced as evolution invades our backyard. Political activist groups Righteous America and Devout Christian Protestants, as well as the country's official Church of Creatonology, gathered to stop these evil forces as dozens of teachers were arrested and put on trial for their communistic and atheist beliefs, harmful to the unity of our country. Creationism and intelligent design will be the only facts students will learn, as evolution, let us remember, is only a theory, not a fact, unlike our Holy divine Bible where the truth was written 2,000 years ago. People who do not believe in the power of God and democracy do not have high hopes to get ahead in life and it's been proven they have higher chances of becoming promiscuous sexual deviants,

criminals or terrorists. They have to know the facts, especially those of the Church, namely, that God created us 6,000 years ago, that the Earth is the center of God's universe and that we need to be ready for His love. Let us help our youth and lead them toward a path of healthy family values and successful, easygoing suburban lives. It's what our Founding Fathers have always wanted, for all of us.

And now, our daily edition of The People Have Spoken, presented by Rita McCarthy. Transmitting live from CMN News Headquarters in the heart of the American Pride, Harry Dushbaugh, CMN News."

"Hi! This is Rita McCarthy, transmitting live from the streets in New York City! Once a dreaded pit full of illegal immigration and African-American gang violence, New York City stands tall today as one of the most majestic cities proud Americans can revel in. It's incredible that CMN News has recently been attacked of being biased as neutrality is our top priority. The People Have Spoken is a program devoted to show you how people actually think in the street and why we represent them in every way! So, let's see all the interviewees we had today and what they answered to whether they accept the theory of evolution being taught in schools;"

"Hell no, lady! It's an abomination! An abomination from Satan! Don't you read anything? Everybody knows Darwin worked in conjunction with Marx to release that distorted myth that we come from monkeys. I'll tell you something ma'am, I don't come from no monkey, and you won't find monkeys in my family. I'm going to keep those satanic communist values out of my family and my country and go to Church every Sunday. I owe that much to Lady America."

"Uh, like, right, so I think that monkeys are animals and

humans are not, so we're not very similar. Besides if the politicians and celebrities keep saying it, it must be like, true, right? They wouldn't lie to us, I think. I'm not sure."

"Evolution is part of the big plan! The big plan designed by scientists and liberals to eliminate God from people's lives! I don't come from no ape! Why haven't they been able to find that famous missing link, huh? It's all part of a big atheist godless conspiracy to take the Lord out of people's lives!"

"I'll tell you something missy, our Founding Fathers wanted Creationism to be taught and we can't go against something the First Amendment says! It's there in the Constitution, right?! The books that haven't been changed by the liberal media! Everywhere! So people, grab a book, and listen only to conservative voices and you'll be alright! Shut off all that you hear from the outside, or else all those liberal Europeans and their funny ideas will get to you! They don't understand how America works! Why should they have a say in what goes on in here?"

"Evolution is a hoax. Everybody knows it. Those promiscuous decadent Europeans and those soulless Japanese believe in it because of how warped their cultures are. I mean have you seen their movies? And those traumatizing cartoons they draw for our children to watch? What values are those? They're trying to instill Islamic communist values to our kids! The government should ban it! I pay my taxes don't I? We need more American movies, about freedom and dreams coming true with happy endings, not that pessimistic depressive European trash."

"So, there you have it people! Our news can't be biased if the people feel we represent them! So stay tuned for more neutral news, only on CMN News, where, like our motto says, the news are just and unbiased! Transmitting live

*from Times Square, New York City, I'm Rita McCarthy,
CMN News!"*

*"Great news, Rita! That's some high quality journalism!
Obviously, liberal media fanatical degenerates can learn a
lot from fair reporting devoid of hidden political agendas
and indoctrination. No sane person will disagree on the fact
that we still have a long way to go in the war against the
blatant bias found in the mainstream media today. Where's
the shame?*

*Coming up next, we go to Donald Perry, who's currently
interviewing demonstrators in Los Angeles, in a popular bid
for people who want the name of the county and the city
changed to The Angels, as many feel its name is blatantly
un-American for such an important region. It's great to see
democracy at work, to see the desires of the people mani-
fested peacefully in such passionate drives so that our freedom can be put into practice. This in turn reminds us of how
different the political landscape was but 10 years ago, when
the violent, criminally psychotic protestors of the anti-
American terrorist cell 'Eradicate Poverty' were swiftly
dispersed by New York's Finest down at Wall Street, some,
as we sadly remember, taken by our Lord and Savior to His
Heavenly realm ..."*

I recalled things in the US being quite bad, but this took
the cake. The US had long championed for an Anglo-Saxon
utopia free from black, Asian and Hispanic influence, and in
order to achieve this the racist theocratic government incarcerated entire populations in overcrowded prisons and deten-
tion camps, where the majority would be deported and those
deemed most dangerous to the integrity of the regime executed under the excuse of being dangerous criminals and terror-

ists. The US had officially returned to its purest state, that of a racist, colonialist, imperialist and genocidal regime where the white man reigned supreme. Being isolated from the world creates that effect I suppose, just like civilizations were before global communication between nations, brutal, sadistic and ignorant. How glad I was that the US wasn't my country, that this mess of a warped society didn't have anything to do with me in any way. This being said, I could not possibly imagine how people like Ryan and Mike could feel; I felt that The Motherland had betrayed me by forsaking Communism, but I could not imagine my own country becoming like the US. Feeling complete and utter embarrassment for the homeland was certainly one of the heaviest burdens.

The country's new official religion, Creatonology, a mixture of pseudo-science, self-help book nonsense, science fiction mythology and Christianity represented Unitedstatian culture so well that it of course became a laughing stock worldwide. It told of how we were created by an Intelligent Creator called Ekab-Malc, who in turn had been created by God to do his bidding, 6,000 years ago, and how Ekab-Malc had to constantly do battle with the forces of Evil to keep the Earth pure and shiny. This science-fiction reject screenplay required members to pay insane amounts of money that supposedly the Church retroactively paid back to the community by doing certain services, like programs to get drug addicts rehabilitated and to educate criminals. It was all a sham. The rehabilitation procedures consisted of practices devoid of any scientific proof and furthermore actually harmed individuals who underwent them. Taking hot bathes and vitamin supplements and the like were what these people put themselves through. Some had their skins burnt while others developed respiratory problems or heart attacks. Others found problems with the vitamin supplements as they

hadn't been surveyed on whether they should take them or not by a doctor. In essence, a disaster. The most disgusting thing was that the organization's High Clerics and Priests owned lavish mansions in Hollywood and had shares in big corporations. Naturally, this church was stopped and tagged as an "organized band" and a scam everywhere except for the US, although many European branches were trying to worm their way abroad in a bid to save more "souls." Progressive Scandinavian protests had begun as an answer to what they considered to be a "censorship on religion." I would have never taken the Scandinavian people for such imbeciles but if this was what the weak and liberal left was up for lately, then I must have gotten lost somewhere. There was more to it, I was sure, but enough of that; let me elaborate on the country's most predominant and long-running set of ideals; racism.

The North American dictatorship, disguised as the world's most functional "democracy" – an ironic title given also to US backed dictatorships during the carnage of Operation Condor in Latin America – had begun to unofficially prosecute immigrants of non-Western European descent for religious or political motives, incarcerating or deporting them with the pretext of being terrorists, infidels, deviants and enemies of the state, same as with people of different sexual orientation, race, color or surname – obviously excluding celebrities, movie stars or TV personalities who rolled the big money and made foreign accusations of racism disappear. The unlucky ones were usually not persecuted in the open, but instead suddenly disappeared from sight to end up in faraway camps like the one they had kept at Guantanamo Bay in Cuba. Others were deported and shipped back to their respective countries or any random nation that would welcome them. This was done in a manner in which the human rights record was

kept at a bearable minimum and also kept the usual human rights watchdog organizations away enough. Inside, the reality was very grim, as leaked by Michael Weinstein; racist lynchings organized by paramilitary death squads resembling the early KKK and ROA vigilantes were the norm, and this created the desired effect of making immigrants leave on their own. Furthermore, other ways of making them leave voluntarily included suspension of health care or educational programs, rejection of job applications and sizeable reductions in wages. Hazing in the workplace and in school ran unchecked, and some resulted in fatal beatings. Houses of immigrants had reportedly been burned to the ground, and women were often raped and murdered. But nobody had the power to stop this, internally or externally. The US remained completely isolated from the world, as its vast army prevented other countries from butting in, and its nuclear arsenal was a serious threat given the fact that Creatonologist zealots had their fingertips on the button. The Unitedstatian Fortress, as it was usually addressed in the media, stood tall and impregnable, luckily also isolating its idiocy preventing it to leak outwards to the scientific, civilized world. Not even the most fascist European right-wingers wanted anything to do with them. They could be racist oligarchic oppressors too, but weren't as straight-forward as Unitedstatians. Europeans have always had a history of two-faced politics. They knew where to draw the line and how to survive. However, it was a psychological war on more than just two fronts. The Muslims in the Middle East were getting quite restless, increasing the Unitedstatian foreign policies to unheard of budgets, inciting armed militias to rebel and overthrow dictators they didn't like or pick. Nobody knew yet how Unitedstatians managed to survive with the enormous military spending of their government, but one thing was certain; the US was so vast it

could self-sustain to a certain degree, and its army was so large and modern nobody was willing to take the first step to WWIII. And thus, it could still gain allies infiltrating their puppet dictators on third-world countries to still see what the political spectrum was like in the rest of the world, and nobody would object directly. It seemed we now lived in the Cold War of the future; the United States vs. the rest of the world.

I often switched immediately to another channel after watching CMN News to cleanse the disgusting taste of Unitedstatian decadence from my mind. Fortunately there was Cadenas Latinas, that is "Latin Networks" in English, but bearing a double meaning as it also meant "Latin Chains," a reference to Latin America liberating itself from the yoke of Unitedstatian meddling. It was Latin America's main informative network comprising several TV channels and radio stations, established as a way to promote Latin American unity and strengthen the bonds between all Latin American countries, and eradicate the subversive division always encouraged by the Unitedstatian Empire and practiced by the pro-Unitedstatian Latin American puppet right-wing parties. It was often my main source of news, as not only they were seemingly the only mainstream media network which promoted left-wing ideals, but they also seemed concerned on reporting the inhuman atrocities happening in the horrid North American society to help balance the scales and debunk the myths and lies always perpetrated by the right-wing news corporations like CMN. They also always broadcasted the reports of Michael Weinstein, which as expected, was like a symbol of what a progressive United States would be like. No matter how many times Unitedstatians hammered the subject, there was no such thing as a left-wing media in democratic Western countries, Latin America being an exception

261

due to its Bolivarian Revolution and the necessity to defend it from the destabilization attacks promoted by the overwhelming media of the Latin American ultra-right and the Northern Eagle. It was an intricate endeavor deciphering how powerful media conglomerates could benefit from spreading left-wing propaganda in neoliberal countries, but right-wingers seemed absolutely convinced of a left-wing conspiracy to take over the world and turn everyone into mindless Communist aliens, or at least, this conspiracy was their main weapon used to dissuade people from sympathizing with an ideology that would topple the powerful from their positions, provide universal healthcare and education and social stability; the ideology of Socialism. South America was rising, that was the undeniable truth, and everyone, from the old ultra-right of the United States to the centrist coward puppet politicians of Europe slaves to the banks – who laughably called themselves leftist – were afraid of a true left-wing, peaceful, democratic and humanitarian movement supported by the peoples themselves and practiced entirely under democratic systems. These cowards were afraid because they knew the peoples could make others wake up and incite them into defending their rights from the wealthy elites, toppling them from their positions of power.

I had actually had an argument with my parents when knowing that my destination would be Loynne's. I was unwilling to come to this disgusting capitalist land, yet my parents were very clear on their decision. South America, the probable true successor of the glorious USSR due to its new way of reinventing Socialism and benefiting the peoples with certain capitalist luxuries while keeping away the psychotic ultra-consumerism of the US at bay, was to my eyes the future. I wanted to live in South America, in any of the beautiful countries that comprised it; Venezuela, Ecuador, Brazil, Uru-

guay, Argentina and Chile were rife with leftist movements. But my parents had been very clear on the subject. The right-wing puppets of the US regime still active, destabilization campaigns had begun to try and topple the democratically elected heads of state with brutal and violent coups, and my parents did not want to put me in harm's way under any circumstance. They didn't care whether they lived or die, but would never cope with their only son being murdered. Choosing the seemingly safest place in the whole world, Loynne's Island was to them the only choice.

On this occasion, I watched as Weinstein informed of the situation regarding the theory of evolution in the US, an old but still trending topic that had most people scratching their heads as to why this was even an issue to them.

"Even with all the overwhelming amount of evidence throughout a great number of scientific fields, many people, especially in North America, still refuse to accept the theory of evolution. If the evidence supporting evolution is overwhelming, why does this continue to happen? The US is on par with some Islamic countries regarding the percentage of its population that rejects evolution. I find that fact very strange as it's totally at odds with the stats for the vast majority of developed countries. What makes the US have a large fraction of its population hold the beliefs of a developing country's superstitious and uneducated population?

As you can assume, there are several explanations for this. One is that the Unitedstatian educational system has done a terrible job in properly teaching about the theory of evolution, and religious organizations are always behind the anti-scientific agenda which makes students harbor completely false beliefs regarding the theory. These organizations misrepresent evolution strategically in order to deter people from embracing it. Deep inside, they know that

*a scientific world would harm their dark and ignorant reli-
gious fanaticism they try to spread, and they have targeted
the institutions that are most likely to destroy them; the
schools.*

*But the root of the problem is not only the survival of a
conservative, anti-scientific and deluded social meme of the
past like religion. The reason why we fail to properly teach
the theory in schools and why religious organizations invest
in preventing our kids from being exposed to scientific evidence is the existence of death. In other words, what it is so
threatening about this particular scientific theory is the fear
of people to die. Recent studies have reached the conclusion
that existential anxiety about death is the cause which leads
people to resist evolution and favor intelligent design or
creationism.*

*The premise is that us humans are unique animals with
the intellectual horsepower to reflect on ourselves, which
enables us to reach the conclusion that we cannot escape the
fact of our imminent mortality. When we are fragile children, we already understand that we are not impervious to
physical harm. We acknowledge through our nervous system factors which cause us great pain, and later as we age
understand how we can be the victims of a violent practice,
a random accident or a disease. As our development pro-
ceeds, we also begin to fully understand how we can avoid
some fatal risks through certain behaviors, all because science teaches us through biology what practices are beneficial for the human body.*

*But eventually we cannot escape the fact that death is in-
evitable. We are the only species on the planet that can self-
consciously acknowledge its lifespan and reach conclusions
about it. Extensive research has shown that this awareness
of death generates a drastic amount of social anxiety caus-*

ing us to create systems of belief like religion which help us escape the inevitability of our fate. Humans turn to cultural trends like religion that suppress the fear of death by telling people that our existence is meaningful and significant. What they tell us is that even though we may be mortal, our existence is justified. We are meaningful beings in a pur-poseful universe, specifically created by an intelligent, be-nevolent and all-powerful entity for us to dwell in. This elevates us to higher positions than simple evolved monkeys which happened to grow smarter. People greatly dislike this idea, and as such favor denial over scientific facts.

What we are left with is simple; the more people believe their lives to serve a greater divine meaning, the less the inevitability of death disturbs them. Summarizing, existen-tial meaning protects people from the social anxiety monster produced by the awareness of impending oblivion.

Since people are aware of their mortality, they often search for a meaning which can justify their sheer existence and the theory of evolution does not offer them the respite they seek. Actually, it ultimately shatters and destroys their equilibrium and offers them the view that life is entirely meaningless, chaotic, random. With religion, humans find the respite they seek through denial and delude themselves into thinking that a guardian angel keeps them safe from harm. But we all know how hypocritical that is. Humans do not firmly believe that a superior entity guards them from danger at all times, for they use preventive measures, pas-sive ones such as seat belts, or active ones such as firearms, to keep danger at bay. Mothers take care of their offspring and often overprotect them. Why would anyone believing in a benevolent and all-powerful entity which looks after the entire human race need to resort to such measures? Wouldn't it be considered blasphemous? But this is where

religion grows exponentially hypocritical and shows us to our faces that it's man-made. With the contradictions in the holy books such as the Bible we are already able to destroy the foundations of organized religions, but we don't even need to resort to that. We can already designate religion as a lie when a priest tells us the nearly infinite excuses of why we cannot expect that hyper-benevolent god to look after us all the time. What we are left with is with a cruel, despotic and childish entity which creates an entire race of beings only to later play with them as if they were experiments, never providing them comfort or communicating with them in any way and simply, leaving them to their own devices. With empirical evidence, given there was a god at all, this is what we are left with; humans who choose to believe in any religion are simply deluding themselves believing in something that has zero evidence only because it makes them feel better. It's the ultimate placebo for social anxiety, and the main antagonist of truth and science.

In any case, I have brought with me several responses from Unitedstatians to evolution, so that you can grasp what a mixture of religious fundamentalism, geographical isolation and lack of education can do to a human mind. The people who made these comments shall remain anonymous to save them the embarrassment. These are answers to the question 'Why do 97% of Unitedstatians reject evolution?' And without anything else to add, here you have them;"

"Humans are significantly different than any animal on Earth that's where your problem lies. If you want to convince yourself you came from a jungle monkey, that's fine with me. But I know I didn't."

"Because there is no concrete proof."

"Evolution was invented by Darwin, a man who despised

God. He now has rotted away along with all his nonsense. Everything he said can be disproved. Even scientists are now finding out that his theory of natural selection has many flaws, and is untrustworthy."

"Because it's merely a theory, not a fact which has been proven."

"I don't accept nor reject evolution; that it has become close to an imperative and is now considered as something close to intellectual impoverishment not to go with the meager concept of it taught in schools leads me to suspect it. When a majority of people are being forced to believe in something, that immediately raises my guard. I don't consider myself intellectually impoverished and yet, I don't feel the same compulsion as others to accept Darwinian evolution. When I read Darwin I sense I will find other motivations/biases sufficiently persuasive that will lead me to further doubt his theory, despite the confirming evidence that supposedly proves it. What I've learned is that no theory is beyond criticism. I've not come across a single theory in my life without flaws or at least rooted in some unfounded assumption. There is always a strange sense of sophism in the rhetoric of scientists. That leads me to be on my guard against deceit."

"As you can see, even the ones who try to provide a semi-intellectual explanation to their denial of evolution fails miserably when the moment of backing their arguments with reason comes. I won't analyze these comments as I prefer the audience to think about what this means regarding education and social decadence. I must offend a few with my firm atheism by saying that fortunately, religions change with the times and ultimately disappear, evolving in newer forms. It's my greatest hope that humanity can learn

to value and respect science for it is the cornerstone of our survival, and without it nothing awaits but our extinction. With religious zealots in developed countries like the US two problems arise; since technology and communications ironically give them a voice, the influence they exercise over average people is amplified massively, and secondly, the strategy they use making themselves victims of censorship and intolerance by claiming that their religious beliefs are trying to be suppressed by an agenda or a conspiracy grant them seemingly absolute political immunity from anything that questions the basis for their beliefs. As such, we have a problem which we are unable to talk about, to question and worst of all, a problem that we know is in people's heads. Until humanity crashes against the wall and wakes up to the realization that no benevolent gods care about carbon-based beings who happen to be ruling this planet until they go extinct like so many ruling species before them, we shall never overcome this problem. People want to believe, they want to feel special and wish their lives to have meaning. Against that, there's absolutely nothing you can do. Everyone's free to believe in whatever they want, no matter how irrational it is. But what we cannot allow is for these people to destroy and question the scientific method, the basis for every single piece of technology we use in our daily lives, what's made us discover the working mechanics of our surroundings in order to understand it more and the only thing we can back up with solid evidence. Science, the ultimate search for the truth, will always prevail, because fortunately humanity is not as stupid as it seems. Hopefully, there will always be someone who analyzes and challenges the establishment in a bid to prove he's correct, and all others are wrong. These pioneers and brave revolutionaries are the ones who religious zealots mercilessly slaughtered when

hearing what they did not want to hear, and now we have the power to make our voices heard so much they will drown the nonsense and the lunatic ravings of religious fanatics. Only we can prevent society to fall in an obscure and ignorant era, and we shall do every single humanely possible thing to prevent it. Remember that sad as it is, my report on evolution does not affect only Unitedstatians, but an important part of Canadians and British citizens. As a Unitedstatian living in Cuba, the rejection and denial of evolution continues to worry me, and I wonder whether the reason lies deeply within their deformed system of beliefs."

This piece of news had stomped my already shattered mood. The world seemed to be taking new steps into idiocy. Idiocy that would put outrageous witch-burning puritans to shame. Nothing good would come out of this. Had the rest of nations been more like the US, I wouldn't have been surprised if a new Medieval Dark Age emerged to suppress all the knowledge and science we managed to discover and send the globe into a plunging abyss of religion, tribal warfare and chaos. Needless to say, everything outside of Loynne's was looking rather bleak; aside from Unitedstatian bigotry, an economic crisis had been announced in Europe, paralyzing the markets and sending much of the world into a deadly recession. But none of this mattered to me at the moment. The world as a whole could burn in that particular moment. So what if the US was getting stupider, the Middle East restless, Europe poorer? Loynne's was alright, able to self-sustain as much as the US and living off the world as an expensive and attractive leech. The Atlantic Switzerland, as it was usually called, Loynne's was also unofficially known to hold bank accounts of influential people all over the world. In other words, Loynne's was as untouchable as Switzerland during

WWII. The world was going to hell, so what? For once, I considered my life to have a meaning, and attributed respect to myself. No more of that stupid useless daydreaming about politics with Wolfgang, about the supposed brand new future we'd give to the peoples of the Earth. The world was rotten and stupid, it was all I could see. Yes, my loyalty still lay by the side of Communism, but I didn't trust my fellow human beings. They were easily corrupted by selfishness and greed, driven by their desires to live luxuriously and without hardship. Each day, I was seeing people as disposable waste with growing disdain, and I wasn't even afraid of admitting it. What else could I do? It was the image they brought down on themselves in the first place. Looking at people in school was more than enough. They would never be interested in others. Why did I have to care for them?

I headed for the bus stop, once more easily dismissing political concerns when the photos of Faye that now adorned my wall below Marx greeted me and pushed any worries aside.

· · · · ·

The air in the school had been lively and different during the time the Prometheus Project students walked among us, when dozens of innocent-looking foreign students strolled around the school struggling to reject the wonderful things Loynner students offered them at every turn, from crude dirty jokes and insults to alcohol and drugs. I often wondered why Loynners had to be so primitive, so straight-forward in their social approach. On these lands corruption was widespread, even in the most microscopic of environments. But their time in Loynne's had expired, and now we were once

again back to normality.

Waiting outside of class with the guys and limiting myself to admire Axel spewing a bunch of nonsense about Realm of Witchcraft to Wolfgang, I saw Ryan duck-walking toward me, in a way I found more pathetic and sorry-looking than never before. It's funny how I sensed someone was missing from the group but I couldn't tell who. I prepared myself to react accordingly when he told me what I already knew. He started directly, without even saying hello to me or the other guys.

"You won't believe it," he began. "Jenna ... it was terrible ... I knew it ..."

"Why? What happened?"

"Jenna was a lesbian, that's what happened you dumb schmuck! I suspected somethin' but didn't think it was possible. I mean ... would you have thought? Could you tell? I couldn't man, I couldn't!"

"Come on Ryan, she did seem kind of tough, and ... not too interested in men. But, how did you find out?"

"Oh, you don't wanna know ... I should have known better ... I'm about to give up with this shit ... I fuckin' hate these dykes, what a waste of a fuckin' female human being ... They're there for us to fuck 'em, you know? I'd be thankful if just once they weren't so selfish. I mean, sure, you're a dyke, but that's not the same as being a gay guy, right? I mean ... women are supposedly bisexual since they're born, but they sort of choose when they mature sexually and fall for cock or beaver ... but Axel said it, there's no such thing as a lesbian, only women who've never had a nice sausage deep inside. It's no wonder there's so many gays around with chicks like these, damn, we have our needs to stick our shit in something, anything!"

"Where are you going with this, you mean you're turning gay now?"

"Hell no! Fuck you! Gay he says. NEVER! I'm talkin' about findin' someone who ain't a fuckin' carpet-munchin' boot-wearin' time waster. That."

"I know how you feel. Even if you don't want to hear it, I went through that all my life. Girls seem worthless until you somewhat reach a certain age and find someone perfectly suited for you, someone who satisfies your every need, physical and emotional."

"Right, and that someone is my sister in your case. Well that's all very nice and groovy but I'm still not getting any, and neither are you the way you're going ..."

Before I could open my mouth to reply, we got distracted by Axel, who was seemingly instructing Wolfgang on how to get a woman's attention ... A nice girl, very foxy with a round butt and enormous breasts passed by, prompting Axel to yell "YEEEEAAAAAHHHHH!!!" following her with his head as she walked past. The girl turned around, Axel smiled and winked at her and she smiled back flirtingly, noticeably amused.

"Uhh ... what were we talking about?" Ryan asked.

"You were talking about how I found the woman I sought in your sister and how it wouldn't lead anywhere, and I was about to say ... 'what do you mean by that?' "

"Well, even if my sister likes you, which she won't, I very much doubt that I'd be comfortable with the relationship."

"What ...? Look Ryan, I know you're the older brother and all that, but you're no one to decide over her."

"Like hell I am! She's only 15! That's rape!"

"Shut the fuck up Ryan, I'm 17 and so are you, everyone rapes everybody at this age by that reasoning. We're not even supposed to be doing this legally until we're 19, at least in Loynne's, so who cares?"

"I know that, I'm only saying she really is 15. Most girls

her age are total sluts but she's not and I want her to remain that way. What if she dates you, then you guys break up and then she learns to love the sausage and sucks a dude's dick here, another dick there? Put yourself in my shoes, would you want that for your sister?"

"Well, I think you know her better than I do, in which case you shouldn't be afraid. If she's a decent person she won't go around sucking dick for no apparent reason."

"You're so calm because you don't have brothers or sisters, putting up with this shit is awful. Don't you see the poor thing, she depends on me for everything. Sometimes I even walk her home 'cause she feels lonely or scared. Or that's what I think."

"You should stop that, she needs to grow up sometime. And besides there's other things to care about right now."

"Like what?"

"Well, weren't you worried about getting pussy barely a second ago?"

"Ah ... oh yeah. Well you know what I mean. Forget it. Let's just go to class. Fuckin' European milk-face Jews ... I'm glad they're all gone now. And you know what, I'm gonna tell you one more thing ..."

We got startled again, this time by Wolfgang. A girl walked past and Axel signaled at her, trying to make Wolfgang do what he had done before. Wolfgang let out a booming, grave "YEEEEEH!!" that sounded like a Japanese command to attack, causing the girl to stare back only to see Wolfgang with his arms crossed and his chin up, smiling vigorously. The girl looked at him in disgust and went away, dismissing him with a hand gesture as if to say "forget you."

Laughing and clapping his hands, Axel patted Wolfgang on the shoulder, trying to make him feel better:

"You said it, Wolfie! No pain no gain!"

• • • • •

Artem Arkazhov cleansed the sweat off his forehead with the usual tissue he carried in his jean's back pocket, and breathing heavily took a gulp of his bottle of water. It always seemed he'd die in front of us of a heart attack or heat stroke, but always managed to recover enough strength to sternly proceed with the lesson.

"Even if you don't believe it, the world wasn't always the place we know now," he began to say with his Russian baritone voice, in the usual somber and gloomy tone. "The world was once divided by ideological struggles. The two superpowers of the time, the then called 'United States of America' and the 'Union of Soviet Socialist Republics,' heavily fought a series of proxy wars indirectly which resulted in political skirmishes all over the world, from South America to Asia and even the Middle East. This is the period we refer to as the Cold War."

"Heh, heh, period, heh, heh ...," Ryan muttered to himself, who was sitting next to me scribbling on his notebook drawing characters from some Japanese cartoon series. I felt insulted by his lack of interest or respect, and trying to hide the utmost disgust I felt for Ryan at that moment I proceeded to stare transfixed into the heart of this Soviet survivor, who had had the pleasure of witnessing the maximum expression of Communism the world will ever know.

"The Soviet Union, as it is most commonly referred to, was a union of several republics under a centralized government, focusing on a planned economy. This means that unlike in the US, the Soviet Union did not engage in free market practices and multinational corporations of capitalistic nature

274

were kept out of the State's affairs."

"Commie retards, no wonder they were so poor," someone behind me had said.

"What do you mean, Dellica?" asked Arkazhov, his dog-like eyes set on those of the girl who had spoken. The gloominess had gone; instead, his eyes were now engulfed in the cold, analytical spectrum you would see in those of a KGB officer.

"I'm saying it's no wonder they collapsed and they had to welcome democracy and capitalism to live decently. I mean why did it take so long for them to find out?"

"Someone as bright as you wouldn't begin to understand." I could not help myself. I really couldn't. I said it without even thinking. Each time you insulted someone in Loynne's while in public in a sudden rush of fury, the person would always back off to preserve his image as a non-violent model citizen in a bid to make you look like the bad guy.

"Oh right, sorry, you only say that 'cause you sorta come from there and you feel offended or whatever."

"I say it because aside from that, I happen to know more than what the free right-wing of the capitalist Eagle lets you know. I happen to know everything that caused the collapse of the most ambitious Socialist project the world will ever see. We didn't allow it to live and this is the reason the rest of the world except for us lives completely under the line of poverty. And us here living on this island are next, so I wouldn't be so cocky if I were you."

"Oh come on, you're telling me communist countries are wealthy and comfy? Why do people from those oppressive regimes flee then? Why do they come here, like you must have done?" I felt fear at these words. I could not let anybody know my identity, and I had to struggle against the urge of telling my incredible story. But I kept my composure. I struck

back.

"Firstly, I'm Moldovan, and many years have passed since the fall of the Soviet Union, so if I came here it wasn't due to Communism, but because of how capitalism basically ruined the lives of millions by increasing the gap between rich and poor, making a few richer and millions poorer. And secondly, many Communist nations have committed atrocities and resembled oppressive capitalist autocracies, using Communism as a way to harness their one-party rule, but being driven by capitalist economies. I do not support Communist governments which do not fight for the welfare of the people and partake in mindless slaughter. But we must be realistic, and judging the history of the Soviet Union and the People's Republic of China, we must admit how without rapid industrialization these countries would have been invaded by foreign powers or remained forever stuck in agrarian economies. Thanks to Communist industrialization, both countries became recognized global superpowers and held their own against the capitalism of the West. Arrests and executions were ultimately the only way to ensure a steady and fast way to progress, it's cruel but true. The Soviet Union defended itself against the psychotic evil of fascism and Nazi Germany, and won the war almost by itself. The measures taken by Comrade Stalin and Chairman Mao were ruthless and resulted in countless deaths, but were only a simple historical need based on the context where they found themselves in. The death of the State, or its preservation. After the initial phases of persecution, both States enjoyed prosperity and peace. In any case, these practices are officially recognized by many Communists today as excessively ruthless and not applicable in a 21st century context, a view I share as well. Communism does not entail death, persecution and oppression; the historical and social contexts of each country determine how much

repression will be performed by the State. In the largely agrarian and under-industrialized East, it proved effective, and as a result the economically growing East is now superior to the poverty-stricken West smashed by recessions produced by its faulty economic system, which allows corruption to reign freely. And lastly, true Communism has never existed in the world. Communism means the disintegration of the State after its peoples reach an egalitarian society, where such state would be rendered completely useless. What we have seen up to now is states politically ruled by Communist parties, driven by state-capitalism, stuck in an initial phase we call 'dictatorship of the proletariat.' We have not been able to evolve past that, because for that capitalist economy worldwide would need to cease to exist in order to give way for a Socialist one. Socialist economies cannot coexist with capitalist ones, and this is the reason why Communist nations often endure hardships; they are strangled by capitalism and the economic blockades imposed by the West, which often results in the collapse of these nations. But you will never hear the West admitting to sabotaging Communist nations only because they do not fall in line with their greedy ideals."

"Preach all you want, but the evidence is everywhere. Communists are tyrants, oppressors, murderers and thieves, and that's a fact."

"Look, given your narrow analysis of sociopolitical issues, I want to be sure, are you or your family by any chance, extremely right-wing?"

"Of course we are! The left is nothing but a bunch of criminals and terrorists who support death, everybody knows that."

"I'm shocked. Can you tell me what the definition of right-wing is, then?"

"Right-wing means the complete opposite of the left, we

stand for true social values that help the people, not like you communist baby-killers say you do. We promote family values and are pro-life. You oppress people, force women to abort and send them to camps if they disagree and execute them without a trial. I mean if you ask me, those communist states are like abusive parents who don't let the children have liberty to do things and treat them bad all the time."

"And Western democracies are like single divorced mothers, who let the children do whatever they want because they aren't concerned with their upbringing and prefer buying their affection with expensive toys!" The entire class reacted to my quick reply by cheering joyfully, and I garnered strength to go on with my rant when feeling their receptive mood.

"Look, since you've pathetically demonstrated how you don't even know what your ideology really stands for, let me shed some light on it. What we know today as 'right-wing' was popularized in the French Revolution. Basically, in terms someone of your mental capacity will understand, people at the French parliament kept fighting on and on and couldn't reach an agreement. People sitting to the left of the president's chair spoke for social upheaval, revolution, equality and held anti-religious views, wanting to separate religion from state affairs, you know, otherwise known as secularism. Those sitting to the right advocated traditionalist and religious views, and any other thing that spells a complete halt to progress. That's where people like you stand. You're the rock blocking progress in society. That's why anyone sufficiently intellectual and qualified enough to understand differences in political spectrums hates the right-wing. The word conservative says it all. You're afraid of change. You can't adapt to it. If it weren't for leftist movements we wouldn't even live in a semi-civilized society like we do today. You're attending a

public high-school. If you were such a fanatical supporter of the right-wing, do what they preach and go to a private one. Give them your money. Go on, go right ahead. Pay for private healthcare as well, instead of freely enjoying the apt system Loynne's Island possesses thanks to universal healthcare reforms brought forth by years of Socialist activism and paid for by money that comes out of your taxes so that everyone can enjoy its benefits. All of these changes which have benefited society were born out of Socialist thinking. You will know more when you work as a waitress or whatever low-end job awaits you. When the union wants to organize a strike because of how bad they're exploited, you'll understand. Because if you had studied history at all, you'd know all these reforms were needed for normal human beings to live decently ever since they were oppressed by conservative forces that wanted profit at the expense of slavery. Higher ups, government officials, factory owners, magnates, heads of corporations, monarchs, and I can go on. As you can see, regular people like you of insignificant wealth do not have anything to do in the right-wing spectrum. You're supporting and voting for omnipotent people who stand for this and will enslave you for money the minimum chance they get. We, the left, oppose those forces in order to keep them from oppressing the average citizen. We make things hard for them so that stupid people like you cannot be oppressed. There is only one way to approach this, and it's admitting the absolute truth that the left-wing cares for the majority and the right-wing for the elites. This is not an exaggeration, but the ultimate truth behind the issue, because as you put it, 'evidence is everywhere.' The issue regarding sexual minorities for example, has become a left-wing issue due to the progressive thinking that is needed for them to be fully accepted and integrated into society, and as such these reforms could not

279

have been possible under right-wing doctrine. Standing by the side of the oppressed, the poor, the exploited, the discriminated, more than being about differences in economic systems, this is the true spirit of the left. So go ahead. Tell me now which side benefits people like you or me the most." Dellica kept staring at me, her generic Loynnerin face seared with the devastating whiplash of a lost ideological argument. Arkazhov remained silent, his body leaning forward with the arms crushing the desk, his bald head looking at the ground. All the muscles in his body seemed incredibly tense with discomfort.

"Students, let us not engage in an ideological debate, as we're discussing history, not politics," he said with a patient but tiresome tone, almost out of breath. "Let's continue with the lesson. Pay attention because you will need to do an essay on Vladimir Lenin for the next week."

"Wait professor, two more things," I interrupted. "Firstly, Dellica, are you Christian?"

"What's it to you?

"Are you aware of the greatest crimes of Christianity, namely the deaths caused by the crusades and the inquisition, the intolerance to other religions, the child abuses committed by priests?"

"... yeah, so what?"

"Can you say that these actions committed by Christians or in the name of Christianity are representative or exemplary of the Christian faith?"

"... no."

"Well ... same applies to Communism. Communism has suffered from bad management, from key figures enjoying too much power and often abusing it, from atrocities which have forever stained its good name and its principles; same as the Catholic Church, same as Judaism, same as Islam,

same as every single type of religion, ideology, government or state of any kind. It is our duty to stay true to our principles and never falter in our way to achieve our goals. We must strive for the well-being of everyone, for prosperity, culture and progressiveness in society. We must strive for utopia knowing it's impossible to reach it, but doing everything we can to get closer to it." Not willing to end my rant there, I turned to Arkazhov, who had been silently observing the debate. I could not go on without speaking my mind, and I didn't care for the consequences.

"And secondly, Mr. Arkazhov ... you cannot discuss history without politics. That is what's wrong with the educational system, and why Western democracies have failed at making students truly understand history. Making politics a taboo subject creates ignorance, and does not let students understand the driving mechanics behind it. But you and I both know the truth, don't we? Western democracies want people to cease thinking, to swallow forgettable knowledge and spew it on an exam. And this is where they have succeeded. We are encouraged not to think ideologically or politically, and thus fail at training the future generations for improving upon society, leaving them an easy prey of the corrupt two-party system of the center-right and the center-left, parties which bow down only to one master; the banks."

All of the students in the classroom, who had followed the heated argument with enormous interest, gasped when I addressed Arkazhov. The ensuing silence and the stares of classmates were what I met when the bell rang, and was later drowned by the intensifying commotion outside, the laughter and yelling of people exiting the classrooms. I marched to the door quickly and left, knowing I had maybe won a small political debate but feeling the sting of the general right-wing mindset of Loynne's. People always confused abundance with

the right. People never knew that right-wing politicians let people submerge themselves in a false state of welfare that soon sinks in an economic crisis when banks and financial entities don't have any more money to steal from tax payers, education or healthcare, when stock brokers, European nobles, Unitedstatian magnates and tax evading celebrities have hoarded all their wealth in Caribbean Islands owned by the colonialist and corrupt British Crown. Then they move the multinational corporations in to bite the dry bones of the dying proletariat and enslave them forever. I had no idea why people always considered this the best socioeconomic system. And remembering my land was undergoing this very same process sent a lightning bolt of rage down my very spine.

That Loynnerin Dellica exited the class with her friends, giving me a dirty look as she disappeared behind the staircase's corner. I could not help myself. I struggled against the urge of racing to catch her and ship her away to the most inhumane gulag in Siberia. I hated how cocky and arrogant people were when given what the West always refers to as "liberty."

"Sonny! Sonny, man! That shit was awesome! I don't know what the hell you said half of the time, but you shut her fucking mouth. That bitch never knows her place. It's so cool when someone shuts her up her from time to time. And you shut that fat fuck teacher up too! Nice going man, real nice." My male classmates were congratulating me on my rant one after the other while exiting the classroom. I was astonished. Firstly Arkazhov had not sent me to the principal's office, and secondly because I had basically defended Communism, a system they associated with repression and tyranny in front of them, and they loved me doing it. Of course, they didn't understand what Communism even was. My rant had fallen completely upon deaf ears. But to them, I had defended my

country and my feelings, and that was enough for respect.

"Sonny, could I have a word?" One of the ex-boarding school buddies of Axel had approached me, shaking my hand like all the rest who thought what I had done was deserving of respect.

"Sure, why not?" I replied.

"Sonny, thank you very much for what you just did ... I know it's very strange to be so sincere about your thoughts here, in front of a whole classroom like that ... it takes a lot of courage. I just wanted to say that ... well ... as you may have assumed, I'm gay ... and I'm very thankful for what you said back there. I'm glad that people like you who aren't gay aren't afraid to speak their minds about the issue and stand up for our rights."

"Oh—Ah ... well ... thanks! I didn't think I reached any-body in there, you know ... I just did what I thought I had to do. I didn't really think anyone was paying attention. I just did what I thought was right."

"And you did ... Thanks, man. I'll make sure the gay com-munity hears about this. That girl, Dellica, the mother's a fuckin' nutjob, one of those religious pro-family values anti-abortion activists who think we're a plague. Shame on her, you did the right thing. I'll tell the community to not believe the lies they spread about communists."

"You should know, Lenin decriminalized homosexuality in Russia following the 1917 revolution, same as with divorce and abortion. By the way, I'm sorry, but I don't think I got your name ..."

"Gary, I'm Gary Fastuosso."

"Well, pleasure to meet you Gary. But you should know that I don't really have ties to homosexual communities or even homosexual friends, I just consider the homosexual cause an example on how the left fights for the rights of eve-

283

ryone who is oppressed, and their integration in society."

"I know that, well, I imagined, you don't look exactly gay. And believe me, us gays can tell who's what."

"Well Gary, I'm proud to help in the fight against discrimination by these right-wing fanatics who hate change and want everything to be the way it always was. My main enemy aside from capitalism is social stagnation."

"Well said, Sonny. Well, I have to go now, I have a class in the photography lab. It's been a pleasure to talk to you and I'll catch you around at school."

"Thanks, Gary. It means a lot."

"Hey Sonny you went nuts back there, haha, it was awesome! What the hell happened to you?! Hey, and who are you?" Ryan asked, when seeing me talking to Gary.

"I'm Gary, I was telling Sonny about how I found it very brave of him to defend gays like that back there."

"Woah, woah, woah, woah ... woah. Wait. You're a fag or you just defend 'em?"

"I am gay, yes. And that's a very disrespectful term what you just used."

"Haha, we got a bear humper in our class! So you're gay, huh ... am ... can I ask you a question? Do you really like ... I mean ... don't get offended or anythin' ... but gay guys seem to get to know loads of chicks ... Do you fake being gay to get some pussy, or you guys actually like choking on cock? 'Cause I mean ... I don't know ... I could never understand what you see in veiny cocks and hairy asses ... yuck ..."

"Mmph ... look Sonny, talk to you later ..."

"It's alright Gary, and ... I'm sorry. I'll catch you around."

"Yeah Gary, see you later! And don't worry man, I'll tell the guys not to drop the soap when you're in the shower at PE!"

"You really know how to make new friends, Ryan ..."

"Tell me, I seem to be on a lucky streak this year, I never got to meet so many interesting people!"

Something immediately sunk the merry feeling of victory though, and it wasn't thinking about the rise of fascism in Europe or the right-wing theocracy of the US, but Artem Arkazhov's lack of insight. I supposed that as a teacher he would stay out of it, and as an individual he could not care less for some students quarreling. But I expected that maybe just one time I had touched his nerve. How could he remain passive toward statements of such magnitude, happening in front of him? Didn't he remember anything related to the Soviet Union anymore? Did he not feel the burning flame of revolution in his heart like I did? Did he not feel insulted and offended by the effective massive brainwash the right still had on middle-class citizens?

But no. It seemed Arkazhov was yet another Soviet defector, someone who had openly forgotten about Communism and the glorious days of the Soviet Republics like the rest of the Eastern Bloc. Someone who had opted for letting the past in the past and embracing a melancholic, sad and somber life. The amount of respect my classmates felt for me that day, was equivalent to the respect I lost for Arkazhov. The Western educational system was laughable; where was the ideology? How could you study history without entering the field of politics? There was no such thing. Failing to teach politics and not encourage students into political thinking was the biggest success of the Western World. Mindless brainwashed drones like Dellica were a living testimony of it, and their inability to analyze sociopolitical issues furthermore drove Western society to its ideology-lacking state of obliviousness. It was no wonder the world was being engulfed by neo-fascist parties that told people what to do and how to think. The incredibly low intelligence of the people surrounding me

seemed frightening, as it wasn't a local phenomenon. It seemed the ignorant, uncultured and self-righteous happy idiot had taken over the world for good. Nobody was willing to think outside of the imposed barriers of the vapid consumerist society. Everyone rested their minds happily knowing everything was alright, at least in Loynne's; there was no need for revolution, no need for dissent, no need to question the establishment. As long as everyone was concerned, Loynne's was a utopia, and the best place in the world to live in.

In the meanwhile, I had no choice but to conform myself with what good had come out of the situation; from that day onwards, nobody dared say a thing in the Cold War history lessons the Russian professor seemed to dread giving. Not even a spoiled loudmouth like Dellica.

As for Gary, the unusual exchange with him improved my mood, and I was glad I had helped someone feel more integrated in society. Suffering Kannovschina firsthand, there was nothing I hated more than discrimination and bullying in a social environment. Defending and standing up for everyone who is different is an undeniably leftist condition, while racism and hazing are rooted deeply in right-wing fascist ideologies. Kannovschina demonstrated that the hatred of something foreign was always due to ignorance and fear, and that the violence that develops to combat what is perceived as evil was the basis for every single conservative ideology afraid of change, fascism being the highest exponent of it.

Unfortunately, after the exchange with Ryan, Gary no longer approached me to speak, and if he did, it was usually quick and swiftly. I felt sorry for someone who possibly needed an understanding friend in this cold world of bullying, but I had to stick with Ryan even though I loathed him. Faye was still my top priority.

. . . . .

Kannovschina seemed to be withering, but some signs of it proved its status to be only dormant. Through that year, we experienced the very last remnants of a practice so common and widespread that just like Unitedstatian meddling in foreign affairs, it seemed it would never end. On this occasion, we found ourselves in the sports fields waiting for the PE class teacher to show up. Mike, Axel, Ryan, Billy, Wolfgang and I had been the first students to arrive, as the others always seemed to be away from where we were, almost as if avoiding us. From Kannovschina experience, everyone knew it was dangerous to hang around the sports fields too much, as it was Kanny turf. Billy, Ryan and I had narrowly averted disaster when we were in 3rd Grade, and had the audacity to dare play football next to them. We did have a good time joking around in the infirmary later, but the three of us knew the humiliation we had been subjected to could not be considered normal in a high school environment, or taken as lightly as we did. However, the oath of silence could not be broken; snitching would result in devastating results, as we witnessed numerous times outside of the school's perimeter after classes were over.

Sitting on the small concrete walls that supported the enormous fences, our peace was bound to be shattered when sighting JC Vega coming toward us with my main antagonist from the 3rd Grade, Joakim Miller. Joakim was a monkey-like being as tall as Ryan, with heavy sun-tanned skin and an athletic sinewy body, like most Kannies had. He had brown eyes and sported a simple military crew cut. He was the kind of person that loved making fun of people arbitrarily and sadistically, but unlike JC, was more methodic in his ap-

proach and less violent and loud. His calculating eyes often foretold the potential victim when he had something in mind, as I experienced when I gazed at him for a second before he purposefully threw a dodgeball with all his strength to my face, being only two meters away.

As JC Vega and his lackey approached us, everyone became silent and uncomfortable, knowing what their presence implied.

"Oh, look who's here, Pizza Face himself! Hey Pizza Face you got more lard on your face than last year, right? Look at the fuckin' floor man, or you'll stain my shirt with them zits ... and here's The Samurai! Hey Samurai, look what I've got!" JC Vega said, as he pulled from behind him a broom handle he had been seemingly hiding to mock Wolfgang. He began doing samurai-like moves with it, shouting and swinging the stick in Wolfgang's direction, only to stop it centimeters away before it made contact with his face. Wolfgang did not know how to react, and as such limited himself to doing what most did in his place, smiling faintly and pretending he was less bothered and humiliated than he looked.

Suddenly, they stopped mocking Wolfgang as if he were not worth the effort, tossing the broom handle lightly at him, which bounced weakly off his stomach. I had been the only one aside from Mike to look at JC Vega in disgust instead of looking away in fear. That did not mean I was any more courageous than the people surrounding me. I had always felt fear at the prospect of being involved in a fight against this violent and psychotic behemoth. But I could not help myself from looking or hiding my emotions. My face seared with the rage being inflicted on my fellow comrades. I unleashed the wrath of JC when he noticed I was not easily subdued.

"And what's this piece-a-shit lookin' at," he said, studying me with his disgusting blue eyes, those of a true brainless

jock. "Hey Jo, this cocksucker's lookin' at me."

"Maybe he wants to fight. Hey tough guy, you wanna fight JC? You're not scared, are you?" JC positioned himself in front of me, his height surpassing mine by seven centimeters. Looking down at me, JC Vega smiled and fixed his eyes on mine.

"Just look at this faggot," he said. "Uglier than that samurai cockbag over there, and that's some ugly looking shit."

"Sorry to hear you don't like me, maybe you should stick with your current boyfriend," I said.

The consequence of this was immense. JC Vega pushed me against the fence, making me lose my step momentarily as I staggered, and when I looked up again I saw how JC had been immediately restrained by Joakim, who could barely manage to repress the violent urge of his friend. I could not hear what he was whispering to his ear, but he seemed to be tense, as if JC's behavior needed to be monitored and any outburst could result in some kind of serious problem for them. I really wondered what sort of worry would someone like JC have, someone so untouchable and impervious to any kind of immediate consequence from authorities around him.

I then noticed Mike was at the vanguard, and JC diverted his attention from me in order to shout at him.

"You OK, Sonny boy? I had to push that dick away from you, I hope you don't mind, this ain't a game of who's more macho here boy, that guy is insane, he'll grab you and he'll kill you, I just had to keep him away, no friend of mine is gonna be hit by that scumbag."

"Thanks Mikey, don't worry, I'm not offended," I said, as I witnessed JC Vega, who shouting from 20 meters away felt like he was shouting right next to my ear. They took off in the opposite direction and headed down for the Main Building, disappearing quickly from sight.

· · · · ·

This was just an example of what everyday life was like for us in previous years, the 3rd Grade being the harshest one. But these small emotional setbacks related to my hated environment were not enough to stop my courting crusade. Faye remained my top priority, and made these infrequent encounters with Kannies at school unworthy of attention. After many hollow and sometimes plain awkward ChitChat chats, in which we mainly talked about her beloved Frank Boy Al and the newest album by April Divine, I finally reached an agreement with her. I told her to meet me by the stairs, the same stairs I had seen her that first time, and she agreed. But it was a trap; that day, I did not show up, and when I came home and logged on, she immediately told me "*I didn't see you today at school.*" "*Perfect,*" I thought. "*She's disappointed.*"

"Yeah, I know, sorry I couldn't see you today, I was busy, but don't worry, we'll meet tomorrow, Tuesday, I promise," I said.

"ok," she agreed.

The next morning, I took care of the small details that might have won me the first impression stage. I had a shower, did my hair as best as I could, put on perfume, shaved and thoroughly brushed my teeth. When I arrived at the school I met with the guys in the first floor of the West Wing by the staircase, looking desperately for her; I was so immersed in my own thoughts, so deeply anxious and hyperactive that I couldn't listen to anyone; Gordon, Wolfgang, Ryan, the entire school population, everyone was simply invisible. But wherever I looked, she was nowhere to be seen. My heart gave a little jump. I was exploding with nerves. The guys were there

with me but ignored that I was on a mission. I finally gave up on her, and when the bell rang, I disappointedly walked to my class on the second floor, believing she possibly lost interest or didn't care for me.

Then, I looked up and saw a tiny figure sitting at the top of the stairs, right where the second floor started. She was reading a book, trying to study, and her facial expression showed frustration, anger and a wish to be left alone.

I couldn't get over the ecstatic childish sensation the sheer sight of her produced in me; wearing a blue jean miniskirt, black heeled sandals and a black and blue tight long-sleeved shirt with horizontal stripes, I amazed myself at how nobody had ever made me feel such a powerful attraction in my entire life. She wore her usual black nail polish, as I noticed when looking at her bare feet, and could not get over how appealing the black color was when contrasted against the amazingly white skin. When looking at her chest I noticed too that she was wearing her US flag cross necklace, but I did not mind that symbol of disgusting Unitedstatian theocratic decadence at all when facing her, or the reason why she wore it. Before her presence, I was simply not myself.

With my heart on the verge of collapse, my skin boiling to a fusion point and my body shocked and stiff, I positioned myself in front of her standing still so that she noticed me. I took a deep breath, already weakened by the irresistible cherry smell that characterized her so well, and proceeded to speak:

"Hi! Faye?" and felt a strong slap on the back. No, it wasn't my dignity awaking, it was Mike, who passed by alongside Ryan, Wolfgang and Axel; they were all smiling to themselves as they marched, except for Ryan, who tried to ignore the whole thing. For not showing the least minimum sign of support and thus looking like a bad friend, Ryan was in for

the bullying of his life, Axel and Mike style.

"Oh ... hi!" Faye said. She had not even seen me. Her face turned red the moment she looked up and briefly laughed in a shy manner, looking at the floor. She knew what was going on, clearly. Her facial expression changed the next second, making me confused about whether she was truly glad to see me or not. I remained certain that she had actually been waiting for me as promised, as she could have been out of sight or walking aimlessly if she wanted to ignore me, but decided to remain stationary in one place for me to bump into her. She also kept smiling timidly from time to time, but her voice couldn't be heard amongst the unceasing laughter and yelling of little kids. Even when speaking as loudly as she could, I could never manage to understand what she was saying. I loved this feature. She was completely different to those loud Loynnerin cows running around and piercing your ears with their crudeness.

"How are you?" I asked. It was definitely a bad moment to hold a meaningful conversation. People ran, laughed and shouted, the staircase brimmed with people walking past and sometimes crashing into us, and it didn't help that her voice was so low. Even so, the entire reality surrounding us disappeared; the laughing annoying kids, the disgusting shithead Kannies, the stupid Loynnerins bitches were obliterated in a clear blinding light where only Faith could be seen.

Faye said something I could not understand, but it sounded like *"good, I was trying to study, I have an exam"* or something like that. She was so cute with her book open on her lap; it gave her such a childish aura that my most passionate feelings broke free from my self-imposed restraint and fully embraced her.

"What are you studying?" I asked, taking the book from her hands and turning all the pages, wanting to seem confi-

dent, overpowering and dominant. "Oh, I did this two years ago, no problem. All you have to do is—"

More kids passed rushing by, and a girl, the same girl Faye screamed at the first time I saw her, whispered something to her ear, prompting Faye to suddenly get up;

"Sorry, I'm so stressed, I can't study like this, sorry, I'm leaving, see you later," she said, rushing to her class.

"Oh, alrig—" I began to say. But she had already left.

I stood at the top of the stairs shocked and completely still. I didn't know what to do, and suddenly remembered I had to go to class. I grabbed my backpack and walked slowly to where my friends were. Mike was talking to Axel while Wolfgang and Ryan listened in, and they didn't seem to notice my little failure. For once, I was extremely glad that they ignored me for the video game chatter; at least they didn't notice the embarrassing incident that had just taken place.

I should have met her alone in a quiet place, but no, I couldn't wait and had to meet her as fast as I could. I needed to be more patient, but how could I? The need I had developed for her was uncontrollable, making me feel strange, numb, and each time I stared at her or thought about her, felt absolute bliss, that unique sensation of inner peace that comes with the prospect of being with the woman you cherish.

My mind wandered off as it sunk deeply into the mediocrity of the conversations lingering on the air that would develop increasingly, from recess until the end of the school day, thinking only about whether she had liked seeing me in person or she had ran away in rejection.

• • • • •

"Look I'm telling you, Cobra Viper isn't confused or what-

ever, it's the Slovodnian jungle getting to him, being a black-ops commando and all … It's a small price to pay for not letting the world plunge into chaos like the commies want to …"

"No way dude, you can't possibly say that Cobra Viper is better than Makarov Cat, the guy has all the moves, even if he is a commie, you know, the way he spins the Makarov around and commands bullets with his eyes …"

"I don't care, what I can't forgive in the game is the borin' fuckin' cutscenes, they're so fuckin' long, you know. I'd go download a movie from 'hackthatshit.com' if I wanted to see a fuckin' movie! Right? Also they're stoppin' you every five minutes to explain somethin' to you. I'm a fuckin' Delta Hardcore Gamer! Ain't that a bitch in games, borin' out-of-place dialogue? I think it's one of the worst aspects of the franchise."

"Totally."

"Nah. I have to disagree. I enjoy the dialogues. Besides … it helps to carry the story."

"Hey Sonny, and what do you think? Tell us about your gaming experience!"

"Well to start off with, you're wrong about that saga, you all are. That saga is not about praising Unitedstatians as it is about making fun of their silly militaristic culture. Do you seriously think a Japanese game designer is going to praise the country that bombed his nation with nuclear weapons? The franchise is only wrapped in a Unitedstatian military envelope to appeal to people like you, but it could not be more anti-Western. Due to their capitalistic culture the Japanese may not really relate to Communism, but I can tell you some of them hate Unitedstatians with passion, and they're waiting until their chance to demonstrate it is ripe. And … uh … talk to you later, I got something to do right now, see you

around." Gordon had gone on and on about this game in conversations like these with Wolfgang, Axel and Claude ever since the school year started. I had finally gathered enough courage to stop his inane digital rambling, though; and all it took was a fleeting vision of Faye, walking in that gloomy fashion next to her idiot friend. Somehow, Gordon managed to notice this despite his general lack of interest in offline life;

"Wooooh ... I forgot! Sonny is on a little date! And I really mean little when I say that. She must be like what? Half a meter tall? 11 years old? What is she Sonny, on 1st of SCE or something? Why don't you date my sister better if you're gonna date little ugly girls, hahahaha!"

"Come on, I thought your sister had already gotten drilled by some older Kanny jerk ... And besides there's worse, look at Claude, for example ... he looks in need of a chick badly. I mean seriously, you should totally help him out. He keeps on like this and he isn't coming near a woman until he's 30 ... or worse."

"Nah, Claude's good ... Got all he need. Seven customized computers built by himself in local network wired for some serious FAP action. Yeah!!"

"So, what about your sister?"

"What about her? She can do whatever she wants, she ain't none of my damn business! She ain't messing with my gaming, that little bitch ... Just me, a nice comfy couch, the 216 centimeter VaniTV, the GamEsprit Drei and I'm good to kiss this life goodbye."

"Don't worry about that, you already have. Anyway, I'm going ..."

"Good luck with kindergarten! Don't get messy changing diapers! Hahahaha!"

"*(Fucking piece of capitalist ignorant right-wing arrogant childish self-confident bubbly happy-go-lucky geektard*

nerd ... go ahead and toss your life away with computers, games and your boyfriend Claude. You'll notice one day how hollow and simple your life is.)" I stormed off, trying to hide my furious demeanor. Inside, I harbored but the nastiest of feelings, the dirtiest of emotions for this creature, this product of the times, this stereotype of a generation.

Faye was nowhere to be seen. I panicked. I had never distanced myself from the group in the openness of recess, in the vast human jungle of school since the 3rd Grade, where I used to cruise around aimlessly looking for somewhere to fit in. Without my friends, this world seemed scary, alien and irrational; little kids who had to be at least 13 years old – the minimum to be in this school – yet looked like 5 played and ran and got kicked in the groin by girls. Groups of Kannies spattered the rest of the landscape, sometimes laughing and traumatizing the little kids when running them over while heading to play football in the fields. Entire divisions of fashion victim girls who looked just like the ad I had criticized with Wolfgang studied you with reptilian static eyes, and sat down on the entrance's stairs looking vapid, moody and self-indulgent. The rest I don't remember, but it was a bunch of screaming, of people running around immaturely and posers walking as if they were important.

My attempt had failed. The bell announced the end of the break and I marched defeated toward classroom 206, slyly dodging a sighting of JC Vega and a pack of his cronies. Life seemed to have reached its peak only weeks from then; but at that moment, it seemed to me as if that very same life had jumped willingly from the top in order to commit suicide.

· · · · ·

"What the hell are you doing here?"

"Huh ... I sure didn't expect such a warm welcome, *Tovarish*." I entered Wolfgang's house with an incredible face of disappointment; not only was I angry about my exchange with Gordon, but about my pointless search for Faye in recess and the way she had obviously shrugged me off. Nothing had turned out positively that day. And the sickly matter with Gordon and video games I now saw in Wolfgang's face as well. As a matter of fact, I saw Gordon everywhere. The world carried the rotten and tired cultural swan song of the video game industry, from the shallow United-statian military right-wing shooters to the confusing and ambiguous Japanese role-playing games of virtually infinite length. Wolfgang was seemingly not so glad about my daily visits anymore. I couldn't get a chance to talk to Faye like intended, and instead decided to drop by and not go back home to bite my brains off.

"You never get any visitors; you should place a red carpet under my feet every time I come here, ungrateful bastard," I said, trying to make Wolfgang feel less cocky, a thing he had begun to develop since Axel was his friend, only because of their shared love of video games. He just laughed the thing off, like he did whenever he was wrong and knew it. I did not quite fancy this new attitude.

"Sorry Sonny, it's just that we were about to eat and you suddenly show up ... Anyway, what is it?" he asked.

"Nothing, I just wanted to spend a couple of hours here; the math teacher said I'm doing really bad and is making me go to these stupid school lessons and they start at around 17:00. Really funny indeed, don't you think? I hope I don't bother or anything," I said, comfortably lying down on the couch.

"No, no problem, you can stay if you want to. But we have to eat now, so stay here. Use the computer or something. I

just finished a race and it auto-saved so it's OK to quit."

I sat down in front of the computer and saw he had been playing this stupid-ass game called *"Tuning Point,"* a senseless, reckless driving game about illegal street races with tuned cars and street douches that could be beaten by basically crashing against the walls instead of steering; lame dialogue, braindead storyline, and null substance. That's just to explain what was going through my head when I sat two seconds on Wolfgang's throne. Playing that for three full minutes, I got an incredible sensation of wasting my time and feeling I'd end up like Wolfgang if I did. It was amazing how much I was rejecting video games now, when they used to be the shelter I needed to escape my miserable reality.

So then I had another idea; I quit the game, logged on to ChitChat and in an unavoidable rush, tried to see if Faye was online, but only Ryan could be seen. Those moments shrunk my heart to the size of a nail's edge. Do you have a Ryan in your life? Hope you never do. I don't think anyone, no matter how deviated, deserves such punishment.

Wolfgang returned swiftly, probably wondering what I was doing since he couldn't hear car engine noises and United-statian jock slang. He had brought some Japanese food he ate with two sticks out of a bowl, and had me scratching my head as to whether he did that to appear more Japanese or because he simply liked it. It had to be an inseparable blend of the two. I also didn't understand why he chucked me into the room for family lunch so as to later keep eating in the room anyway. Was that a Japanese custom too?

"So, what's up Sonny? How's Jay?"

"Jay? What are you talking about?"

"C'mon *Doshi*! Everyone knows that already. You're after Ryan's little sister. Jay, isn't it?"

"It's Faye. Not Jay. And yeah, I am, so what?"

"Mmm ... alright."

"Well ... so?"

"So, what?"

"So why did you ask?" Wolfgang adopted this air of mysterious, Japanese melodrama, looked down with a very somber expression and gave me a piercing and intimidating answer, looking at me directly in the eye.

" *'No aru taka wa tsume wo kakusu.'* "

"What's that?"

"It's a proverb that means 'the talented hawk hides its claws.' Do not let the enemy know of your intentions before striking. Hide your weapons until it is required to act." Wolfgang stared at me sternly, with gloomy eyes filled with sorrow. He was obviously envious. I had beaten him in getting that Lyria girl in the summer not so long ago, and the recent female rejections he was experiencing without even asking girls out was making him aware of his situation. I felt rather awkward and ultimately decided to go out. I'd find another way to kill time later on.

"Yeah ... OK ... now listen ... I have to go now and it'll take me a while to get there, so I'll see you tomorrow at school alright?" Wolfgang said nothing. He turned around, probably with his eyes shut, nodded downwards and uttered something unintelligible in Japanese with a tired sigh.

I got out from Wolfgang's house with an anxious sensation, the Hipp-Man being my only companion as I walked down listening to the tune of "*Warnung,*" a happy-go-lucky single by Green Köontz:

> *There's a weird sign in front of me*
> *What's it say? I can't really tell*
> *All I see is don't do this, don't do that*
> *Imma ignore this one and do what feels alright*

WARNUNG, HOCHSPANNUNG!
WARNUNG, HOCHSPANNUNG!
WARNUNG, HOCHSPANNUNG!

I trespass, so far no harm
I go along, trying to hide from sight
Again, that annoying sign!
I climb the fence just 'cause I can

WARNUNG, HOCHSPANNUNG!
WARNUNG, HOCHSPANNUNG!
WARNUNG, HOCHSPANNUNG!

Well, that was not quite smart
Next time I'll make sure to think things twice
I climbed that fence to feel alright
But sometimes a minefield waits on the other side

I found myself in a very good mood; The Pentagon, the area where Wolfgang lived in, was considerably fancier than the core of Paradise Plaza, because of its proximity to the even fancier area of Alexandria Boulevard, arguably one of the most luxurious places Loynne's Island had to offer. Palm trees spread on the landscape like the occasional flocks of birds among the clear sky; the smell of nearby swimming pools, oceanic salt and the overall peace that always surrounded the district was impossible to ignore. This applied only to daytime, at least. During nighttime, The Pentagon morphed and became home to the lowest forms of human scum from all parts of the world, from drugged European tourists to slutty Loynnerins and drunk Kannies. This was most noticeable in the high season of the summer, as during

the rest of the year The Pentagon's nightlife was significantly reduced. It would have been impossible to lead a life in that neighborhood if so.

A sensation of peace and relaxation overcame me as I stepped in the school's perimeter; the scorching sun hidden, the place brimmed with the coolness of the afternoon shade the building cast on the street, the palm trees moving softly with the gentle breeze. I took a deep breath, joyfully enjoying the scenery, and went through the main gates.

I wasn't sure of where to go, though. The entrances to both the West and East Wings were shut when they should have been open, meaning they could be probably locked, and the Main Building entrance looked inaccessible as well. There were only two people seemingly waiting for the classes to start, a guy and a girl, right in the main set of stairs. They greeted me instantly and I presumed they were people from school I had just never seen, maybe new. I approached them thinking I had to stick around them if I didn't want to miss the lesson. The guy instantly talked to me.

"*Hey qué pasó man, ¿quién tú eres?*" Judging by the way in which he had formulated the question and the accent, the guy was noticeably Cuban. I had to be thankful for speaking Spanish fluently, they barely spoke any English nowadays ever since Kannovschina was mysteriously fading and people began to express themselves, even talking in their native languages openly, or going against the dress code. In this case, Cubans seemed closed in themselves as if they were still living in Havana, and rarely spoke to other Latin Americans like Venezuelans or Colombians. Although not dangerous, they were simply disgusting *gusano* dissidents to me, and as such had always avoided them by instinct.

"Hi, I'm here for math lessons. Do you know where I'm supposed to go to?" I said in English. They knew that if you'd

rather speak in English, there was nothing more to add to the conversation. To be honest, I didn't feel like bonding, and even though I could have spoken to him in Spanish I did not want to socialize at all. It was preferable to have him think I couldn't speak Spanish.

"Oh ... OK, man ... yeah, I think we have to go to that part of the school over there, to the East Wing, but the doors are locked man, so I really don't have any idea."

Suddenly, the girl sitting next to him, looked at me with interested, curious eyes. She wasn't very pretty, short, some-what hairy, rat-faced with crooked teeth and unattractive facial features. Looking at her from the face downwards how-ever, wasn't that bad. She was the perfect example of a Noyllerin. It was an expression that had evolved from people needing an expression for the guilty pleasure of fucking an ugly girl gladly as long as the outside world didn't know about it. It fulfilled its role of filling the gap between a Loynnerin – which by itself already means hottie Loynner girl – and a nottie Loynner girl. Just like Loynnerins were nicknamed Lollies, Noyllerins were called "Nollies."

But it wasn't like Nollies were rejects, not at all. Some of the most popular Kannies could have a Noyllerin condition. In fact, Noyllerins could infatuate guys on far greater scale than a perfect, pretty girl. True beauty is said to consist of a very delicate balance between perfection and imperfection. An ugly person inside and out, with its imperfections, gro-tesque nature and personality, could be a sex symbol to a certain audience. Some guys who were into extremely large women found goddesses in crude and chubby Nollies. Others preferred them like this short and rat-like curvy girl. It was not unusual to see a very streetwise and handsome Kanny king dating a girl with an ugly face and a breathtaking body. The fact of having a grotesque feature that balanced and

established contrasts seemed to be far more magnetic sexually than the bulimic absolutely flawless beauty the vapid media often tried to impose as canon.

Thus, most Nollies thought of themselves as very hot and amazing, also because they could date older loser guys rejected by the Loynnerin jet-set that had crappy cars and jobs. Crudely dressed, not up to par with the designer clothes found in the wealthy Loynnerins, obscenely designed tops with crude sexist messages on the chest, tight cheap jeans and huge earrings were their flag and pride.

The rat-like girl spoke directly to me;

"Ye Califowrnian?" she said, with that abysmal thick Loynner accent, which sounded like a mixture between Northern British, Jamaican and Brooklynite Jew. But only the most brutish and low-level Loynners would talk in this horrible way, as the majority – Gordon, for example – seemed to have learned how to speak with more education, almost imitating Unitedstatian accents. By her pronunciation, this girl had to be from somewhere near Mount Tyler, from a town so isolated by hills and forests that education didn't have a chance. I will try to keep demonstrating as best I can the horridness of something which cannot be possibly reproduced, but it will be the only time. In the future I will simply point out the thick accents without directly imitating them.

The girl was still looking at me with those pale blue eyes that for some odd reason I fancied beautiful. I didn't know why she was so interested in me, but I responded negatively when looking at her face put me off again.

"... no, I'm not Californian. Why do you ask?"

"Oh 'cwause you twalk just like diz guy ah know, Wryan, ah think ye friends widdim, ain't ye?" Even though I wasn't in the best of moods for it, I was forced to continue this dreadful

303

social interaction.

"Oh, so you know Ryan?"

"Yeh, he fwriend of me man, you wouldn't 'appen to know me man is, nay?"

"Err, no, I'm sorry ..."

Suddenly, they started talking between themselves, the Cuban guy being recently thrashed because of his ex-girlfriend, who dumped him the week before. Then, he acknowledged me and sunk me into his vortex of pain.

"Hey man look don't you happen to know this girl called Rosie? Jesus Christ man, she broke my heart the fuckin' bitch man. I had dated her for months and then I was logged on ChitChat talking to her and the bitch barely acknowledges me, man! So I say to her "hey what's the big fuckin' deal bitch, you wanna break this all, up no problem, man" and the fuckin' skank says 'OK' all cold like, man! Can you fuckin' believe her? She's a bitch dude, she broke my heart. So then I go away and I never heard from her again. Listen to me chico, girls break your heart and they steal away your soul, so never trust 'em man, not any of 'em ..."

"Oh shuddup the'are, you feckin' ep the kid's mind!" the girl said, laughing as if I were a slow and mentally challenged little child bound to get traumatized. She redirected her attention toward me one more time, looking at me with seductive eyes.

"Heow 'bout ye tull bwuoy? Ever fall'n 'n luv?"

"I—no, don't think so," I lied, stalling my reply.

"Nev'ah in ye loif? Noat evan wonce'?"

"Er ... we've all fallen in love once in our lives, I think ..."

"Woodn't that be Alana?" the girl suddenly interrupted.

"Er ... no. I don't know any Alanas."

"Alana, this gal fwriends with Wryan, meh-be that's the wone yer twalkin' 'bout luv, ah know eh, she a very good gal

she is ..."

"Oh well no, I definitely don't know her and—"

Suddenly, an Asian looking guy came in and joined us, looking seriously geeky and absorbed by video games beyond the point of no return. However, appearances can be really deceitful. The guy lit up a smoke and started talking about a one night stand he had had the day before, and how a stripper had given him an extra-official "service" in a Cristobal Atoll titty bar. Those people were disgusting me and I just wanted to leave. They were hedonistic trash from Loynne's, the kind that only think about the womb of vice that envelops this island.

"I'm gonna explore here on my own for a sec," I said. "I think I might be late for the classes. See you all around."

"Bah-baye!" the girl said. "Tek c'are ye tull bwuoy!"

Braindead Loynner scum. I was fortunate enough to find a reasonable escape cue. Now, the only thing left to do was finding a way into the classroom or face looking seriously stupid. With the entrances to both wings shut, I tried sneaking into the Main Building, glad to hear the door clicking and granting me access. Everything was eerily dark and deserted inside the lobby. I headed to the second floor via the staircase, trying to see if I could maybe infiltrate the West Wing from above, but proved pointless when I witnessed by myself the double doors were as shut as the ones in the first floor. I thought about what else I could do. Maybe I wasn't even supposed to go to the West Wing. What if I had to go to the East Wing, or maybe the third floor?

I looked at the three scumbags below me from the balcony and settled on keeping a watchful eye on them until they decided to move. Fortunately, they spoke so loudly that I could hear everything they were talking about. If they said anything regarding where the classes were held I would know

immediately.

For once, it seemed as if luck was on my side; a car had parked at the school entrance and an adult man with a brief-case-like folder approached the students. I had to rush to the first floor before I lost them from sight.

However, my luck had betrayed me once more. It turned out he wasn't a teacher, but a student, the Cuban guy began asking him if he had done his homework, and after conversing for a while the man responded with a horrible Loynner accent worse than the Nollie's that "studying 4th Grade of SCE at night school was a tough decision, but my wife is learning to appreciate it."

That was it; they were adults attending night school, that's why they seemed so strange. I had completely forgotten that during the afternoons some days of the week the building functioned as a night school for people who had abandoned their SCE studies. Furiously, I pondered whether I had come to this dreadful afternoon lesson for nothing. I thought that I could seize the opportunity to explore on my own either way and at least enjoy the rare silence of a place I had always associated with absolute unpleasantness. It could be a fun way to break the routine instead of going immediately back home.

I decided to check the basement, descending via the Main Building staircase. Finding myself near the computer class-rooms, the place was completely desolate and sunk in dark-ness, only illuminated by the faint light coming through the windows. I was still curious about whether the West Wing was accessible, and a smile drew across my face when seeing the doors to the connecting passageway completely open, exhibiting the darkest bowels of the basement.

This was such a nice break from the usual school routine that my mood improved just by seeing the deserted corridors,

which were deprived the usual hysterical little kids running around like idiots, a reign of absolute silence ruling upon the entire academic institution. I went in with carefully measured steps all the way to the staircase, fully enjoying the mysterious afternoon peace.

It was something that unfortunately didn't last very long, as when I got to the first floor I could hear screeching voices coming from room 102. *"This is what I get for being curious,"* I thought, not really expecting the school to be populated after so much silence. In fact, I was already planning on visiting the canteen to see if I could make the trip worthwhile by delighting myself with a couple of hot chicken croissants with cold mayonnaise spewing from the sides. Why wasn't I able to hear all this ruckus from the outside? And why would they seal all entrances and have people go through the basement?

Dreading having to think that what awaited me was a classroom full of loud Loynner kids from SCE, I damned my sense of duty for not ordering me to retreat and pretend the school was as empty as I first thought it to be. But what was the alternative? Biting my brains off again at home, thinking about Faye? I chose to give this a chance, and if the atmosphere was too much for me to handle I'd just walk out without answering to anyone. I was already on a terrible mood, and in case anyone decided to bother me I was planning on firing first and asking questions later. The first floor was the turf of JC Vega and his braindead cronies for this year, and in case I bumped into him I would not be Kannied into submission, no matter what the consequences were.

I approached classroom 102 and took a quick glance seeing the door was open at an angle, wishing I hadn't; my heartbeat accelerated so quickly I felt the blood rushing painfully through my neck. Staying right where I was and feeling

shortness of breath, I saw her with her howling-white legs crossed, writing something on a notebook, looking bored and annoyed as always, the little kids in her class probably getting on her nerves.

I looked at her, but she did not look at me. I kept on mechanically walking shocked by the surprise, trying to find an explanation as to how could I completely forget that she attended these afternoon tutorials. It had never occurred to me that this would be the perfect scenario to establish a conversation with her, well away from all the ruckus of the morning classes, and especially, her dreadful siblings.

In any case, if Faye was in that classroom it could have only meant it was a 3rd Grade supporting lesson, and judging by the screaming, there was no doubt about it. I decided to check the other classrooms, fearing them to be all SCE lessons. If access was so restricted it meant that not all classes were active, so worst case scenario I would have to just search the entire West Wing instead of the entire school.

In front of the room Faye was in lay room 101, which was JC Vega's. I hoped more than anything in the world excluding Faye herself that he was not in there. I wouldn't have been able to take it. I found myself with all the emotional and physical strength to murder him in front of everybody else without remorse if he pushed me, which he surely would. But no activity emanated from the classroom, so I decided to go further down the corridor. As I came near room 106, I saw light coming from below the door and heard voices, not the yelling of children, but voices speaking coherently at a reasonable volume. It had to be this one. The rest of the rooms on that floor were deserted, lights out and doors locked, and it didn't seem as if any of the upper floors had any activity.

I entered the classroom and instantly noticed that it was largely unpopulated, containing six people sitting quietly and

pretty far from each other. I recognized some of them that I knew only by sight, all Baccalaureate students. With renewed confidence and glad at the prospect of not having to bear an afternoon of little kids yelling, I walked right to the teacher to get acquainted. He appeared to be someplace from up-North, as he didn't have the distinguishable Southern Loynner accent, but a more proper one, with more refined manners.

"I don't know where I'm supposed to start, sir," I said humbly. "I'm new."

"What's giving you the most trouble so far, kid?" he said, with that tone of youthful superiority and disregard so typical from Nova Atlantica.

"Well, pretty much everything, actually ... We're working with trigonometry at the moment and resolution of triangles, that kind of thing."

"OK, then, take a sit right over there, show me some of the problems you're doing in class and I'll be with you in a sec after I'm done with the others."

"Alright."

I sat at the left side of the classroom on the front row, right where the first window was. I loved sitting by the window in any classroom as it gave me a relaxing feeling when on edge. I took a quick glance and saw that everything outside was unusually calm, a very different feeling compared to that of the morning, the afternoon sun subtly illuminating the structure of the sports center under construction in front of the school, a cool shade enveloping the whole area and the empty street, the gentle breeze swinging the palm trees back and forth with the greatest delicacy.

My thoughts went back to Faye, who was next door partaking in the same time-wasting process I was. How could I possibly concentrate on what I was doing having her just a few meters away? All sorts of thoughts and fantasies began

intruding in my mind. Would I get a chance to see her if I finished quickly? Would something interesting arise from our conversation? I needed to get over the class fast so I could get out before she did and that way, walk her home. It was of utmost importance that I did, because I certainly would never get a unique opportunity to ask her out in such a relaxing and calm setting; after all, the setting was everything for this kind of thing, and the atmosphere of Pilgrim Coast's evening was enough to make anybody feel at ease. During that time of the year night arrived pretty quickly, sometimes at 18:00. Faye probably had arrived shortly before me, and would leave in about an hour or two, the usual length for these support lessons. I would keep watch from the window and then give chase as soon as I had spotted her, depriving her of any excuses to escape from me. She'd be cornered, forced to hear what I wanted to tell her.

· · · · ·

I needn't look out of the window every five seconds to spot Faye. Out of the corner of my eye, I could perfectly monitor everything that was going on outside. The few figures that had walked by the school's perimeter were mostly old British tourists and they were easily identified, sporting square-patterned shirts, vanilla cargo shorts, white socks up to the knees and sandals, holding enormous maps as they walked with the fat, old and bloated hags they had for wives. A depressing thought always haunted me when seeing this scenario of decay; if that was the future that awaited us all, I wished to die before hitting 40 years of age.

I spent most of the time daydreaming about Faye, so it was no wonder I had finished the dreaded exercises without even realizing. Most of them were either wrong or half com-

pleted. My head was about to explode and my eyes were tired and sore. I only wanted to escape from the boredom of that place; after two long hours of solving mathematical problems you can't help but want to crack your head open with a sledgehammer. This was infinitely better than being in stuck with shitheads in the morning or biting my brains at home, but wherever I went it seemed I could not get rid of the phantom of Faye; encounters with her were beginning to become less of a rarity, and sometimes my active imagination pondered the remote possibility that it was actually Faye the one following me around slyly wherever I went.

I looked at the window, leaving the pencil on the table and pushing myself back against the chair, rocking it back and forth. Lots of people started to come out of the main gates, probably the students from room 102. Just when I was starting to wonder whether Faye could be among them, I distinguished her distinctive figure among a cheery mass of immature 15-year-olds. It was time. I could definitely catch up to her pace, which was slow but progressive, and my eyes followed her until she disappeared out of the window's range.

"Sir, I'm leaving, I need to do things at home."

"OK kid, see you tomorrow afternoon."

"Good luck with that," I thought. I didn't care whether these lessons meant thousands of opportunities to meet up with Faye. It just wasn't worth it. I just couldn't go to Wolfgang's everyday to kill time and was not willing to spend my time and money on a bus going back and forth between Montenade and Pilgrim Coast. And I would definitely not walk around the city like a bum for hours waiting for the lessons to start. Also, judging from what I had seen, Faye would surely always be surrounded by her classmates after classes, destroying all possibilities of conversation with her. Simply put, I had to take my chances with my original strategy, working

this out in the morning classes.

I got out through the basement gates, as the first floor gates were still shut for some retarded Loynner reason. The sun had hidden and nighttime covered the curious city, now seemingly more alive than in the afternoon. A midly Kanny-looking girl got out at the same time I did and walked up to a guy on an expensive Yamazaki Samurai racing bike, surely her Kanny sugar daddy boyfriend. The girl herself was the kind I had so desired before discovering Faith; sufficiently thin, pale, dark haired and wearing a mini-skirt and high heels that displayed her exquisite white feet These girls were nothing but whores anyway, and I couldn't care less now that Faith had wrapped me up so tightly, but a man can't help but at least look out of curiosity. Even so, I have to admit that by no means you look at another woman in the same way after you've known true love. At that very moment I thought about my encounter with Viktoria von Östinsel, and felt immune once more knowing this kind of woman would never exercise control over me. Only fools like Wolfgang would have wasted their time desiring and wanting these unreachable worth-for-nothing vapid nymphs.

I walked listening to "*Warnung*" again, still horribly searching for Faye and fearing we would not meet; not by coincidence, not by luck. She had completely disappeared, and not that much time had passed by. I even thought about going to the bus station and keep an eye on the lookout for her in case she was in the area, but what for? She would not show up by magic and even if she did, I was quite sure talking to me would not have been one of her top priorities. No, I'd better concentrate on myself, do things for my own good and take the bus in the regular bus stop, I thought. But, why? Why did I have to? Suddenly I felt a great deal of pressure inside my head, and made a decision which by then was

weird in me; I decided to go to the heavy metal store we had seen with Ryan and Jenna that one day. I could maybe see her along the way and even get this thing out of my head; buying some clothes to fit in that little world of hers, sporting the colors of her flag so that she would see me as something close and friendly she could relate to. Sheer psychology.

I marched immediately to Pilgrim Coast Church & Square, the place surrounded by bars, restaurants, banks and liquor stores I had visited with Ryan and Jenna. The entire place was infested with popular brands like Dominique Bouche, Bassa Donna and Detènte, which competed with each other for the money of wealthy tourists. A very expensive Vulgarowski jewelry store was right on the corner of the square, very near to where the Spin 'n Punk shop stood on the corner of the opposite block.

As I marched through the busy Monroe Street, I found myself looking at the population of Loynne's Island; a group of African people, dressed in colorful robes and archetypical things from their culture strolled across the street I was staring at, talking in a high pitched voice like they always used to, seeming happy and interested in what the other had to say, their white, bright teeth and eyes distinguishing them from the rest. A group of British tourists also walked carelessly through the street, almost all of them fat and above their forties, bear-chested, wearing aviator sunglasses and cowboy hats for some reason, showing proudly their suntanned skin and saggy tattoos. A couple of very beautiful girls, with their Bassa Donna belts, night slutty outfits and other corporate capitalist brand new possessions talked cheerfully carrying several shopping bags to a luxurious SUV, none other than the latest GDW König, an opulent and massive vehicle marketed to executives and businessmen. These girls were surely the wives or mistresses of said types on a little shopping

spree, as we lived in an age where the only purpose of women was to use their sex appeal in order to bag someone rich and important. In front of them, just up front, a group of Colombians with cowboy hats and brown leather boots parked an enormous six-wheeled Forge Patriotic Duty truck with imposing spotlights on the roof and front fender, and loudly proceeded to get off it as cocky as they could so as to impress Loynnerins, whistling and usually yelling an occasional "*¡vente pa'cá, morena!*"

Watching out for Colombians in Loynne's was like a sixth sense. Flamboyant and transparent, their drug cartels didn't precisely hide from Loynner authorities, not even the SKAR. Many operations directed by the SKAR brought down most of these thugs down, but never the central structure. No one could trace the links up to the core since the Cartel itself was a consensual agreement amongst various ghost enterprises and organizations that had missing links almost everywhere. Due to this, the Cartel remained unchallenged as the natural criminal ruler of Loynne's Island, superior to any other Russian, Italian or Chinese criminal society.

The cocky Colombians were sure to belong to the Cartel, seeing that now a fancy Montana Tusk and a Chevraun Suburbia, one of their most beloved vehicles, placed themselves alongside the titanic Patriotic Duty, meaning they were out for business and surely would attend some meeting in the Méndez Center, a place filled with bars and seemingly innocent places where you would pass unnoticed and no one would ever ask awkward questions. Colombians managed more than half of the cocaine trade in Loynne's, and had made sure no other organization could enter the island's criminal circle on its free will. The evolution of the old *thieves-in-law,* the next generation of Russian oligarchs and entrepreneurs, had been buying property in Loynne's,

something authorities had been warned about and had come up with a story involving a soon-to-be turf war between Colombians and Russians. The news loved to spread such rumors. Keeping the population scared with tales of ruthless murdering gangsters was a nice tactic to stop people from joining these criminal worlds, but the propaganda machine ultimately ended up contributing to the fame and lifestyle of the most well-known criminals. However, the Cartel and the damage it did to society with drug trafficking was very much real. In Loynne's, the cocaine bridge to Europe and the US, where the population was always kept under tight control by the SKAR, the drug damage wasn't as heavy as it was in European countries, as their laws clearly paled in comparison. It was no wonder Europe and the US were in the state they were. In Loynne's, drugs were used specifically for recreation out of sheer boredom, and not to escape harsh realities.

Unitedstatian trucks were a bad omen if driven by Latin American types. Forge, Chevraun, Madison, Christler, Washington and Montana were the only vehicle brands they drove, in colors that ranged from olive green to light desert brown, sometimes even in military camo patterns just to show off and laugh at authorities. Average members had luxury cruisers, huge six-wheeled SUVs like the Montana Tusk, the Washington Escalator or the Forge Patriotic Duty. These were used to transport the drugs from the docks, and many said the SKAR overlooked the majority of the shipments, only detaining and prosecuting a small number of patsies to appear active in the drug war.

However, Colombians weren't what you would call smart in business management; they spent almost all of their income in luxurious vehicles and the latest in suits and fashion, their top members having titanic mansions with white Washington Townscape limousines and filled with sports cars such

as the legendary Sforza Contessa and the infamous Sforza Cavaliere, always in white, yellow or red, cheesy and striking colors. As such, it was normal to see in local news incredible mansions seized and all their assets auctioned off, bought by the other, more powerful overlords of Loynne's, usually the Russian oligarchs they hated so much.

I stopped thinking about the criminal underbelly when I took a moment to admire the diversity of the island. In contrast to The Motherland, where I would have never got to see a group of loud black people next to fat British tourists and drug cartel Colombians, it gave me the impression that this was the only place in the world where nobody cared anymore for their own country, preferring to travel, see new places, and live beside other races and religions instead of discriminating them – which there were some who did at times – but you would mostly see them interacting, some races keeping to themselves, and others being very social. The Loynners didn't mind since tourism meant more money in their fat wallets, but having foreigners move forever to Loynne's just didn't quite sit with them. Loynners were lazy by nature, and preferred cheap foreign labor doing the unfortunate jobs while they occupied the best civil servant and office cubicle jobs. Loynners never did low-end jobs unless they were young and needed the money, or were eccentrically greedy, taking into consideration that being greedy in Loynne's wasn't very much useful. Even if you saved money, you weren't going to keep it stored for a long time before you needed to withdraw it, and any vice, property or possession could be bought in comfy, easy as pie payments everyone could afford.

I finally arrived at the Church & Square, which was covered in the usual Christmas paraphernalia. Loynners usually started decorating in November, loving the anticipation of

these holidays. Also, lots of people wandered around in packs carrying shopping bags and conversing happily with each other. These supposed Western Christian celebrations, which appeared to be based on hyper-excessive consumerism, were of no concern to me, but they seemed uplifting enough. I had my goals clear, and I was going to see whether something in that shop would get me closer to Faye before my intentions were made apparent. I already dressed alternatively enough, something that would surely mix with her modern rock likings, but enhancing my overall look into something she'd find more palatable would not harm my cover.

The Spin 'n Punk shop at night seemed cozy and inviting, a refuge compared to the chaos of people going on outside. It was as if those shops were there only for me to visit. The deserted marble corridor guided me to the shirts exhibited outside, and I recognized instantly the Green Köontz ones I had "reserved" during my last visit. The shop assistant, a heavily tattooed blonde girl clad in punk garments, complimented me on my choice as I decided to buy two shirts and a studded belt Ryan told me I needed, just like his. I also got the Hammer & Sickle metallic box. I had no idea what it was for but I felt it was my duty to take it out of that ultra-liberal, foul and ideology-lacking store.

I went outside wearing the stuff I had bought to see if I was comfortable with it. Strangely, I hadn't felt good in such a long time with clothes. I felt I was now a part of something, part of a social group. I was rejecting Kanny subculture while at the same time sympathizing with Faye's world. At the time, I felt it was the beginning of something great.

I considered heading toward the Pilgrim Coast bus station, which was nearer than the school one, but instead marched to the school stop as I felt uneasy in the station. Many strange people roamed at night and I hated the barely lit atmosphere

of the place. Getting there using the same route Ryan used to take to go to school, Pilgrim Coast's night began to mature progressively into its evening charm. The school bus stop at night was always deserted, especially in a week day. I felt incredibly relieved when this was the case, and I enjoyed sitting on the solitary bench that on daytime would always be occupied by Kannies waiting to go to Asiz Valley and Arias Town, talking loudly and laughing at whoever had the unfortunate chance to be noticed by them.

The Purple Wonder appeared after 10 minutes. This was another uplifting scenario; the titanic Forge Monsoon was completely empty. It would get full later on after picking people up at Pilgrim Coast bus station, but the sight of an empty bus was always a good one. I seized the opportunity and sat at the back of the bus where Kannies would always sit to yell insults at the driver. It was exhilarating to occupy such a privileged place even if it was for 15 minutes.

Taking my mind off from the events that had transpired on the course of the day, I needed distraction and my attention was now set on the people crossing right in front of the bus. The uplifting effects that had cheered me up soon dissipated when I remembered how tired I was, mentally and physically, beginning to feel the exhaustion of this Faye situation. She was always on my thoughts in a subtle and unconscious form. I sensed I needed to distract myself even more, and the population of Loynne's was the only attraction I could afford at the moment. My eyes decided to look at the huge windshield when the bus stopped at a red light to let people pass, right on the corner of the Community Center, very near The Crucible.

Unlike the window next to me, where reflection of the bus' lights basically forbid you to look outside and acted as a mirror, the windshield allowed an extremely clear view. Among

those people walking by, my eyes found themselves scrutinizing a tiny, compact and minute figure walking rushed, wearing a striped black and blue shirt and a tight jean miniskirt.

She strolled with a face so frowned, frustrated and bitter she could have intimidated the cocky Colombians on the Patriotic Duty. I remember myself leaning against the window, watching her walk from right to left, until the bus continued to move and I lost her from sight. Where could she be going? I should have gone to that bus stop instead to the one near the Méndez Center, that way I would have met with her and at least talked without distractions. With the face she had at the moment, however, I think I did the right thing.I was left there thoughtful in the purple bus, thinking about how ironical it would have seemed to look at the destroyed expression on my face above the "Paradise Itself" caption on the bus' ad.

"*Where could she be going?*" a voice constantly repeated inside my head. She was gorgeous. Her white skin seemed to glow in the night, and her striped black and blue shirt was like a warning sign designed to let me know the dangers I was bound to come across. I wanted her so much. No one would ever stop my frantic desire to become a reality. She was already mine. The simple fact of desiring her in such a way tagged her as my own and gave me full rights over anyone else.

Faye disappeared among the crowd of colorful robes and fat naked torsos. I felt a strong sense of irony mixed with relief, as she'd never know how I desperately ran leaving aside every worldly care just to maybe catch a glimpse of her, which even though I eventually did, left me feeling emptier than before. My mind began to reminisce about where this obsession was going and if it'd end anytime soon. As the bus ventured further into the darkness of the barren freeways, my

shattered reflection greeted me on the window pane. I closed my eyes and turned the Hipp-Man off, officially tired of Green Köontz for the day.

· · · · ·

I found myself in my room, as usual, looking at my decorated walls. A photo of the Berlin Wall sparked my interest as my sight swept for all the GDR images I had.

I always pondered about the concept behind the construction of the wall. Nowadays, it's enough to make most Westerners cringe with fear and disgust. Who would do that to their own people, separate the ever expanding barriers that divide our Earthly territories? Our common capitalist, savage human ideology? The truth is, the wall was needed. The barrier between East and West stopped being imaginary that day of 1961, on the 13th of August, when construction for it began. The Cold War needed a symbol to let humans know what they were heading toward, to help them understand the circumstances civilization was facing; the alternative to that perpetual, immortal, vicious cycle, that oppressive system that widens the gap between rich and poor wherever it's installed. We have walls separating our houses from the ones of our neighbors, but that's perfectly understandable. A wall dividing completely different countries, ideologies and customs is considered inhumane. It's but a physical representation of the social circumstances; a way of saying we weren't like them, and they weren't like us.

For those interested in the technical aspects of the wall, it measured 155 kilometers in length, containing a death strip with no visibility or cover, 300 watchtowers and 20 bunkers. 50,000 armed guards with trained attack dogs, anti-personal mines, a division of Mil Mi-24 attack helicopters and anti-

climbing measures to ensure nobody would escape or trespass.

But now I found myself in the shoes of the dreaded GDR defectors, the hated traitors that had undermined Communism's possibilities of survival in such a strategic and important ideological battlefield. For the first time, I despised my feelings for Faye.

I imagined myself pressed against such a monstrous wall, begging for freedom, while at the same time crawling back home fearing what I could find outside. Many have described Communism as a "nanny" system that treats its people as children, as kids not allowed to go outside and "grow up" as proper capitalist pigs. It's even been described as a system for the lazy and the coward. The truth is, there's no such thing. We, as humans, learn the hard way every day of our lives. In society, with its unwritten social norms and psychological warfare, at school, where we learn what will make us complete human beings in the future, and in the privacy of our minds, where we learn to separate the garbage from what we deem worthy. That was exactly what my naïve heart was discovering; it knew what it needed, but the wall that had been built ever so slowly was establishing itself, consolidating its position and grip. Faye and I were separated by unknown barriers and emotions that couldn't be matched for the moment, by feelings that would go on unanswered indefinitely. At the sheer thought of this, my love for her soared above the sound of beastly rotor blades, of deafening assault rifle fire, of the barks of fierce attack dogs. What would I do if I were just one man oppressed by external forces? What were the odds of succeeding against kilometers of impregnable concrete and land mines?

For Faye, I wouldn't think twice; I would throw myself at the spikes and dogs and death strips, burning with the pas-

sion of my loved one, chanting individual choice as my anthem. Ahead of me, the promise of a better tomorrow, a clear sun rising from the dead of night, materializing out of my own feelings and decisions. I wouldn't doubt; I would face death or success, one or the other, inseparable, knowing inside that the suffering would be worth the effort once I was at the other side, which I would be; after all, someone like Faye was worth the most extreme hardships and risks in the world ... anything valuable was.

A symbolic, invisible and massive wall had been built between us making any type of approach impossible, and for the first time in my life I wondered what I truly felt regarding the Berlin Wall. A painful electric sensation, as if I had just been shocked with a stun gun, traversed through my abdomen when pondering if depending on a context such as that I would have been one of those disgusting rats crossing over to the other side, abandoning ship. If the situation forced me to choose between my ideology and my loved one, which one would I settle for?

Leaving the mattered unattended, I went to sleep trying to leave my mind completely blank, hoping the question would answer itself in the coming days.

- CHAPTER V -

Iron Curtain

"Sometimes when you stand face to face with someone, you cannot see his face."

- MIKHAIL GORBACHEV -

Soviet Politician, General Secretary of the Communist Party of the Soviet Union and Last Soviet Head of State

---

"In international news, gun hysteria continues to terrorize the US as a mass-shooting in an elementary school resulted in the deaths of 51 children and 12 adults. Although the perpetrator committed suicide, another murder occurred minutes before when armed ROA vigilantes sent to guard the school by the state fatally shot an armed boy who was escaping from the massacre, confusing him for the perpetrator. The father of the deceased boy spoke on his behalf, saying he had given his son a firearm to defend himself in case a shooting like this ever occurred. The nation mourns their dead as ROA spokesmen refuse to give any official comments. ROA supporters claim despite these unfortunate setbacks it's still necessary to use firearms to keep the country safe, especially when considering the uncertainty of potential foreign threats.

In technology news, GlasShack, the hyped newest iteration of online social interaction, has officially been released to the public today registering an impressive 35 million users in only 5 hours. After the gradual decline of social

media and its eventual disappearance with the rise of the intranets last decade, online social interaction is proving to be back and strengthened, as GlasShack demonstrates that open forms of socializing which transcend the intranets will make a comeback. GlasShack's CEO and founder, Teivel Zusman, commonly known as "The Zeev," has worked exten-sively for the intranets of the world to accept it, and negotia-tions have been largely successful in Western countries, as opposed to the governments of most Asian and Latin Ameri-can countries which have largely rejected petitions for the website to be integrated into their systems, fearing United-statian espionage.

Analysts already predict various shortcomings and dis-advantages, namely the frightening return of cyber-security and hacking issues, as well as the lack of privacy inherent to social media. Talks about Muslim radicals using these social websites to perpetuate Jihad are also beginning to be taken seriously by certain governments. However, millions online are already leaving behind the reclusive social past of the intranets in order to embrace a more global and homogene-ous platform. Only time will tell if this experiment triumphs or fails. So far, everything points out to a revival of the transparent sharing culture of last decade."

It had been social networking in the first place what caused this geopolitical scenario of fear. Anyone with an agenda gathered beneath the anonymous curtains of social networking to provoke terrorist acts of all kinds, shielded by the unregulated nature of the old and chaotic World Wide Web. Before the rise of national intranets, the US and its NATO puppets in Europe lived in constant fear due to the uncertainty of terrorist attacks, be it in the form of physical terror or cyber-terror. It took a while for them to notice the

harm social networking could do to them, and finally cooperative measures between all countries began taking effect. Entire social networking Internet based companies collapsed because of this, their parasitic existence of making a living leeching off the private lives of individuals no longer being a legal business. Surprisingly, millions of people around the world felt fortunate at this; no longer tied to the shackles of this cyber social-nightmare, people returned to a type of life more akin to that of the 20th century, a life more oriented toward face-to-face social interaction. Social networking sites and software still existed under the new world of the intranets, although it was government regulated and you could almost make sure that anything you said was being monitored by a government agency. Everywhere except for Loynne's, that is, or at least that was the official stance. Yet, it seemed that now the world would return to social netslacking once more. Under the guidance of this Teivel Zusman Ivy League elitist Unitedstatian prick, the peoples would bring back the globalized stupidity of the old Internet to our isolated intranets. Certainly, the world seemed to be taking two steps back for each forward.

I took a break from watching TV momentarily to gaze at the outside world through the kitchen's window. November raged on. The heat was stabilizing day after day, achieving a nice 20 °C instead of the usual Loynner 29 °C. Cloudy days would appear from time to time, and even the occasional "storm" with raindrops that would evaporate before reaching the ground, lasting an overall 20 minutes before the sky was crystal-clear again.

The days were passing by so fast they escaped my notice. I wasn't doing too well at school, failing all the exams we had had because I wasn't even studying, blaming it all on Bacca-

laureate being too different and unbalanced compared to the SCE. But I could not care no matter how much my sense of responsibility warned me. I was fully enjoying my state of obliviousness, sheltering in my newfound friendships at school. In fact, I forgot so much about things with all the events that had transpired that I even forgot to write back to my parents, getting quite angry responses. When checking my mailbox I was surprised to find two letters, trying to comprehend why on Earth I had completely forgotten to write or check the mailbox. Deep inside, I knew very well the reason why, even though I didn't want to face it.

"Dear ********,

Is everything alright? For some time now your letters have been distant, cold. Is anything wrong? Have you gotten into trouble of some sort?

I hope not for your sake. Remember how important your mission is. We depend on you, ********. We as a family depend on you being alright and taking care of yourself, I can't stress that enough. If anything happened to you, I would never forgive myself.

Sorry, but I have to tell you these things. I don't want to nag but I don't have any other choice. I feel impotent, watching helplessly as you grow without me and I'm stuck here with your father. Sometimes I get scared of what this is causing him. He's not cut out for this sort of rural life and doesn't get on well with the ignorance of the farmers. A man of science doesn't belong here with the peasantry. And your dad has never been much of a worker. Today he locked himself in the small shack we live in outside of the farm because he had a headache and didn't want to be disturbed. I lied to the peasants and told them he was ill. It's getting out of

control, and I don't know if we should go back to the city now that things have calmed down. But we're too afraid; what if they persecute us, what if they find out about our ruse, about you being in Loynne's? We can't afford that, so maybe it's better to lie low for now. Your father can't take much more of this and sincerely neither can I. I'll wait a few months more maybe and then we'll move to the city. Your dad can go looking for work, he will probably get a good one with his engineering degree. Then I'll follow ahead when he rents a good place. Tell me if you think it's a good plan, maybe now you know more of this capitalist things than we do.

Love you,

Mom and Dad."

And here I was, giving myself the luxury and liberty to ignore them as they endured countless hardships for my well-being. Afraid of opening the second envelope thinking it would unleash a curse upon me, I felt the horrible guilt of momentarily forgetting my original endeavor, deluded by this confusing island and my unimportant adolescent urges:

"Dear ********,

You haven't responded as of yet! What are you doing? You want to give your parents a heart-attack?

Your father and I are very worried, please respond soon! We are already thinking the unthinkable and want to rest assured that you're alright!

You'd better have a good reason for this! We're very upset!

Write soon!

Mom and Dad."

Have a good reason ... I wondered what my mother would have said had she known the status of the situation well. She would have most probably called me foolish and selfish. I wrote my reply and immediately dropped the letter off at the post office, feeling as if I had disappointed myself more than I had disappointed them.

• • • • •

At school, my fragile social equilibrium would experience an important shift; Billy and Robbie were moving away to Nova Atlantica City, the capital of the island and its largest, most populated city. I had learned to hate the place just by smelling its foul urban atmosphere, and I had only been there a couple of times. In any case, it seemed that their dad had come up with a business plan there and would settle down for good.

"Hey Sonny boy, how ya' holdin' up?" Billy greeted me, with a rusty and nasal voice like usual. It was one of those days when we had a free hour due to an absent teacher, and were just chilling out in the cool shade on the West Wing's parking lot ramp.

"Oh not up to much Billy, surviving ..."

"Well guess what, ya' fuckin' survivalist, I'm movin' to Nova Atlantica next week." I was really surprised to hear that actually. I would have never expected them to move, especially now that we were becoming friends.

"Hey! Why? When did you plan all of this?"

"Well Sonny, Pops arranged for some business opportuni-

ty there on some priiiime land, seems it's all legit. He wants to sorta move away from this town, it depresses 'im I reckon."

"But Nova Atlantica is a disgusting place to live in. I've been there, and I—"

"I've been there more times than you boy, I know how it is. I've learned to like it somehow. It's got its charm, you know, and there's plenty more things to do; like, gun shops, airsoft contests, paintball, you know ..."

"So what else is there to do aside from paintball?"

"What you think, boy? Goin' fer the pussy too, but, like I say, you know you never know! Damn city girls like to play it fuckin' straight, and can't fuckin' hide the fact that they really enjoy a good nice poundin' like all the rest of us! We boys givin' 'em ... I mean ... that'd be kinda queer the other way 'round ..."

"Uh, yeah ... Well Billy, but you're leaving us all behind, doesn't it bother you?"

"Course it does you goddamn fuckin' faggot, but well, I kinda wanted to invite you to this sorta goin' away party I'm throwin'. Just you, me, my bro and the guys. It's gonna be at this pizza joint called "Pizzanovante," great place. Oh, and Ryan's brother is coming too. You'll get to finally meet him. You haven't met him yet and he's fed up of listening about you. You know what, the inbred calls ya "Danny." Gotta reckon they haven't gotten your name straight 'round 'ere!"

"Oh yeah, well, whatever. Might be nice and all, a not-so-final goodbye ..."

"Yeah, by the way boy, gimme yer number son, jus' in case sumtin' comes up ..."

"Sure, write it down ... User Prefix 54539, Personal Number 76239. What's yours?"

"Alright, pay attention then, boy ... UP is 79233 and PN is 79257."

"Got it, Billy ... I'll be there," I said, thinking that now, half of my school time would entail being around Ryan and Wolfgang, or probably worse, around my classmates. The only certain thing was that I was staring at a steady decrease in the quality of my social life.

· · · · ·

This going away party involved a medium sized group of people: the Nazarethes, The Mantis brothers, Ettore, Wolfgang, Mike, Axel and me. Billy and Robbie would make a very good job telling me every single secret of all the people there in a few minutes.

While having a few laughs outside the Community Center, we noticed a small figure coming toward us with a steady but shambling way of walking, as if his shoulders moved a lot in comparison to his arms. Wearing a long-sleeved black and white shirt, skater baggy jeans and hip-hop shoes with a chain completing its outfit near an expensive belt, this was Dave Mantis. He came accompanied by two girls, of albino-white skin tone and skinny to the point of anorexia. One of them had big blue protruding eyes and light-brown straight hair, while the other had hazel feline eyes, black curly hair and prominent cheekbones. Dave Mantis had marked his position in front of a group of strangers, a trademark he would always use as a sign of pack leading presence from that moment on, the first I ever saw him.

He was noticeably shorter than Ryan, only slightly taller than Faye, with short dark blond curly hair and blue eyes. His hair was done almost in a Kanny fashion, and he even had a shining diamond earring, which somehow ended up bringing attention to his prominent earlobes. He was well-built despite his unimpressive height, and had the body of an athlete,

in top physical shape. He had enviable forearms, a square jaw, rock-hard abdominals, a pointy arrogant nose and a prominent forhead, a winner's smile with perfect white teeth. He was living proof that some people are born genetically better than others. I was sure that women saw in him what I probably saw in Faye.

Dave dismissed the attractive thin cute girl with a cocky *"see ya later, longboard,"* this meaning "tall thin hot medium-sized boobed girl" in Loynner-skater slang. Amazingly, she even surprised me: with almost perfect white teeth, sparkling blue eyes and a sharp, pointy nose, she kissed Dave thrice one cheek after the other as in the usual Loynner style – in The Motherland we would only use handshakes for girls and boys alike – and with a *"see yaaa Daaaave,"* she left with the other girl giggling, these two probably being best friends or something, and we all watched them stroll away headed for the Church & Square via the Dakota gas station, their miniskirts blowing gently with the nighttime breeze.

"Say, and who on God's faggot name were them broads, ya goddamn queer?" Billy spurted suddenly.

"Oh, ah, my friends, Billy. Angelica and Jenny," he said, as if Billy's question was unnecessary and insulting.

"Let me guess, they hang out with you 'cause they think you're gay, right?"

"Shut up Billy, smell a woman first and bitch all you want later."

"Why you hangin' out with them Loynnerins like that, thought you were the one that followed the anti-Kanny policy the most out of the whole herd, you sellout sonuva bitch," Billy barked.

"They're my friends shithead, can't I have friends? Sheezus, now we got another tower aside from Mike here?" Dave had suddenly noticed me with my arms crossed looking

down at him, not precisely in a nice way. With a slightly concealed tone of disgust hidden between my vocal chords and a
cold transfixed stare, I let out:

"Sonny Zharostin."

"Oh yeh, yeh, Ryan told me about you, kid ..." he said,
without adding much interest. "*OK,*" I thought. "*Nice intro-
duction. Especially for a guy that supposedly was asking so
much about me ...*"

Dave had given me a pretty shitty first impression and I
doubted friendship with him would go onward. I also
couldn't possibly take very seriously – or positively – the fact
that a guy who was roughly 1.60 meters tall had called me
"kid." However, the awkwardness of silence was broken by
Billy's voice:

"Right, fellas, movin' on up, headed southbound and
straight for Pizzanovante! Oh, y'all wait! I forgot the 'stuff' an'
my damn keys again. Sonny! Hey Sonny! Come with me and
ol' Robbie. We goin' back to the apartment fer the keys an'
the shit ..."

"Sure, why not ..."

"Hey, Sonny, wait! Where you going?" Wolfgang cried out.
He couldn't stand being left alone with a group of strangers,
me being his best of friends. But Billy didn't doubt one bit ...

"Wait a second lard butt, we only need one fucker fer this
aside from my brother! Y'all juss wait 'ere till we look for the
keys an' the rest o' the 'stuff?' OK? Good ..."

"Don't worry, Wolfie man! You're with the Axe now! Give
Sonny a break or he'll divorce your ass! Haha, jus' kiddin'
Sonny ... I know what you're really after ..."

· · · · ·

The Crucible; an eleven story building with over a hun-

dred rooms, with marveling views and three swimming pools, surrounded by other luxurious apartment buildings, a community center and a public park ... It was not only one of the most centric and privileged places to live in Pilgrim Coast, but the home to two families that would influence me and my behavior for almost three years; the Mantises and the Nazarethes. There was just one little difference between them. Although they came from the same country, they came from widely different states, California and Texas respectively, and they of course had not shared the same lifestyle. The thing is, they only had each other so as to not be prey for the Kannies, and this had seemed to pay off somewhat nicely. Now it was my turn to become somebody in Loyne's, someone with identity, friends, a normal life, without freaky friends but instead with streetwise sharp friends that knew better how the world worked and didn't spend their days locked in a room playing GamEsprit Drei all day, at least. That streetwise sharpness was instantly confirmed when Billy talked again, this time stealthier, in a manner that was going to become quite familiar with him:

"Sonny, fer starters, the 'stuff' is liquor," he began. "And well, the other stuff is having a lil' chat with you about our friends Ryan and Dave here." I started to smell where this was going; they didn't trust them one bit and they could bet their red necks that I didn't trust anyone neither in this forsaken island.

"Look, them two, them Mantises ... you can't trust 'em for shit, Sonny boy. I don't think you've realized so far, but hey, we know each other for like what, two, three years? We've seen you around Sonny boy, we know what you folk from them countries are like, we know you don't trust 'em kind neither ..."

"What kind are you talking about, Billy? I don't under—"

333

"Shut up mongrel, ain't givin' me 'nuff time to talk 'ere," he interrupted. He continued to stare at me with those cold blue eyes of his, that calculated every expression in your face in such an intricate way you couldn't help but look away, with a nervous laughter product of the sheer awkwardness. I have to admit, Billy Nazareth was the only person in Loynne's who I've ever admired in terms of sheer cunning. Admired and feared.

"Listen," he said, finally breaking the ice, taking a little time to breathe deeply. "We both know how you've been takin' a likin' to Ryan these past days in school. Yeah, the jokin', the fuckin' around with Axel, Wolfgang an' the rest of the guys, yeah ... But let's share a secret Sonny boy ... better said, let's open up to each other ... you know sumtin'? Nobody likes Ryan. Yeah, they do at first, but when people get to know 'im better, they realize what a selfish backstabbin' basterd he is. Look, we might be soundin' like a couple of gossip bitchy folk talkin' about others like this, but listen ... I warn ya boy ... don't become his best friend or nuthin' ... it'll only do you harm. And worst of all, he'll try to isolate you from fuckin' mankind like this Wolfgang fucker has tried to do ... yeah, yeah, hold your horses, I know why you befriended him ..." he interrupted me, just when I opened my mouth to defend Wolfgang. "You befriended Wolfgang 'cause you were alone, had almost no friends and didn't want to fit in with the cool folk. Well, lemme tell ya how things work round 'ere son, 'cause you may have not noticed exactly how yet ... You've got all these queer folk 'round, Wolfgang, Ryan, etcetera, well they're people nobody likes to hang around with, and it shows, since they have both seen ya and fixed ya in their sights as the best goddamned friend ever. I know the Wolfgang story pretty well. You started 4th Grade, you knew some people but exactly didn't quite know anybody well.

Wolfgang approached you and talked to you, a sign you considered a nice, friendly gesture, and then began to talk to him associatin' that he belonged to the same cultural class or social group as yourself; an outcast, somebody with sumtin' special to show, that people don't really understand with lots of undiscovered potential ... Well listen, I myself have, and Robbie here has too, fallen to that 'charm' of being in a new land alone with nuthin' to do, and suddenly meetin' all these folk that seem like yourself 'cause these fuckin' Loynners and Kannies and fuckin' rich folk Mafia basterds who should be shot and don't let you in, don't let you integrate. Well, I'm used to that 'cause we were quite the same back in Texas, we used to be quite racist Robbie, Pop, me and the whole family ... but you come to Loynne's and all that changes ... We're not in the old country anymore; rules 'ere are different, and globalization has changed our fuckin' perception of life and things and shit ... We see yanks strollin' alongside ragheads, gooks, kikes, niggers, wops, ruskis, spics, jews, every single pile of shit, you name it. You name it and it's sure to be found in Loynne's. We've got every fucker in the world piled up in this shitty island, and well, let's just say trailer park white trash rules don't apply here like back home. So, Sonny ... back to the point ... I know that's been affectin' you since the very first day we met, and well, this is the deal. WE are YOUR future. WE are YOUR safe haven here. And if you decide to ride with us instead of them faggot cockbags over there, maybe, and I mean MAYBE, we'll have ourselves a fiiiine deal. I don't know much about Wolfgang, so I'll let you know what I know, alright? Listen up ... Wolfgang, well, I can't really say he's a bad person 'cause I don't know him that much, but he's the worst weirdo piece-a-shit you'll come across here ... Being seen with him is almost instant beat up by any Kanny. I don't know why you still on both yer legs ... Must be 'cause yer a

tall, bulky fella ... but listen ... Ettore, Robbie and I, well, we used to be in class with him, like say two years ago ... damn scumbag couldn't get anythin' straight. Half of the classes he spent 'em drawin' them damn gook swords, tanakas, kanatas, or whatever the fuck them little yellow people call 'em, then he said he was a fuckin' samurai ... SAMURAI! Jesus H. Christ!! What's this world comin' to, dammit. He told everybody his dedication was that of a samurai, and that he knew how to kill people usin' a ... whatever, that sword he used to draw, and he spent half of the time speakin' in these weird Asian metaphors ... like, well I don't know what like, but I'm sure you know if you're his friend ... and well, what nailed it was that he was so pure proper grade-A fuckin' clumsy basterd, fallin' down the stairs, doin' fuckin' bad, and I mean FUCKIN' BAD at PE, everyone just laughed at the poor basterd and instead of keepin' his mouth shut and be a silent weirdo, he interrupted like every five seconds or so to say a stupid Japanese proverb. Do you think that's a nice person to share your time with? It's OK. But I'm warnin' ya ... and for Ryan ... well, there's a whole lot goin' on with Ryan ... We met him years ago, when we just came 'ere ... Everyone used to laugh at him and called him "Pizza Face," damn Kanny fucks, I do remember them days, maybe you don't but I sure do ... I haven't forgotten what they used to call me ... Anyways, we picked Ryan up as if he were a fallen dirty, filthy abandoned puppy, we vouched for him, sorta taught him like how to stand up to people, a thing he didn't quite learn not even until today, and well we sorta provided protection alongside Robbie and Ettore. Then the same with Dave. Ryan however, never returned that nice gesture of ours back, and never thanked, and never bothered to see back the person he was back then, and the one he is now; in fact, he simply laughs at everyone and everythin', disrespects everythin' he sees and

never looks up to anybody, he's got like an inferiority issue. That thing makes him unable to thank, to lower his head, to give in his arm to bend, nuthin' at all! No matter what service you show 'im, what gesture, whatever, he WON'T appreciate it, and if he does, it's for a self-interest. He won't ever be honest to you neither, he'll never ask anythin' unless there's sumtin' in for 'im, and he'll never return a favor just 'cause, but depends on what cut there's in for 'im. You get what I'm sayin' boy? Not only that, but he does stupid things you just want to beat the crap outta him. Like when we went on an excursion to Kalysand Lake. Ryan never bothered to clean, help, wash the goddamn dishes, nothin' at all, and guess what! Motherfucker pisses on the only clean pure water canteen we had to make a goddamn first campin' day prank that made all of us go to the nearest town that was like 20 kilometers away for some water and we locked the fucker in the tent all day and sorta beat 'im up. He's DUMB ... he's USELESS ... and he's SELFISH. There's no talkin' to him, there's no reasonin' with this guy, so don't bother yourself with 'im, Sonny ... don't bother ... clear? Good. Now ... let's go." Billy concluded his speech and without any more words led the way to his apartment on the tenth floor of The Crucible building, room 101. His dad greeted us at the door.

I knew they had to be some kind of Texan racists but the dad couldn't be hippier; a man in his mid-forties with a black beard and baggy eyes, with a sorrowful yet energetic expression was holding bottles of several kinds put together in a white plastic bag.

"Hi kids! Off to an 'epic bottle,' aren't we? We'll listen, here ya go ... rum and vodka for today, I don't want ya'll so tipsy you can't even smash the bottle on a faggot's head ... Jus' keep it outta sight, you know how them cops are ... crackin' the skulls of youngsters like yourselves and shit ...

Anyway, guess you're off for the night ... See ya 'round kids, keep standin' on 'em toes!" he said, shutting the door.

"Well ... I sure didn't expect your dad to be like that, Billy ..."

"Oh yeah ... my dad ... The only racist hippie in all of Houston ... quite a misfit he is alright. Don't fit in with Houston folk, don't fit in with hippie folk ... hates everything and everyone ... and is the happiest man on Earth. I wish I could somehow be like him one day, though ... And what about you? You wanna be like yer dad one day, Sonny boy?"

"Well, to be completely honest, Billy, I don't think that's quite of your concern. I don't want to seem harsh, but I can't talk to you about that." At this point, Billy simply smiled and said in his mysterious whisper:

"Some things aren't supposed to be known by yer friends, Sonny boy ... and if you let me, I think a loose tongue's like a noose 'round yer neck. Nobody should cut it off except for you. That's sumtin' you should do by yer own hand. Friendship is not knowin' where you come from, what you done; friendship's gettin' along with the person and knowin' their habits. It's like fishin' or huntin' ... knowin' what you gotta do to go after your prey, and you'll get it if you know it well. And to me, Sonny boy, you're no deer or fish ... you happen to have a mind of yer own, and that's about the most valuable possession you can have nowadays."

"Er ... thanks a lot Billy ... really." Billy and Robbie had a very radical and different concept of friendship than most people. That was pretty clear.

· · · · ·

We returned to where the guys were waiting, and Billy immediately signaled at a tall new figure obscured by the

shadows.

"That over there's Mario, Mario Baglionni," Billy said. "We'll introduce you now."

We advanced toward the group, everyone being entertained by this Mario telling a story. It didn't take me two seconds to notice he was another Axel.

"Hey, how ya doin' Billy The Kid! Hey yous guys find another pal on the way back or what?" Unnecessary as it may be, I must remark that Mario had the most distinctive Italian accent I had ever heard in my entire life. A guido in every sense, Mario sported a very modern hairstyle used often in the Loynne's island clubbing scene, called the "fairhawk," it involved a fauxhawk style haircut with the sides shaven and long sharp sideburns.

Mario's skin was heavily sun-tanned and his facial features were round and childish, but he had a very square jawline, the face of an Olympic athlete. His bulging blue eyes and ever-present smile added to this childish air, which contrasted completely against his sculptural body. Sporting the latest in professional sportswear, it was difficult to stand out beside him. A white thermal shirt pressed tightly against his torso, expensive Detènte jeans and running Unoq shoes gave him a sporty and trendy appearance nobody there could possibly hope to match.

"I'm Sonny," I said, looking directly into his light, cheery eyes. "Pleasure to meet you."

"Huh, we got us a proper made man, eh? See this Dave, this guy knows RESPECT! And respect is everything, boys! You don't say hi to the *capo di tuti capi* like he's your fuckin' neighbor! You show 'im respect! See this wiseguy right 'ere, this man knows *RESPECT*. And he deserves respect jus' for that. Pleasure to meet ya, kid, welcome to the family!"

"(Mario's connected)," Billy whispered when Mario was

out of earshot. "(I'll explain that to you one day ... I didn't tell you 'bout him 'cause I didn't think he was gonna make it.)"

I didn't have to ask twice about that. I had heard that Italian mafias from the US and Sicily had begun to work the Loynne's island underground scene in the '90s, thinking it to be an opportunity akin to Las Vegas, but never really bothered as their hands were too busy locally to think about expanding. Leaving Loynne's on their to-do list, the Italian Mafiosi sought refuge in the wealthy island after police crackdowns began taking place in the land of milk and honey, deporting most citizens of Italian descent back to the old continent, and as such many chose to explore a whole new place instead. The result was the establishment of a Loynne's Island Italian Mafia, but not in the way most people thought it to be. The gangsters had to cooperate with the government on such a level that they were mostly servants instead of the exploiters like they loved to see themselves as. The SKAR played a prominent role in the restraint of organized crime, and instead of vanquishing it completely chose to let it operate as long as things didn't get out of hand. The safety of Loynne's Island citizens was the top priority, and failing to protect it from the violence of the Third World – namely any country that wasn't from Oceania or Scandinavia – would result in a crucial loss of tourism. Tourism was what kept the island alive, and as such had been established as the primordial goal above all else. The SKAR always ensured that these requirements were met satisfactorily.

After a while we marched onwards to the Pizzanovante restaurant, but in the meanwhile I had to get something out of my mind. I needed to speak to Ryan and confirm if everything Billy had said was true; I simply needed to see if that person, someone I was seeing as the best tool that could help me getting closer to Faye, was actually a fake and self-

interested imbecile. I thought about how my strategy would revolve around making Ryan think he could trust me all his self-esteem issues, all his childhood traumas, every single emotional problem that could make him dependent on my understanding reasoning. It was also important because if Ryan was as bad as Billy described him, my possibilities with Faye were close to none.

However, I didn't need to start putting anything in motion. Ryan was quite capable of doing that all by himself.

"Look ... I remember the day pretty clearly. OK, so I am sitting down drinkin' my cocoa, watchin' MonsterPock on TV, and then my dad bursts in the room, all calm like, tryin' to be psychological with me or somethin' like that ... then, he tells me about how he loves me very much and that that's not gonna change ... DUDE! I was seein' it from a kilometer away! It's such a stereotype! MOMMY AND I LOVE YOU ANYWAY! BUT WE ACTUALLY DON'T 'CAUSE WE'RE SUCH DOUCHES THAT OUR PERSONAL HAPPINESS COMES FIRST! I MEAN, COME ON! But anyway ... so then I go ahead and say ... *'you and mommy don't love each other no more, don't you?'* Then he nods and says ... *'but listen ... that doesn't mean we don't love you or your brothers anymore. It's just for the best, Ryan ... we have decided this together, and we hope the change is for the best.'* Well, guess, next thing I do, is rush to the room to lock myself in the room to cry. I cried my head out dude, I'm not ashamed of sayin' it, 'cause I'm friggin' tellin' ya, I FUCKIN' CRIED. But anyways ... that's how I found out." Then, a small figure approached us slyly and said with his head lowered, showing a sort of attitude;

"Why this now, Ryan?" he said, still walking but with his head down, looking at the floor as he went by swinging his too-big-for-his-body arms forwards and backwards violently.

"Dave, don't come here if you're not needed, douchebag, I'm just talkin' to Sonny."

"Danny." He corrected. Tried to, better said. But he knew everything; that's what the tone of his voice always assured you.

"Er ... no, you fuckin' retarded mook. He's called Sonny. You started callin' him Danny because your neurons can't distinguish a douche from a tampon." What was this obsession Unitedstatians had with the word 'douche' anyway?

"Shut the fuck up Ryan, what can you know about anythin', goddamn nerd. Go play some RPGs or sumtin'."

"OK guys, anyway, listen ... was it difficult for you going through that? I had a friend that went through the same long ago ... he was very troubled by it ... especially since all he had in the house were women ... *dve sestri i mati.*"

"The what?"

"Oh, sorry ... I sometimes get a bit confused with languages and throw in a couple of words that don't belong ..."

"What? How many languages can you speak?"

"Four ... Some better than others but overall, yeah, I can communicate in four."

"Jeeeezus Christ, and what did you say there then, dude?"

"I meant two sisters and a mother ... I'm Moldovan and Russian, but in my house we speak Russian and German ... English too, but not as often. My parents speak Russian and German, they both met each other learning English, so yeah ... and I speak Spanish as well, which I began learning when I was about 3."

"Holy fuck dude, I would have never noticed you're Russian, you've got some English skills alright ... Say, and where are you exactly from?" At this point, I was talking only to Dave, who seemed to be highly interested in me all of a sudden. Ryan joined the others in their conversation when he

realized I was not going to give him any preference over his brother, and became notably offended, duck-walking away from me.

Dave and I kept on talking for a long time, about what we enjoyed doing and where we came from, about Moldova, Russia, Santa Monica and California, about his love for breakdancing and extreme risky sports and his parents' divorce, but the ever-present subject came up in the conversation, as I knew it would.

"Sonny, don't wanna seem out of place comin' with this all of a sudden, but ah ... I hear you got some business goin' down that's buggin' Ryan, or so he tells me ... and well I would like to know what it's about ..."

"Dave ... I actually have to be honest with you about something."

"Yeah ...?" He said, not making it sound like a question.

"Well ... yeah, if you haven't guessed it already, it's your sister. I have to be honest ... I've seen her around in school without even knowing she was Ryan's sister, without even knowing Ryan had brothers, when I didn't even know you. So the fact is that, well, I like her. And not just a bit; being sincere, I like her a whole lot. And well, I wanted you to know that I am not a scumbag like all these Loynners, and that I'm not going after the obvious. If you have any inconvenient with this situation at all, please tell me. That's all I want to know." Dave kept on being silent yet seeming troubled for a couple of seconds, and then, decided to break the ice. The changed tone of his voice made me feel as comfortable as sitting on nails. "Sonny ..." He started, with a deep breath, as if to say "*don't bother me with this shit.*" "I don't think this is even gonna go anywhere. I mean. I know my sister. OK? I know her. She won't like you. I'm not tryin' to sound harsh but it's the plain truth and I'm totally positive that this is pointless. There are

a whole lot more girls out there, man ... why don't you try with any other girl? This isn't gonna be good for you Sonny, I know what I'm talkin' about, understand? And this is a dead end."

"Dave, you don't understand ... I don't want to just go out with any easy Loynnerin like these Kannies do, I liked her at first sight because I thought she was different from the rest. I'm not going to give up easily, Dave ... I mean, I'm actually telling you ... I'm going to do everything I can to get to know her, and I'm sorry if you you might not be liking what you are hearing, but I AM going to take the risk knowing she's worth the effort. I'm absolutely positive about it. And if you don't like it, well, I'm very sorry, but this is the truth. I won't let this opportunity slip by me." Dave started to seem a bit more pissed off now.

"Sonny, please, just give up, this ain't gonna happen ... I mean, I AM absolutely positive as well, dude ... you should know what you're doin' ... I mean, you must be certain about what you're doin', and I appreciate the way you talk about her as if she's not just a piece of ass, that's respect and I like it, but Sonny, we barely know each other too, so I would make up for a pretty shitty brother if I didn't protect my sister and let her go with the first asshole that shows up, right? So I hope you understand that Sonny. You're really cool and all ... but I think this needs time." Then, his concerned facial expression completely, and I mean *completely,* disappeared and began talking about other things in such a speed that you'd never swear we had been talking about that uncomfortable subject just six seconds ago. He began telling jokes, laughing at things, doing agile stunts ... Dave was really a hyperactive athlete. And it seemed he had the ability to forget things quickly. My mind rushed to the thought of using that to my advantage. Indeed, Dave talked a lot, but that showed

that he was a man of words and not action. And I was sure that he wouldn't retaliate at all if anything he didn't want to happen happened. He'd just forget it for the sake of friendship. That was one brother out of the way, sort of. But now the matter at hand was Ryan, who aside from being a more sturdy guardian, was a smarter person overall from what I was seeing. He probably feigned his stupidity for all I knew, and that made him incredibly more dangerous.

Shortly before reaching the restaurant however, Tory approached me suddenly and asked me the following:

"Hey Sonny, can I ask you something? Why are you still a communist?" I couldn't believe the question. Why now, of all moments? Only Tory could bring up complicated subjects like that with the worst possibly timing.

"Er ... I am because I still consider the capitalist socioeconomic model faulty and unfair, Tory ... that's the only way I can put it in a nutshell ..."

"Well, I'm asking because you seem to still support a communist system but comfortably live in a capitalist one taking advantage of its benefits ..."

"Tory, don't try to talk to me into your distorted Objectivist views again. You already know we don't agree in anything and that's final. Don't start another pointless debate," I said. The truth was, I didn't want to lose concentration. Faye was my utmost priority at this point.

"What pointless debate? Look around you, look at the triumph of capitalism. You are already seeing it through Loynne's; the people here have enough capital to indulge in buying property, commodities, to pursue their dreams, to lead a satisfying life and enjoy free educational and sanitary systems or pay for better ones if they wish to do so, which they can easily afford. What's better than this?"

"Tory, you know how naïve you sound, right? Look ... peo-

ple like you think that money either grows on trees or is infinitely printed so that everyone has capital. It doesn't work that way. Putting it simply, for Loynne's to exist, the rest of the world needs to be plunged into chaos, which is what's happening right now. Loynne's is the luxurious villa of a powerful industrialist surrounded by millions of people living in shantytowns in absolute misery. Don't you know this already? There can't be a rich person without a million poor ones existing. Wealth needs to be equally distributed according to a Communist economy for people to live decently. Through capitalism, the wealth is unregulated, privatized, freely distributed so that some people hoard uselessly immense fortunes and some never receive anything at all, not even the most basic means. It's been proven time and time again that that libertarianism of yours only benefits the rich. Without state regulation of the economy, businessmen, oligarchs, Mafiosi and other opportunists simply seize the chance to exploit the system and make immense fortunes. Today, entrepreneurs and businessmen hoard the wealth that a devastated world in a financial crisis needs so much. They go to millionaire auctions to buy sports cars, relax in expensive yachts with the world's elite and rule the world as they see fit. This is the world you want, the only world possible through capitalism, a financial system that, like Communism in the 20th century, is already crumbling under its own weight, crumbling because we have not learned how to correctly apply it."

"Purely the fault of communism, you've just said it ... capitalism regenerates, while communism needs not only to be implemented through violence, but it's so unstable that it needs to exercise great authority and state terrorism to be implemented and accepted ... when the grip of the state over the people loosened, everything crumbled ... capitalism may

have periods of economic stagnation, but it soon booms and recovers ..."

"Political socioeconomic systems aren't to blame, Tory. It's what we do with them. I for one would love to see a new world emerging from the ashes of this decaying system, a Socialist one, where the people are put first in front of profits. But the world you see is illusory. You have grown accustomed to property no common man should be allowed to have, expensive devices that through payments and loans you manage to pay after your blood has been completely drained. You've bought the cars only executives drove, you've bought the video game consoles only rich kids could afford, you've spent enormous amounts of money in useless holiday vacations that only gave you pictures and videos in return. People under the capitalist system have not learned to save, to be careful with their capital, to think ahead of time, and this is the result. They're plunging further into chaos, all the while we happily live here, safe from that outside world, on this island, the so-called 'Paradise Itself.' Of course this is paradise. But this paradise exists because in the remaining 99% of the world's citizens are traversing a living hell in their everyday lives."

"No, your point of view is largely incorrect. Given that countries like Scandinavia, Canada, New Zealand and others are not affected by this financial crisis and that other countries are actually emerging like China and Brazil, we can acknowledge this is a momentary lapse in capitalism that will soon be patched up. A change in the current socioeconomic system will only bring more famine and war, less stability. We have to stick to this system because it's the only way it will bring us peace, prosperity and happiness."

"You capitalist types only talk about peace and prosperity and happiness and freedom ... 'No amount of political free-

dom will satisfy the hungry masses,' Lenin said. That shallow defense of what you call freedom, your lack of order, your unregulated economics are proving to be your very downfall. In the West, we have as much freedom as far as our capital can reach. In the Soviet Union, there was sufficient freedom to be educated and make something useful of yourself. But the Soviet Union fell, all because of its inability to keep up with the arms race and compete with the capitalist Western economy, an economy that grew dangerously larger exponentially with the chaotic nature of the free-market, of speculation and unregulation. Isolated in its centrally-planned economy, there wasn't much the USSR could do in a capitalist-oriented world. China resorted to using a market economy so as to avoid this collapse, and many other Communist countries had to as well. But you know what? The US never really recovered from that enormous military spending in the arms race. Right now, we're seeing The US crumbling, testimony to its competitive capitalist nature. No country, no matter how powerful, can keep that kind of competition going forever. It will eventually fall. The US will fall just like the Soviet Union, allowing China, Brazil and India to emerge. It doesn't matter if it outlasted the USSR by a few years. Everyone falls just the same. Socialism builds, and capitalism destroys."

"You'll see, Sonny ... Communism had its era for a reason. It was proven that it was not a satisfying economic model to the needs of people. Capitalism has worked since it evolved from mercantilism. Ever since we've used this system and we're not about to stop now."

"Tory ... you are not reasoning politically. All you do, just like religious zealots, is speak of blind faith. You like to study history, well, look at history, then tell me what will happen. Capitalism goes through cycles, through eras of abundance and poverty, capitalism dies and resurrects constantly due to

speculation, a chaotic free-market and a lack of government regulation. There is no stability in capitalism, and we have learned so through history. The past is the only means we have of predicting the future and not committing the same mistakes twice, and it works every time. Don't try to 'believe' in politics. Faith has no place in the political battlefield, only reason. So don't speak to me about faith, or about hope, or about convictions, we're talking about evidence here, and all the necessary evidence accumulated so far indicates that the current financial system will have to change to serve an over-populated world and to prevent the Western consumer society to fall in disarray. Can you imagine what would happen to Westerners if they went through the same the Soviet people did? Westerners are weak minded and petty individuals, growing up with everything handed to them in a silver platter. They wouldn't have the necessary strength to endure what people in the East experienced in order to adapt to new worlds. In the West, the consumerist types used to an easy-going life would commit mass suicide and mass homicide, panicking in the streets as riots emerged worldwide. A crisis in the West will not be so easy to cover up. And definitely, its citizens won't be accepting a life of misery so willingly. But it's what's happening right now. Not only in the West, but also in the East. People in the East are just used to suffering more, to be stomped on more. They're more submissive, but also more productive and eager to survive. The individualist mindset of the West will be its destruction, while the collective hive mentality of the East, of countries like India, China and Japan, will only make them flourish and lead the world into a new era. Like it or not, this will be the future. And we're already walking toward it."

"Would you two just shut the fuck up with politics? I don't even know what you're on about, damn!"

"I know you don't, Dave. Which is very sad. It wouldn't do you harm to learn more about the world you live in."

"Fuck me sideways Sonny. You think we have a say in anythin' these political big shots do? You think just 'cause you learned how the world works you have a shot at stoppin' what's goin' on out there? Why do you think I give up on this, because I'm stupid? Because I can't understand it? It's because I know we've already lost. You can call that the foundation of my ideology. Live fast, die young. You've already lost and there's nothing you can do. We're little kids. Little fuckin' kids. We ain't the sons of businessmen or politicians, we're just kids. And that's the reason I find it pointless you two fuckin' arguin'. You're goin' nowhere. Just enjoy your youth, you'll have a lifetime of old age to talk about shit like that. Just fuck some sluts and shut the hell up, man."

"You might see it that way, but ... I don't want to sound naïve and hopeful, but there's always a chance. If you look at history, people have become great leaders and icons from nothing. Normal people like you and me. We might be tomorrow's icons. We might be legendary heroes people use in the slogans and pamphlets of the future. There's simply no telling the amount of possibilities if you push yourself too hard, if you believe in what you're doing. Your ideology is that of self-defeat, of giving up before the fight even starts. I don't like it. From where I come from, we believe nothing solves a problem better than a gunshot. If your enemy is dead he can't speak lies against you. Don't bother teaching him a lesson, humiliating him, wasting your time in useless torture sessions. No. End his life and forget about he ever existed. With the problem gone, there's nothing to do except advancing unopposed, unleashed and unstoppable, always on the way to progress."

"And this, Dave, is why Sonny's ideology strikes me as an

inherently evil, genocidal, savage and barbaric philosophy. Communism is based upon the belief that individual rights must be suppressed for the good of the state. Rand's view is that a human's mission in life is living for himself or herself, that humanity is inherently free and that repressing our rightful freedom turns us into little less than animals. I, for one, completely agree with her views." At this point, I looked at Tory right in the eye, turning slowly so as to face him. His utopian imaginary world of "freedom" was beginning to annoy me. I made sure he was paying full attention and that he wasn't going to speak, and told him;

"Tell me something, Tory. Tell me wholeheartedly and without lying that you've never, ever wanted to murder someone if you couldn't get prosecuted for it. If you had a license to kill for one day, tell me how many people who've hurt you you would murder." Tory backed off seemingly disturbed, as if my statement had either touched a sensitive nerve he was trying to conceal or as if he were trying to really put his thoughts in order. With an "I can't believe it" he started to laugh mildly and smile, and this time he looked at me sternly.

"I can't believe what you're saying. I would never want to murder anybody. Not even if I were allowed to, not even if people weren't watching and I couldn't get caught. That's the difference between you and me. You condone mindless killing, I don't. I respect life and humanity. You have to understand this sometime, Sonny. Your ideology is part of a dark side of humanity that shouldn't be allowed to resurface. Fascism and communism killed millions of people, with either war, repression, negligence or hunger. We can't allow those evils to resurface. It's our duty to put a stop to it and create a more humane society."

"Senseless killing, huh? Like capitalism doesn't kill. You

should ask a person in the US who's been denied a life-saving surgery because he doesn't have insurance, see what he tells you. Or children in Africa dying of hunger and civil wars because the West encourages them to kill each other and it's in corporate interest to keep Africa as a weak land to exploit which won't defend itself. Or maybe, and allow me to go a bit farther, you could ask the ideologues behind Operation Condor in the CIA, that allowed countless far-right repressive dictatorships all across South America just so that the US could have a chance at stopping Soviet influence and undermine South American integration and strength. The ends justify the means, right? The so-called 'democracy,' that hypocritical Western morality, the economy-wrecking neoliberalism, everything goes for you people as long as you 'liberate' the oppressed lands and force your ideology on others. At least we don't hide what we do. Repression is not an inherent part of Communism, but violence is. Violence is necessary to overthrow the old rulers and institute a new state, as no one in power will relinquish power willingly, this applies to any type of state. However, repression is a whole different matter. I know your point of view on repression. But repression can also be humanized, as demonstrated in Chinese reeducation centers during Chairman Mao Zedong's rule. Prisons won't rehabilitate prisoners or traitors. Education will. Education that will also make the person fit to integrate society again. You cannot treat ideological criminals with the same methods you punish individuals who will never see the light of day again, such as murderers and rapists, depraved scum who will never care for ideologies and who should be shot and forgotten about in my opinion. The repressions we've seen so far attributed to Communism have been largely the answer to our stubbornness to bend to Western powers, the only way we had of surviving in a world where people do not know

what they want, and sink themselves in financial crises like the one you're seeing now. Say what you will about our humanity, but you should know there's no place for morality when in a matter of life and death. And, just as we Socialists expected, your crumbling system is giving way for a new world where repression will have a whole new meaning. Forget about torture, abuse or murder. The repression of the future will be a psychological one. We'll be repressed by the absolute certainty that we are worth nothing, that we can't change the world according to our vision, be it what it may be. We will turn into the men of the future, unfit to govern, too stupid to think, and we will need leaders who will have nothing but their own interest in mind. Leaders who know for a fact we are a dumb herd of sheep which won't fight back or complain. That's the future I paint for you. And now it's your chance to counter it with whichever hypocritical neoliberal moralistic bullshit you have to throw at me."

"Actually, I—"

"Oh stop it already, stalemate, stalemate! C'mon, just shut up! You guys have different political ideologies which don't go together, I got it, I got it. Just stop the fuckin' chatter, guys. Damn."

"Fine, Sonny. We'll continue this discussion some other time in the future."

"Of course we will."

"Fine, as for now, just loosen the hell up, guys. We gotta be there for Billy and Robbie! Remember? Celebrate! Park your brains and enjoy yourselves, jeeezus ..."

"YEAHHH!" Axel said, coming from behind us and smacking Tory and me in the back of the head as a prank. "BEST THING I HEARD ALL DAY, BITCHES! PARK YO' BRAINS! Listen Sonny man, I'mma tell ya sumtin' that'll cheer you up, look the other day I went to The Pentagon, me and my homie

Zack begin dancin' with these bitches right, so they come with us to the beach, and they start suckin' us off for no reason and me and Zack do a high-five, YEAH! And then I give this bitch the cockchoke of her life, banged that head against my groin so much she started like really chokin' on cock and cryin' you know, all the make-up fallin' down her cheeks, like in the videos, they love that shit, you know what them bitches call it, seein' stars! HA! They all fucked up in the head man, but ... better for us guys! I asked the bitch later if she was OK and shit, and that was the only thing she had to say ... 'I love it when guys make me see stars!' How fucked up is that, Sonny man?!"

"Really fucked up."

"EEEEXACTLY! So enjoy yourself, man! Stop thinkin', start livin'!" I seized the opportunity to talk to Axel about something; Mike had been very quiet, and didn't seem in the mood for celebrating. I deduced he had to be sad about Billy going away, as they had struck up a nice friendship. Nonetheless, I wanted to make sure:

"Hey Axe, is Mike alright?"

"Mike? Sure, man! I mean, yeah, you know how he is ... his ol' man givin' 'im shit and stuff ..."

"I guess ... but is he alright or not?"

"Yeah man, jus' goin' through some trouble at home, and he'll miss these two lil' bastards too, wont' he? Don't worry, I'll cheer 'im up for ya! Hey, yo Mikey, hey Mike! Sonny says he wants to make a pass at your bitch! Haha no, no ... I kid, don't kill 'im!"

As Dave and Axel suggested, we left aside matters that required you to think and had a great time in Pizzanovante. For an instant I forgot completely about Faye, and everyone laughed at my jokes and imitations of celebrities and films. They couldn't believe how much of a cinema freak I had

turned out to be, and I enjoyed being the center of attention, even if it was just one night. At school I usually tried not to be, but between them everything was different. It was extremely exhilarating that people didn't laugh *at* you but *with* you, that they understood what you were joking about, that they comprehended your accent; I felt in a blissful heaven for once ... no matter whether it was Billy, Robbie, Ryan, Dave, Wolfgang, Mario, Ettore, Axel or Mike, I felt they actually understood me and I could understand them back. It was the first time in years that I had felt anything similar to true integration. My mind rested from the shackles of peer pressure, Kannovschina and studying useless things to vomit in exams. Everything seemed alright, fearless and fun in Pizzanovante, with those people who now were a safe shelter for my tormented mind. "*Finally,*" I thought in a calm, ominous voice only I could hear. "*So many things are turning up alright ...*"

• • • • •

With the party coming to an end, Wolfgang, Mario, Ettore, Axel and Mike headed back home. Robbie, Billy, Ryan, Dave and I had something else to do now. Billy's alcoholic surprise was saved for this instance, a moment among his best friends plus a newcomer, that being me. Someone they would "initiate" in the ritual of alcoholism. We ended up in the easternmost part of Crosshair Beach, right at the Citadel Gate Hill.

"Heyyy Sonny! Now for the moment we've all been waiting for ... some nice good ol' rum." We were in a section of the beach where drunkards and the few homeless Loynne's Island could have usually used to hang out, but not that night. It was just us, the drinks and the tidal sounds of the sea.

"Alright," Billy, started. "Now Sonny, this is some niiice shit ..."

"*Harosho ...*"

"Now this, this is the very first step into adulthood boy, aside from fuckin'! Just relax and take one sip!" I timidly took the glass off his hands and attempted to smell it cautiously ...

"Now, what the fuck you think yer doin', boy! Don't fuckin' smell it, jus' drink up, dammit!"

"Wait Billy! Wait ... I got it ... I got it ..." and without thinking, I shove the whole thing up my throat in a matter of a few seconds ... Billy was amused, but also laughing at me.

"You ain't supposed to drink it up like that, son! But it'll do. Here, lemme show ya how a real man drinks this shit up ... you never really had any alcohol before, you queer?"

"Of course I have! Just ... not for kicks ... with friends. Only a beer now and then or a little vodka."

"Hehehe ... well don't worry son, we'll make you a proper man in no time."

But Billy had underestimated my hatred for alcoholic beverages. I regarded them as the ultimate drug of the working-class, a social placebo which had to be eliminated for a proper intellectual society to be born. I turned around and pretended to drink the whole glass in one gulp, drinking half of it and spilling the rest, which would have made it seem as if I had drunk hastily. Good luck nobody noticed the spill.

"*YEEEEE-HAW BOY! THAT'S THE WAY YOU DO IT!*"

Soon, we were jumping and singing around all over the place, me obviously pretending to be drunker than I actually was. We wrestled, ran, laughed and sang, Dave threw the empty bottles at nearby docked boats and walls, and Ryan and Robbie sat locked in a private conversation looking melancholic, without saying much to the others. The stars in the dark sky of Loynne's shone directly in my eyes as my drunkenness delighted itself with every kind of color and light beam from the city's neon-lighted hotels and restaurants.

Being the first time I got something related to being properly drunk, I had the typical alcoholic conversation with Billy, the kind that usually starts with a "I love you, man."

"This guy ... this guy right 'ere you gotta love ... no, not in a queer way you know, Sonny boy you fuckin' fag!"

"*Ia ponyal! Ia tebya lyublyu tozhe!*"

"Speak English, you commie motherfucker! What the fuck that mean?"

"It means 'I got you, I love you too!' "

"Well, let's cut that off before our tube steaks end in each other's sisters ..."

"What do you mean, Billy?"

"Haha, you don't know? Tube steak, Marine slang fer dick ... and sister, Marine slag fer armpit ... supposed to be this gay-ass faggot army practice, where you stick yer cock in another guy's lubricated armpit fer sex simulation ..."

"Oh ... really?"

"Yeah, really! When Marines need some, they go to a fellow Marine brother and they say 'I wanna stick my tube steak into your sister ... what do you take in trade?' But I bet you know that, seein' as you basically said that to Ryan already, hahaha!'"

"Well, one day I'll get to it, with her or not ..."

"Watchoo mean, boy?! Haven't screwed anything yet?!"

"Negative ... I've only gone second base ... Well, maybe halfway between first and second ..."

"What you talkin' about now, son?!"

"I might as well say it, since we're talking about sisters so much ... I have to be honest about something ... I don't just like Faye ... I'm ... I'm in love with her ..."

"Hooooly cow in space, boy! Hahahaha!!!"

"What's so funny, Billy? Anything wrong?"

"You jus' had to go 'n choose the most frigid bitch in Pilgrim Coast High, didn'tcha!! Haha!! Bitch wont fuckin' like you, boy ... and I'll give you a little piece of advice, 'sa matter of fact ... she's fuckin' 15!!! But she ain't bangin' anythin' just yet ... she ain't a whore, at least fer now. Maybe if she's paid enough attention she'll turn into one, but I doubt anyone wants to pay attention to that thing ..."

"I do ... I love her ... I want her ... She needs to be mine! SHE *IS* MINE!!"

"Woah, there, calm down boy! Jeeeeesus ... didn't know the bitch meant so much to you, son ... Thought she was just a piece of pussy for ya, boy. Turns out you actually love the bitch? Man oh man, you don't love her ... nobody loves nobody at this age ... and even less in fuckin' Loynne's Island in fuckin' Pilgrim Coast ... think about this proper boy, 'cause you're headin' to death row slowly like this, right to the goddamn chair ..."

"Probably ... aww, and so what! We're 17, not 30! I have all my life ahead of me! And if she rejects me, fuck the bitch, like you say! Seriously! Not like it's the only girl I've had before! Ha!"

"Yeeeeeeaaah, that's the way you do it, boy! Now we talkin'. Look, look who's goin'." Billy pointed at Ryan and Dave, who were about to leave. They didn't look very pleased and in fact their faces reflected the worst time of their lives. They didn't even say much of a goodbye to me.

"Yeah, it's gettin' late guys. We'll see you next week," Dave said.

"Bye you faggots. You sure know how to end a party."

"Ahh, shuddup you inbred redneck," Ryan said.

"I'll fuck yer mamma when you ain't watchin', you queer!"

When their silhouettes disappeared I seized the opportunity to ask the Nazareth brothers a few questions. It had

been pretty obvious that Ryan's conversation with Robbie also included Faye, and he probably informed his brother after finishing with Robbie.

"Hey guys, what's up with them? Anything wrong?"

"Ohh, never mind them, they get like that from time to time. Damn queer city big shots. They're quite moody as it is anyhow. Listen Sonny, our party ain't over just 'cause we gotta get home now. You stayin' for the night in our house, right? Well listen up boy, there's one thing my dad asked of me, we don't got no bikes now, so if we move to such a big place like Nova Atlantica we ain't got no free urban transportation. Catch my drift, boy?"

"But Billy all the shops are closed now, besides, bikes are really expensive here, do you even have the money ...?"

"You really think I'm talkin' about shoppin' like a little queer homosexual faggot?! I'm talkin' takin', not payin'! Jeeez, where your mind at?! Brighten up, boy!"

"Ohh, right ..."

"There's this little restaurant near here, my dad told us they always leave the bikes outside. It's not unusual here 'cause almost nobody ain't into robbery, and those chains are crappy anyway, very easy to snap, and they probably will be able to afford replacements, but I ain't rich boy so I need me some bikes. They probably belong to some Kanny fucks anyway. So come on boy, you gotta help us out, whaddya say?"

"Well ... it'll be interesting ... if they do belong to Kannies like you say ..."

"Huh, sure they do, boy ... Ever seen normal folk 'round here in bikes? Only Kannies and cyclists ... and these ain't no professional bikes so they can't belong to cyclists ..."

"You're probably right ... yeah, why not, let's do it."

"OK. Let's head out," Robbie said. It was as if for a moment they exchanged leadership. Robbie stood up from the

rock he was quietly sitting on, and began marching decisively out of the beachhead, looking at every direction from time to time searching for possible witnesses. Billy wasn't different. The town itself was sunk in darkness, but it wasn't as if winter attracted a lot of tourism, and the mayor wanted to reduce costs in everything he could, mainly water and electricity. Loynne's produced electricity with ecological means like wind power stations and dams, and did not possess many electrical stations. In any case, it had to be around 02:00, and all the businesses were shut, excluding the DAUCO 24/7 mini markets.

"This is it. There they are," Billy said, pointing at them and smiling gleefully. The restaurant was called "Bayside Restaurant," one of the typical simple seafood joints usually found near the beaches in Loynne's.

"OK, look. This is how we'll do it, guys. Don't go screwing up now. You and Sonny take a bike each, I'll take one too to scout ahead and tell you if the coast is clear. Make sure you make a run for it immediately if anyone sees us. When waiting make sure you look back to see if anyone's coming. OK, let's go," Robbie ordered.

We quietly took a bike each after Billy managed to stealthily remove the chains. In the darkness I couldn't quite see what he was doing, but he had to use a lock pick or some other tool, judging by the clicking sounds. We proceeded like Robbie said. We would take Monroe Street and reach Paradise Avenue, surrounding Poseidon Park through Bazner Avenue and then going to Duarte Street, the street that led to the Community Center itself from the Church & Square. We needed to cross an entire area filled with restaurants and shops where it was hard to tell if people were hiding, and the police was also difficult to identify with their navy blue uniforms. The place seemed so deserted that being cautious

seemed a joke. Who would care about three people riding bikes at night anyway?

We tried to get to our destination as fast as possible, with Robbie signaling from time to time telling us to stop or keep advancing, but we met absolutely no obstacles and managed to cruise through Monroe Street in a matter of minutes. We actually had a blast sneaking and robbing the bikes, and soon Billy and I laughed while racing and carrying them to the destination. Robbie didn't seem to be having fun, he never did, always so deadly serious and objective, but it was as if that was his normal state. I could never help but wonder what Billy and his brother hid from people; just like me, I was terribly sure they had some inner family secret they couldn't discuss in the open.

We made it to the back entrance of The Crucible, not a single pedestrian in sight. Then, Robbie said: "*The watcher will notice us if we got through the lobby. I'll go ahead and take the stairs, then you can pass me the three bikes from the ground floor, then come help me carry 'em.*"

It's hard to explain, but the staircase in The Crucible was like a twisted spiral up to the very last floor that protruded from the building, like a fused screw. You could climb or fall down the lowest set of stairs in the first floor to the ground floor with no damage and that was the section we were going to use to pass up the bikes.

Robbie was already waiting looking down at us from the lowest section that led to the outside. We passed him the bikes and walked inside the lobby up to where the first floor elevator access was, and helped Robbie out getting the bikes inside the small elevators. Robbie went up with the bikes alone and we ascended in a separate one.

Trying to keep the silence alive to the very end, we entered the apartment stealthily without waking their dad up, feeling

incredibly relieved and lamenting only that the fun had come to an end.

"Pheww, boy. That was some good ol' fun. But anyway, we made it. Look, this is the Nazarethes' current household. Stare at it all you can, we're movin' next week."

The apartment resembled the Mantis residence but inverted. The walls were white as well, but the tiles were made of a rough red material which was very common throughout Loynne's. I noticed they had two rooms instead of three, which increased the size of the living room dramatically The kitchen was at the right side upon entering instead of the left side, and the bathroom next to the balcony. They had a small wooden table at the left corner in the living room, surrounded by shelves and stands with books and trophies, and an old computer placed on a desk against the bathroom wall, a small brown couch beside it. It seemed immensely tidier than the Mantis residence, and it struck me how two brute rednecks could live in a house that was nicer looking than mine.

"Come on Sonny, you must be tired, go to the bathroom and clean all that shit and sand and then come here to the kitchen, and we'll have a quick snack before hittin' the sack."

I went to the bathroom, trying to be as silent as I could since their dad was just sleeping in the room in front of it. I looked at myself in the mirror thinking a total stranger was staring back at me, someone incapable of doing such feats. I had always used my time in front of mirrors to reflect on myself, to search for my true identity and my real essence. This time-out from my friends after so much interaction only deepened my philosophical insights about who I truly was and where I was going toward. The face that looked back at me was that of another Sonny, a politically-incorrect Sonny

not scared of society and eager to use questionable means to fulfill goals. This thought had always haunted me. Educated by both parents and State into an exemplary citizen and Communist, the fact of me partaking in situations such as this one and letting myself be influenced by outside forces somehow forced me to emotionally seal myself from the world.

Emotionally awkward after my pondering and hesitant on what I was even doing next to these people, I washed my hands and tried to clean the sand off as much as I could, then headed to the kitchen where they had prepared the meal. Somehow, I now only wanted for this outing to be over quickly. We never spoke much for some reason, which was a good thing as I did not had to lie about my lack of social enthusiasm, but after we were finished Robbie went immediately to bed, enabling Billy to show me something that interested him in the computer in a much more personal way.

"Come 'ere Sonny, I think yer interested in these things, they told me."

Billy turned the computer on; it was an old white CRT monitor with a small gray tower, probably hailing from the distant start of the millennium. Even so, the computer was able to run the Hipps-Tear FOX operating system, which although not being the latest one, was commonly found on non-updated systems worldwide, such as government buildings, hospitals and even businesses. Obviously, this was quite a rare item in Loynne's. However, Unitedstatian immigrants couldn't afford very expensive possessions, as I had learned interacting with Ryan and Mike, and some of them even brought their old pieces of technology to avoid unnecessary spending. It was no wonder that Billy's family had had to resort to this. After the computer booted up, Billy opened several websites about airsoft guns and military related

hardware.

"Listen son, I can't have a *real* gun yet, I love guns but well, this is what I can get so far; airsoft guns. Really nice ones. There's this M4A1 carbine I want there, look. Really sweet, huh? Just the model that kid back home used to shoot 67 people from that pier before the Eagle Eyes shot 'im to pieces. Removable and retractable stock, Picatinny rails to change to different gear, like flashlights, laser sights and scopes, even accuracy handles. How's that, boy? And it only comes at like 300 crosses. Really sweet. Hey look, I think this is the one that suits you best, huh you commie basterd? AK-12, the new official rifle of the Russian Army, Russia's very own M4A1. Reckon' they needed one already. It's got as much customization as an M4, if not more, with the addition of bein' extremely reliable, nice and sturdy like an AK. You can't tell the advantage of an AK playin' airsoft anyways. In real life the M4 would need more maintenance and would surely fail to fire in the most needed moment. That don't happen to an AK, gotta give that to you, damn Russian basterds. Look, we'll go on tomorrow mornin', let's hit the sack fer now."

Billy's room was as big as Ryan's, and had even less space because of them not having bunk beds. Each bed was pressed against the wall in a parallel fashion, leaving a small corridor in between to walk. Looking from the door, Billy's bed was the one to the right. His bedspread consisted of M81 Vietnam era woodland camouflage patterns, while Robbie's was neutral. In front of Robbie's bed there was a shelf with many collector's airplane kits and war-related miniatures, as well as gun replicas, of which in the darkness I managed to identify an FN SCAR-H Mk. 17 in CQC configuration, an H&K G36K and a Steyr Aug A3. A confederate flag hung above Billy's bed like the Soviet one did on mine, with three messages that read "1861 – 1865," "REMEMBER THE ALAMO" and "THE

SOUTH WILL RISE AGAIN."

Just like mine and Wolfgang's, this was the kind of room that reflected the owner's personality perfectly, and soon I found myself insidiously inquiring about the nature of the room:

"You really like carbines, eh Billy?" I asked, admiring his replicas further.

"You noticed, huh? Yup ... daaamn right I do. Carbines are beginnin' to replace assault rifles more and more son, or at least, resemble 'em. Lightweight, shorter, compact, easier to handle, they're jus' like rifles only better. Who cares about bigger range or more tolerable recoil? A carbine's got everythin' a rifle's got in less space an' weight. Nobody wants to carry a big-ass rifle in the jungle or the desert all day long. We learned that with the M60 in 'Nam a long time ago ... hehe, nobody wanted to walk kilometers of rainforest carryin' a big-ass 10.5 kilogram machine gun. Soldiers tend to love their weapon more if it's friendly to them back. 3 kilos, son; that's the best average weight for yer gun. Anythin' above that ain't worth it in combat."

"What's your favorite carbine, then?"

"Well, I gotta say I've always had a thing for the M4A1, but it's seriously outdated now, especially when compared to the HK416A5. I love German military hardware, Sonny boy, always have. But I also have a thing for US guns and the M16 family. It's tough to choose. Visually, I really prefer the M4A1, but I think the HK416A5 has made it obsolete. But the M4 has never gone outta style. It's after all still the official carbine of the US Army after so many years, no denyin' that. They say they should upgrade, but go an' tell the brass to change their main service carbine for one made by a foreign brand. An' what's yer favorite gun then, son? AK-74M, right?"

"The AK-74M is a fine weapon, but it's not my first choice.

I prefer bigger calibers, that's why I like the AK-103. It's a sleek rifle, but like you said, it's like the M4A1, somewhat obsolete now that we have the AK-12."

"Ain't that the truth, son. Believe me when I say these are interesting times. I can smell war. And you know what, as a matter of fact, I'm not really afraid of an all-out war. Who knows, maybe next time we see our faces, I'll be through the crosshairs of these rifles, eh? Hehe ..."

"You mean, you'd be willing to fight for the US and everything it stands for?"

"Haha... if the ol' country decides to start a war, I won't be fightin' for its beliefs. I'll be fightin' to be the first kid in Loynne's Island to get a confirmed enemy kill. Come on now, let's hit the sack." With Billy's rant over, my thoughts went back to the titanic revolver I kept so carefully stored. Due to all the emotions at school I had completely forgotten about it, but it was a good thing; I didn't even want to touch it afraid of upsetting the owner, when he finally came to retrieve the gun. Distracting my mind off of Billy's gun obsession, I wondered one more time who the mysterious owner could be, what *Reviziya 02* could really stand for ...

Billy signaled a sleeping sack with a desert camouflage pattern in the space between the beds and after some difficulty – it was a bit short for me – I finally was ready for sleep. Billy, however, seemed in the mood for talking, which was kind of odd given the situation; nighttime, two guys tired and ready to sleep, the very first time I was in the house, and also the fact that Billy's perspective on life seemed frightening; it just didn't seem normal. A chilling sensation rose through my spine when thinking if I was actually getting to know the real Billy. I reaffirmed myself on my position following this conversation:

"Weird, ain't it ... what you told me before, boy. Are you

really in love with that bitch?"

"Hey, don't call her that, Billy. I may not know what's going happen from here on in but I can really tell I get pissed off if anyone speaks about her like that. Might be a sign that I truly do like her ..."

"Huh ... izzat right. Well ... You know what, boy ... I don't want to let yer hopes down or nuthin' ... but you ain't gonna get this one. And I don't mean to offend you ... but I think that to make anyone like you, you'd better do summin' with yourself first."

"What? What are you talking about?"

"I'm talkin' about you bein' naïve, boy. That's what I mean. Look; it's pretty clear that yer one of them folks that want to live happily ever fuckin' after and fall in love with their friggin' damsel in distress an' shit. Look, the pretty colors don't say nuthin' nice boy, that's a fact."

"What are you talking about, Billy?"

"Hah ... don't worry. You'll know soon enough. For now, let's jus' talk about summin' else other than chicks. They get me pretty pissed off them fuckin' bitches in heat."

"Right ... so what do you want to talk about, then?"

"Well, for example, that you haven't been clearly honest with me, Sonny. I don't take kindly to that. In fact, I don't even know where the fuck yer even from, boy. And don't lie to me. Just who the fuck are you?" There was an awkward silence, only interrupted by my nervous, inconsistent breathing. Billy's friendly tone had washed away and was now insisting and menacing. But no matter how suspicious he could get, he would never have any evidence to back it up.

"I've been honest with you, like I've been with everyone else, Billy."

"Yeah, right. And there's another thing buggin' me, I don't trust for a second yer from Moldova. You could be Croatian,

Serbian, Czech, Bosnian, Albanian, Macedonian, anything but Moldovan, and definitely not from Russian descent. You don't have the features. Yer from somewhere closer to the Mediterranean than the Black Sea, more Western than Eastern. I know that. But I just can't tell what the fuck or who the fuck are ya, boy. I gotta accept you really got me there. You might be from anywhere and I'd still believe it. An' trust me, I'm good with foreign countries and races." I became immediately alarmed at these accusations, and not believing Billy was being entirely serious, I decided to stand my ground and distract his attention with a joke.

"I don't like where this is going Billy, and I don't like you doubting me. If you have a problem with me I'll lock you in an elevator with Ryan after he's had a date."

"Haha, now there's a good threat, boy! Jeez ... you really have to hate the guy, dontcha, all day babblin' on and on. I barely know what the fuck he speaks about nowadays ... we were really close back in the day but last year he believed himself really cool and shit, and we kinda forgot about 'im for that whooole year ... till now, he reappeared again from wherever he was. He used to hang out with these Brit sluts at school, seems he fucked one I think. Damn, that's gotta be the first time he's gotten laid." My joke had seemed to do the trick just fine, but I was still on high alert. In any case, I decided to fuel the subject of criticizing Ryan, as he seemed keen on it.

"Give the guy some credit ... if that's what really happened, that is. I have doubts myself ... do you think any girl would have him? I've seen girls literally smack him right in the face."

"Haha, me too, I've seen girls rejecting that piece-a-shit pus-filled walkin' zit with open hand smacks, lemme tell ya. The guy is incredible. I think I told ya before why you

shouldn't trust him. Robbie and I think friendship is all about siblin' cooperation instead of rivalry. Do you get along well with your brother? Or are you like these two lamedicks?"

"Actually, I'm an only child."

"Look, we're all about fraternal loyalty 'ere and shit, but if Robbie ever crossed me that would be the last thing he ever did."

"Well ... I wouldn't actually know."

"Heh ... yeah, well ... that's why we say that how a person treats his brother tells you a lot to you about 'em. I mean look at them snakes, them Mantises. They compete an' stab each other first chance they get, they go for broke when it's about winnin'. They smack each other, leave the other like dirt when in front of people ... well, but at times they really do seem like proper brothers ... at times. Damn ... it's amazin' how much they actually changed, son. You never really saw 'em much before, but ... before they were more stupid and childish, yeah, but more loyal. Now they're all about looks and stupid gay punk rock, like Green Köontz. Fuckin' yuck. I can see you're wearin' a shirt of 'em, you queer faggot. Do you really like that shit boy, or it's all a front to stick it into Faye's goal, 'cause I think it's not hard to see you comin' wearin' that."

"Yeah well, would you hit me if I told you I actually enjoy this music? It's not just for Faye, Billy ... honest."

"Hah ... guess you're far beyond repair more than we thought. I knew what everythin' was about the moment I saw you wearin' that. What happened to yer commie shirts?"

"Well, I just thought a change would be nice ..."

"They look like fuckin' fags, no offense."

"Well ... not like this is the only music I like. My passion is retro rock, particularly Soviet bands. But I guess this is trendier than putting on a Soviet band shirt."

"My dad, he's all about bands from that era. You should see 'im. Was a friggin' stoner back in the day, but one of the cool ones, not the hippie anti-war ones. Everyone did that shit back then, hippie or not anyway. My dad loved the music but hated what the music had brought forth. The stupid life-style, the anti-patriotic sentiment, pretty much all the bull-shit came with the '60s ... well, look Sonny, we'll talk more tomorrow, in case you forget, we still gotta go to school, it's only Thursday."

"Yeah, right. Don't worry, Billy. Good night."

"G'night mongrel, watch out for Ryan gettin' in yer bed at night! There's some pillows over there if ye ever need to make yerself a fort ... hehehe ..."

· · · · ·

I woke up feeling empty and out of place, looking at the morning sunlight irradiating the room through the window blinds. As per usual, I summarized in my head all the scenes lived the previous day, to see if I had a reason to get up or not. I definitely had a blast with the guys, but after things got personal and weird with Billy I almost thought he was going to call me a "commie" and kick me out of the house. The exchange had left me worried, and I no longer had a desire to remain in that strange and foreign house any longer. I looked at my Hipp-Man's watch and saw it was 10:30, least three hours too late for school; I wasn't about to walk into school in the middle of recess out of duty. In fact, the last place I want-ed to be in, aside from Billy's house, was school. In situations like these, I never doubted what to do. I would just take the day off, go home again and call it a day. This was a bit too much socializing for my anti-social behavior, and I soon felt the need to distance myself from these people as quickly as

possible, so as to be in the comfort of my home and mind my own business. I gazed at Billy and Robbie, who were still sleeping, and pondered whether they would mind if I just left like I often did while at Wolfgang's, that is, without previous warning. They would probably skip school as well for all I knew, as I hardly could see them picking up their stuff and making a run for it, precisely when they didn't have to officially attend anymore. Billy had probably meant the night before that they would accompany me to school, but not going in themselves.

I grabbed my backpack and headed out the door, trying to keep the stealth until I walked out safely. The daylight impaled my eyes as the shiny atmosphere of Loynne's spread over The Crucible and its yellow, creamy beige paint. This was quite unusual for me to do in a day of the week, walk out of the house of some school buddy after a night of drinking and skipping school while heading back home unrestrained by the oppressive nature of school duties, something to just clearly dream of in The Motherland.

Heading to the elevator, I developed the irresistible urge to check on the Mantis residence, but remembered they all had to be in classes, especially Faye. I couldn't see her being late for classes or playing truant. I wondered whether it was a good idea to make sure, as the reward would mean spending an entire morning next to her ...

But no; I ultimately decided against it, choosing instead to take my time and stroll around the uplifting daylight of Paradise Plaza and watch its citizens perform their daily routines, everything seeming like a dream to me. I had only ventured outside the safety of my shelter a few times to stroll freely across Loynne's, and each outing had proven to be memorable, even if it was only due to my inexperience. If you rarely go out, the few times that you do stay forever with you. How-

371

ever, as per usual, I didn't care how much fun I had had or how memorable the outing could have been; I always felt the urge to retreat back into the safety of my dark apartment, far away from the corruptions of the world and the invasive thoughts of others, in this case, Billy's. Even then I was absolutely sure that there was something wrong with that kid, and my first reaction was to mark my distance and try to freeze relations. He'd be in Nova Atlantica indulging in whatever he liked doing, and I'd be in the South perfectly away from his awkwardness.

But as you may presume, that would not be the last I ever saw of him.

- CHAPTER VI -

Vera

"Religion is the impotence of the human mind to deal with occurrences it cannot understand."

- KARL MARX -

German Philosopher and Economist, coauthor of the Communist Manifesto and one of the Fathers of Communism

---

I found myself in class sitting next to Wolfgang, analyzing the people I was surrounded by. Behind me there were two girls, actually very attractive, gossiping about. This moment was tense, as Wolfgang had been for a very long time interested in one of them, the girlfriend of a Kanny Kickboxing Champion of Loynne's Island. Wolfie couldn't pick easier prey.

"Sonny ... Agostea ... it's her ... it's her essence ... I dunno how to explain it ..."

"Here we go again," I thought. Little old Wolfie getting mystical and poetical and proverbial yet another time. Billy and Robbie did a good thing that night telling me about Wolfgang. I now saw him under a different light, as if my eyes had been opened to the truth behind his nature.

Feeling an incredible pity for Wolfgang and his inability to integrate in any level whatsoever, I decided to start a campaign with the objective of making him more "normal." Even though I knew he wasn't going to get the girl by any means, I

wanted to use it as an excuse to reshape his behavior, at least, in a way so that the Kannies in class didn't laugh at him. It was starting to prove dangerous to hang around him out of fear of being as isolated socially as he was. After suffering through Kannovschina, that was no option. I was ready to abandon any friend who wasn't willing to help himself survive the psychological jungle of school. After all, that's what it was all about. Brutal animalistic survival. And I wouldn't be dragged down by a person who with each passing day I felt less and less respect for.

"You can get that girl no problem! Of course you can, *Tovarish*. But first, you need to make yourself, eh, should we say, more appealing. Appealing to locals, that is. Come with me this afternoon and we'll do something about it. How much capital do you have to invest on yourself?"

"Ah … well … don't worry about capital. I'll bring enough."

· · · · ·

We headed to Stockholm Avenue going up the Church & Square, which was where the peoples of Paradise Plaza usually went shopping. We went inside clothes shops of various kinds, trying to find a style for Wolfgang which would suit his personality and make him blend in better, like I had managed to do with my Communist uniforms. Unfortunately for him, Wolfie was too obsessed with Japanese culture to appear as normal as me, and I had to be very restrictive when setting the standard for what he could and couldn't wear.

In any case, Wolfgang spoke his mind about something important, something which had been seemingly troubling him for some time. For the twentieth time, it was related to the opposite sex.

"Hey Sonny, I need to speak to you about something … I

need your insight."

"Alright *Tovarish*, spill it!"

"It's just that ... well ... let's just say that I've agreed to do something, even if it's something that doesn't exactly go with me. Let's just say it's an insurance policy, a last resort emergency scenario should this fail ..."

"What are you talking about, Wolfie? What did you agree to do?"

"Well ... Axel was talking about these sex and drugs parties that he organizes on weekends, and well ... I know it's wrong and uh, it's not like I do drugs, but I'm sincerely so desperate *Doshi*, that I'm gonna have to consider his offer if I don't find someone suitable soon. I can't stand it ... wherever I go, everyone has a girlfriend, or has had sex before ... and I can't stand this sexual frustration either. I mean, I have needs too, you know? I can't just, you know ... be content with relieving myself all the time ... I need the company and the love of a woman."

" '*Vidna ptitsa po polyotu.*' "

"What's that?"

"That's a proverb for you, you like proverbs so much ... it means 'the bird is known by its flight.' You can judge anyone by his actions and surroundings. Don't go there, Wolfie. That's really not what you need. Believe me. Have you forgotten what I told you? You just need to keep searching. It will eventually happen. But you won't get any satisfaction if you decide to fall for what Axel does. Don't become like him. He's not like us, *Tovarish*. He's a degenerate that will fuck anything, like Ryan. They don't want women who cherish them, who are loyal to them, who are pure and honorable. They want sex for the sake of it. We're not like them, and hopefully we'll never be."

"I know Sonny, but ... I dunno ... it's getting critical. You

have Faye to at least, you know ... I know she's not been very receptive up to now, but it's getting there, right? Well, I have nothing. I don't even like anybody. That Agostea girl, she's the typical one that everybody falls for. I'm deluding myself, fooling myself into thinking these disgusting Loynnerins are worthy of being praised and loved, when they're horrible and superficial people, without Honor. But they're all I've got, these nymphs, like you call them. They're all I have."

"You'll see Wolfie, everything will change soon. Just learn to adapt like I'm telling you to do, and you'll be fine. When the outside has been taken care of, girls will be more receptive to what you're like as a person, it's sad but it works that way. Girls are shallow and superficial, and always go for guys because of status. If you establish yourself as a somewhat normal guy, they'll be more willing to consider dating you. That's all there is to it. You'll see that you'll triumph in the end, and someone will value you for what you are as a human being. And I'll tell you one last thing, *Tovarish* ... if you do go to that party, well ... don't want to put pressure on you, you'll ultimately decide what's best for you, but if you do decide to go to that, I'll lose incredible respect for you. A whole lot. *Nikogda ne zabyvay, Tovarish* ..."

"Thanks, *Doshi* ... I promise I won't disappoint you. You're making an effort for me, and I appreciate it."

"Anytime, *Tovarish*. Come on ... let's go inside this one."

•••••

Needless to say, we didn't buy what we were after, mainly because of money. Wolfgang wasn't exactly poor but that didn't make him any more willing to spend all his money on one shirt. As such, we established a budget and decided to buy the cheapest clothes that could be considered acceptable.

But in Wolfgang's case, I couldn't do much because of him simply not listening; instead of buying clothes, he insisted in buying a couple of expensive SKAR special gloves and a balaclava he had been after, for playing soldier around, as well as an army olive green shirt like the one I had.

"Sorry Sonny, I really couldn't miss this opportunity, we'll do the clothes thing some other day, this is a very special exception!"

What bugged me the most was that the next day Wolfgang wore the olive green shirt in school, precisely the day I had decided to wear mine. When he took his jumper off revealing the shirt, I became immediately nervous at the prospect of Kannies looking at us wearing the exact same thing, as if we weren't considered odd freaks enough.

"Wolfie, friend, *Tovarish* ..." I began. "Cover that shirt and put your jumper on."

"No Sonny, it's too hot! That's why I took it off!" He was starting to get on my nerves at how he regarded the situation as not serious. Some Kannies passed behind him and said something like *"heyyy tryin' to keep up with Sonny now arent' you?"* and winked at me as if to say, don't worry pal, we do know he's a dumbass. We'll that was really nice coming from the trendy Loynners, but I was beginning to feel the stress and peer pressure of people watching and laughing at two "pals" dressed the same. I don't usually succumb to peer pressure but if there was one thing I couldn't bear, was public humiliation and embarrassment.

"Come on Wolfie, don't you see you're embarrassing us both? Take it off," I demanded.

"Why Sonny? There's no problem, there's lots of people that happen to wear the same thing in school," he said, not understanding my point.

"Look Wolfgang, people think you're enough of a freak

without us being dressed exactly the same in army shirts, you're seriously going to sink any little respect we might have around here ... so, I won't say it again, take it off fuckin' NOW," I said with such a repressed tone I could feel my veins pulsating in my throat.

Suddenly, Mike, who was next to me overhearing the conversation whilst playing cards with Axel, took Wolfgang's jumper and threw it to his face.

"Put that on you samurai piece-a-shit," he said severely. Wolfgang obeyed immediately, and stayed quiet from there on in.

Mike had made a clear statement regarding my inability to resolve in a manly way the situation Wolfgang had put me in. Things like these made me confirm Billy's theory regarding Wolfgang's mental deficiency, inability to integrate and his selfishness, and so I began to separate my way from his after the following incident outside of the West Wing;

"Wolfgang, why the *fuck* did you bring those gloves to school for ..." I asked, unbelievably irritated.

"Oh Sonny, look at them, aren't they sweet! These are the ones that SKAR teams use for shooting practice, that's why they're colored and not entirely black—"

"Oy, look 'im there man, with dem bicycle glavs on!" Some Kannies from the class had noticed Wolfgang's gloves. I know I said I wouldn't keep reproducing Loynner accents and I'd just point them out instead of imitating them, but I really have no other way of letting you know how horribly crude their disgusting dialect is.

"Didn't know yo' had no bike fwiend, that 'ow you git 'ere?"

"Ya Samurai, you in a SKAR teem yet?" They laughed him off and went away quickly. I simply stood still looking him deep in the eye, relieved that the incident had not derived in

anything serious, and said:

"Wolfgang ... this is exactly what I was talking about. You want to be a pushover everyone laughs at your whole life? That's cool with me. Hey, I tried my best trying hard to change you but it seems you won't ever listen to reason. See you around ... talk to me whenever you decide to stop being a clown." And like that, I left. Up ahead I met with Ryan, who witnessed the incident without me knowing.

"That Wolfgang prick still with his stupid samurai commando shit, ain't he? Poor dumbass. Leave that limp-dick alone Sonny. It'll do you good. I ain't tryin' to say anything but, the Kannies in class and people in general are losin' respect for you for hangin' out with him. Everyone makes fun of him except for you, man. Even I do now, I don't give a fuck anymore. I never wanted to be his friend anyway. Listen, hang out with me now! Sit with me in class instead of with him. You'll see what I mean. And that Axel douche, better leave him alone too ... too connected with freaks now. Kannies don't respect him no more neither. Just listen to me man, and you'll be alright."

Only days later, Wolfgang performed his ultimate failure; he asked the girl with the Kanny boyfriend, Agostea, out for a date. When she spread the news about it, every single Kanny in school asked Wolfgang about its veracity, and laughed at the shocking fact that he had actually done it, something not even they could believe. Between amazed looks of laughter, admiration and mainly mockery, Ryan and I watched Wolfgang stroll between a human corridor of laughing Kannies at each side, who threw at him the little plastic mayonnaise bags that they gave you when buying chicken croissants. It was such a sad view but I couldn't help but think that at times, to succeed in life and in happiness, you need to leave people you don't need anymore behind. It seems very cruel and horrid,

but dragging behind you the remains of someone that is of no need to you, cripples your way forward. Everyone who has had at least one moronic and self-centered idiot of a friend will understand my plight. Well, there's always a first time for everything in life. And this was the first time in Loynne's I would leave a *Tovarish* behind. I reaffirmed myself on this position when, after the humiliating incident, Wolfgang informed me of his decision to attend Axel's party.

· · · · ·

But even I knew that distancing myself from Wolfgang would not be easy. I had tried ignoring him, even when he approached me directly, which was incredibly hard to do and hurt me immensely. Two weeks passed without having any type of contact, and I saw him grow more isolated, a sad expression in a face that was beginning to become rock-hard in that way only isolation can provide. I had indeed tried to ignore him, but it was a doomed attempt from the start; we were in the same class, we had established a bond that went farther than simple school friendship, and as nerdy and antisocial his definition of honor could be, he was actually the only person I could talk to about such subjects people like Ryan were completely oblivious to. I decided I would keep talking to Wolfgang, but I no longer had the same attitude toward him in public. As much as I hated to admit it, I cared too much about being respect. Even so, the following incident helped in breaking the ice for us.

A week had passed since Wolfgang's incredible public humiliation at the hand of the Kanny friends of that Agostea girl. The only person he could turn to, Wolfgang came to me for advice once more.

"*Konnichiwa, Doshi.*"

"*Privyet, Tovarish.*"

"How you doing, Sonny? Anything new?"

"Pretty good, can't complain. And what about you?

"Actually, I wanted to talk to you about the weekend."

"The weekend? Oh, Axel's party. So you went ..."

"No, Axel canceled it at the last minute, said a lot of people failed to show up. I didn't care much, anyway. Actually, I was going to tell him myself that I didn't want to go, I began to feel real bad. I mean ... no matter how desperate you can be, I don't think that's the correct way to go. Taking advantage of a girl overdosing on drugs ... there's no glory, no honor in that. My honor would have been forever tainted. I don't need that in my life. What I seek is something exclusively true, I seek a loyal companion. Nothing else will suffice."

"Well, I'm glad you saw it my way in the end. I mean ... you can't regard women as objects, and I'm not trying to appear more feminist by saying that. What I mean is that, according to what I think, doing that simply brings both you and the woman down to the lowest of levels, down to the disgusting cesspit of sexual debauchery of this psychotic Western society. You said it, there's no honor or glory in that, just vapid lust and a hollow sexual satisfaction that will always leave you feeling empty. Why do you think Axel does this? He's an empty person, without ideology, without values, without moral, ethics or principles of any kind. He's good to us, but I don't think he's good to a lot of people. Why do you think these idiots in class hate him so much? Also, I don't think women like him too much when he makes himself scarce after fucking them or when he takes advantage of them when they're drugged, given he does that at all ... I sometimes can't believe anything he says, he's a con man, a shyster, the best representative of the Cuban pro-Unitedstatian far-right, the *gusanos*. There's nothing you can learn from him, Wolfie,

except how to be a worse human being."

"Thanks Sonny, and yeah, I know. Don't worry. I learned my lesson. This is what, through hardship, life brings us, *Doshi*. Lessons. Teachings. We become wiser every day."

"Well, I'm glad to see you're back to normal, seemingly. I hope that stupid era of Realm of Witchcraft is over too."

"Yes, don't worry, I was becoming too addicted to that trash, I don't need it in my life anymore. I've seen how Axel and Mike get with that game. It's insane. It makes you waste so much time ... I'm going to compensate the lost time reading and meditating, *Doshi*."

"Ah, yeah well ... you do what you think it's best for you. But never let anyone mess with your head again. Think for yourself. I'm trying to give you good advice, but you don't have to do what I tell you either. Just listen to your urges, pay attention to what you truly need in your life. Nobody else will be able to tell you what you need more than yourself."

"Thanks, *Doshi*. It's great to see a comrade such as you is always available."

· · · · ·

During recess, that very same day, I remember going downstairs searching for Faye everywhere, finally finding her sitting next to a friend on the stairs that led to the basement in the Main Building.

Faye was truly stunning, exhibiting her perfect white legs through a black miniskirt I had never seen before, wearing a tight striped black and red shirt with horizontal thin lines, her black sandals, her usual black nail polish and the distinctive US flag cross necklace. Every single time I looked at it I wanted to ask her why she bore it, but always forgot to do so when startled by her unique and astounding beauty.

Accompanied by a friend, they were analyzing this sort of teeny pop-rock gossip magazine called "Krazzzy!" flipping through the pages praising the looks of guys like Frank Boy Al while criticizing others who to me looked exactly the same. Faye was sure having a good time, laughing a lot in that weird manner of hers, her face following miscellaneous and rapid changing patterns from which one could not distinguish her actual emotional state. She was the only person I had ever met who seemed frustrated and bored even when clearly laughing.

"Hey, Faye! Fancy meeting you here!" I said, sitting down next to her.

"Oh … hi," she said, immediately stopping her laughter.

"So what are you up to?" I asked, not willing to let my enthusiasm die out.

"Nothing, just here, messing …" she said this with such an incredibly inaudible voice, not turning to face me and unceasingly looking at the magazine, while her friend had not even acknowledged me.

After spending a few minutes there being ignored, I came to a terrible realization; a 1.84 meters tall guy coursing 1st Grade of Scientific Baccalaureate was simply sitting right there on the stairs amongst two little girlies from 3rd Grade who were half his size and checking out shirtless faggy pop star guys on a gossip magazine. People from my class looked at me probably thinking I was an immature dick, an annoying pathetic vulture, a child molester or better yet, her own brother. I was so ashamed of myself when the guys stared at me, but I simply couldn't go; and after Faye walked around the whole high school out of sheer boredom without a clear goal while I limited myself to follow her around like a dog, I told myself "stop," and went to see my freaky friends feeling defeated and frustrated; Faye was either trying to shake me

off or was as ashamed of being seen with an older guy as much as I was embarrassed of people seeing me hanging out with a 15- year-old who looked like 12.

"Hey Sonny! Where have you been? Look what I got, the official Gears of Deterrence themed GamEsprit Portable, Limited Edition Bundle, see, it's got a special case in the shape of Cobra Viper's handgun holster, and you can even clip it to your shirt for your sudden gaming urges! And not only that, it comes with a ..."

• • • • •

"Hey Sonny, what you doin' after class?" Ryan asked me one lazy day during Tom Richards' class, as he drew a cartoon of him dressed like a shirtless Vietnam GI with a bandana on his head and firing an M60 from a Huey helicopter. You may guess what Richards must have been talking about for nearly half a class.

"I'm not up to much, why?"

"Wanna come over to my house? Dave's got this new game for the GameSprit Zwei that's got this one scene where they talk in Russian and it ain't got subtitles, he was wonderin' if you could translate."

"Yeah, sure."

"Cool! You can stay the whole afternoon if you want to, got lots of shit to show you, I finally found those videos from our campin' trip to Azzure Lake with Billy and Robbie, lots of crazy shit that summer happenin' that summer, we found this dog that sometimes would hang around us, and he would stay and then suddenly leave and such, and we called him different names each time he came by, like, in one video we call him 'Faggot,' in another 'Homo,' then 'Dave,' it's hilarious! I think Billy started it, so funny ... nice pooch though, I felt

kinda sorry leavin' him there ..." As Ryan kept blubbering on, I thought about how I had basically been granted access to a whole afternoon of uncertainty, of maybe seeing Faye, maybe not. I obviously was fearful of asking as I didn't want Ryan's newfound trust and good mood to shatter, but inside I was bursting with anxiety. As I listened to Tom Richards' moronic rant about Russian T-90 tanks being atrociously expensive compared to US M1 Abrams tanks and accusing Russia of shameless militarism, I shut my eyes for the remainder of the "chemistry" class and dozed off thinking about Faye and what I'd say to to get her attention.

· · · · ·

"Alright, here it is," Ryan said, scanning his files. I gazed at his window enjoying the thought of the nice day outside, my mood remaining high during the walk to his house from school, as I thought of meeting Faye. She wasn't in at the moment of our arrival, Dave greeting us instead, but he informed us that she would come back perhaps in a couple of hours. I was suddenly invaded by inner peace when hearing this information, as I had been granted more time to think of something to say to her. In the meanwhile though, I needed to bear Ryan's antics, which on this sunny and pleasant day full of positive expectations, actually felt pretty tolerable.

Ryan's and Dave's room was always cool and seemingly impervious to the blazing heat that usually scorched my apartment from the outside, and the forthcoming positivity of this sensation allowed me to feign interest in Ryan's stories. He proceeded to show me the camping videos as Dave played on his GameSprit Zwei games then considered older than injustice. Since Ryan was boring me a bit, I decided to stick with Dave and see whether he could be an improvement.

Using the opportunity when he informed me of the scene he wanted me to translate, I surreptitiously sat next to him and assured Ryan that I'd be with him again shortly. He seemed kind of grumpy and even jealous that his brother had my attention, but perhaps let it slide because of that being the hook that got me to come over. I somehow sensed that Ryan didn't have enough self-esteem to know that he could summon me without resorting to some kind of bribe or treat, using any of his siblings as bait, obviously preferring not to use Faye as the first option.

Dave played the typical WWII shooters, although his emphasis was in BMX and skating games, like Mark Falcon's Skating Spree, which for some reason, featured a level in Russia which was the one he wanted me to translate. Dave has a very short attention span and would forget everything I told him in favor of asking what the new dialogues meant, so this got me tired after a while so much I actually preferred Ryan's monotonous metallic voice telling me inane stories. Dave, when he paid attention momentarily, filling the gaps by saying something that embarrassed Ryan or something they both found funny, usually mischief started by Billy.

I was beginning to get into the atmosphere and really feel as if Ryan and Dave were my best new friends, the guys I liked being around the most out of all the people I knew, and I certainly appreciated the way they seemed to struggle for my attention. I was also learning a lot about their personalities judging by their camping behavior, such as Ryan being prone to eating all the food and pissing in the only source of drinking water, and Billy dishing out proper punishment using Dave was a bulldog, consisting of locking Ryan in the tent and throwing him upriver wrapped in it.

Just as the stories were beginning to become interesting, we heard the door to the apartment open. My pulse acceler-

ated immediately, my entire body going into full alert.

"Mom, you forgot the fishsticks again," Ryan greeted her in his bored and monotonous spoiled voice. The alert wore off, but my pulse had indeed accelerated so much I was trying not to seem shaken up in front of the guys.

"It's me," a beautiful girly voice clarified, shortly before a tiny figure rushed through the hallway and locked the door to the nearby room. It was her.

"I gotta go say hi to her," I instantly told my friends, who didn't look at me as they were distracted by their respective screens, but their eyes changed immediately, and ceased being warm in order to become icy and sharp as steel, wary and uncomfortable at the presence of their sister and my clear preference for her.

"Don't bother her," Ryan told me, his voice clearly changed. "She's just come in, she don't wanna be disturbed," Dave added.

"No, no, it's not polite, I'll be right back," I mumbled nervously, and proceeded to get away from the room feeling as if they would pull my clothes violently and prevent me from exiting. To my surprise, they stayed as icy and still as they had become with Faye's entrance, and didn't even blink or stare away from their screens as I proceeded to get out of the room and shut the door behind me for further intimacy. Faye was mine for at least 2 minutes.

I found myself standing at the door to her room, and I had to breathe in deeply so as to get a hold of myself. When I pulled myself together, meaning barely succeeding in fighting off cardiac arrest, I knocked on the door and awaited a response. I didn't get any, so I knocked again.

"Yes!" she barely managed to shout, seemingly having said so before and perhaps bothered at having to raise her unhearable voice. I went in warily, opening the door slowly and

even frightfully, and then I saw an image that is still firmly burned in my retina, locked inside my most treasured memories forever.

Faye was lying face down on the bed, a short jean miniskirt revealing her white glowing legs, a tight and revealing top showing off her waist and pressing her breasts tightly; but best of all, something which was undeniably attractive and unimaginably sexy to the point of exaggeration, was the sight of her bare white feet, so beautiful, tender and delicate, as she rubbed them together and raised them in the air while lying down and looking at her TV set with bored eyes.

She had seemingly come back from the Community Center library and had thrown her folder and books aside, turning the TV on almost immediately, somehow making it seems as though she had been in the house for hours. As I entered she didn't even glance once, and I took it as a very bad sign. However, her ignoring me was irresistibly attractive, and I found myself increasingly drawn to her the more she dismissed my presence.

"Hi ... hi, Faye," I mumbled stupidly, smiling like an idiot. I couldn't help myself, and I was quite certain that she noticed. The smell of her Balearic Cherry perfume was overwhelming, and blissfully dazed me as I lost control of all rationale.

I'd say she greeted back, but for some reason I don't remember her addressing me at all. I only remember her staring with cold eyes at the TV set, as she watched her beloved Frank Boy Al perform on-stage at some gig in England.

"What are you watching?" I said, as I positioned myself on her bed beside her, trying not to seem to invasive and keeping my distance somewhat, which was an extremely arduous task.

"Bibles for Bullets," she said, as I strained my ears to listen

properly and not have to repeat myself.

"Oh, the concert they gave in the UK last year, isn't it?" I said, putting my newfound knowledge of Green Köontz trivia to the test.

"Yup."

"So ... you must know this all by heart, am I right?"

"Uh huh." I noticed the conversation would quickly follow one of those unbearable monosyllabic pattern if I didn't choose my words correctly, but I found myself unable to think properly. After a short but awkward silence, I uttered:

"Not tired of it, then?"

"Never. No one could get bored of this."

"No, no, I didn't suggest that," I quickly retorted. "I'm just saying that ... you know ... you must really know this by heart."

"Oh, I do. Every single second. All the interviews and dialogues."

"Why ... why do you like him so much?" I asked, as she seemed not only to open up more for conversation, but seemed to smile when looking at her idol giving an interview with his manly singer voice and his fresh Californian accent.

"Oh, he's just so dreamy," she replied ominously, again, bending her lips in a way that looked like a smile yet not quite. "He's ... impossible."

"What's that mean?"

"He's ... not real. He doesn't exist. Men aren't like him."

"But, I say again ... what does he have?"

"Something. Everything. I don't know. Listen," she said suddenly, as she picked up the remote and started turning up the volume. "This is where he sings 'Wake Me Up When the Draft is Over.' " The gigantic screens in the concert showed the face of Frank Boy Al as he played the opening riff of the song, and began to get visibly emotional, his voice breaking

as he seemingly attempted to carry on and not let his emotions get the best of him.

"He's ... crying?" I asked in disbelief.

"Yeah. Can you believe it? Ohh ... men who cry are so hot ... my poor baby ..." I actually didn't know how to respond to this. Every single sentence she said came off as a provocation, or an indirect statement aimed toward me. Were these guidelines on how I should act to get her attention? Did she actually know that I felt for her things a thousand times stronger than what she claimed to feel for this rock star?

"Oh, come on, all men cry at some point or another, except that we hide it," I said, as if trying to minimize the importance she was giving her hero.

"I know. That's why letting it all out in front of a crowd of one hundred and fifty thousand means so much. He's not afraid of what they'll think of him. And that's hot."

"That's what I mean. I don't doubt the song may cause him to react like that. But come on ... he knows he's being recorded, and that all those people will see him crying on the screens." I didn't know why I was antagonizing him when this clearly didn't get me any closer to her, but I couldn't help but consider him competition, aside from an infantile dream on her part. As long as Faye liked people like that, she would never be content with a flesh and blood man, hich entails by default a fair share of flaws. How I could possibly compete with an extremely good-looking Californian multimillionaire rocker who was loved by millions and also was a peace and animal rights activist, aside from a generous philanthropist, was beyond me.

"Aww, he can't sing the chorus!" she exclaimed covering her mouth in complete awe of him, absolutely ignoring me. I had never seen her so emotional or undaunted to express herself. It was a if I wasn't even there. Her marvelous green

eyes had grown impossibly bigger with tenderness, and she kept covering her mouth in that fashion people do when witnessing something unbelievable. Just as I was about to open my mouth to say something, a yell was heard from her brothers' room:

"Sonny! Come back here! Got somethin' to show ya!"

It was Ryan's metallic voice. I looked hesitantly at Faye, who still looking at her beloved Frank Boy Al, only had the following to say:

"You better head back."

"Uh ... yeah, maybe you're right," I mumbled, seizing the chance of her not looking at me in order to admire her beautifully stubby and curvy teenage body. A powerful force, more irresistible than anything I had felt before, prevented me from moving, and thusly I began to stall.

"Faye, this concert you're watching comes in a disc, right?"

"Uh huh."

"Mind lending it to me?"

"Oh? Why? You want to watch it full?"

"Yeah! I mean, I'm curious now about the rest of the performances, it seems really cool."

"Well, sure ... let me take it out and put it in the case," she said with a sigh, as she got up clumsily and proceeded to hand me the disc in the heavily-worn case. I couldn't believe I had gotten away with it; I had something which was rightfully Faye's, and one of her most precious possessions for that matter. This had to mean something ... why else would she hand it over so easily?

"Thank you Faye, I'll watch it and tell you over ChitChat about it."

"Sure," she said, looking right into my eyes for a fraction

of a second, which was enough to make me melt away completely. She stood there right in front of me as if waiting for me to do something, and then Ryan's metallic and unwanted voice make itself heard again:

"SONNY!!!"

"He seems way too angry, you'd better go," she said, looking at me somewhat amused, yet also weary and tired as if I had been bothering her. It was impossible to read this girl.

"Yeah, sure ... thanks, and bye!" I approached her to give her two kisses, like it was usual in Loynne's. She was seemingly not expecting it, and thus rendered the act somewhat awkward as she appeared to be startled by my advancing on her so swiftly, and she somehow pulled back as if by instinct. The result was me almost head-bashing her as she moved her head clumsily from one side to the other, but it was apparent that at least she attempted to give me the two kisses.

"Should I shut the door?" I found myself saying, stalling everything as much as possible.

"No, leave it open," she replied, lying once more on the bed and returning to watching TV, not even looking at me.

I went back to my friends with mixed feelings, glad about spending time with her and getting her Green Köontz disc, but unhappy with her Frank Boy Al praise and how she had reacted when dismissing me. I honestly couldn't tell what she thought of me. Only the future would tell. For the time being, I delighted myself with the reassurance that she was there, mere meters away doing her little girl things, as her brother showed me photos of his own little girls, the ones he kept lusting after in that dirty and disgusting fashion I could never adopt with Faye.

The minutes went by as I kept thinking she was there,

probably reading her teenage magazines or looking at the rock stars she loved, rubbing her perfect smooth white feet against one another as she playfully tangled her hair ...

· · · · ·

Tired of inane ChitChat conversations that led nowhere, of talking about what April Divine had worn on her last performance and watching her Green Köontz disc to the point of where I knew it by heart more than her, I decided something radical had to be done. Gathering all my frustration and impatience, I set myself to ask her out on a date.

My first official try occurred unexpectedly when I happened to bump into her. She was wearing her sexy blue jean skirt, her black cardigan and a striped black and blue top, aside from her omnipresent US flag cross. Her delightful emerald eyes seemed to be looking for something in the distance.

"Hey!" I succeeded to say without mumbling.

"Hi," she said as she passed me by, doing what she always did, that is looking at me for one second right in the eye to acknowledge me and then immediately looking away. I found it fortunate that she did this. If she had kept the stares, I would have been the one flinching, ashamed to face her directly.

I became disappointed in how she didn't stop to talk to me, but at times largely impossible events do seem to occur. By some inexplicably feat of nature, Faye materialized in front of me, blocking my path and staring into me as she held me by the wrist. My heart wasn't strong enough for this. Adrenaline began to pump violently and I got ready for the best after so much frustrating work in vain. She looked me right in the eye, and I failed to keep contact, just like I knew I

would. I kept it for two seconds and immediately smiled idiotically; this was it. I had completely failed the surprise test. However, Faye began to speak, still staring at me with those green, round and innocent eyes;

"Hey ... I really need to ask you something." My face became completely red, as she gazed into me with that potent stare, as I repressed the joyful need to smile again and restrained laughter at the same time, looking down at the floor in absolute embarrassment. She gasped delicately for some air and continued her weird lapsus, one I was hoping would never end.

"*Lenin Lives ...*" I thought, raising my head and looking right through her. "*Go on, go on, go on ...*"

I waited impatiently for what appeared to be weeks of standing in front of her, my thoughts colliding against each other in brutal, anarchic chaos, as I figured the aftermath, outcome and distant future of this one instance, all the while looking at those perfectly formed scarlet cheekbones, the immaculate skin, the dazzling emerald eyes, the delicate thin neck bearing her mysterious US flag cross, the heart-shaped lips ...

"*She's going to do it. She's preparing to ask me out. This is it ... what do I do now ...*"

"Have you seen any of my brothers? I have to give something to Dave," she said, in an official sounding manner, as if she were on a mission. There are no words that can describe the fury I felt at that moment. Each time I bumped into her she always looked as if there wasn't enough time to waste in silly socializing. I often wondered how she spoke to others, how she behaved in the classroom and other social environments. She was so lonely and self-sufficient that my antisocial side nurtured my feeling of duty even more. I loved outcasts and people who liked to be left alone. However, as

with Wolfgang, there's always a flaw with this condition. And anti-social people, once given enough confidence, can turn into the worst kind of vermin.

"What are you, their private housemaid?" I said, irritated at this waste of time after so much mystery. "Let them get their own stuff and if they forgot it, well, too bad! You can't sort out their lives for them!" I said, in a rebellious, agitating tone, trying to sound dominant.

"No, I have to give this to Dave 'cause he left it at home and needs it for the next class."

"If you want me to I can take care of it."

"Oh no, don't worry. I'll ... I'll go look for them 'round here." At this point, she began circling around me, looking at different directions without going too far. I was confused. What was she attempting? I wasn't simply standing there and waiting for her to do whatever it was she wanted to do. I had to seem dominant and independent and leave without second thoughts. I noticed I didn't have much in terms of dominance over someone so mysterious and unpredictable, though. She wasn't a braindead Loynnerin you could win over with a simple formula. I wanted a challenge I could win with some effort, but not this headache. Frustrated by her irrational actions, maybe due to her own immaturity, I proceeded to leave in defeat yet again, uncertain of what I was truly facing, questioning whether I should give up on my endeavor. When I looked back she was still there, with that stupid servile attitude she adopted toward her brothers and desperately looking for that arrogant dick. Yet I couldn't fail to seize such a golden opportunity. Not being surrounded by her stupid friends or her brothers, I marched onwards and planted myself before that gorgeous and stunning woman, the only person that manged to completely blur everything surrounding her.

"Hey, ah … Faye?" I said, so nervous I surprise myself today thinking how I even managed to gather strength.

"… yeah?" she said, once more staring into me only to later look away, still walking aimlessly as if she were killing time. It was embarrassing; intoxicated by her sweet cherry smell to the point of numbness and intimidated by her unbelievable beauty, I succumbed to my infatuation so much that I failed to ask her the question, instead staring at her like an imbecile.

"Cat got your tongue?" she suddenly asked, raising her eyebrows. It was the first time I had seen her doing something not related to shyness. For a second, she appeared to be toying with my obvious nervousness.

"*Sink or swim,*" I thought. Finally getting a grip, in a more serious and perhaps very severe tone, I violently let it all out.

"Look, I was just going to ask you if you wanted to come with me to the cinema this afternoon. You don't have to pay or anything, I'll take care of it. What do you say?"

"Oh … I … I can't. Have too much to do this afternoon, plus I'm very tired." I wasn't expecting this. Actually, I wasn't even counting on it. I convinced myself that failure was not an option that I found myself unable to react.

"Oh … uh … right. Some other day, then?"

"Uh, sure, yeah."

"OK, bye."

"Bye."

"Wait!" I shouted. I couldn't let her go like that after our bland exchange. She turned, looking more disappointed than excited, or better said, neutral and emotionally sealed off. Her eyes darted some serious negative warnings. It could be fatigue, or maybe that I was clearly bothering her. Surely, it had to be a blend of the two.

"Listen, it's just that it has to be today because I can't this

weekend because I'm going with my friends to help them out on a school project. So yeah, I can't this weekend." I nervously wondered what she would answer to that.

"Well, I already told you, I can't today, I'm really tired and I just want to get home and have some rest."

"Uh, yeah sure, fine." I left quickly, in part to hide in my own shame and self-hatred. "*THE FUCK YOU DOIN' MAN!*" a voice inside my head said, funnily enough with Axel's voice. "*BE PATIENT, YOU IDIOT!*"

She strolled away quickly with her usual uncaring air and walking in that unique fashion, moving only legs and barely shaking either shoulders or arms, as if her torso and hips were separate. She did move her butt though, and in what way. Her miniskirt dangled up and down as if teasing me to reveal what was under, mocking me as the smooth white legs disappeared from my view.

I had to plan my strategy more thoroughly, that was clear enough. I thought if I maybe had to improve my image in any way. I was doing definitely better than last year with clothes, sporting my proud camouflage cargos and my Soviet shirt, with the official SKAR combat boots, customized dog tags with my name and blood type dangling on my chest. It couldn't have been my image. Even if I had customized my appearance to reflect my ideology, it was basically what most people wore. I was doing everything that was expected from any guy in terms of looks. It had to be the fact that she didn't know me too well. We just needed to talk more, but how? I didn't even get chances in breaks because she seemed to avoid me whenever I was near. That paranoid thought, always managing to crawl inside my head, was what actually forced me into leaving her alone for the most part.

I tried to dismiss this heavy disappointment and retreated back to class, no longer bothering to lift my mood up.

· · · · ·

I haven't quite explained so far what the exit was like when classes finished at 13:30. It was actually as annoying as being inside the school itself, if not worse. Little kids ran and shouted, sometimes crashing against you, while Kannies shouted even more loudly and incoherently. Massive herds of annoying Loynnerin cows screamed their heads off with absolutely no manners and spewed all kinds of unintelligible Loynner gibberish with their thick accents, as you already know, really hard to imitate. Also, the school staff never opened both of the entrance gates, instead they simply opened one and expected 800 students to squeeze right through at the same time while piles and piles of human garbage struggled to pass impatiently. When you finally made it out you had to walk to the disgusting bus stop, where the self-assured, self-titled Kanny kings of the school were sure to humiliate you in front of curious crowds of passive by-standers, while the Loynnerin cows laughed at their distaste-ful macho-man jock pranks. All of this happened while the blinding sun scorched your skin and produced this disgusting sweaty sensation of filth.

Also, the ride back home was usually 20 minutes of bear-ing the same thing on a concentrated space where not even the loudest earphones could save you. Kannies shouting at the bus driver was also quite pathetic, as they sat down in the farthest part of the bus and the bus driver would often wait two minutes and shout a couple of things that would shut the Kannies up for a while, only to later being forced to listen to the music blasting on their phones, of all tasteless genres such as reggaeton, drum & bass, techno and hip-hop. The distorted, tinny metallic sounds and their laughs were your

company in *PARADISE ITSELF* while you rode the Purple Wonder back home, to finally relax in the peace and rules of your very own republic. "*To hell with it all,*" you thought after getting home and relaxing in the cool darkness contrasting the raging sun outside, and thinking about the positive aspects of life in a Western capitalist "paradise." No wonder Faye was my relief and hope back then. This routine I just described had been my everyday life for like two years and a half now, and it was mainly the reason I had stopped going to the bus stop and begun to go to Wolfgang's house every day. That way I could talk about other things, get a relief from the noise and the people, and calmly think about my business in peace. It was also nice to socialize a bit outside of the tension and show-off culture that reigned in school. These sessions with Wolfgang were the part when we talked about different aspects of mankind, philosophizing about human behavioral patterns we did not share or understand, girls, sexual experience which never arrived, stupid fads we couldn't get into like the Loynner sheep, politics, governments, ideologies, war and honor.

Wolfgang had however betrayed this temporarily, preferring to sink in the idiocy games like World Defender and Realm of Witchcraft provided. He wasn't my comrade now, just an awkward freak, the kind of person everyone warned me about and still, silly me, wanted to reach the diamond in the rough ... but with Wolfgang out of the picture, what was I to do?

Then it struck me. The bouts of independence I had recently experienced in Loynne's enabled me to walk with my own two feet to wherever I wanted after the hordes of students had gone home, and the streets were clear. That meant nobody would wonder where I was going, but it also meant I would also lose my target from sight. I wanted to tail Faye to

The Crucible and get to walk her home, talk to her and discover who she really was. We had talked over ChitChat for some time now, so I wasn't afraid to face her as before. She was never going to know me for real like that. The time had come.

· · · · ·

I woke up in a hot day of November covered in dried, disgusting sweat, as I fought against the sheets glued to my skin. Only one thing was in my mind at that moment; and the objective sparkled clearly in front of my eyes, directing my steps closer to victory. For that day, I *had* to walk Faye home.

I followed the usual routine; got ready for school, ignored Gordon and proceeded to the dreadful basement where our early philosophy classes in the AV room took place; watching documentaries with people throwing papers at each other showed how education was on the rise. My mood improved once when the face of one of the most prominent United-statian figures illuminated the room, the face of none other than Carl Sagan, one of the individuals the country had managed to produce that was culturally significant and influential at both a scientific and social level. Truly, an icon to admire regardless of your political ideology. Scientists like him were far beyond the triviality of human squabble and seemed inspired to want to improve it with scientific facts.

As the students didn't bother to listen to what Mr. Sagan had to say regarding Johannes Kepler I became seriously offended, but my mood completely sunk when they simply laughed dismissively at his outdated appearance and the clothes people wore in the video. I looked around me as popular Kannies gave the Lolly cows back rubs and sometimes attempted to get their g-strings up their crack, the girls

laughing loudly as they readjusted their underwear. Everything that should of course take place in a philosophy classroom. To make matters worse, the teacher, although well-intentioned, was one of the most powerless symbols of weakness I had witnessed in all my years as a student. The poor man, a fragile, ape-looking little guy with dark skin and glasses, struggled to keep order in a world where he knew he would never possess any respect or authority. He had as such limited himself to reading most of the time while the students did whatever they wanted, and thus philosophy classes went on like this for the rest of the year. Only a few nerds sat at the front rows, obediently talking to the teacher from time to time and doing the homework he assigned them.

Keeping myself invulnerable to this disgusting environment was an easy task when my life had a top priority. I would just have committed suicide if not, as this pointless Western lifestyle was beginning to take its toll on me. Although I fought the feeling as much as I could, sometimes I found myself on the verge of collapse thinking I would never see my parents or my country ever again. But I always reached the same dead end. No matter what, I had to hold on and patiently wait for their arrival; I had to distract my mind for this to become palatable, leaving my existentialist woes and loneliness aside. As such, I focused my attention on Faye more than ever before, trying to distract a sorrow that at times truly seemed impossible to overcome. In fact, had it not been for the prospect of getting more intimate with Faye, I don't know what could have possibly make me want to even get up in the morning.

· · · · ·

Heading to the disabled people ramp in recess, I actually

managed to bump into Faye in the Main Building's lobby. Completely on her own and without her stupid friends anywhere in sight, this was a rare event by all means. After the usual sensation of bliss was held under control, I prepared myself for the eventual conversation, trying not to smell her irresistible cherry fragrance. The encounter went as follows:

"Hey! How are you doing!"

"Oh … hey …" For some reason she seemed smiley and carefree, without the usual sadness printed in her heavy eyes. I was wary, though; unusual turns in a woman's attitude could prove unpredictable, dangerous and potentially lethal. Still, I kept my composure and simply conformed myself with the fact that at least I got to see her.

"What are you up to? "I asked, casually.

"Oh nothin', just walkin' around."

"Can I come with you? I'm just kind of, uh, sick of my friends, you know, getting on my nerves all the time."

"Yeah, sure."

She didn't seem to be interested in anything I said at all, a fact I attributed to her shyness. I had to do the talking while she seemed to walk on forever aimlessly, almost as if visibly trying to lose me in a corner.

"Do you have any idea of where you're going?" I asked frequently. She used to respond in such a low, unintelligible voice I simply gave up on asking, risking seeming incredibly idiotic. Instead, this silence made me follow her around to the small staircase leading to the basement in the West Wing, two floors below where my class was. This was like a complete 5-year-old slumber party, the only thing lacking was the plastic tea cups and stuffed plush toys sitting at a table. Friends from her class, probably 15 years old but still looking like 10 were sitting sporadically around the staircase, laughing like the little girls they were, while I found myself mere-

ly *sitting there.*

My infatuation was clearly out of hand, but I'm only able to see it now. For in the moment, I remember sporting that stupid smile I carried whenever she was around. The limbo, the excitement of her presence, not even the situation could spoil my mood. After a while though, it was clear to me. I felt unwanted. I stood up and turned my back on this sad circus of shame, and while preparing to march defeated, I bumped into the guys. I almost felt like hugging them all when I pretended to just be passing by and treasuring the seconds they took not to see me sitting down there pathetically with the legion of little girls.

"Hey Sonny, where you goin' man?!" Axel asked.

"Oh nowhere, I was just—"

"Hahaha, yeah man, you like the little 13-year-old tight virgin pussy too huh? Pff, I can't really blame ya, they're so tight you get your cock stuck in 'em and can't pull it out sometimes, like an asshole! YEAH! Bunch of sluts these 13-year-olds, know any your friend can hook me up with? Tell 'em I got a driver's license, a shitload of blow and a private residence, all for my own fuckin' self, ha!!"

"Look Axel, shut up before you're held from the legs downwards. Hi Sonny," Mike said. He really disapproved of Axel's out of place, womanizing ways. I always thought it was the fact he had a sister, and that his dad was seemingly abusive of both she and the mom. He had a reason to ask for respect regarding women, and seemed to heavily agree with Ryan on the subject of me liking the sister of a friend, even though he never said anything against me openly. Mike probably saw what I was up to, but he surely knew my motive was true and pure, even naïve.

"Oh yeah, I forgot Mikey! You can't come to my parties 'cause you got that nice chunk of German-English pussy with

the big ass and the chubby thighs and the tattoo and the piercin' at the back of the neck ... mm-hm, yeah, a rare bird, an attractive weirdo ... I'd definitely hit that shit if you weren't like three meters tall and 300 kilos ... and if she had biggger tits that didn't look like hairy ice-cream cones! Ha-ha!"

"I don't go to your parties Axel 'cause I already have a partner, like you know, I respect her and I care for her ... I love her ... you should know that more than anyone ..."

"Oh come on man, you barely see that chubby bitch, what, you see her, once, twice a week, maybe less? I think you spent two weeks in a row without seein' her once, I dunno how you allow that. She really looks like she don't give a fuck if you ask me ... I told you this before man, burn that bitch before she burns you first, they're all the same Mikey, remember what I always say, 'tight lips sting deep!' No bitch is sacred. They all fuck you over in the end."

"I'm not havin' this conversation again, Axel, and I really think you should shut your fuckin' mouth before I bust a cap on your dome instead of smashin' your head against the wall."

"Ah ... THREAT RECEIVED, AND UNDERSTOOD! So listen Sonny, you should come then, dunno the fuck you doin' with the legion of kiddies but that won't make you a man sooner. Maybe a playa, but not a man, know what I'm sayin'? You seriously have to come with me to a fuckin' sex and drugs party man, with real fuckin' women, proper disgusting bitch-es. I mean it's totally cool if you don't do coke but you really gotta try the pussy man, you look like you could use it!"

Suddenly, someone said something unintelligible, grumbling. Wolfgang appeared from behind Mike, and I was surprised I had completely ignored his presence until that moment.

"Hey, if it isn't The Samurai, before you ask, yeah you're invited you fat ugly blob, but don't scare 'em away with your samurai crap and your nonsense. Really man, make some sense sooner or later or I fuckin' kill you, goin' commando on yo' ass."

"I'm not planning on going anywhere, Axe. And I don't want you to invite me to those things anymore." Wolfgang had passed from turning visibly more stupid by Axel's influence to actually standing by his original principles with even more zeal. I found the sudden change to make myself like Wolfgang better for some reason. It was better to have him learn the error of his ways instead of living in denial.

"Ah, who the fuck cares, better for the chicks! Listen you fat fuck, hit me up on Realm of Witchcraft tonight if you wanna see how the pros handle that shit. Ain't that right, Mikey?" But whereas Wolfgang was beginning to get back to normal, I stuck to Axel and Mike pretending to be alright with their little hobby, which was an enormous task I would have to bear for months. Listening to them going on about video games was indeed such a pain you simply wanted to hang them on a bridge and toss rocks at their suspended bodies expecting some sense to be made eventually. Simply put, they hadn't made any sense in weeks, and it was pathetic to behold how gradually this condition worsened by their addiction to crystal meth in digital form. Axel went even further dropping his sex and drugs parties speeches for lengthy talks about *"discerning eyes of the elves* and *exquisite gleaming seals of dark magic."*

After the bell rang announcing the end of the break, we went to the same staircase I had just been in, heading for the West Wing's basement, where the computer class lessons took place with The Perv. We were sure going to go for another fun ride in the teacher's Stringathon, with all the girls'

thongs perfectly placed for him to watch. It was a mellow and relaxing class, considering how he usually spaced out for enormous amounts of time and then proceeded to appear as if he was actually doing something in his computer.

When the class finished, I dragged behind while everyone went out, as the poorly maintained computer froze on me and I had to wait for it to save my files. By the time I had gone out, Axel and Mike addressed me.

"Hey, your friend is waiting for you out there," Mike told me, seemingly not very amused.

"What friend?" I instantly said, browsing manically through my mental friend library.

"Haha, yeah man, your legion of kiddies is BACK!!"

Faye was up on the staircase leading to the basement from the first floor. The guys instantly started to mock me, but left knowing they would sure spoil it for me if they stayed. At least they had the decency to respect me. Or maybe they just didn't care.

"Hi!" she said, unusually cheerful, her US flag cross dangling from her delicate neck as she leaned forwards and looked down at me from the staircase. It was a marvelous sight. Not the cross, but her as a whole; She kept staring at me, not losing eye contact for a second. I had to, like predicted, look away for a couple of seconds pretending I was coughing. I couldn't bring myself to maintain eye contact with her, finding her presence immensely superior.

"Do you know where Dave is?"

"Well, he's not here. Um ... I really have no idea ... I ... I'm sorry." I said, trying not to seem too bitter. I was still mad about her treating me like that before, blatantly ignoring me and seeming distant all the time. However, those eyes ... I couldn't possibly remain mad at her for long.

"Oh well ... no matter. Thanks anyway! See ya later, OK?"

she said, and left hastily in a delicate and cute fashion. It was funny how that encounter wiped all my bad feelings away and actually gave me another reason to think not everything was going badly. She went looking for me. I had to think about that another time; *she went looking for me ...*

Her behavior was indeed difficult to predict. Even though she had in fact ignored me the whole break, or so I thought, now she came looking specifically for me, which meant she relied on me to some extent. It also meant that her shyness was withering. The sight of her waiting for me at the stairs was a gift from Lenin himself and stayed on my memory the whole morning, the picture of the day that makes you remember *why* you had a good day at all.

Another class awaited, and with my mood slightly improved, I managed to overcome the last two remaining hours with patience and a curious sensation of security. Daydreaming about her kept me going and allowed me to ignore my surroundings completely, as everyone else seemed to bother me those days.

Now for the interesting part. Claude usually went to take the bus with me back home, even though I don't mention him a lot. Mainly because of how quiet he was and the amount of interesting conversations with him were minimal. Think of him as that friend of yours who usually blends in the background with the props. He's there but, as if he weren't. And he also isn't dying to participate.

However, that day he did play a special role, one of those moments you never forget.

Since Claude was also annoyed by the amount of people in the bus stop, we walked to the bus station a few block from there, our bus would make a long turn there anyway and buy us some time. It was also what we used to do before with Mike and Axel, but everyone seemed to be unreliable now

407

and the group had sort of disbanded. As such, we all hung out inside the school but outside everyone stuck to themselves.

Many people walked to their houses following the same route, like Billy and Robbie during their stay in The Crucible. Usually, you would walk near people you knew only by sight from other classes as well, creating the diverse melting pot community feeling so common in Loynne's. To get to the bus station, Claude and I walked to the Méndez Center taking Terán Street and ignoring Noriega Street, the street the school was in, which ended right in Paradise Avenue. Going to the bus station instead of to the school's stop through the Méndez Center shortcut would provide us with some cover from the masses of loud and obnoxious students, and grant us a moment of well-deserved peace and quiet after the punishing six hours in that hellhole.

As Claude and I walked in our mellow limbo of silence, he broke the peace with his monotonous voice. It was officially the first time Claude said anything that made me jump.

"Look; there's your friend."

This was so amazing to even describe; Faye was talking to a friend, with her back turned on us, near an elaborate and tall marble fountain that decorated the entrance. I was wondering if she had seen us, as I had this paranoid thought she was near-omniscient, especially when my presence lurked in the vicinity. This moment was reminiscent of a hunter spotting amongst the bushes that precious trophy that needs a well-placed shot in the head, the slightest movement scaring that coveted prey away. I pushed Claude out of the line of vision, and whispered:

"Shh … do you think she's seen us?" Claude seemed heavily unimpressed, even impatient with this.

"Dunno," he sighed. The tone of his voice was enough.

"Look, what should I do??"

"Well ... do whatever you want. But do it now. You're going to miss the bus."

"OK ... well ... here I go ... catch you later," I said, as I felt the blood and adrenaline boil inside me with anxiety.

"As you wish." Claude said. He didn't seem bothered this time, but more like warning me of something. Or even having some knowledge I lacked about past familiar experiences he did not want to share. At the moment, in my euphoria, I only thought: "*Hanging out with you is a first-row ticket to permanent virginity.*"

Without the company of my friend, I could now act the way I was more comfortable with, solo; I marched toward my target full of confidence, struggling against the powerful smell of cherry which was more and more noticeable with each step. Her friend spotted me and warned her as soon as I made myself visible. Could it be that they actually hadn't seen me before?

"Hey!" I began. "What a surprise! What are you doing here?"

"Hey ..." She said. Her friend muttered something like "*OK well, I'd better go now*" and shared a naughty smirk with Faye, as if to say "*you're so telling me everything about this later!*" I felt important. Maybe these little girls saw me as a kind of omnipotent god. Or maybe I was making Faye look socially more popular amongst her friends as an older, bigger guy wanted a slice of her. This situation boosted my self-esteem in inexplicable ways and enabled me to endure the following:

"Hey, so ... how are you?" I asked.

"Oh, I'm fine ... You?"

"Oh well, I was just going to the bus station and I found

you here, so I thought 'let's say hello.' "

"Oh, right," She replied, smiling faintly. The voices in my head were now both cheering in complete unison. With the unanimous approval of the voices, I went on ahead.

"Listen, do you mind if I tag along? I really hate going back home at this time, too early, I feel like walking around a bit first."

"Yeah, sure."

This was our very first full-fledged conversation together, no ChitChat in between. It felt strangely normal at first, as if there was nothing to fear. However, her acute charm began to manifest greatly as I studied her from head to toe, and got calmed by the sound of her voice. Her smell was incredible; the "Balearic Cherry" swept me off my feet whenever it went near my nose.

"Soo, yeah, how are you doing with stuff in general, how are those exams coming along?" I couldn't hear anything about what she was telling me. The noise of cars in the background distorted her voice to unintelligible sound waves not even hearable by bats. She never spoke with a cheery tone either. It seemed as if it was heavily forced and done only to be over with it. I insisted however, and tried to talk about anything I could. My subjects of conversation where actually running thin, and I hated sounding like I was talking because of the sake of it. This needed a turn.

"Ohh, alright. Well, look, enough about exam stuff. I got something to tell you," I said.

"Oh ... what's that?"

"Well, you know. We're all day talking about stuff like this, there's more to life, you know! Aren't you ever going to talk to me about other stuff? You know, personal stuff! What you like doing, what places you go to when you go out, the usual!"

"Oh, well ... I dunno ... I like going out wherever."

"Yeah, well, that's the thing. Where? Out dancing and clubbing? Stuff like that?" I said this to test her; for some reason at that time, I always wanted to find out whether the girl liked to go out clubbing like Kannies did. It was some sort of filter that instantly allowed me to categorize the girl.

"Oh no. I hate dancing."

"You do?"

"Can't stand it. That's for happy-bubbly types like the ones in my class. It's so lame. They're pathetic."

"Well, I can't say it's all bad. I mean, once in a while it's OK to do it, I think." This was another thing I did; to try to make myself appear dauntless and outgoing, should the girl think less of me for being an introvert who preferred solitude.

"Well, alright," she uncaringly said.

"And listen, what about your friends? What, don't you ever do anything with them?"

"Oh yeah, well, just walking around and stuff like that. Nothing special. Sometimes with my friend Chelsea we get so bored that we are up all night until like 04:00 walking around and ripping those stupid kick-boxing posters they stick everywhere, you know, the ones that have all these stupid Kannies in fighting poses trying to look tough, like that Boa chick from Whitedale, she's so stupid looking ..."

"Mmm ... and that's all you do, you don't go to the beach or anything?"

"You're kidding. I hate the beach. Nothing interesting there for me to do. I prefer to do other things. Like skating." I could notice she was actually lying here, so as to not appear lame and dull. She was never up to much, and found herself almost all the time alone or at home. Ryan had confirmed this. So had Billy. I was playing now with information on my part, and intended to make good use of it. I also knew that at this point she didn't skate anymore.

"Skating? Do you skate?"

"Ice skate. Yeah, I do."

"Woah. I mean. I never thought of you as an ice skater."

"Why can't I be one?"

"Haha, well, sure you can! I meant you just don't look like one. I mean aren't ice skaters supposed to be all thin and pretty?" Bombs away. I had totally screwed up there, due to my own brutish, sincere nature. With Faye, Soviet spontaneous honesty went to the dogs. I remained certain that I had offended her severely. But what I meant was that biologically, she didn't share the traits of the usual ice skaters you would see on TV. By 'pretty' I meant generic beauty, and by thin I meant to express how her slight chubbiness and healthily fleshy body held superior attractiveness in every way. But how could I possibly transmit to her how I would have had her anytime instead of those thin pretty girls? It was the biggest compliment I could have ever given her.

"Well, I know I'm ugly, you don't have to say it twice. But I sure can skate." I was surprised she didn't take it so personal. It seemed she took for granted she was ugly for real, it wasn't a stunt for attention. My ass was saved, but I was sure she took it as a personal offense on some level.

"Aww, come on, I didn't say you were ugly! Anyway I'm sure you're pretty good skating."

"Save for pretty, I *am* a good skater. I won last year, first place. But I haven't done it anymore since then. Competition simply bored me."

"You seem to get bored of everything quite fast."

"Sure do. Always have. I hate it when it's always the same, always so dull. I like change, excitement, surprises ... It's always so damn boring." You might assume I always took these statements of her as motivational phrases. To me, this was translated as "*I need a boyfriend to deflower me fast*"

and "*I need to live a lot of morally-dubious adventures involving large amounts of alcohol.*" I could actually provide her with that; it was my main objective to have her think of me me as someone she could experience excitement with and not the boring, generic friend I was temporarily disguised as. I was failing at making her discover the true me and the intentions behind my friendship, even though I thought them pretty apparent and obvious. What else could I do? Confess it all? It was still too early. Perhaps in a few days more. Then I'd do it when I hadn't a thing to lose.

"Listen, maybe you can work that out one day, but for now just try to enjoy what you can about most of life. You know, you're only 15! I mean when I was your age I thought everything was amazing and wonderful. You're very pessimistic to be so young." It was wonderful the way I could present myself as such a happy, optimistic person, or maybe it was the effect she had over me. When I was 15 I endured the nightmare of abandoning the Motherland, adapting to a system I had been trained to bring down since Pioneer School and endure the persistent hell of Kannovschina. I was anything but optimistic.

"I know, gosh, I never said I don't enjoy life, it's just that right now I have a lot of obligations."

"Yeah, I know what you mean. Too bad we couldn't get to know each other in more uh ... peaceful times."

"Sure."

"But hey, when all these exams are over and the first term finishes then we can go and have some fun! You know ... this is Loynne's Island after all. There should be somewhere here you can have fun."

"Yeah, sure."

"I'm guessing the US was better than this to you?"

"In some ways ... I was only little after all, when we left.

The recession had only started and my mom thought it was better to move here, where everything was on the rise. I was 8 when we left."

"So you barely remember anything about the US?"

"Bits. It was seven years ago after all. Many things have happened and it's kinda blurry."

"Well, there sure are a lot of people from the US around here, almost all of my friends come from your country!"

"Yeah, well ... you speak really Unitedstatian for a Loynner ..."

"Uh ... I'm not a Loynner, I'm ... Russian."

"You are? Didn't know ..."

"Yeah ... well, Moldovan and Russian, I was born in Moldova and my parents are Russian, but I have Loynner nationality, my family came here shortly after I was born. I'm lucky I can handle the accent, I guess that's why I always attract so many people from your country ... I've never really managed to bond with the locals, actually ..."

"That makes two of us."

"But the Unitedstatians I know are not really like I imagined them to be ... take JC Vega for example ... that's the kind of people I had in mind the first time they told me this island was full of them ... luckily most of them are good people."

"Oh, he's just an idiot ... well ... at least, one *hot* idiot."

"You ... what?"

"Oh well, come on, he's hot, it's like asking you if you think Monika Strössner or Viktoria von Östinsel are hot ... you surely go around drooling each time they pass you by ..."

"Hey ... no! No way! I hate them both! In fact, I was giving this speech once, and the bitch tried to snag it from me, you know, playing seductive and all that, and I stood there firmly and said 'no,' and she couldn't believe her charm didn't work on me, so she went away offended and yelling at me."

"Are you gay?"

"Wh—what?! What makes you say that?!"

"Well, unless you're gay, which I'm not saying you are, nobody could do that. So either you're really different or really gay ..."

"Well, make that different, because I did turn her down when she asked me for my speech, and I'm not gay ..."

"Well ... it doesn't matter."

"You don't believe me, do you?"

"Well ... I'll be blunt, no."

"I'm not lying."

"Yeah well ... I don't have any way of knowing. I barely know you."

"That's true ... but ... you'll have to trust me on this. I don't like women like those two. I like ... a different kind of woman."

"Uh huh ..."

"But anyway, let's change the subject ... look, I hope you don't mind me asking, let me know if it bothers you, but your brothers trust me and have told me some stuff, you know ... about your parent's divorce and all that ... was it hard to live through all that?"

"Oh ... well ... it was hard. It always is, for any kid, isn't it? But everyone's divorced nowadays, so I guess it can be considered normal. I for one don't believe in marriage, it doesn't work."

"Well it doesn't necessarily have to be like that for everyone. Take my parents, for example, they're together!

"We'll see for how long."

"Hey, what you mean by that?!"

"Oh nothing. It's just that nothing lasts forever. People get bored quick, like me. People get depressed, get dull, get old ... that's what ruins marriages."

"Marriages have to be built on a foundation of several layers, Faye. Tolerance, trust, love, sexual attraction ... well, I guess you know about this stuff."

"Yeah, sure. But eitherways, stuff crumbles."

"(Like the USSR ...)"

"What?"

"Oh ... nothing ..." I couldn't help it. Ryan warned me against it, but I was unable to resist. I had to discuss politics, I had to know what she thought of the world I came from. It would have been blasphemy to me if she had either a negative opinion or no idea at all. I didn't want to associate her with an ignorant little Unitedstatian, an anti-Communist right-wing fanatic or a pacifist Western happy-go-lucky bubble-head hippie.

"Look, see, as you know, the world was divided by two spheres of influence, named superpowers. This historical period has a particular name, *Kholodnaya Voina*, I mean Cold War! That slipped."

"What was that? You speak funny."

"Yeah, that's Russian actually. Sometimes I get a bit mixed up."

"Oh, right."

"You ... you do know I'm Russian-Moldovan, right? Maybe your brothers haven't mention that to you ..."

"Yeah, I dunno, I thought you were Russian, or Russian-Loynner, or something ..."

"Oh ... well, where I was heading toward was that the world was divided like you know, between capitalism and Communism. Basically I was going to ask for your opinion on the subject, your side in the political spectrum ..."

"Opinion? Well ... I hate politicians. They're the main evil of this world. They do nothing but oppress us and lie to us, no matter who they are or what they stand for." Now, this was

outrageous. She was completely apolitical with no affiliations. That was worse than counter-revolutionary activities. She was an apolitical hedonist ignorant.

"I beg to differ. We need politicians. All we need to do is keep them from corruption and privileged positions through occasional popular uprisings, purges without trial and Mass Terror. Lenin and Stalin advocated terror tactics against the bourgeoisie and the far-right imperialists, and turned the USSR into the most powerful nation on Earth. China followed the same path, and it is now the world's greatest superpower."

"Oh, I don't care. Politicians are sleazy and dirty, that's a *fact*."

"And so is the system that makes them being sleazy and corrupt! That's why we have to change it!"

"If you want work, you got work, anyone who doesn't wanna work is just lazy and wants everything handed over to him. My mom was nothing when she came here and with her own hands started her seamstress business and she does very well."

"Yes, with the subtle difference that not everyone is a petit bourgeois like your mom! Intellectuals and revolutionaries like Lenin, Stalin and Mao laid the foundations for true Socialism, we just have to aim toward that goal. Workers, peasants, they build Communism with their bare hands, and intellectuals guide them toward true Socialism! Like Che Guevara throughout all of Latin America!"

"Oh, I love Che. He was a great man."

"Ah ... what?"

"Yeah, he was so brave. I hated my country for having him killed. Fuckin' CIA. I detest the governments and politicians because of things like that. But I admire Che. He wasn't a politician or nothin' like that, and he helped the people."

"Ah, he was a politician, Faye. He laid the foundations for the Cuban Republic and served as Minister of Agriculture for a short time. He did reject further administrative positions in the government but because he wanted to spread the Revolution worldwide, and that's how he was executed in Bolivia."

"Yeah ..."

"But the power of Socialism prevails. His executioner, Mario Terán, a disgusting alcoholic who had personally requested to shoot Che because some of his friends died in a firefight with him, had his sight restored by Cuban doctors, doctors trained as the best specialists in the entire world thanks to Fidel's rule. See? Not all governments and politicians are alike, Faye. You just have to learn not to listen to the distorted propaganda of the West. Believe me, all mainstream news networks are manipulated generally toward the right."

"Che was a great man, but politicians only care about power and money. That's it. They're the same as criminals."

"Well ... I'm not going to argue with you ... but at least I'm glad that you're not so far away like Ryan said."

"What did Pizza Face say about me?"

"Ahh, nothing really, except that you're an apolitical brat who doesn't know up from down."

"Aw, screw that dick. He thinks he knows so much. He's just a prick."

"You guys don't defend each other a lot, do you?"

"Why should I? Screw those dicks. They never defend me or do anything in the house so screw 'em."

"But they claim they do, and that you never do anything!"

"Yeah, to save face, which is all they do. I have to do everything, I'm like a maid. My mother needs a hand you know, and they're incapable of helping just a little. That's why men are lazy sleazes and assholes, all of them."

"Ah ... sure. Right. And what does that make women, then?"

"Women are bitches and sluts. They're sly, fake, competitive and ambitious and use people all the time."

"And does that suit you?"

"Mmm ... sort of. You could say that, yeah."

"Well then, you're fake? You lie? Are you lying to me now?"

"Every woman you ask this stuff to is going to tell you exactly that. That women are fake. So I'm going to be sincere for once and tell you that yes, I consider myself fake."

"Does that mean I can't trust you?"

"Nobody should trust anybody. Trust doesn't exist. People use each other, lie to each other, and then hug and smile. Everyone is fake. So if I were you I wouldn't trust anybody either."

"Not anybody not you, huh ..."

"Yes." It was funny how she tried to express herself and educate me at the same time. I was playing dumb, letting her pour out lots of sincere information, no matter how many times she emphasized her essence to be deceitful. I was the eyes and ears devouring her from a physical and psychological stance, and she was the book slowly opening up. The only thing wrong about this situation was her tense and serious demeanor. I began to wonder if her personality was like that by default or if I could be truly annoying her.

In the end, I seemed to have been proven entirely right by the time we reached our destination; after mumbling a flavorless "*alright, bye,*" Faye turned her back on me ready to leave, but something which had been bothering me above all else, made me call out for her. In retrospect, I guess I simply didn't want her to leave me so quickly, and in such a detached way.

"Wait!" I shouted, stopping her advance.

"Yeah?" she replied while turning to face me, looking concerned and slightly tired, perhaps even irritated.

"Can I ask you something?" Faye became impressively curious when hearing this. Seemingly garnering her full attention, she replied:

"Yeah, sure ... what it is?"

"Why do you always wear that cross?"

"What? My necklace?" she asked, lifting it with her right hand for me to see.

"Yeah ... um ... this may sound odd, but ... are you by any chance ... a religious person?" Faye seemed mildly amused upon hearing this, and for the first time since I met her smiled genuinely, making her look like an entirely new person. Her eyes became impossibly warm and tender, a look I will never succeed in forgetting. However, the joyful facial expression vanished instantly when she gave her reply, turning serious again:

"With time you see there are things that you can't believe in and people who you can't trust ... I don't believe blindly in things, I find it hard to put my faith in anything or anyone, you always get some kind of dissatisfaction ... so to answer your question I'd say ... no. No way. Never. I only believe in what I see, and nothing else.."

"So the cross ... does it have any meaning?"

"Well ... not religiously ... but ... I'll explain that some other day. Promise." Faith shrugged shyly in what I can only describe as the cutest gesture ever performed by a girl, got red in the face and began walking toward me, looking right through me with those brilliant green eyes which didn't seem bored anymore. She stood before me, majestic, elegant and imposing despite her small size, and smiling with glee she presented me her right cheek for me to kiss, in a cute, eager

and childish fashion.

I didn't know how to react, being caught completely off-guard by her sudden change in attitude. Deciding too hastily, I planted two quick kisses like it was usual in Loynne's, the first on the right cheek and the second on the left one. However, she was still presenting me her cheek after I was done, and I comprehended she wanted three kisses, so I kissed her right cheek again. I was left shocked and surprised by this, as it indicated affection above normal; well above normal.

I watched as Faye went away, waving goodbye shyly and walking nervously toward the building's lobby. What did I do right? I didn't know back then. I only knew that walking Faye home had started to turn things in my favor in ways I could not possibly fathom; three kisses could somewhat be used as a way to show phony affection out of compromise, but nobody that wanted to express detached compromise gave you three kisses just like that, instead, they would give you two, and even that was considered affectionate enough. Giving someone three kisses was considered an act of incredible and utmost affection between a man and a woman, second only to a direct kiss on the mouth, and thus it had to be used sparingly so as to not confuse the other person into believing the bond went deeper than it actually did. Many husbands used this gesture so as to express clean love to their wives while in public, as it demonstrated their joy when meeting or parting ways, and passionate lovers used it too. Gay guys used it often to greet their girl friends and lovers, but then again they were truly over-the-top, so it can hardly count. Heterosexual guys with girl friends who could be ex-lovers, on the other hand, used the gesture as a way of perhaps acknowledging their romantic past. As you can imagine, the fact of Faye expecting three kisses from me served only to confuse me more than ever. One kiss between a guy and a girl meant a

very casual and insignificant "hello," usually used by people who met everyday and did not have need for too much proto-col, or between guys themselves as a way of showing very affectionate heterosexual male-bonding. If Faye had expected one kiss, she would have shown me how insignificant I was to her; if she had expected two, she would have complied with normal protocol. But three? She had no reason to set for one or three kisses, only two; by expecting three she either demonstrated how fake and phony she was, and how she hid her true feelings, or how she felt something strong for me. Stubbornly refraining from moving her cheek until the final kiss had been given, she had clearly decided she wanted me to give her three. So, was this the ultimate proof of her sup-posed dishonest essence, her effort at trying to tell me a ro-mantic hint or her cruel manipulative mind at work?

At the time, I did not let my confusion bother me; I was simply too overcome by joy to care. I headed back to the bus station following Paradise Avenue, immensely satisfied not only because the social exchange had turned up wonderfully, but because she had given me just the answer I expected to my question. She was Unitedstatian, yet not religious. She didn't believe the Earth to have been created 6,000 years ago by an omnipotent being no one's ever seen. She didn't believe in the aberrant lies that preach we don't come from apes and that dinosaurs were placed for us to find by the same god testing the belief of his creation. She was above all that de-ranged sociopathy so common in her homeland. I wasn't sure how much being far away from it and under the influence of Loynne's shaped this mentality, but I wanted to deceive my-self into thinking that even in the land of theocratic totalitari-anism she would have remained an exemplary atheist.

Upon hearing this answer, I no longer harbored any

doubts about the situation whatsoever; I now had every reason in the world to justify how I genuinely loved her.

- CHAPTER VII -

Glasnost

"In the Soviet Army, it takes more courage to retreat than advance."

- JOSEPH STALIN -

Soviet Bolshevik Revolutionary and Marxist Theorist, General Secretary of the Communist Party of the Soviet Union, Generalissimus of the Soviet Union and Vanquisher of Fascism

---

"Once again in international news, a protest organized by Unitedstatian citizens concerned about the massive shootings plaguing the North American country ended in tragedy today when police and ROA pro-gun activists alike charged against the protestors, deriving into a lethal fire-fight when someone fired several shots confusing both police and ROA members. The event resulted in 21 dead and 17 wounded in critical condition. Most of them are not expected to live past today.

Regarding the United States epidemic, the UN is consid-ering severe actions if the US government does not prevent this outbreak, which has once again revived the debate of religious freedom or otherwise over health, science and the safety of others, a freedom Unitedstatians staunchly defend but has ignited protests all over the world. Citizens of the globe view themselves as the potential victims of an unstop-pable pandemic unless the North American nation puts in

motion a governmental quarantine, something US President Johnny Marshall and his entire administration have opposed vehemently citing religious beliefs and low popular support inside the country—"

I became glad when hearing this piece of news. The US still had hope after all if Unitedstatians themselves protested against the psychotic derangement of the government, the religious zealots and the ROA fanatics. I wondered how much time would pass and how many Unitedstatians would die until the progressives finally toppled the brutish, racist, redneck, cowboy televangelists in power. But at this moment, I couldn't care less for the news; I took my backpack and headed outside, sporting an unusual smile illuminated by the pleasant morning sun as another day to see my loved one awaited me.

• • • • •

As you may predict, walking Faye home after school became a forbidden taboo blacklisted by Mantis brothers standards. They had started asking me why I was doing it, and why I didn't do it with them instead. I excused my behavior by saying that I was simply walking with my friends and happened to bump into her, and that it had since evolved into a routine. They always gave me a warning and a "stay away" kind of speech whenever I did this. However, I had slowly started to consider it an advantage, as they would ensure I measured my "harassment" and gave her time to breathe. Each time I walked Faye home she seemed brighter and less negative, bursting in a shy and restrained laughter from time to time, or simply smiling more than usual. She still didn't look me right in the eye while walking, but I thought it was

due to her finding it comfier to look forwards instead of sideways and upwards to my distant eyes. Conversations also started to have a less forced tone and arose more naturally due to increased mutual confidence, and each time she left she performed the same gesture of presenting me her right cheek very willingly, wanting me to plant three affectionate goodbye kisses on her ultra-smooth cheeks. Most girls only expected you to kiss their cheeks and would not kiss back, but not Faye; her heart-shaped lips always kissed my cheeks as mine simultaneously kissed hers back. Her kisses were not silent either; one time she even let out a loud and vocalized "*mwah!*" while kissing me, smiling vigorously, true happiness printed all over her eyes. At the end of our after-school walks, she now always waved goodbye at me in her own funny way, in that unimaginably cute fashion of hers, ever so timid, noticeably happier than when I had first walked her home successfully.

At school, our interactions increased dramatically even if it only was for brief instances, and I became surprised at how her highly negativist and overly pessimistic conversations waned almost completely. She would look for me specifically whenever she had time to spare and talk for a short while in between hours, or just simply smile gleefully at the sight of me when our paths crossed. I had established myself – to a still small, but undeniably positive degree – as a trusted, recognized friend, and someone she thought of as an ally in such a social environment. There was nothing wrong going on for me at this stage, except maybe the fact of me turning my back visibly on friends. "*Screw them,*" I usually thought. "*When I'm strolling around school with Faye at my side I won't be needing anyone at all. And that will happen soon, very soon.*"

• • • • •

It was an unusually cold and cloudy November day, more specifically, 27th of November at approximately 11:40. I was about to set my plan in motion, and proceeded with an instinct and accuracy which felt terribly truer to animals than humans.

After the first two classes I walked up and down the stairs in high hopes of finding her by accident. Even though I had predicted the encounter would be front and clear, it turned out to be the opposite when I saw her talking to a friend with her back turned on me, wearing the pink miniskirt and her usual small heeled shoes. A tight black top showed her perfect white naked back to me in all its glory, the "Balearic Cherry" essence almost knocking me out when coming near her. I passed by quickly, acknowledging her by patting her softly on the shoulder while descending the staircase, heading toward the gymnasium. My plans increased in difficulty. I had to keep my looks and smell in check, and as such had decided to rely on plenty of cologne, hair gel and deodorant. For some retarded Loynner reason people were forced to stink for the rest of the classes as we weren't allowed to shower, something they justified by saying we'd be late for subsequent classes, but I thought it was a common thing everyone had begun to accept and cope with. Most people just brought in shirts and poured some deodorant on themselves hoping that'd do the trick, and that was precisely what I had decided to do.

Astonishingly, the usual lack of focus present in unpredictable social daily life was absent for the full morning, allowing me to concentrate on the task. Anxiety and paranoia also vanished giving me a faint sensation of bravery, a dramatic courage nurtured by my different frustrations toward

this disgusting Western life, which weren't a few despite my young age. I focused all my energies in nurturing this unpleasantness even further, always remembering how great the reward would be.

The rest of the classes were a piece of cake, but still further increased the dormant anxieties. Only two more hours until the deadline; at this point I recited inside my head the steps in order, picturing an imaginary me following them accordingly, hopefully achieving the desired end. These were:

1. Remain vigilant of the time and rush to the exit the moment the bell rings.

2. Lose track of Ryan or anyone tailing.

3. Head immediately toward the Méndez Center and wait exactly where she was the first time.

4. Establish friendly conversation, not suspicious, easygoing in nature. Keep this up until reaching The Crucible, at the parking lot entrance.

5. If conversation goes well and she seems cheery, attempt flirty conversation. If successful, get nearer slyly and subsequently kiss.

6. Tell Ryan I'm banging his sister.

7. Laugh at amazingly angry face in blissful glee.

Alternative Plan

1. If conversation was dull or mood was faulty, attempt to cheer her up before deadline. If unsuccessful, lie about having to get Ryan something and follow her.

2. Improvise before she goes.

I had devised the alternative plan as an unnecessary precaution. I was certain that given Faye's attitude recently,

everything I dreamt of would come to pass that very same day. It was only rational. She was sweeter and more caring, seemed to enjoy my company greatly and had even started to meet me at recess just for the sake of talking. There was nothing against me. It was time to act and wipe out all the uncertainties once and for all.

My eyes kept looking at the digits in my Hipp-Man's watch, waiting anxiously with an incredible energy ready to be unleashed. I was losing focus momentarily. My daydreaming fantasies seemed to awaken and played all kinds of situations in my mind. My nervous heartbeats didn't help, and the adrenaline was as present as ever. Maybe I would not find her at the Méndez Center. Maybe she'd take an alternative path. Maybe she'd slap my guts while attempting to kiss her. Perhaps, she would reject me coldly and without hesitation like so many girls before. Or, maybe I could claim the prize, kiss her and go home a hero. Everything was at stake on this one, nonetheless, a voice kept repeating inside my head the reasons why this was a situation to care about:

"(If everything fails there are more girls out there. Don't lose sleep over one more rejection. Several other girls have done this before. Why care now?)"

"(I care because I always wanted true love, a pure and faithful woman who I can share everything with. I care because this might be it. I care because this feels good. This feels the right way to go.)"

"(Do as you must, then. What will you do if what you fear the most reveals itself before you?)"

"(I'll just go on with living. I'll look for another symbol that represents exactly what I want, and then will also attempt to claim it. It will happen eventually. I can't fail on this endeavor.)"

"*(You can, and you might as well fail. Nothing has ever gone the way you wanted except for maybe a few times. Why should it go well now, merely because you wish for it? Be ready for the worst. If this is how you want it, then prepare to suffer.)*"

"*(So be it.)*"

I imagined that whole conversation with Ryan as an inspirational model, I guess. The perfect model for bringing down dreams and hopes. I had to think of every possible outcome, and prepare myself for the ones not even my mind could imagine. *Si vis pacem, para bellum.*

Thankfully, the real Ryan was busy actually paying attention to the class for once. Wolfgang, Axel and Mike sat opposite from me on the front right corner, unusually quiet and looking bored. Axel was in fact sleeping; I found out while playing closer attention. Mike attempted to watch TV from other countries on his phone as he had shown off to us. Wolfgang slyly used his samurai long hair to cover his earphones.

I looked at the Hipp-Man's watch again. 13:22; three more minutes to go.

13:23. I was getting ready to jump at the slightest ring of the bell. I looked around. A headphone plug fell from Wolfgang's ear and I amused myself at his attempt to put it back on in three lightning-fast Aikido moves. The rest of the class was unusually quiet. Tom Richards kept talking about how the US Department of Defense had called him on several occasions to request insight on his scientific knowledge only to later officially deny his involvement.

13:24. Any moment now ... Mike slapped Axel on the back of the head. Axel woke up with a loud "*¡¿qué?!*" and hit Mike

strongly on the arm only to later hiss in pain holding his wrist. Ryan repressed his laughter getting immensely red, choosing to snort loudly instead. Tom Richards asked him if there was anything funny about his story and Ryan immediately became upright and serious.

13:25. *"Come on,"* I thought. *"This isn't funny."* I took a peak at Ryan hoping he wouldn't look at me back. I needed to evade his presence as soon as possible when the bell rang; I would have dreaded coming into contact with him at the chaos that was the main gate. He would obviously ask where I was headed in such a rush, and I would have no excuse, at least, not under his scrutiny. If I met him at the gates, there would be no shaking him, in turn becoming an instant defeat.

13:26. I looked outside the window. People were crossing the street mostly going to the sports complex, surely students who had managed to escape from the school. I remembered how my greatest joy and purpose used to be able to sneak away and get immediately back home. Everything had changed now. But I couldn't lose sight of my current objective. I had to focus and got back to peaking at Ryan, who was now busy, drawing on his sketchbook again.

13:27; *the bell had finally rung.*

I rushed to the exit, avoiding eye contact with anyone and trampling one or two desks on my way out. I ran to the main gates where people were just starting to pile up, meaning I had enough time to run ahead and cover more terrain while I waited for her at the Méndez Center, where I had last seen her with Claude. Waiting for three people squeezing through the gate at the same time, an unquestionable Loynner custom, I walked as quickly as I could repressing my need to run, as it would have raised too much suspicion. Ryan was proba-

bly observing me right now, hidden somewhere between the crowds, and I couldn't afford to give him more proof to suspect me. I crossed the street looking at the now overwhelming crowd of students, which I guessed would roughly reach the 800 student mark. The street was now flooded with people and cars, and it was hard to keep track of Ryan following me during this frenzy. I was glad I wasn't amongst the crowds and delighted myself on the advantage of being already out of the school's perimeter.

I had been preparing for this all day long. Now that I was well out of sight, I pulled out my Hipp-Man and set it to the tune of Kino's "*Mama Anarkhiya*" — "Mother Anarchy" — running as fast as I could to the Méndez Center, my entire body fueled by Soviet energy.

When I reached the place I found myself panting, sweating, hoping this would not undermine my chances at seducing her. I actually wondered whether it would be a factor at all. She wasn't like a girl from The Motherland, a dirty tomboy thinking only about playing football. Faye was basically the most delicate female human being I had laid eyes upon. Of course this had to be a factor in the overall seduction process.

I took a minute to calm down, hidden from sight and patiently waiting on a top floor that overlooked the fountain she had been next to with her friend that day, near the stairs. I waited long minutes, shattering my already fragile nerves. Figures and figures passed by, thankfully none looking up, but none of them was Faye. I had recognized some students and was fearful anyone would spot me and engage in conversation, or even worse, blow my cover.

"*Come on,*" I thought, my desperation growing. "*You HAVE to go through here. You always do.*"

Watching at the figures popping into my field of view, only

a pair of eyes met mine. It was only a friend of Gordon timidly waving "hello" with a gesture. I immediately felt relief at the false alarm, this wasn't a threat under any circumstances. I greeted him back dismissively as my eyes scouted for Faye like searchlights, hoping to spot her approaching the fountain below. Peace returned to the Méndez Center as time passed by, and all students had surely left school. All except for Faye. I was sure now that she had taken an alternate route, for whichever reason. Maybe the brothers, keeping a watchful eye on things, abducted her before my plan came to fruition, like Ryan would do. He was a sneaky bastard and I was sure he'd do whatever he could to thrash my strategy and humiliate me before his sister. He was primal in some aspects, and wanted to maintain dominance in this field.

A few moments passed, moments in which my thoughts told me to abandon hope and probably throw myself out of my vantage point. Just as I moved the first leg onwards to the bus stop, my vigilant eyes caught a glimpse of a lone, small figure holding a pink folder. The joy I experienced at that moment remains unsurpassed to this day.

Stealthily, I got off from the second floor and followed her to the flight of stairs leading to the street level. I approached her from behind trying to scare her like those Kanny jocks used to do all the time with the Loynnerin cows, who usually reacted positively to it. But Faye was clearly not an annoying immature little bitch like your regular Loynnerin. She seemed barely amused, said something that sounded like "*ohhh, no*" in a timid smile, which I didn't know if it forecasted a bad omen – meaning she truly felt like she didn't want to see me at that particular moment – or if she reacted to the "scare" in her own fashion. Or, she could be simply tired from school. I didn't care; today, everything would be cleared once and for all. I struggled to follow her facial expression all the way

through so much hair, fringe and face pointing down exactly parallel to the floor.

"Heyyy, how's it going! Fancy meeting you here!" I said in my rehearsed easygoing and carefree tone. Truth be told, I couldn't have been any other way around her. Joy used to overcome my brain with such force I was transformed into a smiling happy idiot. Luckily for me she didn't look up that often to see it for herself.

"Oh … fine. You?"

"Yeah, yeah, fine too … What are you up to? Why so sad looking?"

"I'm just so sunk in these exams, I'm really sorry. In exam era I'm always like this. I just can't be talked to. I'm like this with everyone." She tried to smile but couldn't get it quite right. She was clearly bothered about something, and I was starting to panic. She had been wonderful up to now. Why this sudden unwelcome change now, of all moments?

"Well, don't worry, you'll probably pass, right?" I didn't want this to start off with a stupid dull worthless exam talk. My thoughts warned me of bad things and each action of hers was like a death wish signed in blood. I was good with human behavior and psychology, and even better when knowing I was making a clown of myself, or that I was just unwanted. This was clearly the situation, but it would just make it worse if I left. Mainly because I wouldn't ever miss an opportunity to be around her, and I'd just depress myself on the way home feeling that magnetic impulse to be at her side again, not knowing when the next chance would present itself. There was also the fact that something was bothering her and she didn't want to tell me. Why would she go back to her old self after so much progress? I had to find out what had happened. Perhaps something personal, problems with a relative, a pet dying, anything. I never bought that exam bullshit for a

second.

Walking her home felt awfully different from previous weeks. I was back to square one. Why today out of all days?! I remember talking to her about Billy and Robbie, where she had met them, if she was good friends with them and the like. I usually talked about whatever came to my mind without even thinking, and she had found herself doing the same, but today something failed. There was even this awkward interval where we walked in front of the entire Community Center without speaking a single word, and she would never look at me, when I had my eyes fixed on every action she performed. She would also walk a bit ahead of me, making me look as if she was trying to get away and I was following. This was particularly embarrassing when you knew the facts like I did as the perpetrator, and felt exactly like a pathetic lapdog following her.

We finally made it to the now familiar rear parking lot entrance of The Crucible. Faye stopped, said something like *"alright ... well ..."* as if to say "so, come on, get going," and presented me her right cheek like usual, seemingly more relieved and faintly smiling. I couldn't and wouldn't let the whole day be ruined after waiting so much for the right time. I actually pondered in my mind whether it was the right time, and if I should just forget about her now that I could, without putting my foot more into it. Then, that stupid voice not a single man should ever listen to went ahead and said:

"(IF YOU LET MORE TIME PASS BY YOU'LL REGRET IT AND WILL NEVER ACCOMPLISH ANYTHING, DO IT NOW AND IF YOU'RE SCREWED YOU'RE SCREWED, AND THEN YOU CAN FORGET ABOUT HER, GO HOME AND FORGET SHE EVER EXISTED.)"

"Well ..." she said, in a way that sounded like "*alright loser, scram already.*" She was still presenting me her cheek and I resisted the inner struggle to grab that face and plant a long kiss in its heart-shaped lips. Instead, I stayed right where I was and said:

"Look, I forgot, I have to go to your house and give something to Ryan that he left in class."

"Oh, well ... I can give it to him."

"Oh no no, it's not just giving him the thing, I have to tell him something as well, so uh ... if you don't mind I'll go with you."

"Oh ... OK then."

"*This works*" I thought, while Faye scouted ahead and went rapidly inside the building, to the main lobby. It's almost impossible to describe the pressure I was feeling in my chest; I could feel my heart rate going up, the adrenaline being pumped, the rest of the world moving around me in slow motion. The moment was approaching and for the first time in my life, I had to act, all by myself, without any outside help or advice. This was my project, my idea and my duty.

I pulled myself together and trailed after her, looking at a sign I had never seen before placed next to the elevators. It said something like "NOT ALLOWED TO RIDE THE ELEVATOR: CHILDREN UNDER 15 WITHOUT PARENTS OR GUARDIANS."

"*Huh*" I said, jokingly. "*You're good to go then.*"

She barely smiled to that. It was as if her lips lost the ability to smile or even bend. I shut up knowing I was probably defeated unless I did something and couldn't bear the awkward silence and the stupid situation I had gotten myself into. I thought of kissing her in the elevator but, that would have been seriously awkward if she had rejected me. And then I would have to explain my behavior to her brothers, in

case she told them. No, I couldn't risk it. It was a rushed and stupid move. Wondering what to do as time passed by, I studied Faye; she lost her interest in talking, as I could see from her absent body language.

My attempt to start talking was interrupted when some guy got in with his dog, completely shredding the intimacy and what was left of the slaughtered mood.

"Oh, hey guys! Haha, coming back from school huh? Yeah, good kids. I'm just coming back of walking my little Marla around a bit, you know, she needs the exercise. Good kids, good kids alright."

Faye smiled shyly and briefly to the guy, a stance very similar to mine. I seized the moment to stare at her; she was as beautiful as ever. A pink miniskirt, a tight black top, her straight long hair hiding her face, her pale skin glowing in the darkness of the elevator, her soft hands holding the pink folder delicately, her nails painted black contrasting against the incredibly smooth and white skin ... It was time. It would have been criminal to miss pressing that tight body against mine, to plant a kiss in those virginal lips just because of nerves, caution, manners, common sense or whatnot. The world could have gone up in flames as long as I got a taste of her in that exact moment. What's more, I would have done anything in my power to get my way in that particular instance of time. I had to make it happen.

The man got off as soon as we had reached the fourth floor. That meant only three more floors to get my act together and act like a man.

Three ...

To be leader and stop following her like a pathetic lapdog.

Two ...

To finally take command of the situation and impose my will.

One ...

The doors opened and she was already walking out with impressive agility. I had to do something fast, no matter how desperate. I quickly grabbed her by the shoulder and uttered *"Wait, don't go, I need to tell you something."*

I never expected her reaction. Predicting an annoyed face, complete with eyes shining dangerously and lips facing downwards in unearthly frustration, Faye suddenly became red as a tomato, laughed gently and looked at the floor in total awkwardness, completely frozen on the spot. I smirked too, perhaps a desperate attempt of a smile before accepting my doomed destiny.

Renewed confidence and strength were born from seeing her reactions. With true nerves of steel, I patiently rested my arm on her left shoulder, feeling amazingly better when doing so, as touching the hot, delicate skin improved my mood exponentially. Then, we walked slowly through the corridor, with very short steps. I gained all the confidence I needed when she didn't shrug my arm off, not a sign of rejection in her body.

"Can't we talk about that later? By ChitChat, maybe?" she asked. My first thought about this was that I had already won. I could claim victory for certain. Faye was the kind of girl who would always talk about these things in the digital world, not having as of yet learned the necessary social skills to face a direct proposal like this one. It was now terribly obvious that she was overwhelmed and embarrassed by an

event which I presumed was a first in her life. I couldn't help but think she had smelled this from my attitude the past few weeks. Was she expecting me to stop the childish courting, and was that why her mood had gone from negative to positive in the last weeks, or was she rejecting it in the only way she knew? I had to find out now or never.

"No, no, I have to tell you this now. Right now. Come on," I said, awfully calm and confident. I wasn't trying to make her like me out of the blue anymore, I was leading her toward liking me, showing her the reasons why. It was pure animal courting, dominating and straightforward. I had been nervous days ago when I was still deciding what to tell her, but at that moment, I could not have been calmer. Her body language made me confident in the last two seconds. She was submissively walking to where I was headed toward. She was fully receptive, willingly listening with all the patience in the world, spending her precious time on whatever it was I had to say. I had her full attention. With my hand still on her left shoulder, I led her toward the baluster. Being in command, my heartbeat started to calm itself down. Even so, my face still boiled hot with pulsating blood, feeling myself physically and mentally attracted to her more than ever before, indestructible, undefeatable, unstoppable.

"OK ... what is it?" She managed to whisper, still holding that gorgeous smirk, looking down at the beautiful view The Crucible provided of the city of Pilgrim Coast, but actually looking at empty spaces, assimilating, analyzing, thinking, feeling, tasting and immortalizing the moment. She placed her folder on the baluster and rested her little white arms on top of it, crossed, later sinking her head delicately between them until her mouth could not be seen. But she couldn't hide her feelings from me. Betrayed by her eyes and cheeks, I could notice she kept on smiling, as if mocking my attempt to

conquer her heart, cowering like the unwilling seductress that she was, now cornered and possibly knowing what I was trying to do, hopefully desiring it too. I began to speak in a low but confident tone, directly to her right ear.

"Faye, what I have to say is that ... well, I don't know how you're going to react, but the thing is, as you may already know, I like you; and I do so not as a friend, but as a man."

She breathed heavily, produced a sudden and incredibly cute nervous laughter, repressed it quickly and got even redder, finally settling for a neutral face, hungry for more, interested in hearing what else I had to say now that I had finally confessed. While I was saying this, I slyly rested my arm on her back, got my body near hers and I felt a sensation which I haven't been able to possibly explain ever since; it was soft, warm, inviting, welcoming ... I knew now the battle was won. She didn't flinch. She was alright with this. And she kept on smiling with true joy; her eyes kept looking at the infinite horizon, the blazing Loynner sun obscured by a towering building, casting a nice shade on The Crucible which had made the scene look incredibly more romantic and pleasant.

I pressed her pubescent, sexy, tight and smooth body against mine even more, feeling incredibly relaxed and comfortable, something I had not felt in a long time. I let my guard down. I wasn't alert or paranoid, scrutinizing the landscape for predators or mistrusting my friends. I was at home with her. All I needed was her shy and sincere smile, her nearly inaudible beautiful soft voice and her warm body next to mine.

Sensing I was dominating the entire situation by myself shut off my survival instinct. My friendly, shy whisper turned now into a manly and well-developed eloquent speech of such

emotive power I knew it would remain engraved in her mind for years to come.

"Yes, I do. I also think that I love you. Each time I think of you I melt in delight ... your warm expressive eyes simply give me an indescribable feeling. I can't look at them because of how perfect they are. You're one of the most beautiful girls I've ever seen, your smile or your eyes are just enough to make me float among a sea of bliss and marvel ..."

As I spoke, her smirk grew wider and her face shone red in absolute glee.

"Faye ... you make me feel and ponder things I have never ever thought about, and I truly want to experience these fantasies with someone like you. I like everything about you, Faith ... from the way you are smiling right now to the delicate, soft and cute gestures that you make. I don't know how many times others may have told you something similar to this before, but everything you do is a hurricane of bliss to me ... I have never met someone like you before, someone so perfect, so lacking in faults. Any word you say, any gesture you make is enough to make me happy. And that's a very outstanding accomplishment; like you, I find faults everywhere I go, in everyone I meet. But you're the definite exception. You are much too perfect, and I can't stress this enough."

Faye smiled even more. I kept her pressed against me, now starting to caress her left shoulder softly, not with lust, not with a masculine sex drive, but with blind and infinite affection. I do not regret it. Touching her smooth skin literally elevated me on a cloud, making me understand why people

often used the term in the first place when discussing love. It wasn't a simple literary figure, it was a very realistic description. I decided to finish what I had started, to put the finishing blow on this matter and claim the prize I so rightfully deserved.

"That's why I'm giving you this chance now, to answer what I've been dying to ask you since I first saw you ... to hear from your lips what some men would kill for. Faye ... are you willing to ... how should I say this ... to—"

CRASH.

"WHAT THE FUCKIN' HELL, THIS GODDAMN KITCHEN, I FUCKIN' HATE COOKING!!!"

It was as if I had suddenly fallen from the building, landing back on cold, hard reality. Something had snapped, exploded, abruptly ended. A hysterical, screeching voice came out of a window behind us. I realized we were right in front of the Mantis residence's door. Suddenly, someone emerged from the threshold in an angle where the inside of the house was barely visible.

"Faye, I didn't know you were here! Can you do me the fuckin' favor of comin' in the house and FUCKIN' helpin' me in the kitchen? Either that or you ain't eatin'! Oh ... ah ... hello there, kid!" Faye's mother, Flavia, a 40-something-year-old skinny and short woman, greeted me when she realized Faye had brought some company. I would have never predicted we would meet in such circumstances. She changed her mood suddenly, grinning with perfect white teeth as I realized at that very moment that she could have heard all the things I said. My bowels shrank in fear and panic, and I

watched as Faye tried in vain to defend herself from this evident humiliation.

"Mom, wait a moment, we were ... *talking* here!" Her face now shone as the sun itself, wanting the earth to swallow her and make her disappear. She wasn't the only one.

"OK Faye, but c'mon, your food is going to waste!! Goodbye, kid!!" she said, still looking kind, but carefully hiding her anger.

We both stayed there quiet and looking at empty spaces, our eyes lost in a void. My face reflected nothing but loss and defeat. Finally, I decided to break the silence, now talking as if I needed to do things fast, trying to keep alive the flames of inspiration, dedication and passion that I started my speech with. It helped that Faye comfortably returned to her original position, expecting to go through this all the way. I had lost my vantage point with the interruption, but however, approached her slowly again, this time, not so cheekily, trying to keep a bit of distance given the situation.

"Well uh ... listen. As I was telling you ... Faye, I do feel these things for you, and I wanted to know your reaction. I consider you the only girl out there that's worthy of—"

WHIZZ.

A blue pen appeared out of nowhere along with a sudden whistle, struck Faye right on the head and landed on the floor. Ryan Mantis duck-walked slowly toward us, almost like floating or gliding, with a face as cold as steel, possibly knowing what was going on. He was also whistling uncaringly, trying to be as noisy and unbearable as his egocentric nature let him be.

"How ya doin', Fatty?" He greeted Faye, grabbing her by

the belly and mocking her by making pig noises.

"*(Oh no ... please not now, not now),*" I thought. But even I knew it was already too late. I had failed, and not because of my own doing.

"Can't you tell you're fat? Lookit this, lookit this shit, my gosh! Sweet Sheeezus! Hey mum, I thought the pork was already in the oven, what's it doin' out here?!" he repeated, making Faye laugh uncontrollably in a mixture of disgust and awkwardness, and perhaps, knowing that bearing her moronic brother was a way of escaping the very same awkwardness I had put her in the first place.

Now Ryan grabbed her in a tight embrace, and she embraced him back, a thing which made my thoughts sparkling clear. Ryan struggled with her briefly and ultimately made her enter the apartment. Amongst the sudden chaos, Faye looked at me and shouted "*we'll speak later on ChitChat*" She disappeared behind the shutting door with Ryan, who didn't even say goodbye.

I stood there looking shocked, stunned and feeling incredibly stupid. Everything happened so fast I could not even remember what I was doing there. Suddenly and without second thoughts, I marched quickly to the back entrance and left The Crucible building, heading to the bus stop going through the Community Center's garden. Along the way, I met Dave.

"Hey, Sonny boy, how you doin'?"

"Hey Dave ... Well, nothing, I just, um ... I finished, er ... I told her all about it," I said, looking falsely happy and slightly oblivious, feigning self-confidence.

"What? You did? What did she say?" he said, looking at the floor, as if that wasn't interesting enough; inside, he was battered with anxiety.

"She said we would talk this over later, I just don't what

will happen from now on," I sighed.

Dave seemed slightly bothered, now beginning to show what he really felt like, his thoughtful suspicious eyes fixed on the floor.

"Let me tell you one thing Sonny, I don't want to bring your hopes down or nuthin', but my sister's real weird, she don't know what she wants, she's immature, she's never had a boyfriend, I dunno Sonny, but I don't think she'll ..." he didn't finish the sentence.

"Oh, don't mind that! If that happens, we'll be friends and that wil be it!" I said, almost believing it myself and all.

"Hope so," Dave said, looking seriously unconvinced, still looking at the floor.

"Anyway, I have to rush to the bus stop, I'm going to be late. See you around, Dave."

"Bye Sonny, we'll catch up later."

• • • • •

I got home feeling as if the world was falling apart. It actually was, but Faye had kept me from feeling the fear of this crumbling, apocalyptic world constantly whiplashed by a failing capitalism. Now that she was gone, now that the search for that special beloved female had come to pass, no joy could ever resurrect me from the decay of reality. I was at the bottom of the pit.

I checked my mail box, not surprised to find my parents' reply inside, and headed immediately to my room to read it. By the handwriting I noticed instantly that this one had been written by my dad, unusual as my mother liked to be the one in charge of writing.

"Dear ********

Thanks for responding. We were so afraid. What if something had happened to you, stupid boy? Don't you realize what you mean for all of us?

Your mother is so upset she couldn't even write to you. She's very angry. She thought you could be dead or deported. Try and think about what you're doing. Focus on studying and get good grades. Nothing else matters. Don't let people get in your way, just ignore them. You'll be glad you did when we're there. You need academic success to get ahead in this new world. It's very important.

Please try to study and focus on the important things.

Love you,

Mom and Dad."

I put the letter immediately in my night-stand, trying to ignore so much truth thrown at my face, and tried to forget what I had just read. I couldn't handle knowing my parents were disappointed enough and would be even more had they known what was actually going on. But I couldn't help it. I couldn't control what I was feeling. Nothing seemed to matter more to me at that moment than Faye.

I tried to hold off the necessity to go on ChitChat. I thought about how she would not be on at this time, but I could wait maybe for an hour more, at four. I turned the TV on to see if I could distract myself momentarily.

The senseless tube set on the Cox Media Network channel, which I used to watch just to know more about the situation in the US. It was a habit that I needed to lay off, as it only served to depress and anger me, which is what it did precisely on this occasion.

"And now, back with our lovely host Linda Joy, in her own unique space 'Christianity At Last!' Linda, take it away!"

"Thanks, Timothy! Well, there are some unresolved questions by our most loyal fans out there, and we wish to answer as many as we can! Starting with Bree, from the recently renamed city of The Angels, California, she asks: 'Why doesn't the Church accept evolutionism? Why is it the work of Satan? Is all science bad?' Haha, Bree, that's three questions, not one! But I'll try to answer them all for you. Basically, think of evolutionism and Darwinism as crutches, crutches these heathen sinful skeptics who like to live in alternate realities need so as to make their existences lacking in sin, sins they know they're committing. Now you listen to me Bree, I'm sure you're a nice, caring woman, and a devout Churchgoer. Think Bree, try to think for one second. Imagine you're in the shoes of these people, with no God, with no certainty of a Paradise welcoming you into the afterlife, with no Divine Book to guide you through God's material test that this life is. How would you feel? It's only natural these people need these excuses to scrape a living! To live decently with themselves, but it's all lies! You and I both know a life without the good Lord is nothing but empty falsehoods! And this is why we must help these people. Right now, to help heathens in Africa, who are in any case higher up in civilization than atheists because they at least believe in spirits and made up gods, they need our help to find about the true God. Atheists do as well. Even if you don't think so and it may be hard to believe, they're people just like us, misguided people. They need our help to let go of these surreal crutches they make up. Oh, but I'm going too far! I'll

make it quick. One, the Church doesn't accept evolutionism because it's just a theory, not a fact, and it has never been proven. Two, anything the Lord didn't say is obviously a cunning device from Satan, so we could say yes. And three, no, not all science is bad. Science that helps us is good, but science that tries to destroy us, our culture and our way of living is very bad indeed! I mean, here I am, talking through a TV appearing right on your screen! I don't quite know how it works really but it's surely something with electricity. And electricity is something you can prove, right? All it takes is to look at the sky during a thunderstorm! And there you see it, the lightning! So obviously it exists, but evolutionism is going too far ... anything that sounds too far-fetched and complicated is almost always a lie. Have you ever heard of Occam's razor? It's a thing that tells us that when there are various explanations, you have to pick the one that sounds less complicated, and that is surely the true one! With evolution, for example, a theory that tells us that animals evolve from others and this process takes millions of years when clearly God created us 6,000 years ago ... it's contradicting! It makes no sense! Besides, has anyone ever seen a creature evolve right in front of their eyes? I mean, what is this, MonsterPock? No sir, life isn't a cartoon, or a movie! And God is very real! Look, it boils down to this; immorality is the crutch of spiritual cripples, of perverted depraved lost souls. They don't know they'll forever burn in the pit of fire, in the bowels of Hell. Atheism is the crutch developed by those who seek an alternative reality to avoid the hard facts of Creation. Yes and I emphasize it! The FACTS PEOPLE, THE FACTS! The undeniable Holiness of God! The immortality of the soul, the demands of God's Law, the inevitability of the day of Judgment, and the fact that we are accountable to a just and Holy Creator. Reject that rotten make-believe that

atheism and evolutionism provide. Face the facts of the real world. A strong Gospel makes strong people. If you're sick, you need a fellow Churchgoer, not a lying doctor. If you're ignorant, you need a Church priest, not a teacher! If you are spiritually lost you need the Savior, not the idol—"

Enough of this. Enough of this outrageous insanity. Enough of these twisted and deranged human fantasies, product of the shock that an illusion they've been brainwashed into believing isn't real. Enough of the myth of man not being just another life-form on the planet, but an entity so special that it had its own glorious meaning in this universe. I turned the screen of fallacies off as soon as I could wanting to never watch the news again, not of the US, not of the world. How much more of this could I possibly take? Why was this world deserving of another chance? I don't know why I didn't take the *Reviziya 02* out of its case in a lunatic rampage, to exact revenge on society for being so outstandingly stupid. The imbecility of religion was spreading like wildfire, not only in the US anymore but to certain circles around the world as well. This was not possible. It was the new age of humanity. The Middle Ages full of war and fanatical religious fundamentalist nonsense were supposed to be dead and buried. This was supposed to be the age of technological advancement and of ideological and philosophical reasoning, the age of undeniable absolute evidence and the twilight of myths and magic. It wasn't. People just couldn't let go of their silly ancestral traditions, of the past, of these obvious falsehoods. And here there was this Unitedstatian white Anglo-Saxon blonde bitch, telling me, that *I NEEDED MADE UP CRUTCHES TO TOLERATE THE BURDEN OF MY MISERABLE LIFE?!*

I repressed the urge of utterly destroying the TV knowing

obeying such a savage, impulsive and primitive act was never a correct form of behavior. Instead, I repressed it all and took the courage from that fit of unparalleled fury to log on Chit-Chat and see if I could immediately sort things out with Faye.

When seemingly endless minutes passed by and she never appeared, all sorts of paranoid thoughts began worming their way into my already shattered psyche, making me think about how right about now she would be undergoing severe brainwash from the viewpoint of her oldest sibling, who would have obviously lots of things to say about the situation. He would explain everything to her, he would ask her what I had done and said, and she would reply. Why? Because she didn't know better. She would talk it over with him because it would mark a first in her life. She didn't know how to handle the situation, let alone what was discussed and said in it. Her mind was too young for such a powerful complex concept as true love, and she would never understand what I intended to say. My dedicated, eloquent speech would fade instead of becoming immortal, the shift in the atmosphere during the uttering of such words would be remembered, the words themselves forgotten. She would remember the awkwardness of the first serious proposal in her life, being scolded by the mom, more awkwardness and having a pen thrown at her head by a whistling, duck-walking impertinent selfish skinny piece of human garbage.

I shut down ChitChat. In a burst of rage I started to hit the bathroom door with relentless anger and fury, until my knuckles were spattered with blood and the skin began to peel off. I don't know where I got the impulsive, violent drive to react the way I did, and even today I ponder about that, but my best guess is I gave in to madness momentarily. I stopped repressing myself and instead joyfully laughed at the irony, at this stupid world where everything I thought was

right was wrong, a place where my ideology was considered inhumane at best, where the individual was unbelievably stupid. On this decadent slope of a society, I would not even be allowed to triumph in the most meaningful and beautiful endeavor I had ever tried to embark on.

I stood still and quiet shouting no longer, my curses smothered by the sting of reality. I fell to the floor, lifeless. I laughed some more, killing the short-lived reign of silence with my insane, sad laughter, indistinguishable from sobs.

Not long after, the crazed laughter turned into furious grunts, as I battered the bedroom door with my fists to sub-side the impotent anger. After my display of fury, an absolute peace reigned in the dark apartment. I wasn't surprised people needed religion when dealing with things like these, when they were at their lowest, when everything they cared about was lost, no immediate promise of hope. I knew of course why people needed make-believe to operate and gather strength. But I took my strength from other sources. Aside from my ideology and my Party, I gathered strength from the best source in the world; the fact of knowing you don't need humanity's stupidity to face your worst moments in life. The strength of knowing that alone, without the company of fami-ly, exiled in a meaningless island filled with pseudo-human beings and facing the rejection of the only girl I've ever want-ed to really know, I didn't need a *crutch* to re-emerge from my decayed ashes. Enough of this pathetic display of weak-ness, I thought. I got up from the floor and headed for my room, ready to call this a day, proud that at least I didn't need an imaginary friend to survive when at my lowest.

My cell-phone. The vibration tickled my left thigh fiercely. I immediately answered without second thoughts, a new dose of adrenaline flowing through my veins.

"Hello, this is Janice speaking! Are you currently satisfied with your FoniTel service? We at FoniTel strive for the best customer exper—"

CHAPTER VIII

Juche

"The basis of the Juche Idea is that man is the master of all things and the decisive factor in everything."

- KIM IL-SUNG -

Eternal President of the North Korean Republic and General Secretary of the Central Committee of the Workers' Party of North Korea

---

"Summarizing, global warming denial is on the rise as the most developed nations staunchly oppose any measures taken to reduce deforestation and the burning of fossil fuels, particularly the United States, which currently produces 10% of global pollution and 40% of the world's waste. The US also spends 30% of the world's resources in such useful things as the creation of firearms and ammunition, military vehicles, nuclear weapons and killer space satellites. Sadly, this can also be said of other industrialized nations such as Russia, where fierce oligarchs, politicians, nationalists and religious zealots deny not only global warming but any type of scientific facts that point out our imminent extinction as a species, all because of the lucrative interests corporations get when belittling the damage they cause to this planet. At the risk of sounding overly dramatic, I don't know what this world is coming to, but each day I have less and less faith in mankind ..."

"That was Michael Weinstein on his report about climate change. More news later this evening about science versus religion in developed nations and the division between people of left-wing and right-wing views, a growing ideological rift which is currently creating an extremely polarized political situation in most countries.

And now in international news; a popular anti-vaccination stance in the US based on the religious foundations of Creatonology, the country's official religion, has started an epidemic leaving so far two hundred and twenty-three dead and five hundred and fifty-six hospitalized in critical condition. Aside from religious connotations, US citizens claim also to be fearful of supposed adverse side effects to the vaccines that could lead to their death. Misinformation like this regarding scientific facts and the consequences of certain practices is often spread by citizens themselves or by the Cox Media Network, something which has currently urged the World Health Organization to act and prevent a global pandemic—"

Even in the most uncivilized and virginal territories on Earth people know they need to get vaccinated. This piece of news saddened me greatly; countless children were dying for nothing, all because their parents were Creatonologist cultists who believed to be created from clay by a god. Poor children. As glad as I always was when hearing of adult Unitedstatian hicks shooting each other to pieces, nothing could compare to children dying, especially in such pointless ways. This newscast served only to distract me briefly from my own selfish personal suffering, which in comparison was obviously non-existent, but as I turned the TV off the sour taste of defeat materialized once again in the dark and gloomy apartment. I picked up my backpack and headed once more to school, this

time officially without any reasons to cheer me up.

· · · · ·

What was produced after the incident at The Crucible translated into one of the worst weeks in my entire adolescent era. I thought I'd be able to live with one more rejection as I was used to girls rejecting guys like me who they tagged as unworthy of attention. I think anyone is at some level, but this time it was different. I liked Faye immensely, yet I did not think of her as superior in looks or social class. I never saw her as the kind of Loynnerin I'd never get, eventually learning to despise her only to finally ignore the situation and get over it. I saw her as something that with a well-placed work and effort, I would eventually earn. She was my friend's sister, and that made her reachable at any moment, far more reachable than those Loynnerin bitches I didn't even know how, when or *if* to approach. The situation was incredibly adequate, and was clearly the very first time in my life I had experienced anything so astonishingly unique. This was a whole new level. We were teenagers and Faye was only 15. The subject of sex was but the most precious mystery in our lives, and something so reachable and attractively positive wasn't going to be ignored.

The day after my confession Faye was nowhere to be found, and wasn't present in ChitChat either. I think you can imagine how desperation can grow on your spine as you become enveloped by anxiety and cold sweat, making you behave in erratic ways you would under other circumstances repress. I was heavily alert on ChitChat but could only find Ryan online. I had to take whatever chances I could get.

I bombarded him with questions the first time he logged in after the incident, sparking a very interesting conversation

in which I amazed myself at Ryan's typing proficiency and his will to write long-winded texts in a chat program, a truly rare and admirable ability in a world where everybody communicated only using 'F-M-S':

"Hey," I timidly typed. What was there to say? We might as well skip the formalities as the subject was bound to come across.

"Hello," Ryan typed, using his usual unnecessarily formal greeting once more.

"Everything alright over there?" I asked, trying to make the subject of discussion obvious.

"You mean about Faye? Well ... of course you do. Yeah she's alright, I guess. In relative terms."

"Relative terms?"

"I mean you scared the living shit outta her the other day. She was ... I dunno how to even describe it ... I guess 'shocked' comes close."

"Shocked? Why the hell would she be shocked? She seemed pretty happy before you arrived ... Actually, she seemed even happier *after* you arrived." I said. I didn't want to ask about why he had chosen to break us apart in such an apathetic and detached way, almost taking pleasure in destroying my plans. He had obviously done it on purpose. I was not going to mention it.

"She was just nervous and didn't know how to react. Nothing to it. She tried to give you the cold shoulder but you didn't catch the drift."

"What? Look, I dunno what it is she told you or what you asked her, but we were doing pretty alright before you showed up. Look, she was basically smiling all the time. She seemed happy. Yeah, she didn't want to talk about it at first, and she wanted me to talk about it on ChitChat, but after I started talking she was alright, listening patiently, smiling all

the time. I don't understand anything."

"Look, Sonny ... women are not so transparent like you think. Faye was probably nervous and reacted in her own way, which is ... dunno, getting stupid. What do I know? She's never had to face something like this before I guess. She didn't know how to handle the situation and well ... I guess she just chose to run away."

"What do you mean you don't know? You mean you haven't talked to her? She hasn't told you anything?"

"Not a thing ... although I did try talking to her. She wouldn't. She stormed off to her room after that."

"So that proves it then! You see? This doesn't mean anything. It just proves that ... well ... I got to her somehow."

"I dunno what it proves, but either way don't get so smug. I don't think it went that well for you."

"Why's that?"

"Well, for starters she did say something before she stormed off. Look, I started asking her what you guys talked about in hopes of dunno, giving her some insight or advice, and she just said that she doesn't know you well and that it would be weird, and dunno what else. In short, I don't think it went well Sonny, really. I'm telling you this as a friend. I think she won't have the balls to admit it to you. And I don't think it's good for you to get all obsessed now that she's basically almost finished rejecting you for good."

"I knew it."

"What do you mean?"

"I knew all along you would do anything to separate me from her. This has bothered you from the beginning, I know it. And I understand it. But I also understand it's not in your best interests the fact of me being with her, or me liking her. It gets between our friendship. But still, I think it's a very disgusting thing doing everything you can to keep her away

from me, not letting her decide for herself. Faye and I should be dealing with the subject ourselves, on our own."

"Don't worry about that, I swear to God I didn't poison her little stupid mind to keep her away from you, I'm not like that, I just wanted to see what she really felt so I can deal with this in a more professional manner. It's frankly a situation I'm quite sick of and I want to end it as soon as possible, be it you gettin' the girl or not. I don't really care how it goes for you two, I just want it to end."

"Swearing to 'God' isn't sufficient to convince me. In any case it doesn't matter if I believe you or not. If she really feels that way, then there's nothing anybody can do, not you, not me. And that will be the end of it like you want. Hopefully for you, this will end soon enough."

"Yeah, play victim now. You almost make me feel sad there. Look, don't worry about all of this. I've told you a million times ... there's thousands of girls out there and there's obviously one for you ... don't give up just yet just 'cause one might reject you."

"Look, speak for yourself. You make it sound as if I were just wishing to get laid. Don't get that opinion of me. I don't know what kind of people you're used to dealing with, but I assure you I'm very serious about everything I say and do. I live by my ideology and my principles. It's my philosophy that a man should answer only to the call of a certain female with qualities that excel above everyone else's, and that someone has become Faye to me. I'm not interested in anyone else, because I'm not looking for mere sex. I wanted something far deeper, a sensation the simple caress of a random stranger cannot give you."

"Huh ... you're quite the poet, aren't you? I respect people who write very well, and you seem to be one. But still it won't get you anywhere. It won't get you over the fact that no mat-

ter how smart, noble or incorruptible you think you are you won't be able to convince a stupid Unitedstatian girl brainwashed by the media to stop getting infatuated with pop-punk rocker sellout fags. You won't win a battle against a 15-year-old brat. She's a brat, Sonny. I don't know what you see in her, but she's a brat and not that attractive now that we are at it. I really don't know what you see in her, you can't see her face 'cause of the stupid hairdo she's got, she's shorter than a midget and she's got no tits or ass."

"Yeah. That's what *you* see in her, not me. Leave me be, I'll think what I want about her. Let's just drop this and let me solve this situation on my own, the way it should be."

"Fine by me, you have my clearance. Ah, who am I kidding. You have a chance as much as the next guy, who knows. She's never had a boyfriend you know. And she did say that thing about not knowing you well enough ... you never know. Don't get encouraged though, it still doesn't mean I approve of this. I'm just trying to be impartial and not letting this get to me as much as I'm thinking."

"So ... I just need time?"

"I wouldn't rely much on that ... but who knows. Like you said, solve it yourself. If she don't take kindly to your approach too much, well ... I'm sorry. But that's life. Live with it."

"Yeah, yeah ... I know. I will."

"Good."

An iron bar collided against my bowels upon reading that. It was a mixture between juggling the weight of the world on my shoulders and being held at gunpoint at the same time. I was panicking. What would I do now? I had played my last cards. There weren't any more chances, I had completely screwed everything up by not waiting for a more appropriate time. But then again, how much time did I actually have

before this turned messier?

There wasn't much I could do. The first thing I needed to do was to talk more to her over ChitChat, get her to know me better given that was really the problem. This wasn't a direct and clear rejection. Maybe I was exaggerating. Maybe optimism would actually save me here.

Still, my patience didn't do a very good job with this situation. I once asked to Ryan in ChitChat, "*so is Faye around?*" I didn't get an answer. And if I did, I only got a "gotta go. Bye." I began to suspect Ryan could actually be working against me behind my back. Surely with the excuse of "helping us both," he was poisoning any chances I had with his beloved sister to prevent our friendship from ending. He needed me. I was the only person that took him seriously, that defended him in school when Kannies were on his back, the only person who laughed at his lame jokes, or pretended to at least. He couldn't lose me, but I didn't mind losing him. It was a cold war now that our masks were off, but if Faye truly didn't like me then I would lose my deterrent. And I wouldn't win anything by shedding my mask and destroying my friendship with Ryan, a friendship that was extremely valuable until Faye's rejection had been absolutely confirmed.

As a consequence, this made me hang out more with my freaky friends and less with the Mantises; I was once again back to Claude and Gordon.

· · · · ·

After four days of not knowing anything about her, I decided to wait for her at the end of classes as if I were going to have a fight. I stood on the corner of the sports center construction site, immobile, with quiet-shy Claude at my side loyal as a dog, who at this point usually walked beside me to

the bus stop, as Gordon would sometimes get picked up by his mother. I waited patiently, my transfixed expression of determination fueled by love and rage, adamant on talking to her and sorting things out. She said we would talk. I deserved to get a definitive answer, even if it was via the cold and emotionless ChitChat.

The 13:40 sun was blazing on my face as if mocking my blindness for her. The stupid Pilgrim Coast High students, with their loud mouths and idiotic grins, began to come out in packs; their moronic and colorful expensive clothes enhanced by the burning sun of the early afternoon. My eyes were those of a hawk, a sniper, a predator keen on waiting for its prey to come out. My facial expression, that of stone. I had never waited for someone with such energy, with such fury, as if the fate of the whole world depended on it. Claude's seemingly infinite patience was growing thin with each passing second, and as people stopped flowing out of the educational artery, told me with his calm temper *"Sonny, I think we should leave now. She's not coming out."*

I couldn't believe it. I wouldn't. Why would she hide from me? I was the first to come out of the school with Claude, first in the line, I knew she couldn't have escaped. She was there. She was there knowing I was waiting, knowing I'd question her and make her feel as awkward as I did that day. I couldn't believe she could treat me like this, especially after I unveiled all my feelings personally, honestly and privately to her. I recalled the sincere, gleeful smile, the embarrassment-filled scarlet cheeks, the eagerness, curiosity and heart-felt will to wait for me to finish my speech. Ryan came to ruin everything. He'd surely also try to brainwash her into not being with me, winning the unwritten personal competition we had set. It was all a question of territorial dominance. I was intruding in places sacred to him, I was a foreign substance in

every possible way. Ryan would fight relentlessly to watch me lose and roll on the ground in pain, he'd manipulate events, lie, feign being my friend, and on top of all, appeal to his status as brother of Faye. This would not do. I had to change my strategy carefully, as I knew now Ryan had a manipulative mind similar to mine. We would never speak about this supposedly invisible secret cold war, but we both, in our minds, knew of its existent and on-going status. We were opposing factions struggling for our own agendas.

I was preparing myself to walk to a distasteful defeat back to the bus stop, this time without friends; no Axel, no Mike and no Wolfgang, only poor Claude, who seemed to have only one friend, this being Gordon, and me to some extent. At least it made me feel better knowing I had someone to rely on.

Unexpectedly, Claude said "look," with that characteristic energy of his. I was about to slap him right in the face for saying it in such a trivial manner; *Faye was coming out.*

But not alone. Her stupid classroom little friends accompanied her walking in an extremely slow fashion, and since we were the only ones in sight from there, visible from perhaps a hundred meters, it was obvious that they had spotted us. I tried to dissimulate and look as if I were talking to Claude, but it didn't work. In fact, they walked all way up the school's street to the corner, without even acknowledging us, and went upwards from there, opposite to us. I couldn't believe it. I just couldn't. Half of my faith in humanity had been shattered to pieces in a split second.

"Let's go," said an already pissed off Claude, seemingly quite aware of what had gone on before our noses. "Come on already. Remember the bus."

I simply let myself flow seamlessly with Claude's lack of enthusiasm and energy in life. I walked mechanically up to

the stupid bus station and then boarded the hypocritical purple Forge Monsoon, already imagining my face by the window above the "Paradise Itself" caption. I sat next to Claude, listening to music so as not talk about the incident, and waved him goodbye with the same energy that he had for everything offline related, and finally proceeded to walk to my house.

I let some time pass by before resorting to ChitChat in order to calm my unbelievable anger at this humiliation. I rested on the couch, had a snack and turned the TV on. When I considered myself fit for social interaction once more, I logged on as my heart raced in a mixture of anxiety and blind rage. It goes without saying that Faye wasn't on; Ryan had to be.

"Hey," I typed.

"Hello," he said once more, with that stupid, formal "Hello" of his. As if he was someone important you had to address with mature formality.

"Listen ... I have serious matters to talk with your sister. She ignored me today. Like a fucking dog. Who does she think she is? Put her on ChitChat RIGHT NOW, I got a couple of things to say to her, I won't let her think she can get away with treating people like that."

"My sister had to go with her friends to do homework for a group class project. She told me personally to say it to you in case you reacted like this."

Ryan had tackled my argument, wiped his ass with it and thrown it to my face, like he often enjoyed doing, savoring the victory of his strategy. Incredibly furious as I was that moment, I had been unable to keep my cool and had as such misplayed my part, giving Ryan ground to hold on to his stupid online formal orthodoxy, which made him look calm and collected and made me seem like a sociopathic lunatic. I

was stunned; I just couldn't believe a little girl like Faye had predicted and prevented the whole event so ahead of time. I wondered if she had actually seen me, or if I was that unimportant to her that I could be standing around like an idiot waiting for her attention without her even noticing.

"And in what way exactly do you want me to react? Well, I'm sorry, of course I am. But put yourself in my place. It's as if she didn't want to face me. And you know what? I'm sure she couldn't."

"And so what? Don't worry ... let her be. I don't want this to get in our way Sonny, really, I'm telling you now. You're becoming obsessed. It's unbelievable you're behaving like this, man. Dave thinks the same and we got a couple of things to tell you tomorrow at school."

"Like what?"

"Just things. Be ready, though. I don't want you to take them the wrong way."

That was it. I had done it. But I was really confused now ... Ryan had acted as if he truly cared for my well-being when inside I *knew* he was merely a selfish bastard always looking out for his best interests, judging by how he had behaved when intruding between Faye and me. Could it be that the matter pissed him off so much that he couldn't bear but behave that way? Probably. But that didn't make it less important, and by then, I was really believing Billy had been right about him all along.

· · · · ·

The next morning during recess, after hours of bearing Ryan being his regular self – trying to be funny and avoiding the little sister subject – my trial had come. Dave and Ryan brought Faye along, but not in the best of ways. The path that

led to the football fields, which segmented to the left toward the parking lot ramp – our little freak gathering zone – provided us with a beautiful view of the people passing by. That path however was usually covered with jocks and Kannies. Ryan and Dave made a show out of themselves carrying little Faye along for me, with brutal force, dragging her violently by the wrist. Faye then, with a loud "*FUCK OFF!*" proceeded to escape angrily.

"Well, this is just how bad she wants to see you. I think the result speaks for itself," Ryan said.

"Yeah man like, stop harassin' her, she don't friggin' like you, get it? Dude you were cool what the fuck happened to you? You gotta stop this now Sonny, really, we've all talked about this, and it's clear that you should stop this and not see her, or talk to her. You're outta hand," Dave said. I couldn't believe these assholes. It was obvious Faye was finding herself in an uncomfortable position and the last thing she needed was to get dragged through the corridor in front of everyone like an animal. The stupid selfish brothers who had never cared about her before suddenly began "protecting" her from some guy only because he happened to be romantically interested in her. A guy who did not represent any trouble, a guy who was a friend, a guy whom you could trust your life to. That's how I saw myself, at least. I was always a friend to my friends. More than a friend, a comrade. I never did anyone any harm. I was the right choice for a lonely and shy girl like Faye, and I was being denied this by people who were experts in manipulating events, creating embarrassing situations for us both and not letting us solve this maturely. I was surprised my temper didn't make me hit any of them in their scrawny Unitedstatian faces. I was astonished I hadn't exploded out of the sheer outrage of the situation and amazed myself at my ability to solve the following conflict using only my tongue.

"Alright, now, how should I say this … I'm not obsessed … I'm not a crazed maniac rapist … I'm not a bad guy … *I JUST WANTED TO GET INVOLVED WITH A GIRL WHO TURNED OUT TO BE YOU TWO PRICKS' SISTER, AND NOW YOU'RE TRYING TO MAKE ME SEE AND FEEL WITH BOTCHED ATTEMPTS LIKE THESE THAT I SHOULD GIVE UP ON HER, JUST BECAUSE YOU TWO FEEL LIKE IT? BECAUSE YOU DON'T FANCY A FRIEND DATING YOUR SISTER? BECAUSE YOU CAN'T FIND GIRLS YOU REALLY LIKE YOURSELVES AND WANT TO SPOIL MY FUCKING LIFE? WELL, HEAR THIS, I KNOW WHAT I'M DOING AND YOU HAVE NO RIGHT TO IN-TRUDE IN NEITHER HER LIFE NOR MINE.*"

"Dude … you fuckin' shocked her that day tellin' her those things. She thinks you a weirdo perverted maniac or sumtin'."

"I don't think that's the opinion she's got of me, *Dave*. You've only been listening to what Ryan's been saying surely. Faye was alright until Ryan showed up and made everything awkward. I was handling the situation really well by myself and she was cool. Besides what kind of twisted backwards world is this, I'm a pervert only because I like women? You two are lucky the only guy who's ever been interested in your sister isn't an Axel Guerrero who would dump her ass in the river if she accidentally scratched his cock with her teeth."

"Yeah, dude, you're cool, nice, whatever, but listen you slob, *STOP HARASSIN' HER, I'M TELLIN' YOU NOW.*" Dave's tone and attitude were way out of place now. He kept staring at me with his sky-blue scammer eyes, the eyes of a self-righteous lying lawyer. I had had enough of his Californi-an stereotypical accent and bossy attitude.

"YOU don't talk to me like that, for starters. And YOU TWO leave me the fuck alone already, I'm gettin' a little

fuckin' pissed off and you won't like me angry. This doesn't involve you after all, it's between me and her. Get it? Between *ME AND HER*."

"Sonny, with all due fuckin' respect, this is of great concern to us, given that *SHE'S OUR DAMN FUCKIN' SISTER!*"

"So what if you are. Get out of my way." And I pushed Dave away, a not too difficult feat, and made my way through the path of on-looking Kanny jocks. If anyone had said anything, Lenin help me, I would have just busted their heads open with an ice pick. Lucky for them, they didn't. They just looked on rather interested, perhaps waiting for a chance to know what was going on and make fun of it later among themselves.

I chased Faye throughout the whole school, and after 20 frustrating minutes at the verge of insanity walking around like a schmuck running over 13-year-old midgets, finally found her near the principal's office, with a friend.

"Hi," I said. She looked upwards and immediately away as soon as she had established eye contact.

"Hey."

"Uh ... what's up, Faye?"

"... what do you mean?"

"Er ... look ... can we talk a bit ... as in ... private?"

"Fine ..." She dismissed her friend with a gesture and followed me to a well concealed place next to the principal's office, where two brown colored couches were placed outside. We sat down, me not wanting to spend too much time explaining what had been already explained.

"Faye, you know what's going on, I already told you. Now, all I've been waiting for is an answer, OK? Nothing else. I simply wanted to talk this over and don't ignore me like a piece of shi ... trash. 'Cause I don't think I've treated you that bad to deserve this, alright? Sooo ... just say it."

"OK," she started. "Well ... I don't think I've known you well enough yet ... and no ... the answer is no ... I don't want to."

"OK," I said. "If that's how you want it ..."

I stood up and left, venting my frustration furiously punching the wall as I marched in defeat. But, after exactly two seconds of turning my back on her, she spoke again:

"You wanna talk to me?"

Stunned by her lovely voice, I didn't know what to reply. I turned slowly, trying to grasp the reality of the sentence. It had to be a joke. She kept looking right through me, her whole facial expression dangerously cold.

"What was that?" I asked in disbelief.

"I-asked-if-you-want-to-talk-to-me," she replied, irritated, her eyes fixed on mine, bearing a stern and severe expression.

"Well ... yeah. I mean, of course I do."

"Gimme your number."

"What?"

"Are you deaf too? I said gimme your number."

"Oh ... yeah, sorry ... ah ... User Prefix 54539, Personal Number 76239."

"OK. Got it."

"And ... what about yours?"

"55645 and 76251."

"I'm FoniTel, what's your company?"

"Horizon."

"Oh, right. I'm only asking 'cause, you know ... if we belonged to the same company, we could have had cheaper calls."

"I know that."

There were two seconds of absolute silence as I saved the

number to my phone's memory. I stared at her ominous presence. She had her legs crossed in a manner I found irresistible, sophisticated and elegant, the black miniskirt enhancing their curviness, her white top, pressed tightly against her perky breasts and showing her delicate stomach, making me lose concentration and rendering me unable to react quickly when she spoke again:

"You got it?" she asked.

"Uh ... er ... yeah. Faye ... why do you want my number anyway? I thought you said that ... well ..."

"That doesn't mean I don't wanna talk to you."

"Yeah, but what's the point in talking to each other if—"

"Look, you wanna talk to me or not?"

"Yes. I do."

"Well, I'll give you a call."

"Er ... alright."

"OK ... go, now."

I didn't say anything else after that. I looked at her one last time, surprised to find that she was looking at me as well. Her emerald green eyes, electrified with irritation and wide open, made me want to get away as quickly as possible. I froze in shock, however. It was the first time I had seen her eyes so clearly after always admiring them beneath the hair, eyelids, eyelashes and makeup. I stared deeply into them, admiring their undeniable beauty. I got a hold of myself after two seconds and left with my head down, embarrassed after coming back to Earth. Why wouldn't she ever look away now?

I went away as ordered, her face still recorded in my mind. I loved her so much. For the first time ever, a woman had commanded me and issued orders that I found to be completely impossible to ignore. I felt greatly inferior in comparison to her awesome presence, and I was often told I had an intimidating one myself. Faye could command me all she

wanted. I belonged to her in mind and body. But my goal had always been for that to be a mutual feeling.

· · · · ·

"Sonny! Hey Sonny boy, that you my good ol' boy?"

"Billy? It's been a long time! I was wondering when you would call ..."

"Yeah, yeah ... kept you waitin', huh? How's things on yer end?"

"Well ... let's just say, exactly the same as when you left."

"Ha! Is that so? Been 'round Ryan and that Wolfgang prick all day, I jus' hope you keep standin' on 'em toes."

"It's alright ... at least it's better than being on my own all day ..."

"Well, you ain't gonn' be alone no more boy, yer officially invited to come to Nova. We settled in quite nicely, and we got us a nice little place in Drabb Boulevard. How's that workin' for ya?"

"Well ... I don't know ... I wasn't planning on exactly doing anything out of the ordinary ... I'll have to check—"

"C'mon boy! In a bit it'll be Christmas season, son! Even you ain't forgettin' that!"

"Yeah, as a matter of fact, I completely forgot ..."

"Heh ... where's that head of yours at, boy? On that Faye poontang again?"

"No, actually ... that didn't end up quite as I expected."

"She turned you down, I'm guessin'."

"Yeah. You could say that."

"Well then, come an' get that depression outta yer system here in Nova, Dave's comin' too. Gonn' be one helluva week-end, son!"

"Well ... what the hell. Count me in, Billy."

"That's the way you do it! I'll keep you informed, boy. Jus' keep that phone o' yours real near you."

Before inviting me officially, Billy spent once again some time telling me anecdotes about the nature of the Mantis brothers. He emphasized how he thought of them both as complete, good-for-nothing idiots, with whom you couldn't go out in public or hang out with adults, because of the simple fact of them being socially awkward and not knowing how or when to behave. It wasn't though as if the Nazarethes hid their true thoughts whilst around them; they were in fact constantly doing it.

As an example, Ryan and Dave had once spent the whole afternoon arguing rudely over why Loynne's economy was going to eventually collapse due to the unstoppable global recession, while having a cup of coffee at some bar with the Nazareth family. Billy and Robbie had been the whole debate shaking their heads shamefully in silence, as their dad looked from them to the Mantis brothers, and simply was astonished at their ignorance; for they had been talking a lot of shit trying to seem mature in a political debate, a set up by the dad to see if their sons' friends were smart and worthy of attention. They had obviously failed, and miserably. Only one sentence came out of the lips of the oddball but wise Mr. Nazareth after that, addressed at his two sons in a moment of discretion; "*never, EVER bring these two to my presence again.*"

Even if they considered them good friends to hang out with, Billy and Robbie made sure their dad never heard of them again, as dictated. But this was an exception. I was wondering what could have happened for the dad to admit Dave Mantis in his household, plus another unknown friend, but I was in for the adventure. Anything to forget about Faye, even if it meant tolerating Billy's incredible awkwardness.

471

Things between me and Dave were fine, if a bit tense, as he soon forgot about the whole Faye incident. My theory was that he needed me in some way, a type of balance or even some kind of school bodyguard to protect him from the bullies in his class, who were now seemingly on him more than ever. This mini-plot served as a nice distraction from the Faye crap, as during that week I managed to completely ignore her at school.

"Hey Sonny, how are ya?" Dave greeted me one day at the usual place where I waited for my class to start, on the second floor of the West Wing. His trademark serious expression signaled troubled coming up.

"Hey, what's with you? You don't seem OK."

"Nothin' Sonny, these stupid Kanny fucks in my class, makin' fun of me and now Faye, I won't fuckin' have that. Look, I know it's not a good time to bring this up, but if you care about her like you say you do, could you do a little sumtin' about this? It's really botherin' me, man. There's this guy that's like taller than you, a total Kanny, he's got me in his sights since school started, I don't even know the reason, stupid fuckin' Kanny prick. Thinks he's someone, he's a stupid braindead dumbass Loynner with like these huge vagina lips in the face. Look, there he is now." Dave pointed at a mean but stupid-looking guy with similar build and height to mine, and the aforementioned vaginal lips comprising his mouth. He gave us a dirty, threatening and self-assured look, then proceeded to walk to the East Wing through the outer connecting corridor.

"That's the guy. He's called something like, Kiko, or Keko, or some shitty Kanny nickname like that, not really sure."

"What's wrong with that guy, you say?" Out of nowhere, the gigantic, even more daunting figure of Mike made its way toward us, and began to interrogate Dave in an almost Kanny

fashion.

"What?! Who the fuck is givin' you trouble, little guy? Tell me, go on!"

"Nuthin' Mike, that guy that I was tellin' Sonny that went across here just now. But look, it's nuthin' serious man , really, chill, don't really want any trouble with these people."

"HA! NO TROUBLE! COME 'ERE!" Mike, as in a crazed, rampaging bloodlust, directed his powerful legs to where the guy had been seen last, and later returned saying "THE MOMENT HE COMES HERE AGAIN ... I'LL BE WAITIN'!"

Dave later went away when the bell rang and I caught an unfortunate glimpse of Faye. "*She'll never leave me alone,*" a gray thought that resounded inside my head uttered constantly. "*She will always be around to remind me ...*"

I went into the classroom feeling the sorrow of the recent transpiring events, which hadn't left my mind. Flashes of the day Ryan had barged in and ruined my moment constantly flickered in front of me as if it were still going on, and the sensations returned with the images. Perhaps Faye wasn't mine, but there was something that was; my passion for her, the rush I felt whenever she was near, the infinite way I longed and cared for what I considered to be my one true love. The early, familiar feeling of the girl you like in school, which in a childish manner making you think of better days, of when you first struggled with infatuation and unrequited love; the daily daydreaming in class, not paying attention to anyone and sinking deeper into the fantasies only your mind could harbor. The perfume of the opposite sex constantly reminding you of the days, weeks and months you so longed to do such childish little things to your target, such as touching her smooth, silky hands and kissing her sweet lips, the privileged moment of being near her body in social situations such as waiting in line in the canteen ... It was all coming

473

back. Everything I felt in my childhood was returning, with the difference that I was now 17, and able to grasp everything much more steeply.

It's difficult to fall in love with someone, especially when people are so shallow and idiotic like in Loynne's. It's even more difficult than making trustworthy friends. But I was sick of my luck by this point; I wanted to change my future all around, and for once in my life claim absolute victory over what I had set to do. Reinventing myself, that was the ideology of the future ... and failing was not an option.

• • • • •

A week had passed, with no clearly visible developing events other than Little Dave almost getting his sorry scrawny-ass kicked. The short lived bullying that he suffered at the hand of an increasingly weakening and dying Kannovschina caused him to come to us now that he thought he owned two private bodyguards. You could say this helped Dave "forget" certain things happened, and also put me in a position to blackmail him with protection he knew needed. He was a bit cold and distant with me more than anyone, but that was soon forgotten with the laughs, joy and passion the teenage life provides in the diverse melting pot a school is.

"Hey, guys ... Look, it keeps happenin', but now they're callin' me a chicken-shit 'cause of being with you two all the time. They're always sayin' that if I have friends they'll call their friends as well, and I really don't want to get you guys into trouble ... What the fuck do I do now?"

"Hah, what a pussy, I don't know how you manage to fuck so many girls without a dick," a cheery Ryan laughed. Lately, he was really, really cheery, which in him was quite unsettling and disturbing. He was the type of person who could draw

smiles on his face if and only if he was up to something odd and questionable to the eyes of everyone else.

"Shut up Ryan, as if you would deal with this in any other way, you stupid hypocrite. Probably lock yourself inside the house playin' role games, that's what you would do, you big-eared fuckin' gnome."

"Aww, as if you even know what hypocrite means."

"Stop fuckin' in-fightin', you two! Listen, the thing now is to have a parley with these guys to know if they're serious or not. I mean, look at this, you gonna let your brother be ordered around by some Kanny jock? The hell's up with you Ryan? If anyone touched any of my brothers they would already be dead and spitting out their livers."

"Oh yeah well, excuse us for not weighin' over a thousand tons and bein' taller than a giraffe, Mikey."

"You shut up you midget prick, or I join 'em in kickin' your sorry arrogant ass. Look Dave, how 'bout we talk to these guys after class now, or else nothing's ever gonna change for ya. You're my friend and I like ya, even though you're a chicken-shit arrogant pussy. But listen, I don't like any of my friends being touched, OK? Just like family. I haven't survived this stupid hell of life and school standin' still."

"Yeah ... Well, fine with me, big guy, let's do this shit at the exit."

At exactly 13:30 we left for the crowded bus stop. It was Mike, Ryan, Dave and me. Dave was surprisingly cocky when protected by others and it was clearly shown in our stand-off, where Mike stole the show. Ryan and I remained as silent but loyal backup to Mike. Ryan was also behaving in a pretty self-assured way not quite normal in his behavior. My suspicions increased dramatically when I saw him simply smile when we met with the enemy pack. Pretty shocked to find out, many of them seemed *Colombian*. That changed the facts a bit.

Loynner's were cowards well known for calling 50-odd more guys at the slightest threat and never being alone. These guys would carve you up and hang you on a meat hook for less than a nasty look.

We soon learned though, the only Colombian features they had were physical. The bohemian, hippie-like clothes they wore didn't exactly spell doom, and whilst they could have passed as common criminals, they didn't have hardcore Kanny tags on them.

Mike accelerated at first sight, heading right for the bench they were calmly sitting on, heading right for them with a self-assured military march. Their eyes flinched on instinct, and so would their bodies if they weren't trying to intimidate him back. Mike spoke with his hoarse, soft voice:

"So ... mind tellin' me what's goin' on here?"

They simply stared back at him, studying him deeply. That Keko or Kiko or whatever the hell he was called – I'll refer to him as Keko from now on – was also there, quite mockingly looking at Dave. Nobody was looking at either Ryan or me, simply Dave and Mike. The awkward silence increased progressively with the seconds that flew by, slowly and tortuously. Finally, a guy with dark skin, long hair in a ponytail, a bandana and feline eyes spoke, looking right through Mike, positively fearless:

"Nothin'. Why?"

Mike stared back, not flinching or moving his massive body one bit. For a second, nothing else existed in the universe except for those two titans exchanging looks, studying each other as if analyzing something we were blind to. The

other guys, couldn't have been four or three of them plus Keko, seemed to be wanting to get out and their eyes looked for the common purple hope the bus was. Mike suddenly spoke softly again, thrice as threatening than if he were shouting:

"We don't let our kind be prey to anyone."

The bandana guy kept staring for at least two seconds, then spoke clearly wanting to maintain dominance:

"Neither do we."

Mike was almost losing patience here. I kept looking with the corners of my eyes around me trying to see if anyone else would notice the tense stand-off being developed there. No one seemed to really notice anything in particular. They would though if fireworks started to go off, mainly knowing how savage Mike was. The story of him once breaking all the bones in some guy's arms wasn't something to ignore. If Mike were to jump on the one with the bandana, by sheer shock the others would flee and the poor guy wouldn't stand a chance. I almost felt sorry for them now.

"If we ever see Dave complaining 'bout something as little as a cold you're done for. We straight on that?"

The guy now seemed to be losing nerve. His eyes stopped being cold and calculating, his weak smile faded for good, and all that was left on his facial expression was a desire for mercy. He then spoke again:

"Look ... where you guys from anyway?"

"The fuck matters where I'm from, man?"

"No, 'cause ... just ... wouldn't you happen to be Californian? That famous Mighty Mike everyone talks about in Arias

Town?"

"You're starin' at him. And Mighty Mike doesn't like being stared at, asshole," Dave said. Everyone looked at him in unison, and then he looked away finally shutting up.

"Mouth shut, Dave," Mike said. These guys clearly didn't know who they were messing with. Mike went on:

"Look, I'm a peaceful guy myself. Dave here isn't afraid of you, he's not a coward, but he obviously is intimidated if his odds are five against one, especially big guys like you. You're the biggest pussies I've ever met, and I've met some fuckin' chicken-shit faggots in my time. Why don't you pick on me from now on, motherfuckers? Unless you want it obviously to be the other way round."

"No, no, sorry man, look, we just thought that Dave was some smartass' brother that we hate and well, we didn't know who he really was, just suspected it. Look we confused him with another Dave, that's all man, for real."

"It'd better be. Well now, we'll leave you alone. If anything happens again though, my buddy here Sonny ain't a pushover neither. And he's Russian. Ever heard of the fuckin' Russian Mafia? Of the Sergei Lyvov Bratva? This guy's got some serious people watchin' his back. You'd better watch your behavior around some fuckin' people here, OK? Anythin' else you wanna add? Good, that's how I like it. Well, gentlemen, I believe everything's settled then, correct?"

"Yeah ... yeah. No problem."

"That's how I like it."

$$\bullet \bullet \bullet \bullet \bullet$$

We left the group of Colombians behind and proceeded to march toward the bus station. Along the way, Dave couldn't restrain his enthusiasm and caused Mike to lash out.

"Haha, you see that guys, see, now they're never even gonna look at me straight in the face again! Ha, all thanks to you Mike! Say, as compensation and all that for your services, I can help get you a nice hot black bitch, they're really on high demand lately, some nice bubble-butt ebony bia straight from the ghetto with a curly-haired pussy and some of the biggest pair of guns you've ever seen—" Mike looked at Dave as if he was about to raise him in the air by the neck and crush him like a can of beer, but instead just limited himself to keep staring at him until Dave looked at the floor in shame, knowing he had gone too far with the comedian act.

"You know what really bothers me about you, Dave? You got absolutely no fuckin' idea of how serious that shit was over there. Wanna hear somethin' that won't let you sleep at nights? Those guys over there, I know them, you don't wanna mess with them, and I ain't just sayin'. They're known for knife fights, drug dealing, you name it. They're petty in comparison to those death-squad sicarios who organize the hits, call the shots and handle the assault rifles, but who do you think the Cartel uses when they don't want their hands dirty? Ever heard of those revenge attacks like the one Tom Richards is always babbling about to make people shut up and behave? Tom Richards is the biggest douche in the world but you got absolutely no idea how right he is. The day you become a stain of blood on the street you're not gonna shrug this off like this, I assure you. Now, open your mouth again you midget arrogant pretentious prick, dare open that motherfuckin' gutter of a mouth again before we reach the bus stop and I swear on your mother's clit I send you straight to Mount Tyler with one punch. Your call." Needless to say, Dave remained very quiet after that. I had been studying Mike closely, and I could see that from time to time, he exhibited bouts of anti-social and sometimes violent behavior.

Something was going on with him that he was not telling us, but I would have never dared ask. In that moment, we just limited ourselves to keep walking enjoying the scenery, hoping Mike wouldn't go on a random psychosis and splatter our faces against the pavement with his fists.

But as days passed by, the results spoke for themselves. That guy Keko was deprived of his stupid smile of victory for quite a few days, and never spoke to Dave again. Dave's mood also increased for the better and he had learned quite a lesson about arrogance and knowing his place, which lasted but a few days as well. But all in all, this small incident at least served two main purposes; made me forget about Faye for a while, and strengthened my ties with the Mantis brothers again, which was always a good thing, at least in my mind.

· · · · ·

The day to go to Billy's house had finally arrived. It was a rather silent 12th of December. Billy himself had been waiting for me near the Pilgrim Coast bus station's kiosk, wearing his hunting gear; an olive green army cap with a sergeant insignia on the front, a crème colored vest, jungle camo trousers and SKAR boots, the "Peacekeeper" variation used for riots. His camouflage pattern, unlike my classic Soviet TTsKO woodland one, was digital. Digital camouflage is comprised of micro patterns instead of macro ones, which up close look like small pixels. However, the theory says that from long distances it works better in confusing the eye to detect the outline of a person's body shape. Billy's version was the MARPAT digital desert variation, that is, the MARine PATtern of the US Marines Corps.

He remained sitting down while I made my way toward him even though he had obviously seen me already. The

blazing sun of Loynne's didn't seem to bother him at all. He gazed up and looked at me with a wrinkled expression, unable to hide his ever-present cunning smile. After staring at me for a couple of seconds, as if to check it was really me, he spoke:

"Sonny, my good ol' boy ... how you doin'?"

"Fine Billy, not up to much ..."

"Haha ... not up to much? You've been up to all sorts, I hear ..."

"Well ... unless you mean Faye ..."

"Heh ... 'course I do, boy. How it'd go with her? Not too well you told me ..."

"Well ... no. I wouldn't say it went well, no."

"But why? Did she reject you? Did she ran away scared or summin'?"

"No, everything was fine actually, before Ryan popped up and ruined everything. I can swear he did it on purpose."

"Heh. Dave told me that he didn't even know what to make of the situation."

"He ... he did?"

"Yeah ... guess she might still like ya, boy. No need to give up jus' yet."

"Well ... I'm tired of these maybes. I just want to know the truth once and for all. I guess I will when I get to know her better, like she says we have to do."

"Yeah ... who knows ..." Billy stared at the horizon with a transfixed expression for a few seconds, before proceeding to talk again.

"So! Sonny boy. We in for some real good times my good ol' friend. The North is fuckin' insane. You never been, have ya boy?"

"Been? Yeah of course. Couple of times. Not for long though, and not deep enough."

"Haha, so you've heard that story too! Fuckin' Johanna, kraut bitch. Well, you have, in which case you should know what I mean. Anythin' you want, you can find it up there. And believe me I wasn't so keen on this fuckin' up-North thing at first. You should have seen me and ol' Robbie when school first started. This ignorant fuckin' Loynners ... we got in the first day, they look at us with our long hair, they shout at us "*look! It's the fuckin' Stoning Rocks!*" Fuckin' Loynner ignorant scum. We showed them alright, we ain't takin' no shit from no isle muncher, fuckin' Loynners. School is tougher up there than down here Sonny boy. Here in the South, everything's handed to you in a silver fuckin' platter. Up there? Nobody takes no shit from you. And you're supposed to be the same or else you ain't survivin'. Life in the big city, boy. I don't mind that, 'cause I hate people ... and love any excuse I can get to lash out at them." He took a couple of seconds to look moody and keep staring at the horizon while I waited, sensing the rant would go on. He laughed mildly to himself and went on;

"Life over there is different alright. Feels like a totally different country. People are hysterical, aggressive, impatient, full of go-getters, ambitious greedy fuckers who would sell you their own mamma just to get ahead, everyone's got a superiority issue up there. You're about to see some crazy shit. Also, if you think you've seen Kannies, wait till you see that. But don't worry yer little head about a thing ... you'll be rollin' with us."

"I can take care of myself, Billy, but thanks for the heads up and bodyguard service. Look, I've been up there OK? I know how it works. I obviously aren't Vietnam vet like you, but I don't come from an exactly peaceful place either."

"You could become pretty dangerous if you had the right mindset, boy. Look at you. Almost two fuckin' meters tall,

strong big limbs and an intimidating stare. Too fuckin' bad about your happy-go-lucky affair with Ryan's sister that's turning you into a sissy. Love? Are you fuckin' kiddin' me? You should drop that shit, join Robbie, Tory and me up there takin' over the world. Score with the hottest broads, make a quick buck here and there, who knows, we might even be able to make enough money to drop outta school and ... well, I'll tell you in time."

"No Billy, you don't need to go any further. I'm not doing any of that. I'd like to stick to whatever it is life has shown me so far."

"Oh yeah? And what's that? Tryin' to still bang Faye? Finishin' your studies and being a fuckin' schmuck like everyone else? Being a fuckin' drone sheep robot? I thought you were against all of that."

"I am ... and I don't intend on joining them. But the ideas you're proposing are reckless and rushed and, come on, face it, you just have too much testosterone in you."

"Yeah? Well then I'm havin' enough for both of us 'cause you sure got none. Where's your sense of adventure, son? Where's your ambition, your courage? Ambition's all it takes. Have ambition and you have the world right in yer daaamn hands."

"Billy, I don't know what sort of weird things you plan on doing but it just isn't going to work. Look at organized crime, for example. It's history. We have a new type of crime nowadays ... the government. The government uses these types at will and send them down the slammer when they're of no more use to them. Look at the SKAR, the undercover units are everywhere, they could even be listening to us right now. I don't know what's gotten into you about taking over the world, but stop it. You're going down hard if you think you're gonna get away with any of that. And before you know you're

gonna have an entire SKAR unit raiding your house."

"You're shit-scared of life, Sonny boy ..."

"No! I'm not, Billy! I'm just trying to make a point about how stupid it is to do something a lot of people have done before you and failed miserably, only to find their lives shattered and messed up all because of making a 'quick' buck. There's no such thing as a quick buck. And if there is, it comes at an even heavier price, Billy. What, you want to end up raped in jail by some orangutan while we're out here enjoying our only-limited-by-money freedom? You really want that to happen to yourself?"

"Shit boy ... they've done to your brain worse damage than I thought at first ... we're gonna have to undo the damage the media has done to you."

"What the hell are you talking about now, Billy? You really should stop it with that Ettore Illuminati crap. I know there's a lot of chances some Illuminati like organization pulls the strings on the world and all that, but come on, you're supposed to know that in this society, capitalism limits your lifestyle with how much you make so that the rich upper hand can still roll in shit while we bottom feeders get in trouble wanting to be like them and get caught with the hand in the cookie jar. Being in jail you make it easy for them. They lure you into consumerism. Out here, you're way more useful. You can flesh out any strategy you want. Inside, what do you do? Try to make the most of daily rapes and beatings? Thought you were smarter than this. A revolution is not fought behind bars." Just when Billy was about to reply, his phone rang. He signaled me to hold my last thought and walked 10 meters away from me so as to not be heard. He came back shortly and said:

"My dad's comin' for us, Sonny boy. He's gonna pull the car up round the Montenade bus stop so be on your toes, you

know you can't park there for two seconds. We'll finish this conversation some other time, for now, just try to be alert if he comes. The car's a white Forge Affaire."

"First generation, second, third, four?"

"What do I look boy, rich? First, Sonny boy, first! We don't do badly, but we don't do that well neither."

"That's a relief ..." A first generation Forge Affaire from the '70s, that would be one uncomfy ride to hell and back, I almost preferred going by bus. The car was a four-door sedan alright but no larger than a regular Chevraun City Car, and the interior could prove to be quite oppressive for someone my size. Mind you, a Chevraun City Car was the definition of small urban car in Loynne's, pretty much the most affordable, cheapest to maintain compact car in the entire island.

"There he is, don't fuck about boy, run!" Billy opened the trunk and was already in the oxidized car when I had just finished putting my bag down. He rushed me to get inside and I clumsily banged my head on the way, which thankfully nobody noticed. To my surprise, little Dave was just in front of me, riding shotgun next to Billy's dad.

"Dave? I thought you were already with Robbie up there ..."

"No man, sumtin' came up and, well, I asked Billy if it was OK to ride with you guys ..."

"You boys alright back there?"

"Yeah pops, all smooth sailin'."

"Alright, then. Kick the tires and light the fires."

· · · · ·

The journey ended up being rather quiet and dull. Everyone stayed silent for most of the trip, and the old Forge Affaire could barely climb the intimidating mountain roads

leading to Nova Atlantica, but once we got to the LI-1 Highway it was just a matter of lying back and enjoying the awe-striking sights of the eastern coast of Loynne's. To the right side of the highway, the sea stretched out as far as the eye could see, only populated by Russian merchant ships and the presence of the miniature isles surrounding Loynne's. Small fishing towns decorated the landscape, each separated by a deserted valley or a rocky hill, sometimes a warehouse. However, the marvels leading to Nova Atlantica were at the west side of the highway; the most famous being obviously Mount Tyler, a titanic mountain over 4,000 meters tall named after John Tyler, the 10th president of the United States. The icy top would always be seen surrounded by clouds in circles, making the massive mountain seem even taller. The popular Tyler Park Natural Reserve was located at its base, housing a considerable number of species in very healthy and safe conditions. Nearby this reserve was the home of one of the most powerful telescopes on Earth, the Mount Tyler Astronomical Observatory, which received thousands of science enthusiasts yearly eager to organize nightly expeditions and study the Loynner night sky. The observatory was stationed in an area where light pollution was almost non-existent, Mount Tyler blocking most sunlight coming from the east. In the northwest — the least populated part of the island with only a few sparse towns here and there — the jet black night sky found itself always riddled with stars. Each year millions of tourists visited all of these different facilities, drove up the infamous slopes with their Montana Tusks, organized tours and expeditions and some sacrificial thrill-seekers even attempted to reach the top. It wasn't rare to hear about a death or a helicopter rescue involving Mount Tyler in the summer.

The rest of the LI-1 Highway marvels paled in comparison to the gigantic mountain, but they all each had indeed a cer-

tain charm attached; an abandoned airstrip, full of airplane wreckage and craters from accidents that had in fact killed dozens at demonstrations; a majestic wind power station located on a meadow completely sprawling with daisies; a collection of old busted bunkers that had hid the British during the war; an isolated four story abandoned manor, built on a now inaccessible area due to the highway and to no roads leading to it from the other side. And last but not least, a lunar deserted landscape.

We continued ascending through the mountainous roads, impressively overlooking entire populations at once. It was beginning to get dark. The car noticeable had trouble climbing and began to make roaring engine sounds, to which nobody paid any attention. The mood was as silent and dull as ever, and nobody commented on anything.

But before I had a chance to start dreading coming along for the trip, we had finally arrived. Going through a curve, the endless sea was replaced by the blinding lights of Nova Atlantica, complete with spotlights aiming randomly at the sky, trying to give it an international atmosphere of glamour, much like Saphron Bay. The skyscrapers concentrated on the city's center, the downtown area, and each of their windows shone camouflaging with the stars on the black sky. The Atlantic Zeppelin, one of Nova Atlantica's main landmarks, flew by illuminated casually by the spotlights below. This was the only place in Loynne's that didn't feel like it, a truly unique environment resembling an extremely balanced blend between New York City and Monaco, reflecting both luxury and poverty, although much more less of the latter than usually found in most big cities.

We went around a gigantic cliff the city hid behind, and immediately noticed the millions of highway signs leading to the huge metropolis. Beyond, Nova Atlantica spread majesti-

cally just as Pilgrim Coast did when viewed from Saphron Highway, with the only difference of being at least 30 times bigger. The towering mountains offered a bird's eye view of the complete city below.

Going round the sinuous mountain roads, we finally descended on the gigantic urban core itself. Spending two minutes in Nova Atlantica was all you needed to sense it brimming with the big city life you couldn't find in the South. Angry, impatient guys in suits drove their Hades-Larsson and GDW sedans through the concrete landmass, speaking with headsets and gesticulating wildly. Instead of riding in cheap scooters doing wheelies, the sophisticated city Kannies raced gracefully through the sea of cars with powerful Yamazaki Samurai motorbikes. Everyone seemed to have somewhere to go, rushing stressfully. People drove irresponsibly, often shouting at each other, skipping traffic lights and honking at anything they could for the stupidest reason. It was a city alright. I laughed at how the atmosphere managed to envelop you, making you wish you were still in the by comparison laid back tourist-oriented South.

We passed by famous landmarks of the city, as almost all of them were located near the coast. The titanic and twisted auditorium of Australian design, the industrial harbor riddled with Russian tankers, the MegaLon Stores shopping mall, the Kapitalismus Mons stock exchange building and the iconic Nova Atlantica bus station. This was the place known as Oversight Coast, Nova Atlantica's biggest selling point and main tourist attraction. Northwest you would find the marginal residential district known as Drabb Boulevard. It basically consisted of blocks and blocks of residential apartments with businesses at the bottom, and it wasn't a particularly nice sight to behold either. Probably one of the worst places to spend the day in Loynne's.

Billy's dad headed north leaving behind the world famous Diamond Coast beach, a crystal clear landmark and probably the cleanest, nicest beach in the entire island. A piercing feeling of nostalgia overcame me; this was the place my old Loynner girlfriend, Lyria, always fantasized about meeting at midnight when we had not even seen each other in person. We would often talk about making love as the gentle tide caressed our hot bodies, fusing with the sand as our kisses became more and more voracious. I amazed myself at how distant events that had transpired only in the last year were at this point. The once coveted Lyria, the one who almost made me lose Wolfgang's friendship, had been rendered a forgotten memory in the chaotic randomness of adolescence.

· · · · ·

The car began slowing down after reaching a roundabout, and pulled over after squeezing through very narrow streets. In this marginal neighborhood, tall gray buildings covered in graffiti obscured the sky and concrete sidewalks littered with trash asphyxiated the land.

Billy's dad commanded all of us to get off and retrieve our luggage, and we followed him to a building which at least didn't seem to be coming apart. A silver modern elevator, very dystopian-looking in contrast to the rotting landscape outside, took us to the fifth floor. A long corridor led us directly to the far right, where at the end of it, a door with the number "56" shone in cheap golden paint.

Everyone was quiet. Dave seemed to be repressing everything he could in his persona, and it occurred to me that Billy's dad intimidated him. Billy seemed quite stern and serious too, hinting a suppression of his true colors in front of his dad. He was no longer the cheery and loud Texan redneck

he was in front of us and must have surely had to sport another set of principles and values in front of him. I still needed time to analyze Billy's dad from a psychological viewpoint though. And I was 100% sure I wouldn't be able to do it fully before we had to go back to the dry South. I was alright in any case for, as of now, he seemed friendly and never stopped smiling.

"Jus' git comfortable, boys," he said, after reaching for his keys and opening the front door. "Show 'em the room, Billy. Your brother must be comin' back with the shoppin' anytime now."

"Right, Pops ... come on this way." Billy led us through an apartment that proved to be a radical departure from The Crucible design. Upon entering you immediately found yourself in a corridor that led to the living room, with a kitchen to the left and the bedroom belonging to Billy's dad to the right. Onwards there was another corridor which led to Billy's and Robbie's bedrooms, which faced each other. The bathroom was located in the living room area, to the left secluded in a corner. Also, this apartment had a set of sliding windows with a balcony in a similar fashion to The Crucible, although this time overlooking the marginal streets of Nova Atlantica's Drabb Boulevard instead of the majestic views of Pilgrim Coast.

"This is my room Sonny boy, here's where you'll be sleepin', on this bed that slides right outta mine by the floor, whatever the hell it's called," Billy began. "Dave will sleep in the other room, with Robbie."

"No way man, this is balls, why does Sonny get to sleep in your room? There's not even an extra bed in Robbie's! Where do I sleep, on the fuckin' floor?"

"What kind of sissy little daisy are you? Sleep on the floor you son of a bitch, Sonny had to when he spent the night at

The Crucible and you done the same a thousand times too. Shut the hell up and hug that floor."

"I'm supposin' I'll have a mattress at least, right?"

"No, no mattress for you, jus' line up some blankets and sheets and cushion yer sorry ass on top o' them, dirty little mongrel. Now git goin', don't wanna hear another word outta yer mouth!"

Dave went to Robbie's room to leave his stuff, quite mad about Billy clearly preferring my company. Dave was just like me in that sense. He didn't enjoy the non-interactive, silent demeanor of people like Robbie. He couldn't stand being still and quiet, like Robbie's company would force him to do.

"So Sonny boy, we're all kinda tired from the trip, we're just gonn' have a little dinner and maybe watch TV, wanna shower first?"

"Yeah that's OK."

"Right, well, I'll have the shower after and then Dave. Get your things boy, and make it quick; I dunno about you but I fuckin' stink."

· · · · ·

"Took your sweet fuckin' time, boy! Now beat it and git to the kitchen, help Robbie make the damn dinner, Dave's totally useless. Help 'im out before we all end up dead."

Billy's dad was comfortably sitting on the couch, patiently watching a Vietnam movie, the smile never dying. I quickly marched to the kitchen where Robbie, who had arrived when I was showering, greeted me with an inexpressive nod of the head.

"What's up Robbie, want some help with the food?"

"Hey, yeah, can you put the fries in the oil, Dave's too scared of burnin' himself."

"Fuck you, man! I ain't scared! I just hate cookin', I can't be doing with it, that shit's for chicks anyway."

"Yeah, yeah … Look Sonny, just do that and I'll take care of the meat."

Soon, we found ourselves at the table, while in an odd manner, Billy's dad overlooked the scene standing up at the threshold. He engaged in some small talk with us, never losing his patient smile.

"Green Köontz?" he asked grinning to himself, looking at my T-shirt. "Now what in the high holy hell is that, boy?"

"Oh, ah, it's a punk-rock band," I said, before Dave had any chances of opening his mouth. I needn't; he was comfortably quiet for once, without any intentions of speaking or being the center of attention.

"Punk-rock? You gotta be kiddin' me, boy … you even know what punk is?"

"Yeah … a movement that started in Britain in the '70s as an alternative to the growing heavy metal scene and the reactionary politics of the government."

"Heh, textbook answer … So can you tell me what's so punk about those faggots in yer T-shirt?" You might think there was an aggressive tone in this, but it shone for its absence. Billy's dad was surprisingly nice in his approach and felt incredibly down to earth, even when asking questions like that.

"Well … it's not so much what they stand for, it's the music they play. We all know in the music industry there isn't a thing like principles and values anymore, only money."

"Oh well, I guess you kids just listen to what yer generation has right now, it's only natural. My parents also thought I listened to faggots when the hippie movement struck the US. Guess I'm gittin' to be just like them in my old age. Jesus … how time passes by and we don't even realize …"

"Sure, Pops ... now stop intimidatin' my fuckin' friends, it ain't their fault they like faggy music."

"Haha, it sure ain't, son ... If yous need me I'll be in the livin' room, Tet Offensive III is on."

"Yeah, yeah, go on already, pops!" After Billy's dad left for the living room, the whole apartment was soon shrouded in M16A1 fire and Unitedstatian voices requesting reinforcements. This in turn gave us the ability to have a little dinner chat without being heard.

"The Vietnam War ain't bad, but the Second World War will always be the greatest to grace the Earth," Billy said, his eyes shining as he smiled at me. He then turned to address Dave.

"So your queer-ass brother couldn't make the trip, huh? Well ... either he couldn't or wouldn't ..."

"He *couldn't*, Billy," Dave started to say, somewhat annoyed. "He had stuff to do, didn't you speak to him?"

"Sure, I did. But well, to each its own. I told 'im the new house was big enough for all of you three motherfuckers to come here, but still, he couldn't make it ..."

"Stop being a dick Billy, who gives a shit anyway if he couldn't make it. I like it a lot better when he's not around anyway ... I'd rather be around Sonny for that matter ..."

"Thanks, Dave."

"You're welcome Sonny. But hear me out Billy, I can really assure you he's not making somethin' up to avoid comin' here, he wanted to come bad, but he had stuff to do, that's all there is to it!"

"Yeah, look, I told you I don't care and that's final. What? You think I give a flyin' fuck?"

"Well, that's just none of my goddamn business ..." this kept on for quite some time. I could tell Billy was offended at Ryan inexcusably not coming, but I wondered why. From the

look of it, he never seemed to have taken Ryan into consideration ever or held him in high esteem. Maybe he appreciated Ryan more than he let out, or was the kind of person that takes offense in anyone, no matter how lame he could be, rejecting his offering. The thing is, I remembered an exchange of words I had with Ryan when I told him I would go to Billy's accompanied by Dave, and he had this to say:

"Nah. I'm not interested. I'm sorry but I don't feel like goin'."

"What's the matter? Think of it! All five of us up there, it's going to be quite a time!"

"Jump off the cloud, Sonny. Don't you see I really don't give a shit?"

"Wait, what's wrong? You loved Billy five seconds ago."

"I haven't 'loved' Billy in quite some time, Sonny. I hate being near him. He's a paranoid wreck. You can't spend two seconds next to him without gettin' somethin' like *'Oh, so, you're not my friend, you're my alternative friend, a friend who's lesser than Robbie and Ettore, who are my brothers, and lesser than Dave who's my yadda yadda,'* enough, I'm sick of it. Let him decide who his fuckin' friends are on his own. I won't be tagged like I'm some product on a shelf."

"Good for you, that was a pretty Socialist standpoint."

"Fuck off. You'll hate it too when he starts doin' the same shit to you, which he will. Just give him time. Fuckin' fake-ass bastard. I always knew he didn't like me, and you'll see when you come back and tell me all the shit they say behind my back."

"What am I supposed to be now, your personal snitch?"

"No. At least, not if you don't want to. But if you happen to hear anything important, just please let me know. I wanna know for sure if that bastard intends on being my friend just because of how fake he is, or if he truly likes me as a friend

but just treats me like shit for the sake of it."

"Yeah. How complicated. You know there's a thing called a phone, you dial some numbers and you can talk to the person to tell him things like these directly?"

"Ahh, yeah! And there's a thing called ChitChat, which he deleted me from, or so I think! And there's a thing called email, which gives me the same results? And there's a thing called "Billy don't give a shit about me anymore" which tells you a lot about how interested he was in seein' me when he was livin' here? Cut the crap Sonny. Just go there have fun and tell me the obvious so I can forget about the fuckin' guy for good and move on."

"Ah ... OK. Sure."

I had the conversations Ryan so wanted to hear right in front of me. I wondered what Billy would have said if he found out his suspicions about Ryan being fed up were true. I felt bad for him. He wasn't the friend I liked the most, but he seemed to be loyal to his friends. For the moment, I decided to keep my loyalty to Ryan, knowing that being alright with him was important as long as I was in love with Faith.

· · · · ·

After dinner, we went to bed immediately as Billy's dad had to go to work early. As per usual when you wake up and follow a morning routine with three other guys, the mood was silently awkward. We had breakfast and barely spoke to each other, more interested in keeping our mouths stuffed than in socializing. I had a weird feeling when witnessing this scene. What was I really doing there? Was I enjoying myself? Were these people actually my friends? My eyes routinely scanned the room imagining the figure of Faye materializing out of thin air, coming out of bed in her loose, comfy pajamas to

greet me with a tender kiss. I recalled a fantasy I had created one afternoon when in the company of Ryan, based on seeing her in nothing but shorts and a top immediately sneaking into the bathroom to avoid being seen by me. I had found the context so undeniably sexy that now half-asleep girls in pajamas, without make-up and sporting messy hair, comprised most of my sexual fetishes. It was wonderful to see how naturally beautiful she was when just waking up. Picturing the juicy rewards of finally succeeding and imagining her as my wife only made my infatuations worse and the prize bigger. It was the first time ever I had thought of marriage seriously. An enslaving chain to some, the promises of civic alliance with a female for life seemed preposterously engaging. Most of the moments I spent with the guys on this trip, the phantom of Faye lingered ominously in the air, and she even popped up in conversations not started by me, like we did at the table having breakfast that time:

"So I hear your brother Ryan couldn't drill that Kraut in the end ..." Billy told Dave.

"Heh, the hell he could, haha. Turns up she was a lesbian."

"Maybe that's just what she told him," Robbie let out.

"Hehe, yeah. Didn't work with Johanna, what made him think he could bang this one? He should really lay off the Gerries. As for me, I got me some nice bitches already, just for fuckin', no questions asked ..."

"Well, isn't it good that at least one of us is gittin' some? Sonny boy here ain't gittin' a lot of luck with your sister from what I hear, haha!"

"I really would rather you not touch that subject again Billy ..."

"Haha, OK, OK, I jus' wanna hear Sonny's side of the argument, all I hear is yours ..."

"What do you want me to say? There's nothing to say," I

had to hurry before things turned incredibly awkward once more.

"Oh come on Sonny boy, this is things you gotta talk about in the open. Look ... fill us all in on what the situation's like right now. 'Cause you definitely have a situation with the Mantis caste."

"You mean to say you've brought us all here to Nova Atlantica just to talk this problem over and try and solve it?"

"Hell no, boy! You both are here to fuck about 'round Nova with us. This is just summin' I want outta the way before we head out and start the fuckin' about business. Now tell me ... what are your true intentions with little Dave's sister here and why is this situation blowin' shit up everywhere it goes?"

"Well ... for starters, I liked Faye at first sight before even knowing Dave, before even knowing she was the sister of them both. I knew Ryan just like I did you guys, but it wasn't like we had a deep friendship, you know. So well, one day I'm strolling around in school, thinking how shitty life is, and then all of a sudden I see this girl and my heart just stops. I was there standing around looking at her for ages before waking up and realizing I had really liked her at first sight. I spent entire days thinking what was wrong with me before deciding to do something about it."

"And that all derived in you askin' her out, her rejectin' you, and now this shitty situation with two brothers that know you totally want to dive into her pussy," Billy stated.

"No, no at all. I mean I know it's hard to believe, but I never thought of having sex with her, not in the first weeks at least. I mean, it would obviously derive into the sexual matter because I'm a boy, she's a girl, and so on ... but at first, look, I know you're going to laugh, but I only thought of talking to her, getting to know her, asking her to the cinema or for ice-cream, really innocent things ... but that's what I wanted to

do with her, maybe kissing maximum. No sex. Just having a good time and enjoying her company. I felt too much in love with her to even think of sex, I didn't regard her as a slut or as poontang, like you would say, in any way. To me, she was different from the rest, truly special, and seemed the kind of girl I wanted for a proper relationship. I felt all of that just by seeing her that time. And I still think and feel the same."

"Mmm ... well ... that's fair I guess. Now let's hear Dave's side."

"I don't wanna speak about it, Billy. Look, my sister rejected him and that's final, and Sonny knows he doesn't have a chance. They're friends, sorta. Yeah, I know he's mad about her ass still, but it'll pass when he meets some other chick better than my sister. That's my two cents."

"Fair enough too. It's decided. Sonny, you'll stroll 'round Nova Atlantica with us in search of some tight pussy. Dave, you'll do the same, and it's not a command, it's a prediction. So Robbie and I will be doin' the same as well, so luckily we'll all get pussy!"

"What if we don't," Dave interrupted. "What do we say to Ryan? I promised him that we'd be already gettin' pussy the first day we got here. He's tryin' to get this Daphne girl to like him but I know from speakin' to her that she don't like him shit. In fact she's only speakin' to him out of pity. Turns out, the sister's the one interested in him. And guess what ... she's 13!"

"Holy cow in space, boy, yer brother has hit an all-time low."

"Tell me about it. But I want the fucker to really feel bad from tryin' to fuck my chances up with Johanna. Payback's a beeyatch."

"Hell yeah. I want payback from his stacked-up fuckin' ass thinkin' he's too good for us. I say it's payback time for 'im

alright."

"If we don't get pussy here we tell him we did anyway. And we say Sonny didn't because of respectin' my sister or somethin' ..."

"Hey! Why?" I asked, startled.

"Because you dumb bastard, that way we can get my sister to think highly of you."

"You ... you'd be willing to do that? Why? You already told me my chances are next to zero ... Besides, what's your take on helping me?

"I dunno Sonny, I guess 'cause I like you and you ain't no bum. My sister could end up with any fuckin' Kanny out there with a car and a license. I think that it'd be better with someone more decent like you."

"Well ... why, thank you Dave, but still ... I thought you guys were really bugged about this."

"We are. We don't like our sister being stalked to death when she's already said no, that bugs us, but if you're sorta givin' up and will let her breathe freely, I got no objections. Some will eventually drill her hole, and that's inevitable."

"Yeah, well ... at least I like the fact that things are alright between us."

"Right. Well, that's enough of that, you queers. Sonny, Dave, get the fuck outta my house and let's start hittin' those streets. Come on ladies, double time it and don't fuck about."

· · · · ·

Outside, the air was cold and thick. Like anywhere in Loynne's, the variations of height between districts located but a few kilometers away from each other was immense. Billy's neighborhood must have been one of the tallest points in all of Nova Atlantica, as breathing the humid air cost me

an incredible amount of effort.

The district itself was intimidatingly quiet as well. It must have been because it was a Saturday, but very few cars passed by, sometimes alarms echoed in the distance and would quickly shut off before turning on momentarily again. You wouldn't see many people and the few you saw where walking rapidly to their destinations, their eyes fixed on their phones. It was soon apparent that we were weird, at least weird enough for Northerners. When acknowledging us, their eyes would not look at anything else for several seconds, and would always look back at least twice. Billy never took kindly to these behaviors;

"Haha, y'see how the goddamn Northerners look at us boy? Imagine this shit at school. I remember, first day of school ahead of us, these Kanny girls just pass by in front of us laughin', and they say 'Hey! I didn't know The Stoning Rocks were still alive!' Ha! Can you believe that shit? They don't even know nothin'. The Stoning Rocks were all black-haired. This is the kind of ignorance we gotta deal with every day."

"You only have to deal with ignorance? That's it? I thought there'd be more interestin' shit happenin' in schools up here than that ..." Dave said.

"Oh, yeah Dave, you think that's the worst thing that's ever happened to us up here? Tell 'em, Robbie."

"These Kanny guys went up to us and skinned us clean of our cash."

"Holy shit! And what did you do?"

"What you think we did boy?! Goddamn fuckin' nuthin'! What could we do? There was six of 'em."

"Six of 'em with a blade and a baseball bat," Robbie added.

"Where did that happen?" Dave asked.

"Outside of school, well not outside of school, very near it,

say the corner. We were just going back home and then it happened," Robbie said.

"And they didn't hit you?"

"Nah, but we couldn't risk it, that's why we did nothin'. What could we do against six guys, a blade and a baseball bat, son? But don't worry. We're gonna get payback," Billy said.

"How?"

"I dunno, but we will, somehow. I already bought me that Ithaca 37 I told ya about Sonny, the riot version obviously. You can leave a person out cold from the pain for hours if you shoot at point blank. And it's got a large barrel, I can pick any of 'em motherfuckers from quite a distance, boy."

"Jesus Christ, Billy ... don't get into trouble. You're gonna get into some thick shit."

"Shut up Dave, just 'cause you never defended yourself in your life don't mean we all gotta be as spineless as you. Am I right or am I right, Sonny boy?"

"Ahh ... sure."

"See? Sonny will be our bodyguard as we stroll through this shitty neighborhood. It's a shit-ass neighborhood, but you know what? I'm just beginnin' to like it. No palm trees, no beaches, no tourists, no fancy crap. This is the real life, boy. Grim, shitty and fuckin' ugly."

"And I'm beginnin' to think you're losin' your mind. What the fuck are you on about?"

"Dave, look, it's eat or be eaten up here. I don't want no Kannies takin' my money every day just 'cause they fancy it. What was that term you always use when talkin' about Kannies, Sonny? Kannosha-what?"

"Kannovschina."

"That's it. Kann-ov-schina. Nice word. Well, that Kannov-schina thing is more alive than ever up here. The South is kindergarten compared to this. If the four of us keep togeth-

501

er, most Kannies will leave us alone. The shit happens when you're only two or alone. Three or more guys are enough to stop most Kannies dead in their tracks. They're scared shitless cowards who only attack in packs."

"Oh come on Billy, you always see everything like it's some kind of war, just enjoy yourself, put the past in the past."

"I won't ever do that, boy. Have you forgotten when you wouldn't even walk with your head raised like you do now, so proud and stuck up? Forgotten that time we almost got in a fight with that shithead JC Vega Kanny going back home after school 'cause he tossed a bottle at Tory which made a good job at cuttin' him up good?"

"Yeah, I remember all of that, but sincerely I don't give a shit now, I don't live up here, I live in the South, and over there things are starting to get better now. It's like now you can do whatever the hell you like. Most of JC's friends, everyone that used to mess with you, are gone. Kannies have backed off and the worst ones like JC have disappeared, maybe they went all up here. I mean yeah, JC is still around, but he don't do much shit anymore, for some reason he's calm, at least, compared to other years. The thing is, just when the thing in the South was getting good, you had to go."

"I don't regret it. This here's my kind of environment. It's a psychological urban type of warfare. I'm right at home."

"I'll never get you, man. You're fucked up."

"And you got no spine."

"Guys ... come on," I said, exasperated at their constant shit-throwing contest. To be honest, I made them shut up because Billy was unsettling me. There was no other fear in my heart right now than to experience Kannovschina again. I just didn't know how I would react. I could go insane. I could outright murder somebody. I would not be sunk in the bowels of the social ladder again now that I had found an idea to

live by, a cause to defend. I had smelled discomfort in the air from the first moment we arrived in Nova Atlantica. And now, Billy was confirming everything I suspected with his propaganda. I put myself on high alert and decided to show the discomfort in my face. Kannies smelled bottled rage, and they wouldn't mess with someone who looked like unwilling to take shit.

As we walked I took my time to observe the scenery, noticing the businesses all arranged in the same kind of Loynner duality; bars and DAUCO 24/7 convenience stores. Occasionally you would see a depressive-looking low-end gym, a cheap clothes shop for women or a barber-shop. This was all Billy's neighborhood had to offer, but we weren't thinking of hanging out through the rotting concrete streets of this area. We would go to Dandelion Creek, the North's cultural capital, the district which housed the now famous Illustrious University of Nova Atlantica, aside from the supposed radical political underground. It was said that Dandelion Creek was home to a large number of both extreme left-wing and right-wing radicals, Communists and fascists who often expressed their respective ideologies with fierce street battles and slogans painted on graffiti. However, I often thought this was another Loynner exaggeration as it was known to be an awfully calm place and its inhabitants the most cultured in the whole island.

We continued marching observing the graffiti of brain-dead Kannies with such sparking mind-blowing messages such as "Moha Da Kin" – Kanny for "Moha, The King"; they would always refer to their pack leaders as "Kings," while Moha was a stupid nickname almost every Kanny seemed to adopt at some point during their lives – and retarded anniversary dates followed by a "Moha I lavs u 4evs." I don't think that needs a translation. We luckily made it out of this deca-

dence fast, no more than five minutes had passed when we reached the streetcar stop, its funny bell sound making it look like a sophisticated and classy city transport. It was a Northern landmark in itself. No trains or streetcars traveled through the dry lands of the South. Tourism and work assistance would be enhanced by such methods of transportation, yet no plans had been made for implementing them. The City Hall was probably busier in spending the yearly budget in destroying roads that were perfectly fine so that they had an excuse for getting more money instead of spending it all in enhancing the island. Loynne's seemed advanced at times, but all the advances were because of tourism's sake. As such, the failure of implementing a train system through the South wasn't because of laziness, negligence or lack of money; it was scheduled. Both the State and the tourism industry benefitted from this lack of transport method. No mistakes were ever produced in Loynne's such as lazy negligence. The money came first, and anything that made them lose money and not gain much was in the way of the higher-ups. Partly, this was the kind of evidence I loved to throw at Tory' smug face when discussing the myths of the Welfare State. Nothing involving money ever benefitted the general population for the sake of it. Never.

The island-wide company that owned every single bus in Loynne's was called Atlans, but the trains and streetcars were owned and managed by the State, by a subsidiary company called "Traynne." Yes, I know. But the name isn't what was so bad about it; the expansion of trains to the South would severely undermine Atlans' profits and they would do what was necessary to stop it. They must have reached an agreement so that trains would remain in the North and Atlans could occupy the South freely. There was no other explanation, but when money is involved nothing really makes much sense. In

any case, with that agreement both outfits could still generate profitable income as well as possess untouchable territories.

"Here it comes ... strap up boys." The streetcar hissed as it stopped precisely where we were standing, and a female voice announced the area's name. We laughed at the sheer futuristic-awkwardness of it. It was simply ridiculous. Who had ever heard of talking vehicles except for in distant dystopias? At least it was quite empty. The moment marked the only time since I had arrived in Nova that we had sincerely shared a friendly moment together as well as a few laughs.

We sat down at the end of the streetcar, seeing no Kannies nearby. It would be a smooth, easy ride. Billy sat next to me as Dave and Robbie sat on the far-right of the six seat row. The noise of other people talking managed to secure the secret nature beneath our conversation.

"So tell me then Sonny boy, about this Faye situation o' yours ... we haven't exactly touched the subject a lot ..."

"Well ... we talk at school at least. She comes to me to talk for a bit. She goes quickly but I think she's really embarrassed about her friends seeing her with me. She doesn't want to fill their mouths saying she's got a boyfriend or whatever I guess."

"Bullshit, boy. That means she's ashamed of being seen with YOU."

"Aren't you a positive person, Billy? Always knowing the right thing to say ..."

"Heh, yeah, that's me alright. Look, I'm tellin' the truth boy, if yer too blind to see it thru that ain't my problem, ya hear? You probably ain't considered a big boy Kanny lord to boot that would make most of 'er friends flash their muzzles. You must be considered one of them freaks, with black clothes and army gear, just like me, don't you see I can sense people treatin' me differently and watchin' me carefully?

That's 'cause of outer appearance Sonny boy, and you're provin' it right. Faye don't want to be seen with YOU. And that's final."

"Yeah, yeah, OK! I guess! What do I know? From what I gathered, she's a very unpredictable girl. She doesn't function like the rest. It's impossible to know what she's going to do next, how she's going to react to a certain stance or action. She drives me insane."

"Mmm ... and I'm guessin' them assholes don't do much to help neither, am I right or wrong, boy?" Billy said, jerking his neck signaling Dave.

"No ... they don't. In fact, they would be very happy if the Faye situation like you call it didn't exist at all. They want to keep their sister forever wrapped in the blankets of innocence."

"Haha, they sure do! And of course they do! If I had a sister, I wouldn't just make life impossible for you, I'd outright end it. I'd jam a 12 gauge shotgun up your ass."

"Good to know. Well, you aren't exactly helping me Billy."

"Haha, I know I ain't. But there ain't much I can do for you neither. If I were you, I'd just disappear. Don't talk to 'er. Forget about 'er. You made your move, she responded negatively, that's it. Retreat. Don't go turning this into a Vietnam for yourself ... or in your case, an Afghanistan ..."

"I wish it were that easy," I said, half to myself, half audible. I looked at Dave and Robbie, who seemed to be discussing the same situation from Dave's viewpoint.

"For me, it goes like this. Guys have to do all the fuckin' effort, they have to hunt, girls jus' have to sit down and wait for a guy to drill 'em, and the bitches know we're pilin' up for it. It's like Rapunzel. Bitch sits in the tower all day waitin' to get rescued by the *MAN*, and it's the *MAN* that has to go through all the wetworks to get some decent poontang. Story of every

man. If they don't demonstrate their worth, their manliness, their bravery, they get fuck all."

"Now that you put it that way, Faye is starting to look a lot like Rapunzel ... except that as soon as I climbed up and showed my bravery she threw me out of the balcony ..."

"Hehehe ... don't feel too bad, Sonny. Maybe the bitch will react in time. Maybe she'll grow to accept you. Who knows, maybe you'll get to give that pussy a go or two ..."

"Don't speak about her in that way Billy, please ... I don't take kindly to it, like you say."

"Haha, yeah, I forgot you were in love and weren't in just for the pussy! My bad. It's only natural, boy ... no man at this age is gonna tell you they love nobody. Shit son, really, you must be the only one ..."

"Perhaps they lie ... perhaps it's all a front. Like yours."

"I ain't got no front boy! What I got is no respect for women whatsoever, except for the woman that brought me to this world, wherever she is. All the rest can smoke my 29 inch smoothbore barrel. Maybe I'll do it the day I rise to power."

"The day you rise to power? What the hell are you talking about?"

"Heh ... you'll see. We'll talk tonight when we're hittin' the sack. I want a little insight into your political mind. I'm sure there's a thing we both could learn from each other."

· · · · ·

Billy's last words left me quite confused, so as to not say frightened. It was a fear that intensified more when finally arriving in Dandelion Creek and staring at the ever-present graffiti that covered the campus district ominously.

Upon descending, we were immediately facing a tall brick wall with a large black graffiti covering most of it, "Die If You

Want To Die" painted in gigantic letters.

"Oh sweet Jesus, not this again. That fuckin' thing is written everywhere now."

"What is it, Billy?" I asked, intrigued.

"Nobody quite knows. But what I know is that the fuckin' goths have started usin' it all the time since some crazy motherfucker first wrote it. I actually think it's a political campaign in favor of euthanasia but people never get these slogans anyway."

"Goths?"

"Yeah, boy, goths! Never seen a goth?! Those leather-wearing faggots clad in black and bondage gear? Goths, Sonny, goths!"

"I know what goths are, I just would have never thought there were goths on this island ..."

"Well, there are, unfortunately. I swear here and now I would have such a fun time if I had me a license to kill and a SOPMOD M4A1. Kanny shooting range, Goth shooting range, life would be a blast."

"It sure would ... What's that one over there mean?"

"The *'Deus EXiste'* one? Hell if I know. All I know is that it means 'God Exists' in Brazilian or some such shit."

"Billy, and what does a dead chicken surrounded by candles have to do with God existing?"

"What you on about, boy?"

"There, just on the sidewalk, look!"

"Ohh ... the *macumbas*."

"The what?"

"*Macumbas*. Brazilian black magic. Fucked up insane these Brazilians if you ask me."

"Sure looks like it. And what does this voodoo mumbo jumbo have to do with God?"

"I heard Brazilians are full of cults that evolved from Afri-

can black magic and Christianity. You know, they grab the Christianity thing of believin' in God and twist it around with black magic and end up killin' chickens. I dunno boy, don't ask me, I'm not an expert in crazy voodoo shit."

"This town is insane."

"It is, huh? Heh, it'll just get better. C'mon, lemme show you around campus. You're about to see the flimsiest mother-fuckers on this island."

Billy led the way as Dave trailed mysteriously in the middle between Robbie and me. The campus of the whole university was immense, and it was awkwardly surrounded by highways. We found ourselves facing the prospect of instant death running between speeding cars blasting their horns, walking on the street due to sidewalks being non-existent and going from concrete to grass as I struggled to make some sense of the architecture of the place. Like everything Loynner, it was twisted, nonsensical and built at the last minute. We managed to arrive where Billy wanted to take us, a main street where student life was rife and varied, surrounded by pubs and bars. I noticed how retarded it was that the streetcar passed by on the middle of this street but didn't have an appropriate stop, and instead had to circle and drop us where it did.

I also checked that what Billy was saying was true. Up on this campus, you became who you wanted to be, even though most people seemingly chose to become stereotypes. Nerds like Gordon strolled merrily on the sidewalks, carrying their stupid Loynner folders and listening to their Hipp-Mans. Some of them had the typical heavy metal band shirts, sporting long curly hair, one week beards and thick frame glasses. Others were dressed in fashions that had not yet made it to the relatively primitive South; tight womanly pants, hip-hop sneakers and sleeveless shirt with nonsensical glittery mes-

sages written on them. The haircuts were a whole new world too. Unlike the football player and military style most Kanny jocks had in the South, people over here would opt for more metrosexual hairstyles, including very feminine fringes. I couldn't help but think that sexual liberties were bound to be more unrestrained over here. I was sure most of the guys we had seen were either gay or bisexual.

"Everyone lookin' like a right faggot, huh Sonny?" Billy let out, reading my mind.

"Eh? Oh yeah. Well ... they do. I guess you're going to explain what's up with that?"

"Heh, no. Not this time. I got absolutely no idea why everyone is a faggot over here. Content?"

"Well I expected a little more insight but it'll have to do. Got any conclusions?"

"My guess is these Loynner fag-lovers decided to become like this in order to get more attention. Their only alternative was being Kanny, right? Maybe they weren't cut out to be fuckin' Kanny kings, so they went for second best, which is being gay and popular, surrounded by women friends. And in the process they learned to love the cock, maybe the beaver too. I dunno, this is too fucked up even for me to figure out. Forget it, they're Loynners. Period."

"And you like living between all this? You hate more than half the shit we've seen so far."

"Hah, damn right I do. It's the best huntin' grounds, Sonny. I'm trainin' myself to know well who the actual enemy is. The South was more or less the same anyway. But this place is even better."

"Right ..." Need I say Billy's mental well-being was troubling me way beyond simple concern? The way he spoke, you would think he was preparing himself for a genocide. I only hoped that I could address this during the night, as it had

been rubbing me the wrong way for a long time.

• • • • •

The rest of the afternoon had gone on without problems. We ate something in one of the bars, me ordering my trademark chicken croissant with extra mayonnaise, which ended up being the highlight of the entire trip. I enjoyed my meal, but nothing could compare to the croissants prepared at school; I didn't know how they managed to get the chicken so tender and tasty, the bread so soft, the mayonnaise so cold and fresh. However, an inferior chicken croissant was a thousand times better than any other type of meal in the world. After eating, we small talked here and there, walking on and miraculously never sighting any troublesome Kannies. We returned to the streetcar stop and boarded wanting to go back to the apartment and have a shower.

Like it always happens when four guys spend way too much time together, we began to get quiet, listening to our own music, sunk in our own thoughts watching the scenery from the streetcar. This was as close as I would get to experience living in a big city. Maybe this was the self-indulgence Northerners couldn't avoid. The feeling of being the center, of ignoring others, of treating them like obstacles in your glorious way to progress, the cold detachment from random generic faces and stereotypes you would encounter daily, the boredom of having seen it all. This seemed to be what was making Billy more deranged. The atmosphere of the place was enough to make you forget who you were. It was easier to stop being an individual in a place like this, where you were easily placed with a tag under thousands of social clichés you subconsciously reproduced, be it by your attitude, your genes or your memes. How many times have you had Déjà vu trav-

eling in public, looking at people and thinking about what generic-looking faces they have, as if all of them were clones? Or the way of dressing, the way of walking, the facial gestures? It's easy to lose your love for mankind when everyone around you looks like an enemy. And I would have never doubted that whatever Billy was experiencing, I was sure to follow in his footsteps if forced to live on this part of the island.

· · · · ·

The night went on in a similar fashion to the previous one; Billy's dad sat on the couch watching Vietnam films. We waited in turns to take showers and in the meanwhile used Billy's computer, chatting on ChitChat. Dave wanted to log in and talk to random girls. My heart shrunk to the size of a nail's head once more when he opened a window with Faye's nickname in it.

"hi u s2pid bich," he typed. "go munch sum carpet."

"fuck u," Faye replied. Dave got bored of this quickly and immediately closed the window, entertaining himself talking to some Lollies.

"Hey Sonny, tell me somethin' cool in Russian to say to this bitch right 'ere."

"Something cool as in, what?"

"Dunno! You tell me! Like … 'what up, girl,' sumtin' like that."

"Try *'kak dela, devushka.'* " Dave waited patiently for a response. Soon, the beautiful Russian girl answered back.

"whre u lern 2 speek russian???" Dave's smile increased dramatically.

"Thanks, Sonny," he said. "Now I got me another one for sure."

"Glad to be of help," I replied, exasperated.

"Stop usin' my fuckin' computer to pimp out bitches Dave," Billy shouted. "You'll get plenty of chances 'ere."

"Ah, it's OK Billy, not like I'm starvin' or nuthin'. You guys should dedicate yourselves to that." It was amazing how cocky this guy was. Billy wasn't taking kindly to this.

"You log the hell outta that before I start tellin' that bitch to start sucking my white freckled Texan veiny cock. C'mon boy, on the double!"

"Ugh, sir, yes sir!"

"That's how I like it boy. Now listen. Let's go an' eat. Fuckin' starvin' 'ere."

We headed for the kitchen like the other day, ready to cook some meat. Robbie and I did most of the cooking while Billy and Dave prepared the table. Soon, Billy impatiently signaled all of us to come round together before his dad interrupted, and we sat eating the meat away as soon as we had placed it on the plates.

"OK, so today we couldn't fish any Lollies," Billy started. "But tomorrow it'll be different. Not like I'm concerned about that, but we only got one day left, tomorrow; the day after you two are gone. Now, about this fucker here, I know he don't have no trouble gittin' chicks. He don't count. But I'm talkin' mostly about us three. You Sonny, you'd better get your shit together and bang some Lolly broad you hardly know before you're officially deemed fag of the year here. We organized for these Lollies from school to come meet us tomorrow at the skate ramps, up in that park near the Colony Plaza. We'll go tomorrow at around 1900 hours and fish 'em up. You each organize your gigs however you like with them in private, and if things go like they should we all get herpes. End of story."

"Sounds like a good plan and all, Billy, but not quite sure I

want to do it. I mean ... I'm not interested and—"

"Ahh, don't worry Sonny. Live a little. Just go and see for yourself, do whatever it is you're most comfortable with. Deal?"

"Fine. Deal."

"Great. Now well ... how did you like Dandelion Creek, Sonny?"

"I don't know ... it was just too weird. Like a big district from a major country, but in Loynner fashion. It gave me that impression of an ultra-modern Western consumer society surrounded by misery and filth, like some cities in America, think São Paulo or Detroit. It was as if, for every condemned building full of trash and graffiti, you had a MegaLon store. Wealth and misery living side by side, but wealth still maintaining a dominant presence."

"Well, that's about right. Still ... you'd like to live here?"

"I don't know. I don't think so. It seems so advanced and complicated in comparison to the South. I guess it's a matter of getting used to, though."

"In a way. But why do you think I'm gettin' to like this so much? It's 'cause of the complicated shit. I was bored of the South alright. Like I told you before, it seems like kiddie games compared to this. And today's been a very rare easy day compared to what it is normally, when the real life strikes. You just came on holidays. In everyday life standards this shit gets amazin'."

"Yeah, well ... I told you already. I guess I like things easy-going and calm. I don't like surprises."

"Borin', aren't ya? But don't worry. I know what yer like inside. Jus' like me."

"Hey Billy, mind if I cut off your flirting? I need someone to pass me the salt, anyone got any salt? Need some salt here, anyone hear me, hello, salt?!" Dave said, interrupting.

"Here, you dumb fuck."

"Hey fuck you, inbred redneck!"

"Anyway. We'll talk later." Billy winked an eye at me and smiled to himself as he continued eating, the sharp blue eyes fixed on the plate.

· · · · ·

After dinner we went to the rooms, and I was thankful. I wanted the day to end already. Even though nothing serious had happened, I was feeling more and more uncomfortable by the minute, and Billy's rants didn't help. Robbie's silence didn't help either for that matter, but maybe it was his way of expressing how his brother was exaggerating. Dave didn't seem to take Billy seriously in any way.

I put my sleeping bag next to Billy's bed and got ready to call this a day. However, I knew Billy wouldn't give up so easily. He had something to say.

"Sonny, something's been on my mind lately," he began. "Something about politics."

"What exactly?"

"Even though I have a certain idea, I want to know exactly where you stand in the political spectrum. That and how far you're willing to go for your ideology."

"Wait, wait, wait," I interrupted. "I want to ask some questions first. Like, why did you behave all day today as if you are going to start a civil war or a mass murder? Why are you so psychopathic and violent and anti-social? This is exaggeration, even for you. You seem as if you're liking it here, but you're acting very strange. As if you're happy because you plan on setting off an atom bomb."

"Hehe, Sonny ... you're not entirely wrong, but you didn't get one thing right either. Well ... I see you have actually been

515

listening, unlike Dave. He thinks I'm just rambling, luckily ... just the way I want him to."

"What's your big plan then? What is it that you want to do?"

"Wait a minute there, boy, I ask the questions 'round here! Look. I'll start so you can open up. I'm gonna tell you some background info, alright? My dad used to be a secessionist, you know, he supported the existence of a Confederate States as an opposin' force to the United States. He hated the Union. He was really disappointed with the way things were handled in the so-called 'United States' and never again wanted to even step on that land. He became seriously disappointed when the Secessionist Movement failed and became absorbed in the Yankee mindset of Washington. As such, he moved here with us. Obviously, when we moved here, Robbie and I began let's say, gettin' ideas of our own. Without the United-statian regime oppressing us, and without a need to rebel and support the Confederacy, we became lost. We didn't have a cause anymore. We were in Loynne's, and as our lives here progressed, the entire country became engulfed in expansion-ist Yankee politics. Officially, the country was nothin' to us anymore. We didn't identify with our land. That's the worst possible thing that can happen to a human being. I guess you must have been the same, first with the USSR collapsin' and then with Russia changin' so much, becomin' so similar to the US ..."

"I guess we can relate in that sense ..."

"But listen ... the thing is, I forged an ideology of my own with Robbie, an ideology I can't be really open about as of yet. Fortunately for you, it doesn't involve killin' civilians indis-criminately. So don't get scared. No blood will be spilled. Goddamn, I seriously wouldn't have taken you for a bleedin' heart liberal that cares about collateral damage ..."

"Billy, I won't say anything else unless you tell me what your plans are or what you want to do."

"Heh ... alright. Well ... as you know, Tory is like a third brother to us. We're not talkin' about being mere brothers out of blood, like Robbie and I are. We're talkin' true bondin'."

"Go on ..."

"We wanted to see if Ryan and Dave were also worthy of being our brothers. But from what you can clearly see, they aren't. They lack many qualities we need. They are reckless, dumb, overemotional; simply put, they're petty people, who care about petty things. Not worthy of even addressing us I might add. But then, we spotted you. And you ... well, you're a different matter. You might have noticed I no longer am addressing you with my usual redneck slang. Heh, good trick huh? I recognize I'm not a distinguished gentleman but I try my best. In any case, I don't care about being an intellectual, a gentleman, a noble or a higher class. I simply want to be smart. And I always do anything within my reach to be it. Ettore and Robbie share these qualities. Being brothers is more than just enjoying their company; it's about sacrifice, involvement, hard work, trust, honesty. We share everything together, all the secrets, even if we betray oaths promised to others who we consider foreigners. Strength through unity, as we say. Nothing farther from the truth. Strength from unity is what has kept us together so long, what has made our little Brotherhood so successful."

"Like Juche."

"What was that?"

"Juche, a political thesis developed by Kim Il-sung which states that the Korean peoples are the masters of the country's development. What you said just made me think about it. Maybe it's unrelated, but I thought it could interest you ..."

"Haha, 'course it can, I like your knowledge. See, this is

what I've been wanting to talk to you about. I considered you a good recruit because of your knowledge on communist systems. We need that knowledge. And we need someone like you. I'm going to summarize my request as best I can. I want you to be one of the brothers. We call this union of ours The Brotherhood. I want you to be our mole, our insider. You'll betray anything and anyone that's not us. If you do betray us, well, aside from finding out, you'll be of course expelled forever from The Brotherhood. I want to make that sparklingly clear now. Which brings me to the topic at hand. Faye. She's the only thing between us. She's the only thing I would think you'd never betray. As such, I cannot trust you yet. But I'm willing to give you a chance. I'm willing to forget that and have you under scrutiny if you tell me and swear now that you'll never betray our cause."

"In case you're forgetting, I don't even know your cause."

"Of course you don't. I cannot let you in on it without your absolute trust."

"I can't promise anything right now, Billy. Not without knowing beforehand what I'm getting myself into. That wouldn't be very smart."

"Hehe, *touché*! I guess it wouldn't. Alright. You'll get your chance, when we get to know each other better. But for now ... jus' make sure ya drill that bitch, ya son-of-a-whore! YEEEE-HAW! And then, and only then ... we can talk."

• • • • •

"Mornin' everybody," Dave said, sitting down at the table with the rest of us after having a shower. Billy studied him with a glare of disapproval in his sharp blue eyes, and concentrated on his meal as Dave spoke again:

"So," he started. "We ready to meet those bitches yet?"

"What did I say yesterday? Don't you listen, son? I said 1900 hours, you fuckin' boy. Don't get me started already."

"Woah, woah, motherfucker! Chill out, you inbred redneck!"

"Shut the hell up. OK guys ... remember what I said last night, right? We go there and we give 'em hell. You, Dave, make sure you breakdance around and do plenty of funny shit to attract attention. You know, like you always do."

"Hey you know, I didn't notice until now how from time to time you talk less and less in fucked up redneck ... must be city life."

"Hah ... well ... it might be," Billy said, winking at me like the day before.

"Anyway today I don't fancy doin' nothin' till 1900 hours, I wanna relax a bit. We'll play GamEsprit Eins all day, like during the golden age."

"GamEsprit Eins? You still got that shit? Jesus, the memories we got from that ..."

"Heh, we sure do, boy. Come on let's play."

"*Oh no,*" I thought. "*Not this again.*"

"Jesus, man! You still got Mark Falcon's Skating Spree 2! You remember how you bitch slap people with the skate?"

"Nah, don't remember anymore ... but I remember how to do the worm with the skate upside down ..."

Billy, Robbie and Dave spent some time playing the game laughing and remembering times when I did not even exist to them, at least not in an important manner. Hours flew by playing with that old nostalgic console from an era when my fellow comrades in The Motherland fantasized only about owning one. Now, it was an old toy, enjoyable only to those who had owned it during its golden era. It was the basic reason of why I never partook in such shallow consumerism; it was a road with no visible end.

It wasn't long before Billy directed us to get ready. How important could this outing be? My heart palpitated rapidly, pressing against my chest as if I had just seen Faye, but for all the wrong reasons. This was a tingling sensation of anxiety, of predicting awkward events long before they ever came to pass. I didn't want anything to do with some "Lollies." I knew where my loyalties remained. No woman, especially a Loynnerin, could ever surpass Faye; her innocence, her purity, every single unique characteristic that comprised her being was what I was attracted to. What could a Loynnerin mean to me, aside from a deep, condescending pity, that familiar sensation of a void which cannot be satisfied? No simple woman would suffice. The decision was made, and not because I was forcing myself; I would never betray Faith. She was my cause now.

Going out to the cold, damp streets proved to be an eerie omen as awful as I imagined. Staring at the beautiful environment, the containers filled with black bin bags, the graffiti-covered abandoned buildings, the spilled beer cans on the floor, the shattered glass of vodka bottles, I let the foul air of the dirtiest place in Nova Atlantica reach me, and not just emotionally. Even in a recession-stricken Motherland you would never see such decadence, the disgusting abandonment of capitalism. Still, I marched on with my fellow "comrades" still remembering about what Billy had said the previous night, and how I wanted to get away from him as quickly as possible. What was he thinking? That he could convince someone he barely knew so easily with his cheap propaganda? That I'd trust him after admitting openly that he had another face, a darker side only his brother and Ettore knew about? I would keep Billy at arm's length from now on, and I knew it would be easy; he was living on the other side of the island after all. How difficult could be ignoring someone that

isn't going to be seeing you every day?

The thought cheered me up, at least for the moment. First, we had to meet those girls. After formally dismissing them, with my usual cold but respectful manners, I'd move on to fully concentrate on conquering Faye's heart once and for all. It wouldn't be hard entertaining these girls anyway, having Dave there. He'd make sure the spotlight belonged to him and only him, and I would gladly step aside as I would surely get the uglier one of the four anyway.

"So, Billy, aren't you gonna tell us anything about these girls anyway?" Dave asked.

"Heh, ye shut yer mouth, boy. Yer jus' gonn' ruin the surprise."

"So ... they're really hot, then? I gotta admit, I wasn't so interested at first ... I mean, I thought you'd probably hook us up with some godawful shrimps ... but now, I really gotta hand it to ya, now I'm interested ..."

"Oh, now yer interested, huh? Well now it's too bad. You waited so long, what's it to you to wait more, you dipshit? Hold on, we're almost there."

I was glad that at least it wasn't such a long walk. Within minutes we could already see the enormous park from a distance. The wooden skate ramps contrasted against the black sky, and the green grass shone with the water drops from the sprinklers. But it was deserted; no people could be seen walking by, and the place would have seemed completely dead if not for the occasional presence of cars that circled the park. It was an odd setting, but at least we wouldn't get bored. Dave had obviously brought Billy's skate with him to prevent this, and obviously to impress the girls.

"Well, we might as well wait for the girls here. Watch and learn, kids," he said, as he stormed off loudly landing on his skate, making the dead atmosphere vibrate with the roar of

the wheels. Dave jumped up to the ramp with an Ollie and began going up and down, holding on to the edge of the ramp with the skate in his spare hand, landing noisily to repeat the process on the other side. Dave was actually a pro, and I wondered why he wouldn't make this stop being a hobby and turn it into a career. My guess was that he simply lacked ambition.

"A natural born skater, huh?" Billy said. "But don't worry. I ain't worthless neither."

Billy ran up to Dave and stole the skate from him, prying it from his hands. Dave was visibly offended, but soon forgot about it to laugh with Billy, shouting at him to recommend new tricks, new variations, truly enjoying himself like a football coach with his star player. Billy indeed had talent as well, maybe just not the easiness Dave did. I did not even want to try, and judging by his calm demeanor, neither did Robbie. As such, we just sat there admiring the antics of our skater friends and proceeded to actually talk, something Robbie would not do for the sake of it.

"So, Robbie ... what do you think of things so far? Dave giving you too much trouble?"

"None that I can't handle," he said, smiling visibly. "He's alright. Maybe a bit crazy."

"Yeah ... crazy. But a good friend, right?"

"Yeah, a good friend. He's just alright as long as he's got a skate nearby."

"Heh ... he sure does. By the way, you don't skate?"

"Nah ... just not my thing. I'd rather do different stuff."

"Like what? What do you like to do?"

"Swimming. And football. All sports that involve teamwork. Obviously swimming doesn't involve teamwork but it's the most complete exercise there is. You could call it the best workout."

"I do weight-lifting. Not exaggeratedly, but it is a hobby."

"Yeah, I can tell ... why don't you get in boxing?"

"Boxing? You mean ... competing, and all that?"

"Yeah ... why not? You got the body."

"Well ... I don't really like sports. I mean ... I hate competition."

"You do? How's that?"

"I just can't be doing with it. Too much stress. I hate the thought of two opponents, or two teams where only one will have the glory. I've always hated it."

"Haha, well, what do you want, for everyone to win the match?"

"Well, why does a match have to exist in the first place? I mean ... take North Korea, for example ... have you ever heard of the Mass Games?"

"No, what's that?"

"It's like the Olympics and a National Parade rolled into one. It involves coordinated sports that only thrill the public but don't seek competition, like artistic gymnastics, choreographies, all sorts. But all done in a way where there isn't direct competition. I think that's the true nature of sport. To be the best without having to be forced into shredding someone. Competition only brings the worst in people. I think you may have noticed athletes on this island are in some ways the worst kind of people you'll ever encounter ... from JC Vega to Monika Strössner ... Narcissistic, egotistical types that only seek glory and to stomp on anyone who challenges them. It makes people elevate to a certain glory no person should ever receive, not for kicking a ball around at least."

"Haha, JC Vega ... didn't Billy tell you about last time?"

"Ah ... no ... what?"

"You know we work during weekends on this shithole restaurant, right? Billy ever tell you?"

"Um, no, I just found out."

"Well, we do, nothing serious, just to get some money and help dad around. Well, tell you what, JC and that bitch-face girlfriend he has walk in and they didn't recognize us, why should they, and we go and spat on the hamburgers and put all sorts of shit in it, obviously without them noticing. I don't remember what we put in 'em but it was just so damn funny. Then they were munching away and we were in the kitchen laughing our asses off, ha!"

"Haha, yeah ... that's ... great." I thought about why Robbie changed the subject so suddenly, but didn't want to repeat what I had just said. In any case, he reminded me of someone like Dave or Mario, only worse ... someone who never listened to what you said no matter how deep your philosophical viewpoint. Ryan could be like that sometimes but only if what you were talking about didn't interest him at all. Dave and Robbie seemed to live in another plane of existence, a more carefree one. I didn't doubt a second why Billy was the leader of the two.

"Hey you two, dontcha wanna skate or what?!" Billy shouted.

"Tomorrow!" Replied his brother, laughing.

"Ahh, screw it. Anyway I wonder why these bitches are takin' so long. They should be here by now."

"Call 'em," Robbie said. "Give 'em a ring or somethin'."

"I have, I have. What you think I am boy, retarded?" Billy pulled out his phone to call once again, a bothersome expression on his face. He patiently waited for the tone to stop and to hear an acute Loynnerin voice, but he kept getting the annoying FoniTel voicemail message instead.

"FoniTel Voicemail on the horn! If you'd like to give the recipient a message, just let it out after the beep! Ta-rah!"

"Ahh, shut the fuck up, over-happy Yankee cunt."

"No answer?" Dave asked.

"Well and what you think, Eisenhower? Would I look like I just took a shit in a spacesuit if there was an answer?"

"So, what do we do now?" I asked.

"Bah ... fuck 'em. Their loss. Let's just enjoy you guys' last day here. Tomorrow you'll be already in that boring fuckin' South. You might as well enjoy the little time you got left in the big city."

"We didn't really get up to much trouble Billy," I said. "It was actually quite easygoing ... we didn't see any Kannies, the streets were mostly deserted, and we spent a lot of time in the house."

"That's 'cause, you big smartass, it's still December!! I told you, remember? Everyone's gone from here. Nobody wants to stay on the shittiest neighborhood in Nova particularly when they're on holiday. Everyone's left for the South for the festivities and to get ready for New Year's Eve, or whatever. You wait till you come when this is in full swing. And we didn't even go downtown where the shit is at. One day, all of us are gonna go to Oversight Coast on Sovereignty Week. That shit is crazier than Brazil on carnival. Then you won't be askin' for trouble in ten lifetimes."

"Alright then, and when will that be?" I asked.

"You know, on the 21st of May. It usually lasts a full week. You gotta go dressed, and I mean dressed. You know the tradition here, just like on Christmas and New Year's Eve people put expensive suits on, so you might as well go and save you a few hundred for a nice one."

"If you think I'm gonna pay hundreds to wear a suit once you must think I'm either rich or retarded."

"Ha, that's how much you care about local customs, huh? Heh, good old Loynner-hatin' Sonny. Well lemme explain it. After Sovereignty Day, meaning the 21st of May, they start

with the real shit. It's mostly parades, fairs and the like. But late at night, it gets packed with people goin' crazy in the streets, never sleepin', never stoppin', everyone dressed up drunk and drugged outta their heads like some kinda New Orleans shit but ten times worse. People fuckin' in the streets, people fightin', police kickin' the shit outta the crazies, it's awesome. You gotta see it. You gotta be there!"

"Ah ... I will ... consider it. It seems ... appealing."

"Heh, you betcher ass! Don't worry son, we'll do somethin' about it next year. This is, I gotta say, nothingness compared to what awaits you. If we had more time we could have at least gone downtown. Well, at least you got to see Dandelion Creek. That's where we'll all end up if we graduate someday ..."

"That also sounds appealing too ..." I remembered how much I had forsaken my studies. I was passing roughly, but still getting bad grades to Motherland standards. I had once been a top student, the best in my class, except for in mathematical sciences. I had been a force to consider in foreign languages, history, philosophy, biology and wrestling. Now, I was a mere shadow of my former academic self. There was nothing that interested me. No glory for my country, no honor to myself. Coming to Loynne's shut off each and every danger sensor I could have regarding my future. Nothing mattered anymore, it seemed. Nothing except returning to my beloved country once again and reuniting with my parents.

But what use would that be? There was no more country to return to. It was completely changed, inside and outside, from its once beautiful landscapes, now riddled with capitalist trash, to the peoples, who would now surely be as dumb as Loynners themselves, devoid of ideology or purpose. Maybe I should wait more in the Loynner bomb shelter. Maybe in

time, the people would get sickened of the capitalist lifestyle and a coup d'état would ensue, the old Communists wanting to get everything to the way it once was. In the meanwhile, I'd wait patiently paving the way for my parents to come.

We spent the rest of the night skating or trying to, Robbie and I both falling in ridiculous ways, a punishment not even Dave could escape. I was glad that things turned out exactly like I had hoped, a small glimmer of joy appearing every time I thought about the dire alternatives. Meeting random Lollies, what a joke. I couldn't believe Billy had been serious about it, and was actually wondering if it had been true at all. In any case, it was no longer of importance. I had survived the ordeal unscathed and could gladly return to the South, dying to see my little Faye again. It was time to set the wheels for the next scheme in motion.

· · · · ·

"Boys! Get ready! We leave for the station soon, y'hear?!" Billy's dad went downstairs to start the messy Forge Affaire. It would be a long trip, but not because of traveling in the uncomfortable old car. Billy's dad would only be dropping us off at the bus station near the coast, and from there Dave and I would have to go back home on our own.

"Robbie, c'mon, they're gonna lose the bus!" Robbie came patiently out of the room with his usual manner of dressing, wearing beach-like sports clothing. Billy had a more civilian type of wear but still aggressively authoritarian. His black hoody had a sergeant insignia on both arms as well as a drawing of a B-29 Flying Fortress on the chest. He wore brown cargos and beige boots to complete the outfit. I was dressed in a similar style but with my Green Köontz shirt, and Dave never let go of his expensive skating wear, including baggy

jeans, a studded belt and a tight black shirt with a Mark Falcon BirdPrey logo on the chest.

The trip to the coast was also silent yet not as uncomfortable. The day outside was still cold and gray, but active. Amidst the tall office buildings and skyscrapers the ground dwellers walked back and forth in typical Nova fashion, always holding shopping bags, headphones plugged to their ears and wearing sunglasses even though it was cloudy. Packs of goths could be seen for the first time ever since I had arrived, their body languages revealing their status as bottom feeders in the social food chain. These weren't after all true goths, but pretenders. The neat and expensive clothes betrayed them. Other urban subcultures had seemingly gone out of their hiding places too, as now skaters could be seen, wearing outfits surprisingly similar to Dave's but more elaborately. Punks with enormous mohawks on their heads sat on the steps of public buildings, tons of beer bottles scattered around them. The Nova Atlantica Police Department patrolled nearby but continually ignored these petty things, something you wouldn't see in the South. It seemed to me that letting these types breed freely was part of the city's appeal, and maybe they had been issued the order of leaving them alone unless they actually broke the law. Had this happened in the South, where a policeman once told us off because we were sitting on a bench with our feet touching where you would sit, it seemed surprisingly clear that either they didn't care or their orders were to leave them be.

As Billy's dad drove through Oversight Coast, I couldn't do anything but feel glad that during my stay there I hadn't really lived the true Nova Atlantica experience. Weirdness intensified as the strangest things in the entire Western World crawled out of their caves; packs of girls in Victorian era dresses holding umbrellas were sitting on the grass in a

public park, seemingly celebrating a picnic; a group of what seemed to be metrosexual men sporting hairstyles similar to top hats; tall transvestites with their bodies completely covered in tattoos and piercings parading through the streets in micro skirts and tube tops. I was no longer certain of my sanity at this point. I could not believe myself when clearly sighting what appeared to be a living, breathing mannequin or plastic doll, extremely thin and white with pink hair and enormous eyes, walking in a surreal and absolutely inhuman manner. But it didn't matter. The sight of the living doll was completely eclipsed when the car stopped at a red light, and a group of what I can only describe as swollen mutant monsters with deformed faces clad in bondage gear strolled calmly through the zebra crossing. I could not possibly believe what I was seeing; their faces were lumped, as if just being heavily beaten by a blunt object, and their eyes were barely visible due to the malformations of the skin. Some of them had razor-sharp teeth clearly visible when they opened their mouths to speak, and others had something black which I guessed to have been latex or some other material sewn through the skin in the back, arms, legs and stomach. Most of them were male, but still wore tight PVC suits intended for women complete with chains, spikes and high heels. I had never seen anything like that before in my entire life, not even in the avant-garde Nova Atlantica.

"Heh, what did I tell ya, Sonny boy," Billy suddenly whispered, noticing my face of astonishment. "The place is completely gone to hell in a handbasket. Wasn't like this a few years back. Fads change quick, I reckon ..."

"What the fuck were those things?" I asked, still in shock, watching the swollen monsters disappear among the crowds.

"Hehe ... those were what I call 'saltwater goths' ... really don't know what they call themselves yet ... they inject salt-

water or some such shit in their skin and they begin to get like all lumped up and swollen, and then they sort of massage the skin to give it form ... Utter complete fucked up faggot gothic shit ... I hope that stuff ain't harmful, so I can pop me a few heads one day with an MAA1 ... *BANG!* Haha! Like a goddamn water balloon! You imagine that, Sonny?"

The others didn't comment on this, and I wondered whether they had been paying attention at all. Maybe they decided to just ignore it. Throughout the entire trip, the image of the enormous revolver stored in my room flickered occasionally, always when Billy spoke about guns. I wondered what he would have said if I told him that possibly the rarest of all weapons was in my apartment. Would he urge to see it, would he seek to invade my home trying to steal it from me?

In any case, the city was too much for me to bear mentally, I had always known so, and was glad I didn't have to live there. Peer pressure was surely incredible, and I considered Billy's behavior to be changing precisely because of his hatred of it. A lot of psychosis can be generated from social stressful scenarios, and I pondered whether I would one day be the witness of a massacre performed by Billy and an M4A1 carbine. As far as my tolerance reached, the capitalism of Nova – obviously shaped after the Unitedstatian consumerist society and the latest Japanese social trends – was absolutely unacceptable, something I could have never coped with. I waved the city farewell as Billy's dad left us at the station, ready to get on the bus which was already preparing to leave.

"Goodbye boys, you're free to come whenever you want, y'hear?"

"We'll do that Mr. Nazareth," I said. At the moment, I had just realized that I never asked Billy his dad's name, nor I had even bothered to learn it. Somehow, I predicted that even if I had asked, he would have changed the subject. Dave didn't

respond and pretended to be looking around at people, clearly ignoring Billy's dad.

"Good kids ... I'll see ya around then, take care!"

"Well Sonny, Dave ... guess we won't be seein' each other till we come down to the South one day."

"Don't worry Billy, we'll be in touch, call whenever you want," Dave said.

"Right, well, get the fuck outta my face before you plant a kiss in it, faggot. Come on, scram."

"Bye Sonny, take good care," Robbie said, patting me on the shoulder and shaking my hand.

"It was good to see you too Robbie, we'll meet again."

The Nazarethes left in the old Affaire and I was once again stuck with little Dave, my favorite hobby in the world. We boarded the bus and sat at the absolute back of it, like it was usual when Kannies weren't around. Surprisingly, Dave wasn't in the mood to talk. He put his headphones on and completely ignored me the rest of the trip, dismissing me with his hand when I tried to engage in conversation, uttering he was too tired to talk and wanted to rest. Something had happened during our stay there, but maybe he was right. I was also tired of so much socializing, and already missed to be in the silence of my shelter. I tried not to think about anything the rest of the trip, enjoying the cloudy and rainy environment of the North as long as it lasted; in roughly an hour and a half, it would completely morph into a scorching wasteland devoid of life.

I became seriously offended at Dave's attitude, but who cared about him anyway? When his sister was finally mine, I would hardly talk to him. That was only part of what succeeding would entail, to never again have to depend on them for anything at all. I would be the big patriarch and they would just have to swallow defeat. This made me think of my previ-

ous conversation with Billy, of my mentioning Juche; to be the master of all things, and the decisive factor in everything. This should be my main attitude, my principal drive to face this struggle.

I had to convince Faye; I had to for the sake of a better, healthier life, and because I couldn't bring myself to focus my energies on anything else. Slowly, she had become my life, my reason to fight. I had never loved anyone so much before who had done so little for me. Never had I felt that inexplicable force love is on its own. Country, ideology, Party, my love for things that had always been dear to me suddenly became smaller whenever I pictured Faye's beautiful green eyes inside my mind. How could I commit such a crime? To want to abandon everything that comprised me only for another human being? But at this point I couldn't deceive myself any longer. I would have done anything for her, selling my beliefs, betraying my friends, forgetting my goals; she was a grandiose purpose on her own. Being with such a valuable woman one day, to earn her love, respect and admiration was sheer glory on its own. I loved her. Her delicate way of walking, her gentle smile, her powerful eyes; how could such perfection exist? I couldn't possibly answer that, but I knew that I wouldn't allow it to slip between my fingers. I would do anything within reach to get to her, and the reward would be unimaginably satisfying. Glory as great as returning to The Motherland under Party rule, as grand as the revival of the USSR, as marvelous as the idea of Communism spreading to every corner of the globe.

In my mind at the time, Faye was worth more than the sum of all that.

- CHAPTER IX -

Defection

"Freedom is always and exclusively freedom for the one who thinks differently."

- ROSA LUXEMBURG -

Polish Marxist Theorist, Writer, Author, Economist, Philosopher, Socialist Revolutionary and Martyr of Anti-Communist Persecution

---

My visit to the North, limited to Nova Atlantica's poorest district and the Dandelion Creek University Campus, had not just been a somewhat boring outing, but an unbearable nuisance. I was incredibly glad I could go back to my own devices. Billy had rendered the entire trip a perpetual awkward nightmare and it goes without saying that Dave, being his usual self, didn't improve it in any way. Robbie didn't count at all.

Billy had unsettled me greatly with his confession of the existence of this "Brotherhood," a circle everyone knew about to some extent under different names, but it only served to make me want to distance myself from him even more if it was possible. Ettore was my only liaison with him for that matter, and he was known to always keep their secrets well. If Ettore didn't insist, I wouldn't meet the Nazarethes because of my own volition. At least, not for the time being.

Alone in my house, always submerged in darkness to keep the blazing sun from turning the place into a greenhouse, I

decided to watch TV after my usual exercise. My mood was quite difficult to describe; a mixture between hopelessness, general lack of enthusiasm and boredom. Seeing what went on around the world could produce either ecstasy or rage, and with experience I had learned that anything that happened in the outside was bound to increase my apathy.

I decided to forget momentarily about my unwritten law and go for broke; I put the Cox Media Network channel on, ready to be blown away by pure US idiocy. I still had time to catch "Most Embarrassing US Moments of the Month" on Cadenas Latinas but opted to watch the real thing instead;

"Coming soon to a theater near you, it's REDNECK SIX: AMERICAN DEFENSE!

Based on the best-selling First Action Peril video game of all time, the Tom Millius novel that started it all takes it up one notch on the big screen.

See our heroes, the CIA's toughest black ops commandos, fight against terrorism not abroad, but home!

An American terrorist group calling itself "Sins of the Founding Fathers" has taken over the White House claiming America is a corrupt and oppressive nation, and plan on succeeding by unleashing a nuclear holocaust in their own homeland!

It's up to the Redneck Six to defend America from its biggest enemy yet; the American people.

THIS FALL."

Well, that had been quite predictable really. I wondered whether Cadenas Latinas would have offered more shocking

moments.

I thought about how Gordon would surely ejaculate all over his 216 cm VaniTV when watching this garbage. That Tom Millius dick and his decision to move to the video game industry from the political thriller business – with but the most jingoist Unitedstatian games ever made – was beginning to really be a pain in the neck. Now, all the nerds and geeks, from Gordon to Wolfgang all the way to Axel, would be wearing the boots of a jarhead rapist white-trash Marine or a CIA agent justifying mass murder for "democracy" and capitalism. What a disgusting rotten world. And we Communists were supposed to be the sum of all evils? At least the world was now free of the cardboard cut-out characters of Millius' pathetic right-wing spy novels and wannabe political thrillers; video games didn't matter because they weren't taken seriously by anyone, and even with clear right-wing messages, all kids ever wanted to do was shoot each other to pieces like idiots. Amongst the people I knew, I never doubted for a second that the most macho action types, like Axel, would consider the LIPD or even the SKAR when studying failed, as there was no army in the island. In fact, I was certain I had overheard several conversations between Mike and Axel over living it up in the SKAR as an alternative to the "schmuck" life. The thought made me feel alone; nobody would ever understand my political leanings. Nobody would ever care, feel curiosity, or even rationalize the basis for my ideology. After all, why should they? They had already been brainwashed. They already thought of anything remotely leftist as an evil conspiracy to systematically turn people into poor peasants being constantly poked at by soldiers carrying unbelievably outdated AK-47s. Nobody was capable of understanding that the old tyrannical versions of Communism ceased to exist, that they had had their place and context in

history, and that new forms were evolving with the times. Nobody seemed interested in dissecting what they perceived to be a uniform, homogeneous enemy called the "Red," and that the "Reds" had various conflicting and different views on Communism, Socialism and even anarchism. But you'll surely know that said reason is because the right-wing does not have an ideology, just merely a loose theory that involves some benefitting more than others, which is to them absolutely humane. Even if it may seem unbelievable to you, some people on this planet do believe that poor people should exist, that their existence is completely justified and that some deserve more luxury than others. Analyzing this more steeply, however, it starts to sound more believable when you comprehend that the only thing the right-wing stands for is personal benefit, the kind of primitive impulse that has always ruled through human behavior. Nothing but selfishness and self-service, absorbed in their own greed, always fuelling their supreme lust for power that keeps people brainwashed up to this day, an inane definition of Fortune and Liberty that just like religion, every citizen swallows as something that must be true if it's repeated often enough. Fortunately, I was unrestrained by the chains that oppressed most mindless citizens. If there could ever be a thing such as a Christian Hell on Earth, it would definitely be a future ruled by a totalitarian right-wing theocratic government. But come to think of it, the US was one already.

Simply out of curiosity after enduring that atrocious report, I switched to Cadenas Latinas to watch less distorted content:

"Contrary to the ROA's claims of a massive left-wing media conspiracy, a new study by watchdog organization BIAS — Bias Investigation Across Society — has found that 70% of

media corporations have a large right-wing tendency.

A study of the main corporate networks and media empires at a global level by BIAS has found an extreme right-wing leaning, especially in the Unitedstatian Cox Media Network, the only media network left in the North American nation allowed to transmit its contents to the rest of the world, and one which many right-wingers across the world use as an example of what right-wing networks should be like. According to BIAS, 70% of these corporations host conservative doctrines without even hiding it, and each one of them often claims a left-wing conspiracy in the media to be behind the scenes, working to silence right-wing voices.

Unitedstatian President Johnny Marshall's claim that there is a vast left-wing media conspiracy doing Michael Weinstein's bidding is a complete and utter fallacy. BIAS concluded that Weinstein received the most negative coverage of any of the talk show guests in the whole country. Marshall received almost universal positive coverage (86%) while Weinstein performed very poorly (14%). Marshall was simply trying to use an old right-wing myth to pump up his own victimization in the eyes of the conservative base. The right-wing strategy to play victim in order to weaken left-wing support is well-known and has been in fact admitted by several conservative politicians, and seizing the control they possess over the media corporations to cause the population to lean to the right is one of their main strategies, claims BIAS.

The United States has become the home base for right-wing messaging and propaganda. The demographics of the guests on networks like Cox reflect those of the ROA. The CMN News anchormen and guests are all overwhelmingly old, white, and male, says BIAS, just like ROA spokesmen and presidents.

Is the corporate media trying to silence progressive and left-wing voices then? The networks will obviously say no, but how can they explain the unbelievable advantage they possess from their own point of view? Simply put, they don't have any evidence aside from putting left-wing reports under a negative light, which according to BIAS is their one and only strategy, but one that works extremely well with their audiences. The established and solid conservative audiences will believe anything networks like Cox throw at them, and the conspiracy regarding a left-wing bias working behind the scenes to silence conservatives seems to do the trick just fine. To illustrate this perfectly, we can cite the infamous 'BIAS DETECTOR,' a CMN News informative quirk used in their websites and television newscasts which consists of a headline flashing in bright red letters, sometimes with the added dark humor effect of an air raid siren, highlighting a piece of news which supposedly has a left-wing bias according to them. Many have denounced this quirk, claiming that it is used to highlight news that do not fall under the far-right ideology of Cox; as a result, the quirk has become a recurring joke among media organizations outside of the US which closely monitor the content in the Unitedstatian network, with many recommending the BIAS DETECTOR flash to be renamed 'NEWS WE CAN'T STAND.'

The corporate media doesn't want you to be awakened to the fact that there is no progressive bias in the media. Talk radio is dominated by conservatives, and cable news channels for some reason are governed by the Cox Network. The real bias is inherent in the corporatization of the media. Our corporate controlled mainstream media uses its resources to promote the conservative politicians and right-wing political parties that protect the financial interests of the networks.

Based on these statistics it can be assumed that these corporations are not only biased in favor of conservatives, but that they are actively working to suppress the left-wing/progressive points of view. If the left-wing activists are going to succeed in their endeavor, they are going to have to overcome the blatant corporate media bias that tries to bully them every day into submission."

As it was usual now, I turned the TV off trying to forget about what I had just seen as it only served to depress me more, and focused on something I had been neglecting for some time. I proceeded to look at my calendar and realized that soon we would go through the inhumane torture of the Annual Social Integration, Peace and Tolerance Day, which was always held on the 16th of December. Starting on the 17th we would get to enjoy the coveted Christmas holidays, which would last until the 6th of January.

My thoughts were interrupted by the vibration of my cellphone. If it was FoniTel again I was planning on threatening them with switching to Horizon unless they stopped harassing me. Phone companies thought themselves to be the rulers of people's lives so much they weren't too bothered by what customers could have thought of their blatant stalking.

But no; the screen was illuminated by the name "Faye," with the numbers "UP 55645 PN 76251" below. I stared at the screen for a couple of seconds, savoring the moment, trying to predict what the conversation would be like before it transpired. Temptation got the best of me and I violently answered, with trembling hands and a racing heart pounding against my chest. I coughed and tried to make my voice remain grave and masculine.

"Yes?" I said with a detached and wary voice, as if I didn't even know who was calling.

"Hey," she said. I didn't expect much enthusiasm on her part. But this would do. At least it made me remain less nervous.

"You're Faye, right?" I didn't just want to make sure, but I wanted to sound as if I hadn't been thinking about her at all. I wasn't used to hear her voice on a phone.

"Yeah, *c'est moi*."

"Huh?"

"It's French. It means 'it's me.' "

"Ahh … *kanyeshna*."

"What?"

"It's Russian. It means 'sure.' "

"OK …"

"Well, why are you calling?"

"I said I'd call, didn't I? Well here I am."

"I know, I'm just asking why … I mean, have you got anything to say?"

"Not really …"

"So why are you calling?"

"'Cause I'm bored."

"That's it? You call me because you're bored?"

"Yeah. What, you want me to hang up?"

"No, no! I'm just trying to … make sense out of all this."

"Make sense of what?"

"Of, well … of this situation. I mean … we've talked before, right?"

"Right."

"And we concluded that, well … that … we wouldn't be … ah …"

"Yeah."

"Right … and … well, I just don't know why you're calling me if you know what's going on with us. That's what I mean."

"Because I'm bored, I already told ya."

"But it doesn't work that way. I'm not something you can just use when you're bored. That's what you're making it sound like. We have a very delicate situation here, it's not like you can just drop right by and pretend nothing's happened …"

"I'm not, but … I just wanted to call. Don't ask why. Just be normal. Chill."

"Chill? You're telling me to chill? You chill! I mean, I'm here minding my own business after days of not talking to you, and then you appear out of the blue …"

"But I said I'd call and you said you wanted me to, and that's what I'm doing …"

"You're not exactly taking something into consideration …"

"What's that?"

"Nothing … forget it … I don't think you understand …"

"No, please tell me."

"Faye, I …"

"Say it."

"No … I can't."

"Go on."

"I … well … I love you. I want you. I can't hear your voice without melting inside. I can't look at you without wishing you were mine. I want you to seriously rethink what I said the other day. The more I think about it myself, the more I want to plant a kiss in those beautiful lips of yours. Please, just please think it over …"

"…"

"Hello? Are you there?"

"Yeah … I … look Sonny I'm sorry, but I gotta go."

I was left there with the phone pressed against my ear, the hang up tone being the only noise in the reign of silence that dominated my dark apartment.

· · · · ·

"Dear ********,

What is this about wanting to return back home? You can't! What's wrong? What has you so upset so as to want to go back?

I'm sorry but you absolutely cannot. We're doing all these sacrifices for a better life. This will be over soon. Try to be strong and wait some more.

We've sent you some more money this month, just so you can enjoy yourself and buy something that can make you happy. Think about what we're doing for you. We're doing it so that we can be together again.

Love you,

Mom and Dad."

My parents' latest reply was just as I imagined it to be. I had written to them in a fiery mood, sick and tired of Loynne's Island, of my situation, of being unable to truly enjoy myself. I appreciated their attempt at buying me a little happiness with money, but I didn't need that. I already had all I needed, except for one non-purchasable thing. I would probably spend the money on a chicken croissant feast or more clothes, never a bad thing on this fashion parade of a society where people seemed to have absolutely nothing else to do aside from checking if you wore the same outfit twice in a week.

But for the moment I had other things to "look forward" to; every year in December they organized the Social Integra-

tion, Peace and Tolerance Day, or Social Integration Day, as it was commonly shortened; a spectacle of diversity and minorities including African drummers, Arabian dancers, Brazilian capoeiras, German rappers, British boy bands, and other assorted activities that could be said to appeal to the youth. After a while of doing compulsory activities, they would let us do whatever we wanted in terms of leisure, playing sports and whatnot, but we couldn't leave the school for a few hours. This cheap stunt was supposed to stop the now non-existent racism in Loynne's against foreigners and bolster their integration, but more than half of the school, so as to not say more than half of the island, was inhabited by immigrants at this point. The locals had been seriously wary and aggressive against them at first, but it had stopped the moment Loynners began to acknowledge themselves as the minority. The reality of immigration was as such now considered normal, part of the gradually fading Kannovschina I always mention.

This forced circus of diversity was what we had to put up with before we could go on and slack off on some shady corner for the rest of the entire afternoon when the show ended. What else could we do? It was like an extended break that lasted from 16:30 to 19:30. A whole afternoon of *that*. Start picturing it in your head and you'll get why I usually had a ton of fake signed justifications of why I had to be excused for an appointment with the doctor. Teachers were however wise with justified absences on days like these, and would do a thorough check before letting you go. Deep inside, however, they knew some kind of trick was going on and the student in question had either received external help from his guardian or step-dad, making them give you this really nasty look until you walked out of the school. The coincidence was just too vast. I had cheek for it anyway. I didn't mind, and all I want-

ed was to get back home and indulge in my own vices in peace. My anti-social nature always shocked bleeding-heart liberal teachers, the kind who were always supposedly concerned about your mental well-being. Dodging the awkward and direct questions about whether I was undergoing bullying, had issues integrating or was having some sort of trouble at home – who the hell wants to go home if he's having trouble there? – I always managed to check up OK and happily stride back to Montenade.

After classes were over at 13:30, we had an hour or so to ourselves, while the show was being prepared on the football field and teachers instructed performers. My classmates went and bought several things from the canteen to bring back to class. It usually started like that; we spent some time in class talking or playing cards and eating while the teachers organized everything outside. The classroom had also been decorated, with the various flags of students' respective nationalities and pansy hollow values like "TOLERANCE" and "PEACE" written all over. I still remembered what I had done on the previous Social Integration Day; I had put some of my war-mongering pictures to decorate the inside of my locker, such as MiG Fighter jets, Tupolev bombers, T-80 tanks, several Kalashnikov rifle variations and military insignias. The physics teacher had looked at me as if I were insane in the head. I turned around and said: *"I'm celebrating war."* She looked at me in horror, with her mouth open and her eyes frozen. She knew my odd nature, but would have never thought I was capable of such an outburst.

"Why?" she asked in confusion. This teacher had always questioned my reasons whenever I did something strange. She knew this wasn't an act of sabotage, but another symbolism on my part.

"You people celebrate your definition of peace once a

year while you continue to wage war. It disgusts me. This is why I'm doing this. I'm celebrating war today because we can't seem to get rid of it. Maybe if more people celebrate and promote war like me, you will feel more inclined to actually stop it. Maybe you will set your priorities straight then." She needn't any more explanations. She looked at me with a sympathetic smile and let me carry on. I wonder what she could have thought if I had said that in in my spare time I amused myself admiring the might of the Soviet Army parading through Red Square because of its sheer imposing image, a force which would have crushed the entire Western Hemisphere 10 times over had it been deployed at the appropriate time. How low my morale sunk when thinking that the Great Soviet Army missed its opportunity to parade through New York's capitalistic 5th Avenue, but if everything went well I still had time to see the Chinese do it instead. But make no mistake, wishing for this did not mean I was a hypocrite. I never lied to the teacher; I strove for world peace and cooperation among nations. But that little hatred for the enemy is a bit hard to eradicate, even more so when your enemy is comprised of the most retarded, ignorant, uncultured and self-righteous bigots on Earth.

My friends returned holding dozens of chicken croissants, a scene which boosted my mood titanically and dropped my jaw to the ground. A Colombian guy, a wiseguy with seemingly lots of money and supposedly Cartel contacts, bought the croissants for anyone who wanted them. Needless to say, almost all of them ended up in me. I ate at least five of them in a row, and snuck inside my bag three more to eat at home, out of pure gluttonous addiction. This was the kind of excess you would find in Loynne's sometimes. People just didn't care about spending. If you were trustworthy and humble, they'd buy you food, drinks, anything you were in need of if

they saw you standing next to them with nothing. That really is something positive to say about Loynners. They didn't have that paranoid, grumpy attitude my fellow countrymen had, always saving every penny, never buying anything not even for themselves and choosing not to trust you no matter the situation. Inside that classroom everything was utopian, even if it was for a short interval of time. There was no hatred, no racism, no war. Nobody was excluded, undermined or ridiculed. There was no cruelty, no desire to humiliate your peers. Just all of us playing cards – excluding of course Kannies who thought themselves too good for us, and Axel's uptight boarding school buddies, who had gone out to jock around in the sports fields – sharing our food, having a laugh as if we had known each other since birth. Needless to say, girls weren't team players in this guy type of socializing. I'm sure it seemed impossible for the people there to imagine girls indulging in our friendly gathering, deprived of their status system, their discrimination through popularity, their calculated and cold selfish social cravings. No, of course the girls weren't there with us. They were hanging out between themselves or with the Kanny jocks, showing their real nature. I imagined how elevating all of these women to the status of celebrities would give us just the kind of woman we were fed up with seeing every day, the woman who memetically teaches the next generations to be as hollow and deprived of intelligence as fashion models, the lowest forms of scum on Earth.

After a while of this, we were called downstairs to take part in the Great Social Integration Day. Like I predicted, first we went to the gym and participated in activities with this mellow African drummers, who had brought a ton of African instruments we could mess around with. Then, we went to the football field to watch the capoeira show and look

at asses in tight pants and legs flying through the air; later we heard Edith and Tom Richards sing with a kid-friendy rapper, and finally, what nobody was expecting; a local up-and-coming rock band playing live.

The name of the rock band, "BAFFLED," was a play on words with the names of the members or something stupid as that. I really couldn't be bothered at the moment with all this crap. I found myself bored to tears, with my classmates not paying a lot of attention to me now that the contextual social utopia of playing cards and eating croissants had ended, being even boring between themselves too for some odd reason. Maybe it was getting to them too and I wasn't the only one anymore. When this band started playing some grunge music, sang by a girl, I decided I had had enough for one day and left, not really caring about my destination. Watching the band playing wasn't compulsory anyway, and people found themselves scattering, with most of them however deciding to stick near the band. My freak recess friends, including Gordon and Claude, were in the same routinary place, the shady ramp behind the right court. I didn't want this, I wouldn't have come at all if I had remembered. I tried to sneak by and enter the Main Building without being seen but it didn't work. Just as I was passing by, Gordon's horrendous voice shouted my name and invited me to hang out with them.

"Sonny! Hey! Look! Remember what I told you about, that thing in Gears of Deterrence 3, you know ... that if you backtrack like five levels and jump 61 times on the first tree you climbed on the tutorial mission, you get the backpack with infinite stamina? Well, guess who doesn't run out of breath while on battle anymore! I'll take you on anytime!" I pretended I didn't hear him, leaving room for Claude to mask my silence.

"What? You got the Infinite Stamina Backpack?! But how did you even know? That unlockable is nowhere on LoynNet! There are no guides on how to get it! People doubted it would be even in the game! How the hell did you manage?"

"Heh, Claude, in this life, everything takes a little patience and Vanity. I searched every nook and cranny, I dug every square meter in-game and I jumped a hundred times on each pixel. I am the first discoverer of this shit, now people will roll on the ground when they see my Milestone achieved. First guy ever to discover this, right in front of you. It raised my Milestone bar 56% with that alone! How's that!"

"Awesome ... let's hook up tonight on the server and you'll show me ..."

"That's alright, Claude ... Now listen, Sonny ... what you think of the new trailer of World Defender: Peace Corps 2? Pretty tight, huh? Haven't seen graphics like that in a long time. Improved AI, physics and gameplay mechanics, new firearms are off the hook too ... Oh, by the way! I got the box from the first one right here! There, take a look Sonny! Ever played it?"

Gordon handed me a copy of World Defender: Peace Corps. The material was smeared with every single concept I rejected. Holding the box with all the rage and disgust in the world, I began to read not quite believing this had come to be an everyday reality people took at face value:

World Defender: Peace Corps

Spear-heading First Action Peril to its finest hour yet!

Feel the heat and realism of battle as you step into combat in an ambiguous land referred to only as "The Middle East." Surrounded by hostile civs that block your way to the LZ,

there's nothing to do except falling back to base and wait for reinforcements. When a car bomb inflicts heavy losses on your teammates, it's up to you to grab that RPG and blow a hole in the ass of the enemy in the name of God and Country. Soldier, you'd better be Oscar Mike. This is payback time.

Features:

• Dehumanize war and the enemy using terms such as "civ," "hostile" and "insurgent" as you justify your ends by any means, and plant the American flag in the heart of the country's capital!

• Play online with friends! Dehumanize war ever more as you turn serious conflicts into sassy paintball-like battles! Enjoy immortality as you respawn after 10 seconds for every 5 seconds of gameplay!

• Force people into democracy while you steal all their oil! Justify your actions saying they had weapons of mass destruction in the first place! Anything goes!

• Sovereignty shmovereignty! Prevent the creation of rogue states and future enemies of the free world by introducing an American democratic political model followed by a laissez-faire capitalist economic system which will help preserve and exemplify freedom worldwide!

• Use a wide variety of weapons, from good old American M16s to commie terrorist AK-47s full of sand that constantly jam. Your gameplay, your choices.

• Be a human weapon! Use your fists and knives to gently

549

dissuade any incoming confused civilian with killer military discipline.

• Play man of the cloth! Join the army's Creatonologist Division and teach little kids the values and benefits of real religion! Then make them join your side! Happy insurgents, peaceful country!

• Increase your Confirmed Kill Count to get points and upgrades! Uploading a total of 10,000,000 kills will earn you a free copy of 'I Killed 2867 People And I Can Confirm It,' the autobiography of Lieutenant Junior Grade Jack James!

I couldn't take any more of this. I exploded and became sincere with Gordon for the first time since we had known each other.

"Gordon, this entire series of games is nothing but trash, cheap recruitment tools glorifying the same old concept of the US military and its Marine lapdogs in ways that sound cheesy to Hollywood standards. Why don't you open up your mind and play something without right-wing propaganda and conservative values for a change? Oh wait, I know why you can't. Because in this shitty conservative world, there isn't such a thing as a purely leftist mainstream media to combat right-wing lies. I forgot that those who harness all the money and power control the media, and those people obviously aren't keen on left-wing principles. Stop listening to those war-mongers who want you to play that stupid game to join the Marines or switch your opinions about the Unitedstatian dictatorship because they're not doing well in their human rights records. You're a Loynner, what do you care about playing in the shoes of a hollow and

boring Marine dick? Is it related to you or your country in any way? Does it have anything to do with your society? Is it your problem? They are doing this purely to condition young minds into upholding US values, they know the reach these games have, this is nothing but a cultural war strategically designed to vilify US enemies, no matter what they stand for! So fuck Unitedstatians! OK?! Fuck them and their stupid little dream of world domination! Stop consuming their shitty warped values and start thinking for yourself, do you hear me, you right-wing asshole?!"

I turned around without even waiting for his reply. I wasn't interested in pursuing further socializing with him in any way whatsoever.

Just when Gordon risked dying a gruesome death by opening his trap again, I saw something my rational side wished I hadn't. Faye and her friend Chelsea were walking right up to the fields, obviously going to see the band playing. This was one of those moments where I couldn't resist the impulse. Besides, I still had stuff to talk about with her as well as frustrations to vent. I walked away pursuing them, letting Gordon speak to himself.

I tried to shake off the feeling of grime and dirt usually developed after being near Gordon thinking about how nervous and freaking out I was supposed to be. Faye's ever-present friend Chelsea was sure to be keeping her company anyway, preventing a successful intimate conversation from taking place. My attempt was doomed before its execution.

I walked toward the right field, looking sideways to the amazingly intimidating crowd surrounding the band. The little concrete wall that supported the fence was where almost everybody had decided to sit down. Others were doing mockeries of mosh pits, like the typical Kannies friends of JC trying to be funny, embarrassing both a whole subculture and

themselves with it, but mostly them. Seemingly ignorant of their environment, the band kept playing in a world of their own, with focused passion and talent, which I remember feeling jealous about to be honest. This was the kind of thing I had always wanted to do, but social anxiety was too much in the way for it. Besides I wasn't an entertainer. The drummer particularly, was shouting and cheering the crowd, a trait I thought I could have never developed under any circumstance. I hated crowds, the blabbering of a hundred people speaking at the same time, being judged by your attitude, clothes or biological traits, having to hang out with some clichéd subculture so as to not be an outcast ... all these things are what made uniformed mass-education hell to me, always since I was a child.

Faye was one of the people sitting down on the little concrete wall, unaware I was coming toward her. Her wannabe goth-pinky April Divine fangirl friend smelled me kilometers away before I could make eye contact with her horrible acidic feline eyes, typical Western European trait, and gave me one of those mocking evil looks Anglo-Saxons do so well. Without breaking eye contact with me, she leaned toward Faye and whispered my name. I could read her lips. Then next thing she said was *"hurry up, he's almost here."*

"Yeah, go right ahead you smelly little suka" I thought. *"Pump more venom into her mind, you wet little rodent."*

Witnessing my sly approach get shattered to pieces by the actions of this vile, immature and disgusting creature, Faye's presence seemed to cringe and crawl back to her safety shell. This was bound to happen the moment I opened my mouth or she realized I was next to her anyway, but I hated snitchy-bitchy friends who cling to their protégés as if they're married to them, knowing how worthless they are without their approval and disdainful cold distant chatter. I had to get rid of

this bitch fast. I'd eventually think of a way to scare her off for good.

"Hey gorgeous! How are you doing!" If Faye responded, I never heard her. All I could see was her mouth mumbling something unintelligible and immediately shutting itself again, seemingly for the rest of the day. Her bitch little friend kept staring at me, probably studying my reactions to such an obvious public humiliation. Her hazel eyes, like those of a snake, feasted on my disarmed attitude toward Faye's oblivious demeanor. It seemed she was back to not acknowledging my existence. Maybe it had always been like that and I had been too wrapped up in my own thoughts and feelings to notice. I didn't care. The only thing I cared about was getting rid of this bitch friend as quickly as possible, and talking to her alone.

"So, having fun then?"

"Uh, yeah, yeah."

"OK ... so ... you know what, this is boring me, the band's not that good anyway, so come on, let's go somewhere more interesting ..."

"Why don't ye geh't somewha more interestin' alone?" Faye's friend suddenly said, irritated.

"What? What did you just say?"

"Oh, ye 'eard me big man, ge'ht lost. Can't ye tell when a girl ain't interested? Even less if the guy's sum weird-lookin' Wrussian in ahmy gear, my Gawd ... an' buy yeself a language luv, we don't use that language 'round he'a ..."

"So this is it, huh? This is the kind of trash you surround yourself with? Ballerina girls trying to be goth? Please Faye, I know you don't have a lot going in terms of friends, but even you can do better."

"Pff, wha'evah, crweep. Why don't ye go back to yo frweak little loseh frwiends oveh the'ah? 'Cause those are ye

frwiends, wright? Gawd … ye ah no one to tell ha she can do bet'eh, mate."

"She can do better, gothy. And those aren't my friends. They're some loser assholes who I can't shake off. And you, you are the lowest life form of the lowest of the bottom feeders I've ever seen in this place. Get out of my face before you really bug me, you ugly corpse wannabe. Go back to your fucking coffin and don't get up until Lenin does, you hear me? Come on *suka*, go right ahead and get out of sight before you really end up dead." She looked like she was about to reply, but Faye stopped her. The British bitch went away giving me a defying look, and wandered alone before trying to fit in with the posh girly Loynnerins of her class. It wasn't long before she was on her own again, and disappeared behind the wall heading for the Main Building.

"Fucking gothic cunt! Can you believe that shit? I still can't get it inside my head how you can hang out with such human waste … and why … why are you looking at me like that?"

Faye was looking at me straight in the eye. My manly pride was shattered immediately. I pretended I wasn't looking, trying to seem interested in the crazy environment. A short, chubby chick with enormous breasts was trying to flirt with the drummer of the band. At first I thought it was Viktoria von Östinsel but her skin tone was darker, she was shorter in height and her breasts weren't as big. Still nice though. I envied the drummer. The dirtbag probably got all he wanted and there I was, thirsting for a girl who would not even give me the time of day.

Kannies started playing football now that their interest in the rock concert had withered. The Kanny wannabes, not Kanny enough to become worthy of playing with them, decided to play basketball. I witnessed how JC and his cronies

stole the basketball from them and began playing football, laughing wildly while the basketball players just stood there, impotent. After a while, JC got bored of this and threw the ball with all his strength out of the school perimeter, laughing like a sociopath. Nobody dared say anything, and the wanna-be Kannies simply left, looking slightly scared.

Suddenly, Faye's voice seemed to thunder and echo through the school's atmosphere, annihilating any trace I had of recent images. My head turned quickly and found those brilliant green eyes, stern and icy, completely fixed on mine.

"Are we gonna go through this again?"

I couldn't do anything except staring back at her like an idiot, my mouth wide open trying to think of something to say.

"I ... I thought that ... well ..."

"Go on, don't have all day."

"I know ... Look, I know we've talked this over already and all that. But listen, I just wanted to tell you that I just want to hang out, OK? No bad intentions, no hidden meanings, nothing at all ... alright? You too know how well we used to get along ... I mean I admit it, I know I'm really dense and obsessive but then again what guy isn't? Let's just start over again, shall we? Let's leave all this shit behind."

"Mmm ... you serious? 'Cause I'm telling you ... I don't wanna be with anybody ... OK? Nothing personal ..."

"Uh, yeah, sure ... Listen, why don't we get the hell out of here and go to your place?"

"You don't mess around, do ya?"

"Ha ... no, listen ... OK, first things first; I hate this Social Integration 'look at how rad we are' boy-scout parties; they're fake, they're forced, they're too happy, I just can't deal with it.

Secondly, I want to spend some quality time with a person I actually do appreciate, and thirdly I'm just unbelievably bored. So come on, let's not beat around the bush and get out of here already."

"Well ... and how do you suppose we're gonna escape from this cage, bad boy? Have you got us a jailbreak plan outta here? You know that everything's locked up and that not even a signed permission will get you out of here on a special school day ..."

"Yeah, I sort of run out of those anyway ... I had loads of them signed by my parents so that I could skip school whenever I wanted to ..."

"Who wouldn't want parents like that ..."

"Hey! Not like they're slacking off their parental duties, spoiling me rotten or anything like that ... they understand my pain thoroughly and know that I'm going through an unfair, scarring psychological process which is uniformed, elitist, classist mass-education. So give a guy a break, OK?"

"Hey, I wasn't getting at your parents! Who am I to get at your parents anyhow ... I should tell ya about my mom. She's never in the house, she spends most nights at that shitty café down the bus station ..."

"Yeah, I've noticed the absence of parental presence somewhat ..."

"Tell me about it ... I have to do everything in the house ... dishes, washing, cleaning ... you name it. And those two fuckers won't ever help. Ryan's a self-centered hypocrite, and Dave ... well, Dave is just Dave ... for all that's worth. At least he's out all day and he has an excuse as to why he doesn't do anything."

"Dave's not bad, but ... he does seem to evade household responsibilities in the same way your mom does. Ryan seems to be the only one who keeps it real, unfortunately. He

doesn't do anything, but at least he doesn't hide from the fact. He sits on his flaws and takes ~~doesn't take crap~~ from anybody, all the contrary ... he actually wants to make people swallow his own."

"I guess that's Ryan in a nutshell ... but believe me, Ryan's better than Dave. Dave doesn't seem to be such a devil with that cool laid-back attitude, but he'd sell me for two palms only to get rid of me and score with a girl in the house. Ryan would have more manners ... he'd at least pay me to get out. Or just plain throw me out. But Dave is a coward with no values whatsoever. He'd sell himself, Ryan, mom, the dog, me, anything for whatever it is he's infatuated with at the moment ... it could be scoring with a girl, getting invited to a breakdancing contest or a party, you name it. But he'd do it. Ryan would at least work it around a few times before eventually selling out."

"You know your brothers alright ... at least it sounds like them to me."

"The stuff I could tell ya that they never will. But don't worry, there'll be enough time for that ... as of now, let's get outta here already!"

"How, genius? You're the one with the breakout plan now?"

"You wanna bet?"

"I dunno ... do I?"

"How much?"

"Aren't you a capitalistic greedy compulsive gambler! Do you seriously want to bet?"

"Yeeeah ... why not? It'll be fun."

"Didn't your brothers ever teach you it's not wise to seem so convinced when you're betting on something?"

"Oh well, too bad for me then ... Come here ... I'll show you a trick, Baccalaureate boy ... can't believe I'm gonna turn out

to be more streetwise than you after all ..."

"Come on, I'm dying to see you in action ... not in the way you think I do, you know ... although it would make my day ..."

"Hahaha ... sure. Anyway, look ... this is all we have to do. First, we go to the parking lot ... I'll explain more on the way ..."

We passed in front of Gordon's crew, and my chameleon eyes saw him pointing and laughing with his friends, as I felt a humiliation superior to all others, humiliation by bottom feeders. Wolfgang was there too, facing Gordon on the other side of the railing and grinning in his own way, a facial expression he used to have whenever he thought had outsmarted an enemy. Wolfgang mimicked a handgun with his hand and aimed at me, signaling with Makarov Cat's gesture, and then "fired" at me. I saw Faye slipping between my fingers walking further on, but I didn't care. I remained exactly where I was, mimicked a gesture as if I had stopped Wolfgang's bullet with my hand, my fist clenched as if I had it trapped the bullet at the last second. I then slowly extended my fingers, showing him my palm, as if letting the bullet fall on the ground. Gordon and Claude didn't say a thing, as they probably thought we were messing around. Wolfgang looked at me as if he were impressed by my reaction, and performed yet another of Makarov Cat's signature gestures, the "Dusty Beret." He mimicked putting an invisible beret on his head, then raised his hands, putting them up at head level showing me his palms, as if to say "my hands are clean." I amazed myself at how smart Wolfgang actually was, and how he always let nerdyness get the best of him. Wolfgang had understood the whole situation perfectly; this was his way of letting me know he felt brushed aside and envious, yet at the same time felt respect and admiration for me. I had to return the

gesture. This time I mimicked one from Cobra Viper. I did a quick and dismissive military greeting, almost a casual one, as if waving goodbye, while following Faye into the Main Building's lobby, who as per usual behaved as if waiting for me were a secondary objective she had been forced to fulfill. Wolfgang just nodded to himself, in his own unique Japanese savvy air, looking at empty spaces and muttering proverbs profoundly, an expression of absolute satisfaction and release on his face.

The school lobby was now deserted as everyone was supposed to be on the fields, and people were told off if they hung around the building itself for too long. Some nosey tutor was bound to appear out of the blue, always with the task of enforcing fascism and meddle with the lives of students who weren't up to anything, instead of hassling the ones that were. I was the kind that got harassed by these type of teachers; someone rebellious looking, foreign, misfit and defiant. Little innocent girls like Faye were also the perfect target for this kind of hassling, but with other objectives in mind. Lonely degenerates could be found aplenty in the teacher body.

Running only into some other Kanny rebellious youths, smoking and talking about whom they had fought last week and what bitch had pulled some other bitch's hair, we got to the teacher's parking lot exit. A long green electric automated gate opened by a buzzer was the way to freedom. The gate would automatically move outwards like a normal door when it was buzzed and eventually close back after a few seconds, but the teachers had figured out this trick already, and had started to wait a few moments so that the gate shut fully with a dry "clank" sound. This was the way I used to do it before with my friends, but it was impossible now.

"So, Sonny ... given up yet?"

"Look, I'm not going up there again with that annoying band and the drum-playing Africans. Giving up is NOT an option. But if some teacher passing by in the car figures us out, it's game over for us. We're going get told off and forced to go up there again."

"That's what you think ... just sit and wait."

"Alright then, mystery girl, go right ahead!" Faye sat further away from the gate, leaving enough distance to see if cars passed by and immediately run after the car had exited the building, and seizing the opportunity of a fancy large GDW Graf navy blue sedan going through, she sprinted after the car was outside and flattened herself against the wall next to the gate. The car had already driven off when hearing the door shut itself, the teacher seemingly not thinking anyone would be lurking nearby. But the gate hadn't been fully shut. Faye had slid a pen between it, and gracefully with one hand pried the gate open. I was astonished; I'd never taken her for the action type. She had also done it skillfully, almost surgically. I kept forgetting she was very prolific ice-skater.

We went up to the corner of the sports center, still immersed in our fluid conversation.

"I so wished I had convinced you to bet something now ..."

"And good thing you didn't ... I was starting to think you would convince me of jumping off a cliff but I see some things never change."

"Ha ... as if. I wouldn't make anyone jump off a cliff not even if I paid them. Maybe if I spent the whole day with them ..."

"Oh come on, give me a break! Your act isn't making anyone weep for your sorry existence, OK? Women know they have power over men and are too hypocritical to even admit they do. Look, it boils down to this, OK? Women are like Rapunzel. No, don't laugh, let me finish! Look ... women only

have to sit on a tower all day waiting for a legion of guys that fight with each other for the right to rescue her, and then she gets to pick who she wants to be rescued by. Out of the thousands of candidates, only one will go through that adventure and effort rewarded. Think of it in biological terms ... an egg cell does the same. It just waits for stupid sperm cells to race for the right to fecundate it. All the rest die, unrewarded, forgotten. All because men pay attention to women in the first place. Can you imagine what a world would be like where men are capable of controlling their urges and suppressing them to entice women into being less picky? Women would rape men. They would be desperate just as we are to get the chance of sexual intercourse. Women would fight for men, they would actively hunt for a partner like we do ... but anyway, there you have it. Men and women are like sperms and egg cells, only on a bigger scale."

"You sure let your imagination fly, don't you, *Sonny boy*?"

"Er ... yes ... *Fatty*. It doesn't mean I share the viewpoint I'm describing. I'm telling you my experience plus those of other men of the world. Me, you know me already, there's nothing to say ... I don't like the idea of sexual promiscuity, this debauchery so commonplace in the Western World. I'm an old school romantic. I'm straight, honest, delighted by the female existence and extremely enticed by the sexual content beneath it. I want exactly what I want, or nothing at all. And that's the reason I'm not going to rest until you awake from your current frigid state ..."

"Sonny ..."

"Sonny! What's that even supposed to mean? 'Silly Sonny, he'll never learn?' Or perhaps something like 'Sonny, I'm flattered! Keep going! Ask me out!' "

"You do know I'll have to go more for like the first one, right?"

"Yes, that's life for you ... throwing a pie in your face from time to time, to you know, keep the audience laughing mildly in the sitcom."

"C'mon, not like you're hungry for girls ... I think Ryan told me you had a girlfriend not so long ago, in the summer?"

"Yeah, I did ... poor Lyria. We didn't exactly leave it in the best of terms but, is there ever a good way?"

"I don't think so, no ..."

"Well there you go. Besides ... we lived far away. She lived in Nova Atlantica. I could never see her."

"So what did you used to do with her? How many times did you see her?"

"Ah ... well ... how dumb do I look if I say that's classified information?"

"Very ... like, a lot. Total nerd. Like your friends!"

"Very low blow, girl."

"Well, so?"

"So, what?"

"How many times did you see her?"

"Well, I wasn't exactly counting you know ... and besides ... why does she matter? We're talking about us ... I can ask you the same question ... have you had any boyfriends before?"

"Me? Well ... I'll assume my brothers have told you already that ... no."

"So, no? Nothing at all?"

"No. Well ... unless you count this guy that ... well ... oh, forget it, it's too embarrassing and stupid ..."

"What? Go ahead!"

"Nothing, it's just ... we were kids, I guess, 11, 12, I dunno ... he kissed me and that's it."

"Er ... OK."

"What?"

"No, nothing, nothing."

"I know that's not very impressive, and that it doesn't really count at all, but it's the best I've got ..."

"Well ... I would count it ..."

"Oh come on, someone like you must have done better things so as to count that ..."

"Me? Well ..."

"What? Cat got your tongue?"

"It's kind of intimate Faye ... don't you think?"

"Well ... if you want to earn my trust you'll have to tell me certain things ... and I'll have to as well ..."

"Well, what do you want me to say?"

"Haha ... well ... what's the ... naughtiest thing you've ever done?"

"Oh, please, do I really have to say it?"

"Why, 'cause you've done really gross stuff?"

"No, it's just that ... I don't think I'm ready to talk about these things with you ..."

"Why?"

"Because ... you are ... and I am ... well ... you know."

"No. I don't know."

"Oh, please ... look, I just don't think this is the right thing to share, of all things ..."

"You don't trust me, is that it?"

"What? No!"

" 'Cause if that's what's goin' on, you can tell me, you know ... I won't be bothered."

"Faye, it's not that ... I just ... I want to forget about everything I could have ever done with a woman that's not you. That's why. I know it sounds stupid but ... I want to start with a clean new slate, as if I had never had a girlfriend before you ..."

"Come on, Sonny! Yeah, I understand what you're trying

to do, I might add it's even kinda cute, but you know how things are … nothing will happen, OK? I don't want to hurry it up and be cruel and say not now not ever 'cause well, you never know what's gonna happen … but look, you're a good friend, alright? And I see you as just that, a friend, nothing else … I'm sorry, Sonny … but for now I don't want nothing to happen …"

"Mmph … fine … But I'd really be more put off or forced to flee if you were more drastic than that, you know? You're not letting me in on the bigger picture. How come we can't? I mean, we haven't really known each other a lot, I give you that, but it's not like girls give it too much thought if they really like a guy, and I think we're past the point of being total strangers but not complete friends, so friendship won't be ruined, because we're just building it … so it'd be like breaking a small wall you just started to build on your garden … yeah, it's got some effort put on it but it can be destroyed as easily as it was built … and don't give me that crap of ruining a very fruitful future friendship, isn't life supposed to be about experimenting and seeing what's good for you and all that? Look, let's just try, if it doesn't come out right well, at least I'll have learned my lesson, we'll be friends, everything will be fine! Trust me!"

"Sonny, you don't get it … it's not that simple for a girl … it's not such an easy decision to make like you guys think it is. For us it's more about being true to our feelings, not taking into consideration what others think, or what the person asking you is feeling. Yeah, I know it seems completely selfish and cruel … but it's how we work. We don't do nothing, ever, if we don't feel it's right. You guys do the same in some way … why me, Sonny? Why choose me amongst all those nicer, hotter girls out there? Your girlfriend was probably hotter, easier … why'd you dump her?"

"I told you! I didn't feel anything for her, and besides there's the distance thing and ... look, to be honest, I knew I could do better, OK? I knew there was someone out there I could really look up to and admire as a person. And here you are now, right before my eyes, the most awesome, beautiful woman I've ever laid eyes upon, and I'm being denied this because of cheap excuses ... Look, yeah, I do know your rationalization makes sense, but what about mine? I'm being true to my feelings as well, being as selfish as you women seemingly are when it comes to love, and the difference is that men never get the girl they truly want. Girls have it so easy. You can get any idiot you want. What kind of guy rejects an easy to get along, good-looking chick? Only gay guys, or really faithful guys but that's a rare bird nowadays. Or, guys like me, the rarest bird of the flock, the only guy who would be true to you no matter what, never even lay eyes on some other supposedly superior girl and ONLY because I don't even feel like it! Faye ... since I saw you that day ... I can never look at women the way I could before, I'm being honest ... they all seem so shallow, so ordinary, so crude, so Loynner ... can't you see you aren't just looks? Yeah, I do like you and all that, physically I mean ... which is important ... but it's not just that, I love your personality, your attitude, your essence ... anything that means Faye does it for me ... and that's so hard to get. I have never felt like this before. I just won't let this pass because you thought it wasn't right or whatever. I do believe in this. Believe me, from where I come from, we have convictions, ideals, the fire of revolution boils in our blood ... and we're true to that. Our ideology dictates it. And my whole humanly being right now is dictating me to go for broke, to crash and burn and make you not mine, but a mere part of me, of my whole organism. And I also intend on the same happening on your end as well if possible. I want to be that

special someone that appeared out of the blue and made your life interesting, which I already have but you won't admit to that."

"Sonny ... look I think it's best I just go home and you probably should too ..."

"Why! I mean come on, just answer me that one question, why can't we try and see what happens?"

" 'Cause I don't feel it, OK? I don't feel all those things that you do ... I wish I could, but I can't ... you're a great guy and the best friend a girl can ask for, but ... I don't see myself with you, don't even ask why ..."

"So ... what ... what now?"

"Look, I'm up for hanging out with you but not until you've chilled out and moved on ... I'm warning you ... I don't want to hurt you but I will if you make me ... please don't make me, I beg you ... it's for your own good."

"My own good to entail being apart from you then, which is ironical since there's nothing I want more for my personal benefit than actually being around you all the time. Faye, can't you just consider this—"

"NO! Look, I told you no!! No means no! Don't you get it?! NO! I'm sick of this subject! Goodbye Sonny, I'm sorry but I have to leave, NOW!"

"Faye! Wait! *Chyort* ..."

There was nothing else I could have said to patch it up. Faye rushed for The Crucible, while I stayed talking to myself on the corner of the sports center construction site, walking without direction. It was an awful day alright. Raindrops poked my head randomly, and a cold wind shattered my nerves, one of those unusual days in Loynne's where it was ridiculously freezing and cloudy all of a sudden. I wondered what I could do with myself the rest of the day now that I was on my own, abandoned by my impossible true love on a dem-

ocratic free nation where your actions were only limited by your wealth. Going back home to turn into Gordon playing video games and eating candy like a baby? No. Wandering around Paradise Plaza like a bum hoping for something unusual and miraculous to happen? Not likely. Going to The Crucible, checking on Ryan and seeing if I could maybe find Faye? *Kanyeshna.*

· · · · ·

"Hey, Sonny ... come on in."

Ryan didn't seem hostile, and that alone improved my mood. He immediately went to the room expected to be followed, as per usual. I checked on Faye's room but the door was shut. I wondered if she was there at all.

"So ... what's up?" I said, trying not to mention Faye under any circumstance.

"Well, fine ... I just feel glad I didn't go to that schmuck Social Integration Day thing ... did you go?"

"Ah ... no ... I was slacking off around Paradise Plaza and wanted to drop by ..."

"Sure, sure ... You didn't see my sister, did ya?"

"No. Why?"

"Oh, nothin', 'cause she just stormed off to the room and I wondered if you guys had argued or somethin' ..."

"Ah, no, not at all ... I thought she'd be at the Social Integration thing ..."

"Yeah well, it seems she escaped ... must be that stupid Chelsea friend she's got ... always a bad influence ... I don't trust those rug-munching goth dykes for a second ... If my sister don't end up with you she'll end up chewing a lot of carpet the way she's goin' ..."

"You think? And I'm quite sure about what you would prefer between those two options ..."

"Don't be so sure ... I'd rather my sister be with you a million times than ending up a dyke. I fuckin' hate dykes."

"And fags."

"Yeah, I know. Excuse me for being a homophobe, woo, shoot me. Fuckin' liberal teachers. Ain't tellin' me to go and respect and tolerate that. That's disgusting. That's just ... wrong. That's why I hate that 'tolerance' thing day so much. It's fuckin' stupid. Nobody will tell me what to respect and what not to hate. I can hate on whatever I want."

"I don't like to press the issue of homosexuality because being heterosexual I find it wrong of me to speak about their social issues, just like feminism, but they're a minority to defend and as such all the left-wing parties now have absorbed this cause into theirs. That's what social progress is about. I mean, I've never ever felt anything for a man, not even curiosity. Personally, I think it's a completely intimate subject that's entirely up to people, and should not intrude the political or even public life. Many people partake in strange sexual practices but are not turning this into an entire sociopolitical problem. But now, all the sexual deviants, from homosexuals to transsexuals all the way to sadomasochists and in short, every single person with a fetish or paraphilia, is suddenly uniting and getting support from left-wing parties, just because of what they enjoy sexually and the harassment produced by society, which does not approve or understand these practices. Is it really surprising that most people reject the practices sexual minorities enjoy? People are not interested in what starts your engine, be it what it may be, like you, you mental degenerate, who knows what goes on in your head? I for one am not interested, and will reject whatever practices you take part in if they seem too

aberrant for me, homosexual or heterosexual. If you ask me, I'm not interested in who you sleep with or what you do when you're at it. The issue of homosexuality is simply sex-oriented, and I can't take part in it aside from defending the rights of the people and fight for their integration in society. Let them do whatever they want, but don't let them make an exhibition of sex just because they're different. I'm heterosexual, and still would not approve of heterosexuals hyper-sexualizing society more than it is today and doing whatever they like in public. There has to be a standard of decency and education in society, especially in public."

"Woah, woah, wait a minute pal, who you callin' mental degenerate? Just because I like the pussy a lot? A *whole* lot? Ha ... you don't know what you're on about. I hate gays 'cause they're the absolute definition of evil in society. Every single thing they do is perverse. I mean, they're all about perversion and degeneracy ... have you ever imagined it? Suckin' veiny cocks? Drillin' some guy's hairy ass? Are they sane in the head? Who would ever do that out of choice, like doin' time inside? And that goes for dykes as well ... Yeah, I'm a man and I like to watch two women goin' at it, but that's just fiction, fetishistic fiction ... Imagine real dykes, like this couple I saw the other day, they looked like the fuckin' Stoning Rocks, you know, with that hair from the '70s? Shit ... it was so disgusting ... I was gonna yell somethin' at 'em but I thought, nah, I won't sink to their level ... I'm above that ..."

"In Soviet times homosexuality was a crime, same as vagrancy. Throughout history, it's been considered a behavior to not be exemplified in many different cultures. I sincerely doubt that, unless the parents are already gay, parents want their offspring to turn out gay. It's not beneficial for any species if you think about it on a reproductive level. I think it's nothing more than a biological condition we've designed for

population control. I think homosexuality in our society is a response to regulate our species. And as such, we need to accept it. People think that when I say things like this I seem like a fascist, ironic isn't it? But bear with me, listen ... just as we have children dying during birth, children born with malformations, mental retardation, I think it's only natural that biologically we fail as a species, as no life form on this planet is perfect. If we were in a normal wild environment, with nothing to defend ourselves but our bodies, those factors would play a very intrinsic role where our numbers would be balanced. Now, gays don't only want to get married, they want to have children using other women as substitute bodies. The same issue happens with old, sterile women. It's wrong in the fact that nature deemed them homosexual or sterile so that they cannot conceive. It's a natural species regulator that we're blatantly ignoring. So from my point of view, homosexuality in itself is harmless and I don't see any reason to hate it, except when they want to have children and choose not to adopt abandoned ones. That's what I think. But you hate them because they disgust you, like fat people ..."

"Hey, it's because they piss me off! I don't know if you've noticed, but that Wolfgang prick sometimes messes with me, makin' fun of me for being slim! Well what's up, nature, like you say, deemed me slim! That's it! Respect me!"

"He doesn't mess with you for being slim, he just defends himself when you attack him, you jerk. And what about your brother? Don't you think he suffers from being short?"

"Well, of course he does! That's why he's an asshole, so stuck up and thinkin' he's better than everybody else. He needs to make up for the inferiority complex."

"I think you have a mental inferiority complex not related to your biology, but to your personality."

"What?"

"Yeah ... look at you. You've always been put down and made fun of, in this stupid society. We've all been through that. But now it's time to let all that hatred go. Just vent it all out. Don't hate on gays or fat people. Just ignore them if they piss you off. I'm sorry the experiences you've had with those types were negative but there you go, the perfect excuse to avoid them. Just forget about it and try to hang out with people you do appreciate ..."

"That's the problem, there's none. Only you and you are crazily in love with my kid sister. Story of my fuckin' life ..."

"Well, I tried. Anyway ... what are you planning on doing now?"

"Now? I'm jerkin' off to these pictures of Daphne at the pool and her amazingly chubby freckled body, and if I still got juice left, to some of the best piss-shit-puke porn ever ... which marks your exit cue ... Come on Sonny, in any case my mom's gonna be home shortly and you know how she hates to see the house full of people ... sooo yeah, good to see you man, but come on now, scram, the wood under the desk ain't gonna stain itself full of jizz on its own, you know, I gotta add more stalagmites to the pile!"

"Disgusting ... Anyway, you don't even wanna go out for a while?"

"Goin' out, now?! It's 18:30 if you haven't noticed. I just wanted to jack the ripper and take a nap, why you gotta be so—"

"Hey wait a minute, you told me your sister was in the room, right?"

"... yes."

"Oh great, well, since you're busy I'll go ask if she wants to go out—"

"Hey, hey hey hey! Sonny my friend! I just remembered I have to do some paperwork at the Méndez Center, heh, how

could I forget? Come on, let's hit those streets, what you waitin' for!"

"I should have known ..."

"Come on don't make this harder than it already is ..."

"You are lying, aren't you?"

"No ... I really have paperwork to do. I was leaving it for tomorrow, but this is an emergency ..."

• • • • •

Ryan and I parted leaving Faye behind, a thought I fancied amazingly hard to ignore. Faye was there in that room, all by herself, and asleep judging by the silence. She was surely wrapped comfortably by the bed sheets irradiating a nice, seductive heat from every single pore of her tight, tender body. I wondered why I couldn't simply sneak in there and get in bed with her, give her a gentle and loving kiss on the cheek, caress her hair, stroke her smooth skin with my fingertips ...

"Don't you feel an incredible amount of freedom here, Sonny?"

"Uh ... the what?"

"You deaf, pal? Do I really gotta say it twice?"

"Sorry, uh ... keep talking."

"Ugh ... I said freedom. Don't you smell it in the air, can't you feel it flowing through your veins, the joy of absolute freedom?"

"No. Besides, I couldn't care less about freedom. Freedom is illusory. Lenin said freedom was a precious good that had to be carefully rationed, not exploited and abused like in Western capitalist societies. Besides, we've never been free. We're always oppressed by external forces, of which we have absolutely no contr—"

"Oh, shut up! Look, shut up with the commie shit for a minute. Look, just look at this, enjoy, breathe, relax! Would you look at this perfect sunset, it's 18:49 in the afternoon and we have a perfect view of Paradise Plaza, look at all those little ants out there ... it's as if the city was ours. Simply ours."

"Ryan, I don't know how you're going to take this, but this sounds really similar to what I told your sister the first time I hit on her. And we're at the exact same spot."

"Ah, yeah. I knew you wouldn't let me enjoy the moment, not a single moment. I can never enjoy myself because there are always spoilsports like you willing to ruin it for everyone else. People like you who feel so good about themselves that don't ever need to escape, to breathe deeply and enjoy that we have this little moment in time here, in a peaceful place, without nothin' bothering us rather than small time things that have easy solutions."

"Ryan, this is your last warning."

"OK, OK! Look ... I'm tellin' you all of this because ... well ... I'm ashamed of sayin' it ..."

"Don't ask, don't tell. That's what they say in your country's military. It mostly works, I think."

"Shut the fuck up, this don't have nothin' to do with gay faggot shit. Look, what I'm ashamed of sayin' is precisely, how ashamed I actually am of my country. No, shut up for a minute, don't say nothin'. Look ... I'm embarrassed enough. I've just been realizin' things livin' outside of the US. The kind of stuff that's very hard to realize living there, surrounded by like-minded people, deceived just the same as you. I've woken up in Loynne's, Sonny. This land has no alliance to no one, no true patriotism, no specific way of thinkin', this is the true land of the free. And I realized livin' here how warped Unitedstatian mentality actually is. All my brothers have too, I think. But it's time to take it to the next level. I don't want

no country, no religion, no authority tellin' me what I should think and who my enemies are. I want to decide for myself. Over here, I can do that."

"And why this all of a sudden?"

"Sonny, don't you know that the harshest thing for a Unitedstatian to do is admit that your country is a sham, in every sense of the word? Why do you think that we are the only place in the world were we have poor people that think that if they're homeless it's because they deserve it? What other country in the world has a religious cult where you have to pay 10 million dollars a month just to be eligible for salvation? What other country in the world has a TV show about some sluts from Los Angeles tattooing people with their feet? Oh, and by the way, did you know that they got it renamed in the end?"

"Yeah, I heard. Look, the United States is a retarded country and nothing good comes out of it. We have always known so. What else is new?"

"That to reject that retarded country, or at least to admit it openly, is to doom yourself to a lifetime of accusations of communism, treason and heresy. That."

"Yeah but you don't live in that retarded country anymore. Now you live in another retarded country."

"Retarded as Loynners may be, they do enjoy total and absolute freedom. Well, as much freedom as you can have without having a license to kill. So it's good enough for me. Do you know under what pressure you have to live in the US? All sorts. First, TV drives you insane, and no, I'm not talkin' about some 22 non-stop minutes of ads when you're watchin' somethin'. I mean it basically runs people's lives, subjects of conversation, everythin'! You're nothing without TV! You are instantly bombarded when you turn the damn thing on not only by stupid-ass publicity, but by sickenin' cult-like presi-

dential campaigns, conservative news channels tellin' you all sorts of lies and makin' it sound as if we're the masters and defenders of the world, then the usual stereotypical bunch of crap with sex and sluts and drugs on the Cox channel, then ... well you get me, right?"

"Yeah, I get you. So far."

"But when you think you're sick of Unitedstatian society, it just doesn't stop there. It never stops. Imagine that say, you go to school or work. What do you think people talk about all day, all those long hours? What they see in the TV you almost threw out of the window. They talk about all the stupid shit you thought was so idiotic aaaaall day, and then you simply want to grab a gun like so many do and start killin'. I'm not surprised it happens all the time at all. I would have been one. It's horrible, it's either adapt or die. There's no room for one who thinks differently in the US, no matter how much they talk about freedom of expression, freedom of the press, etcetera. It's a disgusting country, and I really no longer recognize it as my own. I wish I dunno, were Canadian or somethin'. At least nobody hates them."

"I really don't want to break your rant or anything but, why are you telling me this and where is this leading toward ..."

"Wait, lemme finish, I tell you it's got a point, just be patient ... OK, so you're sick of people with sheep mentality, sick of TV, sick of the media, sick of absolutely any form of entertainment because it's filled with what you think is utter bullshit, like movies, music, etcetera ... and what are you left with? With absolutely fuckin' nothin'. You have a normal shitty life, with a pointless humiliating job, with friends you don't even like, and what's worse, not even gettin' some because girls over there are so stuck up they wouldn't fuck you not even if you paid them. Not counting actual sluts, of

course. So not only are you under a sort of omnipresent persecution on the part of society because you think differently, but because you reject everything your country stands for. You're a defector. It's as if you hated everything communist and lived in a communist country, exactly the same. They wouldn't take kindly to it, would they?"

"No, you would be sent to the gulag, to a re-education center if lucky. In your country, aside from that and death row, you face the prospect of living the shitty pointless life you described."

"It is. I would rather be sent to a concentration camp than living in in the US again, which nowadays is quite similar. It's absolute hell. But well, lemme get straight to the point. Sonny … Loynne's Island, after everything I've told you about my country, is not my second home, but my only home. And I love it here. Because in here, I am actually free, free to do whatever I want, to think however I like, and don't have to be under the social pressure of Loynners because I'm a foreigner. They won't judge me, outcast me or accuse me of treason because I'm not a local to begin with. They don't care about me, and would actually prefer if I didn't want to be a part of their society. This, to me, is absolute paradise."

"But Loynners mess more with foreigners than with locals, what are you talking about?"

"Well … you're seein' it in relative terms. Like, you think Loynners are bad here? You should see how in the US classmates treat each other. Worse than what Loynners used to do to foreigners like us … why you think kids kill each other all the time and commit suicide … besides, Kannies aren't really as bad as they were before, have you noticed like we can almost stroll around anywhere in school untouched? You couldn't do that in previous years …"

"I guess … We'll, what's the point of what you're trying to

say?"

"The point is the US fuckin' sucks and this is way better, want more evidence than all the shit I just told you? And that don't even scrape the surface. School is heinous. You wanna know something about school? You think Kannies are bad here? You think nothin' can get worse than JC Vega? Look, lemme tell you something pal ... the first thing you see when you enter the stupid school is the fuckin' school mascot, with a message like 'Go Wildcats!' or some such shit. Then you think, fine, these people like sports, right? Think again. They don't like sports. They ADORE sports. They can't LIVE without sports. Sports is what fuckin' makes school hierarchy work. And it goes up all the way to the principal. Who do you think gets the school money? The chess club nerds? The photography club chicks? No, fuckin' sports. It goes a bit like here, sure, but over there it's simply indescribable. The fuckin' jocks have these special jackets, you know the kind, to make people understand they're better than anyone else and above all society. They have their own parking spaces, they get their grades leveled with how well they do at sports, meaning they don't flunk any subject whatsoever 'cause teachers ignore it, they bully and harass and make life hell for everyone, they fuck the best chicks, they become class president and turn the whole fuckin' school into a popularity FUCKIN' CONTEST ONLY BECAUSE THEY KNOW HOW TO THROW A GODDAMN FOOTBALL AROUND, AND THAT GETS THEM MONEY, CHICKS, FAME, RESPECT AND THEY END UP BECOMING MILLIONAIRES ALL FOR BEING THE WORST FUCKIN' SCUM ON THE PLANET!!!"

"Ryan ... uh ... calm down ..."

"Think that's bad enough? The medical system is horrible, just horrible. If you don't have money they leave you rotting on the streets. Religion is everywhere, like a plague. People

577

believe the Earth was *'created'* 6,000 years ago and that some omnipotent faggot entity no one's ever seen simply created us snapping his fingers like a motherfuckin' genie, and those are the cultured ones. People can't find England or Spain on a map, they think Russia is still communist, they think that everything the government does is a conspiracy theory to destroy liberties and rights … they … they … they think UFOs and Bigfoot and the motherfuckin' Chupacabra exist!! How can anyone get so retarded?! I mean how old are we, 5? The Tooth Fairy is real too, right? And dragons? Or even Santa Claus? I'm sure some people believe in it, I just know it …"

"Ryan I … well … first, you're not telling me anything I didn't know already … and secondly, why did you just start to feel like this just now … why this all of a sudden? You've never talked about this before …"

"Because this moment reminded me of when I left for Loynne's. The airport was something similar to this. It was the same time, the same sun was casting. And I just took one last look at my family, who were waving at me and knew inside that wherever I was going to, I'd love it more than anything else. Because I finally had a chance to escape that fuckin' jail of stupidity, mediocrity and self-righteousness. And I was right; it is society what causes you to behave like that. It is peer pressure. And just like that, when you shift societies and live in a country that's not your own, you become who you were supposed to be all along. You become your true self. This is what I am now."

"I can't say anything on this moment of clarity of yours. Anything I say will sound like cheap Communist propaganda."

"You don't need to say anything, you surely already knew all those things about the US in your country. They used to teach you this kind of thing in countries like yours, right?

About the evils of capitalism, all that shit ..."

"They used to. There's no more Soviet Union anymore. And by the way, my parents didn't even bother to let's say, teach me those things. I became a Communist on my own. Nobody forced me or indoctrinated me. I decided to do some research about the system we had left, the alternative to this world of today. And everything during that investigation led me to become what you see now. I am not a Communist because my country has a Communist past. I am because I know humanity is destined to a very imminent downfall if we keep allowing the wealth to go about distributed unequally."

"You sure have a point there. But well, just like you weren't forced to become what you became, I also had a choice. But unlike you, that choice wasn't to become what my country expected me to be. I became the complete opposite. And sometimes I hate myself for it. The word defector is such an ugly one. But I can't love the country, as the country is the people,and I have absolutely no respect for people there."

"You don't need to feel guilty. Sometimes, I also get bouts of remorse. When I don't agree with certain policies of prominent Communists. When I think I'm revising Marx or Engels. When I think certain things could have been done differently."

"I guess ... but still Sonny, I always thought about that ... Look ... even if communist countries can be harsh, they at least stand for values that are much higher than those in capitalist countries. Well, lemme rephrase that, they at least have values. We have hollow, stupid values that don't mean nothin'. Freedom? Freedom for whom? For whomever is white and rich and connected? For the CEO of the company? For the president? Don't make me laugh. You don't have freedom without money. So what else is there to consider a value? Democracy? When we are always meant to choose

between two political parties and the rest don't mean nothin'? That's like totalitarianism but limited to two instead of one. And both end up looking alike sometimes. And don't get me started on that stupid Unitedstatian Dream shit. Nothing but lies. You come to the US with 15 dollars in your pocket and you triumph in Hollywood as a star. Yeah. If you don't mind getting sperm-hosed in the face by movie producers ..." I didn't know what had changed in Ryan, but his behavior was admirable. Always a disgusting idiot in my mind, my perception of him was slowly beginning to tilt toward a more favorable side.

"Er ... yeah, anyway ... so now that you have woken up so as to speak, what are you going to do? Don't get me wrong, but it's not like you're the brightest light bulb when it comes to politics. You're not dumb but you still got a long way. At least you know how to correctly identify the things that unsettle you and make you feel injustice. That always is good."

"Really? Well ... what I'd do now would be learning more. That's why you're here for, right?"

"Me? For what?"

"To teach me all you know. So I can jump to a conclusion of my own."

"Ah ... yeah. Look. I just told you I did all the research on my own and now you come and expect to sit on your ass while I teach you ... can't you just do this on your own?"

"It's different. Look, if I start readin' everything by myself I won't have a direction. It will be like runnin' around blind. With you at least I have a higher view of the political spectrums, a practical opinion on each one of them, not just a textbook answer. I need the answers from someone who knows, who feels it in the blood, and who's not an idiot."

"So I'll be your teacher on Communism?"

"Don't call it that. It's simply guidin' me toward the practi-

cal stuff, skippin' the unnecessary bits. Knowin' the true differences."

"Right, yeah, I think that's possible. This is really good actually, especially coming from an ex-US citizen."

"The US is finished, Sonny. Look at it now. I can't call that place my home anymore. Loynne's has been my home for years now. And it will remain that way for the time being." While Ryan said this, clearly pouring his heart out, I thought of The Motherland. It was almost the same situation. Could I still call The Motherland my home, my country? I doubted it. I couldn't call Loynne's my home, that was for sure. But The Motherland, the last bastion of Communism in the world had finally been defeated by capitalism. And Communism was what made my land what it was, what made it stand tall above every other nation. Without that, we were just another shitty normal country. No glory, no grandeur, no higher goals. No hopes of ever building Socialism again, of elevating humanity to the next step of social evolution and liberate it from the chains of religion and consumerism ...

"OK, so, what is it that you want to learn from me? What are your doubts?"

"Well ... for example ... this sounds stupid but what's the deal with the word 'Unitedstatian' anyway? When did people outside of the US start saying that instead of 'American'?"

"Well ... it's a really long story ... people from Latin America, who say *'estadounidense'* and not *'americano'* to refer to people from the US, began to campaign against the use of the term, and it was as if the world had suddenly woken up from a spell. It all started when lots of protests in Central and South America started a campaign for the US to change its official name, as other people from the Americas believed them to be appropriating the name for themselves. Then the issue widened, as people began to complain that they had the

word 'America' in the nation's name, which not only is arrogant and condescending to the peoples of the other Americas, but inaccurate. If you think about it, every single country in the American continents has a name for their land from which the names of citizens are derived from; The Argentine Republic, Oriental Republic of Uruguay, Plurinational State of Bolivia, Bolivarian Republic of Venezuela, Federative Republic of Brazil ... they all have in their official names their types of governments and at the same time the land they're settled in. In the case of the US, The United States of America only had the word 'America' to refer to their homeland, and it was a largely inaccurate one. I mean, America? What were they thinking? Not even North America, but *America*. They seized the whole continent for themselves. People who defend the term 'American' as a demonym for US nationals will tell you with very cheap sounding arguments why this matter is entirely wrong to begin with; for example, they will tell you that people in Argentina don't call themselves 'Republicans' just because they live in a republic, or that Russians don't call themselves 'Federationalists' because they live in a federation, stupid arguments like that, but we have to acknowledge that the US is only a part of a larger America, and to be specific, it is located in North America, sharing the subcontinent with Mexico and Canada. Look at Mexico for a perfect example. The full name of Mexico is 'United Mexican States,' and since they're the only Mexican peoples in the American continents, it would be useless to call them Unitedstatians as well. But America, it's just an awful crime to call the US that. Look at Europe ... do you have a country called 'United States of Europe,' or 'Republic of Europe'? Hoarding all of Europe to themselves and their nation? No, you don't have that. Since Unitedstatians didn't even have a local name for their homeland, like Canada or Mexico, several names were proposed in

hopes of finding what could most accurately describe them. Some began to say Usonians, but people didn't really like the term. Some still do but they're not many. Instead, people focused on'estadounidense,' and since they usually refer themselves to as "US citizens" and to their land as the US, Unitedstatian was generally accepted as the most accurate and fair name for them. The country's name was still a problem though, and the UN was under pressure to find a fitting name. Replacing 'America' with a word that sounded more local wasn't easy. They proposed New England, Columbia, Appalachia, but none of these seemed fair as they didn't exactly represent the landmass that is the United States. As such, the issue was postponed and left in indefinite hiatus while they gave Unitedstatians a chance to name themselves with an original name, expecting them to decide on a native North American term which would represent the entire country. In the meanwhile, the official name given to them by the UN was "The United States of North America." But again, this name was disrespectful to the United Mexican States, as it would imply that the only United States in North America is the US. Then, someone proposed the entire country to be named simply 'Midnorthamerica,' with the official name being "United States of Midnorthamerica." But there were problems with this as well, as the country still contained the word America in its official name and its citizens would probably abbreviate it to America, and also the fact that they still did not possess a unique name native to their land or its history. Unable to decide whether the US could be renamed United States of Columbia, Virginia, Apalacchia or else, they decided to make the official name simply 'The United States,' as a temporary measure.

That's it, they thought at the time; problem solved, if temporarily. It was fair, accurate, not offensive to citizens of the

other Americas and accepted by foreigners. In any case, it was the most popular name they had ever used. Nobody in the news referred to the US as America except for them anyway, it was a solely domestic use. Internationally, the US was always referred to as precisely 'United States,' without the America part, and nothing more. US generals, for example, have a US insignia on their lapels, they don't even have one that spells USA. The US Army has never been referred to as 'USA Army.' Military bases are referred to as 'US bases.' Since the US had made this a reality and all countries acknowledged that when saying United States you meant this specific country located between Canada and Mexico, it was widely accepted that 'United States' had to be the name of the nation, at least temporarily until they came up with a name of their own.

But, as you already know, the US never accepted this reality and instead isolated itself furthermore into its bunker of delusion, refusing to change the name wrapped warmly under the belief that it was still a global superpower and that no foreign entity would take the word 'America' out of the country's name ... The world preferred this as its idiocy couldn't contaminate the rest of the civilized world with creationism, the imperial system and every single obsolete cultural thing that makes the country backwards in comparison to other nations. Latin America, Europe and Asia didn't want waves of lazy, fat and retarded immigrants looking for jobs and contaminating their culture with their nonsense, so they stopped the phenomenon quickly before it even developed and prevented an all-out Unitedstatian cultural invasion. One thing is watching their films, and another having them wanting to make changes in the law so as to accommodate their imperial system, their gun laws, their silly religion and their Fahrenheit degrees. Foreseeing this, countries like China worked

hard on stabilizing the US economy to keep the United-statians where they belonged, holed up in their asylum where they can buy guns, shoot each other in peace and worship creationism. That's all there was to it."

"Wow ... I had never seen it like that, so clearly ... but you've opened my eyes, Sonny ... You're so fuckin' blind when you live over there ... I wasn't, but even so, I would have never described this in the way you just did ... Over there, you don't even develop the need to know more about other countries, or to see beyond the US ..."

"Yeah, I know it might sound offensive, but it's actually the way it was then and still is now. Your society was reaching an unparalleled level of idiocy, and it needed to be stopped. Anyway, excuse me if I offended you ... do you have more questions?"

"None taken, and yeah, I do ... for example ... this will sound really stupid to you, but tell me ... who was Karl Marx?"

"Karl Marx is what we call one of the fathers of Communism, a German philosopher and economist. He, alongside fellow economist Friedrich Engels, the other father of Communist theory, wrote *'Das Kapital,'* a very intense analysis on capitalist practice. He also wrote *'The Communist Manifesto'*. In it, he urged the peoples of Europe to reject capitalism."

"Right ... and what did Lenin have to do with all this?"

"Lenin was the first revolutionary who put Marx's theory into practice. He overthrew the aristocratic Kerensky regime in Russia after Tsar Nicholas II abdicated, and rose to power. He founded the USSR."

"And then came Stalin, right?"

"Right ... Stalin succeeded Lenin, but there's a lot of mystery surrounding this. Lenin didn't want Stalin to succeed

him as leader of the USSR because Stalin was too reckless and bloodthirsty. But, he wasn't too keen on Trotsky either. He regarded Trotsky as someone who thinks too much of himself, a very intellectual man without the cunning genius of Stalin. He died before he could make any decisions, and Stalin used all his power to prevent Trotsky from succeeding Lenin."

"OK ... so who's the good guy?"

"There aren't any good guys or bad guys. This sounds like a very generic and cheap thing to say, but get out of that Unitedstatian mentality of good guys and bad guys. Stalin murdered and arrested millions to consolidate his power and to turn the USSR into an industrial superpower. But he acted more like a Russian Tsar running a more totalitarian regime, always using his image to exercise his power. He even told his mother that he was like a Tsar when she asked what he was up to. Trotsky's image was damaged to erase him from the political life, but even so I doubt he could have had the necessary ruthlessness to survive the carnage that was the German assault on the USSR in WWII. Of Trotsky, I wholeheartedly agree with his theory of Permanent Revolution, a theory opposite to Stalin's Socialism In One Country. Trotsky, like Lenin, believed Communism could only triumph when taken to every country on Earth, while Stalin believed Communism should be strengthened internally from the USSR to the rest of the world, given the defeat of all Communist revolutions in Europe at the time, of which only Russia's was successful. Personally, I believe this theory strengthened the Soviet Union for some time, but with the Cold War against the United States, it proved not to function, at least for the USSR, but we can see China followed similar policies under Chairman Mao and China is still standing. These are my opinions though, you don't need to think with my mentality. Communism,

after all, is about thinking what's best for the Party, for society and for the world. There are a million different opinions, and a lot of branches. Communists and Socialists argue amongst themselves all the time, and this is partly why the left doesn't rise up to the right-wing capitalist system. We are just too busy fighting amongst ourselves instead of leaving differences aside and slay the dragon. This is why the disgusting right-wing triumphs; they have no principles, and no ideology guides them except for animalistic greed."

"What about socialism? What's the difference between communism and socialism?"

"Socialism generally refers to an economic system, and Communism to both an economic system and a political system. The means of production are publicly owned in both systems, but the ways that money and resources are distributed are different. In Socialism, each person is allotted resources according to his or her input, or amount of work, and in Communism, each person is allotted resources according to his or her needs. Many people consider Communism to be a more extensive form of Socialism."

"So a socialist is a moderate communist?"

"Well, something like that."

"What about anarchists?"

"An anarchist is someone who thinks that there simply should be no government or state, that the people should govern themselves, freely. But anarchism doesn't refer to an economic system. There can be anarcho-capitalists, anarcho-Socialists, etcetera. But anarchism doesn't go well with Communism. In Communism, the state is basically all-powerful, and anarchists don't like that idea. Even if the ultimate goal of Communism is for people to govern themselves, just like anarchists want. That's what's called a Socialist Utopia. When people sustain themselves with what they

produce and everything's voluntarily shared amongst the people. Historically, this has proven to work in modern times, for example communities known as Kibbutz in Israel are basically Communist in practice."

"Huh ... so ... what's the best system according to you?"

"All my life I've tried to be strictly Marxist-Leninist, that is, Marxism as theorized and practiced by Lenin, and sometimes understood that by extension, Stalin. But over time I've learned about many injustices committed under Communism that even though they don't represent the Communist Movement as a whole, have clearly damaged its good name. As a result I consider myself now an internationalist Marxist instead of a strict Marxist-Leninist. I do agree with most Leninist policies, however. But even then sometimes I don't have as much faith in the proletariat; I generally regard people as dumb sheep who can't decide for themselves; look at Loynners, or your fellow Unitedstatians ... do you think such ignorant people are fit to decide for themselves, to exercise the right to vote of all things? Yet I find it too cruel for them to be coldly murdered or imprisoned, no matter how much I try to convince myself that it is inevitable in revolution, and beneficial in the long run. I find it too cruel and I definitely would not support it, but I think those viewpoints change when you rise to power. Up there, those people must seem like meaningless ants, as bothersome as plagues. Perhaps they are, but we're too emotionally attached to know otherwise. What I mean is that what's best for the world in the long run might be traumatizingly cruel if it's put into practice. But as we've learned through history, humanity's greatest achievements have been accomplished by a mixture between pure lust for power, greed and war. All the luxuries and comfort we possess today, you can be certain that were born out of the necessity to slaughter the enemy."

"I still don't understand what the best system is. I mean, if capitalism is all that bad, you can still have a lot of joy and comfort that you can't in communist societies."

"That joy and comfort comes because there's millions who don't have anything. Possessions and money do not grow on trees. We're overpopulated, there's and elite that hoards all the money and you have to conform yourself with leftovers. Capitalism is anything but fair. The basis for it is for some elitists to hoard all the resources for themselves, and keep you alive with the minimum things so you keep working for them. That's why capitalism triumphs. People always think they'll do better and will be at the top. Yet, in this time and age, that's increasingly difficult. The ones at the top have already consolidated their power so much within this system that the only thing that would remove them would be to topple the system altogether. And from what I'm learning, that's also next to impossible."

"Why's that?"

"Well, the banks control everything now. Governments are puppets dancing to the tune of banks. Multinational corporations have also taken the form of unofficial governments. They provide us with necessities and produce capital. But all of this generates immense, wide-spread poverty, aside from pollution but I won't get into that. Banks and corporations are like the Mafia; they serve themselves, they enslave workers and they rip on the benefits it produces. Organized crime, mafias, are like this as well but on smaller scales. Corporations and banks are legal oppressors."

"Funny way to see it ... you would never think about these things in the US ..."

"Of course you wouldn't, just as you wouldn't have learned of Trotsky in the former USSR."

"Well, I'm glad to see my eyes are open. Now we just have

to continue learning."

"Yeah ... I learn new things everyday as well ... but the more I learn, the more I think humanity has no chance. We're too corrupt to create a perfect society. We would need to evolve millions of years from now to do that, and by the time we do that we'll be already consumed by our idiocy. Either way, every species is already dead. Every species is destined for extinction, no matter how well adapted. Sometimes, the more adapted you are the less you survive when your environment abruptly changes."

"How do you know so much? You seem to know about anything! I would have never guessed ..."

"Well, maybe we should just say that Communism, with all its flaws, has an exemplary educational system, which the Russian Federation inherited. In societies like yours, accustomed to 'freedom,' people usually get more rebellious when having to learn things."

"I guess ... well ... enough talk. We have a place to go."

"Where?"

"I told you, to that office, remember? I gotta do this paperwork, it's right round the corner, come on ..."

I followed Ryan as he talked to me about punk bands and how he'd love for a naked girl with reindeer antlers to look at him straight in the eye while finishing on her face. When we had just crossed over to the Méndez Center block, a corpulent black haired girl with rosy cheeks greeted him with a crushing hug. The girl had to be almost my height, and twice my size.

"Ryan! So good to see you!! How you doin'?!"

"Ahh ... hi ..."

"Remember me?? You haven't forgotten, have ya?"

"Oh ... of course not! How could I?"

"Hehe, I knew it! Anyway ... you've gotten stronger, are

you going to the gym?"

"Oh, ah … me … yeah … Listen I'm just going to a restaurant to have dinner with my dad, you know I only see him once a month and it's like, real intimate, you know, and he's right there waitin', so if you don't mind …"

"Oh … yeah … well tell me who's your friend real quick! Aren't you gonna introduce us?"

"Oh, yeah, Sonny, yeah he was just gettin' ready to say goodbye, Haha … not like my dad wants a friend to break up the privacy of father and son, huh? Yeah well, this is my friend Sonny … and this is … woah! Look! My dad's over there! Bye I'll see you later, I gotta run!"

"Bye! Call me!" The girl left us as she kept walking on the opposite direction, and I waited until she was out of earshot to ask.

"What was that all about, Ryan?"

"Shut up I'll tell you later … Is she gone?"

"Let me see … yeah, she's just gone around the corner."

"Good … Look, let's hang out around here for a while, you know how things are in this island, you meet every single motherfucker you've ever known just two minutes after you go outside."

"Right, look, let's just go over there, not like she's looking back …"

"Anyway, that fat bitch … that's … well …"

"Alana."

"Huh? How did you know?"

"I don't know … lucky guess?"

"More than a lucky guess … who told you? Come on man, be honest."

"Oh well, don't get like that! It's not like I'm hiding things from you, it's just that it's long and embarrassing explaining how I found out … I didn't even find out, it's basically associ-

ating and guessing what I just did ... it was a guess."

"Just tell me who told you!! Billy?"

"No! Listen ... I was going to math lessons not so long ago, I only went one day anyway, couldn't take much more of it ... so at first there were these guys waiting at the stairs, and I joined them thinking they would be going to my same class, so this girl starts talking to me about you, thinking I was Californian like you, and she began saying if I knew an Alana or something like that, and well I guessed it had to be this girl, because obviously you've been close ..."

"Yeah ... more than close ... well as close as you can get with a woman ..."

"You mean ... you ..."

"Yeah ... I'm not a virgin anymore."

"Really? And when did it happen? Why didn't you tell anyone?"

"Come on, Sonny ... what did I explain to you that day, before you completely destroyed my life telling me you'd like to completely marry my fuckin' sister? I was telling you to grab the first fat bitch you can and drill her and sweep her under the carpet, right? Well, it wasn't an analogy, it actually happened ... I was goin' to tell you about it at the Church & Square when we were hangin' out with Jenna, it happened before the Prometheus Project, I just never told anyone 'cause you know ... it's embarrassin', you just saw her ... not a prize to go around showin' off ..."

"Well ... I think you're the first out of us to do this, then."

"No. First goes Dave. And he's done it a thousand times. It'll be hard to topple him from his position."

"Don't feel bad about your brother. The time will come for you too."

"Aww, just stop it. I don't need your pity. Anyway the thing is, I was so excited that the first person I told was Billy

... so well, I explicitly told him not to say anythin', and well, I guess he kept his promise ... which I expect you to keep as well."

"Come on, she didn't look like such a bad girl, what is there to be ashamed of?"

"Everythin'. She's fat, Sonny, fat. You know my stance on fat people. They repulse me, ugh. It took me a whole deal of effort to even get it stiff enough to drill her. Then she wants me to go down on her and that shit smelled like seafood on display. Ugh, rotten!"

"Alright, I don't need to hear more. Well ... but what happened later?"

"Nothin', she was just here on holiday, so I never saw or talked to her again. Now I find her here ... She's tried to contact me lots of times and supposedly gave up but well, now I hope she don't call again."

"And who's that girl then, the Nolly?"

"The Nolly's this best friend she has, dunno, real dumb if she's still tryin' to get outta 3rd Grade of Compulsory. I mean she's like what, 24? Anyway, I bet Dave will probably still be in 3rd Grade when he's 28."

"So you're not going to see this girl anymore?"

"No, Sonny! She was a one off! Now that I got rid of my virginity I want to actually fuck a girl of my choice, you know? A girl I like, a girl whose cunt smells of cherry and flowers, not of Galician octopus."

"Yeah, I get it ... What about Daphne? She's given you any signs?"

"None that I consider important. But if she hasn't yet it probably means she's not interested. I'm not gonna barge in where I'm not wanted. From now on I'm gonna do like this blitzkrieg tactic with chicks, like hit on them at lightnin' speed and if they reject me handle the rejection forms like a

motherfucker, record time speed."

"Sounds good to me ..."

"You should be doing the same. Forget about my sister. She's only gonna give you headaches. Get a better bitch. You interested in Alana? I can introduce you, you saw how interested she was in you. Throw your virginity out the window with her and then you'll be glowing for a week, maybe my sister notices that and pays attention for two seconds ..."

"Glow?"

"Yeah, glow, Sonny, glow; that's what you call it when you just had hot hard sex with a skank and you're so happy from it that you're all day stupid and smiling, all self-satisfied. That's glowin'."

"If I had her seafood for dinner, I wouldn't glow, I would repel light."

"Heh, can't take the smell of cunt, huh?"

"More like because you've already been there."

· · · · ·

The Christian celebration Westerners live through the year for had finally arrived. But I didn't have a family reunion like they did, not even a letter from my parents. After all, we didn't have such as celebration in The Motherland, it simply meant nothing to us, and it wasn't like we needed it. During this period, we simply had a public holiday and enjoyed days off from school and work, which almost everybody used in order to go to the countryside or the beach, as in my country the weather was quite hot in December and January, something which contrasted heavily against the snowy Warsaw Pact states. Still, we had our traditions; one was obviously of Soviet origin, and consisted mainly in gathering the family around for dinner and watching films on TV, particularly the

1976 romantic comedy "Ironiya Sudby, Ili S Lyogkim Parom!"
— "The Irony of Fate, Or Enjoy Your Bath!" — which was
always on during these holidays, as it had become a real phenomenon, a landmark of Soviet culture and identity. In case
you haven't heard about it, it tells the story of Zhenya
Lukashin, played by the hilarious Andrei Myagkov, who after
visiting a banya — a traditional Russian public bath — with
his friends and having a few drinks, gets sent to Leningrad,
now Saint Petersburg, by mistake. The joke is that in the
Soviet Union, starting with Khruschev and continuing with
Brezhnev, architecture was so uniform and bland that not
only buildings looked all alike, but there were many streets
with similar-sounding names (Revolution Avenue, Workers'
Street), adding to much confusion. The director, Eldar Ryazanov, thought of the story as something that could hypothet-
ically happen, given a chaotic context such as this one. Zhenya makes his way to his home thinking he's still in Moscow,
and goes to the same address finding a building that is exactly like the one where he resides, even his key manages to
open the door. After he passes out on the bed, the tenant, the
beautiful Nadya played by Polish native Barbara Brylska,
arrives. When she finds Zhenya on her bed right when she's
supposed to be making preparations for celebrating the New
Year with her lover, a lot of hilarity ensues, much of which
has stuck for ages in Russian culture, including everyday
quotes and sayings. I must say, the film is truly beautiful, and
you should watch it as well if you get the chance. It truly
stands on its own merits, and has an undeniable charm of old
Soviet glory, certainly a film that could never be produced
under current conditions. That was film-making at its prime,
beautiful, simple and showing exactly the true Soviet spirit,
energetic, optimistic and humane.

As I watched poor Zhenya get tossed around and slapped

by a righteously furious Nadya, I found myself alone in my apartment, surprisingly longing for Faye more than for any member of my family. I didn't know how to feel; so much time had passed, I felt I wouldn't recognize my parents the day I had them in front of me. It sounds cruel, but I had accustomed myself to living without them and not relying on their love. I had already shed enough tears of solitude, and it seemed my heart had completely hardened. I felt an empty void inside myself, the first signs of apathy; strangely, I found myself not caring for anyone except for Faye. How I longed for her to be next to me, to hug her and have her head rest on my shoulder, watching TV sitting on the couch, eating junk food, laughing like a good normal couple. But it was not to be, and what I had was my own self to fill this enormous emotional void on a time where everyone was celebrating with their families. And New Year's Eve would be even worse; far from the shenanigans of Zhenya and his incredible tale, mine would entail sitting on my own watching films once more with nobody to come and comfort me, the only joy to look forward to being receiving a letter from my parents.

I looked at a draft I had left unfinished when writing Faye's Christmas card. I had convinced Ryan into making sure she received it with the envelope sealed. I had also convinced him that I didn't say anything out of order and that it was a formality I fancied to be incredibly respectful toward her. Ryan saw it as a sign of being a gentleman as well and agreed. It was weird how such a perverted mental degenerate could see the beauty in having respect for formality toward women.

The card went as follows:

"Dear Faye,

I am sorry if you do not receive this letter under the best of impressions. It is not what I expect, nor is it what I intend on. However, I am honestly obligated to transmit this message.

Faye, from the very first day I saw you, I shivered with the kind of emotion that's impossible for a man to describe. Women do not know the power they exercise over men, nor do they succeed at appreciating the power behind their undeniable charm. It is precisely this unstoppable force what possessed me, what drove me frantically to behave the way I did with you. It is a power I intend on deterring. However, I find it an increasingly difficult task. I do not wish to lie to you, and as such will tell you nothing but the absolute truth; you belong to a class of woman unsurpassed by any other. I know you don't share this view about yourself, and I also know you doubt whether any other man aside from me does. I don't care for that. As an individual, I consider myself able to discern when another human being is worthy of my attention, when a person gathers certain particular features I cannot help but find appealing, suitable, impossible to ignore. It is not common for a man to stumble upon these qualities in such a random manner so easily. Fortunately, it has happened to me, but your heart did not answer in kind. I wonder if it will some day, and as for now, cannot do anything except wishing for the best.

In any case, the reason I find myself writing this letter to you is simple. I am writing to merely express my best wishes to you on this celebration that is Christmas, a holiday about equality, goodwill and peace. I want to express my peace with you on our newfound problem with this letter. This isn't a time for resentment, angst, discord or worries of any kind. Take this as an unofficial truce for the time being.

I cannot refrain myself from saying it, so I'll have you know that I love you very much, and wish you all the best. Please enjoy this holiday with your family, and I will expect to see you soon.

With love,

Sonny."

My mind began to ponder; was it possible that Faye was at her house right now, doing absolutely nothing? That her family was leaving her aside like usual, and that she longed for someone to reach out to her? It was worth a shot. I would call her.

But no. I stopped myself when my thumb was already pressing the "call" button. The last thing I needed now was for her brothers to use this against me, to remind me how my obsession was alive and well. No. I would call her on New Year's Eve to wish her a happy new year with a legal reason. I wondered what she could be doing though. Going out to some restaurant, like Loynners used to do? Having dinner with the family at home? Whatever she was doing, I hoped it'd be a safe, family-oriented event. Nothing would have hurt me more than to see her falling for the simplistic pleasures of capitalist life as well, like a common disgusting Loynnerin. She was above that, and that's why I had fallen in love with her. She had qualities unsurpassed by any of those absolutely inferior women. She had self-respect, purity and dignity. She was a real woman, and the only one that had awakened in me the desire to spend the rest of my life by her side.

CHAPTER X

Ostpolitik

*"If anyone believes that our smiles involve aban-
donment of the teaching of Marx, Engels and
Lenin he deceives himself. Those who wait for
that must wait until a shrimp learns to whistle."*

- NIKITA KHRUSHCHEV -

Soviet Politician, Soviet Army Political Commissar,
Great Patriotic War Veteran and Hero, First Secretary
of the Communist Party of the Soviet Union and Premier of the Soviet Union

---

*"The situation in the US keeps getting worse as many
countries claim that the isolationist and militaristic nation
has completely lost touch with reality. In a society who
many claim is in full and steady decadence, warped values
impose themselves mixing supposed constitutional rights
with teachings from the Bible and a zealous sense of patriotism. We will proceed to analyze a speech from an anonymous spokesman of the ROA in a bid to understand this
sociological phenomenon of paranoid fear that reigns in the
North American nation. This is what the anonymous
spokesman had to say:"*

*"The right of the American people to keep and bear arms
is an extension of the right to self-defense. It is specifically
isolated from governmental interference by the Constitution*

*and has been up to now the main deterrent to foreign tyr-
anny. Yet the spineless liberals in the government stand
ready to use their coercive power to interfere with the exercise of that right, as unlike us, they do not concern themselves with the duties we carry on our backs as Proud Americans. They are ready to abide to the will imposed by foreign
tyrants who seek nothing but our complete apocalypse, our
destruction as a nation and downfall as a culture. When
Thomas Jefferson wrote in the Declaration of Independence
that we are endowed by our Creator God Almighty with
complete and utter liberty, he was blessing the nation with
undeniable freedoms which cannot be questioned by any
form of terrestrial government. We seek to carry his vision
into the future and prevent any enemy of America from
destroying it, be it foreign invaders or our very own government. We were created in the image and likeness of God
Our Heavenly Father, and as such are as free as He. Our
freedoms are not political and come from our humanity, not
from any type of government, and as our humanity is ultimately divine in origin nobody can strip away the rights
and duties from the American people. That is what the
Founding Fathers of our Great Nation America decreed, and
if anyone wants to take that freedom away from us, they
will have to pry it out of our cold, dead hands!"*

*"Good morning from New York City, I'm your host Larry
Wiseman, here at Independence Radio we bring you the
latest news in national and international politics. Today we
have with us activist Michael Weinstein, a journalist exiled
from this country by the government, who has been analyzing the Unitedstatian phenomenon ever since its first crisis.
Michael, a pleasure to have you here again."*

"Pleasure's all mine, if you'll excuse my manners let's get

right to the point please, as I've been informed my presence here is causing protests outside."

"By all means, Michael. What would you say about this speech by the anonymous ROA spokesman earlier today? Do you think it's aimed at telling the world the cultural values of the current Unitedstatian society?"

"Absolutely. We don't even need to analyze it to reach that conclusion. He starts by saying that owning firearms is an extension of freedom based on the Second Amendment, a Constitutional residue of the Revolutionary War when the US didn't have a proper army and it was dependent on popular militias. As historical evidence points out, this is a leftover law from an era when the US government didn't possess the incredible self-defense capabilities against a foreign invasion it has today. Those paranoid of the government and of the governments of other nations claim they need to defend themselves against a potential occupation, a completely unrealistic situation in the context we're analyzing. The US Army, with its current military technology and concentrating all its might in the country, could wipe out any resistance whatsoever even if harassed by relentless guerilla tactics, or not completely eliminate it but keep it in check until it did not represent a major threat anymore. Also, no government needs armed hicks and gun enthusiasts like those of the ROA when in possession of a nuclear arsenal that would deter most countries from invading. Besides that, nobody is interested in invading the US right now; Russia, its main rival, wouldn't benefit from it, and China wouldn't benefit from its collapse. The US is an important economic factor at a worldwide level, even though it has lost its former hegemony, and it's essential for the rest of the world to integrate and not exclude the North American country. The main problem here is that the US doesn't want to be just

another country in the world, it wishes to be the sole super-power and establish a unilaterist order where it has the final say. Let us move on to something else, quickly now, they're informing me I should leave soon. I want to point out that many people in the US are populists who do not trust the government and see it as an oppressor that wants to take away individual freedom, rights of citizens and collect un-fair taxes in the process, but let the government they hate so much operate freely when reminded of terrorist attacks and patriotic related subjects. This is a strategy perpetuated by the ROA, which acts as a mediator between the citizens and the government, and makes the citizens hate the government and society so as to exercise deeper control over them. In a way, the ROA is the government. The ideology of the US clearly comes from this organization, and the government is used as a scapegoat so that the ROA can keep exercising this power over the nation. About the ROA's Christian funda-mentalism, something almost nobody knows and which is completely verifiable by historical evidences, is that the beliefs of the Founding Fathers they quote so much are com-pletely distorted. The Founding Fathers were religious, yet not ready to impose Christian beliefs in the government, as not only they belonged to different churches but wanted the state to be largely free from religious control, and also some of them, such as Washington, Franklin and Jefferson were theistic rationalists, meaning that in their religious beliefs rationalism was the predominant element and most likely the one they wanted to pass on, as such they would have never allowed the nation to be so intertwined with religion as it is today. The first act of anti-secularism in the US hap-pened in 1864 when Congress approved the 'In God We Trust' motto in two-cent coins, to bolster pro-Union senti-ment during the US Civil War using religious self-

righteousness to assert that they were the good guys. A similar scenario occurred during the Cold War. The country's official motto, 'E pluribus Unum,' was replaced by 'In God We Trust' in 1956, and this began to appear in dollar bills as well, not just in coins. There you have the answer. In 1956, at the height of the Cold War, the US needed a way to differentiate between the values of capitalistic Western democracies and Eastern communist states, which supported state atheism. The 84th Congress passed a joint resolution to replace the old motto and President Eisenhower signed it. You can verify this yourself. Want more facts? What about secularism and the Separation of Church and State? If you're asking yourself this, and are highly upset about how the state violates your right to atheism you will simply have to put up with it, as their official stance is that it doesn't violate religious freedom of any kind. Seemingly, in the theocratic land of creationism, puritanism, superstition, sects and religious scams, secularism doesn't have a chance. This is how the trend of religious mania that has turned Unitedstatian citizens into complete zealots was started. Modern Unitedstatian society was shaped purely by a powerful mixture of anti-communism and religion, flames fueled by the ideological struggle of the Cold War. Mixing Bible teachings and myths, which unbelievably they consider facts, with the constitution and firearms is also something quite new, a phenomenon which grew around the same era. Officially, the US is a secular nation, but good luck having a Unitedstatian admitting to that. Sorry if I can't explain this in full detail with more historical facts but I must once again leave quickly due to security concerns ..."

"The words of Michael Weinstein ... Tonight we'll have a special report about the culture of fear and firearms in the US and how the media effectively perpetuates it for its own

ends."

Disgusting. I couldn't bear to hear about the US anymore. Each report by Michael Weinstein filled me with rage and as such I always resorted to turning the TV off without second thoughts. However, I always found myself returning for more news on the crazy North American nation, curious as to what future the country was moving toward. Seemingly, its ultimate destruction. With the existence of this decadent nation, more people could copy their stupidity abroad, no matter how the imposing global majority already had officially deemed Unitedstatians mentally challenged. The sheer existence of the country frightened me. In fact, everything about the precarious global situation frightened me. I feared a catastrophe nearing, something which could probably derive in a Third World War. But I always managed to eliminate my fears with the situations of daily life. No matter how dangerous things seemed outside of Loynne's, the island's atmosphere would always delude you. Nothing would ever happen to Loynne's.

I turned the TV off and headed for school. We were now in February, and Faye had replied to my Christmas card with a message sent to my phone, surprisingly well-written for someone who pretty much didn't care for grammar, at least in the digital realm.

"Sonny, I need time to think. Please don't try to talk to me or call me. I'll contact you."

My distance from Faye had been relentless; I never called or visited her, and she responded in kind. I tried to avoid The Crucible altogether, always finding excuses that sounded understandable to the Mantis brothers. Soon enough, every-

thing had seemed to go back to normal. They predictably liked the change, and even thought that it was the end of it. I obviously never intended on the frozen relations to last so long, but I felt as if I needed to do a test of endurance against her, trying to prove that I was man enough to spend time without her. Had it not been for Michael Weinstein's reports, I would definitely would have ended up harassing her over the phone to reestablish contact. Also, for some reason I didn't fear someone else stealing her away either. I had absolute confidence that she harbored feelings for me, of which she was confused about. Those feelings, which unequivocally always surfaced when we were together, would keep her from doing anything she shouldn't. Besides, there was nothing to fear; if she had not replied, I would have probably been shot up in nerves for weeks, eventually resorting to talk to her again. But with what I had said in the Christmas card, I believed she would understand the situation in a different light, reaching her final and most decisive conclusion. After that, given she rejected me once more, I thought myself able to move on definitely. Enough was enough, and no matter how perfect I could consider her to be, I was ready to say farewell.

This change of perspective also served to better my grades, incredibly low in the first trimester; I had joined a debate club which was exclusively integrated by Lollies, almost all of them from biology class. It wasn't a debate club like the one you must be thinking about though; the objective of this club was for subjects to be discussed, ranging from a wide variety of ongoing sociopolitical issues, and for us to solve them with our eloquence in group, collectively. The profiles of these girls were obvious to the naked eye; 'democratic,' peace loving Lollies who would try to look good in front of the teacher not only politically, but morally. Sex was often discussed from a respectful and intellectual point of view, very diplo-

matically; once outside of the club, the Lollies reverted to their actual personalities and laughed between themselves spurting all kinds of rude sexual innuendos that would have made Ryan proud and horny.

Being the only guy in this club also helped my social status; I now small-talked with the Lollies here and there, not being exactly friends but school acquaintances. People often thought better of you if you were seen with girls like these, and I took full advantage of the situation. Girls like Agostea, the kick-boxing champion's girlfriend, even offered to help me with biology homework asking for absolutely nothing in return, a true sign of the improvement my social status was been subjected to. Others exchanged help if I took care of their German homework. Indeed, life had reached its peak once more; I had absolutely no chances of getting to date any of the Lollies there, not like I wanted to, but it was a nice distraction from my inner conflict. Faye looked incredibly more serious when seeing me joke around with the Lollies – who often cheered my witty utterings – and had decided to altogether avoid walking through the second floor.

Axel, Mike and Wolfgang became my main companions in normal classes. Wolfgang and I had started to talk more to each other, but not as much as we always used to before Faye appeared in my life. He had been rendered a shadow of his former self due to a digital crack overdose; mentally, he seemed to have become as skinny and weak as the body of a real life crack user. His conversations were inane at best, and long gone were the golden days of philosophical and political curiosity. Even so, he was still good to hang around with, at least in the classroom and free hours. We self-imposed an invisible distance we never crossed or talked about, and we were satisfied with it. To some extent, Wolfgang knew he had already lost me in some way, but was unwilling to let me go

for good. I saw no point in distancing myself from Wolfgang fully as we were in the same classroom, and decided to play along even though I no longer harbored any true respect for him. For the most part, nobody could have been able to tell a rift had developed between us.

I was seemingly not the only one losing respect for Wolfgang. It all began one day in school, obviously; Mike, Axel and Wolfgang played Poker as Tom Richards prepared himself for one of his monologues;

"So, look, is everybody paying attention?! Good ... It cannot be, this, guys, all the time, you really want me to get tough and send you all down to the principal's office? 'Cause I can! I can ... you just gotta give me one more little push ... anybody? Anybody wanna push me?! Thought so ... Anyways, as I was sayin', ah, Dmitri Ivan-ovich Mende ... Mel ... Mende-le-yev, God, what a name, I never get it right ... Anyway, yeah, this Russian guy invented the periodic table of elements. Not that an Amer ... *Unitedstatian*, couldn't do it, but in 1869 we had other things to do, such as recovering from the Civil War, so it's only natural ... either way, Unitedstatians did come up with the best and most popular layouts for the table! Ha!"

"Shit, Mikey, stop fuckin' winnin' already!"

"Not a chance Axe, got a full right 'ere ... you can bet somethin' else now ..."

"OK ... well ... I pretty much ain't got nothin' else ... Look, I only got a weapon for one class and items for another ... so you want my Heathen Wizard's Long Rod or my Christian Elf's Silvery Fluid?"

"What the hell are you two betting on?" I said scornfully.

"We're bettin' Realm of Witchcraft items, man! C'mon, you really gotta join someday ... I mean, come on! You already got us as allies ... we'll take care of ya, man! Goin' there

alone is like being alone in prison, and trust me, that ain't cool one bit ... so what do ya say?"

"Er ... not sure Axel ... what's the point of all this? You even have to pay like 45 crosses a month ... that's a bit too much for anyone."

"Yeah, but the game don't cost you nothin'! You actually download the game! I mean yeah, obviously you can go like a prick and buy the whole fuckin' box with one month paid and shit, but it's more expensive, so you actually just have to log in, pay up, and download the shit, man! Then you can join us!!! Don't pay for it, play the free version and then if you like it you show 'em the cash!"

"Well, uh, I'll see Axel, OK? Not like I swim in pools of money like you or anything but I'll see ..."

"C'mon, even Wolfie is in! Ain't too bright though, right Wolfie? Stupid motherfucker gets himself killed all the time ... hahaha! Ain't you clumsy, eh, eh? You fat bastard!" Axel said, as he poked Wolfgang repeatedly on the stomach.

"Leave me alone, Axe ... at least I help you all out."

"Hey, you two, what are you doing? Are you playing cards over there?" Tom Richards said, surprising Axel.

"No, no sir, they fell on the table and I'm pickin' them up."

"You'd better be ... Well, as I was saying, I knew the guy from when I was researching in a team back in the day, we were doing chemical investigation, and the man was one of the few in Loynne's to have a proper, classic white Sforza Contessa with solid gold rims ... Not many were keen on it because they thought the suspension was unreliable for the roads here, too low and it just scratched the chassis, but ..."

"God, here he goes again with that stupid Contessa story ... Look, let's scram after this class, one hour here and I'm already bored to the penis ... You comin' Mikey?"

"Why yeah, on your sister's pie tonight, thanks for askin'

...”

"Haha, sure, silly me! 'Course you comin', you fat bitch ... jackin' it to your Realm elf! Now, who else is comin'? Sonny man!! I see it in your eyes man, you're so wantin' to slack off right now."

"Ah, I'm not sure, Axel ... I've still got things to do after this and—"

"Ohh same old fuckin' square! Screw you then, you commie prick! Hey ... what about you, Wolfbang? Wanna get outta here or what?"

"I told you man, don't call me Wolfbang, OK?!"

"OK then Bangwolf, you comin' or not?"

"No, I can't man, I have things to do as well ..."

"Oh, bunch of fuckin' schmucks! When will you fuckin' learn, eh? Studyin' will get you nowhere!! FACT! Studyin' is for idiots! Name me one guy who ever got ahead studyin'!"

"That guy from Hipps-Tear ... the CEO ... what was his name ... Applegate? Bates? Something like that, I don't remember," Wolfgang said, mumbling.

"That guy did nothin', man ... he dropped outta school and college and university and whatever like anyone who gets ahead in life and goes to where the shit is at. The school of life. That's where I'm goin' now, with Mikey ... so Sonny, either you come with us or you choke on my cock man, not givin' you any other choices ..."

"Look, I can't right now, alright? I've already skipped a lot of classes with you guys, I can't afford to miss more classes, but I'll go one of these days, alright? It's important, I got an exam after this class ... and actually so do you ..."

"Pff, and you think I care, I'm already gonna repeat this year for all I know ... as if I care! After this, I'm gonna go work with my old man in the gamblin' business, make a lot of money and then party with some snow and bitches, I'm sick

of wastin' my life behind a desk watchin' some prick write shit on a whiteboard ... You wanna know what I think of this place Sonny, of the entire academic institution? I think it's all flawed, man. Right from the very start. We go through six fuckin' years of primary education when we're kids, studyin' a lot of crap we don't need and that we ain't never gonna use in real life, only to go through six more years of high school to do the exact fuckin' same, sit behind a desk while some ass-hole tells you to write shit like a little fuckin' baby. Do you think this is right? We can't pick the subjects we want, guys who are good at math are stuck with learnin' philosophy, or history or language, things they ain't never gonna use in their careers! And guys who are bad at math and prefer dunno, languages or biology and shit, are stuck with math! It's fuckin' retarded! We should be able to choose what we want since we're kids, when it's pretty obvious what we're good and bad at. Not everyone is good at the same shit, you know? And then comes university. Fuuuck that. Education right now ain't nothin' but a huge conveyor belt assembly plant where all the robot assholes are assembled, shaped after what the teachers tell 'em to think. They strip 'em down to the bone and make them lawyers and doctors ... yeah, that the world needs lawyers and doctors? Yeah, I know, of course it does, but studyin' for ten years when you should have to study two, learn the fundamentals and get to work immediately? We can't waste so much time in this modern society, man! Every-thing's quick now! And the academic institution has failed to adapt to the times. There's so many people in the world, that what would be best is to specialize in a field instead of learnin' a bunch of useless shit, like a doctor, instead of stud-yin' all the medicine shit, just study to be a brain surgeon if you want to! And all you'll do is that! And for general medi-cine, we'll have doctors who know about that but not how to

operate brains! It's simple! Also, we should be able to study at home with our computers instead of sittin' all day in this kindergarten for adults. LoynNet, ever heard of it? We should be able to study what we want, a couple of years, and get to the streets and apply it in real life. But no. They want us to study useless shit like little kids for 18 years ... 18 years of your fuckin' existence wasted behind a desk, your whole fuckin' youth, only to later get a job with your diploma that involves sittin' behind a desk as well! So you know what I'm gonna do? I'm gonna get the fuck outta here, I'm gonna make money, and prove these fuckin' teacher losers that in real life, you make the money in the streets fast, you live like a king and you get ahead much quicker than a schmuck who does things by the book. And you know what else? The day the academic institution changes and stops being so retarded, I'll get back to studyin'. Promise!"

"And I guess Mikey is joining you in your noble endeavor until then?"

"Pff, no ... he one fat fuckin' square too, but mostly fat ... but I'll convince him, right Mikey? Like I'll convince him of goin' to a sex and drugs party with me, 'cause he always declines! Ain't that right, you gay homo?" Mike looked at him menacingly, with his intimidating stare. He liked Axel a lot, but didn't actually share his promiscuous and partying lifestyle at all, not wanting anything to do with it. Had it not been for Realm of Witchcraft and the video game world, I doubted whether Mike would have anything to discuss with Axel at all.

"Er ... OK ... guess that's a yes ... or will be a yes one day ... Anyways, we're gettin' the hell outta here, see ya Sonny! See ya Bangwolf!"

"I said don't call me that!"

The bell rang, that horrible blend of air raid siren and fire

alarm. Axel and Mike walked out of the class immediately, making their way toward freedom. I went after Mike in a fit of irrationality, and told him:

"Mike, hold on! Look Mike, listen ... why do you do this? You know Axel is just trying to have fun, he doesn't care about studying because he knows he's going to drop out. Why do you let him drag you down like this? You're way smarter than this. I don't mean to insult Axel but ... come on ... you know he's all about partying and sex and all that crap. You're way too profound for that stuff. I don't understand why you waste your time with Realm of Witchcraft and Axel when, I don't know, you could be doing much more with yourself ..."

"I know, Sonny boy ... don't mind me being an asshole, but I think that applies to you too ... aren't you a bit laid back with studyin' yourself?"

"Uh ... yeah, I know ... but that's different ... I have, well, some issues that need a lot of mental horsepower ..."

"Me too, Sonny boy. In ways you couldn't even imagine ..."

"Hey, I wasn't talking about Faye by the way ... I do have important issues. More important than girls, if you know what I mean ... family matters ..."

"Yeah, I don't doubt you. But never mind ... Look, maybe I'll explain one day. As for now, let's just say that Axel is right, Sonny. This flawed and failin' academic system ain't really cuttin' it for me neither ... and guys like Axel, things like Realm of Witchcraft? I admit it, they might not be the best of things sometimes, but they're the best escape valve I've found so far. They take me away from this miserable, pointless life. Call it depression, call it lack of motivation, call it what you will, I just can't really focus on this day-care center for teens they call a school. That's why I barely bother to come here. And it's next to impossible to focus on this petty shit when you have problems like mine. Don't worry about

me, Sonny boy ... I know what I'm doin' ... what you should be really worrying about is yourself. Do you know what you wanna do with your life yet?"

And with that, he left. My usual cynical slits for eyes shut more than normal, studying Axel and Mike until they mixed in with the crowd and disappeared from sight.

"Come on, Wolfie ... we have to carry on with the schmuck life ..."

• • • • •

But Axel *was* right; the academic institution was a complete sham. With his words still fresh on my mind, I sat next to dozens of Kanny losers who would become gas station attendants or municipal gardeners by the time the school year finished. I took some time to stare at the Lolly girls who always got the best grades by sitting at the front teasing the perverted teachers. These girls could only be molded, and thus they never developed independent thought of their own; they only learned by memorizing things they couldn't even begin to analyze, much less comprehend. They were taught how to think by text books and square-headed teachers, and successfully became hollow and empty shells of human beings with supposed successful careers and upstanding positions in society. This was what the educational system perpetuated, sheep mentality, the obliteration of the self and the isolation of anyone who dissented with the group. I found myself surrounded by such beings, doing a stupid language exam which included sentence structure exercises and a hundred-word essay about three given subjects to choose from; "gay rights," "global warming" and "liberty." To simplify such complex subjects in essays of no more than a hundred words

was not insulting, it was sheer provocation on the part of the teacher body. I picked "liberty" to choose the easy path, write a bunch of pro-Loynner garbage and gain the sympathy of the teacher. Effortlessly, I passed the exam with a 8,5. Axel had proven his point; the academic institution was a sham that didn't teach anything truly worthwhile and furthermore praised half-assed efforts and whatever it was teachers wanted students to think. This was no place to learn.

I turned to look around at my disgusting environment; Wolfgang was having some trouble with Axel's ex-boarding school buddies, one of them saying he was occupying a chair that belonged to him, so he began to push Wolfgang out of it, first mad, then laughing, like usual when noticing Wolfgang's easygoing nature. This forced poor Wolfie to leave and sit somewhere else. I remember myself thinking how he could have perfectly exploded at any point those days, as I watched him sitting down violently after the exchange, swallowing his rage with enviable self-control. Wolfgang's decent skill with martial arts and close quarter combat proved more than enough to fight them, with more chances than even I had with brute strength. I wondered at that moment whether this would actually end up badly. Kannovschina had provoked several suicide-homicides, and even though the Loynner propaganda machine swept it regularly under the carpet in order to keep its nice image as a true paradise in every way, there was no ignoring the facts; if left unchecked, Wolfgang's social situation could perfectly turn into one of those cases. Social exclusion is after all, the cause of most murders.

We got out of the Exam Room 2 and I was once again confronted by Faye's presence, and this time it didn't look as if she would ignore me. Wolfgang was immediately repulsed by the mere sight of her, something Axel and Mike had also begun to imitate. They hated Faye for what they perceived to

be a toying and manipulative behavior on her part. They often referred to her as a cruel teaser, but nevertheless always avoided the subject when possible; they knew I found it severely uncomfortable, and as such had opted to ignore the entire situation thinking how perhaps it would make me come to my senses.

Faye looked absolutely stunning: her new wardrobe consisted of very tight jeans to fight the 19 °C of the Loynner winter, plus extremely tight and sexy tops that showed her belly button. Her sides, not fat but slightly chubby, expanded delightfully outwards, outlining her amazing curvy build. This was what I liked the most about Faye; she wasn't fat, not by any means, but had enough flesh to satisfy the enticing voluptuousness men so often seek. The white skin of her firm-looking yet smooth stomach, which she unfortunately almost always covered, seemed to shine.

Seemingly no longer being her usual awkward self, she came toward me at first sight like a magnet. Wolfgang flew past murmuring some stuff in Japanese, irritated.

"Hey Sonny ..."

"Ah ... hello ..."

"What's up?"

"Nothing, I just had a language exam. And, ah ... how about you?

"I'm good. Did you do alright in the exam?"

"What do you think? I never fail."

"OK, OK, geez, sorry for asking!"

"Excuse me, I'm really stressed ... anyway, what did you want?"

"You don't seem very pleased to see me, do you?"

"I'm fine, I just don't know what you want ... I mean ... I never did expect you to come and talk to me ... that is, unless ..."

"Unless what?"

"Unless ... you know ..."

"No, I don't."

"Oh, you do know. Unless you changed your mind. Come on, don't make me say it, you know what I mean ..."

"Oh well ... no, I haven't. You know I haven't."

"See? Well ... so much for that ... I tried my best, really ... see you later."

"What? Wait, where you going?! Why are you acting like such a drama queen for? You're being pathetic ..."

"Pathetic? Me? It'd be pathetic if I were begging for you to talk to me, or if I were following you around like a lapdog, like before ... that would be pathetic. Shrugging you off because you have nothing I want is anything but pathetic."

"Yeah, and you're telling me you feel better like this? To shrug off a friend, a good friend?"

"How many times do we have to go through this, Faye? I don't want you as a friend ... you'd just hurt me otherwise ... I wanted it to be pretty clear on that Christmas card I gave you, and as I'm seeing, it didn't work ..."

"Look, Sonny ... I don't want to be with you, sorry if I put it so bluntly, but I just can't see you as anything other than a friend, and a very good one at that. Don't you see, Sonny? There aren't many interesting and well-intentioned people like you out there ... either they want something or they just hang out with you because they don't have nothing better to do ... and for once that I find one ... It's just so difficult, you know? You don't understand, 'cause you don't have trouble finding friends ... but I do ... and I'm always alone, always bored and depressed ... everything's just so boring, Sonny ... I have nowhere to go, nobody to do things with ... I don't have thrills, emotion ... I just want to end it all sometimes, so I can't be a burden anymore, not to you, not to anyone ..."

"What are you saying?! Are you serious? Look ... you're not going to fool me this time around, you get me? I know your little act ... you act all sad and depressed and then I go and feel pity for you and that's it, I get screwed again. We've talked this over a lot of times. You know well that neither of us is going to change their minds. So what is there to say? Look ... I just want to wish you good luck. On anything you want to do. Sincerely, honestly. I'm sorry but I can't do this anymore, playing this game. You know I want you, Faye ... and I think you should just go away and leave me be."

"That's what you want? Really?"

"Yes! I mean ... well ..." I couldn't say it. I had had the upper hand throughout the whole conversation, and now I was weakening. It couldn't be. Why did she have such power over me? Why did her gorgeous neotenic eyes instill such enslaving control over mine?

"Say it now, Sonny ... say that you don't wanna see me anymore ... I'm used to it ... nobody loves me, nobody cares about me ... men only want one thing and when they don't get it, they throw you away ... you're no different ..."

"Ohh, no. No you don't. I'm amazed, Faye. That's a very low blow. After all these months, after everything I've said to you, all I've praised you, you have the nerve to come and say that I'm like all the rest and that I don't love you? After everything we've been through together, everything you made so clear for me to understand? You may think you have an idea on who I am, but what I'm sure of now is that I fully understand what kind of woman you are. You're a natural-born manipulator just like your brothers. Bye Faye, good luck."

"I didn't mean it like that! Wait!" I stopped my march, hating myself for doing so. Months ago, she would have been the irritated one, urging inside for me to disappear. Now, I found myself in her previous position, and was beginning to

have absolutely no remorse ignoring her, the urge to go immediately after her was semi-controllable. I wanted to put myself to the test as much as possible, and replying to her call just like she had done months ago was fair enough.

"What?" I asked, exasperated.

"Sonny ... I wanna be your friend ... but please ... I don't want to be with you ... I'm not who you think I am ... you just think you like me, but you're fooling yourself. You have like ... an idolized version of me. I'm not that great, believe me. We wouldn't be good together."

"What, are you a vampiress or something?"

"What? No!"

"Well, nothing can be worse than that, can it?"

"Get real! I'm not in the mood for jokes. Look ... all I'm trying to say is that, aside from not being that great, I'm a horrible person ... I mean ... in private ... I'm very unbearable ... nobody can stand me."

"But I don't care."

"But you will! In time. If we were intimate I mean. We would just end up like a failed relationship. And I don't want us to end like that. I don't want to ruin our friendship."

"Aww, come on, Faye! You get real. You think women really think of that when they want to be with a guy? You don't want to be with me, just say it. Don't give me cheap excuses. If you liked me, which you don't, you'd never hesitate like you're doing now. You'd go for broke and just kiss me."

"Sonny ..."

"What ... can't do that, huh?"

"No, it's not that ... it's just that ... look, I'll be honest, OK? It's not like I don't wanna be with you ... but ... I'm really not prepared, OK? Not with you, not with anyone ... I never lied on that ... it wasn't an excuse. But if I ever have a relationship with someone, I wouldn't want it to be with such a good

friend like you ..."

"So you're saying you want to have fun with guys, get used up and then be with me?"

"No! I just mean that, I'll see how it goes gradually, alright? Maybe one day I end up with you, maybe I don't, I just don't know how I'll feel in the future, alright? And please, I don't want you to pressure me either! Just be normal, alright? Like friends ... just be my friend ... don't think of anything else. Please, if you care about me like you say you do, just do that. Promise me this Sonny, and I'll do anything for you ..."

"Anything?"

"Well, duh, not everything! But if it makes you feel better, I'll do anything you want ... as long as it's not, you know ... the obvious."

"What's the obvious?"

"Oh, come on! You know!"

"No, I don't. What do you expect me to ask of you?"

"I dunno ... maybe some weird perverted Ryan shit ..."

"But I'm not Ryan, and with luck I'll never be. You know that."

"Yeah, I know, sorry ... didn't mean to insult you."

"It's alright."

"Well then? What you want me to do? Anything that makes you forget about this, at least for the moment ..."

"Well actually, there is something ... I ... well, how about you come to the cinema with me?"

"To the cinema? Yeah, that's alright! When, and at what time?"

"I don't know ... I'll let you know."

"But Sonny, if you want to do something like that, there's one condition ..."

"A condition?"

"Yeah ... my brothers ... they don't let me go out with you. And if I go out they'll just know it's with you, 'cause I really don't go out with anyone for that matter. So they need to know someone else is coming, so at least it looks normal ..."

"Someone else? You're not thinking of Chelsea are you?"

"Haha, no, no, relax. I don't really talk to her anymore."

"Well, then, who? Not your brothers ..."

"My brothers? Ha! Only Ryan would come, just to crash the party for you ... but no, I don't think he would unless he didn't have nothing else to do ... and I don't want my brothers there! I want to have fun!"

"Have fun, huh? With me or with whoever comes along?"

"Oh don't be silly! Besides, it'll be better ... more people, more fun! I was thinking maybe one of your friends?"

"My friends from class, I'm afraid, wouldn't really come a hundred meters near you. They don't take kindly to you."

"But, why? What did I ever do to them?"

"The same I've done to your friends. That is, absolutely nothing. Hatred for the sake of it."

"Oh."

"So you understand. And I really don't think you want Axel to come along."

"Axel? The Latin guy? Oh no ... please ..."

"Yeah. And well, I have more friends like Tory and Mario but aren't exactly easy to locate ... and forget about Billy and Robbie ... so that leaves us with only Wolfgang ..."

"Wolfgang? Who's he?"

"He's a friend, met him last year. He's cool."

"Well, he'll do!"

"Yeah ... but he's also very, how would you say ... odd."

"Odd?"

"Yeah, odd ... I mean ... it's hard to explain."

"Right ... well, actually don't worry ... do you suppose

there's anyone else who wants to do anything?"

"Well ... yeah, me!"

"Yeah but you know, we can't do this unless it's with more people ..."

"Sure we can ..."

"No, trust me, we can't ... please don't insist."

"Alright, alright ... I'm sure it'd be different if there were one or two guys coming, right?"

"Well, duh ... you know what's goin' on ..."

"Yeah, I am pretty much able to jump to my own conclusions ... see you later."

"Sonny! Oh fine, be like that ..."

Even if I tried to make myself look tough on the exterior, inside I was struggling against the need of rushing back to her and plead pathetically like a spoiled little kid, crying until my demands were met. I simply continued onwards with a rather weird gap of solitude, the kind you think is never going to be filled. Looking around didn't help as the beings which surrounded me proved helplessly inferior and pitiful. The usual little kids running around like idiots, the stupid loud cows with huge earrings and belts howling like dying manatees, and the same old Kanny fucks looking at you badly for no reason and strolling in packs believing in superiority by numbers. This was natural selection at its finest; the very best Loynne's Island had to offer. Being every single day surrounded by these beings, my longing for someone like Faye became incredibly unbearable. How infinitely superior she was in every field. The absolute definition of a woman at her highest; delicate, beautiful, unbelievably unpolluted by the disgusting social environment. I harbored nothing but true love and admiration for her, and still she kept refusing my requests to take our relationship beyond ordinary friendship.

Marching onwards I met with Wolfgang again, noticing he

had been waiting until my conversation with Faye was over. This raised my hopes a little. Seeing such a loyal and pure person in this rotten school seemed almost a joke back then, as I couldn't even rely on my so called friends. Wolfgang could be an idiot, but at least he was loyal.

"*Do shita no, Doshi?* What happened?"

"I spoke to Faye again ..."

"You've spent months without talking to her, why did she come to you?"

"To confuse the shit out of me I suppose ..."

"Well ... so what did you talk about?"

"Well, after breaking the ice we spoke about meeting, but she said that she can't see me if the both of us are on our own, since the brothers might get suspicious or something like that. I don't know, personally I think she doesn't want her friends to see her with me, I can't imagine anything else. Anyway, I've just told her that we couldn't meet with all of the guys, so I asked her if she was OK with meeting me and no one else. And no, she completely backed off. I know she's lying ... I mean who knows, right? But well ... the thing is I need at least one guy if I want to share an intimate moment with her ... well, semi-intimate at least. I haven't had many chances to be around her alone, you know what I mean? It's always either been here at school, with her retarded brothers, with people and friends around ... I'd kill just to be around her sharing a special moment, alone. I think this is where you come in place, *Tovarish.*"

"Me? And what am I supposed to do?"

"Just tag along, don't speak much and try to behave naturally. I'm sorry if you get bored, but I'll owe you if you do this, *Tovarish.* It's the best you could do for me right now."

"Yeah, I know what you mean ... Don't worry ... something will come up between Faye and you eventually. '*Keizoku wa*

chikara nari,' Sonny. 'Perseverance is strength.' "

· · · · ·

With the plan already laid out, the execution was all that remained. I had been preparing myself psychologically for weeks and analyzed intricately every single possible situation in an effort to predict whichever flawed outcome could be produced. I had Wolfgang's back, and her brothers, the only possible ruiners of my desire, were kept at arm's length safely.

The event developed as follows; Faye's birthday was due in a few days, specifically on the 5th of March, and I immediately seized advantage of this golden opportunity, to further develop my plans with Wolfgang. What we decided was to meet in the Pilgrim Coast bus station and head toward my house from there. Faye's birthday was to be held near my house after all, in the warehouse which the mom, Flavia, used for her seamstress business.

During that cloudy and sad 5th of March, time passed by slowly at the bus station as my patience grew ever shorter. Wolfgang suddenly appeared walking in his very own fashion, sporting his out of place Japanese hairstyle and a gift wrapped up in his hands. I had completely forgotten; I never got Faye anything.

"Oh, don't tell me ... I never got her anything! How could I forget?"

"Oh ... well, don't worry, Sonny. People over here aren't usually picky with presents and gifts. Just get her a card or something."

"No, I mean ... I did do something in that fashion. Of my own design, you know what I mean? But I didn't get her something material."

"Nah, don't worry. She'll oversee it. Trust me. And if not she's not worthy, is she?"

"I know, it's just ... see, I'm always trying to impress her, trying too hard ... I still haven't completely forgotten when she rejected me the first time. I don't know where I stand. I don't know what I'm pursuing, what I'm expecting. She clearly doesn't want anything. She showed it before and continues to do it now. I mean, what can I do? I know what I want, that's for sure, and I can't shake off this stupid feeling of destiny, as if this is exactly what I'm supposed to be doing. I feel and know I'm right, but it just doesn't seem that way when facing her."

"I know Sonny, I got you there. Just don't worry. See how things go from now on. I mean if she truly can acknowledge your virtues and values, she's yours for life. Maybe it's true that she doesn't know you well enough yet, or, I don't know ..."

"And what if she never does? What do I do then?"

"Relax, everything will be alright. Look, let's have a good time tonight and that's it. Don't overthink it. Try to relax and don't pressure her too much. In the end she'll budge when she realizes there's no one else out there that loves her as much as you."

"Thanks Wolfie, really. I can't get this kind of support from her brothers, I tell you that. Or from my very own friends for that matter. I'm all alone in this, and nobody seems willing to lend me a hand, not even listen ... anyway, enough self-pitying. Come on, *Tovarish*. Let' go." We took the bus and headed back home again. It was odd having to go there just to pick Wolfgang up and wished he was a bit brighter so as to know which bus to take, but fair enough. At least I had some company and was doing something different. The day didn't improve at all. The weather was cloudy

and cold, and I imagined all the time that it was a reflection of the recent events that had transpired. Many days in Loynne's with cloudy weather were not normal. I was not superstitious, but in my dramatic and subliminal state I couldn't help but draw the comparison.

· · · · ·

I walked with Wolfgang to Kennedy Park, a small public park northeast from my house, in order to avoid showing him where I lived. I uttered an excuse saying my parents were sleeping inside and wouldn't take kindly to visitors. Nobody could be allowed in my apartment. Luckily, I received a call from Ryan shortly after.

"Hey Sonny, you ready?"

"Yeah, I'm here at Kennedy Park."

"Right, well my mom's warehouse is just south from there. Look, do this ... go to the 'AT & AT' cybercafé on Arias Road, and take the street that's just in front of it, it's called Saavedra Street. Head down that street until there's no more road, it's the building to the left."

"Right ... we're going now."

We walked enjoying the foggy day, a once-in-a-year type of day in Loynne's that at times seemed to be becoming the norm, and made off for the direction Ryan described. We found ourselves walking to a surprisingly concealed part of Montenade. The blocks of apartment buildings finished to make way for the deserted hills, filled with nettles, cactuses, geckos and not much else. The volcanic disposition of the island created vast, maroon colored deserts sprinkled with green stinging plants where life was even scarcer than in Chernobyl. Across these deserted plains, you could view some of the Asiz Valley skyline, which was similar in construction

to Montenade's. All these towns where the same actually. The only thing different were the names. Materials remained the same throughout.

Flavia's warehouse was one of these look-alike buildings, only two stories high and occupying almost one third of the entire block. It was right on the road where the desert began, and made for a pretty nice and cozy setting. At the precise moment of our arrival, the unusual yet now common cloudy, cold weather dissipated and a streaking sun covered us, blazing as per usual. Ryan greeted us outside with his greedy smile and Dave soon followed.

" 'Sup Sonny man! Howzit goin'?"

"Hey Dave. Look, I brought this friend with me, remember Wolfgang from Billy's going away party?"

"Yeah, I've actually seen him around at school too, how you doin' man?"

"Hey, uh ... good ... good," Wolfgang said, nervously.

"Hey, what's up Samurai! Got any new Aikido moves?" Ryan had come to greet Wolfgang in his own unique way. At this point, he didn't hide how much he disliked him.

"Oh, yeah, I actually do," Wolfgang said, in his formal Japanese air.

"Gonna roll on the floor commando style while playin' dodgeball, like that time in PE class? Hahahaha!"

"(Just ignore him *Tovarish*, we all know he's a dick.)"

"(Yeah, alright.)"

Wolfgang's docile attitude was a nice contrast to Ryan's imbecility and Dave's arrogance. He was in fact so easy and nice to get along I doubted the utility of my current friends. I couldn't change them to enemies though, or my plans with Faye would be thwarted. I had to hold on a bit longer until the date of the desired end came to pass.

We entered the building, where it was obvious the large

industrial machinery had been magically replaced with long tables, full of drinks and bowls with chips. A chocolate cake with the number 16 was centered amidst them. The simplicity of this birthday depicted rather well Faye's background. Not poor, not rich, just simple without emphasis on grandeur. I judged people by how they celebrated birthdays. This seemed to me the kind of celebration my family would have chosen and instantly made me sympathetic toward it. It felt almost as if being back in The Motherland, with a working-class Italian-Unitedstatian touch.

Scouting for Faye, my anxious eyes met her tender ones as she approached to kiss me. The "Balearic Cherry" instantly overwhelmed my senses. Feasting my eyes and nose on her for the few available seconds I had without raising suspicion, I handed her my birthday card. She said "*thanks, I'll read it later*" with her extremely soft Unitedstatian accent, and went on to greet Wolfgang. My comrade and I sat down, while Ryan and Dave took care of the guests. Worryingly feeling like a grumpy old man, I went outside after having a few beers. While doing this we devoted the conversation to what we were observing. Faye wasn't being molested or sexually assaulted in the open by her eldest brother, and I presumed it had to be because of the presence of family. Faye as such was for once enjoying herself with her family, almost with childish submission, simply standing quietly while relatives and other adult types talked to her mother or father about how much she'd grown – she must have stopped growing at the age of 10 – how beautiful and shiny her hair was, and other assorted compliments.

"Beautiful doesn't even come close, huh? How's that for the understatement of the year, Wolfie?"

"Mmm ... she's your woman, *Doshi*. I should refrain from giving my insight."

"Well, uh ... sure ... better off that way." Faye passed gliding softly like a banshee before us, wearing the new clothes for the party. My amazement grew exponentially. She had outdone everything I believed could be accomplished by her own hand. My jumpy heart hit another bump causing its acid truckload to spill and burn my whole chest in pure neglected desire.

Faye sported a short, jet black party dress which enhanced her breasts, butt and thighs, doing nothing except reaffirming me on the fact that my race toward perfection was right. I was also surprised at how, even in her own birthday she wore her US flag cross necklace. I cursed my bloated admiration to such an individual. Every time I saw her my natural impulse was to make her more than mine; I wanted to fuse with her very own flesh, see the world through her round and gorgeous emerald eyes, walk with her delicate white feet, breath through her perfect Anglo-Saxon nose, kiss with her heart-shaped lips ...

"Kids! Would you like more beer?" Said a cheery Flavia Avellis, with her wrinkled skeletal smile, startling me so much I jumped. Sometimes I thought of her as Faye in 30 years, and a shivering sensation rose through my spine. Though not an ugly woman by any chance, the idea of Faye – and by golly every single one of us – arriving to such a state of decay was unpleasant at best.

"No Mrs. Avellis, we're alright, thank you very much," I said, and she went forgetting about us as soon as she had developed interest in offering us the drinks.

"Truly beautiful, isn't she?"

"Uh ... what was that about refraining from giving your insight again?"

"Haha, no, *Doshi* ... I meant the mother."

"What are you talking about?

"She's got that Italian-Unitedstatian charm, doesn't she? Passionate, cheery and youthful. I'm sure she would be a wonderful wife."

"Which makes you wonder why the husband dumped her for someone half her age ..." As soon as I had said that, Tory and Mario arrived, and we went outside to greet them. A circle of curious pedestrians was formed around Mario, who had brought a football to play around with.

Soon, the streets thundered with the echo produced by the football bouncing off the walls, as we all childishly joined in, with all our natural flaws and clumsiness which would have made any nearby Kannies viciously laugh at us. But there weren't any. Suddenly, without wanting to, I felt deprived of my usual hatred for my fellow human beings; our group of outcasts felt like a really faithful, tight bunch. Each dressed according to his necessity, with military, rock, skate and hip-hop influences and the spirit of hating any genre related to Kannies made our heterogeneous subculture superior in every way. The resounding success of that street football match being played in that small part of the world was an example of our expanding influence across the island; immigrants from all over the world, united by the need to reject anything Loynner and keep each other sane in a society ruled by ignorance and mediocrity. Standing there, having a laugh with my buddies, wrestling Tory' arrogant ass to the ground after a friendly dispute over a joke, seeing Dave perform breathtaking dancing moves, throwing ourselves out of an abandoned shopping cart down a hill, it all proved to be the experiences with friends I had always craved. The right place, the right situation, the right people. Had it been others, I would have felt I was wasting my time on some batshit crazy idiots. These people, however, proved to be loyal aside from friendly. No matter what a dickhead Ryan proved to be, or

what an arrogant little nuisance Dave could be at times, their antics were more than enough to satisfy our need for social cohesion in a hostile environment full of Kannies. I took their faults as inherent parts of their humanity and psychology, and gave myself to the joy of youth and adolescence while it lasted. I used to say to myself all the time: "*In a few years, you're going to miss this. Cherish every second of it.*"

With the guys busy fooling around, I used the blasting music coming from the warehouse's speakers to disappear momentarily and be alone with Faye. She was sitting at the table talking to some relatives and having cake. I approached her and she immediately smiled, saying something to her relatives and sitting on a far away chair, patting the one next to it, signaling me to sit beside her. I still could not get over how beautiful she looked, and my heart started pounding aggressively against my chest with each step forward.

"Cake, Sonny?" she asked cheerfully, smiling and offering me a slice.

"Oh, no, thanks, I already had enough for a lifetime ..."

"OK! Well ... beer?"

"Your mother's already done a good job getting me half-drunk, it's a good thing I never drink on an empty stomach ... but yeah ... what the hell ... just pour the whole thing ..."

"Haha! Mmm ... that enough?" She said, filling the immense jar to the tip and letting it overflow a bit.

"I'm not responsible for what I can potentially do after this, Faye ... you've been warned ... and what about you? You don't drink beer?"

"Me? No ... yuck. Never liked beer. That's for men. Women look like dykes drinking that thing."

"What do you drink then?"

"Mmm ... I don't drink much, but ... I dunno, if I have to, I think rum, or vodka ... anything but beer!"

"Beer's always been the drink of the working man after all … it's a proletarian drink …"

"Uh … yeah … hey Sonny, can I ask you something? But please, don't get offended or nothing!"

"Go right ahead gorgeous … and no, I won't."

"Why do you have like … that really old way of talking? I mean … like I said, don't want you to get offended … but you speak as if you were, dunno, 40 years old! I mean … so polite, so educated all the time … you never really swear, and you use words that not a lot of people could understand …"

"Well, look who's talking … don't take it as a compliment, but you don't speak like a Loynnerin either … I mean, you know … for a 15-year-old Unitedstatian little brat from Santa Monica you speak quite correctly …"

"Make that 16! And ha-ha, not funny at all … Anyway, tell me!"

"Well … promise you won't laugh if I tell you the exact reason why?"

"Mmm … not promising anything … but what the hell, go ahead!"

"Well … it's because of films."

"Films? You mean, movies?"

"Movies, yeah, films. Cinema."

"What you mean, that you get your way of talkin' by what you saw or heard in fil—I mean, movies?"

"Sort of … well, I know you're probably going to laugh, but … Lenin once said, 'Of all the arts, the most important to us is the cinema.' In my love for Communism, I always took that quote very literally, so literally that I spent my entire childhood watching films, from all countries, but especially Soviet and Unitedstatian films. The thing is, I always watched very old films and TV series, from the '80s, '70s, '60s, and sometimes even '50s. You know that actors before used to say their

lines very correctly compared to everyday people, even when they were supposed to play hoodlums and such, so let's just say I learned English that way, and my Russian accent obviously got modeled after that. I never quite spoke like all the rest, not even in Russian. And believe me, Russian is a very dirty language ... it's a language that lends itself a lot to be used aggressively and dirtily, but mostly aggressively. It's got plenty of slang. But I never liked speaking like the rest. I found it to be mediocre, petty. I always strove to be better than my current self and improve upon it. I know it sounds arrogant, but ... I've always hated the thought of being stuck in time, never progressing, never striving to improve. That's all there is to it, I guess ..."

"Mmm ... it's funny, 'cause I was also gonna tell you you have an old type of thinking too ... haha. Guess the way of talking that you have comes from the mind, not just the mouth."

"Let's ... let's just not talk about me, shall we? Why don't we talk about you?"

"Me? Nooo! But ... why?!"

"Oh, come on ... if I hear you say you're not interesting or that you'll bore me to tears telling me about your life you'll start making me think it must be true."

"I'm not lying! I am boring ... I'm not so interesting like you. I don't come from no exotic country, I mean, the US is the US ... I just don't know what other people think it's so special about it ... it's just ... that ... what you see whenever you turn the TV on or go to the movies, what you hear people talking about all the time ... Los Angeles, New York, Miami, Las Vegas ... gosh ... I mean ... every movie or TV show is set in the same cities all the time, you know how thrilled I was when I watched this movie set in London, with people not speaking with Unitedstatian accents? I mean ... not only you

never hear or watch things about other countries on TV, but even abroad you're forced to see our shit, I can't believe the rest of the world is so tolerant with US things like they are, they should be fed up by now ..."

"They actually are as a matter of fact, most countries barely have any US content on TV or in the cinema anymore, now every country is trying to get their own national industry, their own culture, which is actually very good I might say ... no country should dominate the rest of the world culturally ... it's denigrating ... Before the rise of the intranets, when the world was so globalized, yeah, the world was infected by Unitedstatian culture, but then it started to decline ... now only a few places in the world have US syndicated content, Loynne's is an example, China for some reason is another ... I'll never get why they don't get fed up, though ... China is the main consumer of Unitedstatian content ..."

"Yeah, well, but what I meant to say was that living here you don't sense that, Loynne's is just like the US at times, except that some people speak really funny ... But anyway, I never had any regrets moving here to Loynne's ... I was bored of the US, my whole family was, I think ... I think the entire world was at that time, when it began to decline ... that's when I learned nothing lasts forever ... relationships, popularity, wealth, fame, looks, health ... that's why sometimes, I just think there's really no point in living ... we're all gonna die, and before dying we'll be old and disgusting, unable to move because we'll have so many diseases ... and we'll look at ourselves in the mirror and then at a photo and say ... that used to be me ... and now I'm this ugly skeleton ... just shoot me ..."

"Then I'm the negative one ... guess you really are paranoid about getting old, huh?"

"I can't stand the thought ... that's why I'm so tense right

now, I want to live things before I get to that state ... I'd hate it if I reached that age and had nothing to remember about my youth ..."

"But we have plenty of time ahead of us to do whatever we want to do ..."

"I know but ... on this island? There's nothing to do here ... this island only offers you tourist-class entertainment ... things for old British couples, or for crazy Europeans that wanna go scuba-diving, gliding or mountain climbing ... or for douchebags that wanna go dancing and have sex with hookers and get drunk and high ... I dunno ... I want something else from life ... something that's not what everybody else does ... parachute jumping my ass ... that's for all these rebel conformist types that they use in ads for phones and computers all the time ... it's sickening and boring ... so boring!"

"And what is it that you'd like to do, because, you seemingly don't want to do anything ... you used to ice-skate and then you quit because it got boring ..."

"I know! But I don't regret it! Look ... what I want is simply to, dunno ... meet interesting people ... like now, that I've met you! But ... more. I want to live unpredictable things, I hate routine! I want life to take me wherever the wind is blowing ... I don't want to plan or think ahead, I just want things to happen ... whatever they might be ..."

"Is that right, huh ... so you want to be a sort of nomadic adrenaline junkie but without the parachute jumping ..."

"Haha ... well ... if you put it that way ... Look, I don't know what I want from life, but I just want it. That's how I can sum it up best. I don't know what life has in store for me, but I want it all. Ups and downs, sorrow and joy, happiness and misery ... I want to feel alive ... this is no way to live, Sonny ... stuck here in this island prison ... Yeah, I know the rest of the

world is gone to hell and everywhere sucks except for here, and I know how lucky we are that we have the opportunity to live here, but, people manage to live in other places, right? And they have their own lives, and have enough money to come here even if it is to escape ... but that's what everybody does when they're on holiday ... a holiday is an escape ... and if they can be happy here, even for a short while, then they can't be that bad where they live. I dunno ... I just ... I just hope my luck changes one day ..."

"Well ... I guess ... you just need to have ... *faith* ..."

"Yeah ... anyway! It's still my birthday! We don't wanna get depressed today, do we? We'll have plenty of time to do it tomorrow!"

"Yeah ... yeah ... I guess ..."

· · · · ·

It seemed everything was back to normal, and now I could relax and calmly dive into my strategy. Being among friends actually helped and seeing Faye without getting into fights or arguments seemed to have done the trick. Also, the latest reply by my parents made me greatly happy.

*"Dear *********

We're glad you've somehow gotten to be your usual self. Has anything in particular improved? Are you doing better at school now? What about that girl you mentioned? Any progress? I'd love it if you could introduce me to a nice and beautiful girl the moment we arrive on that island.

Don't get distracted though. Remember your original mission. Hold on until we can allow ourselves to move for good to Loynne's. Try and keep getting good grades, they

will be important in the near future, more than you think.

Love you,

Mom and Dad."

My parents needn't worry about a thing. Not only were my grades improving, but also the situation with Faye. I accomplished the amazing feat of making her call me all by herself once more. Our phone conversations, which back then were only about trivialities, managed to secure a solid friendship. We sometimes talked for one hour, and she always had the initiative. I used to make her laugh like no one else could. We were starting to really have something and the moment to strike seemed to be at hand. My sloppy steps in November were already a distant memory. Faye and I had already begun to open up to each other, share, talk and have fun, more than I ever accomplished with either Ryan or Dave.

Walking Faye home was now ordinary routine, not a special extraordinary miracle. But it was one of the best routines available. For guys of my social standing, this was an incredible sign of change, maturity and respect, even if Faye appeared to be 12. Gordon, Claude and those types could only aim to ask a girl the notes taken during their absences. Shameful. Some guys like Axel could have looked at my little victory and laughed right in my face of how petty and trivial it was, but for me it was beyond the glory of respect, alpha maleness and the mere concept of victory. I was making progress with the only girl I was interested in making any progress with. All others could shoot themselves in the head and I wouldn't stop them. For once in my life, at least in the emotional purpose, meaning was abundant. My goal was to live a happy existence next to this special and unique individual,

for whom I harbored so much love and admiration that my sense of alert and paranoia momentarily left to make a thrill-seeking enthusiasm barge violently in. Her company was everything that mattered to me. It made all traces of solitude vanish. It annihilated the void I had always felt, even in The Motherland. It had brought back and enhanced that long lost sensation, the power of positivism only love can bring out in people.

As it was obvious; the Mantis brothers decreed that my presence at their house right after classes was inadequate and abnormal. They wanted to be left alone in order to safeguard Faye from me, to toss forks and knives at each other during meals and yell at their lousy absent mom without witnesses. I knew the feeling; school was a six hour blazing hell that drained your energy away; the waking up, the not sleeping well the night before, the maybe not having time for breakfast, the constant screaming, the dull classes, the journey back home ... it was a ride alright. Having people invading your intimacy and your right to chill out from that hell seemed a bit unfair. I knew I was even worse than them regarding my privacy rights, so I went along with it. That didn't mean I wouldn't take into consideration the fact that I was denied my right to be in their house if I felt like it. I had had enough of that stupid bus stop, of the childish screaming and the bumping into acquaintances you were forced to say hi to like social order dictated. I wanted some "me" time as well. As such, the alternative I came up with was joining Wolfgang in his lengthy stride toward his home in The Pentagon.

Wolfgang led the way through the luxurious Sun Tower building, telling me that his mother, a very authoritarian figure according to him, wouldn't be back soon as she had to run an errand with the dad. Wolfgang seemed extremely relieved by this, and I guessed he was probably very op-

pressed by her. Women could be worse authority figures than men any day.

While walking through the silent residential building and small talking with Wolfgang occasionally, I began to think how after Faye's birthday the only thing left to do was hanging out. She seemed cheerier and happier when off of her tyrannical brothers' leash, and the thought of her enjoying my company overwhelmed me considerably. I decided to talk about it with Wolfgang so we could get a plan going on.

"Wanna watch some TV, Sonny?"

"Uh ... sure, why not."

"I'll go get something to eat, just help yourself."

"Alright."

Wolfgang disappeared and went to the kitchen, returning swiftly with soft drinks and his usual Asian food.

"Thanks, Wolfie ... but I'm not too keen on this food, no offense. I'll pass."

"Nah ... just eat up, give it a go! Look, let me turn the TV on, there's something so bad that will have you laughing for days ..." Wolfgang turned the TV and left it on the RTV channel.

"AND GOD SAID ... THOU SHALL PIMP THY BITCH!"

"Welcome to another episode of Pimpin' Thy Bitch! Today we have Marcellus and Laetitia! And it seems ... that Marcellus here is ready to go to the next level and pimp that ho' up! Here Marcellus, tell the audience what yo' concerns are!"

"Yeh well, I jus' think the bia needs an upgrade and shit, y'know, like when I tuned up the Escalator. You get bored of the same paintwork 'n rims all the time y'know, so I said, this bia needs some pimpin' right 'ere! Bigga lips 'n tits, sum big-ass bubble-butt, all the accessories dawg, jus' pimp 'er

out."

"*Great! Now we go with our fashion consultant, let's see what he thinks of this!*"

"*Mm, mm, mm ... no no, sweetheart! Everything wrong! Would you look at that hairstyle, those clothes? Mm, mm, mm! No way! Where do you think you are cutie, working your corner back at Bronx? We need to redo this whole mess like my name is Fabio! Somebody get me a whole new wardrobe here! And some silicon! This slut's in need of some pimpin', bad!*"

"*PIMPIN' THY BITCH' WILL BE BACK AFTER THESE VERY IMPORTANT MESSAGES.*"

"Is it just me or that's about the most horrible thing I have ever seen?"

"I know, that's why I watch it, it's terrible ..."

"Don't tell me you actually watch this ..."

"Oh, no, not at all Sonny ... just to check how horrible the world is out there ..."

"Say Wolfie, I don't mean to sound weird, but I thought I might as well discuss some stuff with you. Nobody else can help me really, and I'm quite desperate."

"Yeah, sure *Doshi*, what's the problem?"

"Well, you know, I need to start putting the gears in motion. I thought you could help me with Faye again."

"How could I do it?"

"Just hang out with Faye and me until she's looser so I can seize the opportunity to make a move. Know what I mean?"

"Yeah, don't worry Sonny, I'll help you out, I'm sure that when she sees all the stuff you do for her she'll realize what kind of person you are and she'll understand there's but a bunch of truly worthy guys out there. You have to understand

Sonny, she's still very young and doesn't have a lot of experience, you know, like a little girl who's guided by instincts more than rationality."

"That's what everyone tells me! And yeah, I know it's the most plausible explanation. I mean I don't think it's me, I mean you know, for some reason I do feel we have a lot of chemistry. It's as if, I don't know, like she doesn't even want to try it in case she likes me. I don't really know. Girls are harder to understand than I thought. I'm used to simpler, shallower girls. I can't believe someone two years younger is so hard to get."

"Don't sweat it if nothing comes out of this Sonny, remember there's a lot of girls out there just waiting to cross paths with you."

"Wolfgang, it's not that easy. I want this one. I feel like I've been my whole life just waiting to meet this girl. She's everything I could have ever asked for and more. Have you ever felt that? Staring at a complete stranger for what feels like an eternity and spending the following months floating in the clouds? It's horrible ... Before, I only cared about coming back home in one piece, doing the things that made me happy, and that was about it. Rinse, repeat. But now, my expectations of life have become greater with age. It's happened way too fast but just two years is a very long time at this age. I want to do so many things with this girl it's unbelievable. Actually, doing pretty much anything with her is fun, I have the time of my life just being by her side. You know how hard it is for me to find someone I can trust, have fun with and care about like as if she was my own blood at the same time? Picture it in your head. Look Wolfgang, you're a real good friend, we have known each other for quite some time and I can tell there's no one like you on this island, perhaps in the whole planet. True friendship goes a long way and so does

true love. It's time to grab this bull by the horns. I've had enough of being a chump all these years, held down by this oppressive Kanny fad, put down by these nasty Loynnerin two-bit sluts who think are the bomb; it's over. I'm going to get everything or come home with nothing at all, but I'm willing to risk my neck because I know the result will be more positive than anything I have ever experienced. This girl, Wolfie ... she got to me so fast, and nobody ever does that. I've been searching for this time and place my whole life. It feels ominous, forecasted, incredibly right ..."

"If that's the way you see it, I won't say anything. I believe in destiny. It's scripted in your very genes, you're transmitting what your ancestors stood for in the past, just by living. The human genome is the driving force behind your actions now. You could say it's destiny. It's another name for genes."

"You're right. I never saw it that way before. I should try and look at human nature a bit closer like you do. I live in idealism. It's time to look at the biology of the situation and dissect it, see it for what it is, only genes. The search for a fertile female, the action of chemistry in our bodies, pheromones, hormones ... yeah. It's nothing more than that. There's no such thing as love like people understand it ... but ... let me handle the psychological bit better. I'll leave the biological analysis for you."

· · · · ·

The Crucible was as silent and dead as per usual; sometimes I wondered whether the Mantises could be the only tenants in the whole building. I made my way to their apartment on a sunny and cheery afternoon, ready to see my loved one and already prepared to face the consequences of demanding her presence in front of the brothers.

"Sonny! What a surprise! You came to see me!"

"Faye? Where are your brothers?"

"They're not here ... what ... you just wanted them, right?"

"Oh come on, they're the last people I want to see. I came to see you specifically because I have something to tell you."

"You do?"

"Yeah. I've been thinking about what you said, and ... I decided we'll go to the cinema this afternoon."

"What? Ohhh ... thanks Sonny, but remember what I said ... we can't ..."

"There's no problem *Fatty*, someone's coming with us."

"Who? Dave? And don't call me that!"

"Oh yeah, Dave out of all people ... Come on."

"Then who? That friend of yours, Axel?"

"Nah, not Axel! You think it possible to sit through a whole film with him? It's Wolfgang."

"Wolfgang? Oh yeah. Your Japanese friend?"

"He's not Japanese, he just likes to pretend he is. He's a nice enough guy, a bit let's just say, misunderstood ... so I thought he could come with us given that he's the only one willing to. He doesn't talk much and he's a bit shy but he's on the level. Very good person."

"Well, great! That'll do. When do we go? Where are we meeting him?"

"Well, why so excited now? Anyone would say I got you a blind date!"

"Oh, don't be silly! You know it's 'cause it means that now we'll get to hang out! So yeah, let's get outta here, I'll be right back, let me get my stuff. Be a minute, don't go!"

"*(As if I'm going anywhere now ...)*" Faye came back a few minutes later, shutting the door behind her with that delicate stance she often adopted, gliding instead of walking and giving little jumps with her body, making her breasts bounce

gracefully up and down. She smiled gleefully at me, staring directly into my very eyes in a self-assured and patient manner, limiting herself to smiling. Having never looked at me that way before, she made me blush completely; I turned my head pretending I was about to sneeze and she quickly ceased staring. Soon we found ourselves waiting for the elevator, not talking much but enjoying the comfortable silence of our mutual company. We were behaving as if we had been dating for some time, in a time and place where talking proved unnecessary. We got out at the bottom floor and made our way toward the parking lot back entrance, ready to meet Wolfgang outside, where he said he'd wait for us. He hadn't arrived yet, so we waited for about 10 minutes, small talking and behaving as if our company was enough. It was incredible how I could be myself around her. No need to rant about generic cool stuff a girl of her age might find attractive, no need to talk in an arrogant, self-assured voice, no need to be someone I was not. I didn't feel like talking because I was comfortable next to a person I trusted. This was something rare, so it had to be cherished and enjoyed. I'd soon sink myself again in the problems of the past, the present and the future ... my demons would always return to haunt me, but not as long as she was there, simply existing, living, breathing. I froze myself momentarily in time and space as I admired her breathtaking perfection and thought myself lucky to even be by her side. I would have never, ever gotten a chance like this in the past; times were certainly changing.

Faye emulated my wish to avoid talking and enjoying the silence instead, looking at me from time to time, simply smiling. Our eyes would meet occasionally as the waiting for Wolfgang intensified. Gazes that needn't an explanation, a question, an answer. Everything that was happening there, on that little corner of the planet, on that specific moment in

time, was a rare, unique moment between two people. I couldn't be happier. Even with doubts, unfinished business, uncertainty ... nothing managed to shatter that almost infinite moment of bliss.

Soon, however, the bliss in Faye's eyes became extinct. No longer electrifying and vivid, her eyelids went back to her usual lazy positions, giving her that look of chronic depression and boredom she used to carry along with her person. Lost in empty spaces, her eyes reflected a hungry desire to turn the situation around and take charge of it.

"Call him," she said, abruptly.

"Come on, he should be here already, we spoke about this a million times, he couldn't have just forgotten ..."

"Well, I don't care, call him to make sure."

"Fine, keep your g-string on." I called Wolfgang's cell-phone only to get a constant Horizon chatter drilling my ear about his cell-phone being out of coverage or dead. Great. There was nothing I could do, no way to contact him and I was stranded with an embittered Faye that clearly didn't want my company after all, but that of multiple people that could make inflate her ego and make her feel she wasn't wasting her time inside a house thinking about how pathetic and pointless her existence was.

"So?"

"I can't get a hold of him, I just get this bitch telling me his phone is out of coverage!"

"Let me see if I can reach him. What's his number?"

"What? What difference does it make? If the phone can't be reached, it can't be reached ..."

"I don't care, just give me his number and we'll see if we're lucky ..."

"Fine, UP is 7758 and PN is 6550. Now what?"

"Well, we wait till we get him. C'mon, keep trying you too."

"And what the hell am I Fatty, your freaking butler?"

"Are you always this rude toward women? And I told you, stop calling me that!!"

"I'm only rude when people piss me off precisely when I'm under pressure."

"Why would you be under pressure?"

"Come on, as if you're not putting any pressure on me telling me to stalk this guy to death till I do get him, which I won't because he never, ever minds his phone, or anything else for that matter. He's probably in Aikido lessons because he forgot to come with us or I don't care, you know, I don't really give a shit, because what matters is that us both are together and that's all you should need. Be grateful. Nobody wants to hang out with you except for me and your Chelsea skank friend. So you can do one or the other, sweetheart. Go hang out with Chelsea and have fun ripping off Kanny kick-boxing competition ads and kicking trash containers at 04:00 in the middle of freaking nowhere in Stockholm Avenue like you told me you do to escape your house and your brothers, or you can hang out with someone who's just had to turn down almost five offers to hang out today, all to spend time with you!"

"Fine! OK! Go live your fancy life with your little friends while I get bored here and kick trash containers in the middle of the night with Chelsea! That's my life after all, isn't it? I'm going back to The Crucible, goodbye Sonny."

"Wait, wait! Are you seriously not even going to consider hanging out with me after I turned down my own friends? Does that gesture mean nothing to you at all? I'm honestly asking you. Answer me now because I need you to be straight with me. I'm sick of your awkward silences and the way you slip through my fingers each time I want a straight answer from you. Go on! Say the truth! You feel awkward when you

are alone with me, you lie to me, and all I've ever done is being straight with you since I met you!"

"I lie to you?! All I've done is being straight with you Sonny, but you prefer the lie! Haven't I been straight already? Haven't I said no to your proposals, no matter how good-hearted and well-intentioned they could be? I said no and when I say no I mean no! Don't you get it? How many times I have to tell you! No means NO! And I won't hang out with you, be around you or even talk to you as long as you keep that in your head. I like you, yes, as a friend and nothing more! I'm cool hanging out with you but I'd be more if I knew you didn't want something in return. After all, friendship is supposed to be that. Nobody wanting nothing in return, just being friends should be enough. I won't be your friend if you expect something that will never happen."

"And who said I want to be your friend?! Why are you so certain that nothing will ever happen? You never know! That's what I'm certain about. And one day you'll acknowledge what I already know. You'll be sorry you wasted so much time in the end, all to come to the imminent realization that WE WOULD BE VERY MUCH FUCKING GOOD TOGETHER!"

"Look, I'm through talking to you, you won't listen to reason, goodbye Sonny and have a nice life."

"No! Hold on! Look, I'm sorry! Alright? Let's just forget we ever had this conversation and just keep on calling Wolfgang, OK? If that's what you want, seriously, I'll do it. Even if it's just for you. I ... I'll do anything for you. You know it." Faye looked at empty spaces for some time, before nodding and joining me as we walked toward the bus station.

I kept calling Wolfgang over and over, knowing it was the last card I could use for now. I wouldn't have been able to just wave an entire day with her goodbye so easily. I needed a

logical closure point at least, not an angry awkward rant about how we both were feeling toward the other. Aside from making me feel like shit once again, shattering my newfound hope and making clear we were still only friends, my biggest concern at this moment was the future I dissed only minutes ago, in that blissful moment frozen in time. What now? Be her friend and see how she experiments with other people while I just sit there and take it? Cut off our relationship when it was just starting to take off and gain momentum? I hated unfinished business precisely because of this reason; the uncertainty, the doubt and the what ifs would have been demons added to my personal circle of hell, as if it wasn't populated enough. I couldn't leave this hanging and remember it as a traumatizing moment of my life. I still had a chance to fix it and turn it into the wonderful bliss I experienced inside of me. I didn't know how to act or what to do at that time, and mainly just conformed myself with following my most basic impulses. I grabbed the phone and dialed Wolfgang's number once more.

· · · · ·

"Wolfgang? Finally! What's wrong with you?! Why won't you answer your phone?!"

"Sorry Sonny, I was in the shower."

"You have your phone turned off!"

"Oh, no, not at all, it was just out of coverage, always is, coverage up here in The Sun Tower isn't particularly strong."

"Well, look, why didn't you show up? We were waiting for you here! Don't tell me you forgot!"

"Well ... actually, I wasn't gonna go, Sonny. I thought you caught my drift when I didn't show up. It was supposed to be you dating her and taking her to the cinema right? So I

thought, let's help him out and not appear and then you can have her all for yourself ..."

"Ah ... yeah ... look. That's a brilliant idea and all but it's not like I haven't tried that before ... You HAVE to come. Can you meet us at the cinema itself?"

"The one in the Alexandria Boulevard Square Center Mall?"

"You know there are no cinemas in Paradise Plaza, of course I mean that one. Look, we'll meet you at the cinema's entrance. Be there in an hour, you just showered so I won't accept any slacking off. Get to it!"

I hang up angrily while trying to make sense of the entire situation, but was interrupted by Faye.

"Done?"

"Yes, Princess Demanding, your date has just showered."

"Shut up! He's not my date! We're hanging out! All of us!"

"Yeah, we're hanging out because he's going to make it in the end."

"Oh don't you get me started today. I'm already in a fuckin' mood."

"Don't swear, sweety. It doesn't look good on pretty girls like you."

"Piss off."

"I will in a minute."

"Oh come on Sonny, chill out, I thought you really wanted to hang out with me."

"I did, I mean I do. But you seem to like ... I don't know, not want me around unless you're surrounded by at least three more people."

"Don't be silly ... like I said, it'll just look weird if someone catches us hanging out, the two of us alone, people will start talkin'.'"

"And who cares about that? Because I don't ..."

"Don't be difficult, I'm not having this argument again. I'll walk! OK? And you can have Wolfgang all for yourself! I don't mind that!"

"OK, OK, I'll shut up. Let's just keep walking ..."

"Now there's a good boy ..."

"I'm not a good boy!"

"Haha ... 'course you're not ..."

• • • • •

We walked as winter's early night began to obscure the sky. It was but 18:00 and already nighttime. We took Duarte Street all the way to Stanley Park and then proceeded through Oslo Avenue. This was the same route I used to take to get to The Crucible from Wolfgang's house, albeit inverted. Down the slope in Valmet Street, the Sun Tower imposingly stood above all other constructions, overshadowing the McReady's restaurant nearby and overlooking Crosshair Beach in its entirety. If you walked past it, you'd find yourself in yet another classier and more expensive neighborhood than any other to the east of Pilgrim Coast, called Alexandria Boulevard. Displaying features more fitting of a Cristobal Atoll area, this place was where the luxury and glamour of Loynne's started to really shine. Blocks and blocks of expensive stores with the usual brands – Detènte, Vulgarowski, Bassa Donna – plagued both sides of the road as your eyes got lost in the labyrinth of displays, ads and flashy neon signs. The perfect white and pink tiles exquisitely adorning the springing palm trees, the European tourists walking by, the Hades-Larsson taxi drivers having a coffee break, the occasional but not so rare Sforza car cruising gently down the road, it was all a show. Walking on that area was enough to make you feel rich and important.

One of its main landmarks was the five star Cleopatra's Palaces Hotel. Built as an actual proper palace, the imposing construction sported Egyptian pillars and columns, with archers on top aiming their bows at the sky and a statue of the god of chaos Seth in the middle between them. Below, at street level, gigantic fountains sprayed water onto themselves as the cascade effect poured down its step-like structure. This was at both sides of the majestic hotel. In its center though, a marvelous piece of construction, fashioned after Egyptian temples, laid the entrance to the theater. Yes, the hotel had a world class theater where all kinds of musicals and plays attracted tourists and enthusiasts from all over the world. Russian Ballet was one of its main features, and you'd always see many *nouveau riche* Russian scum congregating outside at night for the show.

Shopping malls, beachfront restaurants, VIP clubs, luxurious clothes shops, five-star hotels, lavish casinos, everything was well within reach, but our destination was the cinema. We took a turn to the right and kept going up the slope, eventually seeing the white, imposing building. It was a shopping mall of sorts, with some stores, supermarkets and restaurants at ground level and offices and apartments above. In Loynne's Island, pleasure, work and residence were inseparable. All the constructions seemed to be a perfect blend of shops and apartments.

We descended the steps to the lower levels, past a toy shop and a Unoq Sports store. Immediately ahead, next to a restaurant, was the cinema. We found Wolfgang inside, staring at the TVs hung from the ceiling, showing movie trailers and the like. He turned his head toward us and laughed in surprise.

"*Konnichiwa, Doshi! Ogenki desuka?*"

"(Not now Wolfie, don't embarrass me ...)"

"Huh? Ah ... oh yeah! So ... how are you guys?"

"Well, pretty good to be honest, strolling with this gorgeous monument around Alexandria Boulevard. Should have seen her, turned all the heads along the way, didn't she?"

"(Now who's embarrassing who, Sonny?)," she whispered, irritated.

"Ah ... see? She totally did. Well, maybe they sort of looked down on her so as to not trample her ... er, anyway, enough. Let's go inside. What are we watching? Please nothing Unitedstatian ... no offense, Faye."

"None taken."

"The only thing they have that's not Unitedstatian is the new Armin Metzger movie, Armin Metzger IV: Seine Teil," Wolfgang said.

"Ah yeah, the one about that cannibal guy. You up for it, Faye?"

"I'll just watch whatever you guys decide on."

"Well ... alright! But don't say we didn't warn you ..."

· · · · ·

We walked out of the cinema, quite cheery, commenting on the exploits of Armin Metzger and his gory cross-country road trip through Central Europe.

"Wasn't that brilliant, you know, when he takes over this nun convent and rapes and eats all the nuns for months? Crazy bastard," Wolfgang said.

"You'd be surprised if you knew how many of those things are based on real world events. At least in there they made it look less disturbing and more comical," I said.

"I know! And it was so amazing when he went and seduced that rich college kid on ChitChat, and then tore him in half and fed him pieces of his own body that fell out of his

stomach. That's what he gets for being so naïve!" That wasn't Wolfgang speaking. We looked at each other in utter disbelief, then at Faye, quite confused.

"And what was all that act about covering your eyes? I think this is the part where we ask why on Earth would a girl like you find anything nice about this perverted gore fest for male audiences? I thought our role was to talk about gross shit as the guys we are and your role was to sound grossed out telling us to shut up while we ignored you."

"I wasn't covering my eyes, I just get eye-strain a lot when watching films, I need glasses but I don't like wearing them at all. I don't mind gore. I actually watch stuff like this all the time. My brothers have me a bit accustomed to it. I don't mind the sex stuff in it either because of the same reason. For instance, Ryan used to show me fucked up porn all the time when I was 9. The kind that has crazy monsters like frogs and stuff raping Asian women. In fact, I used to watch it by myself later on, and ..." She didn't finish the sentence, began laughing silently to herself and turned as red as my Soviet flag. I looked at Wolfgang with an astonished, shocked smile, while he plain burst out laughing, not knowing exactly how to react. I kept staring at Faye with childish curious eyes, as she firmly looked at me with warm ones, covering her mouth in shame.

"Shouldn't have said that! Sorry!" she said, as she did something amazingly daring; she came onto me, expecting to be held by my arms, and submissively fell on my body. I hugged her and quickly pushed her back gently, not used to this kind of contact, which made me feel incredibly nervous. However, I was more interested in the psychological side of the situation and thus decided to ask about it:

"Faye ... you said you what?"

"Oh, c'mon! Don't you guys do that as well? Don't go and judge me! You're probably worse!"

"Ah ... that I recall I started doing that sort of thing when I was 10 years old, but then again, girls are premature in everything they do aren't they? But what comes as a shock the most is that ... you enjoy looking at porn?"

"Well, yeah ... I guess it's just to imagine how it'd be. What it feels like. You know, sex."

"I know what you meant! But, did you say that you ... you do something to yourself while you watch it?"

"Haha ... Sonny boy ... you can't watch that and not do anything about it, can you?"

"Uh ... well, I guess you can't ... it sure feels weird talking to a girl that engages in such a practice like she's one of the guys."

"Well, here you have one! What? I'm a freak because of that?"

"Uh ... I guess you are? I don't know ... I'll get back to you when I meet someone who does too! I mean ... aren't girls supposed to like, not touch themselves?"

"And who told you that? Another girl? Haha ... that's to be expected. Girls never admit they touch themselves, don't you know anything? They'd die before admitting to that."

"And why do you admit it?"

"Well, because I can't be doing with all that bullshit. I've never been like the rest. They're just so immature and girly and stupid. So yeah, I admit I do it because I'm no hypocrite. Of course I do it, and I'm OK with it. I love it." Hot flushes began to take my masculine body over as a hormonal hurricane broke loose and rivers of testosterone kicked in. My imagination had been set to work on picturing this in action. I just didn't know how to feel at what was coming out of Faye's lips.

"Ahh ... yeah ... and ... why are you telling us this? I mean how, do you know we're to be trusted, that we're not assholes

that will divulge this womanly secret and all that?"

"Well, because you're just not like that, Sonny. I think I've known you for some time. And Wolfie doesn't look like he would do something like that either. And even if any of you did, nobody would believe you. The standard is that girls never masturbate. I make sure of that in my everyday life. When a girl says 'ewww this filthy bitch masturbates, did you know?' I just go 'ewww' like all the rest. I make sure not to stand out or seem freaky to others. I'm no coward, but it's easier and I like to be left alone. Besides, like I told you … nobody is gonna believe anything I tell you guys. Everyone knows I'm a virgin, and that I don't talk about things like that. The only person that knows this as well is Chelsea. She's been my best friend for years now so it's understandable. We always fantasized about Frank Boy Al together and all those rockstars. We used to describe to each other the things we'd do to him, we still do. It's a girl thing I suppose …"

"Well … girl thing or not, after this conversation I'm going to have to do something about this. You just don't talk to a guy about these things for a reason … we go berserk."

"I know … I know … but you guys are different. I'm not saying you're like girls, but I dunno … I feel comfy around you."

"Isn't that sweet … Well, listen doll, I have to jet to the bus station, so if you don't mind let's accelerate the walking … yeah, you too Wolfie, let's seize the opportunity and kill the raging boners with the walking."

"Haha, speak for yourself Sonny, I don't have a boner!"

"Yeah, sure … neither do I."

· · · · ·

We spent some time talking while waiting for the bus.

Wolfgang went back home after a while, saying he couldn't stay out so late. It was during this interval that we took our first picture together; I've forgotten now what we could have been possibly been talking about, or how I convinced her into taking a picture with me seeing as she hated them so much, but she agreed all too willingly, and I have that picture with me until this very day. I remember how our faces together contrasted so much, me looking so boyish and her looking like such a woman, despite her girly nature. Her blue eyeliner and her auburn hair with blonde streaks somehow made her seem older, in her 20s.

Faye behaved as if she didn't want me to go away, ever; she had remained faithfully beside me until the Purple Wonder vanished from sight. She waved from the window, looking at me with those warm shining eyes. The waving continued until the bus started moving and got lost in the darkness that consumed the outskirts of Pilgrim Coast. I wished I could have gone back to The Crucible with her and plant a kiss in those beautiful fleshy lips, laugh in Ryan's face for a quarter of an hour and go home with the ultimate feeling of triumph. I fantasized about that day nearing soon.

I spent the rest of the bus ride listening to music and reminiscing about my afternoon out. Faye and Wolfgang didn't seem to develop much chemistry but that was alright, not like I wanted that to happen. They barely talked to each other. I was the core of the troika. It was one of the few times that I felt leader and not follower. Usually there's always some smartass; some Axel, a Ryan or a Dave who can't help but dictate where the herd should be going and what's cool and what's not. Someone who just plain doesn't shut up and completely ignores your contribution, as if the sole fact of being fast-talking and wise-cracking makes him able to rip on others and step on their slower words. Being ignored in a group

is something that affects you gradually. It keeps you from developing and polishing your personality further. It's finally when you break free of that social restraint that you shine as someone else, the person you could not be when surrounded by those socially superior. That night, I had shone like I always did when surrounded by the correct audience. I could be myself, or maybe some other self. Another identity different from the one I adopted while surrounded by the Mantis brothers or the Nazarethes. I had always seen myself as a social chameleon, without ever showing my true colors to anybody. But now I was seemingly developing a true form, a comfortable position in society where an anonymous self wasn't needed. After all, what was there to fear with Faye and Wolfgang? They struck me as the minority I could trust and share secrets with, just like Faye had done before. A small group of individuals who really appreciated me for who I was, and how I was around them; helping them with their isolation while they helped me with mine. Like I've always maintained, a true symbiosis is the key to perfection in every field, the balance you need for anything in life. The whole situation just wouldn't have developed without me, but then again, it wouldn't have happened either had Wolfgang not come. At the time I stopped my train of thought right there, I was just happy enough to be hanging out with friends instead of sitting at home fearing Kannovschina Mondays. It was amazing how everything had changed in the span of a few months. The going back home after school routine, the not venturing out at night – mostly because of not having anything to do at night, not like it was dangerous – life itself at school and the people I interacted with and the whole Kannovschina phenomenon quickly fading away, apparently for good. I guess that people either grow up or get tired of their own antics, but the world I once knew at school was changing beyond recog-

nition. And my life had never felt so intense, so full of wonderful opportunities and unthinkable possibilities.

Brimming with the happiness Faye irradiated me with, I sat back comfortably and set the Hipp-Man to Kino's "*Vos'miklassnitsa*" — "Eighth-grade Girl" — once more letting Tsoi's voice illustrate what I was feeling at the time. I laughed at myself when listening to the song, and surely you would too if you knew the lyrics.

As the bus rode further into the darkness, I tried to comfort myself with the usual supportive monologues that I often fed Wolfgang regarding women, hoping I could believe them myself and all.

CHAPTER XI

The Revolution Betrayed

"A revolution is a struggle to the death between the future and the past."

- FIDEL CASTRO -

Cuban Marxist Guerilla Fighter, Revolutionary, Writer and Theorist, Founding Father of the Cuban Republic, Prime Minister of Cuba, First Secretary of the Cuban Communist Party and Commander in Chief of the Cuban Revolutionary Armed Forces

---

The month of April passed by amazingly fast. Faye, Wolfgang and I kept hanging out, always on week days, since Faye lied to her brothers about pretending to go to afternoon classes, like she had religiously done every afternoon before knowing me. They ignored she'd secretly meet with us, and righteously, this felt like more of a rush. It was a shame that she wouldn't meet me alone, but it indeed seemed that she was afraid of getting into trouble with her brothers should they see her exclusively in my company, something which she knew would sour relations and spoil future gatherings between us. Nevertheless, I was suspecting the primary reason was she didn't want people talking and saying she had been seen around town alone with me. Still, it was a good thing that Wolfgang was behaving in a comradely fashion and choosing to hang out with us, even if he sometimes could be some sort of a third wheel, as Faye had a very explosive

chemistry with me and would barely talk to him except for a couple of disjointed phrases. Still, they got along well and I was surprised that even Wolfgang could make her laugh on certain occasions. It comforted me that Faye could also be some sort of a third wheel at times, especially when I got carried away with my typical conversations with Wolfgang. What I was glad about was confirming that indeed, I wouldn't be a third wheel among them anytime soon; I was the cog connecting both of them in this friendship triangle, and this made me feel even more relevant, the de facto leader of our special troika.

Each time we went out we found ourselves doing something different: the following Wednesday we had once again roamed around Pilgrim Coast, yet this time hanging out at Crosshair Marina, at the corner of the abandoned Iroquois Mall, which was an extremely desolate area directly south of the school people wouldn't visit for some reason. It was one of those lazy school days in the afternoon, which I would have spent by myself locked in my house before, yet this time I had reasons to crave going outside into the world. Being a week day during the low touristic season, the streets weren't as busy as they were during weekends, and people went to and fro clearly not sightseeing, but rushing to places, making our loafing about seem even more pleasurable. I waited for my comrades at the Bus Station admiring the purple and orange twilight, which set the mood quite right for our walk to the marina. We had ordered a pizza in a place near The Crucible, and since I had brought my old-fashioned music player, we spontaneously decided to settle down on one of the benches overlooking the beach below and listen to music. As we watched the sun set, the ensuing atmosphere was one of exhilaration, of enjoying each the company of one another, of losing ourselves in the thrill of having found such friendship

in this cold, hostile and dumb society. Faye's favorite bands such as Green Köontz and Bad Alberta played as we fooled around, laughed about Loynners and imitated their crude accent. We never saw any Kannies, and we delighted ourselves in listening to music banned by their regime, and in making this little corner of the world ours. There couldn't have been a cleaner, more innocent type of fun, yet what we were doing seemed hardcore and enormously out of the ordinary; after all, all of us had barely been introduced to night life, or to a social life for that matter. For Wolfgang and me, hanging out with a girl at night during a week day after school was already too much of a thrill, while for Faye, being in the company of two guys who paid attention exclusively to her probably felt the same.

The week after that one we took it up one notch; disobeying Ryan's and Dave's orders about Faye not being able to be out after 21:00, we had gone to Crosshair Beach and walked all the way to Alexandria Boulevard like we had done on the cinema day, but this time cruising around the beach area. Every single thing we did felt new and fresh, and we laughed and talked all the way through as we saw the luxurious hotels and pubs start to pop in our field of view, places which somehow made those in Paradise Plaza seem more family-oriented. The faces of the people in these places were sharp and street-wise, and all of them were in the 20-40 age group. We stuck out heavily, especially with our juvenile and cheap clothes, yet this only made us feel more of a rush at how we were breaking all the established norms of the stupid and fake society surrounding us. Faye couldn't be happier, while Wolfgang, for once, didn't seem to be behaving like a guy who's never seen a woman.

I was glad to be the leader of the group, as they often did whatever it was I came up with for fun. This is also an im-

portant word, and should be emphasized; for the first time since my arrival on the island, I was having fun. Real fun. I was also glad to be the one who came up with the most fun and popular ideas. I could also tell that Wolfgang's and Faye's social awkwardness completely eclipsed mine. Yet, Faye seemed the sharpest one at times, the most savvy in a way. Or at least, she was really good at pretending to be it.

This all showed during the following incident: now wise to how alcohol was supposed to be acquired in Loynne's when underaged, I took my comrades to a DAUCO 24/7 minimarket to buy some Loynner red rum, which was supposedly the best in the entire world. Wolfgang and Faye somehow feared asking for alcohol as they said the clerk would see our age and subsequently deny it, childishly loathing getting into any kind of trouble or confrontation. I went in fearlessly, and with my tall height and cold personality, I managed to make the clerk think I was at least 19, the Loynner legal age to drink. I exited the shop with the drinks as my friends' faces gleamed with joy and expectation, and on we marched to the beach to listen to more music and drown our social sorrows away. The beach area in Alexandria Boulevard was substantially fancier than the one in Paradise Plaza, and the sunbeds were positioned over wooden boards which also included wooden beach umbrellas. Since we couldn't lie on the sunbeds as they had all been piled up one on top of the other, and the staff near the hotel bars kept guard about that, we sat on the wooden boards next to them under the umbrella, and drank and listened to music well past 02:00. Faye's cellphone, a white and gray old-fashioned model with some kind of April Divine logo sticker stuck to it, kept ringing as her brothers wanted to know her whereabouts. She finally picked it up, uttered some excuse and got rid of them. I felt some sort of thrill at knowing they didn't know I was with her, or

what we were doing, and shared a smile of complicity with Wolfgang as Faye made her way back to us and informed that the fun as over.

The third outing was spent around the Crosshair Beach area once more, which we seemed to have gotten an immense liking to, and we had actually roamed around certain houses that were supposedly derelict, kept like that because of important historical value dating back to the founding of the town, yet rumored to be inhabited oftentimes by dodgy kinds and the two or three homeless that could exist in the island. When entering one of these cliffside houses, we bumped into some kind of groaning lump in the ground wrapped in dirty blankets, and we had laughed and exited with a joyful fright. I felt bad for the person living there, but it was rumored that anyone in Loynne's living like that weren't actually homeless but drug addicts or beggars who chose the lifestyle, so I wasn't too bothered.

The fourth and final outing of April was spent drinking once more, yet Wolfgang couldn't accompany us for such a long time as before. Choosing to do something both different and forbidden, we went up to the eleventh floor of The Crucible, to the staircase leading up to the roof access which was always closed with a padlock, and we stayed outside this door sitting on the steps of the spiral staircase, hidden by the wall-like baluster that surrounded it. We did our little party here, and kept drinking the rum left from the other night. Wolfgang needed to go for some reason, so Faye and I were left to our own devices. We decided to go into the Dakota gas station through Poseidon Park, and we entered the supermarket drunk as we were; I don't remember doing anything in particular, but I do remember Faye clinging on to me and us laughing heavily, saying stupid things, glad to be doing what we considered to be so fresh and cool. We exited the super-

market and roamed around the streets until it was time for her to head back, and as I headed back to the Bus Station with a tipsy march and got on board the Purple Wonder, I felt an intense feeling of relief liberating me of all cares, staring deep into the Loynner night at the black mountains contrasting against the dark blue sky, glad to be where I was, living the life I was living. This was a first for me, and I was sure that Wolfgang and Faye went back home with similar sensations. All of us felt in a way like being in our own TV teenage drama, and our smiles kept revealing how much we had been craving such a situation. Wolfgang, Faye and I had been isolated and repressed by this society for far too long, and lacking understanding and comprehension, there was a lot locked inside all of us that needed releasing, a lot of affection to give. This is something which cannot be understood unless you're shy, introverted, sad, angry, sensitive, thoughtful, analytical, or a combination of at least three of these attributes Some people just don't understand what an enormous ordeal society is for some people, not just the waking up and mingling in it, but being good at it, to bond, to enjoy social situations, to come up with things that not only make us happy, but which manage to make others happy too. Some people have it very easy social-wise, and fail to understand the issues others have when it comes to socializing, to find people or activities that make life fulfilling and worthy. Wolfgang, Faye and I were just like that, and although neither of us wanted to speak out about it, it was clear all of us had been hating society and ourselves for far too long. And now, we had finally found a semblance of respite in one another.

Our bond seemed to be cementing itself so quickly and so positively that Faye was now willing to go out with me anywhere in the school, even though she couldn't waste a lot of her time because of studying. She was really responsible

regarding school matters, that was no excuse. The only reason that deterred me from barging in The Crucible and stealing her away all the time whenever I fancied were, obviously, her brothers. It was a very delicate situation, and I wouldn't be the one harming the diplomatic relations more only because I couldn't restrain my need to have Faith next to me. I tried to take it as a test of endurance and emotional maturity; if I could control my need for her company and at the same time not give her brothers a reason to get genuinely tired of the situation, I would have won. The day Faith formally declared how she wanted our relationship to move forward, I would no longer need to maintain diplomatic relations or otherwise with them.

At school, I inflated my ego whenever Faye approached me in the open, even in front of her friends. Sometimes my older fantasies would materialize and she would spend the entire recess talking to me, whenever I could break free of Ryan's harness or Gordon's grip. Wolfgang would not join us as he preferred to stay around Gordon and Axel, fortunately for me. However, I could never be safe from Ryan kidnapping me not because he hated people not paying attention to him, but because he was incredibly envious of the relationship that had developed between Faye and me.

In any case, this marvelous period of my life was only disrupted by a minor but unforgettable incident. Walking Faith home one day, some of the school's Russian hip-hop wannabes started following her. It wasn't unusual for people at the exit to come into close contact with one another, as everyone almost always headed in a similar direction. However, I put myself on high alert when a gigantic and fat Russian began to talk to Faye, seemingly knowing her from classes. I didn't mind this much. The conversation seemed to be ordinary, like any exchange between two normal school acquaintances.

However, the intentions of the Russian giant became apparent soon enough.

"Hey, so listen, me and my friends here, were wondering, you ever done it? Or you virgin?"

"What? Why are you asking me that?"

"So that means yes?"

"Shut up! Leave me alone!"

"Heh. You done it. You slut, right? Maybe me and my friends take turns with you?"

"Hey, friend. The lady said stop it. So stop it. *Now*," I said, trying to repress my anger.

"And who are you? Boyfriend? Brother?

"No, a friend."

"Then what you want, loser? Get your own bitch."

"You will leave her alone now before I break your face."

"Woah, woah, hold on, you tough guy, eh? Yes? You want fight maybe?"

"Bring it on, I'm right here."

"Sonny, stop it!"

"Sonny? That's your name? Sonny? Sonny for what, 'cause you're baby boy, *gavniuk*?"

"Let's hear yours then."

"Heh, you no know my name? Maxim. Maxim Lyvov."

"Maxim huh? Nice ring to it."

"Hell of a lot better than yours, baby boy."

"Alright, enough bullshit. Let's get to it."

"Sonny, I said stop it! C'mon, it's nothing! Let it go!"

"Step aside, Faye."

The Russian giant put his fists up, that stupid smirk indelible from his face. Confident and believing himself superior in build and size, he began to circle me as everyone stepped aside, egging him on.

"Maxy, Maxy! Beat him senseless!"

The crowd did not bother me as I put my fists up as well, not intending on losing to this poor caricature of Westernized Russian. Compared to the rushes of adrenaline I associated to seeing Faye at school, this scenario didn't even begin to impress me, much less scare me. Calm and calculating, I set to prove myself before this disgusting Russian traitor. His malevolent light blue eyes, a good representation of what modern day Russians had become, stared deeply into mine, his mouth twisted in a mocking smile.

The first hit came from the right, easy to avoid as he was incredibly slow. Unlike Mikey, this guy didn't have speed or experience. He seemed to be a nerdy bully used to get his own way by intimidation, not by actual fighting. I needed to play on this to win. Even though I hadn't fought anybody in a long time, it was impossible to forget how to tackle an opponent like this head on.

I let him grow confident, trying to seem scared, dodging his blows or stopping them with my arms. When they began to hurt I unexpectedly punched him right on the chest.

The Russian tower retreated in surprise, as I pummeled him in those huge fleshy targets for arms he had. It was easy to hit him being so massive. I began to hit him on the shoulders like Mike had taught me to do, in hopes of wearing him down. This guy wasn't used to fighting and, out of size alone, believed to have the upper hand. He began to hit back but discovered I was more tolerant to pain than he was. I took his blows patiently, until they began to hurt too much. Lastly, I sent a devastating uppercut to the stomach and pushed him against a car, crushing him against it with my own body. The crowd roared cheerfully. It was amazing how quickly they switched sides. I wanted to pummel each and every one of

them for not having principles, for being products devoid of ideology guided by simple immature emotions ...

"Stop it, Sonny! You're gonna get us into trouble! Don't touch the car! You'll dent it!"

"SHUT UP FAYE!!" I shouted. The distraction served for the Russian colossus to tackle me, throwing me to the ground. He began to strangle me, curiously uttering "what did I ever do to you?" with a red face, not red because of the effort, but seemingly of sheer embarrassment. I had hurt his pride.

I would have never expected what happened right after. The Russian was blown off like a plastic bag, landing with a heavy thump on the ground.

"You alright, kiddo?"

Mike Levanter had grabbed the Russian monstrosity and thrown him aside as if he were made of cotton. I resented Mike's move. I wanted to see what I would have been capable of against such overwhelming odds. Mike didn't even give me a chance to think of a strategy.

"That was a cheap shot, kid. Care to try that on me? Or on Sonny when he gets back up? Come on, he's here, he can take you on. And he don't need to do dirty tricks to win." The Russian looked as if he were about to cry out of rage and impotence. He left with his friends immediately after.

"Sonny, that guy's a fuckin' pussy but still you can't afford to take on guys like that with your experience. On equal experience, only the bigger guy wins the bout."

"Thanks for the boxing lesson, Mikey, a bit too late though."

"Sonny, are you alright? Why did you have to do it? He was going to kill you!" Faye shouted.

"Nah, nahnahnah ... hold on, Midgetella. Sonny wasn't gonna get killed by nobody. Show some respect girl, will ya? Cut him some slack for once in your life. He stood up for you, yes or no?"

"Yeah ... sorry ... can you get back up, Sonny?"

"Yeah Faye, It's alright. He just caught me by surprise, that's all. We were supposed to be boxing."

"There ain't no rules in the street, kiddo. What you think, the guy was jus' gonna obey the rules and lose? Brighten up Sonny, damn."

"He's not very street savvy. He's too utopian and idealistic. He told me that."

"Why don't you ventilate my whole private life now that you're at it, Fatty?"

"Don't call me that. And yeah, sorry, but admit it, you've had it very easy. You're not used to people being scum."

"I'm not used to dealing with people, full stop."

"Look Sonny, it's OK, you were doin' very well there by yourself, I'm sure you would have done it on your own but I jus' couldn't sit there and watch. Besides, I wanted to hit that stupid motherfucker from a long time now. He thinks he's the big boss man 'cause the dad's some Mafia kingpin or some shit like that. Just a load of crap if you ask me. When it comes down to makin' stuff up like that those damn Russians are better than Loynners. No offense."

"Anyway, I don't think he's coming anywhere near Faye anymore now. I did what had to be done."

"What was he doing exactly? Was he insulting you, Faith?"

"No, no ... he was just being a dick, you know, but nothing so serious like Sonny thinks it is ... I mean ... Sonny defends women a lot, all women."

"That's me, what can I say."

"Mmph ... I'm sure. Anyway I think I get what happened.

Look, let's just go to the bus stop Sonny, we're gonna miss it."

We walked together, a very unusual team. Mike didn't like Faye very much, a legacy he inherited from Axel. Both agreed that my stance on the Faye situation wasn't the right one, and that I should have long ago dropped my obsession. Sensing Mike's body language was enough to know Faye's presence bothered him immensely. He tried to kill the discomfort by lecturing me on street life in general.

"Sonny, you gotta drop the act in times like that, man. I mean, I know your angle. You're all about harmony among men, about utopia, about people sharin' things equally and without fightin'. But lemme tell you somethin', and it's the main reason I don't believe in politics of any kind. Back there you saw what people are actually like. They don't care about honesty, about honor, about valor or principles. They only care about winnin' and seein' you spittin' blood on the pavement. They care about glory, yes, but not as in glory to the nation or glory for the people. All they care about is glory to themselves, about being gods to everyone else, they want everyone to cheer their names and fear their presence. That's why I also ain't into religion. It's all the same game, under different names, under different styles. It's all about cheap-shootin' and stabbin' whomever is next to you in the back to claim his bounty for yourself. It's all about steppin' on friends to get the upper hand. That's life out there. In a fight like that, the best example of what I'm tryin' to describe, you can't be this utopian or honorable. It's about survival. Your call, Sonny." I couldn't help but feel as if Mike was lecturing me on my endeavor as well. Faye shut up like she usually used to do whenever somebody's presence bothered her. She wasn't scared, but always knew when to disappear. Nothing she ever did was dumb. At times, I thought whether she had more brains than all of us put together.

"What you doin', Sonny? You're not comin' to the bus stop? C'mon, you're gonna miss the bus!"

"Ah … I'll catch the next one, Mike. I've got some business to attend to."

"Ahhh … 'course you do. But of course. I won't even say anythin'."

"No, Mike, wait … it's not what you think. Look, I'll explain later …" I said, walking away from Faye's earshot.

"There's nothin' to explain, Sonny boy. You do what you consider's best for you. That's not my problem. If you're sure about what you're doin', then go ahead. No one's stoppin' you."

"Uh … really?"

"Yeah, man. We're your friends, we're here to support you, not to bring you down or nothin' like that. But I will still say it … think about what you're doin'."

"Mike, can I ask you something?"

"Sure, what?"

"We've never really talked about it, because I know you don't like the subject too much, but I understand that, well, you have a girlfriend. How did you fall in love with her?"

"How I fell in love with her? Well … I guess it jus' happened, Sonny boy … everyone falls in love now and then. A mutual acquaintance introduced us, and we started seein' each other … one thing led to another, and soon we were goin' out, buildin' a very trustworthy relationship … but, uh … I'm gonna tell you this because I think you are someone who can be trusted Sonny boy, so don't betray my trust … I can't say I'm havin' the best time of my life with my relationship right now, but … I made my decision to be loyal to this woman, and I have to stand by my original decision. She doesn't really make me happy, but at the same time I can't imagine life without her. Sometimes I feel so oppressed, I jus' want to

leave her and get someone else, but I can't bring myself to do that to her. To tell you the truth, I'm not the best person to talk to about this subject right now, man. I'm goin' through a really weird time right now ..."

"But even so ... you do understand what's happening to me, the not being able to be apart from her and all that ..."

"I don't know what's exactly goin' on in your mind, and it's not like I've been followin' what you've been up to ... but ... I gotta say ... I don't think it's particularly doin' you a great deal of good. Jus' my opinion, man ... don't take every single thing I say seriously ... but that doesn't mean you don't have to rethink what you're doin' neither ... that's your decision, yours and only yours. In my case, I don't know if I've made the right decision, but it's a decision I made and I have to stick to it. At least, I know the girl loves me, if not I wouldn't even bother. She's a pain to be with and she doesn't satisfy me half of the time, and it's not like I'm the best boyfriend in the world neither. We are both goin' through a tough time, but I'm workin' to make everythin' better. But in your case Sonny boy, this girl jus' treats you as a friend. There's nothin' to do there, no matter how hard you try, believe me. If there's no sexual attraction, forget about it, that's what I learned. You should focus on someone else who feels naturally drawn to you, without effort. Well, that's all I can say to you, I guess. Mind your own things and don't let anyone mess with your mind. Bye, man ... take good care of yourself."

Mike smiled faintly, almost disappointed, and dismissed me with a wave of his hand, a gesture that seemed strikingly stolen from Wolfgang. That was it for Mike, I thought. No more respect from him. Unless I of course did what was expected of me and left Faye in the dirt. Sometimes I thought whether I should really do it, but that side was always sunk by my other urges. I was glad that at least, Faye had not lis-

tened to what Mike had said at the end, and thought simply that he was lecturing me on how to be more streetwise:

"Sonny ... don't listen to him ... you did alright back there. Yeah, I know you're a bit too utopian at times, but ... who isn't, right? I mean, of the people that are like us ... we're not fighting machines like that guy, criminals or people with troubled childhoods ... we're normal, peaceful people, raised to be good. We're not supposed to like getting into that sort of trouble. That's just for idiots like that Russian prick back there. Don't let this bother you, it's OK ..."

"You make it sound like I'm traumatized by this, leave me alone already! I've been through things far more horrible than that in my life, you know? Not like it's any of your business in any case ..."

"Look, don't say it. I know how men get hurt, their pride and all that. Don't worry. You didn't embarrass yourself if that's what concerns you."

"You ... you really think so?"

"Sure! Now, come on ... before Ryan gets back home. We don't want him around, do we?"

"We sure don't. Where is he by the way?"

"Oh, I dunno, but all I know is he's not getting back in at least a couple of hours. And Dave went away dunno where too, don't think he'll be coming back in a minute. So you can come around if you want to!"

"Oh ... well, thanks!"

Faye led the way cheerfully, making me wonder if the fight had actually changed her perceptions of me. After all, she knew my bulky frame deterred people from messing with me in the first place, even Kannies. That Russian bastard seemed to have been an exception. She had to feel protected by my presence in some way. I showed that supposedly superior Russian guy how I could not be bullied into submission, all

because I didn't tolerate him bothering Faye. If she hadn't been impressed and flattered by this, then there are not many things I could do to earn her affection. That was as "tough" as I was willing to act for her, since directly abusing her – like some women seemingly enjoyed – was absolutely out of the question; I had defended her honor, from a scumbag, and that was all she needed to think about. I wasn't a regular tough guy who didn't give a damn about her; I remembered what she had said about JC Vega in one of our earliest conversations, and tried to ignore the truth about any girl always preferring a self-destructive alpha-male who will abuse them.

• • • • •

"Want something to drink, Sonny?"

"Oh now that you say so ... got some of that red rum from the other day, gorgeous?"

"Haha ... good joke. My mom would find it in a sec."

"It's alright then, I don't want anything, thank you."

"Did you hurt yourself? When you fell down, I mean? You sure you're alright?"

"Yeah, I mean, I don't know. I don't feel anything."

"Let me see ..." Faye suddenly came up to me, and started checking my arms, rolling up my sleeves. I was so ecstatic I didn't analyze the situation as I usually did. I just sat back and enjoyed her wonderful company.

"Oh my God, Sonny! Look at your arms! Your elbows are all peeled from the fall! Let me get some alcohol and cotton real quick! Just sit here!" Faye went to the bathroom as I sat down on the couch, looking at my laughable wounds.

"(This evening's getting interesting)," I said to myself in a low voice. If either Ryan or Dave dared appear through that door I would have thrown them out of the balcony. Nothing

would spoil this moment.

"Here, I don't think I make much of a nurse, but this'll do, I think … give me your left arm!" Faye was kneeling on the floor to my left, as she poured alcohol on cotton and cleansed my wounds. I couldn't help but admire how well-intentioned she was, what a wonderful wife she could have been; loving, caring, delicate, loyal …

"You don't complain much, huh Sonny? I bet Ryan would be screaming like a little girl right about now …"

"Haha, well … I guess I'm one of those people that don't complain much about things …"

"Tell me about it … I have to be here all day bearing these pansies, 'where's my food, Faye?!' 'Why haven't you washed the dishes, Faye?!' 'Why haven't you made the beds, Faye?!' "

"You make their beds?"

"I told you, I have to do everything round here … they don't do jack shit. Can't wait to get out of here, seriously. Sometimes I don't know how long I'll be able to live here without jumping from Hell's Ravine or something …"

"I know what you mean … but … it's a typical thing to say, but as of now just be happy with what you've got … you know this will end one day. Someday your life will change."

"I really hope so …"

"What do you want to do when you're an adult?"

"Oh, I dunno yet … life is so unpredictable … I guess I'll see when the moment comes, but definitely gettin' the hell away from here … somewhere else … OK I'm done with your arms, let's check your legs now …"

"Should I take my pants off?"

"Ha-ha … you're spending way too much time with Ryan."

"Tell me. He's in class with me. Sitting next to him all day, some things rub off … but I really do think I need to take my pants off, I hurt my thigh not my knees, you know … I can't

do anything except pull them down ... look it's OK, you've done enough, besides it's really nothing ..."

"Are you wearing underwear?"

"Ah ... uh ... of course I am!"

"What, boxers?"

"Yeah ..."

"Well, then there's nothing to worry about! That's like shorts. Come on, we're supposed to be adults ... somewhat."

"Ah ... well, OK ... but only because you insist. If anyone catches you here with me and my pants down I don't think it'll be very good for any of us ..."

"Relax, it'll be quick, just don't pull them down to the ground you know, hold them up to the part where you hurt yourself."

"There, it's on the right thigh, I think I—"

"Oh no Sonny, you cut yourself with something! There's blood all over!"

"What? Let me see ..." I tilted my head to look at the wound, a long scratch which seemed to be shallow, but still had bled copiously.

"I must have landed on some wire ... I really don't know how this happened, I mean, the pants are intact ..."

"Maybe you just landed on something sharp that didn't tear through the clothes and pressed against the skin, those are some really thick tough pants you wear, after all ... look, let's go to my room in case these assholes come in and they catch us here with your pants down ..."

"That's what I just said ..."

"Come on, I think I'll have to bandage this one, or you'll get an infection ..." Faye led the way to the room, and made me lie on the bed on my left side, pulling my pants completely down. Although she didn't appear to have a sexual interest in the whole situation — which was to me undeniably erotic

675

— she also didn't seem put off by seeing my body and touching it. I could not believe this was friendship. There had to be something more to two people being so intimately natural with each other, something far more meaningful than a simple friend thing. My mind instantly remembered the second segment of the 1965 beloved Soviet comedy "*Operatsiya 'Y' i Drugiye Priklyucheniya Shurika*" — "Operation 'Y' and Shurik's Other Adventures" — by Leonid Gaidai, starring Gaidai regulars Aleksandr Demyanenko and the lovely Natalya Seleznyova. In the second segment, "*Navazhdenie*" — meaning delusion, suggestion or hallucination — the nerdy and heroic Soviet student Shurik has his pants torn by a dog, while the girl he's in love with, Lida, offers to sew them but he declines, wishing to do so himself. I don't want to spoil it for you, but I wasn't about to try what Shurik did in the film. Instead, I tried talking again while she cured my wounds, in order to get my mind off of putting her pants down as well. I had made so much progress, I couldn't risk losing everything by jumping on her and force her to not want to see me again. Some time had passed since her last blatant rejection, and didn't want to experience another.

"What was it that you were saying before, Faye? About getting out of here?"

"What? Oh yeah ... well ... I don't know ... I'd really like it if I could get out of here one day, out of the island ... I feel so confined here ..."

"Out of Loynne's Island? I don't know ... have you seen the state of the rest of the world? And more precisely, the state of your country?"

"I know, I know ... Unitedstatians who want to return don't have it very easy, they're deemed traitors and rats ... but even they can return if they play it cool. Well, as long as you look white and praise God ..."

"Well, you wouldn't have a problem with that ... I mean, you even have that cross hanging from your neck, that sure won't go unnoticed over there ..."

"Oh, the cross ... yeah ..."

"Remember that day that I asked you why you had it, and you said one day you'd explain? You never did ... I mean, not like we've had time to talk about it deeply like now ..."

"Yeah, I remember ... well ... it's kind of a long story, but it's a gift from my mom ... she gave it to me when I was really little, like 6, and she said it was a gift so that I would always remember how much I meant to her and how much faith she had in me ... but the truth is ... well ... what would you say if I told you I'll explain some other day?"

"I'd ask why. You sure you can't say it now? I mean, how long could that story be?"

"It's not as long as it's complicated ... and ... well, kinda intimate ..."

"Don't worry ... if it's a family thing, I'll respect it, I mean, what else would I do?"

"Thanks, Sonny ... really, I promise one day I'll tell you."

"It's OK, Faith ..."

"Sonny ...?"

"Yeah?"

"I have something to tell you ..." Faye stopped bandaging my wounds and sat on her knees next to me, her hands on her thighs. My heart beating relentlessly, I did not even know what to predict; my utmost fear perhaps, a scenario where she had met someone she desired ...

"What, what is it? Don't scare me now, I've had enough for two months ..."

"Well ... I'm going to the US ... the whole summer ..."

"To, the US? But ... it's crazy over there, we just talked about it! You want your head blown off?"

"Oh that's just the Midwest. It's gonna be fine, things are alright in California, at least ... I'm going with my mom 'cause she needed someone to go with, and my brothers don't want to ..."

"Well ... makes sense ..."

"Are you mad? I'll come back sooner than you think! It'll be quick!"

"Well, I don't care about time, I care about you not being blown to pieces ..."

"That's fine, I'll try to not go to schools or places with high towers, public buildings, demonstrations ..."

"That's actually a very sensible precaution ..."

"I know ... it was in the informational thingy for tourists, you know, where they talk about risks ..."

"Alright ... well, send my regards to Reagan while you're down there ..."

"Reagan? Oh, I should know this ... no, no idea ... who was that one?"

"The cowboy film star you people had for a president back in the '80s."

"Ohh, that one! The smiley one!"

"All of your politicians smile ... but yeah, nobody looked so contorted while doing it. Looked like his face was about to burst."

"What do you mean all our politicians? Are they the only ones that smile?"

"No, but in typical Unitedstatian fashion, they try to smile all the time so you'll like them better and trust them. It's part of your culture, after all. That culture of fake niceness and forced smiles. You go to a restaurant and the waiter who you don't even know is smiling at you like he's known you all your life. Where I come from, we don't like that."

"That is true ... I never liked that, to be honest. I always

mistrust people who smile way too much. I never smile if I don't feel like it."

"You're like us, then. In Russia, for example, you don't smile to people you haven't been introduced to, it's almost impolite. They think that a smile should be genuine. That's why they come off as cold to foreigners. There's even a saying; 'only a fool smiles without a reason.' I never ever felt the need to smile to people I don't care about, or who I'm going to talk to for just a minute. That's why I come off as cold and distant here to Loynners."

"But I've seen people from Eastern Europe and Russia and everywhere smiling and laughing their asses off, I don't get it ..."

"It's not like we don't like to smile and laugh Faye, we do. But when we do we like it to be honest and genuine, that's all. And those kids you see in school are Westernized Russians anyway, like that Maxim idiot. True Russians immediately reject anything Western, they don't like their culture to be polluted by it."

"I see ... but hey, you left me thinking now! What did Reagan do that was so bad? Isn't he like, one of the most popular presidents?"

"To blind deluded patriots and conservative xenophobes, maybe. To left-wing people and especially Socialists and Communists, he's basically the devil. Here's a rundown for you; he combatted leftist influence in South America and the Middle East in the '80s, aggressively expanded Unitedstatian imperialism across the world, increased the gap between rich and poor, crushed worker's unions and their rights, inspired asshole steroid-junkie actors into making propaganda films about Unitedstatians winning in Vietnam because they were butt-hurt about losing, made it look like he led the glorious USSR to its demise on his own and inspired a revival in Unit-

edstatian right-wing politics that currently has shaped your country into the disgusting nest of backwardness it is today ... and because of all these things, he became an icon to a lot of mediocre and ignorant people, same as with Thatcher in England. For some reason, the most mediocre individuals always tend to go against their own interests by favoring these paper idols who will never fight for their prosperity and interests ..."

"Haha, alright, you convinced me, I'll make sure I spit on his grave!"

"No, it's OK ... I don't think your saliva deserves that ... but if I told you everything he did, you probably wouldn't refrain yourself."

"Well, from what you say it looks like he was a really bad person ..."

"Bad person? Well, I didn't know him personally ... I wouldn't say that ... in any case, in politics it doesn't really matter what you are as a person, but the value of your policies and their impact on the peoples. Reagan was just a puppet for all the powerful entities he represented and defended ... nothing but a lackey. I don't understand how anyone can admire a clown like that. We in the left have not only ideals, but the intelligence and the knowledge to defend our ideology. These politicians like Reagan have only three weapons; their smile, their hair and their tales about how if you vote for the left the reds will eat your babies. We have documented facts and a thirst to end fallacy and injustice. They are simply puppets designed to combat us, mercenary dogs who serve the financial interests of a few. I'm actually very sorry for anyone mediocre and ignorant enough who falls for that type of cheap right-wing propaganda ... to me, it's like this; working-class people voting against their own interest by choosing the right-wing make a completely self-destructive decision.

They have nothing to win by voting right-wing, all the contrary, everything to lose. However, rich people voting against their own interests by choosing left-wing parties makes for an entirely noble and admirable act. They choose to sacrifice their privileges to benefit the rest. Mr. Reagan, on the other hand, is among those who choose the worst possible option; being part of the elites and defending their interests with force and lies. All the while without even having the remotest idea of what Communism even stands for. Ignorant actor clown ... actors shouldn't be allowed to become politicians, yet ironically they're infinitely better suited for the job. Anyway, that's life for you ..."

"Haha ... I love it when you get all political!"

"Yeah, well ... somebody's got to do it ..."

"Haha ... oh, and Sonny ... something else ..." Faye suddenly got up and leant next to me, kissed me on the cheek and started hugging me affectionately, not minding the fact that I was still in my underwear.

"Thank you for being my friend ..."

"Oh, ah ... it's OK, Faith! I'm here for you!" I cannot describe my state of euphoria at that moment. My heart on the verge of collapse, I closed my eyes and enjoyed her hug, seizing the chance to caress her hot and soft pale skin with my fingertips, enjoying the smooth texture of her lower back. I did not want to even imagine what it would feel like to kiss her on the lips gently, to hold her hands while making love ...

"OK. Listen Sonny, pull your pants up. The wounds will be OK now, I think. And you should go now in case anyone returns, I don't think they'll take it kindly seeing you here, and I don't want to hear Ryan moan about you again ..."

"Yeah, I know what you mean ... thanks for everything Faye, I'll catch you around at school."

"Listen, take the service elevator in case you bump into

them. It will drop you off at the basement, then you have to take the stairs, just make your way to the ground floor lobby and exit through the main entrance, they never go through there ..."

"You sure know how to avoid them, eh?"

"Well ... that's what I do when I don't want them to see me walk out, when I'm sick of being in the house with them ..."

"Well, I'll try and see if I can be as sneaky as you ..."

"You sure you don't want anything to eat or drink before you go? I got chicken croissants!"

"You ... you do?"

"Sure I do! Two of 'em!"

"Well ... wha—why didn't you say so?! Give them to me!! I mean ... hope you don't mind!"

"Haha, I knew you'd say that! Look, come here to the kitchen ... OK, I'll tell Dave me and a friend ate them. They're his, he brought 'em from school ... I'm takin' the heat for this one Sonny! See how good I am?"

"Oh, you're a complete angel, Faye," I said, kissing her on the forehead. I did it so naturally I didn't even realize. Surprisingly, Faye didn't seem uncomfortable with it, and just laughed joyfully.

"Haha! Well ... I knew you were hungry, I mean, you always are ... I've seen you at school eating these things, you always look so out of it, like possessed. So listen, I'll talk to you on ChitChat if I see you tonight, alright? Go on, run along now! And please don't choke!"

"Heh, I'll try ... *dasvidanya*!"

"What's that?"

"That's 'see you later' in Russian, literally 'until we meet again.' "

"Haha! Your accent is so funny ... say something else!"

"Mmm ... *Ia tebya lyublyu*."

"And what's that mean?"

"Oh ... I don't think you want to know ..."

"Haha ... alright, then ... your momma, just in case! Bye Sonny!"

"Bye, Faye."

The door shut behind me softly, as I made my way to the bus station. I took a minute to enjoy the view, breathing deeply and still feeling the warmth of Faye's velvet hands on my body, the taste of her soft skin on my lips. I had kissed her affectionately, with genuine love and not teenage lust, like a husband who kisses his wife when leaving for work. She hadn't even flinched in rejection; times were surely changing. I knew that one day she would eventually open to me. One day she would be mine, and I would be hers. We would have each other and would combat the evils of Western life living together, making each other happy. There simply wasn't any other person in the world as honest, caring and beautiful as she, and no one would ever convince me of the opposite.

· · · · ·

Even if the situation with Faye seemed on the way up, outside of our little inner circle things were beginning to deteriorate. My bond with The Mantis brothers seemed to be declining. Tory, Mario and the Nazarethes didn't care much about my obsession with Faye, but they were visibly absent as well. Talks about me hanging out with Ryan's little kid sister circulated and I could sense her friends studying me with malicious eyes, laughing inside like little girls do. It was an era where I felt everyone laughed at me. They simply had no respect for someone of my social standing hanging out with Faye. It was a prohibited friendship, a status demeaning situation I could not help. Gordon's gang had never had any

respect for people that wasn't like them, and ridiculed anyone that had aspirations of getting a girlfriend. It was comprehensible; after all, it was their way of dealing with an inability to attract a member of the opposite sex. Axel and Mike couldn't stand my endeavor either. Axel because he saw it as pointless and didn't like Faye, thinking she was the kind of innocent looking woman who uses men for her own manipulative purposes, and Mike because he knew what having a little sister was like, and strove to protect her by any means. In his eyes, I was the evil seed of men, an obscure corrupter of virgins and violator of the unwritten codes regarding sisters of friends. At least Axel just thought I was being a dick and nothing more. But even so, Mike disliked Faye at a personal level as well, only he never said it aloud.

Yet this Faith hate had quite the opposite effect on me. By wanting to get rid of the Faye situation for good, those around me reaffirmed me on my feelings and convinced me that they couldn't be true friends. My official stance began to be that they simply couldn't understand how someone could develop such an affectionate relationship with a woman without actually being with her. After all, they didn't know me. Nobody did. They were no one to judge the situation from afar and dictate a beneficial solution based on simple speculation. From this conclusion onwards, I openly ignored and dismissed anything related to an anti-Faye stance. Having this secret bond with Faye, where no outsider could intrude in, always energized my will. It made my life seem less tortuous, and as such I stopped thinking of my original goal at times. Did it actually matter that I wasn't officially with her? I had never been happier beside another human being. Faye was beautiful as a person, and never did anything that bothered or hurt me. The rest of my friends could not even hope to bring me to such levels of social satisfaction, and it

was terribly obvious that none of them cared about me like Faye did. It didn't matter for the time being whether I was simply her friend or something else. The growing affection she was developing for me was enough to make me want to get up and go to that prison filled with loud braindead drones.

I kept on hanging out with the Mantis brothers, even if it was exclusively for diplomatic purposes. Nothing good would come out of neglecting my friends and finding myself without allies in such a place. In hopes of strengthening my bond with them and making them forget about my infatuation, I tried to conceal my true feelings. I of course intended on carrying on with my secret plans, but for the moment she needed to keep thinking I had laid down my arms for good. Only one thing was certain; I had to hurry. The thoughts of someone rushing to ask Faye out just like I had done – and their feelings being compatible – always corroded the volatile and sporadic happiness I was experiencing.

Soon, we found ourselves traversing through the first days of May. My birthday was on the 9th. During this time I had never celebrated it in Loynne's with other people, and found the concept to be awkward. I didn't think a celebration was needed. I didn't want to be the center of attention for a predetermined reason, and hated parties anyway. From my experiences, birthday parties often brought frustration and rage to the celebrated, as many unpredictable factors could arise. Firstly, as the party is organized and not spontaneous, people can fail to achieve the right mood for partying, the celebrated included. This not only results in a boring and useless outing, but a phenomenal waste of money. And secondly, I didn't ever trust my moody disposition to be fully energized for a birthday with people, and on this particular occasion I would crave Faye's attention more than anyone

else's. Should this fail, I would not enjoy myself at all. No, the concept of the birthday scared me, and brought me incredibly bad feelings. I wanted to avoid the subject altogether, but once again fell powerless to Faye's charm.

Preparations for my birthday began one day, when I dropped by the Mantis' household expecting to catch a fleeting glimpse of Faye, like usual. Seeing her three seconds was well worth spending the rest of the afternoon in the company of Ryan or Dave, and I gladly took the risk. In the best of scenarios, I would be able to kidnap Faye for the rest of the day until the night.

But it was not to be. I was greeted by Mario, a very unpredictable encounter. Dave was sitting on the couch laughing uncontrollably at the TV, and I presumed he had commanded Mario to do his bidding while he indulged in his vices. Had he been born a Tsar, Dave would have been worse than Ivan Grozny.

"Hey Sonny, check it out, we're watchin' Ink Whores!" Mario said, positioning himself to the right of Dave. I remained standing, preferring to keep my distances from Dave as I always did when I didn't approve of his behavior.

"You what?" I said.

"Check it out, it's this show about a bunch of tattoo artists from LA that are always fighting and stealing each other's boyfriends!" Dave responded. I took my time to understand what I was seeing, but failed miserably.

"Yo bitch yoo think yoo can tattoo better dan me? Yoo outta yo mind, sista, imma one 'ard-ass mothafuckin' tattoo artist, 'now 'am sayin'?"

"Yeh yeh aye, sheck dis shit out, no hands, jus' feet!"

"Would yoo look at dat black ho' tattoin' with 'er feet!"

"Dat's the way you do it sister! 'Now am sayin'? Mm

hm?"

"*Ah can tattoo better dan dat Mexican-ass Latina bitch, sheck it out, imma tattoo dis fat ho' with mah own mouth!*"

"*Woohoo, babeh! Look at 'er go!*"

"What is this?" I asked, irritated.

"Dunno, some new reality from RTV. Crazy shit, huh?" Mario let out.

"Change the channel. This is pissing me off," I said.

"No, no, let's just leave it a for a while, let's see what they do next!" Mario said.

"*Up next in Ink Whores, we discover the truth behind Jessie B's sexual past, plus Crystal's very own addiction to meth!*"

"*Ah swear ah loved the motherfucka, he was so gangsta, so reliable, y'know? But he trash, yoo hear me? Trash like all men. Mm hm, hear me out yoo son of a bitch, yoo listenin' out dere imma pull yo cock out, put sum superglue shit over it and jam it up yo asshole, homeboy!*"

"*Ah don't know what was goin' on in Jessie B's mind, but one thing's fo' sho' ... he one crack-smokin', dope-dealin,' mothafuckin' hustla, yoo all got what I'm sayin'? Mm hm?*"

"How does a country that goes around preaching the moral word of God end up having a show like this? And didn't this channel used to be about music?" I asked.

"Nah, they got bought by that corporation, what's it called ... Reality Check. And who the fuck cares anyway, Sonny. It's just a show, sheezus! Give it a rest!" Mario said.

"Give it a rest? Don't you find anything wrong in this? Am I the only sane person left on Earth that realizes they've crossed the line?"

"Since when did you start defending religion?" Dave asked.

"I'm not! I'm just pointing out that they say one thing and do another ... don't people complain? And not only that, TV is becoming stupider by the minute! They're US citizens, they're your compatriots, you should understand how this goes because I don't ..."

"Oh well, woohoo Einstein, welcome to the real world! Unless you didn't notice, that's what most people do Sonny, they say one thing and do the complete opposite ... you think Unitedstatians are all the same? Yeah sure, you got square churchgoers, but then the rest of the people go talkin' a bunch of shit about Jesus and the Book and then they go fuck some sluts and deal some crack in peace. That's the way it is, Sonny. Nobody has ideals, nobody gives a shit about nothin'," Mario said.

"And what about the detrimental state of people's intelligence? I mean don't you feel insulted watching this? I mean ... it's even worse than when TV used to be all about throwing yourself out of a seven story building with your friends in a shopping cart. Because now they do it for free on VapidVidz.com."

"TV's always been stupid, if it weren't this, it'd be some other fucked up shit. You really care that much?" Dave asked.

"Mph, whatever. Forget I said anything ..."

"Anyway, enough of these black hoes, they're giving even me headache. Let's roll," Dave said.

"Why, where are you going?"

"I gotta go to the chinks in Méndez Center to get me a charger for this fuckin' phone, it's dead again."

"By the way, what's Ryan doing?" I asked.

"Ryan's there in the room, but ignore that asshole, come with us man, he's only gonna kidnap you in the room and

bore you to tears with his stupid shit. Come on Sonny you need some fresh air."

"I sure do, I have been roaming the whole city by myself like a bum all day ..."

"Ah, whatever, just come with us then we can come back to the house if you're feeling tired."

"Fair enough ..."

"Hey guys, I'm gonna go hit the gym now so if you don't mind I'll jus' go right to the bus station, a'ight?" Mario said.

"Sure, come on let's head out," Dave said

We walked out of the house and began talking on the way to the Méndez Center, dismissing Mario at the zebra crossing. Dave seemingly had lots of gossip for me and didn't doubt for a second about telling me every single sordid little detail about his brother.

"Thank God Ryan didn't hear you comin' in, I just saved your ass from one borin' ass day. Dunno what he's up to, but I think he's found a girlfriend. Trippin', huh?"

"Ryan? Ryan found a girlfriend?"

"I dunno, but I really think so, and for me to say this, imagine it. I really never thought it was possible. Ha, ain't gonna be better than my Neelie anyway, not by a long shot."

"What? Who?"

"Heh ... Sonny, Sonny ... he's not the only one who's found a girlfriend lately."

"You too huh? Well, that's not very surprising ... how'd it happen?"

"Wait, wait ... let me tell you about him first. I'll get on with it after."

"Well go on, what do you know so far about this?"

"Well, this is one of them things that I think he'll show off to absolutely everyone when he's ready, so I don't think we'll have to wait long to know the full truth. But anyway, I'll let

you in on what I know. I think he's banging Daphne."

"Daphne? *The* Daphne?"

"Yeah. I don't know how he managed, if it's true that is. But I think that he's finally made it for real. I've been on ChitChat talking to Daphne these days and she seems really cryptic, like hiding something. I think that in all fairness we can say that Ryan finally banged something decent."

"Oh well ... good for him."

"Yeah, good for him. He can have Daphne all he wants ... I got my Neelie ..."

"Is that a hint of jealousy in your voice or is it me?"

"Jealousy? Yeah right. I could have that bitch whenever I wanted. She's just not my type. Too quiet and awkward. Just leave that one to Ryan. Neelie's a friggin' model. I have a model for a girlfriend. You know what that means? I'm going up in the social ladder bad. Stickin' to a girl like this is paradise. I get the best pussy and social status at the same time. I'm made for life Sonny. I finally made it. All the other sluts can go fuck themselves. I found a real keeper for once."

"Ah ... good for you."

"The only shame is you. Let's trust you can find a proper grade A bitch soon. I know you think hanging out with my sister is giving you a lot of possibilities but to be honest nobody thinks that. Ryan and I think she's just dunno, going through a phase. We seriously doubt she'll end up with anybody for the moment. Too much of a square and a virgin. She's afraid of the cock. And I don't think she particularly likes anybody. She's too picky. By the time she finds a man she'll grow bats down there."

"I don't want to talk about this now, Dave. Can we change the channel again?"

"Fine, fine, I just thought you would have liked to hear our opinion. You are lagging behind, Sonny. You need some fine

pussy to drill too. What are you, gonna end up like Tory? Get yourself some while you can. Believe me. I know some guys that didn't get laid until they were like 25 and bought a car. That's some sad story."

"Dave, I don't care about 'banging' anybody. To me, this needs to be worthwhile. I don't look forward to sex just for the sake of it. I have to admit it does make me curious, but I don't think I want my first experience to be so conformist and boring. I want it to be an all-out celebration, a magnificent event I'll never be able to forget."

"Ha, get off the cloud again! Jeezus! Those things are for girls, man. First time, special? That's only in the movies. In the real life, what happens is that you just bang someone who wanted to be banged and then you forget about each other when someone better comes along. Women usually get the best out of this 'cause they get experience with some schmuck and then move on. Guys, on the other hand, need to actively hunt for pussy, and these evasive fucks can be really annoying. I was so lucky. This blonde bitch goes and introduces me to her cousin and we instantly like each other ... I know, surreal, right? But it goes to show, Sonny. I was after her, and it didn't work, but she presented me someone even better that I ended up banging! And Ryan seems to be on the same path. Now it's your turn. Maybe my sister can arrange a meeting with one of those friends of hers, just avoid this one bitch, what's her name ... Chelsea, I think."

"I don't think your sister's friends are a solution, but thanks anyway. And I know Chelsea alright. I don't do necrophilia."

"Yeah, I know, she thinks she's one of those friggin' goth undead black metal faggots. I mean is there anything gayer than a fuckin' wimpy pale-skinned freak with black hair and nails and make-up that looks like he's just done suckin' off a

corpse? Goddamn they piss me off. Luckily we don't have many of those corpse lovers here. Mostly in the North, them."

"Dave … look … I just, I don't know … I'll be honest with you … I really think that I could make your sister happy, and the other way round too. I think we could be very good together. You know I would never harm her, and that I can be trusted. If this would get in our friendship, well … nobody can know, but I would do my best to ensure it doesn't get damaged. I truly respect your sister, and well, wish nothing but the best for her. I still have hopes that we could end up together, but I'm not relying on it. Instead, I'm focusing on being her friend and seeing what happens. She has a good time with me, and if she didn't she wouldn't even want my company, would she?"

"Yeah, yeah, I know what you're trying to say, Sonny … I just don't think there's any hope, really. I think you're deludin' yourself. But whatever. Whatever you want. You'll be the one hurt in the end, not me. I'm just watchin' over your well-bein'."

"And I appreciate it, but I don't think I need it. Like I said, I have it under control."

"Yeah … and now … wanna talk about your birthday or not?"

"My birthday? Who told you?"

"My sister's lips ain't as tight as you think they are … she told me it's on the 9th. Why didn't you tell anybody else?"

"Well, because I didn't want to celebrate it. And I only told her because she asked me a lot."

"Why, man? We're your friends, that's what friends are for …"

"I don't know, it's something personal, alright? I just don't feel good celebrating my birthday. I haven't been able to since I … since a long time ago."

"Come on man, we can make it good for you, we could like, go to Crosshair Beach, all of us, get some drinks and shit, you can bring the radio along, pizzas, I dunno, the usual, but on the friggin' beach! It could be awesome! Come on man, don't miss on a great time!"

"I guess, we'll have to see."

"Look, I'll organize everythin' for ya, alright? Just leave it to me. I know how to make parties. And they never come out wrong, I swear."

"Well, if you say so ... but no outsiders. And nobody that I don't trust in there. I want it to be just us."

"Yeah, yeah, I know. Don't worry. I'll take care of every-thin'. But my sister can't go."

"What? Why?!"

"Because I don't want her drinkin' surrounded by men in the middle of the night! Are you stupid or what? I can tell you've never had a sister before ..."

"She'll be fine if it's just us! Come on! Let her go. She'll behave ..."

"It's not her behavior I worry about ..."

"Oh, it's me now, isn't it? Well you don't have to worry about me either. I don't know what sort of guy you think I am at this point, but if you think I'm about to jump on your sister in front of my friends and her brothers just because I'm drunk you can really stop being my friend now ..."

"Sonny, Sonny ... don't get like that. I just don't like that environment for her at this age, alright? There's ... better ways."

"Let her go. I promise nothing will happen. Everything will be alright and we'll have a good time, like you said. End of story."

"Look ... fine ... but promise me no funny shit."

"Promised."

"Well ... good enough, I guess. Come on, we're at the shop already, just 'round this corner. I hope the fuckin' chinks don't follow us around, though ... I ain't snaggin' more than one or two pens anyway ..."

· · · · ·

Dave had taken care of everything, and my only obligation was to bring my absolutely unfashionable, outdated and nostalgic portable radio-cassette player – one of the only possessions that came with the apartment – money for the drinks and some CDs to play. The rest, whatever it was, rested entirely in my friends' hands.

Confident in everything being organized and having only to wait for the time to go to the bus stop, I foud myself watching TV once more. My eyes instantly recognized and became thrilled at the sight of Michael Weinstein's image at a United-statian talk show, an event of surreal properties by any means. Shinaqua, the hostess of the show, was an extremely fake and pretentious rich fat cow always sporting a new luxurious wardrobe in every show, this time going for a black and pink secretary-styled outfit designed to obscure her ghetto upbringing. Shinaqua, trying to conceal her black heritage, spoke in a white accent trying to imitate blue-eyed blonde Anglo-Saxon anchorwomen from CMN News:

"A rare occasion on the show, tonight we have Michael Weinstein, journalist and all-around political activist. Michael is known for his apparent hatred of current trends, his theory that society is in full and steady cultural decadence and what many perceive to be a full-fledged anti-American agenda. Today on the show with you, it's Michael Weinstein! Applause for Michael!"

The camera began to show the audience booing and hissing violently at Michael Weinstein, who strolled firmly and confidently across the stage in his impeccable suit, shaking hands with Shinaqua and then sitting on one of the available couches. His clean-cut appearance made him truly seem one of the conservative pundits usually seen on CMN News, but the expression on his face was one I knew all too well; it was that facial expression you cannot possibly hide under the certainty that your knowledge is vastly superior to the one of your adversary:

"Terribly sorry Michael, please allow me to apologize for the mood of the audience today, I swear they didn't mean any harm to your person."

"None taken, I'm used to it."

"I want to assure you Michael that it's truly a pleasure to have you here today."

"The pleasure is all mine, Shinaqua. But before we begin I'd like to tell your audiences and anyone who may be watching something. I don't have an anti-Unitedstatian agenda. I fight for a more democratic, progressive and humanitarian United States that behaves as a friend to the world and not its police. What can seem like an anti-Unitedstatian agenda from my part is simply due to the fact that I do not celebrate the military and political repression the US has exercised throughout the world since the end of WWII and I strive to end the military culture Unitedstatians celebrate in order to create a more peaceful one. I want a United States where nobody is denied healthcare, where nobody is forced by peer pressure and ostracism into religions or ideologies and more than anything I want a United States that stimulates international cooperation and eco-

nomic prosperity without resorting to full-fledged military campaigns or occupations of any kind in order to force others into accepting its socioeconomic model."

"May I ask then Michael, why is it that you deny America and Americans the right to be referred to as such? Why do you deny them their right to their nationality?"

"Shinaqua, you and I both know what has happened in this country. The name 'America' to refer to the US needed to be replaced, it was a historical mistake on the part of the British and the Founding Fathers who constantly referred to the landmass that is the present US as America out of sheer laziness and simplicity, instead of giving the land a name of its own like all the other American nations have. The first settlers that arrived in what is now the United States simply referred to the new land as 'America' because it was the name of the entire continent, and no official term ever arose to describe it aside from North America. The Thirteen Colonies were officially named the United Colonies of North America by the British, but even them referred to the colonies simply as 'the American Colonies.' Why was the United States named The United States of America then? Because the name stuck for its simplicity. It was pure laziness on the part of the Founding Fathers, and especially Thomas Jefferson, who supposedly coined the term in the Declaration of Independence. Nowadays however, with the undeniable rise of Latin America and its geopolitical importance, the need to stop referring to the US as America has been made evident. When you say 'America' in English you're not being fair to the other Americans, who also have a right to be referred to as such, but you're also making the issue confusing. What is an American? Before there was a time where you said 'American' and it meant 'US citizen,' but with the rise of Latin America people now say 'Americans' to refer to Latin

Americans instead of US citizens. The decline of the US is an undeniable fact, and its influence around the world waning before the rise of European, Asian and Latin American types of nationalism is the reason for this. The renaming of the US is entirely up to its people, and several solutions were proposed but most Unitedstatians didn't want to partake in the renaming of their nation out of patriotic zeal. As such, there is nothing that the outside world can do if you refuse to get on with the times. The times have dictated that the US no longer has the right to appropriate the term 'America' all for itself, and as such anyone living outside of the country will not use 'America' to refer to it, but to Latin America and particularly South America. US citizens referring to themselves as Americans are simply refusing to get on with the times. This could be a golden opportunity for the US to change and create a new type of ideology, a new current that could maybe integrate the US back into the international community under a new form, a new name. Leaving all the old obsolete values behind is a quintessential part of progress, and the US cannot be blind to this fact if it wants to survive. As a demonstration of cultural deterrence, to exercise my right to freedom of speech and expression and to uphold and defend the rights of all the American peoples, I refer to all US nationals, myself included, using the current official demonym, Unitedstatian, derived from the Spanish 'estadounidense,' the French 'états-unien,' the Italian 'statunitense' and the Portuguese 'estadunidense.' The term 'American' to refer to US nationals is not only regarded by the various communities of Latin America to be discriminatory, partial, inaccurate and offensive in regard to their legitimate status as Americans, but to the nation of Canada as well as other communities of the world where the term is considered to be unfair and devoid of real legitimacy in a

changing 21ˢᵗ century where the influence of the US over other nations, be it political, economical or cultural finds itself unmistakably weakening for the first time ever since the Cold War. Americans are each and every one of the peoples who inhabit the American continents, and as such the abusive usage of the term cannot continue to be tolerated. I actively campaign inside the US to have the official name of The United States of America changed, with the word 'America' removed and replaced with a native term chosen by its citizens that characterizes the nation more accurately. Although it is illusory and naïve to expect Unitedstatians to willingly engage in the process of renaming their own nation, we shall express our discontent and voice our opinions in hopes that one day, the term 'American' stands for anybody living in the American continents and not US nationals alone. We will refuse to acknowledge their nationality and will refer to them as either 'Unitedstatians,' 'US citizens' or 'US Americans,' but never 'Americans.' I also strongly encourage countries like Russia and Germany which do not have a unique demonym for US citizens and continue to use 'American', to create a form similar to 'Unitedstatian' and cease use of the incorrect term 'American.'

If the American people are to fight for their emancipation from the imperialistic interests of the dying Unitedstatian Empire, this should be the first step. As long as the United States continues to use the name and ignore the blatant insulting nature of the issue, it will continue to represent a challenge and a provocation to the heritage of all other American nations. They can continue to use the term if they wish to do so, but we will not. I absolutely refuse to keep granting them the privilege to appropriate the term for themselves, and if they understand and defend the liberty and sovereignty of all nations like they say they do, then

they have the political and moral obligation to treat this issue accordingly. Latin America has suffered enough at the hands of US imperialism and the interests of foreign financial entities to be refused this by its abusive neighbor to the north; it is time to rise up and defend the rights of all Americans and continue to fight for true integration and peace, never by surrendering or bowing to Unitedstatian provocation, standing tall with dignity and pride. As long as the United States continues to call itself 'America' and wage war on ideologies, popular movements or socioeconomic systems it cannot understand or tolerate, we will not consider it a friend, and will never do so unless its unceasing arrogance, double standard politics and military hostility stop.

"OK Michael, that's, uh ... great! Now, if you don't mind me getting straight to the point to seize all the available time, will you tell us a brief background on what your latest campaign is about?"

"With pleasure. In the face of the newest Unitedstatian campaign against Latin America, what many call 'Operation Vulture,' I want to use this occasion to increase awareness of what I regard as one of the greatest crimes of the United States; Operation Condor, the CIA's greatest opportunity to maintain the military hegemony of the US in Latin America. I want to make the public aware of how the United States is deliberately crushing the ability of foreign countries to choose their types of government and ideology, and how many continue to ignore the hypocritical side of Unitedstatian politics. There isn't a better way to understand Unitedstatian foreign intervention than this. Operation Vulture is the newest iteration of Unitedstatian intervention in Latin America, and it consists of disposing of democratically elected leaders who do not agree with the Unitedstatian belief that Latin America should remain a US back-

yard. To do this, the United States has resorted to its intelligence agencies in what many suppose are coups from afar, handled through biological weapons instead of direct military intervention. Biological warfare is no stranger to the US government; the CIA has been experimenting with cancer inducing weaponry since the '70s, and chemical weapons like the infamous agent orange used in Vietnam demonstrate how far the US will go for certain military conquest. There is absolutely no reason to discard the theory of the US giving Latin American leaders cancer on purpose. The numerous assassination attempts on Fidel Castro prove this. Over 600 assassination attempts carried out, none of them successful. If so, they only served to demonstrate the inhuman practices of the CIA and the fascist policies of the US government.

Operation Condor, on the other hand, consisted of a military campaign orchestrated by a consortium of right-wing South American groups to suppress Marxist activity in the continent from the shadows with the objective of eliminating every single trace of left-wing ideals, that is, in the form of oppressive military dictatorships. This event remains largely unknown to most people, and the US never received punishment from the other nations of the world for this humanitarian disaster where thousands were imprisoned, tortured and executed for their left-wing ideals. I think it's time for the US to not only admit to these crimes openly, but to ask for forgiveness in a manner where all nations harmed during Operation Condor can come to terms with the North American country, especially Brazil, Argentina, Uruguay, Paraguay and Chile. The US owes massive monetary and moral compensations to these nations devastated by their right-wing propaganda and the influence of the CIA, and it's about time that the UN acknowledges the damage of indi-

viduals who lost entire families to this petty military intelligence race of the Cold War. The massive funding of the CIA allowed for these military coups not only to be successful and maintained for a long time, but also allowed for United-statian multinationals to prey on the decaying body of Latin America like they did with the copper mines in Chile, miners forced to work on the harshest of conditions ever imagined by man, entire nations losing their rich patrimony only to sell it at the low price of necessity. The South American criminals who took part in Operation Condor have been mostly punished and are currently dead or serving prison time. However, the US never received any form of punishment whatsoever, and the people who were well aware of it have remained completely unscathed until now. Well, not anymore. In my opinion, and I'm speaking as a United-statian citizen, it's about time that they hand the people responsible to justice. Like the Nazis, these people need to pass through Nuremberg trials for their humanitarian crimes, and I am obviously talking about one very specific individual who does not need to be named. About someone who has remained unpunished the most, and kept a nice upstanding position in the form of an international consulting firm of dubious activities. That person in particular is the one that I'm targeting. The one who got away completely unscathed, the one who for his acts of torture and murder all across Latin America was rewarded with a Nobel Peace Prize ... although this individual is now dead, I want to strip him posthumously of this noble award to protest the murders in Operation Condor, and as such bring justice to the countless American countries destroyed by the wake of torture, murder and repression in the name of Unitedstatian interests against ideological currents perceived as threats. If you truly value life, if you defend the right of nations to

democratically elect their leaders and harbor ideologies of their own, you are in the moral and civic duty of denouncing the actions of your bellicose government. This is meant to make everyone understand the plight of entire nations abused under Unitedstatian influence, and make you think about what you can do to change our perception of the United States, which right now is largely negative not only in Latin America, but across the entire globe. Citizens of the United States, I formally encourage you to think about this and cast all patriotism, tradition, arrogance, hatred, paranoia, fear and self-righteousness aside as promoted by your culture, media, government and society. It's time for all of us to be extremely self-critical, from whichever nation or political ideology we might be, but you should be more than anyone. The criminal actions of your manipulative government and the political doctrines and the economic theories encouraged, promoted and supported by you have left us in this shattered and fragile world, and it is now time for you more than any other society to take a hard look in the mirror, to analyze your past actions in order to discard obsolete traditions in favor of new ones, and proceed to truly walk into a brighter future. If we are to live in a prosperous, safe and civilized world, certain efforts are required from all of us, namely a true approach to global peace and cooperation, a massive rejection to the elitist interests of a wealthy, powerful and corrupt elite and an absolute respect to the different and varying sociopolitical needs of all nations.

As the citizens of one of the most powerful and influential nations on Earth, you have the duty to make this change. It rests completely on your shoulders, as only you can decide whether your country engages in building a truly stable and peaceful world, or if it will keep trying to police it through war, coercion and violence, which needless to say, will result

in negative outcomes for everyone. This change is up to you. We want nothing but cooperation, peace and friendship, but won't be able to achieve it as long as the priorities of your country's elite – and some of its population – keep being world conquest, military dominance and Unitedstatian superiority. We, the rest of the world, will keep watching, expecting this change more than anything in what can be considered perhaps the direst moment in the history of mankind. And we shall expect this change without as much as a single drop of blood spilled."

"Michael, you've mentioned 'cultural deterrence' before. Can you tell us a bit more about it?"

"You can call cultural deterrence the driving ideological force behind my work. Cultural deterrence is a peaceful, non-violent solution which seeks to combat the dominance by a particular country's culture imposed in the mainstream industry. As such, cultural deterrence refers to the act of producing cultural works from an opposite viewpoint which actively seek to ridicule, demoralize and shatter the foundations of the culture perceived as dominant, which with its existence harms the creative process by making the industry stagnant in tired and clichéd formulas that need to be destroyed for new ones to emerge. When I speak about cultural deterrence, I have a clear target in mind, that is, the United States, and there's a good reason why. While I do appreciate many aspects of US culture, I believe that through globalization, the world has been completely overrun by it. There is not such a thing as diversity anymore, thanks to the blatant unpopularity that comes when a piece of work, be it books, films, video games or music, is not Anglo-Saxon, and particularly Unitedstatian. The same clichés and formulas are being used at an alarming rate, destroying possibilities for innovation and creativity. The industry makes sure to

destroy anything that does not follow these norms as profit is the only thing that matters. As a result, nothing innovative or truly revolutionary ever arises in the mainstream media, as what produces profit is marketing to the widest audience possible, and deviating from the established formulas or producing work for an elitist sector results in reduced profit. Companies are aware of this, but they're not to blame entirely. We are the ones who dictate where they should be headed and what entertainment must be produced, which forms a vicious circle where companies produce the inane works of today and we the audience effectively prove them right by consuming them. As such, artists, authors and developers follow a close Unitedstatian creative pattern since it's the safe way to ensure success for their products.

Before, audiences were ignorant of this issue, and as such tolerated it. However, I've noticed how with social networking and rapid communication recently the audiences are more resistant to the stagnant clichés perpetrated by Hollywood and how they do not under any way relate to characters, stories or scenarios. Why would, for example, a Chinese citizen feel identified with a US Marine, a CIA agent, a muscle-bound commando, anything the industry tries to make him feel sympathy for? But the cliché has rooted itself so deeply in society that we cannot possibly destroy it. As an example, foreign video game developers design games with plots obviously modeled after Unitedstatian '80s Cold War films, with such staunch Unitedstatian jingoism embedded in them that it raises an eyebrow on how either video game developers are completely useless and lazy at the time of being creative or they simply want to follow the easy road to sales and success. In either case, the point is clear. These tired formulas must be wiped out for the creative process to

cease being asphyxiated by what the mindless masses are told to consume.

Through cultural deterrence, I propose two things; first the complete elimination of formulas and clichés derived from US culture, and secondly, to produce works with anti-US tones in hopes of deterring their cultural advances in the rest of the world. While I hate and reject nationalism strongly, I believe countries should not be invaded by the foreign cultural pollution of a country in full decadence, and should instead focus on their own ideas and values. The imperialism of the US does not only arrive in military form, but in a cultural one as well. What I intend on doing is making the peoples of the world aware that there are other solutions, and that rejecting US culture in favor of others, more diverse and varied, is beneficial for everyone. Firstly, this will make the industry experience a shift in power. Value for US artistic work will fall exponentially and other types of creativity will find a way in the mainstream media. We will hopefully see work from other countries not only in the independent scene, and it will make the average citizen of the world want to expand their creativity and pursue their creative goals not deterred by the absolute decadence in ideas the industry experiences.

I believe that as a country, the US is undergoing a massive cultural decadence. I blame particularly religion and right-wing politics, which together have repressively vanquished any progressive sentiment in the country throughout the years, from the industrial revolution all the way to the Cold War. The country's foundations are purely religious and right-wing, that is an undeniable fact. As such, for it to experience what the rest of the world is experiencing, a massive event should arise, one that would change the fate of the country forever, traumatically. There have been talks about

a dissolution of the US just like the Soviet Collapse, a transition where the southern states, especially Texas and its neighbors, would resurface anti-Yankee sentiment and attempt to form their own nation. The coastal regions of the US also express this, as both the West and East coasts are more ethnically diverse than any part of the Midwest. In what specialists suggest would be a rational scenario, the US could be divided into three or four nations. East, Center, West and South. The tensions arising from the way the government is handling current issues is also a great concern, as both extreme left-wing and right-wing groups do not believe in the traditional parties anymore. This is a trend the entire world is experiencing, and not the US alone. Secession, nationalism and separatism are growing ever since the Soviet collapse, and the US won't be different, according to the political analysts. The current recession does not show hints yet of all these scenarios, but historically every major economic crisis like this tends to end usually in rather extreme manners. Don't you believe me? Open a history book. We have been fortunate in the fact that since the Soviet collapse, the West has not experienced many important or traumatizing reforms, but history has shown that no country is free from this. A strong Latin America leaning now more to the left is also a concern for the US, as it is losing strategic allies and gaining strong and ferocious rivals. All these factors should be considered.

But enough of political speculation. You now know the reasons why I support cultural deterrence attacks against the US. I would do so to any country smothering culture with their own ideas. My main enemy is not the US, it is repression, from any side of the political spectrum and any organization, group or entity. I have strong beliefs in the left, but I will never support anything that could stain its

reputation and betray its convictions. We in the left fight not only for progressivism but for everyone who undergoes oppression of any kind. This should be noted, and acknowledged.

Think about all the action military macho-types of the '80s, with their anti-communist propaganda in the form of a hero fighting for everything that's supposedly right? Think about the actors behind the characters, all men of right-wing ideas and immense fortunes, who spread propaganda in their movies as they saw fit? While not aiming to reproduce their efforts, I wonder why we can't have films in the same style which root for the other side. Why haven't we seen, even in times of the Soviet Union, films that desecrated the US in the same style they did with the USSR? Was the socialist nation above these methods of cheap propaganda? Certainly, parodies like the notably obscure 'Solo Voyage,' produced in 1985 by Mosfilm, don't count, as they can be considered more tongue in cheek than serious propaganda. Certainly, in Russia there always has been a sentiment of pity for Unitedstatians who truly look up to their propagandistic war-mongering. Simply put, I think the more-culturally rich Soviets were above these cheap methods of brainwashing. In any case, with the collapse of the USSR, it is worthy to point out how no films were made to analyze the different sociopolitical problems of the deceased nation. What's more, the Soviet Union was forgotten as soon as it was defeated. It was maybe referenced in films of Cold War settings, but that was it. There were new enemies to focus the propaganda efforts on, like Muslim terrorists. Now, I think it's time to reflect on this and counter-attack with our own media. We've had enough of conspiranoid right-wing lies and exaggerations, and it's time to attack their exposed weak points. They have no weapons to defend themselves

with, and propaganda will prove futile, as we have the intranets. And fortunately, the intranets are currently being used by the people to completely shatter their propaganda and expose their secrets, their corruption and their deceit. To further support popularization of the left, I suggest cultural deterrence to counter-attack right-wing propaganda, creating works of our own that while not including mindless propaganda for the sake of it, will attempt with proven facts to destroy the dishonorable essence of the right, and show the common citizens of the world how upholding and defending right-wing beliefs is self-destructive, as it goes against every single interest of the average man. We won't show them propaganda, we will show them facts. They will be free to decide whether to take the blindfold off or to continue with their beliefs in a clear state of delusion. And we will triumph, because the average working-man aware of his reality puts his trust in the socialist beliefs of the left-wing, and the average intranet user, usually young and fueled by politics, leans to the left as well. Nobody who seeks true equality, justice and human rights leans to the right. At least, not on the intranets. The intranets of the world are our turf, and we will continue to use it to spread our ideas in hopes of finally changing this world, which is built entirely to serve the interests of multinational corporations and financial entities. This world is not built for us, but we'll fight for it. And we will make it subdue to the needs of the majority ... mmm ... and now if you'll accept my apologies I must leave immediately, as they inform me there could be a security problem caused by my presence here ..."

"Well ... ah ... harsh words coming from such a well-versed political activist! Thanks, Michael. Next up, we have a woman you will surely recognize from her trouble with law enforcement and feminist collectives alike! Her name is

*Amber Keplazcki, and she has just been released of the oper-
ating room sporting the biggest pair of breasts ever carried
by a woman in history! Stay tuned!"*

Poor comrade Weinstein had willingly stepped into one of
the usual traps set for him by the Unitedstatian government.
This is the reason why someone like Shinaqua, who would
never, ever let anyone eclipse her awesome presence, let him
talk all he wanted. It was a game of feeding the hatred of the
Unitedstatian peoples with the image of a defector, a chance
to let everyone take a first-hand look at Michael Weinstein
and see what a disgusting traitor he was. It was a very well-
known fact that most Unitedstatians were awfully ignorant of
politics or how the world is actually run, and their government had always preyed on this. Weinstein had seemed terribly nervous and unable to focus, but he did an excellent performance and could reference the clear untouchable nature of
the US, facts which would be duly noted abroad. How right
he was. A nation which had never admitted to its dark and
dirty past, a pathetic nest of anti-Communist propaganda
designed to have its citizens oppressed under the capitalist
power of consumerism and vapid entertainment. It was
shameful to see culture reduced to such stupidity, to a ghetto
black woman rising from the slums to be an elitist celebrity in
a populist show to tackle issues in the shallowest way possible. But Michael surely knew the show's high ratings would
make the masses hear what he had to say. The enemy was the
uneducated mindless masses. They were the ones to blame.
Their ignorance doomed us all and made the powerful able to
subdue us easily. Shows like Shinaqua's further distracted the
peoples from their political duties and sunk them into a happy oblivion of gossip, vanity and superficiality. What a waste
of a human being. Was she truly inherently evil or was her

power derived from the primordial energies of the people, using it to gain personal benefit and live comfortably? Either way was disgusting. After all, if nobody complained, who would oppose them? That's how Hitler rose to power. A classic example, but the truest form of what happens when unopposed bullies are left to do what they want. Just like Kannovschina.

Luckily, someone like Weinstein will always exist, even if the rest of the human race is too busy with Amber Keplazcki's exemplary lifestyle. Looking at my Hipp-Man's watch, I realized it was time to go and headed outside with a slow march, a foul sensation invading my body as if sensing trouble looming in the horizon.

· · · · ·

The 9th arrived on an unusually cloudy and rainy day. Bear in mind, rain in Loynne's meant very few drops evaporating two meters above the ground. The heat was incredibly intense, as was the humidity in the air. Sweat stuck to your body in ways you found absolutely repulsive, and made your head boil with the unbearable humidity in the air. All this heat daze before taking the Purple Wonder to Pilgrim Coast was a very bad omen by itself.

Montenade was covered under that malicious shade, the absent sun of 18:00, which formed an orange and teal twilight that could have passed for beautiful in some other occassion. The gym burst with activity, the Loynner jocks and Kannies coming and going to the restaurant across the street, having probably done the same since 09:00. The gym rats didn't bother me as much as the prospect of boarding a bus at this time. This was the time where all the trash from towns like mine boarded the Purple Wonders to go partying in vari-

ous areas, usually Pilgrim Coast and Cristobal Atoll. The bus would be sunk in loud, tinny music coming from a hundred phones, all blasting to their tasteless music. There would be shouting, fighting, maybe a part where I would have to get involved to defend my honor. I disliked this prospect immensely. Yet, it paled unimaginably compared to what awaited me at Pilgrim Coast. I felt untouchable.

Luckily for me, the bus was nearly empty. This had already boosted my mood unimaginably. The hard part was over. Now, all that was left for me to do was continue my project.

Inside the bus there was only a sparse unit of Kannies, unequally distributed all over the vehicle. In packs of three to four, the Kannies limited themselves to their stupid stuff and noisy phones and I luckily didn't have to intervene to defend my integrity. I wondered often why didn't they have scooter bikes like the whole damn rest of them.

I entertained myself throughout the ride listening to my own music and staring at the rain drops drawing curves along the window panels. This was very unusual climate for Loynne's, even for this time of the year. Ever since I started 1st Grade, after October, days had been getting gradually cloudier and rainier, more so than ever before. However, the heat never really went away. The clouds seemed to amplify the light of the sun, reflecting and intensifying it to a point where you couldn't even look up. The clouds also seemed to be creating the unbearable greenhouse effect I always tried to avoid in my apartment. This sure wasn't The Motherland; in my home country, cloudy days were cold, like they should be. Sunny days were hot or warm, just like they should too. If this was being caused by global warming I didn't know, but Loynne's had never had a passable climate. My head boiled with the heat, the brute roaring voices of the Kannies at the back, the tinny music coming from their phones and the

powerful V12 engine of the bus. I needed to get to Pilgrim Coast in good shape, energized for a long party, and after stepping out of my house barely 15 minutes I already doubted my mood would change much. It was all up to my friends, starting by Wolfgang, who would be waiting for me at the bus station.

· · · · ·

I got off the bus, my head scanning obsessively for my comrade. He was never very reliable on the timing. I presumed I'd have to walk around the scum that used to roam the bus station at that time of the afternoon, mostly Kannies, junkies, drunkards and bums asking you for bus money to support their habits. Sitting on your own was the worst thing you could possibly do. The best thing to do was walking around impatiently as if waiting for someone, and it was just my situation. Loynne's seemed to be becoming more and more infested with these types in the afternoons and at nights, so I had always preferred to do my things in the safe sun of the morning. Risking any type of trouble could get me deported, and all my family's effort would be ruined in a second.

Wolfgang finally appeared, as the last remnants of the sun's light disappeared in the distance. The sky had now a shade of purplish blue, like the hue of veins. I saw the street lamps all across Paradise Avenue suddenly turn on in random order, which startled me. It was now officially nighttime, and the atmosphere at the bus station would only turn shadier with each passing minute.

Wolfgang was smiling cheerfully and performed Makarov Cat's "Dusty Beret" gesture as he approached me. I remember thinking why he greeted me in that way instead of with his

usual "Gunshot Salute." He was wearing one of his usual party outfits, this time consisting of black plaid pants, a purple shirt and a silver watch. He hadn't tied his hair in a bun, leaving his long black hair loose and dramatically blowing with the gentle breeze, and was wearing a strong cologne. His fake glasses, ever-present in school, were nowhere to be seen.

"*Privyet, Tovarish*," I greeted him. I was not in the best of moods yet, and I doubted I would be at all. In times like these, I only wanted to retreat to my shelter and ignore such a thing as an outside world even existed.

"*Tanjoubi omedetou, Doshi*! Happy birthday, Sonny! Hey … what's up?" Wolfgang asked, concerned. He must have noticed I didn't greet him in our usual way, without mimicking Makarov Cat's Gunshot Salute or Cobra Viper's casual military greet.

"Thanks, and don't worry, it's nothing. I just don't think I'm in the right mood for celebrating today …"

"Why's that?"

"Call it instinct … I don't know … I just don't think that it's a good idea to go out today …"

"Why? Come on, we'll have fun. It's just a matter of having fun with your friends and forgetting about everything else for just one night. Right?"

"I know, I know … but … never mind, it's alright. Come on, let's walk to The Crucible."

"Wait, I have a present."

"You do? Wolfie, you didn't need to …"

"Don't worry, *Doshi*. It's an Honor," Wolfgang said, as he produced a present from one of his pockets.

"Didn't have time to wrap it, but I didn't think you'd mind much," he said, revealing a little black case, similar to that of a wedding ring. I opened it with great curiosity, revealing a very familiar rifle cartridge.

"It's a real 7.62 x 39 millimeter round my grandfather found in Vietnam, of an AK-47. He wanted my dad to keep it, but dad hated it, he just wanted to get rid of it because it brought him bad memories of Asia, he really didn't want it in the house. So instead of throwing it away I give it to you, I know you'll treasure it better."

"*Tovarish* ... this is a historical relic ..."

"I know ... some day, if we ever find ourselves in peril, at war, this may serve to remind you of true comradeship." Astonished by Wolfgang's gift and its gesture, I performed a heartfelt military salute, not caring if people around us were looking. Wolfgang responded just the same.

With renewed enthusiasm and confidence, I began to think about the party's organization as my comrade and I walked toward The Crucible. It involved the same old group of people, which as of now were Ryan, Dave, Faye, Mario, Ettore, Wolfgang and me. Axel had been invited but was obviously busy in some other party, and we hadn't heard about Mike in weeks; as a matter of fact, not even Axel knew where he was.

Wolfgang and I, with true camaraderie, parted toward The Crucible heading for the Community Center, as per usual when wanting to reach the building quickly. We entered through the back entrance and took the elevator up to the now famous 7th floor, the world outside still feeling awkward and lifeless, as if we were in some kind of purgatory. Away from the bus station, the British pubs and the beach, not much went down in Paradise Plaza at this time of night. Streets lay deserted and silent, the eponymous palm trees of Loynne's rocking lazily like corpses hanging upside down, traffic flowing slowly, and the bird's eye view that The Crucible provided confirmed that in fact very little activity was going on in the outside world. However, the color and life

returned once again the moment my knuckles stopped knocking on the wooden door marked 75, and a hard to forget face emerged slowly from the threshold.

Faye was as beautiful as ever; her straight long hair majestically shone and covered her cute delicate shoulders. Wearing a black party dress very similar to the ones used by Loynnerin party sluts but less revealing and trashy, her white amazing legs seemed to shine more than ever before, the smooth skin invitingly soft and warm to the eye. Her stomach was exposed as well, the navel covered behind a transparent section of the dress. Everything about her appearance was mesmerizing. The blue make up around her emerald green eyes illustrated perfectly what I fancied so much about her; that exotic, unique and rare blend of artificial Western beauty and natural female allure.

She greeted us joyfully, and we walked inside in the warmth of the Mantis Residence.

"Wait Wolfie, go to the room, the guys are all there, I wanna speak to Sonny if you don't mind ... if Ryan asks tell him you came alone, OK? Don't tell him we're outside or he'll come and bother us!" she said. Wolfgang muttered something in Japanese and went away again with that mysterious aura, seemingly jealous of Faye hoarding my attention for herself. Surprised of her intelligence, I followed her outside, as I hoped Wolfgang's presence would serve as a diversion.

"Happy birthday, Sonny! This is for you!" Faye said suddenly, producing a present I never even noticed she had been carrying.

"I even got the paper with your favorite colors ... it's all Soviet styled!" She said, her eyes glowing. Indeed, the paper wrapping was red with a yellow bow, with an image of the Hammer and Sickle and a photo of Lenin she had printed and pasted with glue. This had to be the first time a Westerner

showed me such an honorable and respectful sign of understanding my culture and ideology. A Loynner would have
printed out the flag of Turkey.

I was so impressed with the present I didn't want to tear
apart what she had made with such love, care and effort. I
ripped it slowly and carefully as I wanted to keep the pictures
of the Hammer and Sickle and of Comrade Lenin, and proceeded to unveil the contents.

First I retrieved a picture frame. In it, Faye had placed a
recent photo of her standing on her apartment's balcony at
what looked to be 19:00, the entire pool area with the palm
trees behind her, the orange sky in the background giving a
sensation of peace; wearing the outfit she always wore when
we were first getting to know each other, including the black
cardigan, blue top, jean mini-skirt, black short-heeled shoes
and the US flag cross necklace, Faye never ceased to amaze
me with her looks. She was waving with her left hand at the
camera, in a girly and shy manner, as if terribly embarrassed,
her green eyes shining even more than her lovely scarlet
cheekbones.

"I hope you like it Sonny, I know you don't have any proper photos of me ... and I know you used to love that outfit, but
I stopped wearing it because I needed a change ... well, there
you have it, immortalized!"

I was so happy I didn't know what to say to her, and as
such decided to keep proceeding with the present. I took out
the letter out of its white envelope. It had also been decorated
with Communist symbols, but with a female touch. She had
placed the Hammer and Sickle inside of red hearts, while on
others she had drawn the Unitedstatian flag on one half,
representing her, sharing the heart with the Soviet one,
drawn on the left side of the heart. Other symbols included
the Red Star and the star of the Unitedstatian Army. I be-

came confused at seeing these symbols living in harmony, not used propagandistically portraying either side as an enemy to be destroyed. But this didn't end here. I still had to read what the letter said. Faye was expectant, and while I wasn't looking directly at her, could see her out of the corner of my eye, anxiously waiting for me to open the envelope.

The letter, also decorated with more drawings, went as follows:

"Dear Sonny:

You know how awful I am writing these types of letters. I cannot be nearly as good as you writing, but, if you let me, allow me to express myself my own way.

A full school year has passed since we first spoke on the second floor staircase, among the noises of people you and I couldn't even bear. Who would have known that 7th of November someone like you would appear to change my life forever ...

You always tried to make me feel good ... and you always made it so. I want you to know that you'll always have me with you. Because you are and will always be the best friend I could ever have, you're truly unique, although you already know that, and ... I LOVE YOU!

You mean a lot to me, you've helped me so much and you keep doing it everyday although sometimes I'm not very fair to you ... and I don't want you to worry or feel bad about anything. When you feel even a little bit sad, all you need to do is call me and I'll be there for you like always! And yes, the world is cruel, but with people like you, one feels truly loved. And don't forget that I love you too, Sonny boy! You

give me back the will to go on when I'm down, and just for that you deserve all my admiration, love and respect.

These last months have been incredible. In my life, I had never had such a good friend, someone who cares so deeply about me and asks for so little in return. I love you my friend, I cannot express this enough. I love you for loving me for what I am. I love you for seeing past my imperfections. I love you for seeing right where I only see wrong. Nobody ever cared this much about me. You're the first, and I feel it's my obligation to tell you that you have a very privileged place in my heart. No matter what happens, you will always fill that place, forever.

One day you'll achieve the true 'utopia' you are looking after in your life, one day you will because you deserve it. I can't express everything I feel for you in this letter, but I will try to show you how much I care for you every day. I love you very much, Sonny. You're my best friend. My crazy communist friend! And I hope nothing ever brings us apart. As for me, I will never let it happen.

Loves you with all her heart,

Faye."

Extremely thankful and moved, I turned to Faye, sunk in disbelief;

"*Faye ... is this true ... is this how you truly feel?*" Faye nodded smiling vigorously, the smile making her a thousand times more beautiful.

"Here," I said, having thought of something suddenly. "Keep this." I unchained one of my dog tags, the one written

in English, and placed it on her soft warm delicate hands.

"Oh, Sonny ... you don't have to!"

"No, no, seriously, I want you to have it. It's, let's say ... a part of me for you to keep."

"Thanks, Sonny ... I don't know what to say ..." She lunged forwards and hugged me, as I pressed her tight body strongly against mine. It wasn't an act performed out of lust. That was the last thing I had on my mind upon reading that letter and receiving her loving embrace. All I could think of was how lucky I had been to come across such a superior human being. Her benevolence and love knew no bounds. The admiration and respect she grew toward me seemed to be now at the same level of what I had felt all those first months, when we hadn't even spoken.

We headed inside, fearing her brothers coming out to bother us and ask uncomfortable questions, and because I wanted Faye to keep the present somewhere safe until the party had finished. If we were going to be drinking and on the beach, there was no certainty it would be safe from harm. At that moment, the last thing I wanted was for that powerful and unique gift to be destroyed or lost. I told Faye to hide it in her room and we would retrieve it after the party.

Mario, Dave and Ryan were in the bedroom playing a WWII GamEsprit Zwei game, "Call to Action: Stalingrad Front," a game I used to play on my computer. The self-righteous and pro-Unitedstatian game developers made games portraying Russians as good only in WWII settings, a cliché derived from their alignment as fellow Allies. Good anti-fascist imagery wasn't enough to distract my eyes, fixed on the striking embodiment of beauty surrounding us.

"Heeeeey Sonny!! Good to see ya!! Happy birthday, man!" Mario greeted, losing sight of the Nazi onslaught taking place on the TV screen, as waves of Soviet soldiers bravely defend-

ed their motherland against the disgusting German fascists in the Battle of Stalingrad.

"Hey Sonny, happy birthday," said an overenthusiastic Dave, who gave the game too much priority to mind me at all. But I was accustomed to this now. He was completely mannerless and egotistical to give others that special empathy and priority. Why he volunteered to organize this party and then behave like this was a complete mystery. Perhaps, he was just as me, struck by a sudden instinct that the night would be a total failure.

"Happy birthday, Sonny ..." Ryan was as usual, transfixed into the computer, chatting here and there, opening windows and windows of different LoynNet search browsers, and watching stupid videos on VapidVidz.com. With the same old predictable phrase "*(hey, Sonny! Check this out!)*," he invited me to partake in his obnoxious, weird, boring, and often perverted web searches.

"Hey let's give Sonny his card, right?" Mario said aloud, trying to catch the Mantises attention.

"What ca—Oh yeah, the card! Wait Sonny, I'll got get it!" Ryan said, going out of the room only to come back shortly after, carrying with him a medium sized birthday card signed by Ryan, Dave, Faye, Mario, Tory, Billy, Robbie and Wolfgang. The card itself was a joke, featuring a black gang member pointing a gun at the reader, with the message "ONE YEAR LESS LEFT TO LIVE! ENJOY YOUR LIFE, MOTHER-FUCKER!"

"Uh ... thanks guys ... you didn't need to ..."

"He, he ... I chose the card ... he, he ..." Ryan said.

"Billy and Robbie couldn't come man, but they sent their regards," Dave said.

"Well, I appreciate it guys ... really, thanks a lot."

Leaving the awkward birthday card aside, it wasn't long

before uncontrollable laughter arrived, the kind that can only be produced when in the comfortable company of friends. Ryan kept showing me stupid videos on LoynNet, Mario and Dave laughed hysterically playing Call to Action and Wolfgang seemed to be amused at the general social atmosphere, small talking with Faye here and there, who often tried to shrug him off so as to not look like they had actually hung out extra-officially.

At around 21:00 we went back to the Community Center where Ettore had been waiting for us, as he seemingly disliked strongly being inside the Mantis Residence for a certain reason he had not yet talked about in public. Tory was wearing his usual clothes, sporting baggy jeans, white sneakers and an orange shirt covered by a maroon hoody jacket, unzipped so as to reveal the shirt.

"Hey Tory! Glad you could come," I said, shaking his hand.

"Hey Sonny, happy birthday!" Tory said, proceeding to hug me in a weird fashion.

"Here, I have bought you a present."

"Uh, really? Hey, thanks!" I said, enthusiastically ripping the paper to shreds, only to find that he had bought me ...

" 'THE BLACK BOOK OF COMMUNISM' ?!" Everyone started laughing at my shocked expression.

"Hehe ... I thought you would react like that. It's not a joke, Sonny. Consider reading it, please. It might give you a different perspective on certain things, even if you don't agree or believe what it says."

"Uh ... I am well aware of the historical inaccuracies and exaggerations of this book already ... but alright ... I promise you I'll give it a go ..."

"You do that. I know I won't change your ideology, but at least it's good to see you can consider the viewpoints of oth-

ers ... hey Mario, you should put a jacket on, it's going to be freezing cold later at night, they said it on the weather forecast ..."

"Would you leave him alone, what are you gay for him?" Ryan said.

"No, but it's my duty to inform him. After all, he's the only one in a sleeveless shirt."

"Don't worry about me Tory, I got a jacket here in the backpack, don't be such a *stronzo* man, sheezus, what a drag!"

"Alright, alright ... I'm just saying ..." Tory seemed to care deeply about Mario's well-being more than any of us. In fact, they had begun to bond really well, in a manner in which looked like Tory chased him around just like I did Faye. But at this point this story wasn't even developed. That's later on.

Now that all of us were together, the next step was to buy the drinks. Tory and Mario took care of that, taking advantage of Mario's height and Tory's supposedly effective psychological tricks and maturity when speaking, something we all knew was illusory. I remember saying I could go with Mario as we were both about the same height, but Tory instantly jumped in and went with him. A few moments later, they both returned, Mario laughing hysterically at how Tory had tried to impress the DAUCO 24/7 Nollie clerk.

"You should'a seen this guy," he began to say, with certain difficulty. "He ... he goes and says ... wait, I'm in fuckin' stitches 'ere ... he goes and says to'er, with like this grave fake voice, 'hey baby ... what are you doing by yourself this time of night?' And the girl goes and says 'I'm working here, you retarded?' Hahahaha!! And then he tries to like say, 'no, I'm askin' 'cause it would be beneficial to have a companion to keep you safe,' and she says 'I wouldn't even want your company to distract my boyfriend from beating me up, kid. Just

take the drinks and go.' And she sold us the drinks anyway without checking! Hahahaha!! What a schmuck!"

"Tory, you're the definition of corny," Ryan said. He

never let Tory remain unscathed when he humiliated himself in public, which as of now, I understood was a common thing.

"I don't understand why it didn't work, it was in the Silverman after all," Tory said.

"The Silverman?" I asked, intrigued. "What's that?"

"Oh ... ah ... nothing. Forget I said anything." I soon dropped it like he suggested. I couldn't bear him trying to appear interesting and mysterious when everybody else just thought he was a clown. In that sense, he was beginning to remind me of Wolfgang.

We continued walking toward the beach, passing through restaurants and pubs I had never seen before. It amazed me how Paradise Plaza seemed like an infinite playground at that time, so vast and unknown, every place my friends walked toward being new to me. I was glad to be with people who were so savvy about this grounds I had always considered dangerous, alien and impossible to traverse. I tried to leave Faye alone for the most part, and noticed she found herself walking on her own, Ryan being the only one who paid some attention to her, occasionally doing one of his immature little jokes grabbing a good deal of her body, leaving the impression he had a serious lack of female attention and found respite touching that body I considered so incredibly attractive and sensual. I had always suspected some incest could be present on his part, his perverted nature not pulled back by the most grotesque of sexual acts. I halted my thoughts when the view of Ryan touching Faye's breasts and running away playfully while she tried to hit him immensely repulsed me. How could she laugh and have fun with that? Where was her

dignity? Perhaps she was so used to having fun with that through the years of boredom and loneliness that it proved a hard habit to kick.

Everyone seemed rather detached on the way to Crosshair Beach, as if something else was brewing inside their minds. Tory and Mario carried the food and the drinks in plastic bags, talking to each other vividly. I found myself staying with Dave surprisingly not put off by his arrogance. While not exactly laughing and messing about like Ryan and Faye, I remember us being deeply immersed in conversations I have since forgotten. What we could be talking about is something I'll never remember now, but what I do remember is us being engaged in a conversation no one else there could have taken part in.

However, only halfway to the beach, Ryan suddenly started walking slowly, and separated me from the group in order to talk in private.

"Hey Sonny, I'm sorry, look I'm gonna have to go now, I can't be there for the drinkin', I wanted to tell you before, but … look, I'll tell you later, I know you'll understand."

"What, you have to go? Why?"

"I'll tell you later man, really! It's awesome man, you'll see. Please don't take it personal, it's not like I don't wanna be here, but I really have to go. I'll tell you later, alright?"

"Well, fine … you do what you have to do."

"Hah, I knew you'd understand man! Look, explain to these assholes why I'm gone, I don't wanna go around givin' explanations to people … OK man, happy birthday and see ya around!"

That was quite odd, but immensely relieving. Now I wouldn't have to cope with him when trying to be around Faye. I explained to the others that Ryan wanted to go back to the apartment for his hoody. In any case, nobody was really

bothered about his absence.

Once we got to the cold, deserted beach, I began to put my hidden agenda in motion. The music was set, and as a consequence, the mood greatly improved. The only thing missing now was the direct approach. I was aware that the heat on my person was immense, and that even though Ryan was gone I still remained under heavy scrutiny by Dave.

We sat down on the blue sunbeds forming a circle, and began pouring the drinks; I was immediately put off by the strong smell. I associated it with irrationality, decadence, violence and mediocrity; but I couldn't ignore the atmosphere around me. The desire for disconnecting and partaking in impulsive irrational acts overcame my brain, caving in to my most basic and repressed instincts. Let us not forget, I was very young, and the work of hormones in such a scenario made me cave in.

As a result, I found myself drinking copiously. Euphoria took over as my social inhibition disappeared completely, and effectively threw aside all shame and dignity. Intoxicated, Dave and I behaved like two prankster buddies, riding piggyback to crash against some poor bystander like Tory, and as rosy cheeks and smiley teeth began appearing, the differences between us vanished. Like children, we returned to a schoolyard mentality glad to be free of our sense of embarrassment, obeying only our need for more impulsive acts. Throughout the whole drinking session, only Ettore remained sober, holding a glass of rum which was always filled.

Smiling and laughing as I never had, my inebriated state made me throw everyone down to the sand in a grappling wrestling maneuver. It's impossible for me to exactly tell you what I remember in my drunkenness, but I have been able to reconstruct it further through the disconnected anecdotes told later by the guys. I stood up covered in sand, seizing the

happy moment of my birthday's celebration to distance myself from the heat of the moment and savor it from afar, gazing at the black sea illuminated by the distant lights of Cristobal Atoll to the south. I looked at the guys crashing against each other in piggyback wars and falling on the sand, laughing hysterically. Everything had turned out perfectly; the day had not been ruined, and I was blatantly proven wrong about my instincts. Now that nobody was suspecting me, the only thing that remained was carrying out my plan.

Breaking away from the group to begin my search, I quickly found her sitting on a sunbed and talking to Tory, the only guy who didn't want to partake in sandy wrestling. Tory always drank very responsibly, as he often bragged of how he always took care of his drunken friends when they couldn't fend for themselves. But I seriously doubted he drank at all.

I sat next to Tory, trying to make him understand that I wanted some time alone with Faye. He smiled with his crooked teeth and left, uttering something about "predictable social mechanics."

Faye's green eyes glowed with enthusiasm, as they often did when my presence was near. It was time to test whether the alcohol was having any effect at all. I positioned myself in front of her and lunged forward hugging her, a gesture she returned all too willingly. My chest brimmed with a strange sensation when doing so, feeling her feminine delicate disposition, caressing her soft white back, pressing her tight body against mine. Then we spent quite some time talking drunkenly about things that didn't make much sense but brought about lots of continuous laughter. However, I began to harbor some doubts almost immediately. Did I seriously want everything to be so easy? To obtain her love when her judgment was most clouded, when she wasn't responsible of her actions?

When the situation simply couldn't have been better, Faye suddenly sat down facing me directly, her body leaning forwards and her eyes staring right into mine. Her drunken, green and incredibly round tipsy eyeballs, with her drooping, arrogant eyelids covering half of them, made my stomach shrink, and a passing cold breeze traveled beneath my neck carrying the most dreadful, disgusting fear. I don't remember what we were talking about; something about life in my supposed country of origin, maybe about her life in the US. I don't know, and I don't care. The thing is, her eyes were no longer those of the little innocent girl I had fallen in love with; slightly intoxicated as well, Faye now sported the stare of those Loynnerin Kanny whores I so despised. Her perfect Western features, which I compared to those of a model, laughed at my rough Eastern ugliness, or at least they made me feel so. My most gruesome memory resides in those supremacist, elitist green eyes. As she looked right into me, face to face and almost near enough to kiss, I felt turned down, rejected, humiliated. Her eyes spoke the words her heart-shaped mouth needn't; the disdain, the disgust, the hatred were printed on them while her drunken state loosened their speech. I remembered a thousand rejections by girls who looked at me with those very same eyes. And they all had turned out to be shallow, vapid whores, attention seeking sleazes that stomped on the weak to attract the mighty, driving them toward despair in a bid to generate more reputation amongst the elites.

I remember the instant as having lasted several minutes, even though a few seconds were all I needed to realize she possessed the same traits women used to scar men like me forever. An evil force had possessed Faye, laughingly staring into my being, and spoke through her beautiful, malicious eyes. As I stared down deeper, looking at my own reflection

on the crystal-clear organs, I realized I was the one to be blamed. I had started it all, seeking for vice and lust in her, all for my own selfish gluttony. The night was gradually becoming a punishment. As I sat quietly on the sunbed, ignoring what was going around me, I wondered if Wolfgang would be thinking the same I was. My only thoughts revolved around what the future might bring and how I would get out of this situation. Her eyes had intimidated me immensely. For the first time since I knew her, she had given me a stare reminiscent of Loynnerins'. Like so many before her, she had looked at me condescendingly, as if I were the complete definition of a bottom feeder sinking her reputation just by being seen talking to her. She looked at me as if I were a naïve little boy who would never get a shot at undressing her unless it was with my mind. For what seemed an infinite amount of time, she wasn't that shy and awkward depressed little girl with no self-esteem who hated everything and everyone, who needed a hero to save her from a pointless and boring life. During that infinite interval, she was a woman conscious of her beauty and her potential to rise up, who recognized the person before her as a loser undeserving of attention, someone who would never satisfy her womanly needs. Did alcohol actually do this? Did the social uninhibitor allow her to finally tell me straightly how she actually felt toward me? Up to this day, I don't know how to explain it ... but her eyes screamed "you'll never have me."

I left, uttering an excuse I cannot remember. I didn't even turn around to see what her reaction would be when seeing me leave like that. The guys were still playing on the sand, wrestling drunkenly with each other. They hadn't noticed my absence yet, or maybe they didn't want to bother me. In any case I seized the moment to once again look at the infinite dark ocean, immersed in a self-imposed mental prison of

which I had completely lost control of. I didn't want to get out and confront Faye or the guys. I didn't want to speak to anyone. I would wait there until Faye finally came to look for me.

But she never did.

Concerned, I decided to return to the guys, who were congregated merrily around the CD player. They were all there. Well, almost everyone.

The realization brought forth a devastating discovery. Turning my head to scout for them, I suddenly froze exactly where I was. Mankind, the Earth, the universe, time itself froze for a full minute as I noticed two things in a quarter million of a second, producing an asphyxiating feeling of panic and desperation in my torso.

The sunbed I had abandoned not five minutes ago in the distant dark horizon displayed, to what my drunken eyes could distinguish, two figures, very close to each other. I headed there immediately. Everyone noticed soon enough, and I heard the traitorous voice of Dave, urging the others to stop me:

"DON'T LET SONNY NEAR THEM!!!"

Enraged by the order he had issued to the guys, I threw anyone in my way to the sand with sudden wrestling maneuvers, and soon I could see that the two heads had turned to look at me in unison. I stopped right in my tracks. Did I really want to see that? Did I want to go further?

I didn't have time to think much more. I got thrown to the sand myself by the combined effort of at least three of my friends. I became furiously enraged, twitching uncontrollably on the sand trying to fend them off to no avail. They had won

729

and I wouldn't be able to get back up.

"CALM THE FUCK DOWN, SONNY! IT'S ALRIGHT, IT'S ALRIGHT!!"

"YOU NUTS MAN?! IT AIN'T WORTH IT!!"

The hysterical voices of Tory and Mario went right through me as I focused my eyes on the dark figures, their heads tilted at me now, two sets of eyes shining in the darkness, looking from their elevated, privileged positions. I panted heavily on the sand, wondering what could I have done to deserve that, what went wrong, why would something backfire so much in such a way. I couldn't forgive anyone for this. I couldn't trust anybody ever again. I couldn't place my trust and confidence on anyone, not even the best human being on the island.

I stopped shouting when I noticed that someone else was yelling, surprisingly even more enraged than me. I heard Dave's authoritarian voice a second time, actually, I only managed to hear the segments not drowned by the shouting of my friends, the strong tidal sounds, the wind and my own alcoholic state, which had dazed me so much I was not even hearing well.

"... A FUCK ... THINK YOU'RE DOIN' ... ASSHOLES ... BRACE YOURSELVES ... SORT IT ... DON'T WANT NOTHIN' ... OUTTA HERE ..."

Like a humiliated beast, I kept lying on the sand trying to gather as much information of my surroundings as I could. So far I had heard Dave issuing orders from afar, and the ones who were keeping me in place were Tory and Mario. I

didn't even want to begin to imagine the people together on the sunbed ...

"Let me go. I'm fine. I'm OK. Seriously. I'm fine."

"We can't let you go, Sonny ... not yet at least ..." Tory said.

"Tory ... I'm being extremely serious ... I won't do anything ... just let me go ..."

"I told you that we can't, Sonny," he cautiously warned me. "We don't know what you're capable of doing in this state. We'll let you go when you're more sober."

I tried to convince everyone into thinking that I was only going to talk to them, that I needed some closure to understand the situation, but to absolutely no avail. they wouldn't release me. The unimaginable fury produced from seeing the two figures lying there so close to each other made me want to immediately take action, but my mind was deterred by the sheer thought that this was taking place. Restrained like that, I was unable to act in any way. Too drunk to make an actual effort and weak from the mental stress of the whole situation, I surrendered, and this time, not for the time being. I had officially lost. Everything I had struggled so hard to build with Faye gone, in the literal blink of an eye.

I heard footsteps in the distance, and heard Dave's commanding voice for a third time, issuing more orders to his loyal enforcers;

"Let go of Sonny, guys. It's over."

I was released by my friends, and I got up immediately to face Dave.

"Explain," I demanded with my eyes wide open, out of breath, my body leaning forwards as if wanting to grab him by the neck.

731

"Look Sonny, I know you must be real mad, but there's a logical explanation for all this ..."

"You knew, you fucking weasel. You knew all along ..."

"No, now Sonny, please ... it's not what it looks like. I didn't have nothin' to do with this. Blame them. They're the ones who fucked you over. I knew, yeah, we all did, but what could we do, you know you never listen to reason and all the reasons she's given you you ignored ... it was about time you smashed your head against the wall and swallowed this the hard way ... leave them stupid motherfuckers to do whatever the fuck they want, life goes on Sonny ... forget about Faye, let her go ... this is not good for you, her or anyone ... c'mon on, let's go. We'll talk about this later Sonny, when you're better."

We all went away quiet, not making a single line of conversation, as we headed toward the taxi stop near the bus station. Everyone was quiet, and I was at the front of the pack, punching random objects and yelling at pedestrians I managed to notice in my drunken state. Tory and Mario would soon become my escorts, as like everyone knew, Kannies and British drunkards could be very dangerous if provoked.

I was numb; literally, non-existent. Gone. My guardian angels pushed me inside a cab, where I vomited my foul insides all over and continued to insult everything and everyone, from pedestrians to my very own friends and even the driver. When we finally got to Montenade, they grabbed my keys and proceeded to enter Rot Volka, leaving me to my luck stumbling on the corridor, throwing my gifts beside me. I barely made it to my bed, lonely and forgotten like any man who's failed to succeed in his one and only mission.

I woke up several times in the middle of the night, the alcohol still making my body bloated and disgusting. Before

finally passing out, I pictured Wolfgang's face, without as much as a single sign of remorse. I wanted to rip him apart, stab him, choke him to death, send a flying punch down his stupid face. But even then I knew it wasn't the right thing to do. I waited for cold revenge and the obvious aftermath of this sudden thunderstorm.

· · · · ·

I got out of my room finding the house very dark. The first thing I did was illuminating the entire apartment as much as I could, and then proceeded to take a bath.

The bright colors of the morning painted my sickened face; as in contrast to the dark yesterday, this tomorrow had not a single trace of joy about it. For all I knew, some part of me had died the previous night. I couldn't stay any longer in that dead and silent space, and so I walked out of the apartment, aimlessly roaming around Montenade.

I returned after a while, more cooled off but equally disgusted and devastated. A familiar feeling told me nothing would erase this mistake. Nothing would make me want to talk to my former comrade again. Even if I wanted, I couldn't have been able to. The desire to outright kill him and watch him suffer for taking what was rightfully mine was too much to bear.

Trying to distract myself and not think about my situation, I turned the TV on, setting it on Cadenas Latinas. My eyes, not expecting to see news that surpassed what I had recently lived through in terms of sheer shock and revulsion, opened ever more as the headlines began to sink in my brain:

*"BREAKING NEWS: Unitedstatian journalist and politi-
cal activist Michael Weinstein shot and killed. Suspect still at
large."*

I couldn't believe it. Only the day before I had seen him at
Shinaqua's show. A strange force overcame me as I, barely
managing to repress my anger, suppressed the need to turn
away from the TV off instead of destroying it. The white letters moving across the screen hypnotized me completely as I,
in shock, tried to digest what had happened:

*"Michael Weinstein, an outspoken political activist and
Unitedstatian dissident, died after an assassination attempt
on his person last night, which happened as the activist
attempted to leave for the TAX international airport. Hours
earlier he had visited a television studio to give his insight
regarding Unitedstatian intervention in Latin America in
the '80s and the current Operation Vulture destabilization
attempts in the region, on the program 'Shinaqua's Show'.
Leaving when informed as per usual of probable security
concerns, Weinstein headed for the California Sunrise Hotel
where he was staying, in order to prepare for departure.
The airport had been completely overrun by a mass of followers who were soon joined up by detractors by the time
Weinstein's motorcade arrived. Followers and detractors
clashed violently and shots were heard, making Weinstein's
bodyguards rush him to the motorcade. His bodyguards
could not protect him in time when an unidentified gunman,
armed with what ballistics identified as an Ithaca 37 shotgun, shot Weinstein. The powerful blast immediately sev-
ered Weinstein's right arm, striking at the joint, and there
was also massive damage to his torso. Weinstein was transferred immediately to the Ronald Reagan UCTA Medical*

Center in The Angels, California, and was undergoing sur-gery the moment he finally passed away.

As of yet, Unitedstatian authorities have not been able to identify the suspect, who disappeared quickly in the confu-sion and is believed to be on the run. The shotgun used is believed by the police to have been especially modified to fire at larger-than-normal ranges, suggesting a sniper, even though this kind of weapon is less than adequate for such a role. The mystery involving the shooter and the way the assassination attempt was carried have reopened the win-dow for conspiracy in the nation, some going as far as to correlate it with the assassination of John F. Kennedy.

The tragedy has also reopened the gun control debate in the country as followers of Weinstein, both domestically and abroad, denounce the attack and claim it was part of a cov-ert action by the US government to dispose of their most outspoken and influential political detractor. Widespread gun ownership, aside from firearm modifications performed by owners to make large guns easier to conceal, are so common in the US that it's hard to consider this a covert government assassination, and this remains the current stance of the US government regarding the tragedy ..."

I felt profound sadness within me, but it was a sadness for myself, of guilt and self-loathing. The suffering Michael Weinstein endured to defend his ideals struck me in an in-credibly harsh manner and made me feel guilty about my petty concerns and my emotional melodrama. The ridiculous endeavor I embarked myself on was nothing compared to the life and goals of this man, which were as high as the ones of all the figures I admired. And what was I doing to honor that?

And then, that was when it finally hit me; this man was ready to give himself fully to his cause, to the death. Michael Weinstein fought single-handedly against the most zealous, imperialistic and powerful nation of the 20th century, from the inside and the outside. He had wanted a new US, completely restructured in its ideology, traditions and viewpoints, more tolerant, more oriented toward people instead of profit, a friend to the nations of the world instead of a militaristic and hypocritical bully disguised as a saint. His activism had been such, that he had now officially lost his life for this cause.

I turned the TV off, and after resting my thoughts and letting the death of Michael Weinstein sink in, I looked at my apartment, as if searching for something that could give a context to what I was feeling. I had been jolted and fully awoken, as if cold water had been poured over me in my sleep. I knew now that Michael Weinstein was the key to my new ideology, not just in ideas, but in example. He was the most modern and recent example of a man willing to die to change the world. I knew now that my destiny was not to fool around searching for love in a teenage kindergarten, but to be as great as this man, to follow in his footsteps. But I was lacking context; I needed direction, and I was the only one who could provide it.

Looking at the table, I noticed I didn't remember myself placing my birthday cards and presents on the living room's table; Faye's present was absent, as I had told her to keep it safe until after the party, but Wolfgang's bullet was in its case. I didn't want to throw it away, though. More than just Wolfgang's gift, this was a historical relic. I first analyzed the bullet, looking at its base. In fact, the bullet was of Russian origin, dating maybe to Soviet times. I would have to analyze it further to know exactly, but the Cyrillic carvings around the

diameter signaled its Eastern history. If Wolfgang's story was true, this had been made for an AK-47 rifle of the earliest iterations, before its upgrade into the more common AKM. The Viet Cong was known to use very old weapons provided by the Soviets and the Chinese, giving proof to Wolfgang's story.

Faye's "Bibles for Bullets" disc was still in my possession, and I wondered now what to do with it. I would probably end up giving it to her through her brothers. How happy that disc had made me, the first Faye object to be in my possession. I remembered well the dayI had asked for it, and how beautiful she looked; how blissful it had been sharing that moment with her, even though she couldn't have possibly thought much of it. But it had been engraved in my mind forever.

As for "The Black Book of Communism," it eerily marked its presence in my house, an awkward reminder of something I needn't think about, specifically now of all moments. But curiosity got the best of me. Eyeing it briefly awoke a hunger in me to finally know where the exaggeration and the propaganda ended and the truth began. It was time to give LoynNet a chance, even though I wasn't too keen on it. I preferred my books rather than a computerized underworld where people like Gordon dwelled. But that day I discovered something that shook my mind forever. I began researching on Communist repression, a taboo subject for me, as it always made me boil with rage. I hated how the mass killings had been attributed to the nature of Communism rather than the nature of tyrants masquerading as Communists and the failure of their policies, dictators who prioritized a comfortable and lavish lifestyle instead of developing the theories of Marx in hopes of achieving a true Communist society.

My thoughts wemt to the name of comrade Trotsky, making me remember a conversation I had previously held with

Ryan; Trotsky was the one who had raised, trained and disciplined the Red Army, eventually overthrowing the useless Tsar and thus laying the foundations for the Soviet State. But Trotsky, like many other Old Bolsheviks, would not experience the glee of this victory for long.

Up until now, I had never developed the need to know more about his story other than that at the eyes of the USSR, he had been deemed a traitor, never rehabilitated by the Soviet State. The computer screen illuminated my dark expression as I absorbed the new knowledge about the darkest sides of Communism voraciously, reading what would have once been considered subversive, forbidden and anti-patriotic propaganda in The Motherland.

· · · · ·

With or without Communism, one thing should not be denied; the history of Russia has always been about a brutalized people.

"*The Revolution Betrayed*" is a book by Leon Trotsky, where he analyzes the USSR after Lenin's death, greatly criticizing his successor and former Bolshevik comrade, Stalin. Trotsky suffered greatly at the hands of Stalin, after he had consolidated power and eventually rejected certain theories Lenin had stood for – from internationalist Communist policies to global revolution – with his unnecessary ruthless reign of terror, purges, a rather privileged and comfortable lifestyle – Lenin had led a notoriously frugal one – and an infinitely powerful cult of personality. Even though it's common for both old and modern Communists to feel certain admiration for Stalin – mainly because of his role as Nazi vanquisher, his great industrialization of the country and turning the USSR into a global superpower – I confirmed by myself that his

story hadn't aged well in the eyes of mankind, and he was not to be blindly admired by anyone. In my younger years I also felt engulfed by the Stalinist propaganda, and Stalin's love for his people was a vision which filled you with the utmost motivation and pride. Nothing was beyond him. Stalin could do whatever he wanted, and what he could not was well attributed to his person by others.

Trotsky had been a true revolutionary like all Old Bolsheviks, but found himself living in exile and later assassinated by a Stalinist agent, Ramón Mercader, while living in Mexico. Mercader was sent 20 years to jail for the murder and when he was released, he traveled to both Cuba and the Soviet Union where he and his mother were received with the highest of honors. He died of old age in Cuba. Trotsky only wanted Leninism to spread throughout the USSR and the world, with his theory of Permanent Revolution and World Communism.

Alas, Trotsky was not without "crimes" either. He had allowed for punitive brigades to fight desertion in the Red Army, the inclusion of secret Chekist policemen being a lethal deterrent to combat not only desertion, but anti-Communism and treason. Like Lenin's Red Terror, these measures were desperate and overly lethal, but effective in their endeavor. So, were Stalin's measures necessary in the historical and sociopolitical context of the USSR? Or was he simply attempting to protect his privileged and powerful position? The countless fellow Comrades he executed in his purges, the Old Bolsheviks who had helped establish the USSR, the countless innocent Soviet countrymen ... was all that blood worth it, or even excusable under Marxism?

My mind began to think a curious thought very suddenly; what if all of this was nothing but Western lies and anti-Communist propaganda? How could I be so sure about what

I was reading? What if all of this were simple exaggerations spread to confuse young Communists like myself? If this happened to be true, I could no longer hold "Uncle" Stalin in very high esteem given the circumstances, or look the other way regarding political or fraternal betrayal, but still I found myself unable to remove every trace of the Man of Steel from my room. It was a harsh emotional detachment, as I had learned to respect and love the man immensely. Stalin was the great builder of Communism and the architect of the USSR, which became a global superpower under his direction. I was of course aware of the leftist Communist movement, of which people like Rosa Luxemburg and Karl Lieb-knecht were pioneers. I was aware of the criticism of Stalin by other Marxists. And what about Khruschev? He couldn't have been lying. My suspicions arose new feelings of mistrust. Had Stalin been a product of the time, needed for the survival of the USSR? Or had he left a mark of blood, repression and abuse far more brutal than it was necessary for a simple lust for power? Many say he limited himself to follow Lenin's footsteps, like the creation of the secret police "Cheka" – which was renamed and restructured as "GPU," then as "OG-PU" and finally "NKVD" under Stalin – which employed mass summary executions of political dissidents, reactionaries and anti-revolutionaries like the former capitalists, aristocrats, bourgeoisie, members of the clergy, priests, White Army soldiers and so on. But Lenin was no murderer. He was just rational, and didn't take pride or pleasure in it, something to which I felt quite related to. Lenin simply regarded this as necessary for the survival of the first Communist State in the world. It made no difference to him in front of the greater good. While I didn't advocate the murders of millions, and certainly not if they were my own comrades or countrymen, I did not mind the elimination of a few key figures, obviously

in case they could be attempting to murder me first so as to eliminate the social movement behind my political party, like when Lenin was targeted by Fanny Kaplan. Destabilization attempts are the most common way to dissuade the peoples from partaking in a social radical movement. Fidel had to struggle against this in his very own Cuba, and so did Che fighting in the frontlines of Revolution. Neither of them allowed their soldiers to betray them to the enemy, or to go about abusing their power and rape peasant women, and they had punished them accordingly with respectful and fair executions like in the infamous La Cabaña prison, which saw the end of many disgusting pro-Batista soldiers, traitors, anti-revolutionaries, war criminals, thugs and even agents of Batista's Bureau for the Repression of Communist Activities, the secret police of the Batista regime which just like the Tsarist Okhrana, had a reputation for being brutally lethal. These people met their end with amazingly popular support from the peasants, who were surprisingly eager for Fidel and Che to get rid of them. What's more democratic than that? To further illustrate this, I'll tell you what Fidel said about José Saramago, a Portuguese libertarian Communist and recipient of the Nobel Prize in Literature, demonstrating quite well my feelings toward this entire issue:

"He is not the only one who opposes the death penalty; millions of compatriots dislike it, but not one had the slightest hesitation before the alternative they know very well. He shoould have expressed his disagreement, but should not have uttered a single word to feed the aggressiveness of the US government against Cuba, nor offer arguments that the brutal imperialist system which seeks to justify an aggression against Cuba receives with delight. More troubling is that Saramago, and some others who have acted in good

faith, seem to completely ignore that the planet is rapidly running toward a global fascist-Nazi tyranny. In all likelihood, I think he got carried away by a fit of anger and disappointment that clouded his ability to reason. Or rather something else, perhaps a fleeting trait of self-sufficiency and vanity, nothing extraordinary in a good Communist for many years used to slander and diatribe, who was suddenly elevated to the Olympus of the Nobel Prize."

To every single person that accuses Che and Fidel of being nothing more than cold-blooded murderers, know that class-warfare happens because of the blatant economic inequality and the eventual hatred that ensues from it, and that the poor have all the right in the world to rise up and murder their oppressors, just like in the French Revolution, a progressive movement which was always in the mind of all Marxists. I also laughed at those deluded by imperialist manipulators who accused Che of advocating the gratuitous use of nuclear attacks on the US. Taking his words completely out of context like usual, Che had wanted only for Cuba to defend herself against the threat of Unitedstatian nuclear attacks looming in the horizon, and loathed the idea of ever reaching the point of using nuclear weapons in the first place, for obvious reasons. Lethality and violence have to happen in revolution and war because those who support the rotten system of capitalism will vehemently cling to it mercilessly, willing to also commit atrocious acts to defend it. The difference rests entirely on whether you inflict this violence reasonably and surgically, or you choose to abuse your power.

Lenin had been an advocate of Mass Terror ever since the Tsarist regime had hung his brother Alexander Ilyich for attempting to kill the Emperor Alexander III. When he passed from simple revolutionary to Leader of the State he

didn't look so revolutionary, noble and dramatic inside an office, yet he felt the same; reactionaries and enemies of Communism had to die. Let us not forget that, for example, during the Civil War the rival White Army had started its very own series of atrocities named "White Terror," and their acts were so vile and cruel that Lenin's "Red Terror" was the only way to stop them and eliminate the enemy definitely. Let us not forget, racism was widespread in Tsarist Russia, and the widely anti-Semitic White Movement often organized systematic murders of Jews, something Lenin loathed immensely. Lenin, however, knew the limit to these much-needed acts of repression. Stalin had faced brutal criticism from Lenin due to his violent nature, who deemed him incapable of governing the USSR. Lenin had also criticized Trotsky and the other Bolsheviks at some level, but he considered Trotsky capable and efficient as General Secretary, perhaps even his successor. After all, Trotsky had been the mastermind behind the October Revolution in military terms. Lenin the Ideologue and Trotsky the General had defeated the Tsar and laid the foundations for the Soviet State. Stalin then seized his opportunity and started making a name for himself under Lenin's wing. He was also an advocate of Mass Terror and many ideas about the Cheka and its functions had been his. Lenin simply gave the "red" light. He saw this Terror as pure strategy, as he had learned to separate politics from feelings or personal touches. For him, this was a matter of life or death. The killing of a few to him assured the survival of the State. Stalin took this even further when he came into power, and purged almost everything he came across. This derived in the killings of not only a few thousand, but of millions.

Lenin, however, knew the limit to these much-needed acts of repression. Stalin had faced brutal criticism from Lenin due to his violent nature, who deemed him incapable of gov-

erning the USSR. Lenin had also criticized Trotsky and the other Bolsheviks at some level, but he considered Trotsky capable and efficient as General Secretary, perhaps even his successor. After all, Trotsky had been the mastermind behind the October Revolution in military terms. Lenin the Ideologue and Trotsky the General had defeated the Tsar and laid the foundations for the Soviet State. Stalin then seized his opportunity and started making a name for himself under Lenin's wing. He was also an advocate of Mass Terror and many ideas about the Cheka and its functions had been his. Lenin simply gave the "red" light. He saw this Terror as pure strategy, as he had learned to separate politics from feelings or personal touches. For him, this was a matter of life or death. The killing of a few to him assured the survival of the State. Stalin took this even further when he came into power, and purged almost everything he came across. This derived in the killings of not only a few thousand, but of millions.

What else can be possibly said about this? Every government or state has committed genocide one way or another, organized crime does it today in similar ways and people take justice by their own hand when they see it fit. Nobody would lecture me with hypocritical bourgeois morality. However, I did know where the limit lay. Lenin and Trotsky were at heart good, intelligent people, who would however stop at nothing to achieve the desired end. They did this because they didn't want anyone to remove them from their position, stop their idealized Revolution and start a vicious circle where capitalist systems would rise and fall again. Lenin, on one occasion, said the following; "Socialism is revolution and revolutions are never pretty. We aim to dispatch an autocrat and his compatriots, who are guarded by the state police, and we know their methods of repression are brutal. Those who suffer most under the current system must be made angry at

their exploitation by the higher classes, angry enough to demand their rights and rewrite the class system. We have seen the rise and fall of dissent, of communes, of a half-dozen movements that have never captured the masses because they failed to explain to the people the problems of structural inequity." I believe that sums it all up pretty well. Lenin and his comrades realized who they were fighting, and noticed that the only way to win was to become even more ruthless than the opposition. This was later transferred to the brutal and vicious civil war they had to win in order to stay in power. They believed in an idea, and knew what losing would entail, regressing back into the decadent past. Some people objected to the killings, in the face of such madness, obviously they did; but Lenin pretended not to hear them. What for? His enemies would have done the same. It was a war, a class war. He did ruthless things to achieve the goal he had been waiting for so long, like so many other leaders, kings, emperors, and revolutionaries before him. But history clearly shows that the circle never stops; The Cheka was like the Okhrana before it, and like the Oprichniki of Ivan Grozny. They were sadists and murderers who took pleasure in their work, or if they didn't they simply got used to it by the hand of alcohol or drugs. But even if they caused these atrocities, they did not escape their harm. Most became mentally ill and developed serious psychotic disorders. They were tools used by politicians, and like normal tools, they all ended up blunt and ruined. No human mind can escape the harm of witnessing, or even worse, committing an atrocity. My vision of Communism was completely incompatible with such brutal methods and I didn't think I'd ever adopt them. Oprichniki, Okhrana, Cheka, GPU, OGPU, NKVD ... these forms of repression represent the utmost definition of disgust in my dictionary, and I certainly do not approve of such cynical

organized methods of mass-killing. But is there any other way out for us humans when the opposition is so cruel and relentless? Does blood need to be shed so gratuitously and so abundantly for goals to be met, for society to leave aside the decadence of the past and venture into the future? Isn't there a better way to bring about said changes? Surely, I can say many things regarding the evils under systems not related to Communism, particularly about the history of the United States; McCarthyism was in its own way the Unitedstatian Cheka, and let's not forget about the genocides of natives, slavery, the KKK, the imprisonment and murder of innocent people of German, Italian and Japanese descent during WWII, the atomic bombings of Hiroshima and Nagasaki, the atrocities in Vietnam and the effects of Agent Orange, the rights of blacks and women in the '60s, the CIA crimes and destabilization attempts in other countries including the overthrow of democratically elected leaders and the support of repressive military juntas ... but I'm not concerned about them now. I'm talking about the past errors and misdeeds of something I strongly believed in; and this leads us to Isaac Asimov.

Together with Mr. Sagan, Asimov remains up to this day one of the most renowned, iconic and popular science fiction writers and science popularizers, one of the few Unitedstatians I was able to truly admire, without exception. A humanist that saw beneath politics, symbols, nationalism or parties, and was able to define exactly what humanity needed. But my lust for Communism had blinded me to the point that I hated anything Unitedstatian, considering it flirting with the enemy. Never again. There was no need to be blind and shun others because of their nationalities instead of opening up to the truth behind their ideas.

Regarding the need for birth control, Asimov said that ex-

treme measures would have to be taken if people didn't cooperate and acted selfishly like they do now. Asimov, the pacifist, the optimistic scientist incapable of condoning violence
said it himself. Carl Sagan admitted to it as well, optimistic
and idealistic as he was. Order, peace, prosperity, education,
culture and cooperation will be the ultimate goal. Systems
like Communism – and people like Lenin – aimed to accomplish this.

Some people want to reinvent humanity, make it better,
smarter, more capable, efficient and most importantly, *humane.* The natural evolution to the Homo Sapiens Sapiens has not arrived yet in full scale, but key people in history
have shown through their acts a nature more akin to superior
beings than regular men. By superior I don't mean of course,
a racial or a biological feature. I mean the feature to show
your commitment to better yourself and those around you, to
show what being a true human being should entail. Marxists
like Stalin show little commitment toward making this end
feasible, and moreover leave a trail of excessive and unnecessary blood, pain, repression and destruction which talks of
their actions furthermore, and worst of all, fuels anti-
Communist sentiment and deters people from looking up to
Communism as a viable socioeconomic system. Who knows
what Lenin or Trotsky could have created in the newly established USSR if things hadn't turned out like that? Who knows
if the union between all leftists worldwide, no matter the
party or specific ideology, could have cleared the way for a
Socialist Paradise, spreading globally as people looked up to
the benefits of Communism? Certainly, in post-Communist
Russia, people wouldn't have suffered like they did, living in a
country devoid of ideology or meaning, stricken by Western
influence while poverty raged on and the rich enjoyed themselves buying properties, cars and diamond clad golden cell-

phones. They wouldn't have suffered when organized crime spread like vermin and made its way into the already polluted veins of the decaying USSR. To my eyes, the modern Russian state was still a beacon of hope and pride for all ex-Soviet peoples, especially because of its anti-Western stance, but it remained plagued by vermin. Without the Soviet influence, Russians transformed into ruthless capitalists, racist fascists, sexual deviants, murderous gangsters, imperialistic national-ists and anti-scientific religious zealots, all because of the Soviet collapse. It was clear to me that my Unitedstatian enemy wasn't just guilty of assassinating the Soviet State, but of turning it into the disgusting pile of distorted semi-ideologies and deluded tendencies it became under 'democ-racy,' of stripping the Soviet peoples of their pride, Party, State and Ideology. But it wasn't time to cry over spilled milk, for revenge or anything as petty as that. It was time to think about the future and get over the past without ever forgetting the mistakes committed.

The Soviet Union under Stalin became the only opposition to the Unitedstatian Eagle, a true power to respect and fear worldwide. There was no denying he had been a true Com-munist. It didn't really matter whether it was all Western slander, campaigns to corrupt his image or otherwise. He had turned the USSR back on its feet, turned it into a modern superpower and slain the Nazi invader, all at an incredible cost in human lives, but he had ensured that the USSR pre-vailed. However, that era for humanity was over, and more civilized and peaceful measures needed to be taken, as people would not cope with brutal changes no matter how necessary or crucial. Conclusions like these were what made me mature politically as well as emotionally. I'd leave any type of radical extremism behind and focus on the welfare of humanity and my comrades through science, culture, duty and education,

never resorting to drastic or repressive measures. What kept troubling me was that though bringing forth unimaginable suffering and death in their wake, many massacres and disasters do serve their purpose in making the world better. With war new technologies emerge that end up helping everyday civilian life, with tyrannical oppression come newer political doctrines with a more humane approach to sociopolitical problems. Every single chaotic act by mankind which derives in unbelievable suffering scars the future forever, preventing future generations from repeating old mistakes. And this would be the basis for my new ideology; an ideology which would never forget.

With my mind made up, I continued onwards ready to confront whatever this situation would lay ahead for me, with one thing being brightly clear; I had to survive. I had to succeed in society and reject distractions like Faye. I had to follow the footsteps of my leaders and enrich both myself and those surrounding me with knowledge, camaraderie and friendship, true to ideals and moral. It was the only way I thought of healing my wounds after the devastation a friend's betrayal and a woman's disdain caused in my already damaged psyche. This had been the final straw between me and the Man of Steel, which I was to exile from my heart just like he exiled Trotsky out of the USSR, not to mention the Old Bolsheviks and millions of other innocent Soviet comrades. I learned that having true and complete admiration for every Communist in history, truly heartfelt and sincere, is impossible. Communism must be built and made pure learning from the human practical mistakes of history. Lenin, Stalin and Mao are but examples of Communist rule, each with their merits and shortcomings. Complete admiration is optional, and I decided to exclude Stalin from the group, since no matter how heartfelt his devotion to Communism could be, he

exceeded himself with his power, bringing forth suffering for not only the Soviet countrymen, but for Old Bolsheviks and comrades as well. It was a difficult ideological situation for a loyalist Communist such as I, who sought evermore the truest incarnation of Communism. Inexcusable things had taken place under Communist governments, this could not be denied; and thus, this was the perfect time to learn from them and improve upon them in the future.

It was decided. I would forever separate politics from feelings and move on forwards toward a more virtuous path, toward the ultimate evolution of Communism. It didn't matter what figures of Communism I admired or how much I admired them as long as I learned from their actions and words. I would dedicate my life to the creation of a political movement focused on bringing the most exemplary forms of Communist politics, economic policies, culture and values emphasizing the hard Soviet lessons to every corner of the globe in hopes of fighting the rampant idiocy and constant economic recessions brought forth by the capitalism of Western democracies, countering them with strict military discipline, incorruptible ideals and vast sociopolitical knowledge. I had still a long road ahead of me, but I would continue learning and studying until reaching the ultimate conclusion on how the world should truly function. The left needed to unite and stop the quarrel, the incessant in-fighting between Trotskyists and Stalinists, between revisionists and anti-revisionists, between those most conservative and those most liberal. We were all comrades, all Communists and Socialists, dedicated Marxists and anti-imperialists fighting for social change and economic equality; when this useless fraternal disputes were finally put to rest, we could eventually focus on our sworn enemy and liberate the peoples from the yoke of capitalism. This was the dream of Michael Weinstein.

I would name this movement SOVREV; *SOVetskaya REVolutsiya*.

- CHAPTER XII -

Perestroika

"Life is not an easy matter ... you cannot live through it without falling into frustration and cynicism unless you have before you a great idea which raises you above personal misery, above weakness, above all kinds of perfidy and baseness."

- LEON TROTSKY -

Soviet Bolshevik Revolutionary and Politician, Marxist Writer and Theorist, Founder and General of the Red Army, War Commissar of the RSFRS and founder of the Communist 4th International

---

"You're not gonna believe it when I tell ya, you're gonna trip balls," Ryan kept saying as he dragged me inside the apartment after a long school day, separating me from Dave, who had accompanied me on the way to The Crucible. Roughly a week had passed since the incident, and I had missed school on purpose, turning my phone off and isolating myself completely from the outside world. I was incapable of facing Faye or Wolfgang, but I gathered enough strength to decide to attend that day. Interestingly enough, I never saw either of them during the day. Wolfgang seemed to have skipped school himself. As so much time had passed since that awful night, Ryan seemed unwilling to touch the subject, probably fearful of reopening very recent wounds. Dave

"Yeah …"

"13 since when?"

"Well, her birthday is on, ah … January, I think …"

"So you're going around touching barely pubescent girls?"

"Hey, shut up motherfucker, 13's a good age. I'm only 18, who gives a shit? What is it, four, five years of difference? May I remind you that my sister was 15 when you decided to crazily fall in love with her like a schmuck?"

"I'm 18 since a couple of weeks ago and she's 16 now … that's only two years …"

"Ah, whatever, in case you forgot 19's the age where you become an adult in Loynne's, in every way, drinkin', drivin', fuckin', all that crap. When I hit 19 I'll reconsider my options. And in any case who gives a shit, she's still a girl, ain't she? She has a pussy, she has her period, she gets wet, she sucks dick, she's a woman for all I know …"

"She sucked your dick?!"

"Haha! Hey! So what! Why are you starin' at me like that? Thought you'd be happy for me!"

"I don't think this is quite right, Ryan …"

"Me neither, that's why it adds up to the kink of the whole thing … it's like morally ambiguous and wrong and nice all rolled into one, and she's got some damn nice titties for her age …"

"I'm supposing I'm the only one who knows about this deplorable incident, right?"

"Yeah and I would like to keep it that way. As you may know, this ain't the best of things to go around tellin' people, even though I'm dyin' to show off … this bitch, I tell you, she has like this reputation of being a little slut but she doesn't know a thing, I think I'm her first. Maybe she dared because of my age, you know, maybe she felt like she needed to step up and give a guy what he needs. She probably just dates

little kids or somethin' and now wants to play popular girl and brag about how she gets drilled by older guys ..."

"Ah, yeah ... anyway, I'm proud of you, whatever you want to hear. But next time you give me shit because of your sister you'll know your argument is null before you even open your mouth."

"Yeah, yeah, whatever, as if that's gonna happen. I heard what went down at the party, I'm not deaf. So she completely fucked you over at last. Good. Now we can all rest easy assured that you'll move on and this shitty situation will be forgotten forever."

"Yeah, I don't know what to say. I mean ... I didn't think she was capable of doing that ..."

"Me neither, that's why I almost kill both her and Dave. How the fuck did he allow her to get drunk and get funky with some guy she barely knew? That's not like her at all ... I think this is like, corruptin' her. I know a girl has to at some point get it on with guys and go to parties, but she's just so young ..."

"Says the guy who's just done getting funky with Miss Beauty Pageant Aged 13?"

"That's different, nobody gives a shit about a little slut like Eva, girls like Eva are born wrong from the very start. In a few years she's gonna be Johanna II. If I wasn't goin' around corruptin' her someone else would, 'cause that's what she's lookin' for. Probably will get pregnant in a couple of years. Faye, on the other hand, is smart, she's a good student, she's got a bright future ahead of her if she keeps on the right path ... this concerns me more than I'm lettin' on, Sonny ... if she decides to become some party slut there'll be no stoppin' her ... my mom doesn't give a shit. Well, not quite, it's more like she doesn't have any real power over this family ... and my dad, well, he's not exactly around to help us out ... and he's

got that other shitty family of his to mind, so you know ... it's harsh."

"So in other words it's all up to you because if it were up to Dave this family would go downhill all the way."

"Yeah. That's the way I see it, but who listens to me anyway ... don't care. Now, I finally can do what I've been wanting to do for a long time. Bang some Kraut."

"Well ... and what do you think of Faye spending the night with Wolfgang, given that's what happened?"

"Personally, I think the guy's a spineless schmuck. And secondly, I would never approve of anyone being with her that isn't slightly more successful than any figure I admire. So that's difficult by itself. In other words, fuck that guy, I don't care, she can do whatever she wants and fuck around as long as she don't fuck her life up ... as for me, I got an appointment if you don't mind ..."

"What? You're kicking me out after showing off and now you leave me to rot?"

"Sorry! Get a life Sonny, if you had a girlfriend we could double date or swing or somethin'. Now come on, scram, I gotta lock the house."

"You're a selfish dick, you know that? Now that you have a girlfriend of your own and I have no possibilities with Faye you don't give a shit anymore ..."

"Aww, come on, it's nothin' like that, don't be so sensitive! Come on man, next time we'll do somethin' together, it's just I can't tell how much this bitch wants me around and I gotta taste the moment before she gets bored and dumps me ... surely you understand ..."

"I understand that the day I get a girlfriend I'm going to pay you back in kind ..."

"Look, I'll compensate you for this, OK? We'll do somethin' some time, I'll help you out get a chick, I dunno, you

name it, anythin' as long as you scram now and let me go in peace with this bitch, besides my mother will get back in a while, if not I'd spend the whole afternoon locked in here with her, what do you think?"

"Fine, I'll drop it, but don't forget what you did one ... I didn't complain when you went away with Eva during my birthday, and I didn't complain after you denied me a miserable glass of water when you were having fun with her and I was half dying ... you owe me ... not counting the countless other things I do for you at school, in case you didn't notice, you would have already been murdered by an angry mob of Kannies and Lollies had it not been for me ... plus, I have to listen to ranting you all day long about your romantic insecurities and your sexual conquests, which is bad enough ..."

"Fine, alright, point taken, I'll be less selfish with you from now on and more of a friend ... but watch it, motherfucker ... I could throw in shit about you too, you know, about my sister an' all that, but I ain't gonna do it ... 'cause I let it go. I don't let things like that come between us. You shouldn't either."

"Regarding your sister, you don't have to worry anymore, ever again. Anyway I'm off, I don't want to see her strolling with her boyfriend in front of me."

"Good idea, I don't particularly want to worry about Japanese weirdo schmucks being accidentally thrown from the seventh floor by angry Russians ... anyway, bye man, good luck out there!"

"Yeah, yeah, bye ..."

"Hey Sonny, wait!"

"What? I thought you wanted me to scram?"

"Yeah, it's only quick ... I wanted to ask you, have you seen much of Billy lately?"

"Billy? No, why?"

"Oh ... nothin', it's just that ... he don't answer the house

phone or the cell-phone, and he's never around in ChitChat ..."

"Well, you know how he is, always disappearing ..."

"Yeah ... that's what I thought ... anyway, one thing Sonny ... I wouldn't hang out with him much if I were you ... just a thought ..."

"What do you mean by that?"

"Nothin', just that ... I don't think he's all up there you know, from what Dave's been tellin' me ..."

"Yeah, well ... has he ever been?"

"I guess not ... anyway, see ya man!"

"Bye."

After leaving Ryan's house I realized there wasn't much I could do in Pilgrim Coast, aside from going back home. I exited through the parking lot entrance, the quickest way to the bus station, and proceeded to climb the unnerving slope with the sun completely scorching my face, while listening to Kino's *"Zakroy Za Mnoy Dver, Ia Ukhazhu"* — "Close the Door Behind Me, I'm Leaving" —.

"What now?" I couldn't help but think time and time again. What was there to do now that life returned back to square one? What was there to keep me going until the infinitely long objective of reuniting with my family, which would surely take years, finally happened? Studying? I couldn't care less about studying; I was beginning to become a proud underachiever and outcast, having absolutely no respect for the theoretical academic world and its papier-mâché goals. It felt good to attain knowledge, but wasn't enough to sustain my cravings. I sought something that really made me feel alive, happy. Books can provide that in some way, but they're not everything. Something physical, like the touch of a loved one, is always needed. And I was very much alone.

I certainly needed something superior to attain, but this time I had aimed too high. If the search for the right woman would have to wait, then it was indeed time to occupy myself with the political life, with concerns regarding my ideology, like Michael Weinstein would have done, like Lenin and the Bolsheviks had done before him. SOVREV should be my main concern, not Faye. But I was sick of theory and lack of practice. How could I apply my new-found ideology in my daily life? There was little I could do about that. My status as a legal citizen, which could be shattered to pieces if the police decided to investigate further on how I got to the country, could not be compromised under any means. I needed to stay out of trouble as much as possible, and the political life would only make it easier for them to deport me. No, I couldn't risk it. I had to do something else, something that didn't involve any risk at all. Suddenly, the hype I had garnered with the creation of SOVREV in my head seemed to have deflated, lost in the heat of that palm-tree ridden avenue and those stupid tourists with kids and inflatable crocodiles. Political conscience and violent revolution were a thing of the past. This was the first lesson I had to learn if I was to implement communist ideas in a XXI century context. The world had changed, and so had the needs of the people. It was just a matter of knowing what people wanted, reaching out to them, and providing them with what they thought they needed. Then they would be educated with superior ideas. This thought re-energized me; the world was in a chaotic state, like it had been before either of the World Wars, and it was begging for a change, for fresh ideas that could revitalize human civilization and grant people a purpose. I had to base my political ideas on my personal experiences. What I lacked, what I wanted, what I felt I needed most; people all around me surely had similar concerns, and it was just a matter of

promising that to them. I thought of Mike, an intelligent and capable human being left to rot in a system that couldn't provide him with what he needed or wanted, lost in a sea of mediocrity. Axel was the opposite, a true product of this land, a parasite content only with living it up at the cost of others. Something had to be done, like Wolfgang had said, taking the best of both systems; in practice, strong government and institutions, free and universal quality education and healthcare, with luxury and consumer items to appease the people into comfort. Perhaps, what Loynne's Island already was, minus the inane superficiality of capitalism, which would be replaced by strong political consciousness and a cultured population. Loynne's had the means; I had the ideas. Loynne's could indeed be Paradise Itself if the stupidity of people was wiped out and replaced by superior culture. I smiled gleefully at the idea of turning Loynne's Island into what my parents would have loved, a kind of New Motherland, a paradise with socialist ideas and practices, without the poverty, the bureaucracy, the repression, the isolation, the aggressive state rhetoric, the sabotages by Western enemies, the corruption by greedy officials, the sad and hopeless population in rags dreaming of prosperity. It would be true socialism, a paradise of the workers indeed. The now-deceased European welfare state had managed to provide a well-balanced blend between capitalism and communism. Now it was time to improve upon it, to truly combine both systems to create true equality and prosperity for all.

I was now at the southernmost part of the bus station, making my way to the 202 line stop. It was incredible how much I hated this stupid bus stop, the lost British and German tourists looking uselessly at enormous maps, the Hispanic-looking immigrants chatting loudly and smoking those disgusting cigars, the amazingly hot and shallow girls impos-

sible to possess or ignore, the 40-year-old Kanny bums covered in tattoos, speaking incoherently and bothering people for money to support their drug habits. But as per usual with matters regarding my luck, things were about to get worse, much worse.

Wolfgang, who was obviously heading toward The Crucible via the bus stop, appeared behind the kiosk. My eyes turned into slits as I stared at him from a distance, cold on my tracks, not believing the bitch would allow him into her home instantly when it had cost me an incredible amount of effort to earn the right for it. He noticed me and instantly adopted a different posture, visibly uncomfortable as he obviously didn't plan to meet me so unexpectedly. With a tightened knot around my throat, still remembering his shadowy figure next to Faye's on the sunbed, I approached him quickly without even realizing, walking in an automatic fashion. Now, I only needed to know the truth behind that night, once and for all.

"You disgusting rotten traitor ..." I began, approaching him as if to fight. I wanted to punch him right in the face but something stopped me. I couldn't see Wolfgang as an enemy.

"No, wait Sonny, I'm incredibly sorry ..." He began, but I cut him off as soon as he started.

"So ... this is what you've been up to, huh? What the hell do you think you're doing? Is this how you repay me how kind I've been to you? Eh? The only real friend you've fucking had here, the only one that completely trusted you? You're dead to me as well, Wolfgang. Forget we ever met."

"Look, Sonny ... we need to discuss this. I mean ... there's lots of things that ... well ... that you need to know. Things are not what they seem, don't jump to any conclusions. I've been talking to Faye, and well ... she just doesn't consider you to be the one she wants to be with. And well ... I'm gonna be hon-

est, I began to like Faye for some time now, I clearly know what you see in her, and I feel incredibly bad with this, but ... well, if one of us has to be with her, it's clearly her choice."

"Wolfgang, *comrade* ... you seem to not understand something. I saw her first. I fell in love with her first. SO SHE'S FUCKING MINE, OK?!"

"No ... no ... that's not true, Sonny. Look, this is just like with Lyria, the same exact situation, but I was in your shoes, I was on the losing side. And I had to take it. If there's one thing I know, is that you can't make girls like you for who you are. You're gonna suffer even more fooling yourself this way. You can't change her mind, her feelings, the way she feels toward somebody. She really doesn't feel nothing related to that when she sees you Sonny, she's told me everything. And who are we kidding? You knew all along yourself. From what she's told me, everyone has tried to talk you into abandoning this infatuation but you're relentless. She's tired of it too. She really appreciates you as a friend, honestly, she has a blast with you, but that's about it, those are her words. So you can do two things Sonny, you can be like this, and wish us dead, or you can try to get over this and focus on some other girl and we can leave this behind for good and be friends again. She really wants us all to be friends. She was never yours to start off with. Don't feel like that, like she was yours and I stole her, like you lost, like I defeated you. There's no such thing. I know how you feel and it's terrible, but it's only natural. Some girls like you, other girls don't. I've been there. And for once, well, I found someone who I really like. I hate girls getting between comrades and destroying everything, but listen, she was never yours in the first place, she's never been with you. Understand that before it's too late. Nothing good will happen to you if you keep this up, you'll only feel more frustrated, chasing something you can't get."

"You wouldn't have carried on with this if you truly valued my friendship. Lyria was nothing. She was just another Loynnerin. You knew what Faye meant to me. You knew it."

"I'm sorry Sonny, but there's really not a thing that can keep me from this, I've finally found someone worthy and I don't think it's right for you or anybody to object to that. Would you like that? Did you enjoy it when her brothers butted in between Faye and you?"

"This is one of those moments in life where you have to choose, Wolfgang. You made your choice already. Face the consequences. I am facing them right now. You betrayed me. You both did. That's something I'll have to cope with. Now, I'll move on, without your friendship. From what you're telling me, I've already lost you, and even though it hurts it's something I have to assume. I'll never feel good again beside any of you. It will remind me always of that horrible night."

"It still won't fix anything. There's no escaping this situation as long as you don't beat your infatuation, your obsession with her ..."

"I'm not obsessed. I love that girl ... I loved ..."

"No ... you are obsessed ... you always speak of possession and ownership ... you want to own her. It will be difficult, but you'll eventually overcome this, Sonny. In no time, Faye will be nothing to you, you won't even remember that night. But only if you choose to do it. The power to do so resides within you. Nobody else will make it happen. Come on, *Doshi*. There's tons of girls out there, you will throw your happiness overboard trying to be with someone who you will have to change all over to be with in the first place ... there must be someone perfectly suited for you out there, someone who likes you for who you are and what you look like now ..."

"Wolfgang ... there's nothing else to say. I'm sorry. Thanks for speaking like this, but as of now, we're no longer com-

rades. We can't be. I'm sorry, and at the same time, I'm really not. I hope you enjoy your time with her. You might as well."

" '*Mizu ni nagasu.*' "

"And what is that supposed to mean?"

" 'Let the water flow' ... forgive and forget."

" '*Proshchay, no nikogda ne zabyvay.*' " I replied. "Forgive, but never forget."

I stared at a truly awkward and concerned Wolfgang who was looking down at the floor in shame. He was visibly hurt, and I could tell he never predicted I'd decide to bluntly end the friendship. Throughout the whole conversation, I looked at him as if pleading, like begging to stop whatever he could have started, not as an enemy but as a friend, and old friend who was about to depart forever. There was nothing but the power of mercy and forgiveness in my eyes. But not now. Like he well said, it was an impossible endeavor, a complex situation that would end up not letting me feel anything positive for Faye or Wolfgang ever again. I knew what was going on inside his mind. He hated how the tables had turned and the situation had made him lose a good friend and gain the best girlfriend he could hope for. After all, he was not evil, just driven by the same passions as me. Still, betrayal was the only thing I saw in both of them. They had conspired against me, disregarded my feelings as collateral damage and forced me into moving on. I was submerged in the most intense hatred for the people who once I considered my very best friends, yet had so gleefully decided to betray me. I left without uttering another word, leaving him be. I didn't even want to see him walk toward The Crucible.

The bus stop now laid deserted of anyone I could call a friend, but I found a much more fearsome foe than the prospect of mere loneliness and my own self-loathing; the presence of Jason Clark Vega.

I became immediately alarmed when noticing how near he was to me. Jason was simply sitting on one of the benches, but I knew what his behavior was like. It could turn from peaceful and quiet to clinically insane in a millionth of a second. I had to be careful. Unleashed in the streets, he could actually do so much damage that the prospect of facing him in school was bliss in comparison. You could never know what he could do in the open, outside of the school walls, unrestrained by teachers and fellow students. If there was indeed someone untouchable in Loynne's it had to be him.

Jason suddenly got up from the bench, giving a sudden and athletically graceful jump, smoking the instantly recognizable smell of marijuana. He now seemed impatient and frustrated with something, walking back and forth like a jailed lion. It was weird to see him alone as well. When he wasn't next to Monika, he was always surrounded by his cronies. Seeing him in an odd context resulted exponentially more intimidating. After all, he had the latest Hades-Larsson car available, a brand new, long-wheeled and futuristic red Drakkar V1 equipped with the most exclusive extras and custom-built with the very best features the company had to offer. This was the flagship car driven by politicians and top executives in Loynne's, costing a considerable amount of 600,000 crosses, 200,000 more of what you would normally pay for a Sforza Cavaliere, the fastest sports car in the world at the time. There was absolutely no point in Jason being at the bus stop. I kept looking at him, wondering and speculating as JC himself looked at other pedestrians, his entire head following them rudely as they strolled out of sight. I remember Axel telling me about this behavior before when we were about to exit the school during a free hour, waiting at the staircase by the entrance. JC had been waiting for someone to punish who had supposedly disrespected Monika, but Axel

quickly dismissed this piece of gossip implying he was only looking plain and simply for trouble. Nobody had done anything as Monika would have taken care of the trouble herself, she had no trouble fighting guys. JC was on the lookout purely for frustrations to vent, and this was no exception.

In any case, it was bound to happen; our eyes finally met. Through Kannovschina you simply learned to avoid automatically looking at people in the eye, but the fading of this bullying culture had made me less fearful and more likely to stare at others freely. I had no excuse. I knew the consequence of this and still continued to exercise my supposed democratic right to look at him. Waiting for what at this point had become the Purple Miracle instead of the Purple Wonder, I found myself looking directly into the disgusting blue eyes of that towering example of societal garbage, which right now were looking directly at its target. JC was now extremely pissed off.

"*WHAT?!*" He yelled with his booming jock voice, which often made him seem mentally challenged. He often shouted at people in a way I fancied both incredibly rude and offensive, insulting everything from pride and manliness all the way to intelligence.

"*WHAT?!*" He repeated. Not answering proved to be a fatal mistake, as did ignoring him and looking away, hoping the Purple Miracle would come and save me. I was now, aside from incredibly nervous and nauseated, facing the probable outcome of a fight that would leave me in a hospital for several weeks.

I knew Jason would forget about me as soon as I escaped from the area. He was clearly drugged out of his mind, in a violent mood-swing, hoping to fuck someone up so bad and forgetting about him in the very same way he would fuck one of his whores. I only needed to avoid this and the crisis would

be averted. But now that I had looked at him and ignored the situation, I would have to face him.

"WHAT YOU LOOKIN' AT, FAGGOT MOTHERFUCK-ER?! He shouted, startling onlookers and making everyone look at me in surprise, as if I were to blame from some heinous crime. This was what I had been dreading the most, even more so than being in the hospital two or three weeks. The public embarrassment Jason often submitted his victim's toward.

"GONNA FUCKIN' KILL YOU," he went on, as I focused all my attention on the person in front of me, wishing the bus to materialize miraculously.

"COME HERE AND FIGHT IF YOU CALL YOURSELF A MAN, COCKCHOKIN' FAG," he shouted at the top of his lungs. Even from 10 meters away, I felt as if he had just shouted that right in my ear.

The bus appeared. A pack of people fought to get in quickly, maybe wanting to run away from JC as well, not wishing to be possible victims during their wait in line. I was now wishing for the people to get in as fast as possible before Jason dragged me from the line and finally mauled me. I was literally expecting to be pulled from the line at any moment, but I did not see Jason with the corner of my eye moving any nearer. He was right where he stood up, shouting without actually moving. I was wondering if it was all show, or if he was in the mood for insulting but not for actually fighting. Who knows the substances he could have had in his organism at that instant. Maybe he was too high to fight anyone. I breathed in relief a bit, clinging to that illusion until I was safely on the bus.

"MOTHERFUCKIN' PUSSY FAGGOT, GETS IN THE BUS TO RUN AWAY FROM A FIGHT," Jason shouted. I had had enough.

I didn't care so much about facing Jason as I did for missing the bus and having to wait around for an hour until another one appeared, but still that didn't make me less fearful; my legs trembled as I approached the taller antagonist, the best Unitedstatian representative of everything that was wrong with that nation; the untouchable drug-abusing jock who was admired and respected for being a dumb and aggressive degenerate only good for tossing a ball around. I would not be disrespected by this human form of scum.

Jason, not expecting me to stray from the bus line in order to challenge him, opened his drug-ravaged eyes more than ever, his jaw clenched in fury at this sign of fearlessness from a victim. It was the last thing I saw before everything turned black and I hit the ground.

I wasn't sure how or when Jason mobilized his arm to strike me, but it was swift and frighteningly rapid. My average reflexes were no match to predict the moves of this steroid-abusing sportsman, and as such I found myself on the ground curled into a ball, covering my face with my arms and hands as a continuous and powerful stream of kicks shattered them in a storm of unbearable pain. My stomach and chest received several powerful blunt blows, forcing me into coughing and breathing desperately as if I were drowning. Powerless, defenseless, obliterated before even having an idea as to what was going on, I couldn't do anything aside from keep taking that vicious beating, wishing for it to stop and lamenting I didn't swallow my pride.

But that public display of torture ended shortly after. Recovering from the acute pains, lying on the floor face down, I looked up through my blurry eyes, full of tears, and saw Jason walking away as if nothing had happened. Even though he did not have the power to assault anyone he pleased without being stopped by law enforcement, he had nothing to fear

as he would eventually be released without more punishment than a "hope this doesn't happen again, sir."

I tried to stand up and immediately fell, breaking the fall with my left arm and knee. Nobody helped me back. In fact, the bus line remained exactly as it was before the beating, waiting for the bus which hadn't driven away in order to stare at the spectacle.

I had hurt my foot, obviously not noticing due to the adrenaline. The throbbing pain had me limping all the way to the bus, the people already inside now that there was nothing else to look at.

I paid my ticket not even looking at the driver; I was too focused on the pain. I noticed some people looking at me while I limped through the corridor, and in return I shouted as loud as I could a sharp *"THANKS FOR WATCHING."* Ironically, being scared to death from that particular foe gave me the valor and the strength to face any other human being on the planet. Nobody could hope to be worse scum than JC Vega.

I sat back and relaxed at the prospect of being carried away from that place, knowing by experience that JC wouldn't hunt me down or target me anymore once he encountered another distraction. His social life, his girlfriends and his professional success could obscure the face of anybody that had come into direct contact with him in the whole day. The drugs did the rest.

The journey back home left me bitter and in the mood for nothing. I had been humiliated greatly in such a short interval I did not quite grasp the gravity of the situation. I did not care about an abnormal sociopathic imbecile like JC Vega, as he was eclipsed by the putrid scent of betrayal in the air. My mind would find itself obsessively going back to that same night, the night I had lost what I considered the love of my

life and my best friend, my closest ally in the Faith endeavor. Ending up betrayed by such a close ally, one that Faye fancied superior or equal to her, demolished me daily. I had lost in the worst way possible. They had everything to gain, every reason in the world not to see this cloudy and rainy day as a depressive and punishing omen. They didn't get verbally abused and physically assaulted by all-powerful Kanny jocks, they didn't have to worry about finding that special someone, so hidden out there in the crowds of sheep, fiends and social-ly unpleasant peers. They had found each other and I had no more place in their government. I was exiled, purged, a non-person. I had to learn this as soon as possible; that Faye would never love me, that Wolfgang would see to it that she made him the happiest man in Loynne's, that I would ulti-mately fail in erasing these scars from my subconscious. It would continue to punish me every day, torture me every night, letting me know how wrong I had been in search for that finely crafted someone waiting to be seduced, enter-tained, fascinated by a person such as I in this astonishingly vapid land of distorted values and non-existent culture.

The Hipp-Man's music barely provided a distraction as Montenade became visible in the rocky road, in the middle of nowhere. The half painted houses with the old Hades-Larsson cars from the '70s and the ancient Forge Patriotic Duty 4x4s parked up front, a longtime Loynner tradition, welcomed me as the cloudy and rainy day in Pilgrim Coast turned drowsy, sunny and hot in Montenade. Sweat covered my body as the sight of my house in the vicinity foretold another special blend of obsessive overthinking, boredom and anxiety.

The aftermath of that night marked the beginning of a new era. A Cold War in its own right, the outcome of the party changed everything in such a way I did not know how or if to

react to it. After all, what was there to do? I had lost. It was over. If I needed definitive proof, I had found it right there. I wasn't willing to submissively relinquish that which I had given myself in mind and body to achieve, but I had to face the absolute reality, that perhaps my objective was never to possess Faye. How could such absolute beliefs in the success of something be so undeniably wrong? I had fought relentlessly, forged strategies, fleshed-out entire plans all set to make her realize the possibilities of being together, all to no avail. Now that everything had failed, I could maybe carry on with my life searching for the perfect match in someone else. If Faye had happened, why couldn't someone else dazzle me again like that? Someone who this time would accept me without effort?

The burning sting of betrayal made me cringe inside, but I found respite in hoping that ending any social interactions I could have with any of them would at least make them feel guilty about their relationship. I would never sit back and allow myself to be seen not only as her loyal lapdog, but as a man incapable of dignity still clinging to the hope of seducing her while she had obviously found someone else. No, Faye needed to learn the hard way. I would not continue to be an asset she could use whenever she wanted, and it was time to start maximizing the imposed distance. The wall that separated us emotionally would be fortified, this time ensuring that no one trespassed over to her side.

The hopelessness of having failed in my endeavor sunk me into a depressive state I could not evade. What was there to look forward to? What goal kept me going? I had none. Waiting for my parents to surpass their situation and finally come to Loynne's was something I had started to dread. I did not want them to live here. I just wanted to return, even if everything had been transformed beyond recognition, I did not

care. It was still my land; and I would appreciate it for what it was. Someday, I thought, I would return. I intended on making this a reality, and I would not be mistaken in my choice. Returning to my country in order to be loyal to the end was the best thing I could do now that Loynne's had finally battered me into emotional numbness. Nothing here would make me happy, and the best I could hope for was erasing every single Loynner memory from my mind, pretending this episode of my life had never taken place.

· · · · ·

A few hours later I woke up to the sound of the buzzer, scared of the uncertainty it represented. Nobody needed me at this time. In fact, I was almost sure it was a simple mistake. I decided to see if they called a second and third time, eventually opting for picking it up annoyed at the situation.

"Yes?" I said, trying to sound ambiguous and detached.

"Sonny? It's me Tory, are you available?" Tory? Ringing my doorbell, when nobody had ever found out where I lived? And then, I remembered they had been the ones who brought me home. I must have told them in the cab, in that desperate situation I had put myself in. My paranoia decreasing, I tried to answer as naturally as the situation let me:

"Tory? Hey, what's going on?"

"Nothing, just wanted to see if you were willing to have a little night walk, and we can talk about certain issues of considerable magnitude which have recently transpired."

"Er ... yeah, sure. I'll be there in a minute," I said, and hung the buzzer's phone. What could Tory possibly want? I knew he lived about 3 kilometers away in Whitedale, in the slums, but we never stayed in touch like people who live

somewhat nearby usually do. It was an incredibly distant friendship, as if he lived abroad. I preferred it like that because I obviously didn't like people intruding into my life, as they could put everything I was building for my family in jeopardy. I went downstairs cautiously hoping to engage in a peaceful and insightful walk with Tory, only to find him next to Mario, Billy and Robbie. I pretended to be joyfully surprised at this unwelcome turn of events, and struggled to generate a convincing smile.

"Sonny! Hey Sonny, you goddamn grade-A psycho fuckin' *LUNATIC!!!* COME 'ERE, BOY!!!" Billy hugged me as his words made clear that there had been some talks behind me regarding the subject. Robbie wasn't so eager like his sibling to hug me, but shook hands in a way that showed some respect, his eyes shining mysteriously. Tory and Mario suddenly started shouting and celebrating, making fun of Faye in what I perceived to be an effort to cheer me up and show their support.

"Sonny, you maniac, what happened to your face?! Did you show that samurai cocksucker how they do it in the Spetsnaz or what?" Mario asked.

"No, JC Vega did this ... I had a fight with him at the bus stop, this afternoon ..."

"You did, huh boy? Hehehe ... we'll talk about that in a bit ... but first tell us real quick, everythin' that went down that night ..." Billy said.

"Yeah! Guess what! Have two words for ya here! FUCKIN' ... SLUT!" They began laughing loudly, making fun of me for being ultra-violent and hell-bent. They didn't make fun about the humiliation itself because they knew what it'd entail.

"Dude! Faye is a freakin' slut! How did she ever end up like that! *'Ohhhh look at me, the poor little shy sister of the freakin' Mantis brothers ... NOT!'* Hahahaha!!" Mario was

really having a good time with this. It was surprising to see him so out of his otherwise respectful wiseguy character, although it hadn't been the first time he behaved in similar erratic ways. Tory's behavior was even more unusual. He loved fun just like the rest of us, but his nerdy exterior and outcast nature prevented him from being popular in any way. As such, he had retreated to a façade of intellectualism and maturity. However, he couldn't hide his age and the needs that come with it. Tory, who was now Mario's inseparable buddy, simply limited himself to sing blue-collar songs along the lines of "*You used to rock my world until I saw you suckin' cock*" like he used to when someone had been dirty, and laughed considerably as well. Billy also was very much amused and Robbie, like usual, could barely hold a smile.

"So, Sonny boy ... come on ... Tory and Mario 'ere told us a bit of what happened ... now it's your turn. TELL US!" When the effect of the surprise faded, I suddenly remembered to ask the important question I had previously – and unbelievably – forgotten to ask; with everything that had transpired throughout that traumatizing night, it had escaped my notice completely.

"Hey, Tory... you never really told me how you guys found out where I lived," I said, smiling faintly so as to minimize suspicion. "Did I tell you in the cab? I honestly don't remember a thing."

"Nope, we didn't need to ask. We already knew. Tory's our tracker, son... that's exactly what's he's good at... findin' stuff, locatin' people... followin' people..." Billy said, answering right when Tory opened his mouth to talk.

"You followed me here?!"

"Haha, wait there, Sonny boy! Don't lash out at poor Tory like that! He did good, and he should be rewarded fer that.

Besides, what's it to you if we know where you live or not? Got summin' to hide?"

"No, but it's a sign of mistrust... why didn't you just ask?"

"Haha, this is so you get a taste of how exactly unavoidable we can be, Sonny boy... and I mean that in a good way... yer gonna wanna have us 24/7 when you hear 'bout what we got to say to ya... but first things first ... tell us all 'bout yer crazy night, boy!" Billy was quite happy, actually. I had been very thankful for their support and their way of trying to cheer me up, so in spite of my paranoia and mistrust, I accepted the deal.

"So ... I thought I had everything going for me ... Faye was drunk ... I didn't want to take advantage of her while drunk, but I thought it would be a good uninhibitor, and that it would make what I thought would happen eventually easier ..."

"Haha, yeah sure, and Dave's gonna get a scholarship! Go on!" Billy said.

"So she was next to me ... it was a matter of time I started. But I left for a couple of minutes, and when I returned I went insane at what I saw. Is that how Dave protects his sister? If that had been me he would have killed both Faye and me."

"We were unable to react accordingly, Sonny. When we saw what was going on, we just couldn't go over where you were and point at them to inform you. You were going to be hurt either way, and we decided that you should have found out on your own. Wolfgang and Faye obviously went far away so that it wasn't there in your face, but it just ended up being even more obvious. We simply tried to have a laugh with you so you wouldn't mind much in the end ... but ... we're sorry, very sorry, Sonny ..." Tory said.

"What about Dave? What was he doing?" I asked.

"Dave ... well ... he was really pissed off, about them doing

that precisely when you were there, but ... he did ask us to try to divert your attention so that you wouldn't find out."

"Oh, so he did ask, the son of a bitch. No, don't laugh, I'm going to get that motherfucker," I said, as the boys started to laugh with what they perceived to be my Stalin character.

"He's fuckin' crazy, the fuckin' Ruski, I told ya man! Never mess with Ivan the Terrible! That's what my grampa always says," Mario laughed.

"Hear that, Ivan the Terrible, you gonna make yer friend dead now?" Billy asked. It was very curious that he had asked me that. It was certainly an interesting and attractive proposal.

"I did think about revenge ... but no, it's over. I'm not interested in wasting my time thinking of vengeance and ways to get back at them. I'm not going to get anything out of it. I can see they never respected me, but I don't want to cause them harm either. It's not my problem anymore. As of now, I consider myself far away from anything related to this. This should have never happened, and Faye was nothing but a mistake ..."

"HERE'S A MISTAKE FOR YA! *'OH LOOK AT ME, I'M FAYE, I'M SHY AND I NEVER GET OUT OF MY ROOM, OH WAIT, SOME RANDOM GUY! COME HERE AND FUCK ME SENSELESS, SILLY!' HAHA!'*" Mario started imitating Wolfgang and Faye kissing exaggeratedly with his arms wrapped around his body, shouting obscenities. We burst out laughing and people started shouting at us from the balconies to keep our voices down. Billy reacted by shouting insults back and laughing uncontrollably again. We walked down to the end of the street where the town ended and the desert sections started, sitting on some rocks to continue to the discussion.

"Haha, fuckin' Loynners, fuck 'em all! Go back to livin' in yer fuckin' garages, you island pansies! Hey Sonny, listen, sit

down ... it's time to get down to business ... we got summin' to tell ya about that particular night."

"Yeah? What's that?"

"Well, we ain't exactly sure, but it goes a lil' like this ... take it away, Mario ..."

"Uh ... oh yeah! Haha, when you hear it, Sonny, you gonna go mad, more than you are now! So, deal is, yous were really wasted man, like, real drunk and shit, couldn't even hold your own piss! Haha, that was some funny shit ... and you went berserk man, totally vicious like, when we were carryin' you to the taxi stop you almost get us killed 'cause you kept shouting at people, you know, Brits and Kannies and shit ... but anyways, the thing is that, since you ended up pukin' a lot, Tory here thought it'd be a good idea to go to The Crucible and ask Ryan for help you know, get you some water so that you didn't dehydrate or some shit like that, or that's what Tory kept sayin', so we goes and motherfucker wouldn't come out man, he kept sayin' summin' about how he couldn't let us in at that time of night, and that we would wake the mother up, and we said we jus' wanted him to come out, not us comin' in, and well, he kept makin' lots of excuses and that's that, he left you to dry man. Sad but true. He couldn't give a shit. I mean we explained that you were a wreck and all sorts, but no, he clearly didn't want anything to do with it, we could tell."

"So that's it, huh ... well, so much for him. I don't give a shit."

"Haha, I know you don't boy, but see, what did I tell ya? Can't trust them yellowed-bellied Mantises for nuthin'. Dave scrammed quick too. Not only he refused to carry you when you couldn't even walk straight, but he went to some friend's house to spend the night sayin' a bunch of excuses we didn't understand. Actually, we know for a fact he went to go fuck

this new Loynnerin girlfriend of his. Point is, not only they're assholes, but we believe there was something else cookin' there, maybe Ryan havin' the house for 'imself to fuck a girl, reachin' an agreement with the brothers so that they left him alone ..."

"And what about Faye? What did she do after this whole thing?"

"Ah, Faye, hehe. Faye ... she went to spend the night at some house in Starfish Beach or Little London, somewhere aroun' there, that's where she was headed anyhow. She said it was an apartment that belonged to a friend of the mom that was away on a business trip, some interior decorator faggot or summin'. See? It all makes sense. And he lied about the mother bein' there. The mother spent the night at some guy's house too, hehe, except that this guy was in the house. Seems the whole family scored in the same night ... wouldn't surprise me at all that they all knew what the other was up to and agreed to have some time alone with their respective partners ..."

"Billy ... be honest and tell me the truth ... did Faye go back with Wolfgang to that house so as to also ... er ... you know ..."

"Well ... we're not certain, Sonny. Faye and Wolfgang did leave together and headed for that place, so it might have happened. We're not sure. Considering that the apartment they were going to was not inhabited it could have probably happened, we're almost 95% sure, at least, that's our most accurate assumption," Tory said, answering for Billy.

"Well, who gives a shit anyway, I'm really not thinking about anyone right now except myself, guys. I'm ... don't know how to express it ... detached comes close ... I feel emotionally detached. Like, numb."

"Heh, would not surprise me, Sonny boy, would not sur-

prise me one bit. But hey, you got a lot outta it! See? Now you know for certain them Mantises are pieces-a-shit, all of 'em, including the poor little not-so-innocent sister. They were all in on it, and it seems everyone in that fuckin' family plans ahead to have intimacy for some good ol' vaginal poundin'. Ryan in the house, Flavia in that guy's house, Dave God knows where with that Loynnerin broad probably, and Faye and Wolfgang surely in that empty apartment. There you go. Even nice little Faye was in on it, at least ... We're almost certain that that's what happened. It jus' seems too coincidental, and you'd be naïve to think she wouldn't seize the opportunity. That friend o' yours, Wolfgang, he stabbed you in the back probably a long time ago, and went after Faye himself leavin' you to rot. And her, well ... she's obviously the worst outta them all ... 'cause nobody would have ever thought of her plottin' such a scheme, or at least, partakin' in it. That's life for you, Sonny. I warned ya, everybody did, but you wouldn't listen ... she's a snake, she bit you and you got fucked. The end."

"Yeah ... You know what? I was completely wrong about her. She *was* a whore all along, just like the rest. I don't know what I saw in her or why I allowed her to completely control me like that, but I'll tell you something, if she ever even dares to ..."

Suddenly, a mysterious phone call sent my heart right to my throat. Sensing the vibration rise up from the leg all the way to my stomach, I didn't have to see the caller's name to make a prediction. It was Faye, right on my phone. This single event was too surreal to be believed. My friends' eyes turned ever wider, thirsty for my confirmation on who the caller was.

"It's just my mom," I lied, walking away from the group. "She probably wants me to get back, be a moment." I didn't

wait to see the expressions on my friends' faces, but out of the corner of my eye I could have sworn Billy's eyes shone mockingly, predicting effectively the identity of the caller.

"Faye ...?" I asked, in utter disbelief. I had every reason in the world to be absolutely furious. So far, I had completely ignored Faye and even deleted her from ChitChat. I didn't want her in my life anymore, and the decision was made. The guys were silent, submerged in curiosity, but when they realized it was probably Faye they howled and yelled and insulted laughingly, spurting things like "slut," "bitch" and "whore," and singing to songs with similar sounding words.

"Hello, Sonny ... uh ... what's that in the background?"

"..." I was simply speechless. I could not believe I was talking to her after all the facts I had just learned off the guys, and didn't know how to feel or react.

"Oh ... uh ... it's just some hobos around here, um ... saying some crazy shit to women ... and ... what did do you want again?" I suddenly said, remembering how much I hated her at this moment. Even so, despite everything, her sweet voice managed to eradicate all hatred, sending me into a state of relaxation immediately. At this very moment, I wasn't as curious as to what had happened between her and my former comrade than I was in rejoicing at having her attention. The thought sunk me further into self-loathing. I couldn't understand this effect she had on me, how she could toy with me however she wanted. But perhaps she would explain; maybe she would say that everything which had transpired the previous night had been an awful mistake, and she would finally say the words I wanted to hear:

"Oh ... well ... I was gonna ask you if, uh ... if you didn't mind giving me Wolfgang's ChitChat Address. It's just, I need to talk to him as soon as possible, and it's really important ..." My pulse went dead. I almost let out a howl of frustration, of

strong disbelief and general shock regarding how women could be so cold, disdainful and uncaring.

"You ... you have the nerve to ask me for Wolfgang's Chit-Chat after everything that's been going down? How stupid do you think I am? How little dignity do you suppose I have?"

"I know how this sounds ... but it's about that. I don't have a lot of time. I need to tell him something quick. I'll get back to you in a bit."

"I don't know what this is about and I don't care, but here ... it's '*wolfgang_samurai@hippmail.loynnet.*' "

"You ... didn't delete me, by any chance, did you?"

"Yes, Faye. I did."

"Um ... OK. Well, re-add me. It's '*green_mantis_07@hippmail.com.*' Just to make sure, yours is still '*nomenklatura_1991@hippmail.loynnet?*' "

"No, I changed it. I always delete my addresses and create new ones so people may not keep track of me."

"How convenient ..."

"Anyway ... the new one is '*sovrev_02@hippmail.loynnet.*' Don't go around giving it to anyone. I only have the people I want in there, not the whole island like most do."

"Alright, got it. I'll tell you in a little while after I've talked to him. We'll speak, the three of us, OK?"

"I'm giving you the address because you clearly chose him, you might as well have it. But hear this: I don't want anything to do with you, or with him. You're both dead to me, Faye."

"Sonny, please, wait until you hear me out before you say that. I'll let you know when we'll meet. Come or don't, it's up to you. Good night, Sonny."

"I might as well say good night too, since you sure won't be having a shortage of those anymore."

"Funny. Hope you decide to come. Bye," and she hang up. I noticed the boys were still looking at me waiting for some

kind of big news, so I had to look the part:

"It was ... this girl, I met her a while back. She wants to see me tomorrow night."

"So ... no more Faith?" Billy asked inquisitively.

"No more Faith," I replied solemnly.

"You the fuckin' man, Sonny! Finally ..." Mario cheered uncontrollably, holding on to Tory as if celebrating the victory of his football team. Tory stood with a face of jolly approval, his mouth wide open. On the other hand, The Nazareth brothers seemed to look upon me with newfound respect, like a pupil learning from his wise masters, as if what I had said somewhat raised the respect they could feel for me.

"We're proud of ya boy," Billy said. "Veeery proud, attaboy."

"Yeah well, it's her loss, not mine."

"You know, Sonny ... this has just done it for me. I don't think there'll be a better opportunity. I think it's time we let you in on what's going down. Tory knows it. Mario now knows it as well. Now it's your turn to hear the full story, and decide if to accept or reject it. You up for it?"

"Why not, I don't have anything else to do until tomorrow night ..."

"Don't get cocky with me, you smartass. It goes like this ... long ago, my brother and I devised a plan, something that can bring us a lot of money ... and *power*. It's got enormous ambition and planning behind it. Our plan is to found a political party. A party that we think will represent what the world currently needs."

"Which is ...?"

"I think you might have an idea, but I'll go on. We believe that the world has grown softer with the rise of the so-called 'democracies,' of 'human rights,' of 'freedom of expression.' These things, as you know, cannot be given to just anybody.

Power needs to rest on those capable to lead the world. Giving individuals this much power simply destroys everything. Nobody wins. Everybody sticks to their own ideas and we end up nowhere. What we actually believe in, Sonny boy, is in benevolent dictatorships. We think they're the only future we have, if humanity wants to progress at all. With democracies, numerous political parties and countless different ideas are poured evermore into the social cesspit, and we experience severe stagnation in both social and political progress. The current democratic systems bring forth inevitable polarization, a two-party totalitarian state which could be avoided by simply changing the voting system, something the controlling parties combat so as to not lose power. These two parties struggle for a power that lasts for four to five years, only to lose said power to the opposition, which erases everything the original party created. As such, we believe in a concept that I think you share; deterrence. Deterrence not only refers to cold war and politics of mutually assured destruction, but to other things, for instance, the practice of dividing every single nation in existence in two. Can you imagine it? Just like South Korea and North Korea, South Vietnam and North Vietnam, West Germany and East Germany, we could have countless countries divided by ideology, between left and right. Unlike you, we don't believe completely in the left. Our ideology takes concepts from both spectrums. But we believe that in order to achieve a new status quo, every single nation needs to have its left and right perspective. Countries cannot progress governed by the left only to later be taken over by the right and viceversa in a vicious circle. Countries need to head in one direction and follow it to the end. What I propose is, obviously, for nations to base their ideologies on my political party. But we can't let people in on my true intentions just yet. We need to make them believe we are kind-hearted indi-

viduals concerned about political freedom, proposing not division but a more effective way in which countries can progress in the direction they like the most, under either left-wing or right-wing politics, and coexist with their neighbor peacefully. If every country has a left and right version of it, nobody will have an excuse so as to hate the ruling party. Can you imagine if nations try to adapt this idea? Countless demonstrations might arise if the idea itself proves popular enough. People will be able to choose to what version of their country they want to live in, and nobody will despise the current government or say it doesn't represent them. If you belong to the left you obviously will live in the left-wing country. And it will have to represent at least part of your ideals. It's better than the current democracies, which actually only masquerade as democracies and in fact are just dictatorships ruled by two parties of clearly conflicting ideologies and agendas which take turns to rule. This applies to almost every Western democratic country. One party that is somewhat left-wing and another that is somewhat right-wing. That's all there is to it. Not only that, but the so-called 'democratic' system is designed to perpetuate the two-party totalitarianism. A majority, a ruling party which stands above all the others will always exist, and as such the smaller parties divided cannot win. They unite and form a mainstream party which can overthrow the ruling one. Have you realized how during elections in democratic countries they only mention the ruling party and the opposition? Two sides, all other parties mean absolutely nothing. They could disintegrate and be absorbed by the two major parties, and nobody would notice, nobody would feel the effect. Voting in a Western democracy has effectively become a 'yes' or 'no' proposition, a referendum where you decide whether the ruling party should pass the torch to the opposition or not. That's democ-

racy today. That's the way that, for example, my country has always done things. And look where it's now! Absorbed by right-wing extremists and religious maniacs, claiming to live in the world's only true democracy. That's what happens when you don't have deterrence, one of the two parties takes over completely. Look at your country, Russia, once governed by a communist one-party system and now ruled, just like the US, by a totalitarian right-wing party which masquerades as a fair democracy. If we in the Western World are going to live like this, leaving 50% of the population angry at the results of the election, why not just divide the country and make those 50% live under a government they will actually support? In this polarized world, divided more and more by people of left-wing and right-wing ideals, what we have is government and opposition living in the same pen gouging out their eyes. It's the worst political system ever created, the least efficient, the most dangerous. It creates bureaucratic stagnation, division, protests, intolerance ... It's time to put a stop to it with a new alternative ... in a free country only divided by ideology, where you are not restrained and have the right to visit the other part of the country without border checks or paperwork, people would react differently than as if it were a North and South Korea, two countries always at odds, separated physically and always fighting for supremacy ... if it was established in the constitution that no country can be hostile to the other or engage in acts of war of any kind under the punishment of intervention by the UN or its closest political ally, the issue would be effectively solved and the two countries could be left to their own devices ... they would have in their respective constitutions the obligation to tolerate the existence of a part of the nation which holds opposite ideals, and people would choose in what part of the country they would like to live according to their ideology ... as such, people

would enjoy every type of freedom available, freedom of speech, freedom of the press, freedom to change their ideology, and eventually the country with the supposed better ideology would of course, demonstrate the superiority of its political convictions through how well its population is fairing. Same territory, different ideology. Nothing like that has ever been done democratically. It would be the political experiment of the next century." Billy stopped talking, looking at me with those sharp blue eyes. I was incredibly confused, and perhaps to divert attention from my person, decided to focus it on Tory:

"You support Billy's ideology as well, Tory? What about liberty, free-market capitalism and Objectivism? Aren't you against totalitarianism and dictatorships and all in favor of blatantly selfish individualism?"

"Well," he began. "I have my reasons to side with Billy. Let's just say, there are worse things out there, especially if you know as much as I do. Billy's option is incredibly more democratic than the shadowy supranational governments that seek a new order, a one-government world state. So, suffice it to say, I'd rather side with Billy than with true totalitarians. Billy's program gives people a chance at peace and stability, prevents polarization and grants everyone an ideological zone based on democracy. So I don't know what it is that you see as being conflictive with my ideology."

I was speechless. Indeed, there was truth and reason in this program, but I would have never trusted anyone to do things their own way. How could I possibly know whether Billy had more fascist ideals in mind and he was merely alluring me with what I wanted to hear to join his group? Sadly, there was no way of knowing. I had to take my chances. Worst case scenario, I would be out of the group immediately if I rejected their ideals, and Billy wouldn't bother me any-

more. There was no loss.

"Alright," I said. "I think our paths do intersect. We'll have to discuss political ideologies more, but as of now, I think I sympathize enough with your cause. Let me know what needs doing, and I'll do it."

"Great," Billy said, grinning. "As of now, nothing else. I'm taking care of things myself. When I require you to do something, I'll inform you. But remember this; you don't call me. I call you. Now, don't forget that."

"OK," I said. "But I do hope this doesn't get in my personal life a whole lot. I have other concerns, you know."

"Don't worry. It won't. You'll be able to do whatever it is you usually do and have time for this as well. I can promise you that."

"I hope so."

"Any more questions?"

"Actually, one, yeah ... remember your going away party, at the Community Center when I met Mario? You told me you'd explain something about him, and you never did ..."

"Ah, yeah ... sure ... well, since Mario's here, maybe he's willing to explain for me ..."

"Nah, fuggedaboutit! You explain the whole thing to the kid, you're much better at explainin' shit, Billy ..."

"Oh well, if you want me to ... Mario never misses an opportunity to talk about his family Sonny, this is a rare exception ... we'll, basically it goes like this, either you believe this shit or you don't, alright? We're not shitting you boy, you believe whatever you want, but I assure you this is how the shit goes down, and you'll see it for yourself if you stick around ... Mario's the grandson of Frankie Baglionni, don of the Loynne's Island Italian Mafia, Unitedstatian branch that is. I think you've heard how things go around with mafias 'round 'ere, well, whatever it is you've heard is all true, most-

ly. This is sensitive information we're giving away, boy, believe it, but don't worry. You won't get a bullet through the back o' the neck just by knowing this. We'll fill you in more steeply if you decide to stick around longer."

"Well, don't go on if you don't want to, I've not asked you to tell me the whole thing."

"No, but as I said, don't worry. This is as much as we can tell you without some kind of retaliation should you decide to reveal information. So listen up, Mario's granddad runs this little Italian restaurant in Whitedale, just a front, you know. I don't even know what goes on around there, not even Mario does, but what we know is basically that; Frankie is the boss man, he runs the neighborhood and tries to be straight as can be, you know, with the SKAR and all. There's a lot of shit going on even if you don't see it, Sonny. I can assure you that every single innocent-looking thing that goes on in this dirty corrupt island is bound to have some organized crime syndicate behind it, from restaurants to cultural venues. Now, the Baglionnis have been here for a long time, and Mario's family is a force to reckon, but obviously they don't keep Mario around for the serious shit. Now, how do we know this? Because Mario's like a brother to us, and we're to him and his family, including Mr. Baglionni himself. What we have is a bond forged through honesty, loyalty, trust and respect. If you wish to be on our good side, that's all you need to remember. We may be just kids to them, but don't forget you can also have the entire backing of a proper Mafia family. This don't mean you can stroll around school believing yourself the big man like some Russian dickheads do, but at least you know JC Vega won't be able to lay a single finger on you without some really bad shit happening to him ... or his car."

"His ... *car*? Wait ... I'm starting to remember now ... When I fought with JC Vega I was at the bus stop, wondering

what he could be doing, you know, given he has a Drakkar ... and he was very pissed off, so pissed off he provoked me into fighting with him, and I didn't back down, so I got the crap beaten out of me ... luckily he didn't leave too many bruises ..."

"Hahaha! So he did ... poor Sonny, you muss'abeen scared shitless ... you wanna know what happened that day? Tell 'im, Robbie ..."

"JC Vega made the mistake of actually assaulting Mario, he and his gang punched him for no reason and took off in the car later ... Mario remembered the plates, then called Siggy."

"Siggy? Who's he?"

"Sigge Sauer, they call him Siggy. He's the don's bodyguard and enforcer, he handles a lot of important shit."

"Hehe, he sure does ... he's also the uncle of that arrogant bulldog-faced hysterical cunt, Juliett Sauer, the one that's goin' out with Mike for some odd reason. Ring a bell? Nah, I thought so. Anyway, as I was sayin' ... Sonny, oh Sonny ... you don't wanna know what them fellas did to that poor car ... after they were done with it, you'd think a fuckin' German Landkreuzer ran it over ... there was literally NUTHIN' left ... that's how bad they fucked the thing up ... I can't even imagine how they managed to do it ... JC Vega didn't know what to fuckin' do, hehe! That's why he must have lashed out at you when he saw you, probably goin' to kill you and all ... but never mind ... look at Mario, he messed with him and he got what he deserved ... now it's your turn, Sonny ... as you're currently nobody to us and the family we can't allow such a revenge, but we might be able to send a couple of thugs JC's way ... whaddya say? Time to get even. We're not rag dolls anymore, boy. Not of Kannies like Vega or whores like Strössner. I still remember that one time the bitch hit me in

front of everyone, I had never been so humiliated in my life, hit by a fuckin' woman. She's next on the list, we got something real nice prepared for her. Every single motherfucker who's messed with us is gonna get some nice slice of psychological urban warfare. They're all finished, Sonny. *Kannovschina* is finished. Heh, what did they think, that the people they abused could forgive and forget? Not us boy, not us. We have never forgotten. People like them who abuse others because they hate themselves and can't bear their lives. We ain't takin' no shit from such inferior beings, human forms of vermin, just 'cause they got powerful parents or friends. We got our friends now, boy. And I assure you, there ain't no way in hell they can find out about us being behind these vengeances ... other people take the heat for these things, and they don't even have to worry, this is like goin' shoppin' for 'em. Now, all you need to decide is whether you want to be a part of this or not ... to have the power to get even at all these people that made you suffer just because you were a foreigner, because you were different or thought different ... unfortunately we can't kill them, but that's even better, there's a thousand ways to make someone's life a livin' hell ... you know they deserve it, Sonny ... and you know you want to ..."

I didn't know what to exactly say or feel when hearing this. My head hurting from all the events that had transpired in such a short timespan, I dismissed Billy trying not to seem very detached.

"Uh ... look Billy, seriously, this is too much information all of a sudden, I'm going to have to think about all this, I don't mean to sound disrespectful but I don't want to know too much, just in case ... you know ... it's never good knowing way too much, especially all of a sudden ..."

"I know that boy, but serves you right, that way you'll think about this way more seriously and will actually make

you consider the whole thing ..."

"I know that, Billy. And believe me ... I will."

"Well, Sonny ... then, there's nothing more to add, at least for the time being. Truly, it's been a pleasure. Expect to hear from us." Billy extended me his right hand, which I shook firmly as I looked deeply into his electric, cunning blue eyes.

• • • • •

Pilgrim Coast

Province of Arias

Pilgrim Coast Secondary Education Institute

1st Grade of Scientific Baccalaureate
(Biological Orientation)

Student File

Third Trimester (April - June)

Name: Zharostin, Sonny
Class: 1-B
Course Tutor: Thomas Richards

Subjects:

Mathematical Sciences: 5
History: 9
English Language: 10
German Language: 10
Philosophy: 8
Biology: 9
Physics & Chemistry: 6
Physical Education: 7
Computer Class: 8

I happily looked at my results, shaking Tom Richards'
hand as he lectured me on how I had to better my behavior
and stay away from people like Mike and Axel. Already in
June, it wasn't long before the end of school. We had actually
already finished classes, and nothing would influence grades
now, but for some retarded Loynner reason they wanted to
keep us locked in the teenage kindergarten until mid-June. I
had passed with flying colors, an amazing feat given my varied distractions throughout the year, and my parents expressed their joy in their latest reply, also commenting briefly
on the Faye situation, which they actually had no idea about
and only knew but the few ambiguous details that I gave
them:

"Dear ********,

*Your father and I are extremely proud that you have
managed to pass with such grades, but you should have
worked harder on math and physics. Another year and you
can go to university. Have you decided on what career you
want now? Engineer like your father? Teacher like your
mother? Maybe a doctor like your aunt? Lawyer like your
cousin?*

*I'm sorry things didn't work out with that girl. You can't
have everything in this life. I'm sure there are many more to
come. But remember to be careful. Women are very complicated. Don't let them poison your life.*

Love you,

Mom and Dad."

Perhaps a little too late regarding Faye, but that was not

important now. I was on the right track once more, strengthened and wiser, and that was all that mattered in the end.

We'd have two and a half months of rest until September,
when we'd start 2nd Grade of Baccalaureate, the last year until
university. I wasn't thinking a lot about my academic profile,
and it showed. While I was managing to pass everything with
good grades, these scores wouldn't ever impress a university.
People that didn't have a perfect 10 or 9 in all subjects were
instantly dismissed as a waste of time, and had to pay almost
double than an all-10 student, university being expensive
enough, even though it was supposedly managed by the state.
What would I do then? Get a shitty job as a waiter? Do some
gardening course like the Kannies who had miserably failed
in life? I had at least a year to think about my options. And
my parents would probably arrive by the time I was done
with high school. They would force me to get a job if by that
time I didn't successfully enter a university. But I wasn't sure
whether I wanted to keep on studying. Four or more years of
doing exactly what I had been doing up to that point in my
life was a gruesome future. Sitting in front of books and desks
studying things only to vomit them in exams and forgetting
about them later, what kind of life was that? To do what? To
become a lawyer, a psychologist, a school teacher, like my
mom said? No. I didn't want to do any of that. Suddenly, the
concept of university started to feel nothing glorious or re-
markable, but, like Axel Guerrero had so wisely said, a cold
assembly plant forging generic professions out of hollow
human shells who had absolutely no interest in the professions they were studying, only in getting a life and making
money to go through the mediocrity of Western capitalist
existence. And then what awaited? A family unit, a midlife
crisis, a mortgage, disappointing offspring, a divorce, sexual
frustration, random sex with strangers, depression, boredom,

old age and then death. In the tombstone there would be nothing written except *"Here Lies Some Human, who lived and died like all the rest. He never did accomplish anything important, or relevant, and he won't be doing it now."*

No. I wouldn't ever let that happen to me, forgotten in a sea of mediocrity, anonymous to the future generations. I didn't know as of yet what I would do to leave my mark in this world, to transcend death and leave a lasting impression on mankind. But at least I now knew my calling. Everything lied with SOVREV. All I had to do was wait until an idea on how to put it into practice was revealed to me. I had everything to gain and nothing to lose. Forgetting about Faye would be the ideology of the next year. That and speaking seriously to Billy and Robbie about The Brotherhood. It was time to discover who I really was, what I really stood for, and there was nothing better than politics for that. Politics is, after all, our essence. Every human being has an ideology and a philosophy, no matter how mediocre, pointless or unappealing. There is no such thing as the apolitical. Deep inside us, lies a politician, an extremist wanting to impose his way into the world and change it according to his needs and view. Knowing how to let that politician out into the world is something not many want to do, as they are scared of realizing their true potential. As for me, I was unrestrained by irrational religions and bourgeois morality, fueled only by the doctrines of Communism and Socialism. It was essential that I gave myself to their cause and not let them die. I felt that if I didn't do it, nobody would. The world seemed to have forgotten about dreams of utopian states and equality, and there was no more room in this conformist world for revolution. But people like me knew this world was illusory, vapid, withering until its eventual implosion. It was our job to get ready for the fallout, and to spread our ideas when the final debris

engulfed the land. It was our job to get the blindfolds off of people's eyes, that is, if they had any eyes at all.

I thought one more about SOVREV, this time under a new light; Loynne's Island had politics reminiscent of conservative states such as Estonia, Lithuania, Latvia and the United States before its theocratic takeover. As you know, there was no such thing as a ruling left-wing party in the US, thanks to their propaganda. The Democratic Party was as right-wing as they come, with the only exception that looked noticeably left-wing in comparison to the awful Republican Party. The Democrats were center-right in politics and economics, and somewhat left-wing in social issues, but still a far cry from being a true left-wing party. In the Baltic countries, same as with many ex-Soviet states, parties were in the majority center, center-right or utterly right-wing, with your typical lone slightly left-wing social democratic party. Loynne's didn't even have a Socialist party. The main parties were the Loynner Coalition, the ruling party for almost three decades and undisputed as the one which had brought Loynne's to its state of prosperity. Of liberal economic policies and conservative attitudes toward politics and social issues, nobody seemed to challenge the Coalition's rule, as even opponents somewhat agreed that they were doing an excellent job with the island. The modern Loynner state was modeled after this party's beliefs. It supported Loynner nationalism and an isolationist policy, meaning that it openly admitted tourists into the island but persecuted immigrants whenever possible. The Democratic Union of Loynne's Island was a party of neo-liberal ideology and social policies, with an interest in opening Loynne's more toward international superpowers and markets, especially the United States. It was the second most popular party after the Coalition, and thus it managed to win briefly in between successive Coalition governments. Then

there was a party which although not very popular, always managed to secure a third of the overall votes; the Loynner Nationalist League. As its name implies, it was a heavily right-wing and even racist party. It supported the idea of using the SKAR as force to overthrow the government and create an authoritarian state, perhaps with fascist overtones. Many people were wary of this party as it sounded radical and dangerous, but even then it was the third most popular party, something which sounded even scarier.

All other parties were too small-time to even bother to mention, and included mainly either Christian Democratic and Muslim parties formed by minorities, or liberal/conservative parties which didn't want to be absorbed by the two majority parties. Needless to say, there hadn't been a single socialist or communist party in the entire history of the island. That was perhaps, my shot at this. Perhaps, Wolfgang hadn't been as naïve as I had figured him out to be when he first mentioned the idea of creating a new political party.

SOVREV ... could it be that I could turn it into a modern Communist political party? It was a fact that the program behind it needed to be fully developed before I incited people into joining it, but I was sure I was on the breakthrough of something great, something enormous; and I would reach my objectives peacefully, without ever resorting to repression or violence of any kind. Long gone would be the stigma of violence and authoritarian oppression associated to Communism and Socialism during the 20th century, and a new element, containing civil rights, democracy, social and economic equality and prosperity would be born. This would be the true Socialism of the 21st century, as the peaceful and benevolent Great Nation of Venezuela put into practice through its Glorious Bolivarian Revolution. And SOVREV would be the movement designed to eliminate the violent

stigma of authority and the unflinching stubbornness associated specifically to Soviet-style Communism. In any case, I
was now noticeably more comfortable after much pondering
on the subject, especially regarding Red Terror and Communist campaigns of repression. Red Terror, the answer to
nationalist and imperialist White Terror, simply had to be
more lethal and ruthless to prevent the enemy from winning.
In a situation as violent as this, nothing comes out except the
worst in human nature. Red Terror was inevitable, it didn't
mean it was an inherent part of Communism, rather, it was
simply an inherent part of human nature and the way we
handle conflicts. Reds and Whites committed unspeakable
atrocities, acts of torture and murders in this particular era.
But what were we to do? Sit idly while the bourgeoisie and
the elites held on happily to power, while they still kept the
population and the working-class under its heel of exploitation? Yes, perhaps we Communists got too carried away with
red rage. But the more I thought about it, the more I studied
the situation, the more I concluded it was inevitable. That's
why Lenin had stopped thinking about it in moral terms.
There was nothing moral to look at. It was simply winning or
losing, and they had already sacrificed too much in order to
give up and let the establishment remain that way forever.
Revolutions are bloody because those at the top never relinquish their power peacefully. As if Red Terror had been the
worst act humanity has ever done... it wasn't unlike any other
power struggle between opposing factions. Perhaps more
systematic and with clearer objectives, but that only speaks of
the intelligence and crystal-clear vision of society from Communist leaders.

But still, as I always say, that was then. In the modern era,
we did things more diplomatically and with as less bloodshed
as possible. Michael Weinstein, for example, aside from not

killing or inciting others into killing anybody, put his own life
on the line every time he dared speak on Unitedstatian air-
waves ... what was deterring me to give myself fully to my
ideology? What if it was after all, my calling in life? Did I
want comfort and stability in Loynne's, something which
bored and depressed me immensely merely to make my parents happy, or was I to obey my ideological instincts and live
the exciting and adventurous life of a revolutionary? The
second option seemed infinitely more satisfying and true to
my nature, but I didn't want to sadden my parents, or shatter
the stability they were trying to create... what was I to do?

The decision was made. I would choose to side with Billy,
if momentarily. I owed allegiance to no one, but Billy had
initiative and could prove useful. If his plan in fact derived
into something fruitful, who knew the extent of spreading a
new political ideology in a small island? The effect it would
take on people when the bubble had finally exploded in a
worldwide chaotic financial recession brought forth by the
flawed free-market capitalism?

The Mafia family thing worried me immensely, though. I
didn't expect it to be as serious as Billy had made it sound,
and probably he was exaggerating, but you never knew. Who
else could completely wreck JC Vega's Drakkar without fear
of retaliation by his powerful tycoon father? In case it happened to be true, I was looking at a possible future where I
could be respected and even feared, a future where I could
maybe hold something akin to power. It could change my
whole life around, maybe establish me in a better position so
as to welcome my parents in full-sized glory. Maybe the Italians could smuggle my parents into the country sooner,
knowing my gangster countrymen would not dare mess with
them. But I didn't want to get overexcited. I tried to forget
about it and treat it exclusively as an exaggeration of Billy, an

unreliable scenario I should not take into consideration at all. If it happened to be true, then Billy was one smart cookie. Forging alliances with organized crime especially with a political strategy in mind was no joke, and I knew there was more to Billy than he let people see. I couldn't tell how much truth there was under the redneck façade, but it definitely was a genius invention. It always kept you doubtful of his true essence.

Exhausted, I went to bed looking at my redecorated room to distract myself from what had recently taken place. Faye's pictures disappeared completely: the new Soviet propaganda posters adorned my wardrobe, and the part of the wall with random pictures had been redesigned, allowing for every single figure to share a similar disposition to the Soviet leaders below my Soviet flag; the clothes and accessories with Faye-related tastes – such as Green Köontz shirts and studded wristbands – now lay abandoned in the garbage container at the corner, no longer shaming me or my ideology. I had gone back to my original Soviet uniform, never to replace it again.

I breathed deeply and took a minute to look at what I had done. Everything looked so organized and clean. It was, perhaps, a message of things to come. A new era resurfacing, where my judgment and my reason would be entirely clear, without external occlusions. I had learned much that year, and my room needed to reflect it. Stalin's portrait still held its position, but Trotsky lurked dangerously close. The addition of Isaac Asimov, Carl Sagan, Stephen Hawking, Arthur C. Clarke, Richard Dawkins, Michael Weinstein and Charles Darwin provided an excellent way to further illustrate my growing ideology with other figures who although not being politicians or even Socialists, were revolutionaries in their own right. Science and atheism were an essential feature of

Communism, and I would never reject anything from the West that incremented the exposure of science to society. I was no better isolating myself from ideas or key figures just by their nationalities. Just like Lenin, who greatly admired Darwin, I had to separate petty nationalism from personal merits and focus on what features were deserving of being passed on to my own ideology. I knew nationalism was a disease, a bringer of death over territory, an ancient device aiming at separating our borders ever more. Yet, who could ever reject the sacredness of a Motherland?

This is why Communism needed to evolve without borders and adapt to the present times, and I wanted to see just how far I would go to make it true. Had scientists and scholars be actually interested in ruling, they could govern us all through reason and logic, leaving aside the emotional aspects that deteriorate and harm global peace. But even then, they were beyond the trivial concerns of mere humans. They understood that as long as we didn't transcend an evolutionary jump, we'd always be violent and irrational creatures, prey of our own fears. Although I hate to resort to the word for more than one reason, I had *faith* in humanity. Someday, we would be able to achieve a great manner of governing ourselves, for ourselves. Someday, we'd cease to have inequality produced by our own hand. And we would all be finally comrades. It was my belief that only through a very special branch of scientific Socialism this could in fact be eventually achieved.

I lay on the bed exhausted, ready to sleep. Surprisingly too tired to think, I rejoiced at the excitement produced from the thought that, at last, I was free from the chains of Faye's oppression. I had replaced the longing for her purely with my ideology, something I should have never abandoned for another human being, someone who had done nothing for me except betraying me in the worst possible way.

I looked at the solitary dog tag adorning my neck, and took it off. I had completely forgotten that Faye still had the one written in English, and a strange chill ran across my body, a sensation as if she had physically ripped something from me. I had indeed learned much that year, but the best lesson I absorbed was never placing your trust completely into the hands of another individual. And even though I didn't want to face it at first, I came to the realization that perhaps I would never be able to give myself in such a way to another human being ever again. What would have Faye done in my situation? Would she have given herself to her idol like I did with her? Or would she repress in self-loathing until the need disappeared? I'll never know the answers to these questions now, but it doesn't matter. The past is the past, and no conclusion I come up with now will be of any use.

I headed back to bed, listening to Kino's "*Gruppa Krovvi*" — "Blood Type" —. I had chosen to lay myself to sleep to it because of two reasons. Firstly, the lyrics of the song made me remember my abducted dog tag, and secondly, because I found it fitting to end this school year to the ending song of the film "*Igla,*" as I had started it with its intro song, "*Zvezda Po Imeni Solntse.*" Like Tsoi in the film, I had been stabbed and left to rot in the end, but would keep on walking, proudly carrying my wound and not giving my enemies the satisfaction to see me crawling to my death.

As I started to get between the sheets, I remembered something. My eyes redirected themselves to the second drawer of my wardrobe, which housed the impeccable gun case for the *Reviziya 02*. It was time to give it a proper look.

The gun's unique exterior shone by itself, even in the poorly-lit bedroom. I felt its smooth texture between my fingers, gripping the rugged carbon-polymer grip. I aimed and gently pulled the tight and responsive trigger as if to fire,

but refrained from doing so almost as if by instinct; what if it was loaded? I hadn't even been able to open the cylinder compartment. I didn't even know how it worked, although it all hinted at it being a simple double-action revolver. However, the external design hinted at something more complex. Even then I doubted this was a revolver at all. I even doubted whether there was a rotating cylinder inside, as the "cover" wouldn't let me see. I wished I could pry it open, but I didn't want to disassemble it and create an uncomfortable situation for myself. I wondered how the procedure to load this gun worked at all. Perhaps, this was a non-firing replica, a model, merely a physical representation of what the final product would resemble. To whom could this gun have been destined? Who was supposed to be the owner of such fine well-crafted piece of weaponry? This revolver was not designed to be fired, I was sure of it. This was a self-given trophy, something someone had designed to commemorate their own merits in a special manner. The best designed pieces of human craftsmanship in life are not meant to be used after all, but admired from afar, isolated in their own perfection where we can't corrupt them.

I returned the revolver to its hiding place and turned the lights off, ready for some sleep. But something had caught my eye in the darkness. A blinking light produced by my cellphone in short intervals indicated a message had been received.

I looked at the screen blinded by the brightness, seeing nothing but blurry stains. I didn't even check the caller ID, too burned-out to care by this point. The letters became gradually recognizable as my eyes slowly opened themselves, not too happy about what they were receiving:

"Crosshair Beach, alone, tomorrow

00:00h – BRING THE GUN."

EPILOGUE

Noises. My weak heart found itself on the verge of exhaustion as a torrent of adrenaline flowed through my tense arteries and I stopped remembering my story. Noises could be heard on the wall between my bedroom and the bathroom. Someone was knocking heavily and repeatedly on the wall.

KNOCK ... KNOCK ... KNOCK ... KNOCK ...

Nobody lived in this apartment complex aside from me. Nobody could be making such noises. My mind raced to find a rational explanation as my first occurrence was whether I could be gradually slipping into full-fledged insanity under the pressure of the surreal situation I found myself in. Was the slightest noise enough to make me so paranoid? So what if there were knocks on the wall at the other side? And why did I care about the reason? There could be a million rational explanations for the sounds. There was absolutely no need to panic. It could be a rat, something dripping due to the general abandonment of the building, something being pushed by the wind ...

KNOCK ... KNOCK ... KNOCK ... KNOCK ...

No. It couldn't be as simple as that. The long pauses between each knock were deliberate, I knew it. A primal and infantile fear overcame me as the possibility of insanity, the only phobia I had ever had, could be a realistic explanation for the noises. Guilt, remorse, paranoia, insomnia, unex-

plainable and recurrent dreams, I had all the symptoms of a growing and unstoppable form of schizophrenia. The next step would be a complete loss of comprehension about whether something was really happening or not. I feared I would eventually lose touch with reality. After all, I couldn't help myself feeling hunted down for my actions.

I returned to the kitchen, shutting the door behind me and locking it, turning to the window hoping once more that the silence outside could calm me down, breathing heavily and covering my ears.

Everything in the outside world seemed frozen at this time of night. Arias Road experienced very little activity, as one or two cars passed by at moderate speed. Nowhere to be seen were the Kannies speeding and blasting their disgusting music, or the powerful Yamazaki motorcycles shattering the silence with their growls. The restaurant down the street, "Loynner Delight," almost never had any customers in, just like "The Gecko Bar" and "Kate's Oven." I couldn't see the neighbors who lived in front of me, the ones in the double garage building, or the tenants living on top of them in the apartments. Everything was dead. The gym had not blasted its disgusting electro-pop music in days. What was wrong with this town at night? Had it not been for the one or two cars that usually passed by, I would have presumed I was frozen in time, trapped in an infinite limbo.

I stopped covering my ears and breathed deeply. Nothing disturbed the eternal tranquility of the Montenade night. The knocking noises on the wall had subsided.

I was fearful of the night. The worst part is that I wouldn't have been able to check whether during day time this context changed, as I couldn't possibly sleep at all during the night. My sleep had been inverted ever since that horrible incident, and I found myself sleeping throughout the whole day only to

wake up at night, when the world seemed to be plunged in eternal darkness and silence. Nothing disturbed the night, not drunken Loynners or Kanny teens. The whole town seemed desolate.

It was 07:00 as a matter of fact, and the sun was already illuminating the horizon softly. I couldn't go on anymore without collapsing. A massive headache prevented me from going on with my story. I couldn't go on for the day. I had relived the past memories inside my head so vividly I struggled not to feel affected. I couldn't believe those days had actually taken place; maybe they all had been a dream as well. But no, I couldn't fool myself. Who was I kidding? I couldn't evade or ignore my past. The situation was very real, and I had to think something up fast or else I'd go down in flames, like in my dream.

I headed painfully back to bed knowing nothing had been resolved by remembering that year of my life, that no strategies were produced by my desperate insomniac brain and that I had only three days left until they came after me. I had anticipated this anyway, and had just in case, disconnected the entire electric power for the whole building. As such, the buzzer wouldn't ring and my phone had been turned off for days for the same reason. I was the only tenant living in the building anyway. Nobody had come to inspect the apartments in ages, and the landlord wouldn't bother me as I made sure he got his paycheck every month, leaving an envelope in the mailbox.

But this temporal safety didn't dissipate the imminent danger I was about to experience. I still had three days left to think and come up with a plan. Only three days before they came for me.

Wrapping myself comfortably under the sheets, I erased every single haunting image from my mind trying to prevent

more nightmares. I sunk into the void of obscurity produced by my eyes, and wrapped myself around it as tightly as I did under the sheets. I had to treasure this comfort as much as possible; soon enough, I would never be able to enjoy it again.

Only three days remained ...

END OF BOOK I

'The Faith Endeavor'

About the author

Alexander Sylazhov is a student at the University of Granada, Spain, who studies Spanish, English and Russian translation at the Faculty of Translation and Interpreting. He writes fiction and articles under the pen name Alexander Sylazhov.

The author is fond of studying the history and culture of communist states and particularly of the former Soviet Union, as well as the geopolitical and social effects of the Cold War on our present society. He also enjoys greatly studying Russian history and reading Russian literature and poetry.